ALL THE RUSSIAS

JEFFREY GIBIAN

With an introduction by
Nicki Jackowska

DALEHAM PRESS

Published by
Daleham Press
27 The Courtyard
East Grinstead
West Sussex RH19 3XU

Copyright © Jeffrey Gibian 1999

ISBN 0-953-55530-5

Printed and bound in Great Britain by
Gearings Printing, Forest Row, Sussex

Typeset in Bembo 11/12.5pt

Acknowledgements:
To PALACIO for end maps
To NOVISTI for cover photo of Nicholas II

*To Margaret, my wife, for her
encouragement, endurance, faith and
sense of humour, her book
as much as mine.*

All the Russias is the first
book in a Quartet called
'The Word and the Sword' and
which consists of:-

All the Russias
Three Leaders
On the Streets
A State of Uncertainty

INTRODUCTION

This book could only have been written by a man with devotion so extensive and profound that the text itself has become a living embodiment of a life's work. In saying this, I must immediately make one crucial qualification: here is no authorship as individual confessional, an ego demanding to be heard. There is no pressing home a message, no hint of propaganda. No covert or seductive political or religious stance.

This writer has taken his time and has so fully taken in - or embodied - his material that we as readers are drawn with ease into the multiple landscapes, philosophies, lives and experiences of the text as a living whole, an effortless interweaving of worlds.

What is the material of *All the Russias*? We have many books on its subject-matter:- the fall of the Romanov Tsars, the Russian Revolution, the persecution and relocation of Russian Jews. What is it that makes this book so different and leads this reader to say what cannot often be said: a necessary work. And by that I mean necessary both that it be written, and be read.

To begin with the simplest of facts: Jeffrey Gibian's command of historical material, the forces and individual destinies that played their part in the unfolding of events covered by this volume (March 1881 - December 1887), is so complete that one experience of reading is the unreserved presence of a fully realised vision and understanding. This quality so permeates every aspect of the story that we are unaware of it and take it as our own. Paradoxically, the author's ability to be present to his material in this way, creates a necessary anonymity. He *allows* the events to speak for themselves, while yet being author of them in this form. So can we enter the events directly, ourselves be present also.

Such mediation is very special indeed.

This experience can be taken further. The vast canvas of history is revealed in the telling of public stories: the murder of Tsar Alexander II, the hangings in Semyonovsky Square, the burning of Jews in Ananayev, the people's deaths at Khodynka Meadow, the student demonstration in St. Petersburg to pay homage to the Russian literary critic Dobrolyubov. I use only a few examples of dramas, crises and historical turning points that are the outer story of this book, so vividly told. Yet these events are made even more real to us by the skill and agility with which they are grounded in the movement of individual lives. We are drawn into apartments of state, ante-rooms, street corners, seminaries, bedrooms, prison cells, where the lives of the individual characters are disclosed. This revealment takes many forms – intellectual, emotional, spiritual. The arguments of autocracy, socialism, democracy and religion are realised through the debate and struggle of individuals in such a way that the reader is taken to the heart of each and every point of view. We move, as it were, with the argument itself between one and another, so that each man or woman's philosophy or belief is lived and laid bare for us, and therefore also *by* us. So is our understanding of the wider movements of history expanded and deepened.

The author does not shy away from the difficulties of ambiguity and conflict, the languages of hate and prejudice.

Another of his gifts is the freedom to allow us to see and continue to turn the matter over for ourselves. So is this book an objective work. Not objectivity as detachment or disassociation, but a fearless engagement with each and every part.

In these pages, the complexities of the rise of Marxism (for example) are fully shown. As are the multiple ways in which the various points of view, the treacheries and allegiances impinge on the religious beliefs of the characters. Such thought and belief is traced through from its inception as interior birth and becoming, through to action itself, and back again – with all the anguish and internal struggle that this can involve.

We are party to this in the lives of the Tsars themselves, their officers and ministers, key figures in the rise of Marxism such as the Plekhanov family, the Jews of Vilna and Vladimir Ulyanov, Lenin himself. In all cases the author locates the characters within their family and social group so that we see and feel the loyalties, identifications and severances that permeate their lives. Yehuda and Aaron Liebman, as they struggle with orthodoxy, materialism and the very core of their own faith and identity.

We have here the greatest gift of a writer – interiority. Jeffrey Gibian is able to enter - by what skill or grace, I wonder – into the very quick of experience. This is at its most powerful in times of individual extremity - death or birth. Almost at random I mention the birth of Rosaliia Plekhanov's child, and also the slow moving-back from life of Ilya Nikolayevich Ulyanov - Lenin's father.

Here, there is a further disclosing. The individual soul in intimate battle - or collaboration - with life itself, beginning or end. And here also is language called into action, again para-doxically, both servant of the event and its supreme master.

All the Russias is the interweaving of narratives born of a consciousness able to range from one end to the other of the human condition. As such it is adequate to its task - to travel the time-bound events of an historical period wherein the very foundations of human community and collective organisation are argued and examined from the ground up, happening in front of our eyes as though for the first time. And to travel also in another dimension - inwards, to the core of conscience and morality. Or to the extremes of love and hate. Or further still, to brush with the edges of individual existence and identity itself.

There are many locations for the narrative voice. Yet it remains single, steady, resolute. The author moves from observer to the heart of an individual, in one breath. Speaks for each and every aspect of an argument and then for the group itself - a crowd in St. Petersburg, the Jews of Vilna, the Bunin factory workers. One might expect such a vast tapestry, such distances - both temporal and geographical and also the unspeakable distance between vision and action - to make for a difficult read.

Not so. In a way I find hard to describe, Jeffrey Gibian has married together a depth of knowing and a profound simplicity. Nothing pious here, nor histrionic. From first to last we travel in the book's embrace. The pace never falters, whether the language is rich and detailed in its depiction of parade, riot, marriage-feast. Or pared to the bone where a solitary consciousness almost breaks under the weight of the moment's significance.

All the Russias, for all its scale, is the first volume of a quartet. This living work has suspended me within its own spectrum. I leave its terrain with something like bereavement.

Nicki Jackowska   May 24th, 1999

HISTORICAL CHARACTERS

Alexander II.	Tsar (1818-1881). Reign begins 1855.
Alexander III.	Tsar (1845-1895). Reign begins 1881.
Alexandra Fedorovna.	Princess, wife of Nicholas II.
Alexander Ulyanov.	Eldest son in the Ulyanov family, hanged for attempted assassination of Alexander III.
Andreyevsky.	Rector of St. Petersburg University.
Andreyushkin.	Student conspirator hanged for attempted assassination of Alexander III.
Anna Ulyanov.	Eldest daughter in the Ulyanov family.
Axelrod.	Marxist socialist. Co-worker with Plekhanov.
Bakunin.	Leading Russian anarchist.
Baranov.	Naval officer.
Botkin.	Court doctor.
Catherine Pobedonostsev.	Wife of Constantin Pobedonostsev.
Delyanov.	Minister of Education, appointed by Alexander III.
Deutsch.	Marxist socialist. Co-worker with Plekhanov.
Deyer.	Judge. Court President.
Dimitri Ulyanov.	Youngest son in the Ulyanov family.
Dobrinsky.	Police colonel.
Dobrolyubov.	Literary critic and revolutionary socialist.
Dolgorukaya.	Princess. Mistress of Alexander II.
Dyorzhitsky.	Police colonel.
Emilyanov.	Member of the People's Will Party.
Frolov.	Public hangman.
Galitzyn.	Prince.
Generalov.	Student conspirator, hanged for attempted assassination of Alexander III.

Goldenburg.	A confessing terrorist.
Grinevitsky.	Member of the People's Will Party.
Helfman.	Member of the People's Will Party.
Herzen.	Radical journalist and political thinker. Exiled abroad. Publisher of 'The Bell' in London.
Hess.	German socialist and father of Zionist Socialism.
Ignatiev.	Minister of the Interior.
Ilya Nikolayevich Ulyanov.	Head of the Ulyanov family. Chief Inspector of Schools, Simbirsk Province.
Kashkademova.	Close friend of the Ulyanov family.
Kerensky.	Director of Simbirsk Gymnasium.
Khalturin.	Member of the People's Will Party.
Kibalchich.	Member of the People's Will Party.
Kremer.	Jewish Social Democrat – creator of new agitational strategy.
Kruglevsky.	Court doctor.
Lavrov.	A leader of the revolutionary movement abroad.
Loris-Melikov.	Minister of the Interior.
Maria Alexandrovna Ulyanov.	Mother of the Ulyanov family.
Maria Fedorovna.	Mother of Nicholas II. Wife of Alexander III.
Maria Ulyanov.	Ulyanov younger daughter.
Martov.	Jewish Social Democrat.
Mikhail.	Grand Duke. Uncle of Alexander II.
Mikhailov.	Member of the People's Will Party.
Mikhailovsky.	Radical Russian thinker.
Morozov.	Member of the People's Will Party.
Nekrassov.	Poet and editor of 'The Contemporary'.
Nikolai.	Minister of Education.
Nicholas II.	Tsar (1868-1918). Reign begins 1894.

Olga Ulyanov.	Ulyanov daughter.
Orlov.	Statistician.
Osipanov.	Student conspirator, hanged for attempted assassination of Alexander III.
Perovskaya.	Member of the People's Will Party.
Peter the Great	(1672-1725). Reign begins 1682.
Pinsker	Jewish physician, author of 'Auto-Emancipation'.
Pisarev.	Radical social thinker and leading Russian nihilist.
Plehve.	Director of police.
Plekhanov.	Founder of Russian Marxism.
Pobedonostsev.	Procurator of the Holy Synod.
Prokopovich.	Archbishop.
Rachkovsky.	Police official.
Rosaliia Plekhanov.	Wife of Georgy Plekhanov.
Rysakov.	Member of the People's Will Party.
Sergius Alexandrovitch.	Grand Duke. Brother of Alexander III. Uncle of Nicholas II.
Shevyrev.	Student conspirator, hanged for attempted assassination of Alexander III.
Solovyev.	Philosopher and theologian.
Strakhov	Philosopher and literary critic.
Tikhomirev.	Member of the People's Will Party.
Varvara.	Nanny in the Ulyanov household.
Vladimir Ulyanov (Lenin).	Brother of Alexander Ulyanov.
Vyshnegradsky.	Minister of Finance.
Witte.	Minister of Transport and Minister of Finance.
Zasulich.	Co-worker with Plekhanov for the creation of Marxist socialism in Russia.
Zhelyabov.	Member of the People's Will Party.

THE CALLING

From Russia
Mother Earth called to her Lord.
Lord Christ!
No longer can I carry
Men who commit such crimes,
Fratricide, lying, slander, theft.
Lord Christ!
Bid my depths open
And swallow lawless man.

O Mother, moist Mother Earth,
Our Lord Christ answered,
Of all creatures thou art most in pain,
By the sins of mankind thou art stained.
Have patience yet a little while
Until I come again.
Then shall thou rejoice.
Then shall thou shine forth
Whiter than snow.
I shall change thee to a wondrous garden
Where Paradise flowers shall bloom.
Rejoice o ye my chosen souls,
Rejoice!
My way shall be your way,
Temptation, suffering, sacrifice, death
And resurrection.
The Sun of Righteousness
The Sun of Truth.
Your radiance, your warmth, for all mankind.

CHAPTERS

I

St Petersburg

Sunday, March 13, 1881 dawned over St Petersburg to tell at last and once again, of that light above and beyond, the radiant blue. The icy winds, whirling snow, heavy skies, were no more. Only that presence above of radiant blueness, its brilliance. Spires, domes, snow laden branches and frozen Neva gleamed and sparked in new sculpted purity.

Everything called upwards, etching firm, man, stone, dome, into the surging blue towards that heart of radiance. Calling upwards, strengthening hope. Vast momentary glimpse of that sun.

Peter's city.

Peter's will, the One Will, Supreme. Absolute, challenged, enduring still in the lives, the buildings, the streets.

Emperor and Autocrat of all the Russias.

Tsar of Moscow, Kiev, Vladimir, Novgorod, Kazan, Astrakhan, of Siberia.

Lord of Pskov.

Grand Duke of Smolensk, Karelia, Tver, Perm, Viatka and other countries.

Lord and Grand Duke of Lower Novgorod, Tchernigov, Riazan, Polotsk, Rostov, Yaroslavl, Belozero, Oudoria, Obdoria.

Each a people made known through the forceful unity of the whole. A jewel in the crown of that Power.

Here, at Neva's mouth, the Swedes beaten, to seize this moment so keenly felt, breathing in deeply the tang and taste of this wind and water's life that takes us out into the open.

Yes, a fortress to make secure but more, more is possible. Open horizon calling outward, outwards Russia! to that whole wide world of the West. All possible in the fiery moment of this new present. Build your ships Russia! Fill your sails with this fresh breeze. Glide along great Neva's back, out to all that world. Show yourself. I will.

Dream on – a port to receive them – a city to forge my space – a capital for my new-born Russia.

Swamp, swirling mist, wildness, desolation – only the hardest, the most enduring – yes, yes, – and we victorious Russia, will do it.

Stone. Stone alone. Stone on stone. Base and sure foundation for the open, the future.

Far, far from that foul darkness of Muscovy this new beginning. Far, far this power from those bloodied vaulted chambers trembling fear and humiliation.

From this hostile emptiness, wild endless marsh to make a limit and a threshold, a barrier and a meeting with the West. That, the challenge of this vast grim swamp, savoured in the salt air, the sweep and beat of Neva's rushing flood.

To begin, at any cost, ordering, inspiring, punishing, terrorising. These swamps must be overcome, his people, great whole, strengthened, formed for the future.

Down and down keep driving the piles until the bottom is reached, touched, known, sounded. Then only can the building begin. A ground must be found. Then at last will Russia stand firm, prepared, resolute.

Plans in hand, his huge steps raced along the emerging quayside, no detail escaping his grasp. Following breathless, slipping, falling, fearful officials, bewildered, amazed by these forms, new world arising so swiftly, forged in the furnace of his will.

Down, slowly down, the wooden piles driven, through the thick coiling ooze, to and through the firmer, more resistant, down, deeper down to the hard, the unyielding, the ground. Each booming echo, pulsebeat of his expectations and demands. The final blow, stern ringing note, jarring, joyful, foundations revealed. Dreamers awake! Sea mists retreat! Here now on earth we make our home, organised, enduring. Earth's master.

Urged on, threatened, punished, inspired, tens of thousands dug, hauled the red granite blocks, bent low, twisted, crushed. Stone cutters, carpenters, unskilled peasants, Cossacks, Tartars, Finns. Frozen, exhausted, sucked under, laid low with disease, they sickened and died.

Slowly, harshly, forms arose wrought from this struggle. First and last, on Enisary island, the Fortress. With its cathedral, to His ever present Mercy, its dungeons for all traitors, its treasury for all business, its court for all judgement. Then arising mansions, avenues, canals, bridges, clear measured cooling forms shaping

Russian life into earth's master. Forms dreamed by men from that Southern land of air and light, Rastrelli, Trezzini, Quaranghi. Forms firmly finely here, ordered, an enduring order. But first and last the Fortress.

Spire's golden needle thrusting eagerly into the blue, focused, warning. Sheer, sudden aloft, infinite aspiration from this new grounded earth.

Peter's people, Russia, also to be grounded, ordered, made secure. As granite, fine-grained, fire-cooled, the fire enduring. Slowly, harshly, his people formed by the hammer of his will. I - Peter, I - Peter, I - Peter will forge you anew in this foundry of time.

This Will the One Will, inexhaustible, all consuming.

Russians! Let us sing the praises of our Father, Peter the Great. Russia's Bridegroom, Sovereign Emperor who has led us from non-existence to existence.

Who has enlightened and glorified us.

The sweat of his labours is a myrrh perfuming the glory of Russia to the end of the world.

Peter's people.

No soul to be left ungraded, unnumbered, unordered.

Existence endowed by Peter's stamp.

Every soul hunted out, registered, none to escape.

All tensions and stresses to be balanced in the cool light of this thinking. Light of Amsterdam and Rotherhithe, shipyards and parade grounds, everything fitting according to plan and working efficiently. Each soul, large or small, to be found its proper place. None to belong to itself.

And he Peter the highest servant, no more, no less.

He Peter, like any other man, but in office the highest god.

The *streltsy's* rotting corpses left hanging for all to witness.

That past marked off.

A scourge! A mission!

A scourge striking fiery sparks, igniting all other wills.

No indeed! Not truly human - a god - godlike - a servant of god - an instrument of god - to forge us into shape.

Tremble before him.

Caught up, overpowered, driven to the impossible by him.

The impossible yielding, revealed, released.

A new vigour abroad - a Russian vigour!

Fourteen clean cut steps to the peak, the man-god's all seeing eye. Lowly clerk to Chancellor, cornet to Field Marshal, efficiency, service and talent alone. Granite, enduring the centuries to come. Close grained this bastion, Russia.

Streets, ranks and souls of men, all ordered uniform.

Peter's city arising, Peter's Russia arising. Bearer of the One Will, Father of his people, harshly chastising. Flesh of his flesh, informed by his will, those closest could sniff sedition and impudence in its most hidden guise across the land. He knew his children well. Terror and torture alone would ensure their well being. All defiance punished.

"By nature like any other man but in power and office the highest god."

His Will the law, the state.

The steady beat of the drum from Troitza Square ordered every single soul to hurry along and hear, assembled, our lord and master's edict. Week after week, edict after edict, the steady drumming. Anxious pulse-beat of our lives.

A fearful security ours – but security.

Time was short. The task urgent. Russia to be made a nation like those others, proud, defiant, prepared, advancing, from North to South, from East to West, industry, education, church, army and navy, newly forged into being by his God-graced will.

Earthwards you Russia! Down, down to earth. Her laws revealed. Learn them Russia and raise yourself up! Be imperious, masterful, use her, become skilled, efficient like them.

Everything the others have I shall bring forth through you.

Fools – traitors – pygmies – I'll knock you into shape before I leave.

A nation like them, skilled, efficient.

So he could die, knowing that a beginning had been made.

Over against the swamp, loathsome bloody darkness of Muscovy, he had thrust glittering granite, new foundation.

What those others were achieving Russia would also achieve.

Purpose, meaning and order had been driven into Russia's life.

The Army's Service Regulations, CAP. III. Article 20, inscribed it for all time in stone and flesh. "His Majesty is an autocratic monarch who is not obliged to answer for his acts to anyone in the world."

In the Fortress Cathedral of Peter and Paul, before the bier, Archbishop Prokopovich's words overwhelmed their stricken hearts, orphaned, by this unbearable withdrawal of God's servant.

"Russians!

What - what? - is happening here - that we are burying Peter the Great.

Can it be?

Or are we dreaming?

Burying him who raised us from the dead to the height of power and glory.

Do we know whom we have lost?

Our Samson - Russians!

Who found us weak and made us into a mighty rock.

Our Moses - whose laws are the strongest shield of justice.

Our Solomon - to whom God gave great wisdom, mastery in philosophy, sciences, crafts, the civil laws with their ranks and grades.

Our David - who overcame superstition, hypocrisy, schisms.

Russians! - Russia! - as he formed you - so shall you endure.

Russians! - consider well and long the greatness of this man we have lost - and the greatness he has made of us."

Servant of Satan! AntiChrist! Fool!

Your city and empire are evil!

The secret waters of Russia's life will loose even your stony bounds.

You know them not!

Fresh and renewing, soul's freedom.

The wanderer's way.

Our ground is Christ.

Brother and Friend.

Yet to come.

On Sunday March 13, 1881, Alexander II, Emperor and Autocrat of All the Russias felt cheered by the early morning brightness and looked forward to reviewing the honour guard at the Michael Riding School off Mikhailovsky Square. After a walk with his youngest sons, Paul and Serge in the Winter Palace Gardens, divine service in the royal chapel and a light breakfast, he went up to his study for the weekly meeting with General Count Loris-Melikov, Minister of the Interior.

But this morning's meeting, this signing - now no longer clear?

The arduous discussions in the Council of State of no consequence whatsoever?

Only this questioning - himself in question, very step, mastered, measured by it, through the slow pacing back and forth from his desk to the window facing the Peter and Paul Fortress across the frozen Neva. And shouldn't that swine of a terrorist have been rotting there too - with the rest of that foul brood? Police? - of no avail! Loris-Melikov's dictatorial powers - of no avail! Swine? - Papa had personally questioned the Decembrists - but these swine were not officers, thank God.

A bomb - the dining room - right here! - blown to pieces - he - saved by minutes - so close - so far - so far! - from this place where he stood and answered for Russia - placed by the Highest.

Be damned this shameful fear, petty, petty, this worry about the signing - "Fear not!" - of course - why! - those were Papa's very words last night from the Spirit World. "Fear not!" That Papa's spirit could speak to him thus, be with him thus. God's very mercy and shield. His fortress. Papa's assurance that his judgement was sound, such strength, given, gift. Be wary of all temptation, even Loris-Melikov. Draw strength from that granite word from across the Neva - Russia enduring - fastness - from Papa's closeness - from the blessed happiness with Catherine.

So bright! This glimpse of the review ahead - their trust!

You and you alone dare judge of yourself. You who were called and have answered. No one but yourself. Between you and the All Highest. And what could those others, he who was coming, know of that?

Hold, assured, justified, to what is yours alone before this unease, confusion.

Through you the peasants liberated - local government, judiciary, army, navy reformed for the good of Russia. State and restate it as your own decisive deeds for the good of Russia, as your very own source of strength.

But still the riots - the fires - the killings - because those swine wanted to destroy him - destroy Russia - and that would not be! Russia would endure Autocratic Absolute. Changes would only come from him alone! Russia would only hold together, know unity through this one appointed godly Will alone.

In his carriage on the way to the Winter Palace, General Count Loris-Melikov, Minister of the Interior, allowed himself some optimism, relief. Very soon the Tsar's signature would mean that the new law was on its way. All becoming so wearisome, a deadly weariness, this never ending battle. HM's ignorance. Best like that. He was being hunted like a wild beast! Hundreds involved – Goldenberg had confessed hundreds of names! Well, at least the reorganisation was working – Goldenberg had been caught – State security under firm central control – what more – what more?

Enough!

You must take some cheer. The new law should isolate the terrorists. Should win over the liberal sympathisers. Should. All that covert liberal support should be withdrawn.

A thin, bewigged, green-liveried flunkey stood impassive, holding open the carriage door.

What look was that?

A year, since Khalturin's bloody massacre in the dining room and still, but how else? not to trust anyone, anything here. In spite of his radical police reorganisation – still not to trust anyone or anything here? In spite of his newly trained Corps of ten thousand gendarmes – this was the truth still! for him still – not to trust any of them here.

His cloak was taken and he slowly climbed the marble staircase, a flunkey posted at every turn.

At the far end of the long green corridor, past the aide-de-camp's office, a blue coated flunkey tapped lightly on the door of the Tsar's study and stood aside as he entered. He must summon up good cheer, approaching the desk, opening his briefcase, taking out the thoroughly discussed draft papers, ready for the brief signing. But HM. standing by the tall window, looking out across the Neva, still hasn't acknowledged his presence. Ridiculous, threatening, forced to declare himself, identify himself, to break through to something, whatever.

"The draft laws on the new commission Sire," he began.

"Yes, yes, Michael Taryelovich – but what – briefly – is their aim?" Alexander demanded brusquely, turning towards him.

Stand firm. Don't falter. Of course he knows but wants reassurance. Intimate trusting reassuring do your best.

Reassurance – and end to your dallying too?

Aim? Be bold. It's the constitutional aspect. He's accusing you.

"Then let me declare at once Sire - that the proposed commissions have absolutely nothing whatsoever to do with constitutionalism in any form. The essential aim is to win over the liberals - all moderate opinion and so utterly isolate the terrorists. Police measures alone will never defeat them. The withdrawal of public sympathy in all its forms surely will."

"And your reason for being so confident?" Alexander countered bluntly.

"The Tver Zemstvo Sire. Who more liberal? They've declared publicly their confidence in our measures thus far. Our proposed commission - merely - - (logically) - - refines those measures - an encouragement certainly - but one considered with extreme care - - (all of which you know well!) - consultation but only consultation with certain elected representatives on issues which we alone choose. Nothing of your Majesty's autocratic power is touched. Sire, all educated opinion will stand firmly behind you."

"So, you believe that the draft laws will satisfy them," Alexander insisted.

"More than satisfy them Sire. The Tver Zemstvo declares itself as already looking forward to a happy future opening up for our beloved country." Don't yield. He'd like you to.

"The facts! Michael Taryelovich, don't dare be carried away! We've done everything that we heard was needed year after year and the swine go on murdering!"

He walked away to the window, slowly returning.

"In what proportion - elected?"

"Some few Sire, will find themselves on a committee considering one third of the provisional - - preparatory commission. The whole process frankly harmless Sire - educational if anything - to create a right attitude in the educated classes."

Alexander sniffed a liberal cunning which this loyal old soldier was not proof against. He, he alone, the pivot, as cunning as those swine for Russia's sake. This boundary, burden, to be lived, alone, by him, was him and no other.

"Well then, arrange a meeting of the Council of Ministers soon for a final editing."

He reached for his pen. But there as ever the frustration as he signed, not wanting to yield even a cursory glance at the text.

His purely good intentions were not being appreciated by his people.

Left alone again Loris-Melikov hesitated, uneasy, the moment so inconclusive, before gathering the documents into his briefcase. No chance at all to explain just how delicately weighted the proposals were - that elected third - no ordinary third - the two thirds - no ordinary two thirds - of course they offered something - they had to - but HM. didn't trust it in spite of all the signing, all of it feeling now of no avail. Such dreadful weary thoughts in his carriage. Not his! That a sacrifice was needed to utterly transform moderate opinion - to turn all Russia against these murdering swine and destroy them. Police power could not stop it. God help you Michael Taryelovich! Such a logic! Terrorists' fulfilment - and this other one too!

Alexander waited, listening till the sound of Loris-Melikov's footsteps ceased utterly. He went straight to the apartment of his young wife and mistress till recently, Princess Catherine Dolgorukaya, on the second floor overlooking the Palace gardens. To have it heard, beyond himself, to share it with her, what he had done, was necessity and relief.

She left her letter writing and went to embrace him, to answer and embrace that distraction and appeal.

"Well, at last - I've signed it - if that's what will help - if that's what they want - yes", faltering, and that's how it was, but this precious relief in and through her presence, to be able to so confess.

So clearly, painfully, she must hear his uncertainty, must bear it with him, what she knew he sought from her, this bearing it together, wholly given over, as he to her, nothing less. Just in these moments his family's bitter hostility pitiful, borne triumphant.

"I've ordered Loris-Melikov to go ahead with things. No point, no point at all in waiting longer."

Slowly, of binding necessity, he raised his right hand and made the sign of the cross. Sign, swiftest plunge for her into such black dread, even as they embraced again and he left to change for the review. Warn warn warn - contain this desperation, despair - before he left.

"Sasha my darling - please don't ride along the Nevsky - go by the Ekaterinsky Canal - - for my sake."

"Yes - yes," he turned around by the door, glimpsed that

brightness ahead, the review, but frustrated by her, but from her, that awkward note of her knowing, "I shall – I shall – be assured," his words now measured, keen the trust asserting, through her blessed care for them both.

In the gently curtained light he began undressing. Jacket unbuttoned, his elderly valet waited, puzzled, as his master stood hesitant, preoccupied, facing his image in the sombrely lit full length mirror. Of course well meant but this constriction – challenge from what powers? Well meant – but better she hadn't said it. Unwanted this vulnerability. Not her to blame for that but the urgency heard disturbing.

Responding to his master's mood the valet helped him off with the jacket. Alexander watched that downcast one looking back at him from the mirror. Lost, that other's look. He? Emperor? Whilst old Aleksii, steadiness itself – steady light, that was him, was ready with the blue trousers and jacket of his Colonel-in-Chief's uniform, Chevalier Guards.

This too is you! – and they are waiting. This one standing erect – adjusting the stars and medallions with Aleksii's help.

No image this but reality – yours and theirs, inseparable, enduring.

This too is you on whom they're depending. Never to be betrayed. They know your truth and will die for it! They! – power, will as of old. Such certainty in this knowing.

A flunkey held open the carriage door. Alexander only just recalled before stepping in.

"Along Gorokhovaya – then straight down the Canal street," he ordered the coachman.

No not forced, for her sake alone.

At last on the way to his own, with his own, dissolving all that other in the fullness of this affirmation, his Cossacks cantering close, to the right, to the left, in front. These the men who would guarantee Russia's future. Moving forward in steady unison. In the very flow of their life he, will of their will.

Police followed in two horsedrawn sleighs.

On the way at last to his own by way of the Admiralty, straight on down the Gorokhovaya at the brisk pace he liked. In the gathering fullness of this moment a broad strength flowing from the city itself beyond all that other, gift, given, carrying him through. Granite, marble, shaped, solid, secure. His destiny uttered, domes, spires, bridges, colonnades sounding the groundnote of order and will. Every stone in its right place, confident, proud, part of the greater whole.

By noon, as planned after weeks of preparation, six members of the People's Will party were in place ready to rid Russia of the despot and free the people. From this vision of freeing the people was born an exaltation, unearthly strength, driving, manoeuvring, charming its way through all obstacles. Yes, seventh attempt since the Executive Committee decision at Lipetsk August 26, 1879 to assassinate the despot. But surely the most thorough, the most foolproof.

And something must happen after the assassination. It could only be for the better. A mass uprising? The successor forced to return to those earlier reforms. Whatever it could only be for the better.

The despot only ever used two routes on returning from the regular Sunday morning review. Both were now covered. Along the Ekaterininsky Canal Street - Rysakov - Mikhailov - Emilyanov - were spaced out with their five pound grenades, expertly designed by Kibalchich. If he returned by the Nevsky and Sadovaya Prospect, the underground mine in position after weeks of exhausting tunnelling, would blow him to pieces.

Twenty four year old Ignaty Grinevitsky, posted at the Nevsky intersection had the possibility of effective action on either route. Keeping on the move, acting casually but warily towards passers-by, shoppers, strollers, he heard, repeated with wonder, the words he had written in a last letter to the comrades, this morning, so long ago? fresh, ever present. His own words - but as from another - with such certainty - unearthly certainty - unearthly clarity - such strength - living warmth - pure light - from where had they come? - so swift - serene. Be vigilant! - the task! Be sadly concerned for these around - these here who would never know of this only real fulfilment - know that the meaning of life here on earth was just such a sacrifice allowed him - know with such certainty this earth here and beyond - and all in those words.

"Alexander II must die. I or another will bring about this last terrible blow and the sound of the blow will be heard all over Russia.

He will die, and with him we shall die, his enemies, his executioners.

What of the future?

How many more victims will our dear and unhappy country demand before we have achieved our freedom? I am terrified by the thought, as I stand now with one foot in the grave, that after me there will be many sacrifices, many men killed, in the final death struggle with despotism.

History shows that the luxurious tree of freedom needs blood to quicken its roots.

It is not my fate that I shall take part in that final battle. Fate has revealed for me an early death, and I shall not see our day, our hour of victory, the blazing light of our triumph. But I believe that by dying I am doing all that is in my power to do, and no one on earth can demand more of me."

Words as if dictated. Of such completion, consolation that he knew beyond all possible doubt that having written them he was ready for death.

Vigilance!

That gendarme outside Mamontov's is eyeing you. Wander round to the Library.

Vigilance!

But brother death – yes!

Your bluff called. Your gift recognised.

Yes! – your mission!

This in between posting – the most unclear.

What made him so sure that he was the one who would do it?

Alexander walked towards his coach from the porticoed entrance of the Riding school, "Hurrah! Hurrah! Hurrah! For the Emperor," resounding.

To still bother about which route?

"Same route back – Canal street – Gorokhovaya," he ordered the coachman, feeling obliged to confirm it, to still do as she said.

All that, of little account from this warmth of acclaim from his own as the carriage and Cossack escort with police in the rear, moved off. Gold, with the glint of their upraised swords as they cheered. Soaring, leaving far behind ministers, kin, no I, no You, We together as One. Change yes but from this centre alone.

Through them true consolation.

Flesh of his flesh, mounted, flashing silver and gold, magnificent in the pride of their manhood, this was life's meaning. To have a leader, a father who loved and cherished his own. To defend him with one's life. Him the divinely appointed, protecting, guiding. To be close, smiled on by him. In awe to know his greatness and difference.

To be first for him.

Risk one's life for him.

Be raised up by him.

That alone was life for a man.

All others to be pitied, they would never know.

Cossack escort leading, its canter borne along on this bond of pride. Booted, sabred, ready, eyes sweeping relentless from stern heights. Their lives ennobled by his presence. He knowing himself through them once wild unruly ones whom his father had brought from distant steppes and made a strong right arm. A warning and a scourge. Proud with the pride of the chosen. Matchless that movement of man on horse. Yes, with these at his side the dynasty must endure. Essential this weekly review. Not simply good cheer – but guarantor too! Loyalty – duty – let all Russians learn. The army alone guarantor of right ways – no! – still no! – of what avail Loris-Melikov's draft laws.

Unplanned Mikhailov, Emilyanov and Rysakov, found themselves having to beat out their particular stretch of Canal street at five hundred yard intervals, past the great mansions and warily mingling with the passers-by, back and forth, back and forth, what else was there to do? Rysakov, the youngest, first in line, nearest to the Nevsky crossing, was becoming very anxious as the world about him withdrew, dreamlike, from his grasp, uncanny fear insisting that if the carriage came this way it would pass him by.

Back and forth, up and down, tramping, tramping, into some sticky swamp, from the Orlov mansion to the Nevsky crossing, again and again, vigilance leaking away. Only left, to feel that heaviness in his carpenter's felt bag, tugging at him.

So alone now, just now! So vulnerable!

That they had believed they could overthrow the autocracy – madness! That crazy picnic in the Lipetsk woods – all a madness! Dreadful – turn around, turn around it's the Nevsky crossing again – to question it all now! How had he come to this?

Feel the truth of that heaviness tugging – at you! Coward! – Betrayer!

Make good! – Make good!

Take hold of it! They're coming thank God for this knowing – and hurl with all your might!

Yes – he was the one to have done it – he alone!

Tsar Alexander was rammed hard into the back of the coach by the explosion, then flung forward giddily, knowing so keenly as he grabbed at the door that he had come through.

"Stop! Stop! Stop!" he yelled to the desperate coachman who managed to drag the frightened bolting horses to a halt. Trembling slightly, he stepped out. Police Colonel Dvorzhitsky ran up from his sledge which had followed frantically.

"Thank God Sire for your safety – let's quickly return to the Palace."

The Tsar, looking back, to the still rising smoke, hearing the shouts and screams, one young scream again and again, knew he must return, back, through the debris-strewn snow to that place on this earth where he must stand again. That he had survived this latest attempt! No quick return to any Palace. Seventh attempt that place of divine protection for the sake of Russia. Spiting her warning yet failed.

Past the dead, the badly wounded, the cheering and bowing survivors, to this young voice screaming, dying, his delivery basket, the fresh baked rolls, forlorn in the blood-soaked snow. By his side they knelt, tearful. May I bear these screams as mine, know the cost, still on this side, his soul crossing, may the God of Mercy bring him peace. Only thus, amidst the wounded, in agony pierced and torn by the flying shrapnel, to be close, let it all work through him. Only thus in this place, on this threshold, amidst these his people.

"Where is the Tsar?" a Cossack officer called out anxiously from somewhere in the rapidly growing crowd.

"I'm safe. Thank God," Alexander answered immediately to reassure him and all.

"We'll see whether you're safe," shouted back Rysakov, infuriating the gendarmes who held him tight.

So close – still here the despot – then speak direct – let them hit him again.

Alexander turned towards him and approached. So close. Everything so close.

"Leave him alone!" ordered the Tsar as a fist slammed down on Rysakov's bruised mouth to draw blood.

Rysakov watched, victorious, spoken as an equal, drawing this

14

one towards him. But closer came the friendly stranger. Tsar? enemy? identity drifting away, only that stern pressure from his captors, wrists gripped tight.

The Tsar wondered at this mere youth - hunted?

"So you threw the bomb," he said, restrained, curious, not hostile his look.

"Yes!" answered Rysakov spontaneously, the obvious, but seeking defiance and pride, to somehow make this conversation surrendered from him, a continuation of the battle.

"What is your name?" asked Alexander, caught up, in this first ever encounter with one who had done it.

Indecision, despair took hold of Rysakov. That it had failed. That this man was alive speaking so easily. That others instead had been injured. That screaming boy was dying. All his work! How was that possible? Screaming accusation. Always the innocent. Never this one!

Alexander sensed Rysakov's bewilderment, resistance, sudden show of bravado, and shame. Who was this facing him? Who was trying to destroy the dynasty? In whose power this unknown boy who knew what of him so well.

"Nicholas Rysakov," he answered with relief and surprise.

"And what is your father?"

"A worker - in a timber works -"

"And what do you do?"

"I'm a student - a student of mining."

With each question and answer Rysakov drawn, knowingly, in spite of himself, felt a tenuous bond forming with this stranger. So vulnerable, dangerous, that bright clarity of purpose, life-resolve, dissolving, abandoning him.

Still needing to search out and accept, fully accept the earthly stamp of his destiny, Alexander asked Colonel Dvorzhitsky to show him the exact place in the road where the bomb had fallen. Colonel Dvorzhitsky heard the request and began leading him to the crater near the Nevsky crossing, through the milling, shouting confusion with increasing desperation, helplessness, that none of this was sensible! - right! - moving about like this - that everything was out of control. Yes - yes - this was H.M. as ever - pale - dragging his leg along - staying with his people - his presence the courage for all - but something was out of control - this dullness - this dark crowd following so close - H.M. should not be here!

With relief as the Tsar and Colonel Dvorzhitsky moved away, Rysakov's bewildered captors punched and steered him towards a police sledge.

Grinevitsky, pretending interest in a jeweller's window near the Nevsky intersection, heard the explosion but checked himself from running in the direction of Canal street.

Think what you're doing! But you must find out exactly what's happened and let them know here on the Sadovaya so they can clear off quickly. Wait till you get there. No conclusions. Disappointment? Who d'you think you are? They've got him at last damn you. Don't hang about like this – join them! Join them!

More and more strollers hurried anxiously along. The pace quickened, almost to a run. No one spoke. Sunday morning – this hour regularly – the Tsar's return from the Riding School.

He too must appear deeply concerned, as he kept pace with them.

Just ahead now and into it. The groans, injured being tended, stinging cordite fumes, the screams – and cheers – cheers? – to his right a crowd gathered, cheering! surrounding whom? – whom? – by the parapet.

He edged his way to the very front.

Rysakov had done it! cleared this space for him – confirmation – assured success of his mission. The truth of his whole life confirmed in this timeless moment.

Brought thus close. Beyond all earthly interference.

We both together!

That you have been left free to do it in purest awareness. Morning's truth. So now your faithful witness.

"God be praised!" they shouted just to see their Tsar, some crossing themselves, so thankful for his survival as he inspected the crater and damage with Colonel Dvorzhitsky.

"No! too soon to praise your god," Grinevitsky shouted back, threshold crossed to the far shore, both of them, reaching into his bag, raising high the grenade and hurling it down at the Tsar's feet, right in front of him.

Alexander felt the man advancing and heard the words, plunged into a violent ocean of flaming noise. Furious waves of destruction engulfed his blind, dumb wreckage. Flotsam barely floating on these livid waters as he rose and was returned, rose and returned. Rose into great expanding whiteness and returned to this shrivelled wreckage. Gamely it floated, settling lower, leaking, purest pain. Yet he no longer of it, rising and returning. All around a veil of shimmering red.

Amidst the dead and the dying, the groans and the screams survivors fought their way through an impenetrable silence, to return, back, far back, remembering, fought their way through a knowledge of their utter helplessness and vulnerability, to look for him!

Remember! - what we were.

With dread, one, and another, and another, found their way to him and stood with dread before what they found.

That is him!

Convince yourself. Have faith.

Look - reverently - and kneel - and pray - that - that - bleeding torso - no! - take it all in now - it is all him - that bright fountain of red life spurting from the gaping stump. Left leg blown askew. His bright red life spreading in runnels through the gashed snow. That face his, all bruised torn bleeding. That left eye resting on the cheek. That jaw partly exposed. All his. The right eye still, but waxing and waning. Through it alone dare we focus and search.

O Tsar - Tsar - where are you?

Who dares bend close - words - words, he is sounding.

Captain Kulebyakin broke through the dread to what was needed here and now, to protect, conceal, with his cloak, gently.

Grand Duke Mikhail, the Tsar's uncle, forced his way through the crowd and bent very close.

"Alexander -,"

"Take me to the Palace - hurry - I want to die there," so strange, so familiar the voice.

Captain Kulebyakin held fast to the obvious, the overwhelmingly urgent, ordering two Cossacks to bring a sledge near, and others to go to the Palace, fast, prepare them for the Tsar's arrival. But hesitating, "Tell them - - the Tsar is - - ill - - wait! - - make sure the Heir is informed." And - and - no end to this.

"For god's sake - take His Majesty across to the mansion - he must be treated now - now!" howled a voice in desperation.

That redness creeping through the snow - what were they helplessly watching?

"No!" sounded the Tsar with such force, familiarity, drawing

Grand Duke Mikhail down low again," - to the Palace - hurry - I want to die there," he repeated clearly, knowing that none of this could touch it - feeling to be with her beyond all this freezing loneliness - such distant voices - that would be enough.

The sledge drew close. Somehow, keeping him covered, cradling his head, they managed, gentle gentle, but so urgent that this wish of his be realised - but he knew with his hurry and would forgive them - to keep him up between Captain Kulebyakin and Grand Duke Mikhail, before driving off.

Only as the sledge moved away did the crowd yield to the truth of that man's dying, with bitter screams, shouts, fervent singing of the national anthem, and his blood made ours, revered, as we soak our handkerchiefs with it, surety of our love for him.

In the Palace, the direction and time of the two explosions created deep anxiety. The Cossack sledge drew up in the courtyard and two Cossacks hurried to the entrance with the news. Flunkeys and courtiers quickly gathered.

"The Emperor is on his way - he's ill - the Heir must be informed."

Someone shrieked with dismay.

Catherine, in hat and cloak, ready for their promenade after his return from the Riding School, hurried out onto the landing and looked down the flights of stairs to the gathering by the entrance.

"The Tsar is ill," called up an equerry.

She rushed back, grabbed an oxygen balloon in each hand for his asthma and ordered a servant to bring more. Not that then O Lord!

An equerry hurried to the Heir's study in the east wing.

"The Tsar is ill Sire - and on his way to the Palace -"

"How - ill?"

The equerry stood his ground.

"That's all we've been told Sire."

Both knew well what they meant as Grand Duke Alexander strode rapidly ahead. Swiftly gathered the guilt from the long estrangement.

The growing gathering at the entrance, ladies-in-waiting, aides-de-camp, equerries, flunkeys, stared hard at what was approaching, straining to believe, that pitifully shrunken one, held between Captain Kulebyakin and the Grand Duke, deeply shocked, as somehow by some, the Tsar!, this dying man, was lifted up and carried, in silence. Grand Duke Mikhail knowing what had to be done, knowing well with Captain Kulebyakin that it is the Tsar, ordered, "Up to the study!"

Three on each side, hands joined for a human stretcher, hands stained, wet with blood, as Doctor Kruglevsky, Surgeon Extraordinary to the Tsar, and Dr Botkin, were fetched. Somehow to hurry, that help was possible, hope! Gently, only gentleness dare touch this fragile hope, but hurry, hurry.

As the awkward climb began those gathering became aware of Catherine, and the Heir, and the Heir's son. A way was made for them. A way was made for such awkwardness, hostility, forced together by the dying one.

Two Tsars present. Catherine become nothing.

Such dissolution threatening.

Catherine blindly followed the cloaked enigma, not yet her Sasha, behind those cradling the bleeding stump and twisted leg.

Grand Duke Alexander followed two stairs behind her, sensing that at any moment she might topple backwards on him, but her! like this! – peace! – some peace towards her! – in the presence of that dreadfully shrunken father, still father! your blood this, drop by heavy drop spattering the marble, bitter flames.

Thirteen year old Nicholas found his own way there behind his father, so needing to be near him. One step right behind him, pained with this awful knowing of his father's loneliness and his own. Once friendly world a bleak shadow and these huge gleaming blobs from Grandpapa's life.

They laid him down on a couch near his desk and lifted away the cloak to prepare for the doctors.

Catherine knew who it was, there, in all his fullness, for her, through her, never to let go that all.

"Sasha, Sasha, Sasha my darling," she knelt and kissed and fondled that poor torn head die she would with him.

The good eye unseeing, the breathing very faint.

"Sasha! Sasha!" she screamed into the darkness.

"Princess, have courage," said Count Baranov, gently holding her arm, "let others do what they can – he's still alive."

He helped her up and led her to a chair, as two valets de chambre tried to undress the Tsar. The rags of uniform stuck stubbornly to the torn flesh.

Grand Duke Alexander watched intently, wincing, resolved

that the Army - indeed the Army would make good - very good! - all this, knowing through the bitter bond of this pain who he already was.

Those watching knew as an act of faith that it was him, in the face of all they saw, consoled by that tall giant in their midst, towering, by tradition new Tsar at the moment of death. Their continuity. This tired blood wasting away. But the Heir in our midst, seed, a ruler born.

But this powerlessness.

This dreadful exposure - bones! - raw naked gleaming flesh - never meant thus to be seen - that once proud body brimming with energy - tall - handsome - so strong.

Unbearable dread all our life exposed - such a seeming - so frail - vulnerable - easily shattered.

That torn flesh slow ooze our own shattered shrunken form binding us so close, freezing.

Tall one in our midst soon to release us from the spell of that shattered shrunken form - dear dear Tsar.

Hurry! Hurry! Dreadful our exposure!

Scissors were used to cut open the Tsar's jacket down the back.

"Nothing can be done," said Dr Kruglevsky after a brief examination.

"No! - no! - you must do something to save him," Catherine insisted frantically.

To console her Dr Kruglevsky took the proffered bandages and began to bind the bleeding stump. Catherine sprinkled water on the Tsar's face and brought the oxygen balloons close to his nose and mouth.

Grand Duke Alexander was gripped by guilt, over a terrible thought which would not leave him, savage spectre, his, him, that all this was justified! Seek his forgiveness - never closer - seek forgiveness!

Everyone sought out that one unseeing eye, and listened tensely.

The head had begun to move slowly from side to side as if by itself. Dr Kruglevsky's fingers remained on the Tsar's pulse.

"The end is near," he said.

The priest began the last sacraments. An uncontrollable trembling, shaking, flung away from him the golden spoon holding the mixture of bread and wine, to lie forlorn on the blood stained carpet.

The new Tsar is with us. This one, whom we know is made differently, very differently.

Dr Kruglevsky gently let the Tsar's hand down onto the couch.

"The Tsar is dead," he announced in a loud voice.

That means the Heir is now the Tsar - long live the Tsar!

The words, the loudness, brought Grand Duke Alexander into his own, this harshness of his destiny now demanding. A standing forth for the task ahead beginning now. The waiting over. Had he been waiting then? Accept that!

Catherine lay fallen on the floor in a faint after screaming out. Grand Duke Alexander's equerry, quickly attuned to the new order of things left the study and ordered in two palace guards to carry the young widow to her private apartment. Grand Duke Alexander found the business very distasteful, she become once again, intruder, outsider, enemy. But she had given his father some happiness - enough! - leave it at that!

One last look was demanded, as a son, before he left the study, where Doctors Kruglevsky and Botkin, remained with two valets de chambre. As a son, his father's work over, with a son's tearfulness he knew the way he would go, tenderness, respect, becoming recast into iron resolve. To live this deed as done to himself. To strike back, assuage this guilt, seek recompense, heal Russia. Taken into himself as absolute duty his father's martyrdom. No rest till the swine caught, hanged, seen hanging by all Russia.

Outside in the corridor Police Colonel Pisnaya approached.

"The police await your orders Sire," he questioned anxiously, well aware of his men's catastrophic failure, to the very last.

"The police! - Orders? The Army will take charge of the situation! I shall confer with my ministers at once in the Anichkov Palace," Alexander snapped, leaving him abruptly.

No! That, Merciful God, was not the Emperor, on the couch.

He would show them who the Emperor was. Let them tremble.

Russia would be brought back onto the right path. No more ambiguity. No more confusion. All blessing to his father's gracious memory. But his father had yielded to the Melikovs.

That was over.

The Autocrat's will could not be destroyed by bombs.

Let the mourning begin. But he must take stock away from this Palace, this city, these people, all become hateful to him.

Pobedonostsev's advice teaching assuredness faith, as a rock now. That, amidst the grief, shock, real enough, he was ready for it. How well armed he felt - plans! actions! work! the work ahead with Constantin Petrovich the friend.

Pobedonostsev's words never faltering, consistent, that this liberalising was not the way. With clenched will, implacable resolve he would burn out utterly all opposition, knowing confidently that such sacrifice was a necessity for Russia's salvation.

That shrivelling ghostly trunkform etched indelibly, never to forget.

Rumour and speculation spread rapidly. Coincidence? That on the very day of signing the draft law which definitely was intended to increase public participation in government - he was killed. Very strange coincidence! And that the police and Cossacks wandered around the place with him till the second bomb was thrown. Very odd!

Clear enough that the Court party had every reason to act, to stop once and for all the whole Melikov reform business even at this price.

Or, was it really conceivable that the terrorists were in such absolute command of the situation? Then woe betide Russia!

Or, with our new Tsar - woe betide the terrorists!

The following day a printed manifesto from the People's Will party appeared in the city and was made known to workers throughout the capital.

"Today, March 14, Alexander II, the tormentor of the people, has been put to death by us, socialists: He was killed because he did not care for his people, burdened them with unauthorised taxes, deprived the peasants of their land and surrendered the workers to the mercy of plunderers and exploiters. He did not give the people freedom. He did not listen to their griefs and their tears. He defended only the rich and lived himself in the utmost luxury while the people went hungry. The Tsar's servants, from the village priest to the high officials, plundered the people and barbarously maltreated the peasants. These servants of the Tsar were especially protected and rewarded by the Tsar. Those who stood out for the people he hanged or exiled to Siberia. So

he was killed. A Tsar should be a good shepherd, ready to lay down his life for his flock. Alexander II was a ravening wolf and a terrible death has struck him. Now a new Tsar, Alexander III climbs to the throne. He must not be allowed to behave like his father. May he proceed to hold general elections in all the villages, towns and factories. May he recognise the sorrows and deep needs of the people and go forward into the truth."

The Winter Palace was surrounded by guards of the Preobrajensky Regiment standing with fixed bayonets at twenty five yard intervals. Guards were stationed at several government buildings including the Admiralty and War Office. The police had barricaded off a large area along the Canal route on rumours that mines were planted beneath it. Orders were drawn up for Cossacks and police to start house-to-house searches. The general mood was for punitive action. Action at whatever cost. To do something, to do anything. To show that the authorities were in command, were the authorities. Soon the whole city was draped in black with guards everywhere. Exposed, raw, was a deep unease, people looking at one another in diffident ways. The city was becoming small, unfamiliar, shrunken around the explosion.

Amidst hectic orders, confusion, Alexander, on impulse, decided to go away on his own for a short while. He sent for Colonel Prince Yuri Galitzyn, in command of the Preobrajensky, confidante of many years. One of the few with whom he felt at ease.

Galitzyn hurried to the Tsar's study from his command post in the western wing of the palace. He knew with pride and relief that to this man now Tsar he would gladly give his all in loyal service. No more doubt. He knew where this man stood and his life would be at his disposal. A strong Tsar, a strong monarchy, a strong Russia.

The study door was posted by two Guards Chevalier with fixed bayonets. They saluted. One knocked on the door, opened it and announced him. He entered and declared affirmatively, "Sire!" They both tasted its unfamiliarity, accepting it till then on first name terms. Alexander reached out for a handclasp at once pledge of unity, witness to the past, renewal for the future. Knot of sacrifice, fusion of lives.

Colonel Galitzyn felt an unfamiliar strangeness, felt as never before this man's vulnerability, burden, isolation. He would protect him to the end.

"Yuri!"

Still Yuri!

"I must get away from here. Come with me."

Question? Order?

"Of course Sire."

"Then let's go, before dark."

"But where?"

"Gatchina," answered Alexander on impulse.

"Gatchina? – alone – just you and me – now?"

"Why not?"

Why not indeed?

"But the matter of your safety Sire?"

"My safety? All right then – a detachment too."

Colonel Galitzyn hurried back and ordered the immediate assembly of a large detachment. Led by their Colonel and their new Tsar they set off at a fast pace into the crimson light of the setting sun. Yes, they knew who he now was and that Russia too must be shown who he now was. His power their power. Their power his power. His power their strength and pride to sweep forth against Russia's enemies. Emblazoned, watchful, advancing.

They skirted the city onto the roadway running some twenty five miles south west.

To be in the saddle with them, amidst them, was relief, easing the anguish. Borne, easily, spacious, on the wave of this thrusting life. The one surging wave carrying them all beneath the darkening sky, the open road ahead. Away from that city, that life, that deed. This plunging and soaring flight binding them all. Onwards, thrusting onwards through the stark, cold air. For ever like this?

As they approached Gatchina Palace, gently silhouetted by a fine rising radiance against the night sky, he knew the rightness of this impulse. This was the place. Still here as of old. The woods, forest, grassy banks leading down to the lake's edge, all so still, firm, as it had ever been. And the Palace itself, stern, stark, resonant with some absolute necessity.

Here, to be alone, coming into his own. Treading as of old through the grounds with Yuri, knowing that he had met with his destiny. Now to realise with awe and acceptance who he was. Acceptance – Gatchina's gift to him. Necessity this – Russia couldn't afford to lose two Tsars in one year. Necessity too that the relatives – all of them – would be stopped from calling too frequently. Even at all! Necessity too away – right away from the capital's hateful life! All to be taken care of by blessed Gatchina.

But – isn't this some damned cowardice – being forced to retreat before those swine – what! for life? – after facing the Turkish guns!

Rising early he wandered through the grounds of his youth. A space was forming around him, a clearing, charged, grim. The place where he could begin his work, take up his destined task. A new strength was arising to face that dread. Let him call on God's guidance and wisdom. Nothing less would do. Firm. Firm as these mighty firs. By Gatchina standing firm.

The troops stood to in the chill morning air outside the Palace and sabres were raised, to glint in the steepening light. Calm, clear, was the dawn ride back. Yes, a flight, but a flight to take soundings. Within their sheltering space he was returning, determined, assured.

At Police H.Q., Chief interrogator Colonel Dobrinsky's concern, now more than ever, was that painstaking preparation, so necessary for the waywardness of individual souls. The Tsar wanted results quickly. He wanted them all caught tried hanged as soon as possible and confidence restored to the nation. Torture might yet be necessary if only to convince that everything possible was being done. That no scruples stood in the way. But torture was primitive. These men were not ordinary criminals.

He could not afford any error of judgement over this one captive. First, habitual, he must gain as accurate a picture of the event as possible, letting it kindle the feeling that something important had occurred at that point. Then, responding to the individual soul – ah! that responding! – gently to explore. To stand back impersonally. To intervene so subtly that the soul itself revealed the key to its own unlocking. There, the sweetest challenge. Tact, flexibility, patience, he instructed his subordinates, but knew that the essential could not be taught.

After hearing accounts from two gendarmes who survived the explosion, he felt a deepening significance in the meeting between the murdered Tsar and Rysakov. He felt it to be of decisive importance for Rysakov but what the 'it' was exactly, remained beyond his grasp. He questioned the two gendarmes again, to approach the scene from different perspectives, to create, refine, a more living image. The Tsar's look, steps, gestures, tone of voice, especially noting the unexpectedness and bewilderment experienced by them over the Tsar's behaviour. Even hearing resentment and anger in their recall of the Tsar's order, 'Leave him alone!'

The unexpectedness, which they intimated had somehow affected Rysakov. The unexpectedness, there the key, for probing, delicately probing.

What had happened he would never know. That something essential had happened he felt certain. Relating himself in this faithful way to his trusted insight, he would patiently explore.

The blinding blast of Grinevitsky's bomb, the knowledge that the deed was done, had flung Rysakov into a serene, radiant place, looking down at the consternation of these shocked, frightened creatures who snatched desperately at the body they thought was him. Radiance with him still, challenging the very stoniness of these cell walls. Radiance dissolving time, so many fighters for the people's freedom together with him in this new now blasted open by Grinevitsky's bomb. A new beginning was possible. The regime shown vulnerable, naked, would be forced to yield. Momentous – fire – the beginning – that decision in the Lipetsk woods to assassinate the bloody tyrant.

"The new Tsar wants it done in style – the whole city to watch it – the whole bunch strung up together –,"

At first from a great distance, such words during the day, permeated the space around him, fixing a limit, staining the stone with hardness, earth reality, grim. The radiance dwindling. The stale familiar congealing.

He reached out and touched the walls, the stone of their reality.

From this sombre depth someone unexpectedly emerged.

The one who had approached him, spoken to him.

One?

Who was that man?

He could not hold it off.

It was not as they had declaimed so rousingly after the failure of the railway bomb – the personification of hypocritical despotism. That if he goes the system will collapse.

He had tasted bitterly, in spite of himself, something different from that in the one who had approached him.

Swiftly from the uncanny silence fear of the end closed in, unbearable. He would hang. Glorious vision of a better Russia now ghostly hope. Wildly the potentiality of his youthful life burned brilliantly - proclaiming a vast unrealised future. Not to be.

He did not want to die.

The stony silence pounded at him.

The cell door opened and men approached to lead him out.

Men! Fellow men. Faces - bodies - walking with you. Where had he been? Where was he going? as they moved through the labyrinthine passageways of this shadowy underground ascending, clearer, brighter, wood panelling, door quietly opening into the comfortable well furnished office.

What world is this?

Only fitfully a thing here - a voice there - no cohesion.

What did this man want?

This greying man calmly approaching from behind the large mahogany desk piled with documents and files.

Not another word.

His end was certain.

Let him be as one dead - fitfully torn by the jagged fragment of his life.

These were beings from another world.

And this one?

His mouth is moving. Sounds issue from it. So far away. So tiny, dwindling.

You have bidden them goodbye.

Why then through this emptiness does he make these silent gestures?

Don't dare unclench from your numbness.

He wants something from you. The comrades.

Colonel Dobrinsky gently indicated the two waiting chairs. The challenge of this impassive stare from the one opposite demanded an opening move which would hopefully indicate an orientation.

"My dear Rysakov -"

Rysakov made no effort to connect these words with himself, they were so utterly unrelated.

"I am Colonel Paul Dobrinsky and my concern, my life's task.. "

Life's task! groundnote of his existence too!

"..is the future of Russia. And you my young friend are part of our Russian future."

The speaking, the words, simply meant for Rysakov to hear.

Colonel Dobrinsky sensed with the most fleeting scrutiny, a lightening, an alertness in the other's look, no more, a lightening, but still set in stony posture.

Rysakov's numbness was giving way – "friend" – "our" – "Russian future" – "this Russian land here for all men of goodwill who want to work for our nation in the right way."

Here? – amongst men again – bliss – of what he could do – might do – myriads of deeds – starseed – fruition.

Colonel Dobrinsky allowed himself to look more directly at Rysakov, knowing that he was listening, even with concern, knowing this gently brooding light through which he was moving forward, holding to its insight, sense of direction, way of approach revealing, way forward one with this light revealing.

"Nikolai Rysakov, I am a man, like yourself. No more and no less. Our late Tsar was a man too. Murdered. To what avail? The Russian people have already made clear in their thousands all over the country what they feel. Utter revulsion. And remember Rysakov – how could you ever forget – that his very last conversation was with you. And what did you meet in him – a wild beast? How did he speak to you – his intended murderer – as a tyrant, merciless, hateful – or as a Christian, in mercy and forgiveness?"

Colonel Dobrinsky felt ever surer of his direction, born of instinct and experience, gently moving forward, holding to this insight, way of approach revealing itself, way forward one with the light revealing. He still watched keenly as Rysakov shook his head sharply to throw off that bewilderment when the Tsar had approached him.

"Our new Tsar is merciful too Rysakov. And forgiving."

Forgiving? Forgiving? What could that mean but?

"I too was a student once. We can all make mistakes. But we can redeem our mistakes for the sake of Russia. Make good what we've done wrong. More," – enjoying his fervency, noting the other's moistening eyes, "we can prevent others from committing the same mistakes – from spreading what we know to be wrong. We owe it to our country. Murdering an innocent man is wrong. Our Tsar is merciful. Give your future to Russia Rysakov, but in the right way. Go on with your studies. Work with the men who have Russia's future at heart, not against them. And did you know, Rysakov, that our late revered monarch had signed that very morning a draft law, granting his beloved people more freedom?"

Forgiveness – mercy – mistakes – just signed!

What was he supposed to do?

Prevent others from spreading these errors.

How?

Names! Names! Addresses.

Our Tsar is merciful not a wild beast.

Rysakov was moved to a light, comfortable cell. The books included a Bible and works on mining.

Soon he was attacked by a violent consternation. But it was too late! But then nothing could stop him doing it again. But then what! – the whole bunch strung up together – God of Mercy – help!

Colonel Dobrinsky ordered that his treatment be most caring. A brief, well earned reward for his penance. On the basis of his information all the others were arrested within three weeks. Alexander was delighted. The trial was set for April 8th, merely a formality before the public hangings.

After a tiring afternoon advising and assisting petitioners from all over the country, who crowded into the special room which he had added on to his apartment for them, Constantin Petrovich Pobedonostsev, former Professor of Constitutional Law, returned to his study. Tiring, but fulfilment, rightness, savoured deep, beyond all such weaknesses of fallen man. Men and women needing funds for a convent, needing government permission for building a railway, needing publication of a manuscript, needing the transfer of an incompetent priest, needing advice for the establishing of a new school. All of these needs to be scrupulously dealt with in the light of that ultimate goal, the hope and the prayer never yielding, for a Christian Orthodox State.

Work for the Lord.

Hour by hour, day by day, work!

Life given from Above, life dedicated in return for Holy Russia, Holy Church where he had been placed. Yes, in spite of, in the face of death, time's flight – wretched Russian man!

From the countrywide Church reports carefully arranged on

his desk, financial, demographic, complainant, two issues demanded resolution before completing his first annual Church report to the Tsar, as recently appointed Procurator to the Synod.

How many non-Orthodox were there? And what to do about these wretched sects?

And the Jews! Now, as Procurator, become a concrete, practical issue, with regard to a completely Orthodox Russian State. Completely!

Constantin's wife Catherine, at thirty four younger by twenty years, looked down into the street below from the window of their plainly furnished living room for long after the last of the petitioners had left and the all too familiar silence returned, those voices, the lively conversation, that tide of life so rapidly receding leaving her helplessly stranded in this sad void. Those lives in the street below - contentment? Could not be anything like this. Such bitterness- from where? Such black guilt. Lord! Lord! Help me not drown.

Let me remember - my Constantin.

Constantin - tutor - intimate friend - mentor of the future Tsar - Procurator of the Holy Synod - mediator for needy souls from all over Russia!

But from him to her - came nothing at all!

Had it ever been different?

What was she getting at? Why this dreadful confusion?

Books articles reports papers meetings never a moment left - for what?

He didn't need her!

Wretched wretched Devil's thoughts flaying her like this. Lord help me Your faithful servant.

What was going on down there?

Little groups gathering, people hurrying out to join them, words here and there - but staring at one another.

What did any of that matter to her?

Don't dare Satan to consider yourself as one dead.

Rouse yourself. Go!

Several people were standing quietly at the entrance to the building.

"What's the matter - whatever's going on," she demanded,

"The Tsar's been murdered - dreadfully murdered - "

"Torn limb from limb - "

She hurried back up the stairs, that Constantin must be told immediately. Immediately - now? - actually to interrupt him whilst working? That had never been.

But, this was the first absolutely justified occasion for interrupting Constantin and she must take advantage of it. Why! even more than justified.

Must - with the breath of that smile - Captain Baranov's smile Captain Baranov so much lit up by it. This fearful seeing forced on her - that smile beckoning - that for him - she was not showing herself as she really was. This terrible comparing - forced on her not wanted. Forced to see by the light of that handsome smile, this thin bald black-garbed dry one - as stranger beholding spellbound. It should have been him! It should have been Baranov!

It wouldn't be silenced - but not - not she! had thought this. Lord save her in this house!

Pobedonostsev added and re-added the bishops' figures. It meant, even allowing for a large margin of error, that the sects accounted for at least fifteen percent of the population. That explained a great deal with regard to the country's moral malaise. Yes, it was good that at last he'd got hold of these firm numbers. So much they told.

Stern action would be necessary and he would set about it. But, but, that dreadful impiety of the Tsar himself. The Tsar had confirmed his appointment. From Above then - to be his conscience!

And the Jews? At least the chance to make him more aware of the problem. To declare bluntly that there was no hope of spreading Christianity amongst them. Their chosen race idea - strong family ties - age old religious traditions - all as stiff-necked as ever. A few converts a year but they precisely, very questionable.

Thus much for the Tsar's attention.

But - now helpless as ever before the real problem presence of the Yids - this bitter pain - their vile threat to Russian life. Over four million of them! All, despisers of Our Lord.

Then for what could one possibly hope, with these four million?

How? that they be effectively cast out from Russian life.

Emigration - assimilation - a dying out - all such feeble hopes - four million!

But something must be done.

Her footsteps approaching?

The sanctum threatened! His very breathing checked.

What did it mean? How could it be?

What could have made it possible?

Who was that?

Why was she standing outside the door like that, and he reduced to this helpless uncertainty? So hauntingly glimpsed – some unfamiliar power yet to come into its own.

Catherine's pleasure at being absolutely justified in interrupting him at his work, in breaking down the barrier, deserted her at the very threshold for trepidation and grief – torn limb from limb!

To flee?

So much involved now as she ventured a timid knock. To tell in whatever voice available, and withdraw. He, after all, was the centre of it all.

Might it bring them closer?

She opened the door, stepped in no more than a pace, found a voice, restrained.

"The Tsar has been murdered – brutally murdered – torn limb from limb – " she said, not looking directly at him, tearfulness forcing her to withdraw, shutting the door gently.

All well and good!

Of course she'd had to tell him.

Fully justified. Stand stern against her tearfulness. Russia's life the issue here. Not the pitiful way of a misguided Tsar.

Her message – the word from Above.

Hold firm against this furious thrust of pride. All is as you have ever believed, followed and taught your prince. The false way now proved to be so – that all may know and see. A pitiful man whose will was clearly exhausted.

God has judged. That he's been guilty of wasting dishonouring the power and authority entrusted by God. His private life flabby, immoral. Your faith fully justified by this word – revelation – command from Above.

The waiting is over, for you, your prince and Russia.

After the silent evening meal he returned to his study. Urgent the need to reassert, confirm from now on as living reality, protect from any slightest possible threat leaving nothing to chance, all that lived between them over the years and was now come to pass. To strengthen from this very moment his prince's will against any possibility of its weakening, before the daunting task ahead.

As frank as you've ever been with him, your truth is his.

"Sire, be warned in this grave moment. Never to consider the Loris-Melikov constitutional proposals. They'll all be singing that old siren's song that it is necessary to be calm and to continue in the liberal direction. That it is necessary to yield to so-called public opinion. For God's sake Your Majesty, do not believe and do not listen! It will be the ruin of Russia and of you. This is as clear as day to me. It is necessary to end at once, now, all the talk about freedom of the press, about popular meetings, about a representative assembly.

These are all lies spoken by superficial and weak people. It is absolutely essential to reject them for the good of the true people."

More, so vital, spell it out to him, as you spelt out so much in the past and he perfectly attuned - writing now as one whose words are becoming Russian destiny - to one through whom these words must become deeds.

"Sire, there is only one way, the true straight path. Stand on your own feet and without waiting a minute begin the struggle, the most sacred Russia has faced. Loris-Melikov's proposals and his supporters must be destroyed root and branch."

Two days later Alexander called him for a meeting at the Anitchkov Palace. He was ready. He was surely being asked to guide, to point the way ahead. He must be careful not to confuse or overwhelm. Patience. All now clearly the working of God. No human hurry or arrogance would avail.

Now for the first time to prepare for the possibility of going beyond what belief, conscience and duty had always dictated. The possibility of indicating in some detail the ways by which this true Russian future could be assured. Possibility? More than possibility if God so willed it.

Deeply reassuring this call from the Emperor. The Emperor. Strange. No - a familiar resonance long present! - only now to realise that prophetic feeling - that things could not go on like this forever and that God would find a way.

When he arrived at the small Anitchkov Palace on the Nevsky, which Alexander had moved into with his family, troops were everywhere, mounted and on foot, checking all visitors in and out. Guards were posted at twenty pace intervals along the front. Good! That was the strength Russia needed. But it was irritating to be kept waiting in a small side room until an aide appeared who knew him only by sight and who brusquely led him to the Tsar's study.

The guard's questioning stare sharpened his irritation. Unwillingly he proffered his name. The guard knocked, carefully opened the door and announced it. The Tsar approached, welcoming with outstretched arm, and Pobedonostsev regained his composure as their handclasp, his dry, bony hand almost enfolded by that warm, huge grip, confirmed the trust, the living bond. Yet touched with strangeness too. Confirmed yet different.

"My dear Constantin Petrovich you have been proved right, absolutely right," began Alexander when they sat down.

Never had Alexander felt so right in wearing the Chevalier Guards uniform. As a soldier he would mourn his father. As a soldier he would lead Russia against the enemy. Pobedonostsev looked protectively, compassionately at him, now burdened with this immense responsibility, yet all in God's will. Anxious for Alexander yet - what lack of faith was this?

"My humble condolences Sire," he said, glancingly drawn to a portrait of the late deceased behind the large mahogany desk, and crossing himself. Alexander crossed himself. Both acknowledged the need but with an embarrassment.

Slowly and carefully!

Take nothing for granted despite that absolute rightness. Despite as pupil taught only in the ways of the same God who had called both, whom both served. He may not at all stand where you think. In belief, feeling, yes perhaps, but give him time to make this new situation his own.

"Constantin Petrovich these scum have shown just how far they're prepared to go," said Alexander, "but they've made a big mistake. They thought they chose my father but they've chosen me! - The Zemstvo legislation will of course go through. That was my father's dearest hope - to bring about harmony for his people," he continued with provocative intent.

"No! No Sire!" Pobedonostsev responded vehemently, his letter of no avail?

"The Zemstvo legislation was the last nail in your father's coffin. Nor is he to blame. His naivetè was being used ruthlessly."

Alexander heard gladly in that voice the resolution of his

ambivalence. Whether to allow the legislation, in reverence to his father's memory and appeasement for his remorse, even though it was in absolute contradiction to all that Constantin Petrovich and he himself believed in.

"Let me be frank. In Russia we see two types of men. True Russians and those who masquerade as Russians, but who want to bring about Russia's destruction."

Listening gladly, knowing that nothing could turn aside this voice from the path it believed to be right, for both of them.

"Your father's weakness was to surround himself with the masqueraders. You Sire, must gather round you the true Russians. Go into the holy Russian temple and in the name of Christ cleanse it! The Zemstvo legislation must not go through! That whole Loris-Melikov machination must be stopped now!"

Alexander listened intently. Pobedonostsev knew the time had come.

"Very soon Sire, you must come to close grips with those vilest of all anti-Russian creatures. The real destroyers and subverters who make Melikov's lot look like beginners. I mean those who have it in their very blood."

Alexander felt that certainty as a sheltering power. This man would stake his life on these words. Their meaning was charged with his life as one who had the truth.

But unfamiliar was this passion, urgency enlivening a dryness which had long both attracted him and repelled him. Behind the horn-rimmed glasses Pobedonostsev's eyes, face, brightened with some inner fire.

"I mean the Yids, Sire, the Yids!" only right sounding name for their loathsomeness. "Our Russian life is being poisoned – slowly, deliberately. Liberalism – constitutionalism – socialism – revolution, all from the same source. They're determined to destroy the Christian heart of Russia."

"Indeed!" said Alexander, never before having heard such an absolute indictment from Constantin Petrovich, such a flame burning through that dryness.

"They control the periodical press and the financial markets. They even try to control scientific thinking and keep it outside Christianity – and no one says a word. Even our own press is becoming Jewified – Russian Truth – Golos – organs for the Yids."

"The government hasn't even begun to take the matter seriously. Who knows what bribes were involved under the late lamented's flabbiness - laxity - " he swept on, " You must take the lead, Sire. The people know well that these stiff-necked haters of the Faith would destroy us all. The people must be given a lead. A plan must be drawn up to eradicate this problem, once and for all."

Plan, task, impulse for action, its challenging rightness strengthening him for the future, his father's portrait wan, distant. No hurry.

No hurry. He was the master now. In his own good time he would take it up. But no evasion any more.

"Until the source of the poison is dealt with all other measures are superficial," continued Pobedonostsev, "The Russian people want the Jews out. The Russian people want to see the dynasty served by true Russian representatives. Men who know that to be a true Russian means to be an Orthodox Christian servant of an Orthodox Christian State. For or against! The pure strong light of Christ, or the evil of those who crucified Our Lord and spilled his precious blood."

They sat in silence.

Pobedonostsev wondered whether he'd gone too far too fast.

Awkwardly, unexpectedly Alexander felt pressed to stand back, to distance himself from Constantin Petrovich.

"Whom do you suggest?" he asked, wanting to hear yet uneasy.

"At the key post for this battle - this sacred battle, Count Nicholas Ignatiev. Sound instincts. A Russian soul. Held in high esteem by the simple folk. Begin immediately with him. No more uncertainty Sire - you must act immediately. This uncertainty is the greatest evil. Melikov - Abaza - Grand Duke Nicholas, must all be removed as soon as possible. Ignatiev at the Interior - utterly devoted to Russia - proved on the battlefield and in the embassies. Energetic - able - and hates the whole liberal gang. And for the security of this city - Baranov. Great initiative. Certainly a touch of roguery - but discipline, organisation - and dedication to the dynasty first and last. That's Baranov, and they're the kind we need from now on," he continued with a rare enthusiasm, "real Russian men. Not those eunuchs lacking any firm will, any ardent spirit. Vacillators - traitors - who held a weak Tsar in their power -"

Yes, let him say it all, cleanse, purge.

"treason - that's how the common people see the

assassination. Those madmen who killed your father must be fought to the death - as Ignatiev and Baranov will. Both of them men who know that a constitution is basically evil - - Sire! you've been chosen to lead and win the most sacred battle in Russia's history."

Alexander was convinced and delighted. Such clarity, fearless, selfless judgement, only for Russia's good. God be praised.

"I shall think it over my dear Constantin Petrovich," he said, feigning cautiousness. "Rest assured, I see the struggle ahead just as you do. From now on you have my complete backing in all Church matters."

Pobedonostsev shut his eyes, serene, touched with the gentlest tremor of a great force.

"Sire, may we with grace further God's holy purpose."

"Constantin Petrovich, please take as your first task a draft for my Accession Declaration. Make it absolutely clear - in words that can't be misinterpreted, what I stand for and intend."

After Pobedonostsev left, Alexander felt himself at a threshold with Constantin Petrovich's words, the power, the vehemence, yet - to be held off, that vehemence. So deeply needing to hear, yet, to draw back from. Constantin Petrovich as ever, like granite through and through. Yet, dimly, the need to nurture that distance felt in his presence for this first time. To nurture, maintain, guard - but always to have him speak absolutely freely - essential.

Alexander looked back at the portrait before leaving, to sense at last some peace in the separation. Pobedonostsev, back at his desk to begin on the Accession draft, knew now that his words, each one, bore the weight of deed and destiny for all true Russians. No longer simply belief - faith - ah that 'simply' - elemental truth you fools! - but even as he wrote on - as scribe - servant - drawing down the grandeur of the building - its ancient sheltering power held so firm in these words - to summon forth a new willing - deeds - deeds! - for true Russians everywhere.

No! Not his words - but the word of a servant of God.

"We, by the grace of God, Alexander III, Autocrat of all Russia" -

This 'We' - let it resonate - as groundtone of that new unity - now to become deed - held fast at this both beginning and end. This 'We' - be allowed to feel the intimacy of your pupil and yourself - thus called - thus calling - and that All! - which now must be inscribed in Russian life.

"Tsar of Poland, Grand Duke of Finland, pronounce to our loyal subjects" – words ever present of the timeless power

"that God, in His unfathomable will has called the Emperor Alexander III, to Himself.

The Emperor died at the hands of sinful murderers who saw in him Russia's great protector, and very rock of her might.

Before Divine Providence we bow.

We offer up our prayers for the soul of our much loved father.

We take up the throne of our forefathers, the grand dukedom of Finland, the Tsardom of Poland, connected with it inseparably."

remember! inseparably!

"We take up this great burden, relying firmly on God's help and guidance for the welfare of all our loyal subjects."

But not enough, not at all enough!

Not a question of misinterpretation but where was the deed—the challenging will?

So thrusting these other words pressing in – words for from Alexander – as soon as the hangings done with – words his and Alexander's demanding utterance now. That,

"The voice of God commands us to stand bravely at the helm of government, trusting in Divine Providence - and with faith in the power-" power! *"and truth of Absolutism."*

No misinterpretation possible here – Absolutism!

"We are determined to strengthen the State against any attempts to weaken Our power and this We do for the benefit of Our people."

D'you understand?

These words sound the true beginning, and only the beginning. What possibilities then pressing! To think of such word–deeds as now within his power regarding the Jews!

The Tsar was greatly reassured and encouraged by General Baranov's memorandum on security measures. Incisive, comprehensive, determined, the way forward, and to know that such men were there – right, Constantin Petrovich! and again right! And how quick the response, as though, as though – and why not? – that Baranov had long thought in this way – and was only waiting.

The city should be surrounded with Cossack patrols to check everyone who entered or left. A Grand Council should be set up to watch over all members of the Imperial family wherever they be. All cabdrivers should list and report the addresses to which they took their fares. All landlords should keep scrupulous watch over their tenants. All servants should watch and report anything suspicious about their masters and fellow servants.

A real tightening up, all well and good. Of course the only real security was in submission to God's will, nevertheless everything humanly possible must also be done for the sake of his subjects' sense of security, in that he himself was secure. Of course, the very least humanly, to continue sleeping with the pistol under his pillow.

General Baranov insisted that the Tsar should leave the city and take up residence in Gatchina. Its seclusion provided the best possible security for the Imperial family. The Winter Palace with its quarter mile frontage along the Neva was impossible to guard adequately. From now on every royal journey through St Petersburg must be regarded as a dangerous undertaking.

Excellent!

Gatchina! not at all forced out from this wretched city, but for the safety of the dynasty, for Russia.

Thousands of troops were moved onto the Gatchina estate. Dozens of small encampments were set up and the whole area ringed with sentries at twenty-five yard intervals, changing over every four hours. Specially chosen agents in plain clothes were to discreetly observe all palace personnel, all palace guards, all visitors, and send daily reports to the Ministry of the Interior. No one was to be admitted without a permit bearing a photograph of the holder on the reverse side.

A railway battalion was formed whose duties included the checking and guarding of all the routes on which the Tsar was to travel. On every trip two Imperial trains were to be used and nobody except the guards would know till the very last moment which train would carry the Tsar and his party. For those visits to St Petersburg necessitated by ministerial business, an armour plated carriage once belonging to Napoleon III, stood ready.

The Tsar ordered a quick trial and involved himself in the details of the hangings as a duty.

If it were only possible - every single Russian should file past - day after day - till the bodies turned to stone. Hanging there forever. A memorial to evil and its defeat. Better still the whole nation assembled together and watching. To see - to feel - to know - that they're being well protected as of old. One people, united, strong.

On March 23rd he was shown a copy of a lengthy open letter circulating in the city, from the Executive Committee of the People's Will party and personally addressed to him.

"Whilst fully comprehending your deep sorrow - - the issue remains unchanged - - revolution inevitable - - or the voluntary transfer of supreme power into the hands of the people - - we too have cause for bitterness - - you have lost a father - - "

How dare they mention – utter such words!

"We have lost brothers fathers wives children dearest friends - - we do not impose conditions. These have been imposed by history. We merely state them. A general amnesty for all political crimes as those were not crimes but rather the fulfilment of social duty - - the summoning of the representatives of the whole nation - -

And so Your Majesty decides."

Decide he would!

Show these stubborn lunatics he would that he had the God entrusted power of life and death.

The trial date was announced for April 8th. Great relief was felt everywhere. Only days then to the hangings! For so many the fear, the vulnerability so brutally exposed, the awful guilt, were subdued, thrust back by the news. The omnipotence of the dynasty, of the established order had as ever – dared doubt? – proved itself to be the fundamental reality of their lives. A secure hierarchy, each in his rightful comforting place, and God's eternal justice to annihilate every murdering madman threatening it.

With tremulous words of praise and adoration they could kneel in homage to their Tsar once more. Divine justice had triumphed, as ever. Justice for the Tsar, and for the one who was martyred in the Calvary of the Ekaterininsky Canal. Now already they could begin to follow in the hallowed footsteps of the One, the Invincible, the Sacred Hope, the August Leader who had succeeded to the Throne.

But the nightmare was not done with yet. And the guilt was very real. That wound gaped open still. Not till the rope bit deep and the body dangled would relief be theirs. Only then would the terror be purged, of that miserable freedom which the swinging corpses had dared to awaken. A purging of that evil with which we helplessly felt akin. But already, before the hangings, that fearful dream lived through, and beyond and we returning to the normal the habitual and secure.

On the opening day of the trial Vladimir Solovyev became increasingly preoccupied with its significance for himself and Russia. The implications for his lecture that evening on contemporary education far transcended any lecture. Something here felt of absolute significance. Something that would have to be done - to the murderers. Murderers murdered Tsar new Tsar hangings people watching, wider and wider reaching out in anguish this ceaseless shedding of blood crying Halt! No more! Peace!

Such distress for Russia!

Everywhere the call for bloody vengeance.

Such fury and delight that blood for blood would be theirs.

That the Law ruled absolute, and their life thus secured.

Exultant at this victory of the Law.

And there, just there each time, ever living memory of Her blessed Presence - heart's radiant blueness - drawn, drawn to the All in all.

To feel for the first time, urgently, through this ever-living memory of Her presence - encouragement, world-knowledge - pure joy of primal creation -

all of it as preparation for a deed.

That blessing freely given of Her presence, now as gravest duty felt, inspiring his free deed for Russia.

He - alone - puny - feeling only - groping - but urgent.

Feeling, still only feeling that the decisiveness of this moment for Russia was in the mending - restoring - somehow - of the unity - union - living human bond - so human bond - with those murderers - on earth.

Pardon - forgiveness - begins here, alone - yet in the presence of that memory - living memory of Her - to make possible the bearing of this deed.

Only one could do this! The Tsar.

He - puny - alone - it was all impossible

The hall of the Mutual Credit Society was crowded with an eagerly waiting audience. Since the outstanding success of his lectures on Godmanhood, whose audience included Tolstoy and Dostoyevsky, the hall was always crowded with enthusiastic admirers, whenever a lecture by this young philosopher and theologian was announced. They heard an original, profound, eloquent speaker telling of Christ's world-redemptive task in co-operation with man. Clear thoughts were weaving a life-giving substance, tender, serene, a yearning for man's highest. They sensed that resonance of an all-embracing wisdom sounded with that yearning, saddened before that primal day of creation, roused by that challenge from the future, that task which only Christian mankind could achieve.

They left knowing that his word held life. Not mere thoughts but the lifeblood of their spirit pulsing anew.

As he spoke, this evening of the eighth, he had to bear the presence of another speaking awaiting urgent. He felt his customary speaking as comfortable, all too comfortable. When he finished, the familiar applause only sharpened his awareness that this speaking which till now he had done, would not change anything!

He purposely chose to walk back to his hotel room alone, after friendly words, greetings, goodnights.

Everything to know that the vast Semenovsky Square was to be the place of retribution. He made for it through a world of burning flesh sweet to the ancient god's nostril, reeking, smoking, this Petersburg sky. That, made null on Golgotha. Forgive them Lord - for they know not what they do.

No! Not that!

Only to this No holding fast, still in this darkness of faith, made ready for the deed that must be done. Nothing could still this city's fury unless inspired from above. Unless revealed by the Helper, the Radiant One.

The frenzied to be calmed, gratefully. The eternal foundation revealed, recalled once more on which alone Russians could build their lives - forgiveness - very ground!

Only with strength from Him to turn against this raging tide.

To calm this seething blood with tenderness and peace.

The reality of Christ's power on earth.

During the early hours he awoke at his desk, in fear and trembling, the risk standing sternly, confronting.

Life or death - alone - a trial.

To prove - himself.

Who he really was.

Such fear as he had never known.

The deed that must be done, hinting at such a fearful aloneness yet - through it he would know who he was.

42

Sensing through it - the pure doing - in belief of its rightness - a turning point - a new life - nothing less. Through it to come into his very own. The deed would make it so. Anything less, a betrayal of himself - of Russia.

Turn to that radiant blue of Her being, all-embracing.

Unity with the Tsar - but too - unity with the terrorists - and hadn't he himself been a materialist - socialist - communist - atheist - destroyer of icons - so starkly recalled - judgement? - compelled to unity with them!

In the dawn light gently revealing the world of this struggle he stood up, went to the samovar and made some tea.

He must not let go.

Hours counted. Time too must be challenged.

Somehow, somehow, it would be done through the concluding lecture tomorrow evening.

Only one had the power to end this ceaseless shedding of blood and he must be approached - appealed to.

First! absolute! orientation by that deed-to-be-done.

Deed-to-be-done sounding so keenly the desert of silence around him. Not a word from the entire Church!

Was he mad with the call of this deed? Made to stand against the entire Church! - and this city's rapturous murmuring over the gallows.

Only that one had the power to end it, Tsar! chosen by God.

He? alone? puny? Being asked in perfect freedom to find himself with that one - with that one? - yes! - two deeds were calling - two persons - the two deeds one.

To be so close to the Tsar whom he knew not.

Two deeds approaching, seeking them both out as one, to become their deeds. Destiny deeds, inseparable, his and the Tsar's.

What?

That he would have to spell out what the anointed of God must - could - only follow God in his way - the way of forgiveness!

Only he could forgive them and through him Russia.

He? alone? puny? being asked - to what? - to dare remind? that one of the Living Truth who had elected him.

Everything now in Russia to be tried by this Truth. The Tsar's very anointing!

Only the way of pardon - forgiveness. Nothing less would do.

This was the risk, the trial beyond all doubt.

Of course it was impossible! But nothing less would do. No letter would ever reach him. What words could he ever use?

But it must be done - and he must do it. For the sake of the deed alone.

Or at least, the very least in daring, to present the Tsar with this as possibility.

Yes! A magic was needed, called on, Christ's magic. Fear and Fear not!

And yet again to think through in His Light - gain courage - more certainly - forgiveness.

Forgiveness by the Tsar means - that the living bond with them on earth where the Christ set foot, is mended, renewed -

means - trust - hope - an exemplary deed for Russians by their God-appointed representative -

means - shine Light, shine! - that the ruler of earthly power will transform it - sacrificial deed - to restore the bond of Universal Humanity.

The fire of his will burned pure but he must reason it through.

Just because the Tsar had the power of life and death as God's representative so he alone could reflect God's mercy on earth. Just this mercy, transforming power, would break the endless cycle of vengeance.

Forgiveness alone would reflect the Tsar's Christian election.

Heart's deed to reform, reorder in a Christian brotherly way. This seething chaos appealed for order through the life-giving deed which called men to Christ.

He would have men as himself, knowing that bliss. For always the two worlds. The cold shrunken substance of this earth and the soaring space of the heights - meant for all.

As long as the monarchy appeared to rest on earthly power alone it would be vulnerable to that same earthly power. This deed of pardon would reveal its spiritual foundations and prove it unassailable.

On the morning of the 10th he knew that it must be done tonight, in public, before men. Only this simplest truth which all knew in their hearts. Nor would be protective reasoning here of any avail. That if all knew it, why such anxiety? That it was nothing but arrogance on his part, that - and that - all, endlessly all of no avail before the challenge to do this deed in freedom.

Planning ahead for it led nowhere. No amount of fiddling about with this concluding lecture would - could! lead into it. Just so! Only possible to imagine, to prepare himself for an absolute break, yes absolute in that this much he knew, he would be calling through this deed, calling for deeds from them too and somehow from them to the Tsar.

Before leaving the hotel room he prayed that Her healing peace would guide his words, that all sting of judgement be drawn from them.

As he finished speaking familiar applause began, gathering, some on their feet clapping, grateful heads nodding, his familiar satisfaction dreaming - dreaming! awake awake! break through this temptation, spell!

"An evil senseless awful deed has happened," he went on, still on the rostrum, to everyone's surprise.

"The Tsar has been murdered. Those responsible have been captured. According to the law death awaits them as a retaliation, fulfilment of a pagan law, eye for an eye, death for a death -" borne, borne he knew, with this surging strength to utter it.

What? What?

Where is he going? taking us?

"But how should a truly Anointed of God act? The highest amongst us who bears the impulse of a Christian society -"

What? What is he daring - mouthing this treachery - mouthing on - can you hear it? - daring to touch this most intimate sacred place in our soul - to violate this our sacred tsarplace - now of all times to be guarded - daring to threaten us!

"how should he act towards those who have committed such a grave sin? He should provide an example to the nation. He should turn away from the pagan principle of retaliation and the intimidation of men through the fear of death. He should permeate himself with the Christian principle of pity towards the insane evil doers - "

He should! He should! How dare he!

What Christ was this he dared fob them off with!

That the scum shouldn't forfeit their lives?

"- the Anointed of God without in any way justifying the crime should remove the murderers from society but without destroying them -"

Good, good, let him go on with this treacherous babble -

indulge his real self – indict – incriminate.

"– the Tsar should bear in mind the criminal's state of soul. He should place them under the Church's jurisdiction. Through this deed he would prove that within him resides the supreme spiritual might of the whole Russian nation."

Prove? It has not to be proved!

He challenges it, doubts, threatens it from the start.

So! Tall thin mystical dabbler revealed for what he was – one of the scum himself!

"The Church alone is capable of healing them morally."

Finished then has he?

Gaze directed downwards before him Solovyev knew an evermore absolute finality for this deed.

"The Tsar can pardon them – the Tsar must pardon them!"

Must, uttered with an authority given him, earnest with the task that must be done, with the change that must be carried through if Christian man was to survive.

In the tense silence that 'must' sounded direct attack. Screams of rage, murderous fury, intended to kill, were hurled at him, from all present, so quickly swept into loyal support, all, except for the students at the back of the hall, immediately provoked into shouting approval, battle lines drawn with relish.

"Traitor!"

"Terrorist!"

"Murderer!"

Many were on their feet, snarling and jeering at this long thin trickster.

Solovyev slowly returned to the rostrum, back from his seat, every step needing to be held firm, silencing all with this possibility that he dared even answer them, even utter another word. During the onslaught two names alone had yielded some sense – Traitor! – Terrorist! – could only mean they thought he was condoning. At least, at the very least, colleagues, friends, all!, was it possible? as he stood before these stern glaring ones.

"Please be assured. In no way do I condone the terrorists for their murderous act. That would be a complete misunderstanding – that – "

Misunderstanding? Pathetic, that he thought he could get away with that now. Understood all too well! Even, that the dreadful murder had forced this traitor in their midst to reveal himself!

Solovyev's superior at the Ministry of Education, Baron Nikolai, was on his feet, to bring this dangerous nonsense to a halt.

"I strongly advise you –" he began sternly.

That's more like it!

"for your own good – to"

Absolutely!

"drive straight to the Ministry of the Interior and explain yourself fully."

The truth my crime! Silenced – framed – no way out there – simply to fight back with the strength given you.

"I'm not acquainted with the Minister of – "

"Be careful! This is a public matter not your private affair," warned Baron Nikolai.

Solovyev glimpsed vast implications in this complex skirmish. Confirmation too that the deed had been done!

Stubbornly still, with this same strength he stood his ground to renewed fury, to Baron Nikolai's frustration that instant bureaucratic procedure for such insubordination was not working, that he was being made to look a fool.

"It could happen," he threatened, "that instead of driving yourself to the Ministry of the Interior – you will find yourself forced to travel to Kolimsk."

"Well – one can occupy oneself with philosophy even in Kolimsk," Solovyev fought back. Siberia? Certainly the deed!

"Traitor!" screamed an elderly respected liberal lawyer jumping up and pointing wildly, "you should be hanged first of them all!"

"Absolutely right! Semenovsky Square for him too!"

The students knew the moment's calling as they stamped along the central aisle to surround Solovyev.

Students! on the platform – what else to expect – all obviously planned!

"You are our leader!" declared the students, lifting Solovyev onto their shoulders and carrying him out through the hall to a carriage.

Awakening, still at his desk, from a sleep broken by obscure conflicts, he made tea and sought to recall, let live what had happened. Beyond all else that 'can' and that 'must' resounded now with an authority truly not his! Through it to glimpse the necessity of that murderous fury.

Baron Nikolai's public – private – of course! That authority had made the distinction of no account. It was speaking through the Tsar to all men at all times. That fury – a denial, fear of the truth.

This truth – holdfast holdfast as its life-vista nothing less for you – daunting exhilarating, enter ahead – timeless moment – holdfast – enter courageously as it yields – no not imagined – borne on the wings of this swiftest flight – this revelation – appeal and task.

It meant! – in this new day's light giving back body to each thing – drawing him down to this present room – it meant – withdrawal!

Withdrawal from all! – that till now had been his – comfort! – his very self – Church – Monarch – whole Slavophil way – all known now as – so strong, so extreme the indictment by this Truth – this authority – failure!

That was the meaning which he dared not hide from, betray.

That was the revelation. This knowing beyond all doubt. That it would, must be so.

Gift! Gracious gift. That he might somehow prepare himself for an utterly new destiny.

Christ's Universal Humanity as practical life task. Meaning that he must work for unity wherever it led.

In the Church – unity.

With the Jews – unity.

With the terrorists – unity.

Unity the All in all.

Wherever and whenever.

A familiar flapping of wings drew him to the window. He gently drew back the curtains and watched his pigeons pecking at the bread he'd put out the previous evening. Below the first carts to market were slowly trundling past. But the friendly pigeons, the city's stirring life, all of it, silenced by the point his gaze held steadily, across the street, through the apartment block opposite, through all the city's substance, westward, to Semenovsky Square, ghastly heart of all Russia, the five scaffolds, the condemned, the knotted rope secured.

So inevitable, for him too!

Sucked into that ghostly place.

Russian ghastliness!

The five hanging together.

He too! made to imagine it. So conditioned, as foregone conclusion.

O Russia, this inevitable ghastliness of my very own too!

Sharpest point of the struggle - furthest awakening - that I too still take for granted their extermination - can only be in this imagination as somehow justified.

Forced to question from this place of mine in the crowd on Semyonovsky Square.

Listen! Listen!

Why did I speak thus - risk all thus - for men I do not know?

Listen - listen to this voice - let it have full play - for a Tsar I do not know.

Why have I sacrificed a perfectly honourable future - a successful prominent future - for what?

That's it!

That's me!

That's mine! - dark brother - never done with -

but - I am with you always - too!

From you - dark brother - my own - in that crowded hall of ardent admirers - from your so-called Orthodoxy - of course! not misunderstanding - your elemental power -

You were challenged and found wanting.

Your Tsar's Christian kingdom was challenged publicly - to your fury found wanting - cosiness and careers in this implacable light.

Only now through you to know the absolute incompatibility of Christ's God-manhood with this Orthodoxy - national - particularist - earthbound - powerbound and earthbound - an aberration - utterly inaccessible to the Kingdom.

To realise just how distant Russian society was from that Godmanhood envisioned, declared, appealed to in his lectures - the call truly from Him - yet his own.

Where was he being taken, that he could see all this, the endlessly new? What door opened into the Universal Humanity now and thus to be experienced, painfully, yet such a source of new strength in knowing it, living it, as the certain Truth.

That audience too. Such ugly faces - scaffold sneering! Colleagues? - friends? - supporters? - the unrecognisable glimpsed in that moment - and - good it was too this awakening - this illusion exposed - of all our lives.

The Tsar too.

The murderers too.

'Lord forgive them for they know not what they do.'

Then he must forgive the terrorists. He alone.

Absurd!

No! In this very aloneness the strength, the truth of this deed – seed for his – their – Russia's future – in all humility – for nothing less would do.

Somehow, somehow to stay with them – with – this frailest seed of unity – that Unity – which must be nurtured.

Staying with them – could only mean acceptance – and of their sins too – how close? – how close? –

as his very own!

How close? how close – to the scaffold – to the moment of death – and beyond?

This aloneness – mystery, gift – purest resonance of freedom in Christ as Redeemer for all!

Only now to realise that the condemned were with him only as mere abstractions. Now into that 'with' he must pour his life.

Christ is that 'with'.

Christ is that 'with', saying your life and theirs must be united. Their deed as though you had done it, and seek forgiveness from God.

Impossible! but nothing less will do.

That they unknown have met you thus, at the heart of Truth, at the foot of the Cross, all known in our fallenness – rejoice! The Comforter is with us too.

That they have met you like this, each one of them, and the Tsar, unknown! But thus to be made known through this deed of the yearning heart.

Dark brother take note! The firstborn man a fratricide – but not to suffer death at the hands of men! The Lord set a mark on him lest any finding should kill him.

He would indeed be in Semenovsky Square amongst the thousands, that glimpsed future had spoken of inevitability. But how? How would he be there? How would he stay with them?

Distantly the gentle tapping on his door persisted. With warm embrace, tearful relief, he reached out to Anton Vasilyevich. Not that alone then, with this dear friend together once more. To start here then, this moment's Lifegift – the so very human – this brotherly immediacy – against that vast historical complexity

- such bitter disillusionment.

Kireyev, a colleague in the Education faculty, his loyalty put to the test, saw, felt, a fragility, the pain. Delicately he must calm down this eagerness, to ensure that Vladimir Sergeyevitch knew just how awkward let alone dangerous his situation was.

"My dear friend, good to see you. Here, some fresh rolls. Yes – some newspapers too – just to keep up with what's happening."

The facts. No pretence, no comforting. That he was here sufficient.

Kireyev poured himself some tea and handed Solovyev a warm roll to take with his.

"I'm sure you can imagine. The papers are full of it. Everyone's having a go," he began awkwardly, feeling in the presence of something unfamiliar, so vulnerable, yet still his very own Vladimir Sergeyevitch listening, from that far place, always leaving such a space for him to be.

"Please go on. You've busied yourself on my behalf – tell me exactly," said Solovyev, his friend's presence the resounding reality.

Grateful for the encouragement Kireyev began anew.

"Most of the papers are wallowing in it. They attack you for duplicity – treachery – excusing the murderers in such a roundabout way. Did you take your loyal – that's it all the way through – loyal loyal loyal audience for fools with your arrogance – and so on and so on. Nowhere I've read your actual words at any length. Everything out of context. The general mood is very ugly no question. Even described you as a terrorist for attacking the Tsar."

Whilst speaking he tried not to look too intently at Vladimir Sergeyevitch. Somehow to ward off what was there?

"Go on – please."

"I decided I must take soundings personally. I've been to see Petrovsky, and Radlov – that would be sufficient indication for the moment."

"Agreed."

"Well, they both said they understood what you were getting at. They were obviously embarrassed – very embarrassed over the whole affair. Of course we understand what he said – but no need to create such a rumpus. Meaning of course – we have to live in the real world –"

Kireyev almost stopped, barely able to recognise it for what it was, so startling, from the thick black hair that reached to

Solovyev's shoulders, a fierce patch of white! So deep then had it gone! So hard hit!

"They hate you for it. They can't bear to hear it. Your word pierced right through. Like wounded creatures – career bonhomie routine – through and through. They can't believe you put your future at risk over such a matter. Nikolai's threat of Siberia – same old phantoms!"

"On the way from the bakery I decided to knock on Dubovsky's door. I know he's in. No answer."

He must speak to the Tsar as one present whether or not the letter was ever read. This calumny, misunderstanding, however called – he must speak himself to the Tsar.

To rely on nothing now except, and precisely where that except pointed was the way. All supports withdrawn. To attempt a new beginning.

To declare himself directly. His voice speaking.

Your Imperial Majesty and Most Gracious Sovereign: Undoubtedly Your Majesty was informed of the lecture which I delivered on April 10th, but probably in a perverted or at least exaggerated manner. I deem it to be my duty, therefore, to report the matter to Your Majesty as it actually occurred. Trusting that only the spiritual might of the truth of Christ can overcome the forces of evil and destruction, which in our days are manifesting themselves in such unprecedented dimensions; trusting also that the healthful organism of the Russian Nation lives and is moved by the spirit of Christ; believing finally, that the Tsar of Russia is the supreme representative and the herald of the national spirit, the bearer of all the best in the Nation: I dared to profess this faith of mine from the public platform.

At the conclusion of my speech I said that the painful contemporary conditions present an unprecedented opportunity to the Russian Tsar to show the might of the Christian principle of supreme mercy, and that this act would constitute a great moral exploit which would exalt his power to an inaccessible height, and would establish his authority upon an unshakeable foundation.

By granting pardon to the enemies of his own power, contrary to all the calculations of worldly wisdom, the Tsar would rise to a superhuman height and would demonstrate by that act the divine nature of his imperial authority, proving that within him resides the supreme spiritual might of the whole Russian Nation, by virtue of the fact that in the whole Nation there would be no one else capable of so sublime an act.

This is the essence of my speech which, to my great sorrow, was interpreted in a manner quite contrary to my intentions.

Your Imperial Majesty's faithful subject,

Vladimir Solovyev

Granting pardon?

Yes.

Impossible officially to come any closer to the act of forgiveness itself – which the Tsar alone could do only as man before Christ.

On the second day of the trial Pobedonostsev spent the morning in Volunteer Fleet committee work. Later back in his apartment several petitioners sought his help. Through it all a deep unease at the trial's progress would not leave him. Thankful at least for his choice of Chulkoff as Synodal observer. The fellow missed nothing of real import, almost as if there himself.

But the fact that there was a trial at all! Forced to conclude that this government was sick, with such false sentimentality – or with such cowardice! – as to prevent the only true response, summary execution. The possibility of public unrest? The public! That filthy, lying newspaper invention. The public! That liberal concoction of mass ignorance. That excuse! – sheerest cowardice, the very same rotten weakness which had made the outrage possible.

He was forced to remind himself, bitterly, angrily, just how unaware that whole lot were of the nature, the fundamental demands of a truly Christian Russian state. All of them would eventually have to be cleared right out that a truly Russian order be established once again.

The last petitioner, an elderly widow from the provinces, left with expressions of profound gratitude, through which Pobedonostsev knew humbly the furtherance of that Christian state, every right word, every right action counting, receiving its meaning from that goal alone. He returned to his study to wait for Chulkoff's report but was given over to a sudden fury. They should have been put up against the wall days ago! They should have been purged right out of Russian life days ago! And that at his prompting – intolerable – all of it intolerable – anxious – anxious – still this same anxiety! Alexander Alexandrovich yielded to the absolute necessity of urging – ordering – hopefully that old fool Fuchs as president of the Court would know it as an order from his sovereign lord – that condign punishment be meted out – condign! And that – intolerable! – so weak – false had Russian life become – one couldn't even take for granted that condign punishment would follow as night follows day!

Because he didn't trust any of them!

That men simply couldn't see this – God help us Russia!

In faith God help Thy lonely servant!

Catherine's footsteps – at the door!

Again!

"Professor Strakhov is coming to see you this evening. He said the matter is urgent, very urgent."

"Strakhov?"

"I told him you weren't likely to be free till at least seven o'clock."

"Strakhov?"

The doorbell was ringing.

Catherine hurried to greet Chulkoff, the charming young Secretary of the St Petersburg consistorial chancery, Pobedonostsev's Synodal representative at the trial.

Strakhov? – Tolstoy's editor – Tolstoy! – that madman!

Chulkoff entered the study, quickly aware of Constantin Petrovich's preoccupation and unusual failure to eagerly acknowledge him.

What the devil was Strakhov coming for at this hour?

What was going on?

Chulkoff sat down quietly on the solitary wooden chair, to look vaguely at the worn carpet.

Turn to Nicholas Ivanovitch – take hope from him – one of your men – for the future – for what must be made to come about.

"Constantin Petrovich, a dreadful day. This Zhelyabov's making complete fools of the court. They simply don't know how to deal with him–"

"Zhelyabov?"

"Yes, arrested several days before the murder. Everything you foresaw is happening. He gives speeches – continually interrupts – asks most impertinent questions. I watched him closely – smirking, sneering, plotting his next move. I was asking myself where's it all going to end –"

"What? What d'you mean?"

Chulkoff heard some threat in that, glimpsed a carelessness, a straying on his part, altogether an obscure confusion. The facts only for his superior, future's guarantor, bald head sternly poised, stone.

"During the morning recess," he recalled with relief, "someone questioned whether Rysakov, as a minor, could be hanged –"

"Could?" repeated his superior, in fiercest breath released, but stone.

"– but of course," he hurriedly resumed, "it was decided that he could be hanged," feeling confusedly that somehow his superior was mixing him up with those idiots he was reporting on. "Oh – yes, yes – I couldn't believe it. When Zhelyabov was asked his religion he actually declared that he honoured the teaching of Jesus Christ. He said he believed in the truth and justice of that teaching. Constantin Petrovitch," he went on excitedly, "I watched the court assessors – everyone did. They went silent – pale – utterly confused – they –,"

"That's it Chulkoff! That's what we want to hear! That's how he speaks, the Adversary. That's how he has to speak. His arrogance must have its say. Now we can be sure whom we're dealing with – puppets – tools – he soon finds them – these weak corrupted souls who must be purged utterly from Russian life. Good, Chulkoff. Return to your family. Be there again tomorrow. Your observations are of utmost importance."

Chulkoff left, greatly relieved.

Pobedonostsev knew for certain that something drastic must be done. Dark forces were at work. The only possible ending to this trial was no longer certain. Even an actual plot to keep them alive – as poisonous germs to infect other weak corrupted souls? Russia's future was still in danger. He would have to give voice to this awful anxiety, confess himself nakedly to – even to – Alexander Alexandrovich – whatever the risk.

These creatures must be hanged.

The deed exemplary for the Christian future of Russia. But the doing of this deed by no means certain enough.

He, of all men, at this moment, to be extremely alert.

Stern the will to establish a new order that would make this farce of a trial forever impossible.

The study door opened much too briskly.

"Strakhov has come to see you," said Catherine awkwardly. But the man was already right in his study, at his desk!

Strakhov felt he had waited long enough this day. Russia could wait no longer. The hours counted. This letter from his beloved Lev Nikolayevitch, anyone could feel – see – hear! something very special – Russia's salvation joyfully ringing in these words – very own heart beating bursting with them – and it could only be so for all others – heart to heart – to the hearts of all men.

"A matter of the greatest urgency Procurator Pobedonostsev – Count Tolstoy knows that your goodwill will ensure that this letter reaches His Majesty immediately," said Strakhov handing over the envelope.

Pobedonostsev, forced back, repelled by this unbearable effusiveness, took hold of the envelope, feeling momentarily outwitted. In silence he pointed to the wooden chair placed well away from his desk. Very slowly he took the letter out and unfolded it, gathering his sharpest guard for this mad blasphemer.

He began to read, incensed by Strakhov's impatience, impudent intent that it would be passed on automatically to His Majesty. Strakhov, watching expectantly, felt increasingly baffled by the impenetrable distance separating him from that rigid black garbed figure. Distance stifling all ardour very life itself.

By the end of the first sentence Pobedonostsev disdained any need to read carefully through the lengthy outpouring. One comprehensive, critical, glance was sufficient to reveal the sickness treachery vile threat – the sentimental wallowing intended to weaken Russia – and this aristocratic oaf thought he could get away with it! Merely glance after glance to reveal this rottenness for what it was.

' .. a third way .. that of Christian forgiveness .. not yet been employed .. on your hands is no blood .. O Monarch forgive them .. I would become your willing slave .. only the ideal of love .. forgiveness .. sufficiently strong to contend with them .. '

Such sickly-sweet temptation of that gifted scribbler – from his heart indeed – of hypocrisy – vanity – arrogance.

"I'm unable to present this to the Emperor. These opinions of Count Tolstoy are in total contradiction to Russian principles."

Strakhov quickly left the room, glad for the freedom to come to terms with this bafflement, helplessness, before the man he'd been with. Tall thin pale black – black! Were those eyes hooded, behind the thick spectacles? There was something - making it impossible to reach that man. Dryness. Such a dryness. Never a hint of movement towards him. And that pitiful wifely creature so nervous.

No matter dear Lev Nikolayevitch - your inspiration - courage - the true Russian principle - they can only give way - yours is a godly inspiration.

As soon as the door shut Pobedonostsev knew for sure that all of it was part of the comprehensive attack, and that he must now think it through unflinchingly for the danger was great.

No chance in any of this. Count Tolstoy was a madman out to destroy the Church and now in his unbelievable arrogance the very foundation of the State.

A madman! who else invents his own Christ? - a weakly phantom whom he called Christ!

Sentimental fool! his talents the greatest danger - one more tool!

Fool! Know that our Russian Christ is a stern judge of men!

' .. innate goodness of every human heart .. ' - dangerous sentimental fool!.

Purest fantasy - dangerous fantasy - that Levin a scribbler's fantasy.

All men are lies - a nothingness - except - except! - through family Church and State. Only a national Christendom under the Tsar's absolute authority.

Russia needs certainty and security at this moment, not these sentimental fantasies. All of them - Tolstoys - socialists - dangerous puffed up deluded fantasists - own religions! - own social orders - own own own! Wretchedness - such wretchedness before the Divinely ordained.

That man Strakhov had felt so assured. How possible for any sane person to come thus to him - in the context of Count Tolstoy's insane attacks on the Church? Were others involved in this?

One thing immediately obvious - that letter would be copied and very soon be in circulation. Many could be fooled by that sentimental rubbish. It could reach Alexander Alexandrovich by another source. He had been the chosen source.

Thank God it had reached him first!

Dreadful this fear.

What was he afraid of? - if the letter reached Alexander

Alexandrovich by another source.

What?

He must bring it to light this fear, glimpsed as he looked to the loud knock on the study door, but glimpsed to the quick, an Alexander Alexandrovich who was not his!

Mokievsky, an industrialist and close associate on the Volunteer Fleet Committee, hurried straight in.

"Pyotr Antonovich? Whatever is it?"

"You must know this Constantin Sergeyevitch. Before a large audience – what? – two hours ago Constantin Sergeyevitch. Something must be done immediately. The wretched man must be stopped. Who are these people? Who allowed it? What is the Synod doing? In whose name dare this traitor speak?"

"Pyotr Antonovich, please! What are you talking about?"

"His talk – d'you understand?" almost threatening, the tone, "Volunteer Fleet? – English naval threat?" pointing hard at Pobedonostsev, "here – right here!," slapping his chest, "is the real enemy," sucking breath in fiercely, dropping down on the chair, exhausted. He waved a hand at Pobedonostsev to clear a space, trying to collect himself.

"I've just been to a lecture attended by hundreds of people. One Solovyev – a Faculty member! – openly attacked the Tsar and the Church – insisted the Tsar's murderers were innocent – should be freed immediately – and all this in the name of Christ! A Faculty member trying to undermine the dynasty by sheer treachery – all dressed up as religion. How is it we don't know about him eh? – eh?" he shouted angrily, "and then so blatantly – so obviously a planned provocation – absolute outrage – the students rushed to him and carried him away. Even now, I can't believe it –"

"Thank you – thank you – action will be taken immediately," Pobedonostsev said, simply to appease him.

"Things can't go on like this Constantin Petrovich!"

"Rest assured, they won't. There will be changes, big changes. And soon, I assure you. That man's word is foul and sick. I assure you he will be stopped."

He accompanied Mokievsky to the door of the apartment and thanked him again. Solovyevs, Tolstoys, no real problem. Excommunication, banning all publications inevitable. But this now – called on to express, expose, this overwhelming fear to Alexander Alexandrovich himself no matter what the risk. And no matter the awful implication that he didn't trust Alexander Alexandrovich, didn't take for granted any longer that Alexander Alexandrovich could only act in one possible way.

All that to be thrust aside.

Only to reveal nakedly – purely – his deepest feelings. Appealing – yes – having to appeal – to an independent Alexander Alexandrovich – an uncertain – unknown – unfamiliar what was it? independent – that was it! bitterly was it – no longer to be taken for granted – nothing to be taken for granted. Russia was at a turning point and everything had to be risked, even, no, above all, his so-called dignity. Whoever and whatever Alexander Alexandrovich he was appealing to – how strange to have come to this place – would – must hear this.

April 12, 1881

'Sire,

An idea that fills me with horror -'

Horror? Yes! Hold back nothing. Express – voice – this ultimate – nothing less will do – no matter what weakness revealing – for the sake of Russia. And that – Alexander Alexandrovich, Tsar would hear this – same voice – from same friend – teacher – and guide still.

'An idea that fills me with horror has just begun to circulate. People are capable of such mental aberration that some of them think it possible not to execute the murderers. The Russian people are already beginning to fear that monstrous schemes may be submitted to Your Majesty to incite you to pardon the criminals.'

Pardon – pardon – what! forgiveness here – the very sound ugly – unruly – bitter for Russian ears.

'No, a thousand times No; in this moment, with the eyes of the entire Russian nation upon you, it is unthinkable that you should pardon the murderers of your father - that you should forget the blood that has been shed.'

Of course Alexander Alexandrovich would never forget. This warning then from on high – against all possible temptation in this hour of crisis – even the unthinkable.

'Blood for which everyone, apart from a few weakhearted and feeble minded individuals, is crying vengeance, and people are already demanding to know why the sentence is so long in coming. I am a Russian.'

Yes – so it declares itself! Tell him – remind him! Bind him to you with it.

Not at all obvious – there are those who think it easily handled – like one's coat.

'I live among Russians and I know what the Russian people feel and want.'

Absolute – absolute this voice – his voice of theirs.

'At this moment they are all eager for punishment. If one of these wretches should escape death, he will immediately begin to hatch new plots for undermining the government.

For the love of God, Sire, do not listen to misguided sycophants,
  Your loyal servant
        Constantin Petrovich Pobedonostsev'

Igor Tikhomirov, who with Nikolai Morozov had drafted the People's Will Charter after the decision to assassinate Alexander II, wrote a long letter from prison to the new Tsar. The recently formed Department of State Police ensured that it was on the Tsar's desk before the trial began.

Colonel Eshevsky wanted not simply that it should be brought to the Tsar's notice but to hope, to ensure, that the Tsar should take it in and act accordingly. That the one who could bend a horseshoe straight with his bare hands would act accordingly.

The letter addressed His Majesty as an equal, no less. It arrogantly insisted on the inevitability of what had happened. It insanely fantasised that the revolutionary movement represented the urge of all Russia towards new social forms. And that unless a government was – elected! – a bloody upheaval must follow.

It dared to address the Tsar as – fellow citizen!

It actually denied what was obvious – the threat in it all and then declared that the only way out was a National Assembly. Yes! Let it be right in front of His Majesty's own eyes before the trial began.

And, not to forget that this voice even though imprisoned – even though the hangings were a foregone conclusion, this voice itself – sounded with the authority of a successful regicide. An authority that had achieved its diabolical aim – an authority that enabled the assassination to be carried out successfully. Not at all to be in any way underestimated.

Only let it strike home to all of us – day by day, fully, to learn our lesson by now.

Essential that the new Tsar heard it, still in all its arrogance, and never forget it.

Since the assassination and then the announcement that all the terrorists had been arrested, the Palace had been receiving hundreds of letters and telegrams, condoling and congratulating, declaring profoundest loyalty and most loving devotion, from private individuals, public institutions, aristocrats and other royal houses from all over Russia and Europe.

From his first hasty perusal of the letter from Colonel Eshevsky, the Tsar was yet drawn, implicated. Annoyed with the Police Department for sending him such rubbish, impertinent outpouring, outrageous insult to the memory of his father's death, he yet sensed contradictively that through facing it, listening seriously to that voice, so clear, assured, again and again, something of great benefit to himself and Russia would come about. The letter was held down on his desk day after day by two large brass paperweights.

He realised that his first wild explosion of anger was being forged into an absolute conviction, lifelong, implacable, by this yielding to the full measure of what he was up against. He must allow himself to take this full measure of them, in order to make trial of himself, in order to know just what strength was available to him in and through this voice of theirs that there be no possible illusion.

"It is a process of the social organism and the scaffolds are as powerless to save the outgrown order of things as the Crucifixion of the Saviour was powerless to save the ancient world from the reforming triumphs of Christianity."

We shall see how powerless the scaffolds are when you scum hang from them.

No greater blasphemy possible!

Deranged - mad - dogs!

Father's torn flesh - the martyred one!

"A revolutionary earthquake, a tremendous bloody upheaval will complete the destruction of the ancient order."

Deranged ones - threatening who with your fantasies? Not yet grasped that we have the power of life and death? A terrible power for the well being of all Russia - and that our resolve is as iron - you swine.

"Fellow citizen"!

He was their Tsar - and they would have to atone with their lives for their fantasy.

"- the government deserves to be called a set of usurping gangsters -"

Exactly what you are! with your indiscriminate murder of innocent people.

In the fire of this merciless wrath, this iron resolve forged, their hanging bodies alone, burned deep into the watching thousands, could begin to atone for Father's shattered flesh.

Yes thankful - so thankful that his awful guilt towards Father - all the criticism - anger in those secret letters with Constantin Petrovich - all that - all that - somehow eased - even redeemed? - by learning from Father's good intentions - learning the hard lessons.

Let it be that Father had good intentions - that I have learned from them - taken his good intentions to heart.

Those shattered - remains! - unapproachable still!

Veiled - veiled - still the despair that it was not his Father - not the Tsar.

' .. the murder of a Tsar is popular in Russia.'

The hanging of murderers - you shall learn - is even more popular?

But accursed even this compulsion to answer them.

'We turn to you as a citizen ..'

Then as citizens you'll hang!

' .. two conditions .. a general amnesty .. a National Assembly .. the only way.'

Conditions eh?

He? to whom the ministers daily reported. Whose every word was sought, awaited, on matters of life and death. He now emerging from his father's pitiful ending. Allowed to witness that martyrdom - and given the power to avenge that martyrdom. His country - his people - and this insufferable voice.

Rage - rage on! - fire flame freely! - to consume them and their like wherever found on Russian soil.

Rage on for Russia's sake that he could be thought of in such a way.

Whose voice?

Whose voice?

Never daring to forget as he read each word again - murderer's voice - who had torn Father into that pitiful bleeding hulk.

Madmen's voice.

Madness! No not their daring to threaten him but madness

– an evil madness to be burnt out from Russian life. Its very measure awakening this fullness of his strength and resolution.

That they who had done this thing imagined they could deal – set terms for him – with him – evil madness!

That pitiful bleeding hulk would judge all his answers from now.

Pobedonostsev's letter marked URGENT was delivered by courier to Secretary Pypin. Alexander read it through, surprised at Constantin Sergeyevitch's upset. Horrified?

This newly forged resolution, keen in the pride of its strength would immediately allay dear Constantin Sergeyevitch's surprisingly deep upset.

'Rest assured, no one will dare to come to me with such a request, and I promise you that all six of them will hang.'

I – I alone.

Secretary Pypin was ordered to send it on immediately.

That Constantin Sergeyevitch had even imagined for one moment?

That he was in any doubt?

Pardon? Constantin Sergeyevitch – unthinkable indeed that word? daring to challenge the sword of retribution – ordained.

But then he had put Russia first, his truth first, beyond all pain of exposing his deepest feelings – and – and – so deeply trusting in me too – to thus express himself. You are Russia's voice as ever my dear Constantin Sergeyevitch – and this resolve is Russia's assurance for the future. Have no such worries poor Constantin Sergeyevitch – the power is mine – for Russia. But indeed you were right – I – and I alone from now on.

Six were condemned to be hanged in Semyonovsky Square on the morning of April 16. Gesya Helfman, the daughter of a wealthy Jewish manufacturer, was confirmed as pregnant and her sentence commuted to life imprisonment.

As the hours passed on the evening of the 15th, Vladimir Solovyev knew with deepest knowing that his letter had been found unanswerable. That silence, finality, demanded fullest acceptance now of most painful reappraisal. Glimpsed as possibility but now surely the reality. A reappraisal so radical and comprehensive that he dared hardly contemplate it, and yet, already in feeling he knew that accepting, even embracing, the very bitterness of this disillusionment would lead to a purification, clarification of his task. Already, even as his thoughts held firm now, in prayer, to the terrorists themselves, away torn away, from self-pity, pain at shattered hopes. Tsar, Church, Orthodoxy, become painfully unfamiliar, questionable. But now, and through the dawn hours till he too would make his way with thousands to the Square, the challenge, venture, demand in the face of all that other – to stay with the condemned – that name itself but mask – we are all condemned – live through these hours with them – as one of them – to forge a bond that could not be broken – and with the Tsar too!

But who are these condemned – who is this Tsar?

Not so! – clever Tempter.

No abstraction this, you know them well – Rysakov, Mikhailov, Emilyanov, Kibalchich, Grinevitsky, Perovskaya – again no abstraction this – for we are all condemned – and saved, through His Grace and Truth and Love.

Through this very demand to stay with them, which will not let go of me – which demands my all – I know them as I know myself – this Light which so unites is His.

The condemned were allowed two days for appeal. Rysakov alone wrote in desperation. The others knew, venturing into the deep silence of the Trubetskoy Bastion in the Fortress. The gentleness of the guards – not common criminals these, dignity in this readiness to forfeit their lives! apart from Rysakov, unconcerned, so normal their behaviour, reading books, studying, the Kibalchich one working on problems of flying machines! – padding about in felt covered boots, the thin trees in the little triangular garden, the aged bath house, everything here bearing its burden of ending.

The whole area, cells above and below ground, surrounded by the high redbrick wall, steeped in perpetual shadow and silence. Silence advising. Take your rise from beginnings again, know the Nothing. Be recalled. Remember. The light not to be taken for granted. Sun. Silence threatening. Speech to doubt itself – to become a muffled thread sucked away. Threatening to exorcise man as the being who speaks.

Words only allowed them during the exercise minutes, morning and afternoon. The words, as the guards looked aside giving them extra time. The words, whatever words, yielding to this greater, purest, simply being with one another, silent ground.

Ending, endings - that beginnings be! Courage, courage, dear friends. Flame of the future, radiant, warming, and who would want to live thus, forever?

Yes, yes, breathe in with love the tang of this clear spring air. Tang telling of seeds - and furtherance. Still taste of this eagerness but from here known too as a gift, as passing. This walk an earthly doing - the price which would balance the books - long calculated.

We've done what we had to do and can leave this place this field of action. Strength, strength in this distance, this vista, furtherance of these seeds.

All this surely being dreamed - for ages - for ages and ages - we've known and will be with each other.

And him? Those swollen eyes that pleading cowering face, demanding our every effort at dignity, to the very end.

Yes - betrayer, Rysakov! - but ensurer - that our destiny is fulfilled. As from the beginning, in case, just in case we thought to evade it.

Forced to turn away from you, wretched Nicholas Borisovitch, as the guards watch.

Each one of us forced.

For you are what we had to overcome.

From within, from so deep within dear Nicholas, we hear your scream for life, but know it too as passing - passing.

Never to yield - be drawn down by him - the Lord of Death their equal - servant of their deed. They had chosen - stand firm beneath this blue spring sky - I am - death my equal - in my fullness - and to somehow cleave to this strength upright to the very end.

"No! No! No!" shouted Rysakov as each of them turned aside at his approach.

At whatever he looked, branch, grassy patch, broken bathhouse door, yes resounded from the joy in its existence.

He would not let them tear him away.

He hadn't chosen this.

He'd been tricked into the action - tricked into informing.

"No! No! No!" he screamed, face blotched, moist, ragged with despair.

A guard quickly stepped across and led him away to his cell.

At eight o'clock the priests appeared, to receive Confession.

Zhelyabov, settled on the iron bed, his back hard against the grimy brickwork, was alerted by the Judas spyhole's slightest click. Deeply immersed in Kluchevsky's portrayal of Peter the Great, in Russia's enigma, to this last, very knot of their destinies right here, he glanced towards the door.

It opened slowly, creaking. Father Joseph, ruddy faced, heavily built, bustled in to do good things for this poor sinner. The guard, under strict orders from Captain Ignatovich, kept the door part open and stood by it.

Zhelyabov stared at the page, motionless.

Father Joseph came closer. This stubbornness from such a sinner, very cry for Christ's Mercy.

Kluchevsky's words, made fainter by this approaching shadow enveloping large, trembling, cast by the waning oil lamp from its niche behind iron bars, Zhelyabov took up the challenge, read on fiercely, each word resounding, made his very own, motionless, as one dead to that other, his god not that other's.

Motionless, till that creature withdrew with his Christtricks hypocrisy. Yet glimpsed, that cosiness, comfort of that yielding to this self-righteous, warmly padded creature.

Father Joseph felt forced to step back, right back, out of reach. Only was left to pray for this proud lost soul, Christ's Mercy ever prevailing.

He nodded sadly to the guard who shut the door and turned the key.

Zhelyabov read on, the test passed, the cell cleansed, his own destined world. The oil lamp's gently wavering light sufficient, comforting. In the time remaining, to reconfirm his truth, his god, from the calm of this sure knowing that his was a destiny from the beginning, soon to be fulfilled. He could have done no other.

This the law of my god – who will surely judge me justly.

In this time still granted, thinking through again and again, to know as an ultimate knowing that no other way had been possible.

Sinful indeed this taking of life – but which had to be.

Bitter indeed this destiny – but a greater, a higher prevailed.

The work could never have remained peaceful, the enemy had seen to that. But not to have followed it through to this would have been self-betrayal. From the beginning – to so so much, we had to say No! And this saying but seed of the deed which had to be done.

Great circle shrunk back to its centre.

That this calm I can say it sought tomorrow.

Sought out death - as justice and friend.

Calm in this full acceptance of paying with our - dearest friends! - own lives.

Own?

Who chose? - The greater speaking?

It is over.

Our leave-taking began long ago dearest friends - Sophie - Timofey - our lives - as one - inseparable - our deaths - as one - inseparable - all in and through each other.

And are we not all sharing these thoughts - could it be otherwise?

Soon after midnight prison guard Ivanov reported to Captain Ignatovich that all the condemned were sleeping peacefully.

They were woken at six for the busy day, given mugs of steaming tea and ordered to dress.

Everything to be kept on the move.

Out of their cells, single file, a guard to each, along the vaulted corridor, into the world outside, keep moving there! this the journey beginning then, on and on, grey grim block of the Imperial Mint every window double-barred teeth bared who dares, keep moving! drawn up up into what heights of this genial spring light, needle point of the Cathedral's golden spire aspire - yes us - up up and beyond into that blue, is ours, we already know you, know the place you tell of, unseen unheard by these below, streets, shops, guardposts, troops and officials everywhere.

Halted, in line, the sergeant ordered them into the drab prison waiting room, and withdrew shutting the door.

What then?

Could only be those five black heaps of coarse material set out on the long dirty table in front of them.

Sophie Perovskaya shrank back sharply, catching her breath.

What could this mean?

The new day's first sign.

The door was thrust open noisily. The sergeant watched them, still, silent.

"Get on with it," he shouted, urgent, threatening. This business was very serious, the timetable very important, thousands involved, many companies of troops, Cossacks, gendarmes, and important persons present.

He withdrew again. Something made him reluctant to stand over them. But they'd better get on with it. Anyway this lot so far had shown no trouble.

Zhelyabov moved to the table, took hold of one and let a wide, voluminous gown-like thing spill down to the ground as he raised it shoulder high.

So! thus to appear before the world – enfolded – stifled – hidden in this heavy black shapelessness pulled down over his clothes.

Tightlipped, he stood, to let the others know exactly what the thousands would be watching, wanting. Yes of course – mockery in all its fullness.

Of course that's what had to be done – black buffoons – ballgowns of death – grotesques – no longer human. To make of us figures of fun – to persuade, convince that we, our deed not human – but creatures demanding derision – laughable – to quell their shame and guilt.

"Don't weaken Sophia," he called to her tearfulness as they too realised through him the intention.

"they can't touch us with any of this," as they watched him, shocked, fearful, rescued by his strength.

The intended mockery and humiliation challenged them to call on that being of dignity, even as they drew down over themselves to their knees this black attempt at effacement. We shall not yield. The truth of our being brighter still through this clowning garb.

Our ending must be worthy too.

Upright.

Unbowed.

We shall not yield to this black derisive annulment.

An official from the commandant's office appeared amongst them and began with Zhelyabov, stringing round his neck over the black gown, a large placard of thin wood, to rest on his chest.

TSARICIDE it read, but awkwardly, the letters trailing away in black ink that had run and blotched.

Each was placarded in turn.

Surely meant to ensure that all knew what they were? Yet the hasty blotched letters seemed to question something. Rysakov did what the others did, numb, somehow being with them.

In the courtyard two carts were waiting. On each a specially constructed platform to which benches had been fixed.

Zhelyabov and Rysakov were ordered up onto one, their backs to the horses. Sophia Perovskaya, Mikhailov and Kibalchich to the other. Zhelyabov knew this as no chance arrangement. Accept! but not to acknowledge Rysakov's presence in any outward way.

From all around great busyness, orders, conferrings, anxious check-ups, by officials and officers, of gendarmes, police, Cossacks and troops, everyone drawing into the fullness, the very power of his own part, participation in this great rite of the nation. The condemned, momentarily fascinated by the troop movements, the forming up of the procession reaching back to the cathedral – for whom? for what? – drew back, to each other, perched high on the benches as five blue uniformed gendarmes approached carrying chains and handcuffs. Brusquely, deftly, the feet of each were shackled together, the arms forced sharply behind backs and handcuffed.

Had we still not grasped?

Never again to stride out freely through this world.

Hobbled trussed delivered up.

Fortress Commander Major-General Schaeder appeared. All sound and movement ceased. The Cathedral bells rang out the hourly canticle chime, "How glorious is our Lord in Zion." Major-General Schaeder waited patiently. Eight o'clock precisely – as planned – excellent!

He looked gravely back across the silent waiting procession, from condemned to rearmost military escort. Thus far no hitch on his part – for the Emperor.

He nodded to the drummers who took up position close by the carts and began beating out a regular, steady roll as the high Petrovsky Gate slowly swung open. Regular steady roll to drown out any speeches dared by the condemned. Backs to the horses, they from their high platforms could watch the carriage behind them packed with priests, then a cart carrying five unpainted coffins, the Cossacks, the troop escort, all slowly advancing towards Semyonovsky Square in the sharp spring air.

Trussed.

Only watchers now.

All this for them – watchers from afar.

This stiffness, awkwardness, no longer of the earth.

Only, as black buffoons stared at by all these hurrying people, eager to take up their places in the Square, only to call on that being of dignity, that one who still stands upright.

Since bright spring dawn thousands hurried from all over the city not simply to ensure a place in the vast Semyonovsky Square but quickened with the hanging's very necessity for their presence, fiercely drawn, streaming into that myriad footed WE, I these others, these others I, surging into the Square, ordered into position by hundreds of armed troops, to face from all four sides that radiant centre, black stage, in dark joy, in righteousness.

Secure at last, kept well back, now to watch intensely that black high wooden platform from which two black uprights supported a crossbeam. There, right there the six hooks, ropes hanging slack, perfectly still.

"They've let one of them off?"

"One of the women – they said she's pregnant."

"She's a yid."

"Never!"

"Yid tricks as usual."

Those six hooks, ropes hanging, the steps leading up to the stage, the black railings, the three wooden posts to which manacles and chains are attached, the Cossacks and Guards drawn up to face us – all so far – so near – uplifting – but this fear – terror! – rightly so! Those stern hooks, still waiting ropes are what we are here for – WE! To praise – to fear – to be confirmed our myriad presence.

WE – called to be the nation's witness.

WE – called into being, reborn, exalted. Deep and strong the call. Myriad-eyed watcher of our very own story.

WE – knowing with dark joy that our presence is what gives to the hanging its meaning it and us one.

But – but – how exorcise this wretched ghost, this I daring to be admidst the ceaseless murmuring, the chatter, banter, waiting hush. Wretched I living through the end to come in terror. WE WE WE – the name, the voice to which hold fast! To watch, in every detail, to the very end, to watch, participate, create.

To watch with eternal gratitude hero hangman Frolov, cleansing sword for the Tsar and us, as they go about their task with such assuredness.

Since half past seven hangman Frolov, an ex-prisoner, burly, florid, and his assistants, had been greasing and testing the ropes.

Chief assistant Stanislav Yelfinov was very uneasy. No question, the chief had drunk too much. Far more than the official ration permitted. He stank of it, was almost swaying. Be prepared for the worst – the knot!

Strangulation instead of a clean dislocation. And all that damned jumping about on the end of the rope. And all that wretched croaking. Be prepared – with all those thousands – the whole world watching – God help us all!

And five of the bastards!

God help us all!

The hushed silence of itself telling, at last, the steady drum rolls louder, fiercer – they're coming!

Mounted Cossacks slowly led the two carts into Semyonovsky Square.

It has begun. The waiting is over.

Watch! do nothing but watch whatever you can. Cherish every detail, be greedy, devour it as a lifetime's treasure. But quick, so much is happening, on the left that blubbering one, and the priests, and the white coffins, and the frock-coated high-ups gathering round the table with documents.

No – not yet.

They're chaining them to the railings. Some official stuff here. They're reading something out.

"They're reading out the sentences."

Nearly half an hour of it!

It's becoming absurd.

Why don't they get on with the real thing?

So far away – so near.

For the official business, the detailed reading out of the crimes, the sentences, the flourishes of the muffled drums reminding of the end, omnipotent, grave, a timelessness prevailed.

For the condemned, chained to the railings, costumed, facing thousands, a timelessness prevailed.

What you see, watch, seek to contain you thousands, is not us, borne, out of your reach to this calm, safe, serene. The dross of flesh purged away. Something greater than mere life, this shining forth, this silent beauty and strength.

For us it is already over. Fulfilment. What had to be done has been done.

The sketch of our own life shrinking, you shrinking too. Yet here in this space – yes we know you! You know us! This timeless moment had to come, witnessing seal burning us into your souls. This watching – witnessing. You yourselves have done the deed – this sealing within.

What draws you is not what you think.

In us you need to see yourselves– duly punished – with righteous indignation.

We are the sacrifice, that you awake from your stupor.

Our time is yet to come.

Russians! your time too is yet to come.

The frock coated, top hatted officials bent down to the table and carefully signed all the documents. The waiting priests, from the previous evening, climbed the steps and held out crosses to each of the condemned. Mikhailov and Rysakov alone kissed the crosses and received their blessings.

Unchained from the railings they were all allowed last farewells. Zhelyabov, Kibalchich, Mikhailov, hobbled in turn towards Perovskaya and kissed her. Rysakov had to be torn away from the railing behind which he had somehow dug his feet, barnacled life. They dragged him screaming, echoing in every participant likewise, that absolute finality.

"They're all refusing to look at him – eh!"

The assistants placed white cowls over their heads.

Handcuffed, fettered, cowled, each was prodded into position directly under one of the hooks. The cowls were fastened and all now was under the expert eye of hangman Frolov who took off his coat and handed it to Yelfinov.

At last something really happening!

Every gesture of hangman Frolov now lived by the watching thousands. Through him, in him, with him, they would bring about the end. With him yet apart from him. Being him yet watching him. The crossing elusive.

The four stood upright with that serenity still, challenged to sculpt with courage a dignified image of man. That must not be denied, for that their sacrifice too, living emblem, upright, dignified, proud, through all this black disguise.

For the watching thousands their stand was strongly cast by the sight of Rysakov's trembling, swaying flesh, now knowing that it was to be offered last of all. Frolov ordered an assistant to keep close by him.

We stare in righteousness and disgust at their sin and shame that dared threaten our mighty WE, in all its strength and glory ringed with the pride of these glittering bayonets.

But - uncannily - the flame of their life - those four - burns calm in this final meeting - we cannot deny it.

We watch - condemn - as our Tsar exhorts, but this too we feel.

Kibalchich was the first, trussed, cowled, only able to look straight ahead, gazing at the distant, far distant thousands, feeling the well greased rope pressing its way through the slit in the cowl and Frolov's thick fingers drawing it round, right round, securing the knot, perfectly placed, to assistant Yelfinov's relief as he glanced up its slack length to the steel hook. Even tipsy - the boss could do it! So shut your mouth - or you'll bring bad luck!

Hangman Frolov, to teach that lot exactly who was the master of this whole show, allowed himself a long pause, glancing around to take in everything, to ensure that the whole affair was going well.

A really big affair this eh? and they'd come to him.

The tabouret was placed in front of Kibalchich who knew that as the first, his way, for all of us must be exemplary dearest friends, never more together than now - it is not so - this yielding - and this freedom - for that light to come.

Hangman Frolov nodded to that bigheaded idiot Yelfinov, who held on to one of Kibalchich's handcuffed arms, steadying the condemned man who managed to guide his shackled feet up onto the stool. Dearest friends - balanced here - you all!

Hangman Frolov glancing up along the rope's length for final check, grabbed the stool and dragged it sharply away. Kibalchich jerked back, quickly into that darkness as the drummers drummed loud and long.

A silent cheer resounded before such skill. No resistance, no struggle, that one must have known how right it all is. Such timing, all so smooth, quiet. And there it hangs down what stood upright, so still now, facing them.

Hangman Frolov went straight on to the next, off to a good start, no stopping now. Steady old pace. Little bit misty so what! The audience with him. Come on there! up onto the stool - and here we go!

"Wake up! he's already doing the next one -"

"Get it now the swing of it - really - quite humane."

"You can see - they all know they deserve it!"

Chief assistant Yelfinov watched that knot with alarm. Definitely out. Right out!

Mikhailov, heavily built, was jerked away to finally hang suspended from the hook. But blurred, slow and blurred this world, still here. So painfully, numbly here.

Hangman Frolov watched, impatient for that stillness. Sometimes they were stubborn. Could be one of them.

The rope broke clean apart.

Mikhailov, trussed, shackled, gowned in black fell face down smashing himself on the platform.

Hangman Frolov was upset.

People screamed.

"Glory to God!" shouted one.

A miracle – this man saved by God!

Hangman Frolov felt under attack.

Chief assistant Yelfinov somewhere readied, rushed for the ladder and a new length of rope. Some opposition out there! – The troops might be needed. This new rope – tested? – tested? – untested? – God knows what's happening.

Hangman Frolov an urgency striking, fiercely hauled the bleeding, dazed Mikhailov onto his feet, to get straight on with the business.

Mikhailov had heard the screams, this judgement, as assistant Yelfinov helped him up again onto the stool, very uneasy over this whole messy business. At least he'd acted quickly. But that rope had been thoroughly tested! Well beyond this man's weight.

Hangman Frolov dragged the stool away again and watched intently, waiting for that first stillness which he knew so well. The crowd held its breath. Some hidden fragility revealing itself? That an even greater power was about?

The assassination had been successful?

Mikhailov, bruised, raw, but still himself grimly. Still to stick to that bargain and tread that very own path of theirs with discipline.

The tens of thousands watched for this final judgement. Unbelieving they saw Mikhailov falling to the platform, on his chest, with a loud echoing thump. The drummers began drumming, unordered.

Hangman Frolov watched paralysed, beyond all understanding amidst the screams, the shouts for release! – justice! – compassion! – mercy! – from all over the Square, at the officials on the platform. Fearful of the thousands, bewildered, some officials even dared to whisper their disgust.

God help us when the Tsar hears about it - who for god's sake decided on this drunken bungler?

Hangman Frolov felt completely cornered by the incomprehensible. Enraged he must fight back.

Troops everywhere stiffened against the jostling thousands, soon contained by an overpowering fascination.

What would this wretched hangman do next?

Who would prevail?

A veil now rent.

Some spell broken.

Ugly gap - two powers?

But have we forgotten - are we forgetting - a Tsar was atrociously murdered.

Poor devil! what must it be like for him - he's trying to hang the wretch and he manages to keep falling off the rope - some game here.

"Frankly a disgusting business!"

Some awful power here - think it! - think its lightning flash - those fibres refusing to hold together.

We We We - now being forced to pass judgement - on a tawdry bungling show! - and a dangerous business. It's becoming dangerous, admit it. We're watching now a drunken oaf disgracefully playing about with the lives of human beings.

God help those responsible - the cast out are coming very close!

Mikhailov, lying in severe pain, unable to move, was manhandled by panicky assistants up onto the stool. Hangman Frolov, sensing direst danger, that this game was getting very rough, vowed in his rage that whatever happened this swine was going to hang.

Assistant Yelfinov broke through his stupor and automatically climbed the ladder once again replacing with yet a new length of rope. The hanging must go on, but he felt they were being accused.

Hangman Frolov, relieved by Yelfinov's momentum at keeping things going, and by the two who were dragging the swine back to the stool, knew that he needed something extra! - to settle this one's hash even if it took all day.

On the edge of chaos, charged by this fury with utmost will

to finish the job. Fury that anything dare stop him, stop the Tsar's orders – brilliantly, fiercely alighting on the certain means of victory.

That empty hook was it!

The very next one! The Yid girl's hook – empty – waiting!

So! you laid the trap – and gave me a way out – evens then again!

An end to this swine's nonsense once and for all!

Grabbing the ladder away from the bewildered Yelfinov and shoving it under the empty hook, intended for Gesya Helfman, trembling with fury, he shouted for "Rope you fools, more rope!" Let everyone hear watch and decide.

The ladder teetered as he stamped up it, fixed the rope to the empty hook, and stamped down.

Get him down, get the swine down. To force this second rope through the cowl slit – right round – force! force! and knot – and there.

That's it you bastard! you thousands!

Try and get out of this one!

Up with him idiots!

Two ropes you bastard – and see what you make of that!

And three – and four if necessary!

But see! This time he's staying put! – Yes, jumping around a bit – but Frolov's got him!

An army doctor amongst the officials could not hold back. "Bloody disgrace! absolute shambles! the man should –"

Hangman Frolov swung straight round at him. "There!" he stabbed upwards at the hook intended for Gesya Helfman, "room for you too!"

He was back in command. The show was still his.

The thousands, the troops, the officials, had long gone silent before this sheer doggedness, ingenuity, extraordinary contraption.

Yes, hangman Frolov had done it at last. But would those dreadful convulsions never end, jaw jerking up and down, face torn livid, body impossibly springing right over from left to right and back again.

What awful puppetry was this?

Ghastly that cry, telling of something dreadful – humanly dreadful.

All of it saying no! no! no! to this awful incompetence.

Bitter taste of a badly staged show.

Something was wrong.

Resound - yield! Their dignity - to the last.

Not in it but watching - this bitter watching.

Every watcher was somewhere thrown back on themselves with disappointment. That was not why they'd come.

Real concern was felt for two remaining condemned. When Perovskaya went quickly still, there was relief.

At Zhelyabov's long drawn convulsions in spite of Frolov's precautionary double knot, only disgust.

Rysakov, last, struggled to the very end but quickly went still after hangman Frolov, feeling threatened again, pulled the stool away, cursing loudly.

The bodies were taken down, examined by the doctors and the death certificates signed. The Prefect announced that justice had been done. The bodies were packed in the coffins and carted to the railway station for burial in the Preobrazhensky Cemetery. The Prefect ordered the scaffold to be taken down.

Solovyev strove through his keenly watching awareness of all that was happening out there, to maintain, create beyond all appearance, the eternally binding. Striving for that sternest of purification, always I - and - You - one - to any end - still - amidst this vast We ever threatening to overwhelm. To be - to stay with them here where Christ's Light shines as Light of their light - and compassion - for this myriad-faced's despair, confusion, need for redemption, furious gestures of apparent strength.

No!

Striving to seek out stand firm resist - be touched - be healed by the peace of that unity - which will surely come.

No! - still - as he watched. Frolov in good humour snipping pieces of rope in traditional fashion, for the highest bidder, and the many gathering round to make a good humoured ending, a memorable event, something to take home for one's offspring, a piece that put an end to the Tsar's bloody murderers.

Louder sounded the anthem from scattered groups.

"God save the Tsar!

Mighty and powerful!

May he in glory reign over us.

Reign that our foes may quake.

O Orthodox Tsar, Orthodox Tsar,

God save the Tsar!"

No! Not to yield to the dark delight of that awful distance but somehow still–

"Got 'em at last eh? Good old Frolov – give him his due!"

– to keep striving for that unity.

To the very end thousands watched with a confused curiosity, to see, to know how it finally was finished. Prefect, coffins, officials, hangman and assistants, all gone, and still reluctant to leave, watching, waiting, for what? – some satisfaction at having seen confirmed, death's as the ultimate power, as the end, but.

Solovyev moved off only when those around him began moving. But yes, in this fullness and lightness he knew that he was with them. Sealed, as task for the future. Serenity. Strength towards that reappraisal.

Poor, vulnerable earthly flesh – your voice – your whispered appeal. Looking back for the last time before leaving the Square. The troops watched everyone threateningly. Delicate the bond amidst this surly crowd as he sought with this final glance to seal within that stricken flesh hanging, so enigmatically. Forms refusing all finality, all one with the executioner puppets from some unearthly hinterland where man was mocked and despised. Poor wretched, crucified flesh – but – through the path it had taken, in the ripeness of this moment, with the strength now flowing from that bond, the battle was joined.

"All those buggers up there were Yid faces – weren't they? – you can see that."

What could be simpler?

And what could be simpler than a bloodletting – the hints – provocations! in the loyalist broadsheets these last weeks.

All the evils of Russia attributed to the Jews. The deterioration of the climate – the rivers getting shallower – all – the work of the Jews.

The Jews again from that same hinterland of grinning spectres.

Bugles sounded from the Square. The troops were leaving.

So strong that bearing on the scaffold – but – fanaticism?

The autocracy fanatical too? Each possessed by inhuman powers?

Drunken hangman – man? puppet?

They destroyed the man. Tsardom they have not destroyed.

Tsardom they have strengthened – their dreadful destiny.

You must carry them in freedom as brothers.

The Tsar is forced to carry them as destroyers.

From the seated area specially cordoned off for dignitaries and foreign journalists, Vyacheslav von Plehve, recently promoted from the Department of justice to Assistant Chief of Police, watched the proceedings with zealous official concern and out of a personal interest. He wanted at first hand to gauge the feel of the huge crowd's response and note precisely how police and gendarmes were carrying out their duties. Beyond this he felt the need to pay his respects to Rysakov, that blubbering lad, the need to see it all through to the very end. The very least he could do considering how much had resulted at this very time of promotion. The Tsar's great pleasure at his achievement in so quickly rounding up the terrorists augured well for the future of his new career.

Yes, that you and I, my friend, are responsible for this whole momentous awakening, strengthening, new resolve of the nation – for these thousands their enthusiasm hopes – for the Tsar's pleasure – for his confidence in the future – for – why! no limit to it! You and I – and of course Colonel Dobrinsky who would always have fullest backing for his considerable skills. Something else too involved – hold on to it! don't let it go – some key here for the future – that – that – even in this tight linked chain of dedicated terrorists – one link – you! – blubberer – proved to be weaker than the rest. A law then for his work – revealed. Guiding rule then that every chain had a weakest link – to be expected – looked for.

Gift, lad – to the very end – and acknowledged.

"Disgusting! A quite disgusting display!"

"Good God! he's stringing the poor devil up with two ropes."

"That damned hangman's drunk."

"Those in charge deserve to be strung up."

Calm, Vyacheslav!

What a cosy sleep! keep absolutely calm – and vigilant!

Hear it! not just the disapproval – but sympathy – no doubt about it sympathy for the condemned.

Reason indeed to be here and face this ghastly mess.

Look to it Vyacheslav – that future – and his wrath!

You are directly involved – and this could not be chance.

At last all hanging and still, so leave with dignity. Face out this threat of farce, of Russia a laughing stock around the world.

All these damned journalists. The questions already waiting on your desk.

To whose advantage this mockery?

Question everything again from the beginning for your beginning. You are defending your own.

Who chose this hangman?

Who chose the rope?

No detail too small.

An enquiry to begin immediately.

Time is on your side.

Make the correct gestures and bide your time. When you are there, beholden to none, you'll show what you can do for Russia.

Solovyev became aware that attendance at his faculty lectures was dwindling. Appointments with colleagues were somehow not kept. Information about committee meetings reached him too late. Manuscripts accepted by the printers were mislaid.

Pobedonostsev reluctantly forced himself to read Solovyev's lectures concerning Godmanhood, but soon gave up, appalled by this by this mystical metaphysical rubbish, dangerous rubbish. And all accepted by those damned liberal professors. What unbelievable delusion. Little to choose, from the outright socialists or the liberal Yid effrontery. In fact more sinister – in the guise of more Russian than all of us!

Pobedonostsev called a meeting of the Synod to spell out the implication and give a stark warning.

Just think, members of the Synod – Solovyev's father, the eminent historian – his grandfather a pure soul – an Orthodox priest. Not the slightest breath of suspicion there. On the contrary, only loyalty vouched for. And his brilliant academic record – examined, praised by professors and all manner of superiors themselves all supposedly – yes – now he had to name things by their right name – supposedly –men who knew what was what!

Was the Procurator warning – threatening?

What was he getting at?

"Members of the Synod, isn't it clear – the enemy is within! Each must look to himself. If those chosen by God to be ultimately responsible for the destiny of Russia – through loyal service to the Emperor – are not themselves purged and purified, then indeed the AntiChrist has already won. Strong measures must be forthcoming. Let all inwardly and in all solemnity prepare themselves in the name of Christ."

Enigmatically he left it at that before opening a general discussion on much more mundane affairs. That much he could and must say at this moment of trying to come to terms with the deepest meaning, so elusive, contradictory as yet of the Solovyev Tolstoy business. Deepest meaning, to do directly with Russia's orderly future. The question – riddle – of thought – of thinking itself. Question, at once so obvious yet so hidden. So simple yet so overwhelming.

Thinking itself was the real issue and that whole business a destiny sent challenge. Those all too clever ones in their malicious ignorance – both of them long infected by the European disease of reason – of a so-called logic – which led straight down into the Adversary's abyss of nothingness – had served God's purpose in awakening him. In fact – and here right here – a decision must somehow be made – be enforced! – all such ifs and buts cast aside – back into that same abyss where they belong – that only the few were wise enough, pure enough in heart to prevent this gift of thinking from being exploited by the Adversary in order to extol the so-called glory of man, of satanic man. And that only the few could accordingly be thus authorised. The rest, that vast ignorant herd must be protected from such dangers – an absolute responsibility here.

Something long-term, all embracing was leading him onwards into a new place, stern, exhilarating. To this lonely place led for the nation's spiritual security. Vision yet reality. A stronghold. A building in the spirit, of the spirit. Yet to be, vision, beacon, it would need refined skills to create, that it endure invulnerable. That was the shining in this desolate place. A new vision.

For sure, others too on a path to this place in a crude way. Ivan's black knights burning with zeal for their task – emblazoned banners of doghead and broom, sniffing out, sweeping clear all treason, subversion. Ivan's holy terror – its protective power – through elemental fear.

Nicholas' Third Section – a great advance – so very close – barely grasped in its audacity – 'to enquire into all matters whatsoever' whatsoever! – very foundation of the citadel – very strength of its builders and defenders – but made a feeble nonsense by liberal corruption.

A new order must be created equal today to the Adversary's guile – equal – and more – to the Adversary's present terror tactics. An organisation that would lead all Russia to this citadel – that would guard this citadel. Only the mad, the accursed and the Yids would resist it.

A new purging, refining, strengthening of all Russia demanded.

Organisation, and again organisation. The State first, Church second, family third – and last – very last – the so-called individual.

Now was the time to measure up to the task and show what could be done. For their own good, men's thinking must be disciplined, contained, purged that they hold to the right task.

Now there were men about who could carry it through. He knew men, and that much he knew. Since the assassination and hangings loyal voices were demanding a new way forward. Men awaiting the challenge, seeking the inspiring vision, the all embracing goal. He would make it his business to see such men. To speak with them out of this truth fearlessly, as he had done with Alexander Alexandrovich. A return to the foundations, the enduring.

Spiritual goals – his especial task and responsibility. But inseparable the organisation needed for their achievement. To think one was to think the other. No boundaries from this standpoint.

Organisation organisation – von Plehve – von Plehve – the name persisting. The name mentioned more than once by Alexander Alexandrovich with such pleasure for his quick round-up of the terrorists at such a vital moment for the State. Von Plehve who'd restored such confidence in the State's strong arm.

No chance in any of this. No chance in any configurations or individuals in these critical moments of Russian destiny.

Alexander Alexandrovich was surely implying that this was the type of man now needed for Russia's future – a policeman!

Is that what he himself had in mind? – that he had been thinking of a policeman? – – of course!

Policemen – of a new type – who else – from this standpoint?

And this man had served long in the Justice Department. Who better to deal with this higher justice calling?

What else – dedicated – conscientious – all of it coming so rightly together. One good thing then from Loris-Melikov, this man's promotion just in time.

He would meet with von Plehve.

Absolutely no expectation as yet. Down! Damp down all fanciful optimism says this vision, demanding extreme caution. The stakes are the greatest - a nation returned to its truth.

Let it be policemen but of a new type.

To simply see.

A loyal clever policeman, praised by the Emperor, who has rid Russia of poisonous scum at a crucial moment of her destiny.

To simply wait and see.

When von Plehve received the request to meet Pobedonostsev he was surprised and curious. No reason for the meeting was given, Pobedonostsev was a name of power, very close to the Tsar. Count Ignatiev was already strongly rumoured to replace Loris-Melikov as Minister of the Interior on the advice of Pobedonostsev. That was very real power. A man so close to the new Tsar was seeking him out. Call things by their proper name! the man in charge of the Church's affairs wants to meet a policeman.

Make sure of your ground! He's the Tsar's one-time tutor, and close confidant for years. He hates the Jews and the old Tsar's liberalism.

No problems here!

But stay cool, watch every step, observe, evaluate as never before - something is at stake - you?

After checking that the address given was in fact Pobedonostsev's he grew more curious. Since his appointment a year ago personages of high rank had sought him out to make certain investigations but the meetings had always been in out of the way places. Here then was absolutely nothing to hide.

From the beginning when shown through the apartment, so still and silent, by Pobedonostsev's pale wife, he felt that this was no simple first meeting. Entering the study he sensed the challenge to enter intimately into this other's world. Such gloom, crammed bookshelves, worn carpet, icon, this other opposite, their focus, feeling overpowered - by what? drawn too close - to what? draw back! observe, hold off.

Bowing slightly he sat down in one of the two chairs set before Pobedonostsev's desk. Preparing to take some measure of the man a sharp sense of unease had to be mastered. A warning sense demanding recognition. Behind his gestures of practised ease he must observe more scrupulously than ever. But how to observe this which was ebbing and flowing.

Listen! He's begun - he's speaking. Of course no need for introductions for appreciation at your appearance - this beyond all that - he knew.

"This recent affair which you dealt with so energetically - thoroughly - well we know for sure now the full measure of those who would bring down the State. But I've seen what you and your men can yet achieve," said Pobedonostsev, straight into it, nothing personal here, if this was his man.

Von Plehve's intention to watch his every step was becoming a sensing, a quickening, what was it? Tone - content - an authority - in some way decisive for his advancement.

"- cleansers of Russia - a real force that will keep every Russian on the right path - trusting no one - suspecting everyone - with ceaseless watch to stamp out this madness! Von Plehve it must be - must come - if the State is to be really secure - that thoughts count as much as deeds. Which can only mean that we - you and your men - know what people are intending."

Intending? Borne this far so quickly - yet not unfamiliar! - here the knowing. His own deepest thoughts but uttered so fearlessly by this other - the lurking suspicion of fantasy vanquished, dispelled.

"That would ensure security. To know, to strike before the deed occurs. Only then will the State be secured. Only then will the true Russian people be protected from subversion. That, will be your concern - responsibility before God. Of course the Jews Liberals intelligentsia are the main subverters, we all know that. But we - your men - must go further and include everyone. Your men must be able to reach further than ever before. This disease of wrong thinking must be prevented from spreading. Their so-called legality, need for proof, is a complete aberration. Our justice can only be that which ensures the State's security. And the State's servant and master is the Godly chosen one."

He stopped, knowing himself youthfully anew through von Plehve's confirming presence, this other so with him through all that was evolving, knowing himself as the one - of course who else? - who will advise Alexander Alexandrovich, and lay down the guiding lines for the new constitution which will must take into account just this very possibility - actuality of deciding - for that is what it must be - deciding! - what men's intentions were - deciding - deciders - and the powers of the deciders.

In the silence von Plehve glimpsed an extraordinary horizon. Such possibilities, such a new reality posed. Depth - boldness - comprehensiveness.

Intentions?

What men intended?

"And of course," Pobedonostsev eventually continued as though musing to himself, "everyone must eventually be involved."

Everyone? Was he serious?

"Everyone?"

"Of course. No one is to be trusted. Not you nor I. The Adversary lurks in every soul. What makes you or I different? Only that we know His presence - His power. We've looked into the abyss and not succumbed. By no means have most the strength to resist. We must protect them in spite of themselves. That's why our work, your work, is essentially a high work. The weakness, the errors have to be corrected. Your men will become guardians of the State, on which all else will depend in Russian life. Your men will ensure that good thoughts will replace bad thoughts."

Von Plehve felt uneasy, confused. Strongly drawn, yet somewhere along the line - this Adversary - this high work - uneasy. Yet - beyond the context, that tone, manner of speaking, authority, as from another world - so strange - so familiar!

Pobedonostsev felt greatly encouraged. With this other he had brought to expression those difficult, uncertain ideas and now felt their reality, their power.

With this other.

As even now, but for him alone, the shaping source of utterance sketched a final picture. No afterthought but keynote of the whole. For him alone. Keynote he knew it, conclusion, but so puzzling. Impossible - but must be - if the State was to be secured. A Law of laws, against independent thinking!

Both men sensed a building, as fellow servants of its master-builder. A building, spectral as yet, which they would embody through the substance of men's lives.

"We are of course both agreed on absolute secrecy - - you don't think this remark necessary - but our personal feelings are of no account compared with the task ahead."

Von Plehve, irritated by the merest indication of mistrust,

nodded in agreement, increasingly respectful for the other's sense of what was going on in him and able to express it in a way that bound him still closer.

Pobedonostsev's secrecy spoke truly enough, beyond the words. His own very sense of self now felt changed by this new prospect.

Delicate, intimate processes had begun and must be protected.

The busy world below began to thrust at them.

"I find it incomprehensible that Loris-Melikov let the traitors get out of the country – the Plekhanovs – Axelrods – Deutsches – and spread their lies from abroad," began Pobedonostsev, already testing the new ground.

"Then we too must go abroad," responded von Plehve almost immediately, this new 'we' inspiring, empowering, "we too could have men stationed wherever they are, trained, vigilant, ready and able to use whatever methods are necessary – I too ask – was Loris-Melikov's reorganisation after the Khalturin affair just a liberal smokescreen?" Yes, this to be risked now about the man who had promoted him.

Indeed they were speaking the same language – even that the same language was speaking to them engendering this intimacy, this intimate recognition.

Pobedonostsev nodded in agreement.

Von Plehve ordered his coach back to his apartment.

He would not spend the night with L.

He must be alone tonight to take in, taste to the full all that was happening. Such a vista, such opportunities, new men, new methods, new goals – surely? Such a strength, purposefulness through Pobedonostsev from the very centre of affairs – to which he could be led. And all turning on this puzzling, provocative intending. Everyone's guilty intentions! And that Pobedonostsev had spoken with such authority – implying what surely – that he himself would could ensure that new powers were available.

Nothing absolutely clear but to stick with him.

Only that he was the man – that he was indicating a new way forward – and that he believes I can do it.

Why wasn't the coach moving?

Good Lord! is this your place?

How strange such uncertainty.

The coachman was puzzled by his master's long wait.

Von Plehve vaguely opened the coach door, went past the

dvornik, ordered his servant Paul to bring him tea, then went straight to the study.

This intending - men's intentions - how? - just how?

Was Pobedonostsev fooling him?

Right! take a man! - a suspect - here - X - ring him with red - - then smaller red circles for all his known political contacts - then green for non-political acquaintances - then brown circles for persons in contact with friends but not known to him personally - then - contacts between the friends of his friends - and this for everyone - the whole population.

But all this - is not intentions.

Intending - intentions?

Anything! Everything could be judged a bad intention.

Vast this vista.

Vast this power - to make Russia secure.

Is that what Pobedonostsev was getting at?

But of course he's right.

That idiot hangman, nothing mysterious about it, just rotten organisation. That's what Pobedonostsev's pointing to, a new kind of organisation.

Jurisprudence in practice.

Realistic jurisprudence.

We are all guilty - he and I?

Such objectivity can only be trusted.

He's right - if the State is to hold firm - a discipline, a fear - men's intentions towards it are crucial. Then we must have the power to decide whether those intentions are bad or good before they become deeds.

It is a high work - he's right.

But why this unease - bodily - bodily! whatever it was - not the utterance - that was purest bond.

And that - hold to it! Pobedonostsev was in some way superior to the new Tsar himself - superior.

The Tsar, settling down in Gatchina with his wife Maria Fedorovna, and four children, Nicholas, George, Xenia and Michael, was eventually informed of some hitch in the hangings. He did not demand details, it was still extremely painful. But any hitch was typical of the present lot. Anyway, he'd assured Constantin Petrovich, they'd be hanged and in spite of the hitch they'd be hanged. Couldn't be soon enough to have new men about him in every ministry for the new way ahead.

This draft, from Constantin Petrovich, of a manifesto setting out the ruler's intentions, was perfect. Every word, phrase, tested as he went through it many times, sounding as his very own voice.

> '*In the midst of Our grief the voice of God commands Us to stand bravely at the helm of government, trusting in Divine Providence and with faith in the power and truth of the Absolutism We are called upon to defend; and We are determined to strengthen the State against any attempts to weaken Our power, and this We do for the benefit of Our people.*'

Loris-Melikov, Abaza, Minister of Finance, and Miliutin, Minister of War, only knew of the manifesto when it appeared in the Government Herald. Clearly Pobedonostsev's fanaticism had proved decisive for the new Tsar. Coming so soon after Pobedonostsev's savage indictment of the reform policies which they had long served, left them no alternative but to offer their resignations. The Tsar most willingly accepted. The first lot to be rid of. Pressured by Constantin Petrovich's anxiety for quick, decisive action to check all public uncertainty, Tsar Alexander completed the ministerial changes within two weeks, with a new man in every ministry. The message was clear.

When Count Nicholas Pavlovitch Ignatiev, envoy and ambassador for the previous two decades, was appointed Minister of the Interior, those responsible for the violent attacks on the Jews in southern Russia and the Ukraine during these last few weeks now knew that they would have official backing at the highest level. The journalists who had been hinting since the murdered Tsar's funeral that the assassination was part of a Jewish conspiracy against the Motherland; the officials who unexpectedly appeared and vanished in cities of the Pale of Settlement, rural area where most Russian Jews had been confined for one hundred and fifty years; the police who colluded by remaining inactive during the violent destruction of Jewish homes and shops, killings, and maimings, and the Governors like General Drenteln of Kiev whose equivocal hints implied that the Tsar wished to see the Jews suffer retribution for the assassination.

Pure chance that Helfman had got off? She was a Jewess!

They all knew that with Ignatiev at the Ministry the way was wide open and that all this was just the beginning of a real, long awaited confrontation with the Yids. And there was more, from the very highest level coming through. The new Tsar's marginal comments on a police report from Warsaw quickly went the rounds.

"I'm glad in my heart when they beat the Jews but it must not be permitted."

So! make of that what you will- gladden H.M.'s heart – and let the beating continue!

Count Ignatiev was appointed after several long conversations with the Tsar and Pobedonostsev. The Tsar had been emphatic about the complete failure of all attempts at forced Jewish integration since Alexander the First. Count Ignatiev was delighted to realise that not only did his long held views on the Jewish question absolutely coincide with the Procurator's, but that now he was in a position to take practical measures which would finally and thoroughly deal with it. Even a great privilege this. A free hand, Tsar and Procurator fully behind him.

A key issue emerging in the conversations was the economic one. Everyone knew that throughout the Pale, where segregation of the Jews was originally intended to keep Russia clean, that even there – in the rural areas – the Yids had come out on top again with their money cunning – sucking the life out of the peasants with their age-old thousand different Yidtricks.

"Then start there!" declared the Tsar, stating what was obvious for himself.

In late August he issued a ukase signalling intent at the highest level. It 'declared unambiguously' that relations between Jews and Russians were 'abnormal', and that 'injurious' Jewish economic activities would be thoroughly investigated and brought to an end.

So! loyal Russians, make of that what you will, but Yids beware!

Professor Vyshnegradsky, Minister of Finance, was not at all happy. The nuances were far too crude – almost indifferent. Were the three concerned at all that the Paris Rothschilds had already withdrawn from the consortium negotiating the half billion franc loan because of the recent anti-Jewish disturbances – and what that signalled to the Bourse!

The Jews read the ukase as an unambiguous warning.

Count Ignatiev held to the Tsar's 'Start there!', with enthusiasm and relish. Straightforward as that for His Majesty – and it must be so for him too. Think as simply, honestly, straightforwardly as His Majesty – that in the Pale the Jews must be forced out from the hamlets – small towns – from which they carry out their parasitical activities – their centres of alien culture. And then some hard facts – in a memorandum to H.M. irrefutable facts which will strongly influence H.M. in utterly rejecting Count Pahlen's Commission on the Jews – the umpteenth! We don't want any more Commissions on them – crazy advice that enfranchising them would help resolve the Jewish Question.

So!

Laws! – to force them out of the Russian countryside into the cities of the Pale – and – at the other end – all the Yid climbers – Yid professionals – so-called respectable Yid tradesmen – who'd managed to wheedle and push their arrogant way up in our cities – due to Liberal idiocy and plain treason – they too must be severely dealt with – yes – suitable laws to flush them out too – back into the cities of the Pale.

Yes, it would all be possible with H.M.'s full backing.

Enfranchisement as an answer – God help us! Pahlen's either mad or a traitor!

From now on the war against the Jews must be a war of extermination – not more futile attempts at conquest.

From now on let the economic basis of Jewish life be destroyed – ensuring that they died out completely.

Not Russianisation but that every Jewboy should feel keenly and never forget that he is an outcast. Once and for all an end to these too well-intentioned efforts. From now on Russian Jews to be wiped out. An end to the Jewish Question.

A straightforward memorandum to H.M. right now. The momentum must be kept up.

'Sire: the main cause for the movement lies in the economic situation. During the previous twenty years the Jews have taken over trade and industry, purchased areas of land by sale or lease, and by means of their unity succeeded in exploiting the main body of the population, particularly the poor, hence arousing them to a protest which has found distressing expression in acts of violence'.

Alexander found it irrefutable.

After weeks of discussion between the Tsar, Pobedonostsev, ministers and high officials, Pobedonostsev drafted legislation which the Tsar signed on August 14th. Legislation above all, intended by Pobedonostsev to safeguard the security of the Russian state. It gave provincial and city governors absolute powers during states of emergency which they alone could call. All political activity was to come under the control of the Corps of Gendarmes. Not subject to any juridical supervision, they would have the right to search, imprison and exile on their own authority.

Whilst drafting, Pobedonostsev came to see the Corps of Gendarmes as the vital organ of the State's living unity. These men alone, chosen, called, beholden to none else, would determine guilt, who was guilty. Simply knowing that, everyone – everyone! – would surely be on their guard to ensure in turn! the State's security.

This the building's sure foundation – deeper one couldn't go. Foundation for the Russification of the non-Russian territories, for education – for the press.

And – within the year surely, only logical conclusion – that the Gendarmerie must have the right to declare any citizen as subject to overt surveillance. And the power to pass sentence autonomously.

No necessity to prove, to justify anything to anyone else.

For von Plehve who since his appointment had taken over the old Okhrana organisation with its agents provocateurs, cryptography experts, large pool of informers, this new power was decisive, just as they had talked it over together. Everyone, just as Pobedonostsev had emphasised, would think twice about the way they – comported – themselves. No one could be sure that they weren't under that eye. And powerless – no one to appeal to if arrested and hauled away. The very minimum purely for form's sake, justification.

And this power now at his disposal.

His new gendarmes. Theirs the absolute right to determine intent. Not restrained by excessive formalism – able to restore order quickly – to fight revolutionaries at a truly professional level. Secret agents – spies – informers etc. – all of great value but only now with this new foundation to come into its most effective own. And this power to subject any citizen to surveillance – can only lead – to the refusal of trustworthiness to any citizen – which leads – everything leading logically – juristically eh? – to the – when necessary of course – barring of attendance at institutes of higher learning – and in particular –

of employment in public institutions.

Eventual - then must and will be - the State's control and direction of everybody.

Firm foundation indeed Constantin Petrovich!

Von Plehve and Colonel Dobrinsky worked closely to implement the new legislation. They considered two aspects as basic for this great calling of State guardian, natural gifts and a thorough training. The ideal, a harmonious blending, was rare. Each tended to note more particularly one aspect in the choice of aspirants, and their complementarity strengthened the resources of talent in this new, formidable war against subversion.

Thorough training and experience were essential but not to be overrated. The confidence generated could even prove illusory, dangerous, and men who depended on them alone though generally assured of a certain minimal efficiency, could still make crass mistakes. The born gendarme could sniff out the stench and track it through delicate, obscure reaches. That unique odour given off by all those sucked down into anti-state activities, some original source of corruption. Ideal was the born gendarme, thoroughly trained and experienced. Rare birds! Life being what it is, von Plehve and Colonel Dobrinsky were resigned to the fact that most gendarmes of the new force would continue to be average, loyal, well motivated men ready to learn from their mistakes.

Since September new, younger faces were appearing in the St Petersburg gendarme Headquarters. Some old hands, who had taken for granted the sitting out of their last years before being pensioned off, found themselves unexpectedly posted to provincial backwaters. Uncertainty reached the higher ranks. Those unaffected tried to wrest some pattern from the comings and goings which clearly signified an extensive reorganisation. Younger men definitely seemed to be favoured for the rapidly expanding departments specialising in dossier compilation, interrogation, blackmail, cryptography. The new boss was hot on specialisation and facts - more and more facts. But where was this new lot coming from? What were their backgrounds? Some seemed to have appeared from nowhere.

I mean what about that Rachkovsky fellow? - his bow - that's what gets me - whatever is he doing with that little bow - that's what it is - a bow - all over the place - so helpful - so hardworking - of course I keep it to myself - a climber, anyone can see that – Antoshin's usually right – one from the other side – something to do with the Drenteln affair – of course I know the approach – but can you really ever trust them?

Von Plehve and Colonel Dobrinsky wondered whether they had one of those rare birds in Rachkovsky. As a member of Colonel Dobrinsky's team chosen for investigative work soon after the assassination, Rachkovsky's dogged concern for detail and his patient determination to follow through the finest nuances of a discrepancy, had all proved richly rewarding. His hunches were proving remarkably fruitful, certainly a man to watch for the future. Though chided about his obstinacy and time wasting he bore it with cheerful resignation. Composed, concentrated, he slogged his way through piles of reports from everywhere, in spite of the constant pressure and anxiety engendered by the Tsar's ceaseless demands for immediate! urgent! results!

Rachkovsky knew this composure, almost timeless waiting, as essential for the task of sensing the life behind the words on these piles of documents. Until, forcing nothing, expecting nothing, subduing all preconceptions and judgements, the demon of seeming relaxed and revealed itself. Through this composure he was learning to recognise, evaluate and trust this intuition.

Rachkovsky knew that extremely tedious tasks were often being pushed onto his desk. He took it all in his stride, prepared to learn from it all as much as he could because something was telling him of the future and he was daring to listen.

Many more than the five accused and executed were now under surveillance due to his work and with the new powers, could at any required moment be taken out of circulation, for good if necessary.

And yes, he had been tempted to the other side. And now he was their man for the future.

In the light of Pobedonostsev's revelation, von Plehve had come to learn that such men – and Pobedonostsev had emphasised how their numbers would be increasing in such critical times – who had succumbed to temptation, precisely such men, when they were returned from that nether world, often proved most extreme in their loyalty to all that was true in Russian life. Loyal to the death. For they had seen farther than most and their gratitude for the dynasty, for that whole sacred order, was intense. They burned with a flame of most earnest resolve to ensure that the dynasty endure against all its enemies.

Sometimes when Rachkovsky raised his eyes from the files and glanced round at the others, making the little bow to each and all from within, the resonance of that life pledge took strong hold, eyes down, work on, recall, relive, but work on, that moment demands even now here, shadowy but more real than all this which is its fruit, life pledge, terror born, sustaining, empowering all this work.

Head down, be seen pondering gravely, but forced now, even here it insisted on full recognition - that then now he had is nothing - it was absolute powerlessness, eighteyes stare alone existing - he nothing - forced to relive it - move your pen on

"Yes - we were friends -"

down drop deep into eighteyes' abyss - but - but

"but - I knew nothing whatever of his intrigues -"

saviour's word from where?

eighteyes heard, recognised were ready. They heard that note, beyond the words - vulnerable - no longer his own - that bitter-sweet note familiar - warning - of confession - guilt.

"then you can help us - -"

suggestion?

question?

order?

deliverance from the abyss - a light shining -that you thus allowed to become as one of us - the empowered - to reach here be here where the power is - such relief gratitude life seeping back - present happiness with all you around me - that voice from afar called back into being - himself again but a new self - a knowing self - eighteyes stare vanished all relaxed genial.

So swift who had done it? - plucked from the abyss salvation - enduring pledge that never again - never need again to endure such terror. Only to be at all times where the power was. To be something someone.

"Rachkovsky, have you come to any conclusions?"

"Yes indeed," he answered readily, handing over a substantial report to his departmental chief.

Many conclusions, as I work through file after file, statement after statement, that never again will I be that victim. Never again pierced by that eight-eyed dagger spread-eagled in frozen terror.

That here, working here, the line drawn taut - that terrible innocence - remembered - unbelievable - ended. Living live this - innocence - indifference - neutrality - not sustainable - either for or against.

Forced to come to terms with life.

Here - spell it out again as you glance round - never too often - no place for friendship's innocence - simply one of them - accepted as one of them - simply the recognition - cautious appraisal - that we all serve the same master. Ah this dark height reward enough.

Reward enough never again to be victim,

Friends? - only others.

"An excellent report Rachkovsky!"

There there! all servants - but sharers too in his magic - this omniscience raising us above the mundane daily life.

Bitter-sweet this knowing but a knowing, not an innocence. A knowing which side you were on. That the only side to be on for survival was theirs.

Well, no longer quite his own.

But something has to give.

Survival is a very serious matter –not for dreamers - eighteyes' lesson - for which some thanks!

Quietly immersed in the dossiers and files hour after hour, day by day, mastering chaos with order, endless facts with the meanings of power, Rachkovsky felt himself increasingly in touch with an intangible something. Here was work for a lifetime, so watch, learn and keep silent.

Here much was left unspoken. They recognised one another, respected one another, yet were wary of one another. A great mass of information was collated and shared.

But that other more intimate knowing was decisive for the real embodiment of the order. All knew that.

Late September, von Plehve and Colonel Dobrinsky had decided that the question of émigré activity outside Russia, intensified since the assassination, must be seriously addressed. Instead of depending on chance information trickling through from various unreliable sources, a security network of trained, trusted agents must be organised, to penetrate, counter the émigré groups, which included terrorists who had fled the country and other political opponents. Of immediate concern were the former members of Land and Liberty, who had split from the terrorist faction and were active in Switzerland under the leadership of Plekhanov.

Rachkovsky was one of the men chosen for the new security organisation to be centred in Paris. His movements were surprisingly light and quick for such a heavily built man, as he entered the office for his interview. That bow also, correct but – never mind – his record excellent – hear him out.

"Absolutely essential," Rachkovsky answered immediately, confidently, as one already fully involved, strange feeling this, "London – Geneva – Berlin – Paris – we should have our men in all of them. Paris the best placed. Take Paris for instance –"

Von Plehve felt himself listening to one who spoke with authority – strange!

"with sufficient funds the concierge class will prove invaluable. As for penetration we must go much further –"

Much further?

"not simply –"

That 'simply'.

"inciting revolutionaries to commit violent actions and then ensuring their arrest. All too long drawn out – wasteful of time, energy and money. Our agents should be encouraged to plan – carefully – their own bomb attacks and carry them out – – If innocent people are killed? –"

Von Plehve heard that innocence in question – that there were none such for him?

"whatever discredits the enemy is justified – surely?"

Where was this man taking him? – so absolute the power?

"That won't be difficult for me. I was once seriously involved in opposing the dynasty –"

Was this man interviewing him? Making him complicit, to what?

"an experience I feel deeply grateful for – something of a privilege –"

"Penetration?" recalled von Plehve.

"So – yes – to return – penetration – I for one would be well prepared to use especially for my bomb throwers – revolutionaries – men who had given up their cause for any number of reasons – redeeming work for them eh? Yes, Paris would be the best centre."

Rachkovsky felt an extraordinary confidence, even superiority over this other man who was listening, watching and trying hard to keep up with things.

He left von Plehve's office - on the way - to more - much more than information - agents - concierges - on the way to power!

Subdued, before the unacceptable immensity of this vision but for Russia - yes! but for himself too!

Let von Plehve feel him so - beholden to him- be moved by his trust through that confession.

No - not Geneva - Paris! - what a vista!

At Gatchina, hour by hour, day and night, thousands of troops, Guards, Cossacks and police, patrolled every inch of the way. Inside the palace each of the several hundred rooms were constantly checked, and outside, the gardens, parklands, lake, woods, fields. All these watchers to be watched in turn by plainclothes agents, holding innocuous positions on the palace staff including administration, and reporting directly to von Plehve. He had decided that passes and familiarity were not enough. His special agents were chosen and trained to deal with a really determined adversary.

Everyone coming to the palace on official business, of whatever rank, however familiar, had to report in the guardroom with their official pass and photograph.

The life of this us to which this pass admits you, draws from His power, and His presence, which we guard. His power, remember, even you high-ranking passholder, His power alone, keeping each in their rightful place.

General Baranov tirelessly drummed into the duty officers involved that this reporting by visitors must never be regarded as a mere formality. In truth, even the passholders, though identified as one of us, yet each time, the act of identification should be carried out as if for the first time. It had come to that. Each time in truth as if the person presenting themselves to the officer on duty, was wearing disguise! Never a formality. That would be to treacherously underestimate the enemy.

That would be the most dangerous feeling of all, certainty, even an absolute certainty - that's for God alone. We here at Gatchina, guarding His Majesty with our lives, can only be as certain as possible, which means every conceivable effort must be made, even if we have to question well known persons of highest rank for the common good, that is - for Russia's good, not at all a personal matter.

Thousands of eyes, trained, watching for the least sign of irregularity, anything not in its usual place, anyone not on their usual round. Any embarrassment on your part, any arrogance on theirs – of no concern. Here if anywhere in Russia all are equal! Clear enough now eh?

Every shadow of doubt to be dealt with immediately. Question! Investigate! Record! and inform one's superior.

All existents under the stare of this omnipresent eye, that uncertainty be made certainty. Gatchina a bastion of certainty. But ever lapped by lurking waters.

How can we be sure?

Can we ever be sure?

Space, that everywhere, whose appeal is to freedom, now become sole enemy, threat of threats. Mind staggers. Yield. Obey simply obey. But what are we looking for? That which we cannot see!

Our myriad-eyed watch General, never slacking, all-seeing presence, pressing hard, close. Nothing ever to be unseen, unwatched, and we too, each for the other, fixing, pinning down, penetrating, not to be withstood.

Our thousand-eyed being, wall, barbed, guarding the treasure which holds the whole together.

Of course we're all watching one another – but with the watch, of the One which we are. Russia's shield.

Nothing to be left unseen, lurking threat.

Everything forced to be what it was before the heavy thrust of this watch.

Everything must be seeable seen – the seer too.

Nothing to be taken for granted after Khalturin. The enemy must be assumed present everywhere.

If not above ground then below ground.

Each midnight the duty officers were to assume that the enemy had not been detected, no more than that!

General Baranov conferred daily with his duty officers and reported daily to the Tsar.

Pobedonostsev had learned to accept, to justify the discipline. Of course the distaste, irritation, of course they know who I am. But precisely, the safeguarding of the Emperor's life no matter what measures are needed, ensures – is inseparable from that who I am.

Baranov's measures could not be bettered. In him at least I

chose the right man, fully measuring up to the enemy.

All those of highest rank had to come to terms with these unprecedented security measures, accepting the necessity, almost.

But of course everyone knew who they were.

But that wasn't the point.

Just here, as the bit of paper was being checked, certainly yes with the respect due – one was actually being made to feel that everyone was equal before the Tsar.

But in a somewhat painful manner be truthful, very rank at this moment felt as given by him – and equally – able to be taken back by him.

But even that closest one Pobedonostsev, showed his pass and photograph – some consolation there.

All at Gatchina knew an eeriness, a void, a nothing – something, flickering everywhere in this play of uncertainty. Some enduring fear beyond this mistrust of each for one another. A helplessness.

Alexander's dread and uncertainty since the assassination, was muted, contained by this fortress yet never silenced. Baranov's security measures had begun to establish a routine which though chafing allowed a certain contentment. Not to visit St Petersburg was no real restriction let alone a challenge to his power. Even providential justification for withdrawing utterly from that hateful St Petersburg stew. The traditional excursions throughout the year, to Livadia, Peterhof, would still be possible through Baranov's security plans.

And it was good that the children would grow up in this place where he had once known happiness. Life here would be healthy and natural for them. Surroundings to shape character that must see straight to the heart of things, beyond all that infernal deceit and corruption that from now would be done with. Providence was at work as Constantin Petrovich insisted, if only one would humbly acknowledge it.

Well, the boy was dutiful enough, but more was needed than that.

Always that damned more whenever he thought about him – forced to think about him – very seriously right now! Hadn't he become Tsar without any warning? In spite of that future held out by Constantin Petrovich's Providence – Constantin Petrovich's confidence – the thought that Russia's future, as it were even now – harsh! harsh! – but very strength to acknowledge even that truth – make it his own with Russia's destiny – hovered over that boy likewise! – would not be denied.

In spite of this whole protective presence around him, these loyal soldiers everywhere, well armed, ever watchful, saluting with pride, he knew that his was to be a life always under threat of destruction by the enemy. And that's how he would live it – to the full – as one condemned to be attacked – but taking it on as a fighter – in good heart – and in spite of everything still reverence for Papa. You good Russian soldiers stand firm with me! Destiny – destiny – but it was little George who so clearly had the spirit – liveliness – strength that would be needed. Nikki was so diffident, out of reach somewhere – what was it, that felt so uneasy about him.?

Tsarevich Nicholas, in his thirteenth year, delighted in the move to the vast Gatchina country estate, far away, safe they were all saying, from that dark place in the city. Why had they done that to poor Grandpapa – would no one ever tell him? Dark crowded crying room where something terrible was happening to Grandpapa. Good God's gift! that here was going to be their real home.

Lake's gliding waters, shading woods, open endless sweep of sky above, so different, dear, calling, befriending, hinting adventure – beyond all the soldiers everywhere – the guarding – far far beyond the barrier of their kindly watching, something else calling.

Along that rough track, leading away from behind the stables, after family lunch, on – and on – alone! unwatched! – unseen! – this was for him! – that he could go on, like this, so far! his own world awakening.

Unseen except by those round him trees hollows mounds creek green light fusing.

Called to be alone in this unseeable place of himself.

No one else in this vastness, so far reaching, living silence but him.

With this new power, new knowledge, to turn back now, hold fast to the glimpsed gold of his own, and plan a venturing forth right into the heart of this new world awaiting.

To plan as he hurried back along the muddy track, returning, gratefully returning, to plan to get to know just how far he could go, alone, unseen, trying out himself to get to know who he was, secretly, with this new strength. The two of them, seeker and sought, riddling hide and seek.

Not missed!

Unseen!

Unseeable!

Ages passed!

Move warily! round the stable corner into the glare of everyone's seeing now, and join George for games in the playroom.

Wilder, more daring the plan. He would do it again but during lesson time. Such pain, a wrongdoing, but this way only it had to be done. Such upset cause but his worth prove. Upsetting Papa! but must do it. His own worth prove.

Yes, during lesson time. That really would be himself. During that barrier forbidding all questioning, all life of this quickening self.

This lesson learned, only to repeat day after day what a Tsarevitch has to know, a proper pupil acceptable to Papa.

Leave questioning alone.

Christoph Engelhardt, Pobedonostsev's middle-aged appointee to tutor the Tsarevitch in German, sat waiting for his pupil at the bare wooden table, books, dictionary, lesson notes meticulously set out ready. Quiet moment in this restrained autumnal light before his diligent, reserved pupil appeared, always on time, boding well. A good providence here working for him, model pupil and just recompense for such responsibility, State pension assured.

Nine o'clock - and the hand moving on - no footsteps approaching.

To think that the time would come when his pupil would be Tsar of this immense empire!

Moments of freedom unveiled - for himself! Just to muse for himself! But - but - don't dare! So stark this voice of His Majesty. Very first instructions so stark, not allowing for the slightest deviation.

"Treat him exactly as any ordinary pupil! He must always be on time and work hard!" Why, if anything, right now that tone seemed to imply even more exacting standards than for any ordinary pupil.

Well then in these respects his pupil simply could not be criticised.

Five minutes past nine -no approaching footsteps - the silence deepening along the corridor.

Exactly?

Until now it had been so.

Ten - eleven - twelve minutes late - and it grows!

Stop staring out of the window - address the issue - my pupil isn't well - not feeling well enough to attend - then why haven't I been informed - ridiculous this anxiety - what tarnish on me? - lessons have always gone smoothly - we get on very well together - then why hasn't someone come to tell me?

but yesterday

now!

now you'd better remember yesterday - have you been wanting to try and forget yesterday - only yesterday? was it?

watch your step!

this post is no ordinary post

nothing here to be taken for granted

those soldiers through the window - tramping around - looking - looking - all day - every day - fully armed.

Yesterday's lesson! don't let go of it it's telling you something very important - for your own good - wasn't listening properly - mumbling answers - wasn't there -

and - you let him get away with it - were taken by surprise - didn't know what to do -

wasn't there! - no longer interested at all -

he's not coming! - no longer wants to come - dreadful this certainty - but insistent

and - and - and -

this dreadful judgement on himself overwhelming

that he had been utterly fooling himself - that the Tsarevitch was in fact fed up with his lessons!

Where is he?

Nine forty seven - on and on -

very serious matter - he was staying away on purpose - where?

where turn? - where turn?

who would know?

that his pupil was hiding from him!

And - at whatever cost to himself he must report raise the alarm - that the Tsarevitch was - missing!

not to make it known immediately, unthinkable

to inform the Emperor His Majesty - nothing less would do.

Dreadful this paralysis, entanglement.

You should never have accepted this post – no pupil this but Russia's future – the pride – terrible temptation – the responsibility! Wrench out some coherent facts for God's sake to put to His Majesty. Your guilt grows by the minute.

The Tsarevitch has not appeared for over an hour.

No one has come with any explanation

then the Tsarevitch is – missing – is not under anyone's watchful eye – has escaped surveillance

everyone knew this was lesson time

But

to inform His Majesty immediately could cost him his post whole reputation

not to inform? the same!

Hurry hurry along these endless corridors – no stopping to explain – risk the guard's threatening gestures – fly past them. "I must see His Majesty immediately!"

The armed guard stood firm outside the Tsar's study, gripped tight his rifle barrel, before this breathless, desperate man.

"I must see the Tsar immediately!" shouted Engelhardt.

"What's going on?" shouted the Tsar.

"Engelhardt! Engelhardt! Your Majesty a very serious matter." Engelhardt shouted back, relieved through the contact.

"Let him through," bellowed the Tsar, angrily leaving Pobedonostsev and striding to the door flung open by the bewildered guard. The Tsar, not shifting his massive bulk from the doorway, looked down hard at his son's tutor.

"It's the Tsarevitch Your Majesty – – I – – I don't know where he is," Engelhardt managed not daring to look directly up at the Tsar.

"What d'you mean?" the Tsar threatened, bitter that hint of an insecurity.

"Mean Sire? – yes – indeed – I mean," as the Tsar yielded way for him into the study and confusedly he noticed Pobedonostsev, "that it's over an hour – and the Tsarevitch hasn't come for his lessons – and no one has informed me of anything – and – and I think – I can only think – what else can I think," he stammered timidly, tearfully, "– that the Tsarevitch is missing."

"Missing?" bellowed the Tsar at him, making him tremble,

"– we'll see all about that!"

He shouted for his aide-de-camp, Colonel Pogodin, in the

adjacent office, to fetch General Kudrinsky the Palace Commander, immediately.

Missing? with these thousands of so-called guards.

Missing?

That such was possible?

So soon! General Kudrinsky's assurance that every inch every person was under ceaseless surveillance.

All illusion!

So soon! and Nicholas himself the proof - of all and any - Nicholas himself!

"Engelhardt! When should the Tsarevitch have come to you?"

"Nine o'clock Sire," answered Engelhardt so relieved that everyone was involved now.

"So - you've waited over an hour to tell me - that's a very long time Engelhardt."

"Don't dare speak to me," he bellowed at General Kudrinsky struck dumb by the open door.

"the Tsarevitch is missing! If your valiant watchful troops don't find him within the hour - you too will be missing. Vast is Siberia - get out! Find him!" he threatened, shoving General Kudrinsky hard, back into the corridor.

Engelhardt desperately took the opportunity to follow quickly behind the stricken general. The Tsar slammed shut the study door. Pobedonostsev continued to be engrossed in some documents. That was how it should be!

Alexander stood by the window, furious, and annoyed that the boy could cause him so much trouble. Again again his son! and Russia's future - infuriating entanglement when all seemed on course with Constantin Petrovich's encouraging assessment of the new appointees' progress in all departments.

Tsarevitch Nicholas knew that here, furthest edge of the woods, tender shade of ancient pines, ripened corn beyond, waiting, just here he was free of them. Just here in this wood's silence whose every tree was for him. Just far enough away from the palace from Papa. Just far enough away to taste this freedom - himself!

Just far enough away to stand by this sea's edge, own horizon yearning, own.

Just far enough away to avoid too much trouble. Palace sounds still heard.

Of course the pain to come, but deeper still to drink of this delight and strength – so brightly awake with this sparkling life.

To wander unseen I alone called by each and all here in this my world – so far away from Papa's reach.

This gentle humming air is sound of me.

Lost yes lost to them in this secret place of himself – yes! he knew it was himself. Unknown. Unseen. Yes – to be lost unknown unseen in this my world – challenged endurance courage – in this uncertain world.

"Tsarevitch Nicholas! help is near! help is near!" called Lieutenant Samarin, slowly advancing with his Cossack platoon towards Nicholas.

The whole wooded area was ringed by a huge cordon frenziedly ordered into place by General Kudrinsky, and thick with soldiers beating, poking, stamping about, wildly swishing around with sticks, rifles, swords, fearful, earnest, everything in sight suspect, trees, dead branches, wild shoots, clumps of bramble, fallen cones, the very air, all threatened with direst punishment if they failed. And the Tsarevitch when found, to be dealt with extremely carefully – whatever that meant, every officer briefed, these words and God help you no other, "Your Highness, the Tsar orders you to return immediately to the palace."

"Are you here? – Are you here?" called Lieutenant Samarin closer, desperate to know, to find the right words.

That was him too, being called, to turn around, away from the cornfield, the beating, swishing, stark echoing raps on the wood – painful – no need to treat them like that, closing in. Lieutenant Samarin appeared with his men, from all sides encircling, all halting, hesitant.

But they had found the Tsarevitch, nothing else counted.

"I lost my way," said Nicholas. Lieutenant Samarin smiled gratefully. Such relief all round as the Tsarevitch straightaway stepped it out with them back, oh yes back, returning to Papa, trembling.

Where had he been? stepping it out with these smiling Cossacks, returned to the world of men, safe, friendly forms – world of Papa's huge shadow.

Straight to Papa's study through these thickets of fear, he leading them – simply that Papa sees you knows that you're here – trembling victorious – trembling he'd won.

Back to that world he must go, called, no matter. Go with

them but different, fearful but different, knowing this newness about himself but returning.

Lieutenant Samarin and his men were delighted.

Who was going to ask the Tsarevitch how he'd done it?

How could it have happened?

Alexander's anger was becoming uncontrollable. Back and forth he struck out from desk to window, staring blankly at the lake, his boyhood boat at its mooring. His hands, whole body sought relief.

"What are we going to do with him?" he snapped at Pobedonostsev, still studiously concerned with the documents.

Alexander snatched at a report on his desk then slapped it straight down.

"The sooner you take him in hand the better. But four years to wait – that's a dreadfully long time. These wretched tutors – he's making fools of them."

Pobedonostsev knew to keep calm till it subsided. With measured intent it sought its target and relief relief.

Alexander picked up a brass poker near the burning logs. The wild consuming power him yet not him, challenged, challenged to bend – back – back – to break – to break it – to break himself – glimpsing proudly his strength, power, his power, yet afraid of it. Compelled to master it for wild it sought anything a whole world to destroy. Bending to break, bending with gritted teeth and back, bending and back, to snap in two, two wan lengths, let drop to the floor. Never before had this strength thrust itself up with such violence, desperation.

Pobedonostsev knew well what was happening. This too was the strength Russia needed. But the intensity of Alexander's upset over the Tsarevitch greatly surprised him. Very much more was clearly involved than he ever suspected.

Hearing the timid knock on the study door Alexander struggled to compose himself, to ensure that the danger had really subsided. He grunted something, vaguely aware of what presence might be there. Nicholas entered, fearful, dumb, his Papa so near longed for but across such desperation.

Alexander now knew who he was, that he had come, that he was there! But he did not want to look at him. Nicholas, trapped in uncertainty, dreading Papa's displeasure, stared down at the carpet. He sensed as never before Papa's dissatisfaction with him but too a new note, life's seriousness.

So distantly Papa was speaking about him. He must listen most seriously to these words, life of his life, they are coming from Papa.

"From now on you will study properly - -"

So glad that Papa's great friend is there wizened one told off in front of him - but he'd done it!

"Every morning you'll be at your lessons on time. This nonsense will stop. You'll become the Tsarevitch - my son!"

Relief, even to hear rightly so Papa's anger - terrible anger - but Papa's.

Unseeing Alexander pointed to the door.

Nicholas withdrew, trembling, bewildered.

"Constantin Petrovich we must make something of him. I'm under no illusions. Anything can happen. At any time. And I'm not happy, not at all happy about the Tsarevitch."

Out then, for truth's sake, for relief, that something had come to a head. But what was it about the boy? Something he still couldn't get hold of. As though he didn't belong not quite one of them - so ugly such feelings!

After Pobedonostsev left he stood by the window, to watch the reflections cast by his boyhood's boat, touched with rippling tremors in the autumn dusk. No not boding well for the future. Would whatever he achieved be carried through by that boy?

Well, Constantin Petrovich knew it now - that too a relief.

II

The Plekhanovs

Soon after the June 1879 meeting at Lipetsk when eighteen members of Land and Freedom, led by Zhelyabov and Mikhailov, decided on a strategy of systematic terror, directed first to the assassination of the Tsar, a conference was held at Voronezh for the whole movement. Two distinct groups emerged. The People's Will led by Zhelyabov and Mikhailov. Black Repartition led by Georgy Plekhanov and Pavel Axelrod.

The People's Will put politics first in that the execution of the Tsar would force the authorities to grant civil liberties, when the serious work of preparing the revolution could begin. Black Repartition decided on peaceful propaganda among the peasants for a just redistribution of communal land. For them the evolution of the peasant commune and agrarian socialism was the only possible and just social future for Russia.

From his considerable experience as agitator in the St Petersburg factories, as manifesto writer on behalf of many groups and individuals severely treated by the authorities, twenty four year old Plekhanov concluded that although the city workers would certainly have a role in the revolution, the countryside – the earth itself – and how could it ever be otherwise in Russia - its voice of justice would be the heart of that revolution which must come about. The peasant question was Russia's essential question. The village commune's future was Russia's future. Steady agitation for a just division of that earth was the only way forward.

Dark earth.

Dark people.

That darkness, which Pavel insisted on despite the old Land and Freedom party's so-called failure, that still our task as propagandists is to transform ourselves, so as to feel one with them. Ours the task still to leap that abyss and become one with real Russia's millions. And the good Russian earth would have it so.

The unsuccessful attempt to blow up the Tsar's train by the

People's Will party in November 1879 and their ensuing defiance, "A Declaration of Implacable War!", forced the police and gendarmerie to take the most urgent measures. From his recent record they had reason to regard Plekhanov as a prime instigator. Informed thus by a sympathetic official, successful identity papers were drawn up for him in the name of a provincial nobleman. He shaved off his trim red beard and moustache, and with his wife Rosaliia closeted himself in a quiet quarter of St Petersburg, reading, writing and taking his meals from the landlady.

Revolver and knuckle duster finished with. All hope vanished of a scientific career by way of the Mining College. The word now become the weapon to fight for Russia's future. A word rapidly maturing in the cut and thrust, explosive targetting, bruising violence, cracking impact of polemic.

In ideas the real explosive power, unconfined by space and time, indestructible.

Learning to accept that his fervour, dedication, will to sacrifice, was become this study, this writing. But painful coming to terms with this seeming passivity, no less! This standing back, being thrust back unwillingly that the given be revealed for what it was. That Russia had reached a turning point and that the way forward be found through study and word. Word honed by an evermore sharply refined awareness.

Word ultimately, yes ultimately, the only victorious weapon.

A sympathiser warned of a full scale crackdown by the police, very soon. The papers of everyone in the city would be scrutinised. It was voted in committee to send abroad Black Repartition's four leading members, Plekhanov, Axelrod, Deutsch, Zasulich, until the crackdown was over. Switzerland was chosen, Zurich, Lausanne, Berne, and Geneva for Plekhanov. All places with Russian contacts, where Russian exiles and students had settled and studied for the last three decades.

"Well, the chance to see Lavrov while you're there," said Nemtsov to Plekhanov, "rue de Viollet, don't forget," he continued, not really serious. Yet. Yet – some need to come to terms with Lavrov?

They left separately but it had not been an easy decision especially for Plekhanov. He insisted that they could easily evade the police for a few weeks hidden by supporters in Pskov. The first number of the new paper would be off the underground press in a few days with his leading editorial emphasising their solidarity with the old Populist aspiration for an agrarian revolution to divide all the land among the peasant communes. A Russian agrarian socialism, Land and Freedom! to remain our fighting slogan. These two words enduring, fullest expression of the people's demands. And it was essential for him to know the members' responses.

In turn the committee insisted that just his safety mustn't be risked, he having achieved a firm theoretical foundation for their work. But even while arguing the point Plekhanov knew with trepidation the possibility of a challenge to that foundation. At this very moment! But he would not yield easily.

Apparently, at first glance, this book of Orlov's just out, 'Communal property in the Moscow District' presented statistical facts proving the decline of the village commune. The main cause apparently, a growing clash of interest between the poorer and the more affluent groups in the commune.

Prove?

Orlov was a zemstvo statistician!

Well, he was good enough at figures too. If they insisted on Switzerland he'd spend the short stay there with no other task than those Orlov figures. Figure by figure nothing less for already everything seemed at stake. Yet somewhere, leaping past that already with a strength glimpsed - a strength glimpsed that would carry him through and beyond this whole Orlov confrontation. A strength glimpsed which sensed this confrontation as inexorable - destined - and which made it so! Strength which - yes - enabled - accepted this burden of leadership - of responsibility for lifedeeds - sacrifices - all knit together in a most subtle yet real way.

He responded almost casually to Deutsch's and Axelrod's concern, even dismay over Orlov's findings.

"A few days will do to go into it. Figures can mean whatever you want them to."

But he sensed in that effort at casualness an acknowledgement of profound implication.

Settling down in a corner seat of the second class compartment on the Warsaw express as the last passengers hurriedly bustled aboard he knew this as very beginning of a questioning task to gain some certainty, for himself, about himself. Task even needing a strategy, this arming with several newspapers, this necessary aloofness. This threatening hostile something which only now, at the very moment of departure, declared itself. Something so intimate, so me, which now felt threatened at the coming separation. Which now felt drying up, cut off from an ever present source. In spite of all the evils - as nothing, mere temporal defects, in the presence of this life which we call Russia.

Rousing - dedication to their liberation, that mighty unseen all - heart of his existence but so too his intimate bond with the comrades.

This whole moment, as doors slammed shut to the guard's whistle, the train pulling away to the vigorous blare of its horn, now revealing itself as one in which he must somehow on this journey West, find himself. Glance up then to acknowledge the young couple opposite! That was that. Return. Somehow to gently encourage the presence of the recent past - fragments - wholes - constants - constants insisting - Kazan - Voronezh - Kazan - Voronezh. This countryside a blank.

Somehow through the confrontation with strangers - the changes - Warsaw - Munich - chaotic memories - anxiety - unreality of it all outside - an ever more constant resonance of those before him - as they were now becoming - Bakunin-Mikhailovsky - Lavrov so many who had all made this journey. Voices - hounded out - their cry of anguish - Herzen's bell tolling - to - into - Pavel's people - cursed Russian abyss - but bell ringing out - always from the West as the train steamed on - was he? to be one of them - extraordinary thought - from where? - the facts please! - to counter any such anxiety from this corner window tucked far back - the facts - his actual situation - a temporary strategic move - a few days? - weeks? at the most - but - but - this actual movement away - as the train steamed further and further away - and in these circumstances - drawn together with all those voices - inexorably. His facts please! Fight to get at the facts of his recent past. Live through his own recent past and bestow some certainty about himself. For none of this strange voyage was arbitrary - all decided out of a necessity.

It could only be Kazan.

Kazan the beginning. Leap from his mouth that utterance - making him state-criminal Plekhanov - or iron decision from whence? - could not be otherwise - deciding his whole future.

And Voronezh.

Kazan.

Essential this reliving through to make sense of what was happening.

Lavrov! – why! – there could be a meeting!

Just shut your eyes – pretend to be dozing.

Orlov – yes Orlov – a reckoning to come – waiting there for me – that I take you on.

Yes deep the pain, but resolved.

Forced – forced out temporarily – by his own destiny
with the crowd outside Kazan cathedral
in his very heartbeat now caught up
a leap!

A leap – that's what it had been – onto that ledge – flash of redbrick narrowness – to speak – very leaping up of such unknown life in him onto the ledge – into this destiny – above the crowd – new presence leapt into – leap of a new Georgy Plekhanov – rousing – declaring – amazing – all those unknown ones around him become we – amazing all – and to realise only now that he had escaped! – been allowed to escape! – looked after – a purpose – a beginning – so clear now against the boy's arrest. Who was that boy? Who were those other youths – all ten year sentences – and the girls – all long sentences – he – rousing – declaiming – escaped!

Escaped – leaping into Land and Freedom with revolver and knuckle duster so quickly.

Warsaw!

What meant that name so blank!

Compartment emptied.

Against the rhythmic pounding of this journey West – return to Voronezh! relive – confirm!

Another leap! These leaps – from whom? – whence?

That Morozov's call for widespread revolt was a madness – nothing less – to him – as a lightning its unreality – their silence at his denunciation of such madness – his walkout, no compromise possible – all from that same unknown life, in its certainty – leaping – alone. Now at this moment grateful away – to feel the empty temptation – fever – in Morozov's call. Of course the dedication – courage – sacrifice – of his own too – in those leaps till now – but a darkness, needing to be transformed in a thinking way – and all before Orlov's challenge.

all unplanned unexpected

out of an inexorable purpose – no other way
to see and know that now!
only now!
thus to be carried forward
but now to know it

this much, fruitful – this journey – to have come this close to himself – that it could not have been different – an inevitability – and so standing firmer in this   present –

Prague

Munich

names telling of what? for him – all this excitement bustle children luggage porters – what? had it to do with him – still still why was he here? could – would make no connection – that would be yielding to the temptation – that it could might be something more than temporary. Many had taken this journey West and never returned home. Yes precious their voices – but never again our Russian voices.

Live as though still in Russia – talisman obscure – stakes high – spell, your life.

Skirting the lake south from Lausanne the train steamed slowly into Geneva's Cornavin Station. Still with him as he made his way to the Charushin pension in the rue de Berne, was the flash of the water's pure light through all this around him – mere temporary refuge.

So strong its radiance.

Don't yield in any way. Your purity be guarded!

Lavrov nearby – Voltaire, Rousseau, already insisting they've walked these neat streets too. This one that is you – forced here only – for a temporary stay.

Spell not to be broken – still in St Petersburg – in Russia – surely a dream what was happening.

No yielding to the stranger's allure. To keep purely to the task in these few days. To confront the Orlov challenge with all his strength. Orlov's numbers – numbers! – challenge? – engage – but warmly positively. Numbers? – then that will be a firm scientific way of challenge – then to know one way or another – surely – what is going on.

This is it! No. 19.

"Monsieur Plekhanov?" asked the neat elderly Russian lady.

"Yes."

"Please come in. I'll show you to your room. Please don't

hesitate to ask for your needs. We eat at seven. Breakfast is at eight."

He followed, to a small room on the second floor. He stood listening as she went down the stairs. The house was very quiet. He opened his suitcase and took out the Orlov. Through the window he saw on the other side further up a large estaminet called Soleil-Levant from whose fascia board a cheery faced sun flamed.

Mme. Charushin, no questions asked! Others had been here. She knew. Her purity good for work. Letter to Rosaliia on safe arrival, then to work.

Straight into Orlov's figures and conclusions. Hold firm to his link on link. The dessiatines have been measured, counted, dessiatine by dessiatine, cool, crystalline, and the roubles have been counted, rouble by rouble, kopeck by kopeck, and the percentages have been extracted, one hundredth by one hundredth. No guessing, mood, feeling – only method, step by step, objective, self-evident – no hopes, expectations, confused strategies. But bracing now, the challenge that from the figures only one conclusion to be drawn. That – fear not! – in the last resort fear not! Somehow the numbers themselves were encouragement. The fact that numbers – the certainty of counting, had been brought to bear by Orlov, somehow told of a return despite their immediate threat.

Walk it out! early each morning away from the small talk, politeness at breakfast, away, from these strange streets surrounding the lake and into the countryside of his own space as of old at home on their estate in Gudalovka. Lonely ardent walk of youth spacing out some grand perspective, unknown future calling.

Returning each evening to the amiable chatter of supper was a relief, hoping for news. Nothing of town or people to be seriously acknowledged. No! Not to accept Orlov's threat to their entire agrarian programme – their very life. Certainly a shift inevitable but something still to hold onto. The commune could surely be saved if the peasants could be moved from passive expectation of a general repartition to an active demand for it.

He must be back in the St Petersburg reality to continue the struggle anew, yes even with Orlov's challenge.

Descending into the town from such distant heights. Strange this reality of buildings and people. Descending from that harsh loneliness of thinking, bewilderment which had to be endured. Thinking which had to be. Lonely ascent, dangerous travail - well, pride that he had come through. Familiar this old experience. Bitter-sweet. To leave men. To think for men. And to return - from that enchanting wilderness.

Men!

Which men?

Those he knew - was united with in St Petersburg.

The paper was out by now and he would soon be with them.

Day by day waiting to hear yet not wanting to be recalled.

How - why - should this be?

Torn away thrust out from that in him which was Russia.

Walking as of old to assuage the pain.

Only to be back in the thick of things before it was too late!

What was this, lateness bearing down on him?

Too late?

Too far away?

Peaks goals - and that parting of the waters. Wood's gentle presence saying 'Here to be helped!'

Then to let this countryside bear him along.

Day by day, logical step by step with Orlov, each now so tested, its certainty assured. It meant, beyond all doubting, that the very idea of agrarian socialism, the commune as Russia's salvation - was utter illusion! And his planned future, very self-image - the same! Don't dare deny it!

This is your truth! Pure light granted that alone can carry you forward - at whatever cost.

The editorials and articles ready for the next issues, the grand guidance for comrades - all based on illusion. Such warm feelings for the people but dreams - not numbers! Orlov's numbers could not be faulted. Inscriptions in tablets of stone.

Something else must come of this somehow.

A friendly strength this, for pure light's deeds which would carry him through. To trust in this strength which hinted that all this was necessity.

Day by day and in the walking forced further away from that fairy tale. Walking in which he heard the pace of his very own life resounding.

His so-called leadership, firm foundations - illusions!

A leader of dreams - sentimental nonsense.

Orlov had taken nothing for granted, not been carried aloft, looked coolly at the people – true foundations. He'd noted carefully the increasing numbers of peasants who invoked the name of God to be freed from the land, the commune with its injustices. Counted carefully the increasing acreage becoming private property, and then drawn his irrefutable conclusions.

Take courage!

This is your beloved science recalled.

From these pure numbers must you be able to forge a new true foundation.

A new beginning.

From the calculable.

To stand back now thus before that self-assured Plekhanov is to know that it is finished with. Then he must let the others know immediately, Lev, Pavel, Vera. Not to go on in this stupor one moment longer, or else wait till the return and at the very least in some way prepare the group for the change.

But if not the commune – only the urban workers left!

To begin again but how?

Groups newspapers programmes – of no avail whatsoever unless somehow built on this firm Orlov foundation.

Breathing deep the mellow autumn sweetness, the journey took him along the Northwest shore of the lake, through fields, vineyards, past farmsteads and hamlets, sensing day on day something about the way these men were working. A difference, drawing him, but felt as that other world around him. Stance, pace, thrust of arm, call to fellow, passing greeting to himself the stranger, all in this sweep of feeling's divination telling of something different. A strength informing these heights. A strength setting a certain space between men, calm, dignified, upright. Mountains woods lakes men beginning to claim him from out of that fastness.

At the end of a winding mountain road, ahead on the further curve, Nyon's five towered castle, the town. The castle alone, towers poised pointing into the blue. The castle alone, all else dim. Castle alone hovering over the lake, sufficiency, fulfilment, journey's end.

On the sixth morning he awoke early. News must come any time now. This wearying theoretical uncertainty could only be resolved back in the reality of St Petersburg. He must be on the move, dressing, quietly downstairs. On the small bamboo table by the hanging mirror, letters, some unclaimed for several days. But there it was! His name. A strange handwriting. The envelope postmarked Bremen? Bremen? And a strange hand? Not the letter he'd been expecting. What matter. Contact. And he would soon know what was happening. Not here though. It must be alone - a solemn moment to hear the voice of that living bond.

The lake's calm waters were solace and strength as he strode towards Nyon. Solace and strength the letter in his pocket, voices of them all and Rosaliia.

A vision before him on the further curve, hovering vision, light woven, all substantiality fled, or stony stronghold of sombre power? Which was it? Very set, texture, rooted in this place, this whole living configuration of lake, hill, wood, vineyard. He knew that he was called on to steep himself in it, acknowledge it with the fulness of his presence in a most solemn way. Some profound inner gesture which he had to follow through, attuned to that compact presence, so settled, yet hovering over the waters. Reassured, his aloneness, rejoicing too, strong in that proud castle.

Ready now to open the letter - what indulgence was this? with men labouring all around him.

Indeed it was time to return.

The neat handwriting in widely spaced lines informed of furniture and other goods on the way from a Bremen warehouse as ordered.

As ordered?

Good god Georgy! Wake up!

Both ways the winding mountain road empty. He held the letter against his thigh and awkwardly rubbed spittle between the lines, right down the page. Holding it high against the brightness pale signs could be made into words whose ghostly gist was very clear. 'All Black Repartition arrested printers press seized Rosaliia free S.' S? - Shashkov! - always dependable. What was he doing in Bremen? Rosaliia free. They were letting her finish her medical course - it must suit them.

Such a reckoning then!

You did sense something eh?

Don't let go already step it out!

Turn and back to the town. Keep walking through the stream of this helplessness rage that these few faintest words signs have shattered your existence into such confusion.

Yet voice calling to accept even this and fight on - purely

willing yourself to endure - even through this nothingness, stubborn will of this walk insistent in its driving impulse, a becoming a strength being forged. Strength, a movement, sustaining. Answering no questions, potent for some future turning, turning hard towards this place, surroundings where the challenge must be taken up anew.

In this affirmation a rhythm sounding harmonising with all out there, very heart of the mountains distance setting sun. Old vast fusing. Men gone, only echo and reflection. Not wanting to leave this vibrant space. Peasants - terrorists - commune - articles - what for? Why? in this sufficiency, silent surge and certainty, calm and purity of this starlit dusk.

We!

Amazing! this we of those lines speaking - that boy reciting in secret - first very first of leaps - in secret.

"We - in the heat, in the frost, strained our sinews.

Toiled with our shoulders eternally bent.

Lived in mud hovels, were sodden and frozen.

Fought with starvation, with scurvy were spent."

This we! - its strength

its voice

through Nekrassov

This we! - these words - as fresh enduring - whole life's word.

Stop! turnabout to know the space of this freedom, to know so keenly as pure deed of your will this pledging anew out of this new-born strength. Turned to the crescent moon - the stars, the unknown town. Such a fullness and with him no fruition only fragments, promises, stops and starts, dazzling glimpses - led astray.

But - We!

Returning past the vineyards, knowing that pledge thus renewed as most real deed. Knowing that beyond all failures schisms arguments - beyond - his goal remained - the people's liberation.

Yes Nekrassov - he remembered. Reality of that pledge - in its potential for creative renewal by him in freedom.

Back, on the quayside, approaching Mont Blanc bridge this whole town, country itself, was wanting to be known by him! That he had been sent to just this place now beckoning, so many, all the exiles who sought justice, freedom, human dignity human rights for all Russia. All those who had thought here, worked here, walked these streets, and he now too so unexpectedly. A rightness, a calling in it.

Small beneath that shimmering radiance from above, yet cleansed, connected. Simple echoing footsteps, one with these others here. Held in this tranquil night. Small timid hesitant but a man amidst these fellow men. Freed from that arrogance. Thus alone, feel assured that you are truly admitted into the ranks of the fighters. This is the price they have all paid. Till now you have paid little.

The people's liberation – in this loneliness?

To get a whole people on the move – from here? – but – shattering this hammer – only in this aloneness – can the reality of this pledge be drawn forth – conjured – no outside help persuasion suggestion – only this pure hammered pure – to give my life its meaning fulfilment – hope.

That he had despised exiles for not being truly Russians any more! Westernised and all that!

Lavrov! So close! just streets away. The man himself. How strange. The very one whom he had so recently attacked over his failure to recognise the absolute necessity for action – and he himself now in the same position. Then on your knees!

Go! Yes go!

Pay your respects to the one whom from the beginning has insisted that mass agitation is the foremost task for Russian socialists.

Orlov!

What would Lavrov make of Orlov?

This wretched Orlov business!

What why was he wanting to ask Lavrov about that?

Why was he wanting his help?

Orlov! – then why not?

You and your so-called sacrifice of a scientific career!

This man was a professor of mathematics! Thirty years of his life given to the cause – from here! so far away – so unRussian eh? – his voice – his call to us all sounding so pure – so near – and you dared even imagine that he'd lost his Russian roots!

Yes! Go! Ask for his help.

There the reality, the need, to discuss Orlov. He must – and who better than Lavrov?

You have nothing to be ashamed of.

Your record stands firm too.

Kazan.

To factory agitation – successful pamphleteer and yes, acknowledged leader.

A supplicant? Never!

He could go as equal to equal.

He would meet Lavrov with respect, great respect, but as a fellow fighter, in the same great cause.

This wandering up and down the Rue du Viollet – Nemtsov had known? – in such painful indecision, must stop!

and this pride must be overcome

and he needed help.

Never – to go back to the pension and ask Madame Charushin for Lavrov's number.

Recalled!

Recall!

Take courage – he is the one – his are the binding words for us all.

'I shall release myself from responsibility for the bloody price of my development – for the blood and labour which has been spent on it, if I use this development to minimise present and future evil.'

To meet him as brother through these words which are my life's pledge too.

There we know each other.

There we are together.

They are our ground.

Seek him out from this beginning with courage!

Ask someone! – most basic – no short cuts. Right here – this house!

Retired engineer Monsieur Beaulieu slowly opened his front door to face the well dressed foreigner of fine bearing.

"I'm looking for Monsieur Lavrov – can you please help me?"

"Of course – you are from Russia too?"

"Yes."

"Not far to go – my friend – number twenty four, just further down on this side."

"Thank you for your help."

Simple enough, yet such an encouraging sense of help, answering help.

The ground floor of No. 24 was in darkness, bay windows emptily glinting back the street light. Above, light seeped from a heavily curtained room on the first floor.

He tugged at the brass bellpull, listening hard, confused. How to introduce himself? What had he come for? What was he wanting?

Ridiculous! No right way yet he must. To force a way in, such was his need.

He tugged harder, heard movement, wanted to flee from with this weakness this wretched need.

So steady those footsteps descending, approaching, he must now stand his ground.

"Georgy Plekhanov," he said immediately to explain somehow before the calm, friendly way of the slightly built man, spectacled, with thin silvery hair and a trim grey beard.

"Plekhanov! - well, well," said Peter Lavrov, looking intently at the stranger, very surprised, sensing much difficulty for this young man, "do come in. Have you been in Geneva long?" easing the way as he led upstairs to his study.

Plekhanov followed into the well lit room, walls shelved from floor to ceiling with books, folders, papers, an absolute certainty telling in waking dream that this was the world of his immediate future - the world of study learning knowledge. Future? - the francs in his pocket wouldn't last a week.

Embarrassed, awkwardly silent he sat in the green wicker chair.

Lavrov tried again to ease the way.

"You're staying in Geneva?"

The purity space, Lavrov's openness acceptance - made possible why! - some kind of a purging confession. "It must seem odd -" he began, "that I - who have knocked on your door - I who - -" he trailed off.

"Not at all, be at ease, we all have our own way to find. None of it's easy. The paper I founded has just kicked me out - no! None of it's easy," he went on, wondering, Plekhanov, the razor sharp critic, wounding, ruthless, and this young man sitting with him in such painful confusion.

Confide Georgy! let go! the truth!

What then, to speak right out of his despair?

"I'm afraid at the moment my situation is impossible. The entire Black Repartition group has been arrested in St Petersburg. The press has been seized. Myself with three other members left stranded here. But that isn't the worst. At this very moment Vasily Orlov has shown – proved irrefutably – that the commune is in irreversible decline. Proved, with statistics, in strictest detail. So what is left Peter Lavrovich? What is left? For all of us – any of us?"

That all, needing to draw Lavrov into this desperate reality.

Let Lavrov good Lavrov, answer now to that distraught fullness of his heart, to that bitter truth striking them all down.

"Georgy Valentinovich," responded Lavrov, sounding this new note of intimacy, so encouragingly, confidently to Plekhanov's bewilderment.

"– four years ago you led that first great popular demonstration outside Kazan Cathedral. An historic deed. Your agitational work in the factories, an historic deed. And now your group arrested. Be proud! Know just how real a danger the autocracy sees in it – and so just how important it is for Russia's future. But your destiny is catching up with you. What you've told me about Orlov's findings can and must lead you to the only possible way forward – for all of us! They corroborate absolutely Marx's law of historical development. That the revolutionary impulse will take hold through the urban workers. Not, definitely not, through the peasants. Iron laws which Russia too must follow and which you must master. Iron laws based on reason, as night follows day. Hard thinking, deep study is needed. Something we Russians have to learn. Nothing else will see us through. Sound clear thinking that's what we must bring to the people! Clear logical thoughts so that actions based on them must succeed. Heroism, sacrifice in plenty, always has been. But they're not enough. All this energy and dedication, all those deeds simply peter out into wastelands time and again. We must find the right basis for our deeds. Absolutely unshakeable foundations – and they exist! Scientific socialism is such a basis. And this, my dear Georgy Valentinovich, you must master. All good Russians are natural socialists but our socialism must be put on a truly scientific basis that now exists. We must simply continue to learn from it."

All so warmly binding, their common background too. Both fathers, officers in the artillery. Both fathers, devoted monarchists. And they both had been students at the Mining Institute.

Plekhanov returned very late to the silent pension. He would risk the most timid of knocks but was ready in this new-found strength to spend the night on a bench by the lake, anywhere. Madame Charushin quietly placed her book on the bedside table, drew on her blue dressing gown and went down to let him in.

"It went well with Pyotr Lavrovich," she knew.

"Yes, thank you," he agreed, relieved, surprised.

Every day he went eagerly to Lavrov, to question, discuss, learn, to hear from Lavrov of his meetings with Marx and Engels, of his experience with the Paris Commune and of his thoughts for the future. He felt at home in this place.

Read! directed Lavrov to book after book on his shelves. The Communist Manifesto as priority, as first and last, of course, but he had read that years ago.

Read! repeated Lavrov, the note warning, insisting.

Reluctantly he turned to it, hearing in the opening words, potency of absolutely new life meaning. The opening words, no need to go further, "The history of all hitherto existing society is the history of class struggle."

Peter Lavrovich was right. In such reading to learn – who you are! What the world is!

"The history of all hitherto existing society is the history of class struggle," as in a childish dream was that previous reading, an old naive Georgy knowing action alone as meaningful – these as mere words – now charged – powers for the world's future.

And that – all.

'All' – thought through with intensest application – come into its own through the thinker as a living creative energy – to transform – destroy – build anew –

the final leap – absolute – potential for total transformation – deedground of a revelation.

Light of this 'all', active knowing – burning away appearance as chaff.

Class! as key – as law! – restored, his inmost yearnings in this recognition, revelation. With Marx socialism become a science!

This moment so charged with personal destiny – with him.

That just now, when for him, through Orlov, the issue of Russia's future had become so uncertain, this science, these laws would explain in full clarity, and point the way forward.

These words spoke with an absolute authority revealing the laws of all social development.

As revelation – yes! But of reason itself, every step provable, what must be, absolutely determinable as with all scientific method.

From the beginning Lavrov met Plekhanov's earnestness, dedication, application, as equal to equal. He withheld nothing in response to Plekhanov's incisive, dogged questioning. Even though feeling uneasily that somewhere Plekhanov was at times pressing close, perilously close to his own painful dilemma regarding the conflict between these very laws and the idea of individual autonomy.

This place was becoming Plekhanov's new home. These buildings no longer threatened as temptation. Smugness, but too a beneficence, this space in which unharassed, one could become oneself, claim what was truly one's own. Move speak think read freed from that constant presence, threatening, accusing, preparing to punish. That ceaseless Russian vigil of mistrust. Dark care! Yes, it was that from this place of lightness looseness.

But this painful indifference between men here? It was care for all Russians but dark suffocating. Here, so awkwardly feeling one's way. 'Keep your distance – don't come too close.' This closeness new realm to be painfully learned.

Slowly to get some balance – to make the best of it – no easy entrance – a subtle threshold. Each one standing here on own marked, bounded ground, facing as equal to equal. Affirmation, confirmation of each other's presence freely bestowed in mutual recognition, painfully learned but learned.

This place becoming a new home, guard dropped, affirmation begun of his surrounding's reality, as he ranged freely through the libraries, discovering, pursuing, validating, grounding abstractions, checking wild flights, collating, gaining historical perspectives, all in the light of the fundamental law. 'All history is the history of class struggle!' These rows of silent texts waited humbly, available to anyone! There for all men. Intended, ready to speak to all men. The only hiddenness here was not through censorship but the lack of one able to bring to light, enliven all that lay silent. Me!

In Russia the freely uttered word threatened.

Here it alone bore weight, substance, trust.

Here at last to discover the real questions and to follow wherever they led.

Lavrov felt strongly that this young man was bearing something essential for Russia's future. In Georgy Valentinovich's gesture, tone, was pride indeed, the pride of a power well aware of its far reaching ability, its pride justified, in having made itself over, like his own, for the liberation of his people. To this young man he must give freely of his experience and knowledge. His alone, surely by now learned, was the concern for justice and truth, the searching itself, beyond any call for political leadership. To explore, to teach was his task beyond all else. And with Georgy Valentinovich to show that Marx's work not only explained what was happening, but when fully understood would help determine what was happening.

As a result of the St Petersburg arrests, the financial support arranged for Plekhanov, Zasulich and Axelrod during their enforced stay abroad was now unavailable. Lavrov found Plekhanov a tutoring post with a wealthy Russian family, which enabled him to move to a larger, more comfortable room.

In spite of Lavrov's bold attitude over his expulsion from Forward, the paper he had founded, daily meetings with Plekhanov assuaged the pain of an uneasy isolation. That Plekhanov had sought him out at this moment was a good fortune, no doubting.

The more intensely Plekhanov studied Marx, the more vigorous his questioning of Lavrov, the stronger grew his doubts about Lavrov's position. Through the testing of every new concept, theoretical formulation, for its consistency, cutting edge, he became convinced of Lavrov's confusion, of a confusion in Lavrov's thinking. A confusion. A superficiality - yes! It must be called by its right name or the goal will never be achieved. And not only Peter Lavrovich, but in this brilliant light so many dead but not buried. Most serious the effect of these false teachings, leading so many astray.

False.

Name it as you have seen it. No hesitation despite what it must mean, a grave weakening of this friendship. Russia's future first. The differences becoming become! unbridgeable contradiction.

Each time, the same barrier reached, the resistance felt, the sentimentality nothing less! Nothing clearer now, the old guilty feeling. Clinging on absurdly incongruous besides the laws. Clinging on, and for himself too - be clear about that!

That for himself, towards himself too, on this question he must be hard. So deep it went, one's very identity inseparable from this need for the peasants.

In deed

and in one's thinking

to see in them the only possible future for Russia.

And to have gained objectively this self knowledge, precisely through the laws.

To stand back thus from oneself, little by little, unyielding, this very hardness a new strength.

Likewise Peter Lavrovich's illogical conviction about individual autonomy and freedom. Either his 'free deed of responsibility' is outside the law of social development or it isn't. And he couldn't make up his mind. But even – and even precisely for his 'free deed' the social structure was primary. His so-called individuality, precisely, can only reveal itself through the structure of class conditions. Just there! the vacuum of his 'nevertheless' – and his 'possibility'. Not to press Peter Lavrovich further, but to know this as the point of his own parting – need for his own resolution – subsuming all under the law of class structures which themselves provide the means for individual realisation.

His own destiny inseparable from the social context, which shaped him as an individual, and which he in turn was preparing to shape.

Be hard!

No more misgivings.

No more of his own sentimentality over friendship – disappointment – not really wanting to accept that Peter Lavrovich – they had come so close – really couldn't see the contradictions in his position.

Was it that he lacked the courage to follow through the great teacher's logic – to action – to revolution? That 'nevertheless' of his – when pressed hard – decisive – 'My dear Georgy Valentinovich revolutions can't be artificially provoked – historical development – not independent wills – decide – nevertheless' there! there! – 'nevertheless' – 'the revolutionary path is most probable for Russia.'

That in fact, in truth, Peter Lavrovich had never come to terms with Russian historical development – as revealed by the iron law of class struggle.

Let it go!

The task was his alone.

Alone.

Peter Lavrovich wanted his own private version of Marx's laws which would comfortingly include continuous peaceful propaganda amongst the peasants. But for the great teacher, the peasants were not instinctive revolutionaries or even the chosen people – but idiots, plain idiots – that's what Marx was saying. The reversal, contradiction, rethinking needed – absolute. The great teacher could have used that word, chosen it, without any personal feelings involved. A cool scientific naming – 'idiocy' – wrapped in a world of their own – that 'idiocy of rural life – doomed by economic evolution' – then four fifths of Russia's population lacking all political consciousness! The going to the people an illusion! The workers, certainly his experience of the factory workers, had revealed a dreadful naiveté over the Tsar. But his experience was purely subjective. Marx's laws made clear that precisely through the factory system itself the worker's self-consciousness was being forged and at the same time the unification of the working class as a whole. A new class.

Russia was indeed no different from Western European nations.

A way forward then after so many illusions – vain heroic sacrifices – to bring Russian socialist aspirations into harmony with the great historical laws. Then alone it could and must succeed.

From now on all available revolutionary energy must be devoted to the working class, the new industrial proletariat. Nothing of this precious and dedicated strength from Russia's best must be wasted for a single moment on any more illusions. The iron law of capitalist evolution determines bourgeois constitutionalism through political struggle and the eventual political power of the working class through this same constitutionalism.

Leading again but unease.

He was the one who'd split the first united revolutionary movement. Now again he was compelled to attack – it must come to that one way or another – the man who had done so much for Russian liberation – and for himself! But the man who still supported terrorist action and the People's Will. Naively confessing it - naively - unaware then - best supposition rather than glimpse a horrible hypocrisy - of this unbridgeable contradiction.

Once again through him, attitudes perceptions lives would

have to look to a new way forward.

How bitterly he'd been attacked for that split. But he'd had no alternative then, or now. He had not chosen to lead. But he knew he was leading and could not pretend otherwise.

Axelrod, Deutsch, Zasulich eventually found work. Zasulich, badly paid secretarial work. Axelrod with his wife began an enterprise to provide fermented milk products for the Russian colony in Zurich. Together with Plekhanov they began to meet in Geneva and Zurich. They listened with respect to Georgy's enthusiastic appraisal of Marx's teachings and took note of the works he acclaimed but their basic attitude remained unchanged. They continued to maintain contact with the populists who supported the peasants. They began to resent his new-found certainty, its arrogant tone. He held firm, not for the first time pained by their failure to see what he could see, and by a personal animosity so alien to the truth of his argument.

They, like most of the Russian émigrés, were elated at the news of the Tsar's assassination. But they were shocked by Plekhanov's stern criticism of the action and by his forebodings. Stern criticism even though the dead resonated sympathetically in him – nostalgia for that so very direct action – but now the absolutely necessary activity – was thinking. Of course the revolutionary will was crucial – its fire its passion but that fierce wild flame must be tempered to a focused real knowledge – not wildly spending itself in flashes of subjective fantasy.

He was sure that the authorities would respond with a fearful repression which in turn would only intensify a general hopelessness and despair.

The new Tsar's 'implacable' declaration and appointment of ultra conservative reactionaries was proving him right. The three began to follow in his way. To learn that social classes were the driving force and that the working class was the leading class for the future. That the old commune forms had no potential for serving as socialist alternatives in the light of capitalist economic development as reasoned, discovered, by Marx.

And his way meant shifting Russian socialism onto a scientific basis. To understand the law-determined historical process independent of human will. The purest determinism. The individual? – to recognise and work with this law is freedom.

The distortions of terrorism and populism reflected in this pure mirror.

The terrorists unaware of the need to create a mass movement.

The populists unaware of the need for political activity.

The political rights struggle and the socialist economic struggle no longer an irresolvable contradiction. But – as reasoned revelation – that only by way of political struggle could socialism be achieved.

At last a thread, unbreakable thread through the maze of social historical enigmas, darknesses, will o' the wisps, till Centre and Exit were clearly identified – vantage point for comprehensive survey of the whole – survey in Space and Time – the Future outlined – yet to be made – a bright Future – and for its making a comprehensive strategy.

The terrorists?

The terrorists simply – now simply substitute – this in thought as firmer grip still – more absolute attempt still to come to terms with their ongoing life and his own so recent past –

the terrorists simply substitute conspiratorial skill for historical development – but – taking his stand on this now granite foundation – and speaking – declaring – with a ruthlessness hardness – as it must be – 'the laws of history cannot be violated with impunity' –

But – that 'simply' – that 'simple substitution' – no longer as it once was for him sacrifice of one's life for highest ideals –

But – lingering – extremely diffuse – but lingering – an unease at this unarguable transformation – of that 'simply' – so spontaneous from this new place – yet?

When the Police Department realised that the four most important birds had flown, it was decided to leave Rosaliia Plekhanov at large, untouched by the swift roundup of the whole Black Repartition group. She would be a useful source of information about the four especially Plekhanov who must surely contact her soon.

From the start she had been uneasy, distressed, over the Swiss plan, arranged so hurriedly. She tried to hide it, well aware that Georgy was not at all his usual confident self regarding the work. But why abroad – why Switzerland? The four could easily have laid low for a few weeks with sympathisers away from St Petersburg. Now that the worst had happened, she assumed that Georgy and the others would be returning as soon as possible to build up a group once again and try to make contact with the arrested comrades.

By the end of the second week she had become familiar with the informer staring up at her second floor apartment, as he dutifully padded past every afternoon around three o'clock. She knew too that her mail, including letters from her Jewish family in Kherson, was being opened. None of which seriously mattered if only she knew what was happening. This break, silence, unexpectedness, was dreadful. They two, she and he, had never been cut off like this before. Only these echoes over a closing waste flitting about her. Heart's challenge! Flame of my being our being endure!

To grapple with my studies more fiercely than ever!

To forge a strength that will suffice us both - reaffirm, celebrate our bond.

She must not give way to the bewilderment doubt threatening from these brittle surroundings. But why hadn't he written? What had happened to him? There could not be any excuse for him not contacting her by now.

Was he even alive?

From where - this question? so brazen!

Almost to extinction this pitiful flame of myself - fight for your very breath - very breath - such sadness - such a weak fragment.

"To die for the cause!" - once - so long ago - so casual! - through this knowing right now that his death would be her death too.

To kindle into tender life through my gaze and touch this his chair, this his notebook - to reclaim them from the deathly grip. Life life - to kindle.

He and she and to know so keenly now their abiding together, bond, bound, lifedeed, life's deed. This mysterious him - and her. Mystery that she would keep to herself with joy. Her life's meaning in and through him. As faith. Burning as this faith. In spite of this silence, raw fragment of herself - what she did now - how she bore herself would be life substance for them both, present and future. Would create out of itself in faith, the present and future of that reality in which they both stood. Yes! to create and maintain from out of herself a substance from which together could ever draw. In calm enduring faith - in him - in the cause - not knowing yet knowing, she would finish her studies, alone yet ever more with him.

Throughout the five years of intensive study her grades had been excellent. Once qualified she would be assured of economic independence. More, she would be able to help support him in that revolutionary work to which she too was wholly dedicated.

Plekhanov's letter to her written soon after his meeting with Lavrov, merely to confirm that all was well with him and that he hoped to be with her soon, had been held back by the Police Department for several days due to bureaucratic indecision. Seized on eagerly at first, its contents proved disappointing. It confirmed his whereabouts but no plans for the future could be discovered in spite of expert analysis. Apparently he was simply describing his new surroundings and telling how relaxed he felt on this unexpected holiday.

One morning on her way out to the University she was handed it by her landlady. In the street she began to tremble fiercely hurrying straight back. She placed the letter on the table before her and let the tears flow bitterly, joyfully. Simply the letter itself, fragile paper, reality of his life - confirmed! Enough in itself. Simply to abide in that, before this messenger of his existence in all its fullness. Through this messenger in bittersweet fullness, come to life, tearful, trembling breathless joy.

Not yet at all wanting to open the letter, even painful the thought. Only to feel its presence, to see with loving care the date stamp, the envelope flap obviously re-stuck, telling of police fingers and eyes. Its real life aflame in her untouchable by their pathetic groping.

Fools! who saw so little and so much.

Who thought they could nail the words down with their stupidity. Never would they have passed it on to her had they suspected what stupendous life-kindling magic -encouragement for the future it concealed.

She left it opened out on the table and in the days that followed would walk over to it, sometimes merely looking, sometimes re-reading. Beyond confirmation, celebration, she knew he'd written it with the censors in mind. From the date she assumed that he would be back in the capital and make contact very soon.

Two weeks passed and instead a second letter appeared from Switzerland. Agitated she tore it open. She was right! She knew it! He spoke about the need for a longer holiday. The doctors had advised him to have a thorough recuperation. And then in due course he would be fit enough to get on with his work once more. So would she think seriously about joining him as soon as possible.

She wrote back immediately in anger, near panic. Doctors - recuperation - holidays! enough of the round about talk. Of course their letters were being read. What difference? Let those police idiots know what they thought about them. He must tell her by return exactly what was happening.

Was he afraid to return?

Had he lost his nerve?

Shameful when all the comrades were in prison - What use to the revolution staying a minute longer in Switzerland. Russia! here! this was the place!

And did he really imagine that she was going to give up her studies just like that after all these years with the end so near.

Unbelievable! That Georgy had never really sensed the depth - the seriousness of this calling - actual calling of healer - medicine - still not mentioned?

Had he completely forgotten their pledges and plans?

Who was she writing to? Her Georgy?

Answer immediately! and no signature.

Such dreadful confusion this blind bitter cry which she posted off straight away, to be rid of it. So ashamed, afraid of what she had said done. But no! stand firm erect - fight hard for your very life. Somehow - somehow - from here to recover a faith in that life - lifework - together.

"As soon as possible?" That he took so lightly her studies - her calling knowing well that the culmination of five years was so close - and that even when she qualified she was simply to run off to Switzerland? Were they short of doctors in Switzerland? Here was the calling, from the beginning - for her to practise amongst the people, the poorest.

An incredible selfishness? self-centeredness? - to which she had been blind?

How else could he talk like this.

Such bitterness, emptiness - yield! let the tears break! recalling - dear heart - mercifully recalling - message - from another world that he had sacrificed his entire vocation for the cause.

Entire vocation!

What selflessness was that?

His cowardice? – he who in late youth had led the first great demonstration – been hounded – on the run ever since – never holding back from danger.

Dreadful weakness.

How had she dared think such a possibility?

He had never let her down before?

Plekhanov, shaken by her letter, answered by return telling of his discovery, guided by Lavrov, that in Marx's writings he had found an unshakeable foundation for their work. That in Geneva he could study unharrassed to one end only my dearest, our work together. But now the foundations would be impregnable. She must forgive him his unthinking remarks that had so hurt her. He was as ever totally supportive of her vocation. It was after all only a matter of weeks till her qualification – then new decisions could be taken. Either she joined him in Switzerland or he joined her in Russia. But together they would be.

From then on they wrote weekly which sufficed her till graduation. Yet whenever she thought seriously of their future she could not accept his need to remain in Switzerland. Nor could she contemplate going into voluntary exile without feeling it as a betrayal of the immediate revolutionary aspirations in Russia. His new theoretical studies? never any problem about this before! No! Russia alone was the place for their work. All talk of Switzerland remained unreal, ultimately always seeming some subterfuge.

The Police Department maintained their censorship eventually satisfied that State criminal Georgy Valentinovich Plekhanov was in fact settling down to a conventional life, tutoring and studying some theoretical German mishmash. A good riddance to him – and long live the Swiss! But as for her, a little lesson needed there. Just so that she should know once and for all what was what and who was who, her examiners would be consulted accordingly. That, by the grace of our Tsar alone does anyone become a doctor. She is by no means entitled to that particular working of grace. Her five years' student work does not in itself provide justification for expecting such grace. Indeed, judging by the work alone can lead to false conclusions. She herself must be approved as worthy, and that is altogether another matter.

The days following her final examination were exhilarating.

Sweet the air around her, an irrepressible power rising within welcoming all. She had proved herself, kept at it, begun to show the world who she was becoming, what she was.

She kept recalling the Practical and Theoretical papers with amazement. It was as though they had been drawn up for her alone, to prove just how able she was. She saw her name in first place at the top of the list, dazed in that height. Only remained to decide where to practice. St Petersburg itself? Kherson? home ground where she could gain such wide experience in a district she knew so well. Georgy? then she would go to Geneva and talk it out with him. Her new status would require that he listen in a more serious, less overbearing - for them both - more fruitful way.

The graduation results were customarily posted up in the Main Hall at nine in the morning of the third Friday in September. The ritual entailed a clerk, followed solemnly by Faculty heads, making their way up to a mounted wooden board and the pinning to it of a large framed golden card. Rosaliia had watched it all the previous year when she stood with Anna Mikhailova, close friend from Kherson days, amongst the large group of anxiously waiting students and friends. Apart from Anna, Rosaliia had been extremely careful in her friendships, so much was at stake.

She set off at quarter past eight giving herself plenty of time. More than once she had acted out her smile, even slightest bow, in acknowledgement of what must surely be their, perhaps reluctantly granted respect. Yes, she would acknowledge their respect with humility and dignity. And how proud Georgy would be of her at this moment. For he above all was the one who'd insisted 'Never give up!'

As she approached the entrance she met up with Anton Lemke, one of the few fellow students with whom she felt fairly at ease. Heavily built, with shambling step, he called out cheerfully, "Well Rosaliia, now at last we'll know - not that you've got any worries."

As they went through into the great hall itself, beneath the richly decorated ceiling, across the gleaming wooden floor, past the portraits of Tsars and eminent teachers, she felt something very odd. The absolute emptiness. No students awaiting the entry of Faculty members. Nothing. She turned to Anton who looked puzzled. Standing still, on the edge of this echoing emptiness her heart began to pound as straight ahead there gleamed the golden card on the wooden board. She advanced through a mist and stood square before it, the ground gained, breathing awkwardly, till she was able to bring the copperplate flourishes into focus. In one flash of knowing she saw it all. Not daring to look any closer she knew that at the very bottom, in those depths was her name. With a supreme effort she focused on it. She had to. She had to prove to herself that this nightmare was real.

Theory: Parts I and II – Failed.

Practical: Parts I and II – Failed.

She fought her way back through the emptiness of the hall dimly aware that Lemke had vanished, wondering whether he'd ever been present, trembling with fury and amazement at her innocence. All of them, faculty and students – all their gestures words glances – for months – tainted – none of it – none! – as truthful.

Through a blind willing reaching her street her block her apartment her room – and her chair – scrap of refuge secured.

Such a fierce need to protest – to hammer on walls – to scream out against this injustice. So suddenly shrivelled, stillborn, pathetic.

Was she mad?

Beat on these walls their walls absorb all human sound!

Gratitude – fiercest gratitude to them, they've reminded you who you are!

This pain is the raw wound of yourself exposed to their hatred.

Yourself – Georgy's wife!

This pain is the punishment for being Georgy's wife – which is you. Had she forgotten, pretended otherwise? Then they had made it absolutely clear branding her forever with this knowing.

Good! Then she would be Georgy's wife once and for all.

If that's where they attacked, from there she would fight back.

Dreadful this power which could so cast her down, damn her, annul this potentiality, her deepest impulse, to heal the pain, sickness of others, unsullied by any consideration of financial recompense.

Professors faculty students – craven, shrunken into this cruel blind power denying mankind her offering, her meaning. Her life's yes! to that healing call from all. That 'all' one with the healing power and promise.

The meaning of her life was at stake. She would fight back.

Only one thing now, to be with Georgy as strength, refuge, certainty.

The beast's blindness! Of her, this one aroused now to implacable bitterness, it was unaware. This one already vowing lifelong opposition, to destroy it.

She must be out of this land.

With books and clothes stuffed into a couple of trunks she took the train to her family in Kherson. Her father, a Jewish merchant, was not especially surprised. His concern, unease, about the Jews' future in Russia was justification for his sympathy toward her political involvement. He was extremely bitter about her treatment and promised to provide her with a small regular sum of money. Could she begin all over again in Geneva and qualify there? She would be in familiar company, amongst Russian students, so many of whom like her were from Jewish families, due to the *numerus clausus* in higher education restricting the Jewish intake to five per cent. If she was so prepared to begin all over again, he would back her up.

"The history of all hitherto existing society is the history of class struggles."

That 'all'!

Only the truth could speak thus.

Trust in that 'all' which could be thus revealed through the teacher.

That 'all'!

Fructifying energy, by night and by day, at his desk from eight in the morning to six at night, iron discipline. Father was right. 'We shall not rest when we die!' And damn the chest pains.

Steadily beating, the pulse of this knowing, never to cease – it's 'all' – till everything is transformed.

Never to leave him, this knowing's power, intent on involvement in every aspect of what is human. Nothing to remain beyond its reach, its drive to make part of a new whole. Nothing whose contradictions can't be resolved, this knowing's light, raying, raging to furthest horizons.

New science of man for all times.

Such an encouragement, unfolding, enrichment of his talents, questing drive. Analysis, synthesis, no detail too small, no whole too large.

No need to feel so guiltily changed. The idea, the real idea of the teacher has forged the change. Thrust, attack destroy now with finest subtlety. Most comprehensive weapon of all, this awakened consciousness. This most real power - ideas - no longer confined to space and time but everywhere, indestructible!

The teacher is speaking to me - calling to me. Awakening me to the truth of my life, its enduring purpose and meaning.

In the rousing warmth, this fire of my will - a way cleared for the future.

History and men known newly. Himself known newly.

The power of this thinking, this knowing for Russia's liberation.

This then was Switzerland Geneva Lavrov!

Long hard study.

Long hard thinking.

To define with utmost precision in this new light, our differences. To discover - create - through this quest not only what is, but also who we are.

Differences? Surely unbridgeable contradictions? These differences are of worlds. And that only one of us can be right!

Through the light and fire of this knowing, anarchists, terrorists, populists all scattered to the wind, with their labyrinthine chaos of contradictions, their fissions, fusions, will o' the wisps. Of course each was justified through the dialectic - through this final meaning given by scientific socialism. Justified and extinguished in the same brilliant moment. Of course justification for all that came before. But all now finished by real History, itself the Lawgiver. Real freedom possible only by acting in harmony with its laws.

Light revealing.

Fire consuming.

Power enforcing.

Nothing and no-one could hide, resist its exposure by the light of this thinking.

Anarchism, terrorism, populism, their time over. Superseded by that towards which each groped this truth, this final conclusion. Scientific socialism. Only now was meaning given to History itself - the real action of classes. Real action, strategy, future.

No longer the partial.

No longer the abstract.

But the whole – the concrete – the action grounded in truth. All.

'Collective ownership by the working class of all means of production –

'The radical economic revolution will render unnecessary all those social organs which have developed as the weapons of that struggle for existence between individual classes and whole societies –

'The impending revolution necessitates the participation of all civilised societies –

'Scientific socialists must aim at the necessary political reforms by all means in their power.

That 'all' itself informing his knowing at every turn.

He would do the same for Russia as the teacher had done for Europe. He would show irrefutably, those illusory gropings for what they were. With goodwill but with ruthless intent. This fire, the burning edge of this brilliance would consume every last vestige of utopian mentality, and clear the way for scientific socialism in Russia.

Ruthlessness and severity, as his teacher's, towards false ideas which must not be a minute longer. False ideas spreading amongst Russia's finest, so destructive of those youthful energies needed for building Russia's true socialist future.

Some months after Rosaliia joined Georgy the four met regularly to work out a programme for Russia's immediate needs. It included: the distribution of Marxist literature; translations of Marx and Engels; analyses of Russian social and economic life; the establishment of a base, to train agitators for work amongst the proletariat, to create working class groups for a future Social Democratic party, to prepare such groups for struggle in the cause of political liberty.

In the late night quiet, alert for any sound from the bedroom, Plekhanov read through several times his final version of paragraph 4, for the Emancipation of Labour draft programme to be discussed at tomorrow's meeting of the four.

'4.   Introducing consciousness where now there reigns blind economic necessity, replacing the present mastery of the product over the producer by that of the producer over the product, the socialist revolution simplifies all social relationships and gives them a purpose, at the same time providing each citizen with the

real possibility of participating directly in the discussion and
decision of all social matters.

This direct participation of citizens in the management of
all social matters presupposes the abolition of the modern system
of political representation, and its replacement by direct popular
representation.'

Emancipation of Labour.

Producer over product.

This naming surely new beginning.

Think through again to ensure your inmost confirmation!

Yes - emancipation! Not peasant emancipation but Labour itself. That same Labour sweat and blood which Peter Lavrovich had pledged his whole life to redeem.

And Labourer - to become human. So far back known! - the floggings on uncle's estate - his embarrassment, shame - felt by no-one else in the family?

Producer over product - let all hear that - all workers!

His new weapon finely forged - ideas!

Each word, concept, phrase, sentence, finally tested, finally left. No further movement of any avail in the quest for clarity, definitiveness. Familiar this threshold of intractability, circularity, very force of language and meaning thrusting him back, holding him off.

It held firm, proudly self-sufficient before the strength of this feigned criticism.

No further moves possible. Enjoy the craftsmanship - striving for perfection - quickly enjoy - not a word more - or less possible uncertainty but such a slow business. But such a seriousness guiding him.

Sigh! - a sigh from the bedroom, sign, groan? - she'd told him not to keep on worrying - he'd know the real thing soon enough.

She - essential part of that which united them all - and Gankin? Deep pure their presence felt Vera - Pavel - Lev - Rosaliia - the coming one - and Gankin? To feel so keenly that all - each - must be present if the meeting was to confirm its inmost truth - and Gankin? Sensing in all its fullness the uniqueness of each - and that these the individuals alone exist - and can work together.

But very pain this Gankin business. And right now it was dreadful. It was tainting his very concern for her well being, tainting his welcoming hope for the little one's life!

Little one coming to what! - forced to follow this what's dark mood - money? - work? - no reliable news from Russia - food! - dependence - loans and more loans - utterly dependent on Lavrov - a falseness there - such unease - uncertainty - what welcome was this?

The treadmill again, no stepping off - victim of some fatality?

But she his very life too he knew that - not just the work but himself was her love. Her being there at his side very strength.

Why did she so dislike - hate? - mistrust Gankin?

No more whys!

At this time of all times simply enforce it.

She, not Gankin.

That he had to argue it out like this!

Gankin's background - university - disillusionment with the terrorists - etc. - etc. - all familiar, straightforward. And when pressed she accepted Gankin's earnestness dedication generosity - all so awkwardly having to be emphasised - she'd agreed it was so. All that. But he was still for her a leech. Leech!

That he'd had to keep on defending Gankin - his support and understanding for the new programme - and she'd agreed - but still was not yielding in her dislike and mistrust.

That was a deadly seriousness on Tuesday, simply that he knew it must never be mentioned again.

"I don't want him anywhere around, anywhere near me, until it's all over!"

Still with him guiltily the unease, sadness, negation in that 'it's all over', tainting, tainting as Gankin's fault, as sounding thus because of Gankin, because of his friendship with Gankin, as though - he'd heard it clearly - that she was saying her life and that other new life - were at stake!

He'd had to yield.

He must yield.

And after all perhaps, after her terrible experience at the University - was it that? - who could she trust? But the others didn't trust Gankin either! Pavel had clearly implied it. But how well Gankin had taken it, to stay away just for the time being.

All in Gankin's favour even more.

Those approaching footsteps to the front door were Gankin's!

So well he knew them!

At this hour?

Rosaliia must not know!

Down the stairs as quietly as possible to unbolt before Madame Castelot was involved, fatal to upset her anymore!

It could not should not be!

Off with him at any cost Rosaliia first!

No disturbance to be risked on the doorstep straight up into the kitchen with him.

Quietly drawing back the bolt and opening the door before any knock occurred he angrily snapped a warning finger to his lips and led Gankin upstairs into the kitchen.

"Didn't you understand me? What are you doing here?" he whispered loudly, almost desperate but, wondering as he looked at Gankin what it could possibly be about.

Careful! very careful!

He needed this man, Gankin's help absolutely crucial, nothing of it to be risked.

Gankin smiled weakly.

"Of course, of course" he whispered back.

Confused lonely fled here for respite, succour.

Threatened by something dreadful he was losing his grip.

"Forgive me Georgy -it's been on my mind for days - I - ," he could only put the folded franc note somewhere on the kitchen table and hurry away from Georgy's upset which he so painfully felt - even guilty! Georgy was staring at him like a blind man! Quickly, quietly down out driven. Numbly, fearfully to find the way back to his lodgings. So desperate this need to be with them near them at this time of the birth. A madness, knowingly endangering everything so delicately successfully achieved - but this need!

What! tearful!

Just at this moment to cease the spying and be with them both - truly fond of them both for the little one's birth. Dreadful place of no return and he knew it.

Get down to the weekly report for Rachkovsky down to it! Stop this whining!

Too late to change anything.

But what would Plekhanov make of it? Had he blown it?

Had he wanted to blow it?

"- - the four to meet at Plekhanov's in Geneva to continue work on the Emancipation of Labour programme - -"

He'd been with Georgy himself - so purely at that moment

– stupid confrontation – he had!

"Plekhanov's financial situation continues to be extremely difficult. The editors of the German Social Democratic journals delay paying him. I continue to help financially. Birth expected any time to Rosaliia Plekhanov – – "

This was not about the man he had wanted to be with.

This whole mess not his fault.

Tsar – State – times – Russia – entanglement in all that, not his doing.

No need to blame himself. What left but to make the best of things. All of us entangled. Plekhanov too – that's why he takes the money – without a word.

Of course no turning back.

Rachkovsky could never know of this.

What then – what? was he dreading.

Why not – why not straight to Paris and tell him a thing or two – if he still existed – ghosts all of them – bits of paper there and back every week – bits of paper – what would he tell him – prospects of a steady career! promised that joker – but this bloody loneliness – so bloody lonely – he'd never mentioned any of that – "most important the Swiss network" – to hell with the Swiss network!

Plekhanov went back to his study relieved and confused. A Gankin he hadn't seen before – and what had been on his mind for days?

"Just like a leech!"

Dreadful, Rosaliia saying that.

Like some curse – you don't understand.

Extremely painful this entanglement.

The others didn't like him either? So what! What did they know? and how should they? Why hadn't he told them? All too difficult. Dependence independence damn the money business. Nothing to be ashamed of. Gankin was dedicated to the cause – looked up to him – and had money. What was wrong with that? And he would take the money until those damned German editors coughed up. And he wasn't going to Lavrov again, much too embarrassing.

Of course Pavel could make his usual big noises. Of course it wasn't absolutely clear where Gankin's funds came from. Of course Gankin's story wasn't absolutely consistent. But whose was! Who could afford to be absolutely consistent at this particular moment? Pavel's absoluteness not at all practical. Only to have a few more like Gankin, modest, eager to learn, to help.

No more money from Russian parents.

No more credit from Carlweiss.

Tutoring small children – when he felt called on to change the course of history?

Thankfully dozing off, drawn away from the wearying strife. From those voices living a life of their own.

Harsh moans from the bedroom called him to Rosaliia's side from time to time. He went in a daze, to kiss her strained flushed face, his hand gripped by hers. Faintly she smiled. Dimly he divined what was happening, dense the veil beyond word, thought, but his divining knew. He withdrew to the study, stretched out on the sofa, and slept.

He awoke soon after dawn, made coffee in the kitchen, took some to Rosaliia and stepped out for a brief break into the sweet dawn air. Just to be away from it all, along the lakeside, away from that oppression grown so strong in these last weeks of her pregnancy. A turbulence, engulfing, loosening his grip, making him question what they were both doing here.

The fragrance, bird song, awakening earth, fields on the lake's far side in pale radiance, all, healing, restoring.

He must justify their presence here, way of life, for the sacrifice grew harder, the debts graver, the anxieties more acute. Even though she had pledged herself to his destiny, freely, asking nothing in return. This guilt and uncertainty insisted.

A joyous birth? – joyous! – instead of this ceaseless worry.

Then damn this destiny!

No more credit even for milk or butter – except this two franc note!

Was he mad?

Could any good possibly come from their being here? Shouldn't they try and creep back?

He sat down on a bench by the lake, helpless before this destiny too hard to bear yet impossible to throw off.

From the ground, that ground he gazed down at, calm, firm, a deep resignation, a strengthened resolve, became his own. Earth's sympathy renewing, hints of that joy which She had revealed so long ago at Gudalovka.

No hopes.

No expectations.

Do simply what must be done.

Serve, renounce, plod on!

Never cease till you're finally crushed.

Nothing achieved by a valiant truthful heart is ever lost.

That youthful leap! known then, the task's immensity – impossibility.

Plod on – the flame does burn steady.

Rosaliia knew that it was beginning.

Knew that the ardent longing was reaching its culmination, outside her, far outside her.

She could not speak not tell him not utter it yet, but she knew it was near, very near.

Those Gankin footsteps blackly threatened this temple.

She knew that now was the fullness of time as mighty rhythms approached, as the waters of life broke free.

"Georgy, Georgy," she silently murmured, calling.

The space of the pain of that longing, infinite yearning had ripened to living form. Heavy with pain of its substance. Ardent determined fierce, to wrest itself forth from the darkness and gain the light of mansworld. "Georgy, Georgy," was her silent call as she drifted, he not there she not here, stranger outside this vastness which was her.

Dipping down to taste this dawn freshness, then away, away as the mighty rhythms tread out their shoreline beat. Waves, murmuring swell of waves approaching. Pulsations inexorable, incoming tide swifter wilder surging. Away, away from this sweet relentless grip, drowning, cruel fire. Up and away to flee this embrace with the wild sweep of my wings.

Georgy Georgy where are you – how leave me to this?

Rending dissolving, the pain that is me.

Turbulent grip of the clashing waves rising and falling.

I skim them again.

It's beginning Georgy. Beginning this yearning ripeness for life – life! – in mansworld.

Calm are these waters now for I am the waiting.

Here, in this peace, on this bed, serenely alone, I am the temple at whose portal the stranger knocks to be led forth.

Gentle insistent knock within this strange space of herself – to be tenderly drawn away in a sweet exhaustion yet – resonance of a fierce challenge to come.

Returned crying out with the shock of this pain, fierce oppressive power. Twisting and turning. Pressed so hard by the stranger within, determined, relentless. Fiery life expanding to fill all space. Yield!

Yield!

Joy in this that it must be so!

That a greater than she was present.

Such strength this longing and such strength to bear this pain.

Mighty power determined that the stranger shall enter that life shall be.

She now the earth of its striving and flowering.

Yield!

Become earth for this new flowering.

Sweep your wings up and over the turbulent waves of new life.

Yield to this mighty stranger's power risen up.

Power – from my darkness – risen up to overthrow me.

Joy in its rightness, in the acceptance.

Plekhanov returned from his walk, listening, waiting. His life's meaning, task, rekindled through that resignation.

A rasping strangled cry violently jerked his whole body. His writing hand, underlining, annotating, struck a long fierce line across and off the page. He stood up holding on to the desk, knees trembling as the cry, pitched in desperation, tore out yet again and then again.

The note so dreadfully strange – not human – to hear it repeated!

He rushed into the bedroom and found her lying on her stomach boring her head into the pillow, frenziedly biting at it, flinging herself from side to side without stopping, till the pain subsided.

"Get Madame Brissot," she gasped jerkily, drawing in breath, her pupils dilating, a gout of vomit spurting. Plekhanov found a grubby towel to wipe her chin and cheek, repelled by the sour odour, touched to the quick by a growing helplessness as he bent over to kiss her hot, sweaty forehead.

"It's all right – but go," she murmured, straining herself to nod reassuringly through the sweat drenched, tearful blur towards his pale, anxious face. He hurried off relieved by that gesture but the panic did not leave him.

A huge iron grip was squeezing her womb to cast that life

forth.

Then merge!

Don't fight against it. Yield to the greater than you in you.

Sink into this power so ruthless unyielding.

Yes – yes – so quickly learning so thankfully not simply to yield to go with it, but to temper even to guide. To help, to tame, to touch with her nature as from below, from distant depths of herself, the gate of her being opened this living gift of her ripeness preparing to journey forth. Inmost sanctum forced open so willingly now as he pressed forth, ripe fruit of her desiring, as tenderness charged the shimmering light around her.

Yes – yes – she was willing, willing it. Alone – she was sure that her doing was right.

But the flow the warm flow of her yielding was suddenly blocked. Again and again as the waters built up and she yielded, no culmination, no promise fulfilled. Only a dry merciless void. A wall of densest darkness.

Desperate now and sensing death, alone.

So heavy this stranger's desire to be. And she would surely die crushed by the pain of its denial.

Desperately she sucked in air trying to join with that power. Again and again and again it went on relentless. Bruised and torn she lay dazed on furthest shores. Released. For a while released as the wildness withdrew.

Knowing, gently knowing this room this self.

What reality timeless, touched, at the heart of the world's becoming!

Plekhanov returned with Madame Brissot, a calm, kindly woman in her fifties whose husband was a cobbler in the Rue de St Jean. Her mother had also done this work. She liked these Russians for their generosity and warmth, but found them odd and suspicious. They were constantly changing addresses and partners and their means of existence was a mystery. When Plekhanov appeared, breathlessly, her husband discreetly reminded her to demand payment on the spot. This one looked just like the rest of them, as though this was the first baby ever born.

As soon as they entered the house Rosaliia's cries tore at him, such yells so vulnerable – humiliation – forced to yield in such a way! Madame Castelot standing in the hallway, greeted Madame Brissot with relief and pointed her head upwards in the direction of the Plekhanov's room, screwing up her nose in disgust.

Madame Brissot followed him up the stairs.

Here it all was. Same as usual with these Russians. Books papers. More books and papers. Piles of this and that. Very little furniture.

When Plekhanov took her into the bedroom he was shocked at the change in Rosaliia's distraught appearance. Her features seemed twisted, somehow unrecognisable.

Madame Brissot immediately ordered him into the kitchen to boil up a kettle of water, to make ready a clean bucket, basin and towels. He was only to come to the bedroom when called for. Shutting the bedroom door and rolling up her sleeves, she went over to Rosaliia and drew the blankets away. Carefully she felt, sensing the baby's head, firm and wide, but too a constraint from the pelvic bones on either side. This gate would not open easily. The girl would have to work hard. But she looked fit and strong enough and should do it.

Rosaliia drifting tide, gratefully drifting on a gentle tide, loosely mingling with room with the stranger at the worldcentre felt Madame Brissot's firm hand on hers and the calm friendly voice. "Now then my dear when it begins again – ah – come on – come on now – push hard – push hard," Madame Brissot encouraged as the flesh strained, stretched wider, drew aside to reveal the light of that glistening dome. Again and again Rosaliia heaved, pressed, with Madame Brissot increasingly impatient, anxious, chiding, warning. Merciless this power – she would die dissolve away could do no more. "Now come on – you must do better than that. Now here – hold my hands – press hard against me – –" voice from across the void.

Rosaliia flat on her back, pushed and pushed with her feet against Madame Brissot's shoulders, Madame Brissot herself tiring with the strain. The very sap of Rosaliia's strength was leaving her, as a wraith. Hands stretched towards her, words seeking her but she utterly alone, desperate, in the shadow of some doom.

Plekhanov waited in the kitchen by the steaming kettle, agitated by every sound and word from the bedroom. Bleak in this burning present, all time sucked up on this endless strand of her pain which was his pain.

Those yells victim so vulnerable – no no not to have to yield like this my dearest – generations to come they surely would be victorious – and her pain for that too!

A great fear growing from Madame Brissot's words. Both of them trapped. Why had it happened so? A darkness encompassing all.

That was a knock at the front door.

But all meaning was draining away leaving a bleak, empty shell, eerie steps approaching.

Since early morning, after a sleepless night, distraught, as one possessed, Gankin had walked the streets, bought newspapers, drunk coffee here and there but finally found himself returning to the Plekhanovs. Simply to see to speak with Georgy. Confused, panicky, he knew he was losing his grip.

He knocked again, less timidly and waited, till Madame Castelot appeared, staring at him unpleasantly.

"Monsieur Gankin again! Well –" but she did not move and there was barely room for him to squeeze past.

"Aren't the women in your country used to having babies?" she stabbed a finger upwards, "I've never heard such a bleating in my life."

Madame Castelot's attitude and the realisation that Rosaliia was in labour halted him at the top of the stairs with one foot set tentatively on the Plekhanov's landing. Rosaliia's moans and Madame Brissot's anxious voice held him back. Compelled to glance quickly into the kitchen he came eye to eye with Georgy, sitting immobile, staring straight back at him, through him. Seared, scared, by this void, denial? he hurried out of the house.

Fleeing ever wilder through a world of stony rejection, his feet alone led him to the edge of the lake. Everything was receding from the touch of his gaze, only the water's open embrace could quench this despair. Welcoming waters, gripped in this stony vice.

Lost!

Through the fact of this little one's coming, strength of their life together which he could only observe!

Let him be found out – be found – but somehow be with them he would.

No! Not to be drawn by that glistening green enchantment, feet alone pressing urgently forward along the lake's edge.

There must be something to live for.

This wretched dog here lives so why not I?

And dare I ask what I'm doing here how I got here?

No - no!

Not at all that whole business with Rachkovsky - vetting - encouragement - training - not any of that - but I - I - I - this I -

He must have gone soft!

That he was running away from Plekhanov when the man's fate was in his hands! Remember Rachkovsky's line - keep your finer feelings for Russia - these bastards are Russia's enemies. Draw the line firmly. You'll be on your own. But I want results. A good career ahead - a responsible job - could be a posting in Paris.

What the hell then - Russia's enemies!

That look on Plekhanov's face - the man simply wasn't himself.

He'd never shown the slightest suspicion. Simply overwrought. The whole baby business - thank God she was out of action - damned pest.

No! Nothing personal involved.

He could be pleased with his tact these last three months.

But he must know.

The usual provisions! and he'd know with more certainty than this.

Madame Brissot was alarmed by Rosaliia's ashen colour and the blue tinge around her mouth. The girl's strength had given out - and anyway more exertion could risk rupture. Sweating hard she wiped her hands down the sides of her apron and prayed fiercely to the good Lord for all was so clearly in His hands. The girl could might survive. The baby very doubtful.

She pulled out a small flask of brandy from her bulging bag. After a long swig she gently hauled Rosaliia up, and sitting on the bed tight behind her as support, pressed the flask against Rosaliia's mouth, insisting that she drink some.

Within a bright new space created by the radiant sweep of this uprightness Rosaliia was suddenly given back to herself anew from out of the abyss. Words language came now within reach. She made a supreme effort to speak.

"Like this - like this - I can do it," shuddered the words from her throat with desperate intensity.

Out of the darkness shattering, Madame Brissot's action had awoken a knowing, a certainty, an answer. With Madame Brissot holding her up like this her whole being, stranger filled bodily being, was loosening to life, hope, as myriad streamlets began to pulse, flow, that ancient slab of darkness shattered.

Tell her. Tell her again!

Rosaliia mouthed more silent words, willing sound and meaning into them as she turned away from the brandy bottle and shook her head.

"Keep me up – like this – not down again – I can do it."

Puzzled by this up but relieved by the startling change, Madame Brissot kept firmly supporting Rosaliia. The girl knew something.

This knowing, conjured forth by Madame Brissot, streamed fecund through Rosaliia's body making it strong, able, to emerge afresh as it kneeled, swung back on its haunches, the flesh easily swiftly parting, wider, wider, glistening thrust of that fleshy dome, Madame Brissot, surprised at the suddenness of it all, delighted, stood upright, firmly supporting Rosaliia under the armpits, as the baby's head, pressed on forward into the world of man through fierce, rapid final contractions. Fierce, yet friendly, deeply bearable, taking all before them in this final offering of herself. Nothing now could stop it.

She asked to be let lie prone. Madame Brissot relaxed her hold and quickly turned to the foot of the bed, alert, confident now, her cupped hands gently guarding, guiding, barely touching the baby's head. Rounded fullness of new earthbeing from our Father's gracious answer. Forceful, thrusting this little one – sensed already as he – as she gently held back the yielding flesh to finally free his way.

Carefully she disentangled the cord from one leg, unsealed the eyes and throughout praised the Lord for his mercy. A cry, his cry punctuated her prayers. A raw healthy cry and she knew that all would be well.

The large red protuberance on the head, like a livid wrinkled horn, where it had been stuck and bruisingly gripped for so long, would sure enough go down just as it had with the Violet youngster. A matter of weeks.

Rosaliia heard the freshness of that cry, so pure, right an answer, binding note of exaltation, triumph for them both. A sudden surging wind of warmth whirled through her, emptying, cleansing, afterbirth shedding itself, humblest substance of her ripeness, fine veined fleshly love. Deftly Madame Brissot slipped it into the dented bucket.

Rosaliia's body returned to itself from afar, relaxed, healed, breathing a wistful serenity. All heaviness gone. The new one a tender presence around her cradled in its swaddling clothes.

Together now, a sweetness, last echoes of that mighty, turbulent dream.

Madame Brissot settled Rosaliia comfortably, washed her hands, took another long swig and went into the kitchen.

"Well now Monsieur, just make sure this is burnt," she said putting the bucket down. "Everything's all right now. Just let her rest, she's had a hard time. You're very lucky. But the good Lord's got his own way of doing things," she went on, looking at Plekhanov with some misgiving, pity, as he stood there smiling stupidly, the tears flowing full since that first cry, sheer fact still that a new being was here.

"Pull yourself together Monsieur! It's her you must think of not yourself. If only you men knew. And don't disturb her yet. She's sleeping – and she needs it. Busy yourself Monsieur! Prepare something for her."

She looked keenly around the kitchen disturbingly concluding that the jug of milk and portion of loaf on the table were the only food to be seen.

"She'll be very hungry when she wakes," she emphasised. Or did he think air would feed her?

"I don't know," she sighed.

"Monsieur, I must go," she warned briskly, waiting, watching him, still tearful, with irritation, puzzlement.

"If you please Monsieur," she insisted.

Plekhanov stood there making little of her words. Rosaliia was alive! The baby had been born! All was well! But the pain, desperate anxiety – not entirely gone. He listened and watched Madame Brissot from afar feeling the goodness, comfort in what she said but why was she still standing there instead of leaving.

"Thank you Madame Brissot for everything – oh for everything – thank you!"

He felt the rightness of these words though they floated away so elusively. But still she persisted in standing there.

Madame Brissot had noticed the franc note as soon as she entered the kitchen and assumed that Plekhanov had put it out ready for her.

"My fee Monsieur," she hissed with annoyance. What was he playing at?

"Fee? of course Madame! Fee! But how can money repay for what you've done," he responded fervently. Fee? but he couldn't pay her!

"How Monsieur? Like this!" she deftly picked out the note, folded it slowly and pressed it down into her leather purse. He witnessed her taking it with confusion and relief. That he hadn't picked up that money which Gankin had left last night – how very strange!

"Excellent excellent!" he called down the stairs where Madame Castelot stood waiting.

"You're right – him too a bit crazy," said Madame Brissot on her way out. Madame Castelot began thinking seriously about more suitable tenants.

Plekhanov went to the bedroom. Nothing was any longer the same. New balances had to be struck. Only here, at the foot of the bed, with them could he begin the return to the everyday world which had aeons ago withdrawn beyond this fiery place of new creation. Only to be with them both amidst this new reality. Simply to follow out of this joyful intuition, to know this threefold presence, newly living in him through which he lived and the world out there withdrawn greyly. From somewhere, soon, to do with this living present, the comrades were coming. In this serene stillness he could hold the greyness at bay with a joyful strength welling forth from this threefold presence. And the fecund centre of it all was this little one here. Nothing yet all!

Nothing this little one yet all, in his sudden fullness – fullness of his embracing future pointing to what? – Paragraph 4? – the Paragraph 4 meeting – yes! there they all met – mysterious yet real place.

Yes, ready now to turn to the grey, weak world and begin to work for its future with hope. With this new strength, clearer about essentials.

How dreadfully bare the kitchen, not a scrap of food anywhere – but this lightness of heart! A new strength – work plans everything around still dreamlike in the dazzling light of this new one.

Yes – nothing else for it but to go to Carlweiss once again pleading and begging – but with a good heart now! A good heart my friend! A good heart to see this thing through – this business of being human. God knows how we go up and down! A good heart out of this fullness. No longer just the two of them. But something new filling the place with a richness, well being.

"Gankin! my dear fellow - amazing - what have you brought us!"

Gankin smiled vaguely and began unloading from the two large bags crammed with cheeses, sausages, sweetmeats, fruits. Plekhanov could only watch with delight and gratitude as the table made welcome. Tearfully he took hold of Gankin's hand for some while, looking straight at him, smiling. Dear to him this man.

Gankin smiled back with relief. Plekhanov did trust him. Crazy, that flight had been.

This embrace his welcome back into the world of fools - but not to become entangled. The man had been distraught. Keep a cool head and get on with the job. Nothing to worry about but don't go soft again.

"Aleksy Vasilievich she had a hard time - a really hard time. But it's all over now. So much is happening! Here - we can't have this around - please take it down to Madame Castelot for disposal - Pavel! - Vera! - Lev! - amazing! - amazing!" he shouted hearing them below.

The three had arrived at Madame Castelot's within minutes of one another, a happy omen, greeting and embracing noisily outside the house. The door was opened by Monsieur Castelot, a thin, quiet man, retired government clerk whose sympathy and respect for these Russians was discreetly restrained. They all nodded politely to him and hurried up the stairs, forced to halt halfway by Gankin descending, holding stiffly before him the bucket covered with its white enamel lid. They tensed as he pressed awkwardly past, his faintest smile annulled by their hostility.

Plekhanov heard clearly the restraint in their response to his greeting and saw uneasily the way they stared at Gankin.

They were very dismayed that Gankin was still around. That their hints - strong hints - were - would be no longer enough.

Each in turn embraced Georgy on the landing but the unfamiliar stiffness was upsetting.

"What's the matter with you all?" Plekhanov demanded, bewildered, staring into their faces.

"What's he still doing here?" Axelrod demanded, furious, to hurt, yes to hurt Georgy. That, he willed now and nothing could stop him. That creature below was a betrayal.

"Not that again," said Plekhanov, bewildered, by the violence, hatred.

"Georgy I'm amazed – and I think I'm speaking for everyone –" Deutsch and Zasulich nodded bleakly in confirmation, "God alone knows what hold he's got on you but I'm telling you now – and I don't care what the others do – it's either him or me. Take your choice. We don't and never will accept him here with us."

"Amazed are you?" shouted back Plekhanov, incensed by that 'hold on you' the unsavoury dependence dared imputed, the absolute casting out. Feeling challenged on many levels he lashed out, swept forward helplessly yet pained by the viciousness.

"Of course he's not one of us. He's got money for one thing. Money!" he shouted, "that's the hold! Mind you – my dear Pavel," he thrust into Pavel's grim face, "I don't expect you to understand that – but where is the damned money coming from for all our fine projects eh? Eh? Or have you suddenly found some? Or Vera? Or Lev? And – it just happens too that he understands the Programme – about as well as you do. But of course all I'm after is his money. Oh yes – and I know, don't I Lev – I'm after his adulation obedience – you know – my pride conceit arrogance – eh? Comrades?"

Hoarse, trembling, he stopped abruptly. He sensed behind the fury some weakness lurking, but the surge of this violence towards Pavel, so naked! Pavel? Dear Pavel? And he no longer master of the situation.

Deutsch was shaken. It could only be through Vera, those words were his very own. She stared down helplessly at the floor. Axelrod held firm, letting the words pass over, out of his love and respect for Georgy. Precisely for Georgy's sake he would hold firm. Let Georgy twist turn torture himself into these histrionics, he would hold firm.

"You can mock, threaten as much as you like," he said, trembling slightly, "My mind's made up –"

"Your mind," flung back Georgy, "always your mind – and I'm supposed to be the arrogant one – Vera! – Lev! Can't you speak up for yourselves? Are you afraid of him?"

"We agree Georgy – on this we agree – absolutely," said Vera on the edge of tears.

"It's a sad business – dreadfully sad – that you can't trust me," said Plekhanov with an ultimate resignation yet desperate at the void opening up – why! – he would call Gankin straight back to confront them.

"Not you – not you – him – it's him down there we don't trust," shouted Axelrod in despair, pointing fiercely down the stairs, determined that Gankin should hear.

The man was no longer there.

Feeling threatened by their hostility he'd reached the bottom of the stairs weak at the knees, furious with himself. Beyond all doubt he should never have appeared here today at all. What madness! A madness – unplanned! forcing him here not once, not twice but now three times!

But now he knew!

It wasn't working out. That damned Axelrod!

But Georgy still trusted him. That was enough to hold onto for this wretched moment. That row was getting nasty. Interesting to hear what the dear comrades really thought of one another.

Standing far down the dark hallway outside a door leading to the Castelot's private quarters, consoled by the row raging above, his gaze was caught by the foot of the bucket which he had set down on the blue and red tiled floor. Through a minute crack something red-tongued viscous was seeping away, shot through with cloudy streamings, creeping along stealthily, drawing him into its uncanny life. What awful hiddenness was daring to expose itself like this, lapping the solid world with its vile tongue.

He dared not yet must know.

Bending down, gritting his teeth, he pulled up the lid violently. Exposed, searing, was a seething bloody jelly, purple veined alive, alive. A giddiness overcame him, an anguished upwelling, a cringing dread, disgust, making him retch. Swaying, impelled by some terror to pull himself back from an abyss, he managed to hurry away out into the streets, safety, the known. That horror was never meant to be revealed. That shame, sadness, filth of man. Walk walk walk somehow beat down this terror tumult from that bloody pulp.

That's what we came from? that bloody seething mess creeping crawling.

Hidden – it should have stayed hidden never to be seen.

Bloody slimy waters – from Rosaliia her revenge!

From that dreadful wound between her legs.

Though silent they still stood on the landing. Plekhanov felt it sadly, something preventing them crossing that threshold into his home which had always been their home. He felt all resistance waning, no longer at the centre, glimpsing a strangeness, frightening, a stranger in Pavel.

"Pavel Borisovich," he said in a low almost pleading voice, "tell me – because you've never told me yet. The facts. The plain facts please against Gankin."

"Facts?" answered Pavel, feeling it all so burdensome, yet this too must somehow be brought to some resolution.

"Not facts – fact! One simple fact, only one but it's enough for me. The man won't look you straight in the eyes. He fails the test – my test. D'you remember my suspicions about that printer – the same test – and are you absolutely sure you know where he gets his money from – have you checked? – bothered to check. And what d'you mean he understands our programme when we ourselves are still working on its meaning – and –"

On and on he went, always the last to yield. But all knew that this was no resolution. That there could not be a resolution. And they felt trapped. Vera felt torn between her devotion to Georgy and her respect for Pavel's very practical way with life. Deutsch was summoning up the courage to simply remind them why they were here.

"Georgy! Georgy!" called out Rosaliia's voice anxiously from some other world.

Georgy hurried to the bedroom leaving the others exposed, despondent, called to wondering where they really were.

"Rosaliia?" Vera uttered the word, the name, involuntarily, in puzzlement, reminding them of that which was so distant so near.

When Georgy entered the darkened bedroom in which the curtains were still only part drawn to allow a soft glimmering light on things, Rosaliia strained to sit upright. He quietly shut the door on a world to which he did not want to return. She, from her newly achieved knowing, confidence, serenity, had been carried through a gentle rhythm of sleeping and awakening. Returned for ever longer moments to gaunt old world.

Sleeping and awakening.

A journeying, blissful enrichment with a strength from that upwelling source. And the returning each time to the bleak, weary, sad. And dreams, meetings, dimly known, resonant, colourful, with helpful friendly ones.

Raw sounds of their voices outside searing – a violent flame of meaning – their identity discord rage. Searing with pain, dread, waves of destruction beating at her, threatening the one at her side.

Something was terribly wrong!

"Georgy! Georgy!" Desperately afraid for Georgy she called out amidst the surging bitterness to remind him, simply remind him that she was now here too. In dread his voice had reached her, distorted, like the others.

He sat on the bedside, to kiss her and beyond the kiss this knowing of one with the other, succour, haven for both.

He did not want to return to the comrades – those outside.

Let them leave him.

This strength encompassed all, deep, true. In this affirmation, purest gratitude, he could have dwelt, he yearned to dwell, blissfully yielding, forever – the three of them – completion.

She felt the need, urgent, to break the spell, reach out to that bitter brittle world beyond the door.

Georgy must return. That world needed him, must be helped. Georgy must return bearing with him this strength.

He dreamed into her eyes, would dissolve into her presence. With effort, yielding yet resisting she gently called him back.

"Georgy."

"No!" he answered, compelled by that tone, threshold irrevocably crossed, already back in it, the door no barrier, the drifting apart, familiar selves, the quick of single being, task, freedom, burden fused, rough hewn.

"It's hopeless. I can't get through to them. We're stuck. Frozen solid."

"Yield Georgy – yield – and take us with you."

Her eyelids closed. Beyond their veil of tiredness she willed him to return.

In the strained silence which stretched out interminably with Georgy's quiet closing of the bedroom door Axelrod was beset by a nervous embarrassment. He felt guilty, forced to break through the tension with bravado. He made a noisy move into the kitchen, familiar kitchen, their kitchen, gesture intended to prove how normal everything was. It failed. Some void sucked swiftly at all action, everything withdrew, nothing here declaring itself as they knew it and Georgy still so far away. Zasulich and Deutsch followed him in, very surprised at the bounty crowding the table but feeling as never before with Axelrod, that here they were not at home. He mouthed words intended to lead them out of this limbo.

"It's ridiculous - quite ridiculous," it sounded a queer high pitch.

Zasulich and Deutsch stared glumly through to the gleaming bottles of wine, the apples, cheeses, and rolls, lying just as Gankin had dumped them down. Zasulich dimly remained with Rosaliia's calling voice. Throughout the grip of this silence which had thrust them so far apart, it sounded on, yearning reminder of Georgy's greenest presence. Branching tree, and that they could nurture, green presence of a life that belonged to them all.

When the bedroom door opened at last and Georgy, resigned, reluctant, returned to the landing, then into the kitchen, she asked, so simply, from a long forgotten stricken self.

"Georgy what is it with Rosaliia? Isn't she well?" hoping, so hoping to reach him.

Deutsch and Axelrod were stirred, dimly stirred by her question, remembering, feeling a loosening truth.

"What is it? Rosaliia's had her child," he answered, looking into Vera's wan face. He shut his eyes as the tears welled, glistened, then turned away, wiping them with his fingers. Vera received the words nodding sadly. Her tears broke forth greenly, warmly, so helpless before what was happening.

Awakening, they heard so clearly his bitter reluctance to tell even that to them - to them! What had this done? - so wounded him!

In shame they were seared by his vulnerability, his fear of exposure before them. Seared, purged by this fire, tender fire, cleansing of dross, returning to that old renewed simplicity, sharing all on the way together.

Swift the return to this old new world as Pavel embraced Georgy, finding himself in the warmth of this simplicity embracing them all as one, Georgy Rosaliia and the child.

To re-centre the circle, refocus the trust and the power. To hold firm. To keep back that encircling threat. To face one another strengthened and cleansed, eye to eye once again.

"Georgy," Pavel began but could go no further, the word so laden, comprehensive, name telling of the life together, such a sharing, in which each lived through the other.

Lev found the words, straightforward enough, out of such need to name the crisis and seal the return. He shook his head in disbelief.

"We must have been mad to let things build up like that."

"But we've come through it. We've come through it," insisted Vera, smiling through her tears.

"That's it Vera! We've come through," declared Pavel, "come on then – the wine's here – the food's here – let's drink to it."

"– and to the Emancipation of Labour," said Vera as the bottle was opened

"– and to Rosaliia – and to the baby – and to the work." said Lev as the drinks were poured. Georgy knew it as out of some deep necessity, simply to be endured, wait, a test, the bond with Pavel tested and greatly strengthened.

They ate and it had been made good.

Before the work began on Paragraph 4, they went to the bedroom, raised glasses and drank to mother and baby. They had to see Rosaliia and the child returned to their lives. Georgy lived through it as a necessity which had to be endured, a test, the bond with Pavel tested – and greatly strengthened.

Stepan Kovnator was one of the few People's Will members who escaped the big round-up after the assassination. Several others turned informer besides Rysakov. The police net was cast wide.

He shaved off his thick beard, cut short his shaggy mane and slipped south from city to city, helped and hidden by sympathisers with money, rooms, connections, information. A story about Gankin turned informer – could be in Geneva – make of it what you will. But – if he was going to Geneva – and he was! – and if Gankin was there – then.

In Vitebsk, Eisenman had heard that Novitsky, Bendel, Gerson had all turned informer – a whole bunch of the bastards! Well well! How extremely deep this commitment went, much deeper than life or death. That men could so lightly? give themselves to a cause. Not know? That only lifepledged could anything real exist. They, they too, would have to learn that the price for betrayal was inevitably their own life.

Real commitment or betrayal – a life – each time a life.

In Kursk, Malinin mentioned a new organisation set up by von Plehve. Second time Gankin's name mentioned – in Geneva to report on Plekhanov and Co. Idiots! As if Plekanov and Co. were in any way a danger to them! The betrayers only endangered the real revolutionary future of Russia.

He knew he had survived the round-up for one purpose only – to carry on.

Before so many comrades imprisoned exiled he alone – one! – this one! – himself! – was here, at large as the swine would have it – to show that something greater than numbers was involved. To bear witness! – exactly dear Zhelyabov, as you would have it. To bear witness – just as you did, that the truth, the cause, concerned one, one alone.

One was enough, to carry on, to begin anew.

And a deed to mark this new beginning. As ever – a deed!

At any cost, this particular deed so charged with necessity to make known this new beginning.

The deed, beyond all withdrawing now, pledged, given to it, creator created by it. This the betrayers would never know, this rare realm, on his own, fire in which the strongest alone could survive. Rare realm entry gained through the hard lonely way.

Indeed yes of course, well meaning, dedicated, industrious, but never reaching further than mere words. Here where he stood no turning back, turning about, playing around – untold forces, lives involved.

Such a warmth here, a brilliance, for the chosen and called – those with the greater vision – called – to take fire – burn – burn out – burn away – cauterise with deed after deed.

Deed – swept out into will's great tide far away from self.

From this eager brightness – sparks! to leap, to ignite that yearning warmth throughout all Russia.

Only to purify oneself through the truth.

The Executive Committee was eternal. Diamond essence resuming its task through the deed.

One good kick indeed Pisarev! and this rotting corpse of autocracy would crumble into dust – only a seeming life – which the deed will make manifest through the clouds of moulding dust.

Time was of no account.

Only this pure brightness to light up glowing Russian hearts. What must be!

He the shining torch, instrument, inspired.

He must make his way to Switzerland and pay his respects to

the real betrayers, Plekhanov and Co. Betrayers who would infect Russia with their false ideas intended to lure the best of Russia from its true task.

Intended to confuse with their cunning cowardly articles.

Paid by just whom? Used by whom in that Swiss haven?

That too he must seek out.

He would confront Plekhanov with the truth – himself! The truth that could not change. Only Georgy with his rotten cowardice had changed.

And that Gankin might be in Geneva? Gankin turned informer would account for a lot of the comrades. If – – if – – what a paying of respects that would be!

That wretched Rysakov an infection – one! always only needs one to start it.

Plekhanov and Co deserved it! Very just price for rottenness – but – he would if – if – remotely imaginable – on the contrary – do imagine it! – imagine it! – a force here – imagine that he would if he could – respect that if! – but master it – make it yours – and so settle that matter of Gankin too! with this his deed.

Gankin – such a miserable name – best finished with.

He arrived in Geneva late April to stay with the Steklovs incognito as a visiting cousin. They would very soon be travelling to their estate in Kharkov province for the brief annual visit. Only a few days then for him to get that necessary feel of the place. What it was that had so tempted, undermined Georgy and the others. This Geneva city of so-called freedom – or sleep. Well he'd give the comrades a chance to wake up. Yes yes he could feel it too with these good Steklovs so sympathetic, generous, to the cause, but living in a comfortable world of their own. But they at least weren't claiming to lead the way to Russia's future.

Yes if he stayed here long enough, he too by this lovely lake, these orderly clean buildings – that surely was it! – so clean so dead – the churches monuments hotels people, a tranquillity smoothness – all problems questions solved away – dreamed away. No depth here – no bent backs, hard destinies. No resistance here – bent bent, so low to the earth, Russians. I know it these flights to Geneva Paris London – betrayals – escapes.

From Russian soil, from the children of Russian soil, from their never ending anguish, deepest darkest lifequest, true freedom will yet come.

No! They shall learn from us not we from them.

Every step of my feet on this earth rings strange, stays apart.

Yet, just here by this tranquil lake to have known so clearly this truth!

The day of confrontation at the Plekhanovs was decided for him. The Steklovs were packed and leaving tomorrow.

He set off across the city late afternoon, turning down the Rue du Bois, deeply grateful that he had been sent here to know for himself that in this place Russians could only dream dreams. If only he could be right now, opposite the Plekhanov's apartment, he would call all Russians, wherever they were, back to Russia, there was so much work to be done. Rouse up! rouse up! just you Georgy, have you forgotten? how you were called too then, to lead the first great demonstration - for freedom! pointing the way - just you - take the lead! come home! - return.

Let it be known this strength and call rousing through him, gathering pace to cross the road.

"Return Georgy - awake from your stupor!" That's what he'd say. To the point. No yielding to wordy discussions and cunning debates. No creeping about. Let these smug Switzers know too.

Let all know that the struggle in Russia had hardly begun, that Russia was calling her prodigal sons to return for her needs - for the work, banged the ram's head knocker hard once twice three times, and could have gone on on to rouse this whole smug street city country.

Everyone in the house heard the furious bangs.

Monsieur Castelot at bezique with Madame Castelot was shot out of his wicker chair by the frightening bangs. He hurried to the front door.

"Who is it? What is it?" he called out.

"Kovnator, Stepan Kovnator," called back Kovnator, smiling to himself, familiar vigorous note of himself, " for Monsieur Plekhanov please," he added, as Monsieur Castelot opened up to this heavily built, clean faced man - what was it with these Russians? - whose large friendly eyes smiled generously and who bowed low so graciously. Confused, distressed by his wife's angry approach, he pointed limply up the stairs to the Plekhanov's rooms.

Staring at Kovnator and intending that all above hear she shouted, "They're impossible. I won't have it. They'll give me a heart attack. And what's this - what's this?" she screamed out at the white dented bucket. She grabbed at the lid, let it drop, backed sharply away.

"Animals! they're just animals," she clutched wildly at her husband's wrist, "d'you see what they've left here - the whole day! decency - common decency - they haven't got it - don't stand there like that - call them down! make them get rid of their filth! - I won't stand it any longer - let the rooms stay empty. A month - a year. They must go!"

Beside herself she hurried away, slamming a door behind her. Monsieur Castelot stood trembling, unable to move, Kovnator, fascinated, picked up the bucket causing so much trouble, nodded sympathetically to the poor husband and began up the stairs, aware that all four! were present, gathered on the landing at the commotion and looking down at him. All four here together, what a rightness!

He smiled back, of course they're all here, living proof of his inspiration, never never after this dare doubt it that it speaks for Russia. Yes yes - all their exclamations, astonishment but meet them - let it be open warm - for them! Yes yes - shake hands all round.

"Impossible!"

"Amazing!"

"Kovnator - you here!"

He felt their shock pleasure wariness.

Of course it was Kovnator - not imprisoned -not silenced - some oblivion they had consigned him too eh? - uncanny! Shaking hands to ensure that he was really here. Still uncanny. His face the same but changed. Beyond the odd beardlessness, the short cut hair - the voice exuberance all no question Kovnator - that booming voice could only be Kovnator. To what comforting oblivion had they banished him?

"No ghost! comrades," he said lightly, grinning, enjoying their confusion, wanting discreetly to assess their situation.

Comrades? what was he up to?

Georgy was confused by the bucket, by the sight of Kovnator with the bucket. What was he doing here?

What was he doing here?

"No ghost this, comrades - I smell good food - and drink," he said enthusiastically, stepping towards the open kitchen door, in charge already, that 'comrades', distinctly sarcastic.

"Well well," he went on, beaming at the food and drink crowding the table, "this is the life eh? Georgy," he commented breezily, pouring himself a glass of wine, and letting them catch up with their memories, yes indeed let them. Remember the last meeting – uproar – bitterness – threats – remember! – years? ago – still now.

"Excellent wine. The real life eh? for a Russian revolutionary. No wonder they all come here – Paris – London – everywhere except where they're needed."

The change of tone, attack, was immediately felt.

None of them yet could properly draw breath. Kovnator's presence, gestures, words had awoken such a painful past – and that lest they dare forget – the issue of the deed – still not – never to be completely resolved.

"Kovnator, what the hell are you doing here?" demanded Axelrod in desperation.

Georgy, over the shock, felt the need for considerable caution, a curiosity, the touch of alarm. Not to expect malevolence from Kovnator but prepared for anything in this mood.

Kovnator nodded seriously as he looked around the kitchen. "They were right then. Who'd have believed it? – real fighters all of you – come to this. Sitting on your backsides stuffing your bellies and reading more books. You've sold out my friends plain and simple. Don't be too ashamed. All the others have done it too," he gestured expansively to the city, the country, the world.

They were furious at his daring to presume that he was still one of them, an equal, in order to lecture criticise – destroy them. Axelrod and Deutsch heard it, took the measure of him now, to somehow destroy them, that was it!

Georgy, sensing danger, held his hand up to caution, to pacify. "Let him speak – let him finish," he said tensely.

"– and now they tell me," this damned 'they' he kept on about, "you're preparing a mighty onslaught – mighty theories and powerful words – eh?" he went on, frowning severely.

They sensed that he was not really talking to them.

Georgy, confused, drawn to the man they had all once worked with warmly, admiringly, felt compelled to begin a meaningful exchange. Some balance must be restored, some resistance. Kovnator had caught them by surprise, seemed to be taking them over. He must hold it off, restore.

They all felt the change, strangeness in this man, an

164

indifference, remoteness, yet, in the uneasy silence, a power, an authority.

"Well Stepan Ivanovich you can call it words if you like. We see it as the need to educate a mass consciousness – to change a mass consciousness – a slow –"

"More words," Kovnator sneered, "Consciousness? What d'you know about consciousness? God help us all! that you still don't know what the bomb – the presence – the sight of that mess of bloody flesh – I'll tell you – listen! listen! – everyone there by the Ekaterininsky Canal – everyone in Russia whether they realise it or not doesn't matter – knows now somehow that they themselves – are creators of the Tsar – the so-called real Tsar – that's consciousness! That's how you change consciousness. And that was done by Grinevitsky's moving arm – not theories, not words – but deeds! Real deeds to tear people out of their dreadful sleep. Everyone – in time. Whenever those exalted bones lie scattered on the road something happens to those who see it, hear about it. Something absolutely crucial," he shouted excitedly, "As for that scum on top – they're waking up to the fact that they're also under the same tyrant – fear of death. The worm's entered their guts. They trust each other less and less – no you can't even say that – they don't know what trust is. Better, they suspect each other more and more. Did you see what Delyanov said about their late revered master, 'his death was a blessing – if only the circumstances had been less cruel.' So much for the divine autocrat! At the top it's everyone for himself. Hang on to your power whatever the cost. But they know the end's in sight! They've met men who can't be controlled by the fear of death. Of course the peasants were outraged by the killing. But I tell you – their consciousness has been changed – what you're pretending to do. They know that death from the hand of man comes even to our Tsar. Even! That these men and women hanging from the gallows aren't afraid of it. Did you see them hanging there – the way they lived their end? That's what'll bear fruit for Russia – the time when the peasant's children will themselves kill the Tsar. Free themselves from this incubus. As for your so-called workers – working class – who are they? Your own creation!"

Throughout the tirade each of the four prepared a counter-attack.

Vera intended to emphasise the autocracy's savage reprisals

which had wiped out all serious opposition – as everyone well knew! But for any of them, how argue back with him? The peasants? His peasants! – they were accusing the nobility! – for the assassination in revenge for the Tsar's emancipation of them!

Plekhanov dared to think of mentioning Gankin – that even once committed terrorists were seeing the light – but impossible to mention Gankin.

By the end of the tirade each felt, sadly, that this man was a stranger to them, living in some world of his own.

Axelrod unable to hold back, felt the need to respond was justified, as forcing Kovnator to face reality. But softening, generalising, he felt himself talking into a vacuum.

"Kovnator we also get some news you know – that the Executive Committee of the People's Will doesn't – hasn't existed for a long time – if that's your 'they'."

"Exist? D'you think its a question of numbers? One is sufficient for existence. Purity – that's what's needed for existence – and that, we shall maintain," he said as if to listeners far away. "Enough! Enough!" he exclaimed abruptly and was on his way to the landing, hands thrust into the pockets of his coat which he had still not taken off. His right hand rested gently on his revolver, his left on a small package, the touch of which made him smile, halt, turn about and call out to Georgy in a changed almost familiar voice from the past.

"Georgy – for the little one when it comes," he said, tugging out a small package, looking directly at Georgy.

They could only watch and wonder. So unexpectedly close, so distant.

He was gone. They could breathe more easily.

Gone, yet as presence itself such a sadness. Such a disturbing quiet, emptiness. Emptiness, sounding his dreadful isolation.

Their unity, so challenged, now re-centred, on all that Georgy stood for.

In the sad space of that absence a pathetic figure wandered through a doomed world of his own. Wandered with that unfamiliar limp and haggardness glimpsed.

The soundness of Georgy's position was reaffirmed through that spectral appearance. And yet to know too that Stepan Ivanovich and they, his task and their task, his destiny and their destiny, somehow still remained inextricably woven within the great destiny of Russia.

Wandering blindly up and down the lamplit street in dreadful indecision, back and forth past the Plekhanov's door, Gankin panicked and fled back to his lodgings when Kovnator opened it to leave. Kovnator's enough! enough! returned him to the task ahead, burnished him finely in the flame of this rightness. Go! be finished with these naive idiots.

Opening the door Kovnator saw, flash of a turnabout and off! and knew immediately – as in a vision that it was him! As in a vision, to keep moving, to follow him – having to – dimly connecting it – that one in front with himself – his exit – but connected it stays – to think – assess – follow well back – sufficient to keep him in sight – connected it stays – having to – trusted voice.

Almost running the one ahead –must – could only be him.

Voice from that deepest source – don't doubt. Comrades – such a rousing name – for those naive fools?

Excuse me! excuse me! good citizens of Geneva – sorry good sir! – but that one ahead I have business with!

He turns left – turns right –nice living round here – stop! – stop! – well back – straight in through the front door very useful – first floor – light on – it all goes according to some plan – calm down – steady yourself – take every precaution – instrument indeed! – but with extreme seriousness!

Idiots! don't even imagine they're being watched – planning Russia's future – already sewn up! idiots! that Russia's future was in their keeping! Morozov's attack on him for being too suspicious – eh? Nikolai Vasilievich – a little compensation then for me in your apartment under the Neva?

Gankin sat at the table, trembling, staring helplessly at the whiteness of the empty report sheet waiting to be filled in. Last two reports – just managed. This whiteness refusing all approach – brilliant void.

Flee! for good.

Surely someone would come to his aid.

So damn tight this breathing! Force it out! Force it in! Air – air – air!

Pack the job in – get out!

But they had this hold on him. Remember when he asked about whatever happened to Bodemann and was answered with a blank look – blank – dawning the utter stupidity of your question – what happened to Bodemann is whatever you think happened to Bodemann! But don't expect an answer – for there is no answer to this particular question.

Everything around him, once so comforting, there for the plucking, become ghostly.

Listen! life returning in that measured tread approaching your door – someone visiting him! – was it her? Helena lovely name – for her – madman! she doesn't know where you live – respond – answer to that friendly knock – one – two – three – come on – answer it!

"Kovnator!"

"Yes – that's right – it's me Kovnator."

Kovnator seen the light! One of us too! – come to help him out of this mess.

"My god I'm glad you've come. I knew you would I knew it. But I don't mind admitting – the situation's getting tricky. Different though now you're here. Actually they're fools. Plekhanov for instance he's completely taken in. In fact the work is easy. Take your coat off Kovnator – make yourself at home. Yes of course, pour yourself a drink. No shortage. Fancy. Just the right day. They've had their meeting you know – so there's the report to do now. A lot to tell you Kovnator – not sure where to begin. Why don't you take your coat off? How long did it take you? You've never been out of Russia before? But thank goodness you're here now."

Stepan Ivanovich, be extremely wary of this babbling trembling! This very comfortable room, distances, angles, report sheets stacked neatly – everything so neat, be wary! One end only for this creature.

Pitiful! Pity – never!

"– you see Kovnator we already know everything – so just a question of – well, tactics – maintaining their confidence – and –"

The words stopped, withdrew, vanished, he, left in a soundless space, staring at the still point of his life, the dull metallic aperture of Kovnator's revolver barrel through which his life was being remorselessly sucked away. The revolver, which Kovnator had never ceased pointing at him, poised from that ample fist, its indictment absolute.

Cruel powerwords booming through time's abyss.

The revolver pointed steadily as Kovnator glanced at the paper on the table.

"So! your new work eh? Well paid? – a very neat worker! –

very pleasant surroundings – but my dear Gankin you simply haven't realised the seriousness of what you're doing – the choice you've made. But you will. I shall help you to,"

Gankin heard with dread, relief, utterly in Kovnator's power.

"– well written – very orderly – they must be very pleased with you in St Petersburg. But my dear Gankin the game you're playing is a very serious game. For most – sooner or later the cards fail – they won't fall right. And with you it's sooner."

Gankin felt himself bound tight, in some dream that had been was there all the time.

"But you see Gankin, we don't know everything. Take your betrayals. Do you know what they achieved – who on the gallows? – who into the dungeons? – who to Siberia? No Gankin not at all – gallows – Schlüsselburg – Siberia – they're all here – right now! I've become many Gankin since their deaths – entombments – exiles – all your achievement Gankin – Gan-kin – Gan-kin – Gan-kin – that's not a real name, something odd about it – like dry bones. No ring. Nothing there! Grinevitsky – Mikhailov – Kibalchich – Zhelyabov – Perovskaya all real names! Gankin, I'll do as much for you – give you the chance to become a man – to get a real name. But time is short. Put your coat on! We're going down to the lake. Your last walk. A bit like theirs so make the best of it. Just time to find out who you really are. Not everyone even gets that chance. Who knows – you might even achieve it. Not die a spy after all – an informer – police scum – mankind's shit – bloody shit! – but a man – die a man! – die? – born! – you'll see – get going! – straight down the stairs – no tricks! Gankin – if we meet anyone on the way out, act naturally or I'll blow your brains out on the spot."

Gankin led on relieved, his thinking unexpectedly attuning itself to the reality, Kovnator's revolver back in his coat pocket, seconds there sprouting!

A low heavy mist hovered over the lake and was creeping through the city. Soon, approaching the Quai de Mont Blanc they were right into it. Kovnator sensed danger as the form in front kept vanishing and reappearing. On either side house fronts loomed in elusive presence. He willed intensest concentration.

Gankin was moving mechanically. In the soundless swirl he no longer heard steps behind him. Both men felt alone, ghostly to each other.

"Stop! Stop walking!" Kovnator snapped out, jabbing his

revolver hard into Gankin's back, relieved at the impact.

"Walk forward slowly - slower! or I'll blow you to pieces."

That jabbing contact woke Gankin into life edge calculation. Mist, slowness, friends now. High waters slopping over the quayside at their feet for immediate action.

"Kovnator they've set a trap for you - my life for the details," he whispered hoarsely, hardly able to find his voice for this last mad throw.

"Turn round - slowly," ordered Kovnator, relieved at being face to face with Gankin on the edge, his back to the lake.

"Life? - And what could you do with life," he began musing. Gankin felt that barrel point waver, an infinite moment of loosening, life-filled flash, kicking up with all his might towards the gun. Kovnator staggered back pulling on the trigger before the gun fell from his wrist. The shot pounded at Gankin's forehead. Dazed, off balance, he toppled into the water. Kovnator scrabbled on the path for the gun and watched tensely.

The still body kept close to the edge. Balancing as best he could he kicked hard at it to force it away, right away. But it moved little.

He must get going, in this friendly mist, across the fields and back towards the station, back to Russia and the work. Those waters pure enough to receive that creature and take care of him.

Many days later a body was found by a fisherman, trapped in some reeds, never satisfactorily identified. Axelrod, Deutsch, Zasulich, felt reassured, relaxed, but discreetly, by Gankin's failure to appear. Georgy found it difficult to come to terms with.

Reports reaching Rachkovsky all pointed in one direction.

A pity! The man's reports were significantly detailed and regular, fully justifying his recruiting policy. The Swiss files were really beginning to take on some substance and shape. The real pity was that the new forgery project had pointed to Gankin as the most useful and likely operator. Never mind, others were coming forward all the time from nowhere.

III

Ananayev

"Jews! To the bath-house!" called the elderly Shammas, called out, named, warned, making his Sabbath Eve round through every Jewish street, made and unmade, of the Jewish quarter in Ananayev, eighty miles northeast of Kishinev in the southern Ukraine.

"Jews! to the bath-house!" sounded the timeless order to obey the Commandment from Sinai, making us present with Moshe Rabbenu, ending the tension, heralding the break, bringing relief.

Call - called - the calling.

Each of us on his own together dealt with, addressed. Sun setting, shadows deepening, streets narrowing, but the glorious Sun, the Law, of our very own world His world arising.

At last and again glance high above to the hem of His robe, before his first lights kindle at the Sabbath Bride's approach.

Let go, thrust aside, wash away this world's grime of care sadness humiliation - pain pain pain!

Rinse off, be cleansed, enter the Sabbath world, hand in hand with the Sabbath Bride, Israel's enduring hope!

"Remember the Sabbath day by keeping it holy. Six days you shall labour and do all your work but the seventh day is a Sabbath to the Lord your God" words voice engraved within forever - of our new life beginning as the Shammas, our own, makes his way.

Stern that call to my duty, my answering for all Israel. But joyful the promised release from this world of deepening shadow below.

Call to our burden as the Chosen, call to the Covenant with Him. Father of All.

His lights above and we Ananayev's Jews, His Children below, called, forever called till the time of the end.

Hurry! Hurry!

Shopkeepers! stall holders! innkeepers! beggars! Yeshiva bochers! Rabbi Melnikov - himself! Porters! Sweepers! Well-off and poor! But now we can be what we truly are once again,

Ananayev's Jews! - each as of the One.

Children of Israel His Chosen One. Sons of the Covenant - glory - greatness - this Ananayev exile - simply the exile - ordained - endured until the homecoming - Jerusalem! Zion! His Holy Place! Here but tents, husks. Zion our true abiding, which is, yet is to be.

Hurry, hurry home, and to the place of cleansing, His waning sun ordains the time is now. Time of His Will, His Word, Revealed.

Let this spark of our deepest joy be kindled as we come into this place of our truly own.

In my heart be kindled this now of our renewal.

Sharply to draw the line between their time and ours.

"Jews! to the bath-house!" calling our difference into all its fullness and glory - and the burden to be endured.

Hurry home and tremble that on my heart's intent and deeds depends right now the Covenant.

Rise up Jews to his call, to our true stature, remembering who we are and what awaits.

Why! - pity! - such pity for these goyim awoken by my Shammas' call. The ones who had not been Chosen. Who had not the words of the Only One. Who have vodka only to quench the thirst of their souls.

Who have not the Law and can never yet know Right from Wrong, Good from Bad.

Hurry home, take up your Sabbath clothes, to the bath, and then to Shul before the sun sets.

Called to the painful joy of being born a Jew for the whole world's goodness.

Born to life and redemption, our life's calling, nothing less.

Tested, testifying, testimony is our life.

Wash away the dirt of this earthly exile, the worry and sadness!

But so stubborn this worry right now!

before daring to enter the joy of His Creation.

Such power our Shammas' call! To make our way to His Holy Place with all the strength of our hope. To make ourselves ready through this enduring Sabbath Life to bear witness, even to the very end.

Yes - Yes - "I believe with all my heart in the coming of the Messiah and even as he delays - nevertheless - I expect him every day."

But it's not so easy, dear Shammas this Shabbas eve – is it?

Aren't we hearing that other call through the ages coming from them?

Not so easy, dear God in Heaven – Moshe Rabbenu, we'll need your help.

Not so easy to turn away.

This worry refuses to let me go free for the Sabbath Bride's embrace.

Listen Our God!

Do You know the facts – then you'll make allowance.

You'll hear me. You must know how it is.

They're getting ready for something – isn't it so? – and we're going to need Your help.

Even to hold it together makes my throat go tight – it's Our story all over again. But I tell it to You – Our story – Who Else?

Who Else must know that the rumours won't let go? And I'm putting them to You God of Our Fathers. Israel's Lord.

Take Bender – has he ever been known to lie? Hasn't he seen on his rounds in their parts – strange men from Odessa – talking to them in little groups – and how those strangers watched him – and they themselves began looking at him in strange ways – and he knew that something was happening!

And our good Halkin – didn't he grease those greedy palms as usual to find out what was going on? – Rubbish Jew Halkin! Stop making trouble! We are fully responsible for His Majesty's law and order in Ananayev. Go back to your quarter! Get on with your own Jewish affairs – – but our good Halkin saw smirks – with the truth of the eyes You have made us – good Halkin money they took but the clerk was smirking – that ignorant pig of a clerk knew – was enjoying all – our helplessness! – given over Moshe Rabbenu – helpless! – we need your help.

That's not all!

You should know all the facts.

As good Halkin left that office, one from Odessa walked in – made very welcome!

And – – Zuskin, back from peddling his stuff to Balta, heard of the men from Odessa there too.

But what's all this God of our Fathers compared to Steinberg's news – back from Odessa itself on Wednesday – Who more pious more truthful than Steinberg? – whisper! – whisper I must – the CHMIELNICKI madness! – that story be resumed – whisper

whisper I must – murder rape looting arson – lying in wait to smirk at the Sabbath Bride.

But to You I cry it out – yes! fearful helpless.

In Odessa the Jews were being blamed for the assassination – blame that was coming from on High! Blame then requiring – what else – what else? from Haman – action – revenge – could it mean anything else?

whisper it whisper it

but You can already see it for Yourself, God of our Fathers when Steinberg came back yesterday from Odessa – that everyone knew men were on their way from the city to stir up trouble.

Do You see why it isn't easy?

Why I struggle to make a space for the Sabbath Bride?

D'you hear me O God – doesn't the Shammas' call tonight warn instead of the ageless hate?

Is not all in Your Hands – Only One on High. Who spoke the Words of our Life from Sinai's lightning and thunder. Who inscribed the tablets of stone that set our bound that holds us firm and seals our life with Yours.

Then fear not! Jew that I am and have been chosen. Timelessly put to the test.

Willingly sacrifice then for the sake of the Covenant – for this speaking with God – this sharing to change the world.

But it isn't easy tonight.

Avram Lieberman's two young assistants were very surprised when he ordered them to bring back inside, the hardware and foodstuffs, in barrels, sacks, bottles, on boards, racks and trestles, displayed on the paving outside his general stores. So early! At least an hour before the Shammas comes round –he's already checking the book?

So! it's not been the usual eve of Shabbes trade. Usual? unusual? so what! Who's complaining? – Kantor's putting his shutters down! – Davidov's shut! – so what! alright alright. So! – there may be some trouble.

"Yes Mr Lieberman we are getting on with it."

With the last wooden crate containing tongs and choppers dragged inside, Lieberman handed them their wages and told them to be off, to get ready for Shul!

Of course get ready for Shul as they checked their wages –

same as usual! – Who dear God could fathom the ways of our boss Avram Lieberman?

So wanting to be alone, to come to terms with what was happening to him in the dim light of the shuttered shop, Lieberman snapped shut the ledger. Such pitiful weakness before this anxiety!

You – lack of faith?

You – So blessed with such sons – lack of faith?

Then here – in this emptiness – you will stand – and wait – and repent O Lord for my cowardice – nothing but cowardice?

That Josef and Nathan could only know from what I did, some terrible weakness – the Evil One's victory! and I will fight back O Lord, before the young – before the young.

Avram Lieberman you will not leave this shop until the Shammas calls!

You will face with all your strength your cowardice – face Him now – and seek His forgiveness – Our God is a forgiving God – repent!

Eyes stop lying those hatchets and knives are means for life only!

He is our Rock of Salvation – not – not – spell it out – those hatchets those knives –here! – hiding here! – is your lack of faith.

"Jews! to the bath-house!" at last, from what distance heard, succour.

"Jews! to the bath-house!" called now right in front of the shop, Shammas Liptzin's familiar acknowledgement of the store's importance and of the Lieberman sons, sign, blessing for all Ananayev's Jews. Yehuda and Aaron Lieberman, Ananayev's sons Ananayev's pride, Ananayev's future treasure for all Israel. Avram and Dorah Lieberman blessed, to prosper, with earthly and heavenly goods.

"Jews! to the bath-house!" struck hard the call releasing him, to hurry away from the desolate street and join with all Ananayev's Jews hurrying homeward from wherever. Stall-holders, artisans, bakers and tailors, journeying merchants, itinerant cobblers, hurrying homewards, to be cleansed and in Shul before the sun finally sets.

His sons! For him to know on his way with such sharp joy this blessing of his sons as a new future – made to know it at this very time. Made to know that if the news was so! then only for God's purpose – only for Israel's good – chastisement –

purification – his! shortcomings – failure to keep the commandments – he to blame so more than ever now make Shabbes true pure deed in faith standing before Sinai – security and hope with those timeless ones against this anxiety – achieved! Always the price to pay, reminder for being His Chosen Ones but – next year in Jerusalem – our Jerusalem – the end time would come!

Yehuda and Aaron Lieberman, fourteen and thirteen, watched out expectantly in the front room for their father's Sabbath homecoming. Each eager to spot him first, to open the door, greet him with a kiss, hand over his clean fresh Shabbas clothes and all off to the bath-house. This delight, after the long hours immersed, day after day in higher Talmudic studies at the bare, ill-lit Gemoreh Kheyder room. Hours spent reading the Book written by Moshe Rabbenu, teacher and prophet. Reading, memorising, engraving, interpreting, true life in the true homeland. A reading that kept the world steady on this wordground of salvation. Kept, through their life absorption in this struggle and clash, point against point, question and answer, wrestle and dance. To know, to already know, as sons of the Covenant, in the pride of their budding gifts, that everything around them was ultimate captive to the Torah's true naming, everything. The goyim's naming only a noise, appearance of an ignorance. Already to know proudly this kindling, consuming of oneself to ash, eyes forced to blink back bitterly at this world's forsaken daylight beyond the study room, beyond the Book. To feel the proud acclaim enfolding, the burden of expectations, that on their future the Jews of Ananayev somehow depended. To know that in the Torah were the answers to every possible question but only when one wrestled with all one's strength as Father Jacob wrestled for our very life.

Our pride aflame in this knowing, our zeal, our love for these words.

Our duty as sons of the Covenant to discover God's Will for our People.

Exhilarating this ceaseless flashing up. Voices speaking off the page, off the very line. Rabbi Bizna ben Zabda in the name of Rabbi Akiba who had it from Rabbi Nahum who had it from Rabbi Biryan who was reporting the words of Rabbi Bana'an – – voices sounding so clearly round the bare wooden table – this story – their story – a swaying – a song. And then by some magic the final weighing. Boundless the All in all yet, in each, in just this particular case, the fence to be clearly staked out. This particular one – the ultimate exhilarating challenge.

The Lieberman brothers' exceptional powers of memory, ability to analyse, synthesise, contrast in fine shades, soar, balance out the intangible 'but ifs' – regarding Temple law, divorce, animal sacrifice – developed so rapidly as to often leave bewildered their teacher Mendel Tversky. He must admit that with him they were chewing on nothing. As soon as possible they must go to Vilna and be with their equals. Not a minute to be lost for Israel's sake.

Yehuda respectfully handed the sweet smelling, freshly laundered Sabbath clothes, to his father. Clean shirts, underpants and white woollen arba kamfas with its knotted fringes. Take! Take! Be bright to your boys – be with them! Listen to Aaron's tale of so many things they had done today in that study room. Enter into all that be cheered. Life of your boys, meeting and greeting friends and relations on the way to the bath-house. How the boys so loved it, looked forward to it from the week's beginning, the excitement, mysterious transformation, how it comes about?

The steamy drift enfolding, the warm yielding, the letting-go though pressed for time. But a cheerful pressure. Duty of purification but such a pleasure too. All laid down but with such a rightness. The easy dreams, chat, life and play of streaming gasping water all as a gift before the seriousness, before the new man was called fully into his own, strict and strong before God. New Sabbath man taking hold – new Sabbath clothes. Tender vulnerable skin but we shine towards each other. Greet each other anew shining. Grime of that earthly week's work washed away. No longer that 'for a living' but Life itself.

As soon as they entered the large brick building, and made for the cubicles, they knew. Everyone was already here! it was crowded, but so quiet!

Not at all the usual mood and they knew. Knew just how to bear themselves. No indulgence possible tonight. No bodily pleasure justified – some commandment at work as they undressed and carefully laid their clothes, old and new on the wooden shelving.

Something demanded of them as they dipped down into the

water's warmth, not to yield, not to yield. Demanded by a wary warning guarding guardian. All felt so keenly, this need to act with such restraint.

From somewhere in the thicket of steaming heat chat tried to begin but found no response. No one in the mood for basking, only the ritual immersion and the prayers.

In truth this Godgiven time of reverent pleasure shouldn't be affected. But it wasn't easy tonight, none of it.

Clothes changed, skin changed, but it won't let go its grip.

They hurried back home with their old clothes and drew on their Sabbath caftans of black silk, girdled around the waist with a black silk cord. They covered their heads with black hats and hurried to the Synagogue in Avner Street.

Since Wednesday Rabbi Melnikov had felt the deepest calling of Ananayev's Jews to hear something from him. He made preparation through constant prayer that the right words, from his mouth sound forth for the Sabbath.

They were waiting to hear from him.

He must with God's help calm the anxiety, light up for them the glory, the joy of their sonship, their speaking with God.

Since Wednesday's news from Odessa he dared to feel that there could be an attack on the Sabbath Bride Herself, on that citadel of Jewish heart, test indeed.

Then the Sabbath itself would be his only concern. Life itself – Bride of Israel's consummation. Sabbath itself, true home, not these husks of Ananayev, fleeting earthly tents but to the firm house of the Sabbath he must bear witness, establish anew their anxious faith in Him, will that from this fearful shrinking Israel's strong We burst forth anew.

The synagogue in Avner Street, standing for over a hundred years but in need of much repair was unusually crowded and silent. Everyone in their correct place waiting.

Since when so many suddenly come to Shul? Some strange faces too! It wasn't as though it was Yom Kippur. Wasn't it?

Yes we in our places looking over at you on the Eastern side – you pious learned wealthy ones. Of course knowing who you are, who we are – but waiting, pressed shoulder to shoulder, feeling something else too – those never ending differences – a veil – illusion. No! – a much greater gathering telling my heart of something else. We! my heart is saying to burst – beyond fiercely beyond all this that I see. We! it speaks me – this anxious moment is Mine. Be lifted up gathered embraced – I have chosen you – fear not!

Yes we in our places looking over at you on the Western side – common poor unlearned shiftless but this silent waiting tonight tells my heart of something else – the difference going away, never closer never stronger gathering this We. Come on come on dear Rabbi Melnikov – so old pale tired you look tonight. What will you say, offer, confirm?

Can anything be said?

Can this awful silence be thrust back?

At last – Oh at last – begin dear Rabbi Melnikov – the pounding of this We is my trembling heart.

"Come forth my friend the Bride to meet!

Come O my friend the Sabbath greet."

Keep singing my heart sing sing this We to hear itself sounding forth, but none of it's easy tonight.

"Sabbath to welcome thee joyous we haste

Fountain of blessing from ever thou wast

First in God's planning though fashioned the last

Crown of his handiwork chiefest of days."

Sing, sing, try and sing! my heart – this We to hear itself sounding forth, but none of it's easy tonight.

Rabbi Melnikov left his seat next to the Ark and stood on the Bimah, at the centre. Calm, slowly he turned in all fullness from the Western to the Eastern side.

To begin, with steady strength, assuredness, surprising freshness, addressing, confirming, reminding.

"My dear Jews, it is told by our sages that God said to Israel, if You accept my Torah and observe my Laws I will give You for all eternity the most precious thing that I have in my possession."

Israel asked, "What is that precious thing Thou will give us if we obey Thy Torah?"

And God answered, "The future world."

And Israel asked again, "But even in this world should we have a foretaste of the other?"

And God answered, "The Sabbath will give you this foretaste."

"And the prophet has told us dear Jews, 'Ye are my witnesses saith the Lord and I am God.'

Now dear Jews know that – and fear not!"

Stern the imperative as he looked around.

"We are his witnesses – on us alone it rests. Hasn't the prophet told us?

This is the nature of the Covenant nothing less.

It is so!"

He was warning - warning.

He'd stopped.

That was all?

But that was it - and we know it!

So brief but it alone spans the abyss. So brief - but this quickening of my soul. It alone, and he will not waver to right or to left.

That I - am a Jew he declares calm strong together with and through the Lord of All who is my God.

He's blazoned forth this truth -in this blazoning it will prevail - sustain me - cast out fear.

That I - Jew as the fullness of my being is Rabbi Melnikov's voice and words.

That the pain wound glory of this fullness he tells of - speaking - walks before us - to emulate - as what lies before us.

He's telling us we must live with it - hear it - ponder it - at this moment my trembling heart recalling us all here as that One Israel - exiled tortured murdered - but faithful. Rabbi Melnikov's calm, the ground of our strength, telling of the enduring which we alone are called to uphold.

That witness a warning?

No one wanted to be the first to leave their seat.

Rabbi Melnikov, looked round at everyone, gently raised his hands in blessing and walked slowly into that world outside, followed first by the Cohanim, and then, so orderly and quiet, everyone else, making space and place for each other in unfamiliar ways.

Stirred, sustained by Rabbi Melnikov's words, by Rabbi Melnikov himself, Avram and his sons quietly exchanged "Good Sabbath!" greetings by the synagogue entrance before returning to bless and welcome the Sabbath at home. Stirred, to hear the glory of that talking with God, of that very own timeless world, untouchable by these barefoot goyim children, walk straight on! by the taunts from somewhere by this roaming pig snorting and snuffing for good Jewish waste. Returning through yes Jewish streets - but with this unfamiliar vigilance.

Entering the house each called a loud "Good Sabbath!" to Dorah whose cooking embraced with its warm assurance that everything was in its Sabbath place – as usual. But unfamiliar, uneasy, restraining, this feeling of the usual. For all of them something that couldn't be pushed aside. Something restraining the joy and devotion of the Sabbath way.

Everything as usual thank goodness in the Sabbath front room, the candles burning in their silver candlesticks, gentle radiance blessed by Dorah, the blue embroidered napkins, the polished boxes of spice. Everyone knowing what to do thank goodness. Father's usual greeting, "Peace be unto you, ministering Angel, messenger of the Most High." His prayer praising the virtuous wife, for Mama herself. His Kiddush prayer, each sipping from the silver goblet. The washing of hands. The chollah's radiant whiteness blessed.

Yes – yes but this awkwardness.

The spiced fish, juice as sweet as ever, the chicken soup, such sweetness warming. The chicken itself, "Lovely Dorah – eh boys? just melts in your mouth."

Between courses when usually the boys discussed their studies, or the portion of the Law to be read tomorrow in Shul, an awkward silence threatened. In that painful place of restraint Yehuda and Aaron struggled with unfamiliar questions. What did Rabbi Melnikov mean? What was this witness? – some awful danger felt in the Rabbi's words.

"Well then," Avram began uneasily, "the portion tomorrow!"

Yehuda answered all that easily enough with some relief. Leviticus – purification of the lepers after healing – Metzora 14:1 – the two live clean birds – the cedar wood – scarlet yarn and hyssop – seven times sprinkled – the dead bird's blood over the leper – the live bird released in the open fields – on the seventh day – on the eighth day – on – and on – when suddenly it demanded utterance, and that, before Dorah came back with the first bowl of compote and raisins.

"Why do they hate us so?" looking straight at his father, face to face, with and for strength.

Dorah heard it as she came in.

The bitterness of that goyim hatred penetrated.

Yehuda was embarrassed and relieved to have uttered it but somehow it was not from him. A mysterious I – myself.

It's good that he's said it like that – of course he knows why – that we're the Chosen ones but that 'so' of his – that lingering 'so' – that Yehuda knows – hear it from him – it tells of living with death as a Jew - the boy knows - did he know what he was saying to us all? Be humble here Avram Lieberman - to you too who might have forgotten, your son's 'so' - son - boy - man - Jew - only God can fathom this.

At last with a brave effort, the songs praising God as the candles burned low. Time for the boys to go to bed. Aaron found words for his pain since leaving the synagogue.

"I couldn't see Yitzhak anywhere in Shul," he said, surprising his brother and father, that till now, how possible? they hadn't given Yitzhak! any thought.

"Yitzhak? - - he can't be feeling well tonight - what else?" answered Avram wanting to reassure, to assuage that odd forgetting.

"Yitzhak would never be away from Shul on Sabbath - don't worry Aaron. We'll soon find out - my boys. Good Night! - sleep well with God's blessing."

As soon as he felt the boys settled after hearing their nightly prayers from the room above he turned to the blackbound Torah, book, very source of life. Life, to issue from Moshe Rabbenu's own world set large in the centre of each well-fingered page. Life to issue from the oases of surrounding commentaries, set in ever smaller letters. Rashi, always the first which he must grapple with, taste drink from. Rashi's words on tomorrow's portion from Leviticus, for the morning's discussion in Shul. Most decisive duty this, to respond, bear witness to our great teachers.

But Rashi's words, page, book itself withdrew before Aaron's innocent indictment. Yes, an accusation felt, guiltily felt and he must get to the bottom of it. What had happened? What was this forgetfulness? - forget? No - never!

He had known all along that Yitzhak wasn't there! - and now - to know that absence as his feeling of loss - that ominous feeling throughout the service - a sign! Where did he end then and Yitzhak begin? - and the boys too - and at this moment of all moments! The life with Yitzhak essential life of our We. So much so that now - so opened - with such warmth he would break out and tell the world - the name - the story - the story of Yitzhak. Why! - as a very challenge to this that was breaking in on them from every side. Even now to begin thus to think of Yitzhak was to expand, to know a pure joy.

Rashi there calling, duty, but this other story not yet told a duty too! Commanding too! The story of Yitzhak. To tell the whole world that here in our town we have such a man. Hadn't Rabbi Melnikov said that he was a blessing to the whole town, goyim included. That what pious men strive for, he was naturally. Didn't people feel ashamed of themselves with him. He showed up your weaknesses - self-deceit - but always in a good encouraging, yes encouraging, way - as an equal - never more than an equal. Yitzhak about whose origin no one seemed certain. Yitzhak who had confided to him such wonderful things. Well the whole world should know! If he Avram Lieberman could write like Mendele Seforim what a story he could tell. It would begin like this - how else?

"In our town of Ananayev - -"

but the town wasn't really ours!

Our quarter perhaps - not even after two hundred years? This 'our' business was worrying. Mendele Seforim surely didn't worry about things like that?

Our - our - our - the whole story that was ours! - not mine nor Yitzhak's but ours! Yield then, surrender to this great story first - it must be so - where our road to Ananayev began. This great story will not let you go even for Yitzhak. Even? This was the beginning of Yitzhak's story too. The real beginning. Exodus - Sinai - Babylon - Second Temple - Crusades - pogroms - Inquisition - Egypt Babylon Rome Greece all gone - we here surviving in Ananayev - but surviving only through the living Covenant.

How could you write any story without this real beginning? That's why he wasn't a writer like Mendele Seforim. To be a writer you had to dodge this business of beginning - real beginning.

And how good he was with words - always the right word here and there. Tough, honest, that made people think - made them turn. You asked him to mend the roof, the door, the fence but something happened. In a few words. A turning for you. Firm gentle words starting anywhere - and your story would come out. He would show you to tell it better.

And there was only one real beginning for any story - the beginning of all beginnings - 'In the beginning God made the heavens and the earth.' - Moshe Rabbenu knew that was the only way to begin.

Fool!

Stick to your shop!

Well no one could stop him telling it to himself – and a sip of wine would do nicely after all this business.

Who was Yitzhak?

Startling – so strange this question.

Whooo? – echoing strength – uncanny – surprise – richness – that till now he'd thought he knew Yitzhak – all these facts that he'd like to tell the whole world – that for odd jobs he could put his hand to almost anything – woodwork – plaster – tiling – but the way he worked! Everything must be made good again – restored – mended – found its proper place – no hurry – no point otherwise.

All of this dissolving as appearance – to reveal the enduring – in this radiance was Yitzhak – this Who warming within – joyful radiance – of the absent one – Yitzhak – warmth of goodness that All is well – is good – no separation – here the true Sabbath – a strength beyond all this anxiety – beyond Rashi – heart of Torah itself?

Listen – listen – to those words – speaking once again. Seek to learn their secret, the depths over which they hover.

"Avram you must make a holy temple within, serene and spacious. There the holy ones will speak with words of life. We have a great work to do we Jews but few will find their way to it. Avram – the Torah isn't a book but the fire of creation itself. A mighty flame which can burn away man's dross to leave him as gold. Whatever you do Avram, do it for God's glory."

He felt the need to draw the curtains, open the window and look along the moonlit street. What! – a scream – a muffled scream!

Dorah, in the kitchen, carefully stacked the dirty plates, dishes, cutlery, and looked over the food for tomorrow, in oven and larder. The cooked chicken, kasha, chopped cabbage and the baked pudding of noodles, raisins, cinnamon – the boys' favourite!

But the boys were going – away – and why hadn't sister Hannah and Nathan come round for the usual Sabbath chat. Why? Everything? in question – such a storm begun raging. But she'd lit and blessed the candles and welcomed the Sabbath Bride in right here.

What was she thinking of?

Dear God give me strength!

Dear God let everything be in its rightful place.

Why were these tears pressing so hard at her?

Why this need for crying out, lamentation?

Sit down! Hold back! Don't dare let Avram be worried by any of this. His only time for study, for rest from work.

Avram heard the hoarse constrained anguish. Such strange sounds from the kitchen.

"Dorah, Dorah what is it?" he hurried in, his arm about her as she sat at the cluttered table, head lowered in sadness and pain.

No, not to utter the real source of her pain that the boys were being taken from her!

"The boys – the boys are going," she managed, as calmly as she could.

"Dorah, Dorah of course it's sad – but it's in God's hands – for Israel." Ready, immediate truths.

"Dorah, Rabbi Melnikov has said publicly that God looks kindly on us both. That He has great work for our sons to do. Dorah Dorah, such a sadness! Given by God – given back to God – given in trust for Israel – for Israel, Dorah – giving giving – such a sadness Dorah." Confused, pained, tearful, he embraced and kissed her.

They were being taken from her!

No talk, no words would ease that, could convince her otherwise. But it was more than that.

Yes! Let Avram say all these things. Wise words always from the men. Such wise words. But they didn't know – never would! And she must brave it out.

Yes yes of course she understood.

Let Avram back to Rashi his Rashi.

Avram went back to the Sabbath room.

That muffled scream? – shriek? – from where in this street – our street Vigoda Street a scream? – had he heard it? – at this time of night?

Rashi stubbornly beyond reach. Only Dorah's unhappiness insisting. Dorah's pain. His words spoken easily enough with authority but no longer at all so clear.

An empty house? – without the boys? Real this loss right now pressing forward to be so deeply felt. The memories – from the beginning – the boys on his knees – sounding the pointed letters after him – such little ones – learning so quickly. What was he yielding to? Such a life there! – Rashi – Rashi!

Listen! listen! down! pounding heart – down!

those footsteps

it's him – hurry.

Yitzhak, to his surprise found Avram waiting in welcome by the opened front door.

"That's good, that's good," he said smiling, reaching out a hand.

Of course it was Yitzhak, but in the moonlight such a weariness caught, such an aging, as he indicated the Sabbath front room whose window was open, the candlelight low, dark shadows flickering about. Avram pointed to a chair, only wanting to hear, to know but Yitzhak remained standing.

"Calm – calm yourself Avram – we're brothers – that's what we are – all men are brothers but not all men know it – brothers – to share burdens with each other –"

Avram knew again that sweetness, that quickening, the greater.

"No I wasn't in Shul. At sunset I went down to the river instead. And when I crossed the bridge over to the other side the air grew so foul, so bitter, that I was forced back. Foul with hatred – bitter with death. A great wave of destruction surrounding us. I saw the mighty king of Russia. His head was a raging demon as he glared at us, at all us Jews in Russia. And vast about him was the Angel of Death."

"Avram," he reached out to hold Avram's hand firmly, "we will be one of the first. But all of us Jews will have to face the most terrible evil. The demons will assault us and tear us to pieces. We shall bear witness to them. Nothing can prevent it Avram, nothing. Till men walk in the way of the Lord. And in spite of all this which has to be endured, the Splendour of God, His mighty and all consuming Glory ever reigns supreme. Avram – death cannot touch the Spirit. Be glad to suffer it Avram. Don't be afraid – don't be angry. What our ancestors felt every day of their lives – one long terror. And should we experience nothing of it? We're their sons. Let's make their suffering dear to us. Be raised up by their glory to sanctify the Name."

Avram gripped his hand tightly.

"Yitzhak – when will it be?"

"When? when?" whispered Yitzhak, "listen! – when else? – now!"

Avram made for the open window, held fast by screaming, some ancient terror, to watch trembling, to know that it was really happening, ancient truth confirmed my God, nightmare reality of the rushing storm, yelling, cursing, torches aflame, horses galloping wildly around.

Destruction and death

Out! Out! candles and lamp.

Made placeless, by the roaring voice of this boundless fury hacking, ripping, pounding, wave on wave, the shrieking, the wailing, hammering on doors, shattering of glass, splintering of wood, the cursing, the chanting. Must stay to listen – must hear it!

Death to the Yids!

Death to their god!

An end to their rule!

And God save the Tsar!

Such a wildness excitement mad joy staring naked through the open window as it advanced.

Jacob the cobbler waited tensely behind his front door, grasping his largest awl, at odds with God.

Some of them were hurrying ahead intent on something with their torches flaming. Iron bars, axes, knives, thrusting ready. Where else could they be making for on this dark night aflame!

Do something!

Break through this mad fascination! Come to yourself!

The boys had woken quickly. Dorah was already with them. Avram rushed frantically up to their room.

"Quick quick down to the cellar!"

Down, down in wild terrified descent towards that sour damp darkness of our refuge. But our very own home turning against us wild mad world! release us! let go! stop banging us! wounding! you wretched tables doors chairs with your corners and stiffness bruising obstructing our desperate search for safety for life.

Down down descending deep into earth's bitterness. Dorah, the boys, Avram, stumbling down the rough hewn wooden cellar steps into the darkness. Forgotten, uncared cavern, ancient webs trembling, forsaken, their spinners fleeing into the further darkness.

Uncared for.

Sole refuge!

Only from that distant grating, light filtered fitfully, barely yielding a sense for shapes and forms. Avram willed fiercely to take hold of this situation beneath the muffled violence threatening overhead.

"Not a word!" he whispered.

Copying him, together they shifted as quietly as possible, boxes, crates, sacks, whatever, to build up a wall in front of the steps. Then, walled in on four sides, their only refuge now in God Himself. But the screams reached them. God knows what was happening to – whom? whom? What were they doing to whom as to us! our own!

In this darkness of terror, taste of death, heart's life streamed through hands so tenderly held all four. The fortress surrounded. This tiny shrinking space. Only this blessed streaming of hands held with Mummy and Daddy to ensure that each of them for all was here. Is God so very angry with us?

Together the prayer began, whispered, but such substance, very life of theirs speaking to Him. Not like in Shul tonight. No uncertainty now. Our lives are in Your balance. We can only leave it to You. Who gives, Who takes back.

Avram's heart beat painfully for the Shul. That's where they were making for! That's what Rabbi Melnikov must have known! Witness! Witness!

Held fast in a dreadful silence they knew from the change in this feeblest light that the grating above was being poked. Then – the Angel of Death passed over.

Ananayev's Jews trembled in their cellars and behind barricaded doorways. Some fled across the bridge to the woods. Some few hurried along passageways and alleys to the Shul with Rabbi Melnikov. For them it was exactly as the Rabbi had said. The moment was now. The call from Below was now. Only one possible deed or else the Covenant betrayed. Such strength, such joy in this fullness of belief, old and young made new, as they ran in their Sabbath caftans between the fences, tassels of snatched prayer shawls flaring away.

Faster faster in through the back way hear the evil ones already inside. Straight to the Ark! out with the scrolls! right in the evil ones' midst how else?

They were pouring kerosene on everything wooden, benches, chairs, shelves, tables, whole rotten stuff of the jewgod's house, den of the murderers who killed our Tsar. Burn it brothers burn it! from Russian life – them next!

Yid fools! that you thought you could do us for ever!

Yid madmen performing such crazy antics to your rotten evil god. A feeble god whom we'll burn with you too.

Rabbi Melnikov and the chosen danced the dance of spirit

fire, consuming, as the smoking choking flame ringed their circle. Holding hands, no way out now fervently singing, contracting and expanding, centre and periphery, freedom's sanctifying space. Zim Zum of life. Wisdom's dance towards the heights. Wisdom's dance towards the depths hands clapping out its rhythm – that

"He is the Lord
Who reigned ere any was formed
After all shall end
He alone shall reign
Who was Who is Who will be."

Fiery this exaltation that we have been graced with this witnessing way.

Treasured heart of Israel in the arms of old Rabbi Melnikov! Such sprightliness, spring, this fire advancing, life of our lives.

To give thanks to these ignorant goyim that we have been chosen to live our People's eternal beginning – to burn with the Glory of the Name – our lives Its consummation.

Torah Torah Torah our partner in the dance. We Your Bridegroom, You eternal Wisdom of our life. These precious scrolls Your earthly garb. We Your earthly sons.

Soon – soon – to know You as Wisdom's Queen.

Soon – soon – the longed-for meeting in truth.

Hey! – Hey! – Torah we embrace You!

Hey! – Hey! – Torah Your sons await You!

Hey! – Hey! – Torah we – –

Hey! – Hey! – Hey! – –

All consuming the fire of this exaltation as the rafters buckled and crashed, the destroyers forced out. The cheering mob outside were forced back by the savage heat, their faces aflame with victory. Roof tiles cracked explosively. Ashes showered down from the April night.

The leader from Odessa stood apart, his hand raised high to the smoking night sky, to the rippling showers of fiery-quick darts ceaselessly streaming upwards.

"Cleansed be our Holy Russia! Well done! Devil's spawn! Let them stink in their yidgod's nose. They'll roast well these pigs. Next time the whole lot must go," he shouted, swinging round in the aura of savage heat and dancing light to indicate the whole Jewish quarter, " Leave nothing standing – nothing at all!"

The survivors waited, trembling, listening for long after the bloodlust had been sated, the yells, curses, beating and screaming still so resonant. In Krochmal Street and Meir Street, converging on the synagogue, surviving neighbours dared to emerge here and there, dared enter the desecrated houses, dared step on the bloodsoaked floors, to mourn and tend the murdered, the dreadfully injured, the dumb petrified children.

Families of the martyred silently trod their way to the smouldering ruins of the synagogue from whose ashes wisps of smoke still issued.

In this silence aware of confronting a terrible power.

No speech could utter it – language itself withdrew.

Ghosts in a strange world, dazed spectators trying hard to reach out to the black charred bodies, all so together, all so alike. But how, how? to recognise, establish exactly who, in the glowing dawn light of this emptiness, all past all bearings torn away, unreachable the life that was beyond this abyss – to establish who was who.

Somehow it had to be done.

Then – to see through the mask of each burned form's blackness, this sight be strengthened dear God more and more – this crumbling mask – you! – as you were and are – not to be fooled, put off, by the Evil One's tricks. No! He never will tear your true face from me!

Dumb they wandered about and around with this seeing, foolishly nodding their heads in eerie isolation till the sudden anguished cry, the gentle sobbing, bitter-sweet rain, as they knelt beside him and tenderly kissed, husband, father, brother, son.

Avram was one of the first to recognise and stand by Yitzhak. Deeper, deeper his gaze was drawn into that form, some revelation hinting, to be wrested, as Yitzhak's words spoke anew, "In spite of all this which has to be endured, the Splendour of God reigns supreme." The Splendour of God, living! wrenching him out of even this detachment to confidence and hope. With courage now to accept whose that body was, with this new-found courage that knows – the reality of Yitzhak enduring still!

The crowd of mourners grew rapidly, standing about, watching, staring helplessly.

Jacob Edelman the cobbler, angry with the Lord, called out in their midst, strong and clear, "Was it for this we were chosen?"

"Fool!" pious elder Nahum Trebnik shouted back immediately to protect the mourners from this accursed attack, "they've sanctified the Name. We're blessed – even blasphemers like you!"

"It's a decent burial they need, not this shame. How much longer are we going to stare at them," insisted Jacob with a sudden authority. "It's Sabbath - they must be buried today - there's work to be done - Shimon! - Moshe! your horses and carts! - coffins! - carpenters! carpenters! - shovels! picks! - to work! to work!" he ordered in his brusque dealing with the Lord.

Sweet April air, birdsong still streaming aloft - have we not all become question?

For most, the call to action was relief. A proper burial before Shabbes ended let everything go into that! Run - run to Yigdal - David - for coffins - a digging party - straight now to the cemetery with shovels and picks every man available - and Nahum of course - to take the service in the cemetery.

The carts laden with coffins appeared at the cemetery gates. Family, friends and younger men with shovels searched urgently around to stake out a space. They tried for some dignity, to calm a desperation that even here - why! but just here! - with those demons anything could happen.

But what after this unutterable desecration could yet be possible?

Bowlegged Pinkhasov, chief grave digger for many years, and cemetery warden Fein, were horrified by the tumult, unprecedented desecration, desperate to establish order.

Pinkhasov stumped his way right through them all and on towards the far western wall.

"Here! I say - lay them all here!" he shouted pointing at the weedy unkempt patch.

"No! never! not in a corner like that. These are martyrs - our martyrs. They must be buried for all to see. We shall find a place for them - right here - in the middle," called out Saul the butcher.

Right! - but of course there was no space in the middle!

To Pinkhasov! Over to Pinkhasov! Then let the martyrs bless this weedy patch - mitzvah indeed for the earth itself. Get digging get digging! - don't stop - so tough so stony this ground - that's just it! that's the whole feel of this hour - don't stop! tear the stones out - keep digging till you drop!

Everyone knew they were burying something else besides the dead. Their whole future existence in question once again. That they were Jews through and through - homeless - exiled - and in question – on this fine April morning.

Anything can still happen!

Let some of us go to the cemetery gate – keep shovels poised as on guard!

Sweating and cursing the diggers went at it.

"Get back! Keep back! Give them room," shouted Jacob angrily.

Reluctantly the crowding families and friends shrank back a little, to the ancient molding gravestones of Ananayev's Jews.

Gravedigger Pinkhasov was not entirely displeased that a few of them should know firsthand what this grave digging was all about – yes sweat on a bit! – your shallow little holes – some skill as well needed, eh?

What kind of a Shabbes was this?

Working harder than ever!

A Shabbes of mourning!

A Shabbes of burying the murdered and loved ones!

Nahum Trebnik, pious elder, in deepest concern sensed the threat, the testing. They had to be reminded. Right now the urgency to speak of it.

"Remember Jews!" he called out, "Remember Jews!" halting all activity, the diggers knee deep in their shallow pits, stilled.

"We bury martyrs – Sanctifiers of the Name. Remember Jews! the Spirit is the work of God – the Soul is the work of God – the body is the work of God. Tenderly – tenderly watch over them all – no need to rush! Dignity – calm – for they are all holy."

Some were awoken by his words, shaken, trembling within, themselves now blessed with glimpsing something of the awesome courage, glory, strength, that must have flowed through the martyred ones – knowing them anew as who? they really were.

Alright Nahum but does that make a joyful restful peaceful Shabbes? Truly – aren't we now on our guard – more than ever?

Didn't you recognise some faces in that mob?

Didn't you hear from your cellar some voices you knew? That they're no longer our peasants but our killers. What can we make of that?

Avram helped with the digging, taking turns till Yitzhak's coffin lay firm at the bottom of the stony trench. At last, near midday, all were ready, as families and friends came close to the open graves. Avram stood with the boys, all in tearful tenderness, when Nahum began to utter the Kaddish, amidst low sobs and mournful cries.

"Let us magnify and let us sanctify the great name of God in the world which He created according to His will."

Joyful serenity pervaded Avram's tears.

That Yitzhak had known!

"May He who made peace in the Highest bring peace to us and all Israel. Amen."

Let the boys see and know that none of this can deflect the task of Israel.

This fallen world which we are to redeem. All life is to Him.

Handfuls of earth showered down on the coffins.

"What kind of God is it?" questioned Jacob sternly, loud and clear before any diggers could begin shovelling back the piled earth.

"Fool! Blasphemer!" shouted Nahum angrily, turning to face him nearby, "don't you know fool that our ancestors assembled before Caligula in their thousands and bared their necks – bared their necks I say! for him to chop off rather than transgress the Law. Don't you know blasphemer – when they tore the skin off Akiba's body he thought himself blessed! – blessed! that he'd been given this opportunity to love the Lord thy God with all – all his soul!"

"Life is sweet," insisted Jacob, facing him squarely, beginning to enrage many.

"Faith in God is a thousand times sweeter," hissed Nahum, serious this challenge.

"Without life there can be no faith," countered Jacob.

For many now, outrageous this desecration – goyim talk – goyim, this violation but so helplessly drawn in.

"Fool! without faith there can't be any Jewish life," spelled out Nahum with contempt, forced to continue the struggle but appalled by what was happening.

From somewhere mad Ruben rushed through them all into their midst, his thin sallow head shaking excitedly beneath the black curls.

"Do you know," he shouted to them all and the April sky, "the Messiah is coming. The Holy Ones are with us. We're blessed forever. Now's the time when we shall all go up to Jerusalem. Dance! Let us dance! Let us dance for joy!"

He jumped about, eyes glittering, embracing and kissing Nahum, running from one to the other as they stood helpless, overcome. He ran off, away, hopping and skipping wildly towards the cemetery gates. They heard him shouting and singing along the streets.

Many of the younger men digging felt untouched, impatient, repelled by Nahum's kind of talk. It was saying we are nothing. That we goyim can do whatever we like knowing you won't respond. This is humiliation. Not a way at all!

Jacob the cobbler's words sound us – no pretending – what prayers for this desolation? – and to whom? – and for what?

These black scattered flakes – the Scrolls – that made us what we are – cursing what we are – helpless hopeless vagabonds – fools! – and they're there! by the gates smirking grinning!

It has come to this!

And we must soon decide. We the younger ones – decide.

Jacob made his special task the burial of the Scrolls. Ashen welded mass, crystalline fragments flaking off, showering away in flurries, as he collected together the bits of wooden spindles, burnt remnants of silken covers, blackened bells, all lying adrift, left there for him, our destiny.

IV

Odessa

After the busy weekdays in the consulting room of his apartment off Odessa's main Primorsky Boulevard, eminent physician Dr Leon Pinsker turned to very different work at weekends. But with as dedicated and serious an intent, if not more so. After nearly forty years of medical practise he felt himself tiring, ageing. In that weekend work for the future of Russian Jews he knew a youthful vigour, a very source of fruitful life.

The Association for the Dissemination of Jewish Enlightenment in Russia was nearing its twentieth year. As President of the Odessa branch he had taken on the main responsibility for preparing a commemoration number of the Journal, to mark the occasion. So much positive achievement! The founders' original initiatives all proven absolutely justified, so right for the times, and so fruitful.

Slowly but surely more and more young intelligent Jews were managing to turn away from that dreadful Talmudic succubus - pilpulistic vampire sucking them dry from childhood, leaving only white-faced specimens with dangling sidelocks - turning right away and in the light of enlightened thinking, find their way to vocational, professional standing in the real world, find their way to a longed-for dignity, acceptance as equals in the real world of today. To stand as equals with our Russian brothers. Eventually for all Russian Jews!

What acumen, courage, determination, Grandfather Pinsker and the others - yes indeed a time to dwell on that beginning - to give it real thought in gratitude - he himself - his destiny - owed to their deed - and so warned, unexpectedly warned! Not to take any of it for granted! That he had been to university - trained in a worthy profession - treated worthily, enabled to enjoy the greatness of Russian literature - all due to their decision - to break out to something greater - beyond the prison wall.

Yes of course he was one of the few! But he knew what was possible. His work in the Association was an absolute moral responsibility, let him remind himself – insist on that. Through his privileged destiny – it was no less – hope for all Russian Jews along this path.

That all this is due to them – all that I am – here – this fine apartment off the Primorsky – all due in some way to them?

Yes – and deeper question still – leave alone! – to fructify. But beginning – actual beginning – how? – that Grandfather and his friends actually broke through that economic barrier from – nothing!

On Saturday mornings at his cluttered desk in the booklined study he went over the programme for the Sunday evening meeting at the Davidoffs' mansion. Warshavski was coming, staying at the Davidoffs to tell them about his latest linguistic research. That the spirit of the Russian language was uniquely similar to Hebrew. Very significant. But what a heaviness it was becoming during the week – no question, some sort of sad resignation – boring? – yes boring! – with these affluent patients worrying over nothing – nothing at all – empty lives? – young Dr Pinsker's enthusiasm! – new world opening up – was it possible? some dream? Sooner or later he must be freed from this heaviness.

Then he himself to speak on the unexpected tribute being prepared in the Archaeological Museum, of a special cabinet containing artefacts discovered by his father, from earliest Greek colonisation of the Odessa region. To be named the Pinsker cabinet! And affixed with a short printed account of father's work on the Karaites. Really truly, a most gracious – why – almost overwhelming tribute!

But this little terracotta bear with its huge basin of a mouth – shouldn't that really be in the cabinet too? There was nothing like it being shown.

No, definitely No!

He wouldn't like at all to be without it on his desk, standing everyday, genial redbrown, to receive what? in that basin of a mouth – freshly dug up by father from Odessa's depths.

Yes it could be significant but always it spoke, warm to the touch, of Father's warmth, encouragement and standing back, stepping forth from an ancient past into the clarity of reason – pioneers – sacred inheritance – torch passed on – we sons of gratitude to light the way for all our fellow Jews.

That huge basin of a lower jaw, smiling mystery to live with.

And what about a discussion on the Karaites sometime at Davidoff's as a tribute to Father's pioneer work on them. Thirteenth tribe? - another mysterious business for the Jews.

And the leak! Discreet mention of the leak.

A very busy evening.

The leak! Very discreet mention. Impossible not to.

Who? on the Commission.

The anonymous source surely could not have wanted otherwise?

He must indicate something tomorrow evening. It was such an encouragement for the work. More, that they and Russian history were moving in the same direction.

Of course the Commission had sat before the assassination. But simply to know that these opinions existed at this level was encouragement enough.

It would and must come because it was the truth. We are equals.

Contrary to the new Tsar's dreadful accusation of Jewish economic exploitation, local bureaucracy held a positive view of Jewish economic activity and that consequently the correct procedure would be gradual Jewish advancement towards complete equality of rights - and that most Commission members had agreed!

That was the truth which would carry them through and they must be told tomorrow evening. But to be kept absolutely discreet - since the assassination.

Next Davidoff on the biannual financial situation. Always the exacting banker, calculating to the kopeck expenditure on the three basic initiatives and which he spells out each time in case we forget! First, Russian language promotion amongst Jews - second, subsidisation of secular education for needy Jewish children - third, publications on natural science, vocational training and any other useful knowledge - and for each to the kopeck!

And Nathan wanted to say something about Dostoyevsky's death, what it meant for mankind everywhere, let alone Jews. Dear Nathan - unstoppable! they'd be there till the early hours - but he couldn't be put off for ever. But just imagine - all Russia's Jews - in every town, village, ghetto community - all! - reading Dostoyevsky one day!

Definitely progress. Of course Russia wasn't going to change in five minutes. But that leak came from confidence in – trust in him what else? Be proud to emphasise, define it. Necessary to define and emphasise it. And one trusts whom? – only an equal. Such Russians were the few but ensuring the way forward.

But in whom did that Commission member trust, regard as an equal?

Me the Jew?

Me Dr Leon Pinsker? – was that it?

Where then lay hidden that equality?

Progress – progress – but always the back and forth the back and forth.

Such a prolonged ringing of the bell – Saturday morning – at this hour – an emergency! another heart attack – Nathan's father inevitable – for goodness sake answer it Mikhail!

Reluctantly he turned away from the desk, stood up and faced the study door as footsteps approached.

Nathan opened the study door but could not enter, that world, work annulled. He faced Pinsker distraught, so tensed only this deedword possible – "Come! Please come – come!"

Dr Pinsker gently touched his arm, looked to comfort, "Of course," and went for his bag in the consulting room. But Nathan was shaking his head, gripping Pinsker's arm tightly and drawing them both toward the front door.

No bag needed. All over then.

The waiting cab drove them straight down the Boulevard and across the main Square.

The old man had suffered enough – basically the programme for Davidoffs' was settled hey! – they'd passed the Aarenson's turning – descending – descending – down – down – passing terrace after terrace – all happening so unexpectedly – turning to Nathan at his side in the gloomy interior to ask – Nathan reaching for his hand, nodding to himself, unable to break through – down – down – past the Armenian – Greek – Bulgarian – to the poorest Jewish quarters close by the dockside warehouses and the catacombs, lowest depths, for long kept distant this Odessa – now being brought to what? – spectre of such ugliness – from the bracing heights the squares – the beauty! of his daily Odessa.

Sharp swerve left – for what? this new awaken ready Nathan! The cab forced by the chaos to a halt, led out by Nathan into what?

What was it? What had happened for these cries wails lamentations burning houses, rubble thickstrewn of broken smashed things and these lost ones wailing - in what dream - whose dream was he?

How very strange!

Whatever had happened?

Bombs?

Ruined burnt out gaping houses blackened thicket of some demented savagery.

Some war!

Then he would ask, ask questions - straightforward questions, immediately - what had happened? Find out the facts. What was going on? This one here now tell me, what has been happening here? He must know what had actually happened to hold off the breath of this threatening terror.

The well dressed stranger and his words meant nothing to her. Lost, all of them, lost amidst the lamentations, smoking ruins, the dead, the dying, the slashed the hacked the beaten. Only tears hoarse cries of helplessness lamentation. O God of our fathers why hast Thou done this to us? His too his too! in this Odessa - struck down, annulled in this Odessa - led by Nathan through this wandering spectres as a blind man choking tears wanting to weep. Cast out into this wilderness of desolation with them, one of them. Unbearable this irresolution of his existence, exposed, burning entanglement in that lamentation too. The shame of it, the cowardice of it that he had wanted to know - to know what? He knew it all, from the beginning. These blinding tears unveiled it all as he was led wandering by Nathan, lost! Lost! Not knowing where he was amidst the sobbing and the wailing for the lost. Here near the catacombs, wretched, backward Jewish poor - ugh! hateful part of himself so tearfully lamented and embraced.

Meeting tomorrow evening as usual impossible! But the question so vast, the gap so great, one could only go ahead with it!

That the years of work had been a mistake, the aims an illusion - unbearable! He would not let such a mood take him over threatening to paralyse, nullify. Hint of something infinitely greater at stake, infinitely. Of course they would meet at

Davidoffs'. But such destruction and hatred – such a force! – then no more compromise – so! – that's what it insisted it was. And had been – something of a compromise – even more? Their utter helplessness – ghosts – utter vulnerability – their – his – and again know it his – story – pattern of the ages enduring still. All denials seen for what they were in this harsh light – betrayals – of the truth – of himself – a self-inflicted wound which must be healed. Enough, surely enough, and thank God for the practice and the patients and all that normality as usual – this reckoning, from whom, by whom, threatening to overwhelm. Of course he would have to come to terms with it. But he too! had rights. One must wait. It was all too vast. For sanity's sake he must do the usual things, the familiar things, grateful for them. But the line thinning.

At the Davidoffs' mansion near the Opera House, everyone turned up as usual. But no one knew how to mention it. The speeches were duly made except Nathan's but no one was really listening.

All were turned to tomorrow morning, in expectation, in hope – but whence this forlornness – of the Press account, and soon, the speaking out, the indictment by those voices, civilised, enlightened voices of the best in Russia – Tolstoy! – Turgenev? – Fet surely – that even Nekrassov – Saltykov-Schedrin would repent? – change their minds. The Liberal Press! – to condemn outright this primitive savagery which – surely? – could only disgrace Russia in the eyes of the world. This they were assuming, depending on, feeling as the touchstone of all they stood for, confirmation of their work, their standing in Russian Jewry. All felt that nothing less than such a confirmation was at stake.

From early morning for all of them, a waiting began.

At the breakfast table Dr Pinsker found himself searching – searching! stupidly uselessly – through the papers, Liberal and Government, not accepting this utter absence of any reference – this silence! No mention whatsoever! Then it must come, the papers would have to make space for those authoritative voices speaking out on behalf of the Jews. Have to! Have to? – on our behalf – such a desperate dependence, such vulnerability – hopelessness – helplessness – this dependency on those others to speak out on our behalf – this – this! somehow key! must not be let go!

At 11 o'clock Meir Horovitz, Odessa's leading timber exporter, was due for a consultation, one of his own. One of his own? what kind of thinking was this?

Soon after breakfast Nathan appeared.

"It's bad. I've just heard that students from the University were involved - seriously involved, and even some youngsters from the Gymnasium. Such slogans shouted! - that the Yids murdered the Tsar - Helfman mentioned, cursed!"

Helfman! that fanaticism - Jewish fanaticism! which the Association had hoped to eventually overcome. Hopeless illusion, all of it.

He had to mention it to Meir Horovitz during the consultation.

"It's never been any different," said Horovitz with the assuredness of a bitter, absolute knowing.

But surely the Education Ministry would be compelled to issue a statement.

By Wednesday the sustained silence spoke to him with utmost clarity - as a deed - as an uncompromising declaration.

This silence was the official response - and they were all officials!

It said - the murderous slaughter and injuring of defenceless Jews is acceptable to us. Read this our silence, learn from it and get out! Clear out!

Yes! That is so. We are not who you thought we were.

And you Pinsker be grateful! You haven't done too badly out of us but now is the moment for you to learn something too.

They are right!

They are telling us we are not them - not! but that nevertheless we are - we are - but in a way that makes us utterly alien. We ever remain an alien people but in what way?

Journey, travail begun in this transformation which must be fought through to the end. No possible way out, back.

Not even Tolstoy! who had dared to intervene for the terrorists.

If not Tolstoy for us then whom except ourselves - lifetime's simple logic no longer to be hidden - and this our - me! Myself - Ourselves - ghosts - frightened ghosts - enter! - take full hold of this body - become at home on this earth like them - with a home of your own. That smashed burning ruin never a home - a death trap - sprung for millennia - to close finally one day -

was a logic insisting?

No! No! beyond all this pain – beyond – to something else – objective! that must somehow be tracked to its lair.

A nonsense, pathetic, this rereading of Tolstoy.

Four five six days and still waiting!

Cowardice!

Fearing the challenge ahead because if challenged everything especially 'himself'.

But feeling already the breath of that keen air – of what it will mean.

No! Not to expect, to hope – to grovel!

From whence accused that naming of behaviour over the years as grovelling?

What door was opening – by whom?

What blind drawn back so sharply in this feeling that it's entirely up to us – us! New sounding, all embracing, he himself-as-a-Jew clasped in this bond.

What is it that this can happen here?

Thankful for the very question's voice, so basic, and not to let it go in all its elemental charge and comprehensiveness.

Something must be done by him but with the only thinking that he trusted in, practised with, lived by.

Not at all a conspiracy this silence but the reality all along. We pretended otherwise.

That University students, high school boys, Narodniki, all participated with enthusiasm in murdering and maiming Jews! This is Russian culture! Not then a question of education or culture – some fundamental irrationalism – a disease – immune to education and culture.

Such illusion? Such arrogance of ours – all in desperate need that we be accepted by them.

Very revelation.

Acceptance!

Anything in order to be accepted!

Acceptance! revelation, this naming of what is engendered by their non-acceptance – their silence.

That the real meaning of the 1871 pogrom here in Odessa can no longer be concealed.

So long veiled this need for acceptance. Open wound now this 'me' and only salve, this urgency of thinking, felt as never before.

This tearfulness won't dry up, let you go. Veil, blurring, bitter source of that upwelling truth.

Such destructive hatred!

My Odessa! your spacious elegant heights – the leisurely promenade – the glorious sea vista and you pretending for years that those Jews so far below by the catacombs – Dreebin Street – Barr Street – would eventually what? in millennia? become recognised as what, as what? – as human beings!

Man, men, the rights of man, civic equality – all burned out rubble here – looted, murdered, raped. So begin again with the only thinking you've got – but this time make it benefit all Jews – use it, work it ruthlessly to that end alone.

Use this thinking which you so pride yourself on – through which you know yourself so superior to that decadent Talmudic pilpul – have been thoroughly trained in, privileged bearer of and all intended well meant to lead your fellow Jews to some Paradise – now use it, return, reunite, reinvigorate, find a way out of this morass.

First the facts. Then deduce the laws. Then the problem's solution.

No longer temptation, illusory privilege but through this same thinking, destiny and redemption in this turn and return.

What is it about them and us? Again and again never ceasing. In the fire of this question caught up, formed anew, drawing closer, leaping Israel as living totality – the Jews in the Association – in his consulting room – in Dreebin Street – in Barr Street – all Jews – them means all of us – the tears are of us all – accusing, challenging, redeeming – Rights? Rights of Man? Then the Jews would have to show that they were indeed men. How? Just how? Question that must be borne – carried through to the very end of this quest and in the carrying through you must be painfully wrenched.

Use this thinking ruthlessly, cut to the bone, sharpest surgery, make that piece of ribbon worthy now of all Jews!

Beginning right now as it eagerly reveals itself, work with its raw thrust – so – beginner's question indeed!

What have they got which makes them 'them' – and which we haven't got – so making us 'us'?

What is it about us – himself – merciless reflection – what he truly – bobbing cork on the stern tide of this truth – this 'he' – what he hadn't got in spite of possessions – position – the ribbon!

– acclaim.

Well – simply – say it simply – and so obviously – all this that you have known, felt, kept unthought, untracked to its lair, held at bay with dread till now.

They have a motherland – their land – we have no land that is ours.

They have unity – all Russians – so taken for granted – so fundamental – we have only the unity of dispersion – diaspora – grotesque caricature of a unity – so much, no, everything essential about us malformed – all an ugly distortion – which makes them fear us –

they have solidarity

our solidarity an abortion born from their hateful gaze – hateful – fearful – terrified –

a diseased entity in their midst which they dread – we must get healthy again – then! we must have our own – own place in the world of men – own governance – own!

Strangest thoughts these – even to imagine – yet so reasonable – fantastic!

His life too a sickness – in tears dread – he one of them.

But to know it thus with such strength resounding –

'We too are a nation!' – but in this ghostly way which terrifies them – makes them hate us to destruction. They cannot stand it – this uncanny entity, held together without a land of its own.

Spiritually we haven't ceased to be a nation.

Spiritually? yes! this bond of tearfulness was spiritual – no less.

Hear O Israel! – Nothing else would do from his youth. No archaeological restoration this but heart's voice – heart's lamentation and tearfulness – their Yiddish lamentation his very own too.

Ourselves – ourselves – being tempered in the question's burning forge. Only in the willing and the doing.

No one can heal us from this sickness except ourselves.

To create ourselves anew as a nation. No other way out. As sane and fantastic as it sounded.

He must set it down on paper as a beginning in all humility and uncertainty- that it withdrew not, vanish not, presume only to be a fantasy, dream – wrenched away – to wrench it away from the millennial temptation of escape – flight into some void.

To name it from the start as it names itself.

Self-emancipation!

His whole life suspect in this fierce light?

Ever present? - the need - effort to be accepted - so hidden till now?

That was its choice too - that decision to disregard, turn aside from the demand everywhere for retribution after the assassination - pretending - not daring to answer the only possible answer - against whom that call for retribution - whom else? - and the whole Press hounding led by your precious liberals - the tone - you knew! consistently anti-Jew - and still that wan echo of feeble justification - that yes of course there's a difference - but that can - oh yes - always - be resolved by men of reason - men of goodwill.

But what then with this 'logic'? - that - as I am myself? - what I know myself to simply be - not acceptable by whom? - by them - then what is this them? a darkness here? - but this light says nothing easy - be specific - less ambitious - and wherever you look - wherever your glance alights in this light - a hidden meaning begins - so much - all? - of that past, a seeming.

How blithely, now, he had started on law. How easily he had turned aside from the implications of not ever being able to practise - as a Jew! - and the change to medicine.

It was not allowed.

It was forbidden.

The change was forced on him from lawyer to doctor and he so quickly adapting, justifying, pretending that anyway he'd make a much better doctor than lawyer. And so it had proved - and he'd gone on - now see it! - to prove himself.

No!

To prove the Jew in himself - the Jew he was - to have to prove that this Jew-that-he-was was acceptable to them. What Father had had to prove, what Grandfather Pinsker had had to prove - all in vain. There was no such proof. The idea of such a proof itself a vain illusion. Somehow created by them, one more cruel trick to make endless the delay - lack of courage in returning - coming to ourselves.

Ourselves?

The medal ribbon - such bliss!

Was it possible?

The seal of seals from His Majesty - the Highest.

Take it out now! from the cabinet - and for the first time feel and know this bit of green ribbon for what it is – and has been.

Guarantor of your immunity from the truth.

Read again His Majesty's commendation for your bravery with the wounded under enemy fire,

"His refusal to leave the wounded during a retreat and under prolonged bombardment was in the highest tradition of His Majesty's army."

Bliss, incense, sweetening the years of study and striving, but no longer.

Bliss, dreaming as perfect an acceptance as possible – but you are not accepted – dear green bit of ribbon!

Bliss – culmination, assurance that the Highest Russian had graced and blessed you these last twenty seven years. Twenty seven? – remember it? – and how once with me you felt certain of your equality with every Russian – as simple as that!

Fatal so early.

What more could any Jew want?

See now for what it was!

Bliss!

That was the bliss, security, superiority – a Jew! – with this decoration – this piece of paper – this bit of ribbon – these precious words from him.

Yes – take me out now – go and face the mirror! – remind yourself of the bliss that never left you till now – as a Jew without the medal – naked thin.

But what exactly had he been decorated for – why had he done it? stayed with them under French fire during the retreat from the Alma river – that it had nothing to do with Jews or Russians! – and the pride, the bliss was only because bestowed by His Majesty.

For twenty-seven years this bit of green ribbon assuring, asking what more could make him one of them?

Fool!

You one of them! while your Jews have been murdered at will?

Fool!

Strutting fool – that 'Russian' I liked to think I was.

Yet beyond all that they came to him year after year as a good doctor, or hadn't his dedication, integrity, yes integrity, helped to maintain the illusion? Of course now their logic confirmed. His skills had made him one of their useful Jews. But this integrity, there where he found an integrity within himself, was a healing impulse, pure, that in truth was for every human being.

Deputy Governor Anton Dnevnik, an old patient, was due at 11 o'clock. Dr Pinsker waited uneasily in his consulting room. Consultation, being with his patients, was no longer so straightforward. He was hearing something different from them.

He knew he was no longer with them in the old way. Something within him was waiting, alert - for what? for what? - from a very different place.

"Thank God one can at least depend on you Pinsker," Dnevnik greeted, through a faintly wheezing breath. He began to unbutton his tunic then took off his shirt and vest, to sit down as usual in the large leather-backed chair, leaning forward as usual for Dr Pinsker to tap, to listen through his stethoscope, all so comforting that this man at least took his life seriously.

Dr Pinsker listened carefully here and there amidst the flabbiness, the overweight frame.

"I don't know what it is with me - such pain every morning - early - yes usual place - you'll be absolutely truthful," said Dnevnik, remembering, forced out of this warm comfort.

Once again, listening carefully, sympathetically, keenly aware of the wheeze, the unsteady beat, the darkening about Dnevnik's eyes, all clear enough, yet, poised, from some new place, something else, a listening, but for what, something else, false move possible, tread warily, some old protective veil gone.

"It's nothing that we can't do something for-" he began, forced to go in that direction, this asking why just now happening after all these months since last visit - careful!

" - are you working too hard again? - you need to take things more easily - to rest more - the medicines by themselves won't do it."

"Rest? - Rest?" Dnevnik shouted angrily, up on his feet, shirt in hand, "with the stinking Jews - terrorists - new regulations from the capital every day of the week - impossible - it's impossible - none of us dare rest - with Russia like this," shirt waving about with each point "- anyway the Jews had it coming to them - the other swine will too I assure you."

He nodded to himself, put on his shirt, feeling calmer, whilst Dr Pinsker sat at his desk, studiously writing out the medicaments for the pharmacist, only once glancing across the abyss opened up by those words, by his beating heart, to somehow take up the challenge.

The I that was no longer wanted here - fully identified - angrily shocked into unambiguous being - what phantom that? crouching low by the entrance door.

This I that was no longer wanted here - that knows this is not our place -

"The Jews had it coming to them?" he risked.

"My dear Dr Pinsker," Dnevnik responded, surprised but immediately launched into the indictment with relish, "they're vagabonds, plotters - they exploit the people - the people don't want them here - the people know how to settle things in their own Russian way - so - the Jews have been taught a lesson - why of course they had it coming to them - they've been put in their place - but we're all under attack - only thank God for the new Tsar!"

And you too learn, this ghostly collusion to the very end, and that's why he still suspects nothing and never will. He'd be puzzled if you told him, insisted, that you were a Jew.

Contain this anger in the knowing now after years before this abyss just what his so easily uttered words actually meant!

Contain! its real strength for the greater cause.

The mutual liking still in place, strange!

"Do try and take things more easily," he said, helping Dnevnik into his coat.

"My dear Dr Pinsker you always give one hope."

He's gone. But catch hold of it - listen! listen to what's being said about them - about the Jews - not about you - this net of his thrown out - wide - wider over the years given into your hands - no letting go now - casting wide - wider - through those unreflected deeps of the past.

Nothing daring to be missed now - for some key.

So much of it! wanderers - vagabonds - plotters - exploiters - daily, yearly you dreamed away 'casual' remarks like this - not now! - now to make something of them - now surely become key to unlock the prison door - miss not one - nothing - dredged up before you - to bring into this light that dark Whole! - against which - projected by - protecting them.

When they call us vagabonds they know themselves as long settled on this land of theirs.

This homelessness - hold to it with calm detachment, to yourself us as they see you us. This homelessness is the ghostliness which haunts them – their fear, terror to be rid of us at any cost.

When they call us beggars – unproductive – shady, deceitful – they know themselves as wealthy with a fullness of knowing that this here is their place – with this fullness no need to beg for anything.

When they call us exploiters – they feel their own wretchedness.

When they call us hateful competitors – they call on that unity and equality beyond all their classes.

Us – always all of us.

An absolute negative whole – the darkness that is us.

So you – I'm addressing myself too – You to whom I speak throughout this daily conversation – You – We – You We – must become and can only become through our own efforts – an absolute comprehensive positive whole.

Are they not recognising our unity – challenging us to confirm our unity in a positive way?

Challenging us to achieve it in a living contemporary way – the way of nationhood – possible only through a territory – government – polity of our own.

All to come from us. To thus be and become ourselves. Equal on our terms. The only equality that is real. Not this illusory equality of rights but equality of nation. Our nation to nation

state to state

power to power.

Reason this? or revelation from that fierce light?

This thinking – beyond purely personal feelings.

Or inspired by the most truthful personal feelings of all?

A healing this thinking.

A beginning of healing for our Jewish sickness, what makes them know us as parasites?

A healing this thinking for a wholesome healthy new birth and body of Jewry. From that same heartfelt impulse inspiring his daily work.

Liberalism and humanism were not the cures.

Only land – and its politically assured status.

Nationhood! Vast the sweep of it but nothing less felt right. Nationhood it must be. Mazzini knew it – exiles – aliens – bastards – all that – but for two millennia! "Without a country of your own – the bastards of humanity. Without a country of your own you have neither name voice rights – admission as brothers into the fellowship of people."

National dignity - in control of your own - only in such a new Jewish way will the world accept us - you - as a power like itself.

We must become that nation which we are - enter history - make our own history - no longer victims of their history.

The Association's acceptable definition as merely a religious sect now known for what it was. Down on our humblest knees! for their acceptance - that two thousand year 'merely' - that fury of hatred and destruction by the docks for a merely!

Their fullness pointing to our fullness behind this ghostly presence, pretence. Their total hatred revealing our totality which that silence resounds with. All unworthiness shamefulness finally they find in us - which is what this silence resounds with. And which calls - Come into your own! Truly own - as deed - as will!

Then the story is true!

A true story - a nation - yet different from all other nations.

He came from this story, from the people who lived this story.

Father's work on the Karaites - the 'progress' illusion and the circle closed by those tears of his.

All-Jews is this destiny, this return to beginnings.

Newfound 'we' - by this very thinking returned to the story.

Newfound we by this very thinking, but a ghostly one, source of their fear and terror.

"If I am not for myself - I Israel? - who then shall be for me?" - or was God waiting for them century after century to act for themselves? Strange thought.

"If I am not for myself" - what fullness, tension of meaning waiting till now? Such an enduring resonance, never silent - Rabbi who? - still with you - will never leave you - the Rabbis - be humble.

"If I am not for myself" - what I is this who asks the question? Ourselves? Israel? Midpoint, turning, play of such forces, very axis of Self-Emancipation.

Secular yes but to ask, and try to answer the question for his people - the People who had made him what he was - even as negation - that 'even' reality's tension.

Of course Hess was right - that every Jew whether he wants to or not is solidly tied in with his own nation.

The so-called emancipation begun by Napoleon hadn't

touched what now disclosed itself as the issue – only this inner emancipation by themselves – this change of themselves by themselves would prove real.

Somehow, soon, a clear comprehensive statement – of all this. To be publicised, to reach fellow Jews as soon as possible.

Which fellow Jews?

Could only be in the West – Germany – even a centre there – a centre! – to begin there, where political activity would be possible, unrestricted.

Facts and figures became known throughout Russian Jewry.

In about 200 villages Jews had been savagely attacked and their property destroyed. At least 100,000 Jews were left without any means of livelihood. At least 20,000 were left homeless. Even in Warsaw a pogrom. Everywhere the attackers well armed. Could only have been organised from above.

Any show of resistance met everywhere with increased violence, outright slaughter. Any! We are the absolute Lords of life here – Here!

Here!

Here!

Here!

Then – that Land There – Here in our hearts and dreams for millenia, for home, and livelihood, at last and once again to become our home.

The Land that seeks our feet, to tread it.

Land that seeks our hands to seed it, flower it, fruit it.

Dream that we make come true.

These facts and figures an ultimatum.

Hated to the point of extinction.

Only future at all – only real future – Palestine.

Survival as Jews the only issue now.

From our anguished heart of Russian Jewry beating out clear and strong – the deed – the mission – life's meaning – a beginning – a new creation.

Earth our home.

To dig and plough our way – no longer only to read it.

The real land calling. The land to be made real.

Our land.

No! The land yet to be made ours. Our will – sweat – hands – feet – and faith.

For these few beginners, no longer emigration, no longer emancipation, but reclaiming our land. Land alone will set us free. Earth. That on which we stand and must make our own.

Pure this call.

Pure our response.

Our life a new creation.

There alone, the freedom to become ourselves.

From young Russian Jews, a thinking, precise, proud, responding.

From St Petersburg. *"There can be no salvation for Israel if it does not found a government of its own in the Land of Israel."*

From Minsk. *"It is necessary to seek out for all the wanderers a special, isolated place where comrades can gather together until, in the course of time, all matters of state, law and administration will be in the hands of the Hebrews alone and everything will be determined by the word of their mouth."*

From the Bilu group. *"The objective of the society is the economic, national and spiritual renaissance of the Hebrew people in Syria and Palestine."*

Secretly they met in cities of the Pale. Secretly they collected money, held Hebrew courses and trained in self-defence.

Some thousands set out, feet to tread that earth into their own. To create anew the bond which would yield a home.

Beyond, beyond the desert heat, swamps, malaria, bandits, Turkish officials – the Land – earth – life – Mother and Father – our hope.

Arising, the settlements, Rosh Pinah, Zicheron Ya'akov, Petah Tikvah.

V

The Railway

The intimacy and trust between the Tsar and Pobedonostsev no longer prevailed. The Ulyanov affair four years ago had raised doubts about Pobedonostsev's higher education policy. The Tsar had even become critical of Pobedonostsev's overall Synod control in which till now he was considered infallible. Pobedonostsev's effective influence was increasingly confined by various bureaucratic means once the Tsar's dissatisfaction had become sufficiently confirmed.

Alexander was increasingly irritated by Pobedonostsev's ill-considered statements and unwanted advice on the newly developing foreign policy for a closer relationship with France, a distancing from Germany and a more dynamic involvement in the Far East. The rift made Alexander uneasy, much more uneasy than he wanted to admit to himself.

Pobedonostsev's bitterness, suspicion and anger focused on one man, a new man appearing in the Emperor's counsel, Sergius Witte, onetime station master, then head of South Western railway, rising to become Minister of Communications and now strongly tipped to replace Vyshnegradsky as Minister of Finance. Witte insisted that change was a reality that could not be denied or exorcised but had to be understood, mastered and integrated into the autocracy. Otherwise it would destroy the autocracy. He had persuaded Alexander that industrialisation must be encouraged and that its expansion could only result in alleviating the peasants' poverty and the declining economic fortunes of the nobility. The newly arising working class were not a threat to the autocracy. On the contrary they would provide the very base of a new powerful industrialised Russia ready to take her rightful place amongst the European nations.

For Pobedonostsev such ideas, let alone their implementation, were madness and meant disruption of the whole social order. The peasants would become increasingly vulnerable to the corruption of the cities and their revolutionary ideas. Any fool could see that. Why couldn't Alexander? This so-called working class was no reality but some phantom conjured up by Witte and his like.

Pobedonostsev was not alone in his antagonism but none dared to mention these matters too openly. Witte had very much the Tsar's ear. Pobedonostsev decided to speak out at the Ministerial Council meeting in March. Deeply pained by the breakdown of his relationship with Alexander, feeling a growing sense of isolation, he blamed it all increasingly on this one man. Publicly then, he would give vent to his revulsion and suspicion of both the policy and the man who had risen so high so quickly, and in whose presence on two occasions he had felt as though confronting an alien creature, unRussian. He couldn't bear to think that this one stood close to Alexander, to his Alexander – but no! –no longer his Alexander!

In Witte's supporters he sensed a new breed of men appearing from somewhere. Brash, well informed, extremely confident. With all the answers but absolutely no depth, no substance to any of them. All statistics but no Truth. A new breed catching Alexander's ear in spite of all his teaching. All of them revelling in their power, so obvious!

At those two meetings Witte knew his enemy, but his confidence, sure and strong came from those hours spent standing at the Emperor's side by the outspread map, very centre of the world, as his fingers traced a line through that virgin emptiness south to cross the Volga, – feeling the Emperor's excitement – through the Urals, on across Siberia, Lake Baikal, and those ever distant ever closer waters of the Pacific, to stop at Vladivostok. Line, great artery which would connect, seal and provide the centre and source of unity to this unformed vastness of lands and peoples which was Russia. He Witte firmly at Alexander's side, at the very centre of it all, knowing it not only in purely Russian terms but as of vital interest to European nations, a trade route for their economies which in turn will bring profit to Russia.

The Tsar had taken quickly to Witte. A real individual, a strong character along with whom Alexander let himself be drawn, as Witte in his quick, bold, direct way drew many threads together pointing to the logical culmination of so much that had happened during the recent decades.

Sergius Witte, a self-made man, rough-hewn, energetic, ambitious, sensed with enthusiasm, exhilaration the new energies of a new future pulsing through Russia. Sensed a vision, needing drive, men, money, power. Onward, breathlessly onward to the waters of the Pacific. And all to be Russian. At last to reach waters of the world. Not absolutely sure where it all led. But the plunge must be taken.

Moments, when he felt his destiny high above these others. The one man now in a position to set this thing in motion. Nothing he could not achieve if given the Tsar's full support and his boldness so shaped as to pay obeisance to his Tsar for making any of it possible, never ceasing to know his destiny as lying in the gift, the grace of his Tsar. The suspicions and jealousy towards him a spur. But once appointed Minister of Finance he would be in a position to plan, stimulate, direct, with the backing of many. He would create a sound gold policy and press on with his plan for a Trans-Siberian railway.

The Council of Ministers had been established by Alexander II to consider comprehensive policy questions, with himself as president. The new Tsar decided to be rid of it, wary of its dangerous potential as an independent power grouping, even a cabinet system. Pobedonostsev persuaded him to let the Council meet just once a year. He agreed with the Tsar's suspicion of this typical example of the late lamented's misguided liberalism. But he also indicated to the Tsar how this one annual meeting, the only time in the year when all ministers came together, might be used to ensure unity and loyalty in a positive way. Each March the dreadful event of 1881 could be commemorated and its lessons reiterated. In conclusion the successful achievements accomplished since then could be enumerated. Alexander liked the idea and a tradition developed for himself to address the session followed by words from Pobedonostsev on a lofty but relevant spiritual theme.

Early this March morning, long before the session was due to start, the Tsar had almost decided to cancel the meeting. He had spent a restless night pitched about in a brooding fury by the intractability of his son over the choice of a future wife.

Damnation! cancellation would mean victory for the wretched boy!

As he began to read from the text of his opening address backed by a full length portrait of his father, gloomy shade today, his ministers soon heard the distant tone. He turned over a couple of pages together and went straight on before realising his mistake. He turned the pages back with indifference. The ministers had begun to speculate on the reasons for his clear discomfiture and were looking forward to an early conclusion of the wearisome ritual. They assumed that Pobedonostsev, should he speak, which was by no means certain, would draw matters to a discreetly rapid close for it seemed obvious that His Majesty was wearily impatient to have done with it all.

Since taking his place in the chamber around the curved horseshoe span of gilded ministerial chairs, Pobedonostsev had been intently taking the measure of each man present with an unexpected clarity and finality. Witte he refused to register as a reality, only a spectre, a turbulent hateful emptiness.

Towards all of them now utmost doubt. Timeservers all. Perhaps - Rostovsky - Danilevsky - just those two he could rely on for support. Good! Better to know it had come to this than any more pretence. That distant tone, brittle irritation, in the Tsar's voice told of the false ways he was treading. Here in this chamber was no unity. And into this he would speak, fateful, alone, never less doubting.

As the Tsar finished giving vent to a deep breath of unmistakable relief, Pobedonostsev rose to offer the traditional declaration of gratitude. Everyone relaxed, barely listening, glancing at the Tsar who was stroking his beard and staring down at his papers. Definitely not his usual assured self. Pobedonostsev began with his customary opening.

"His Majesty has once again graciously accorded me the privilege of addressing you. We all know when we recall that unforgettable day - the day of our late revered monarch's Golgotha," turning his head in the direction of the portrait, "just how much has been achieved by our beloved Emperor as he holds steadfastly to the one and only path of truth for Russia. Yet there are those in the highest councils who think strange thoughts, dangerous thoughts, traitorous thoughts. They tell us that our Russia is not at all what we believe it to be. They tell us of some fantastic Russia where a new class of people has suddenly appeared, called? - the working class! A class on whose future Russia depends. Lies! - Fantasies!" he called out. The anger, the trembling note, all so out of keeping, drew everyone's attention, and especially to glimpse the Tsar's reactions to this unprecedented outburst.

"There is no such class in Russia. Our Russian classes were

created by God in godly times, not created by clever – oh so clever men! Those who speak thus no matter what their standing are in truth socialists themselves, undermining, threatening our Russia, our autocracy. But worse. More corrupt still. These same people tell us that the future of Russia lies in what? – in railway lines! Lines of metal stretching across the country. I can hardly bring myself to believe that there are men who say such things. Yes – that our Russian future lies in railway lines! Very worst kind of materialism. For the future of Russia can only lie in faithfulness to the Church as it has done since Vladimir chose the Christian way nine hundred years ago. Orthodoxy and Autocracy. Anything else is idolatry, destruction. Open your hearts! Doesn't it wound you? Don't you feel how such ideas are tearing into the flesh of our Holy Russia? And these are men who have risen to eminence with such beliefs. They pay lip service to Orthodoxy. They say and do anything to further their careers. Metal tracks! There we hear betrayal, blasphemy. Of course we've heard all the clever arguments. Channels of communication – swift flow of goods – the so-called science and economics of it all. That the Tsar will get to know his people better? That's nothing – absolutely nothing to do with railway timetables – or the movement of goods. We see in truth the swift flow of poison making it that much easier for corrupting influences. We see in reality men torn away from their roots – lured away scurrying about everywhere meaninglessly – at the very time when our sacred roots are more important than ever. This unholy movement will only bring chaos – this mixing. No! Behind all this is Satan! He indeed would have men drawn out of themselves, forgetting themselves – so then would come in the poisoners, the destroyers of Russia."

Witte was ready to counter attack but the tension in his broad jowl yielded to a smirk of incredulity at the old fool's madness. Satan in the railway lines!

Others kept their response more carefully hidden.

Rostovsky and Danilevsky were dismayed, chastened by Pobedonostsev's audacity, anxious, then relieved by his overreaching, or was he possibly reverting to some ancient privilege presuming to be the conscience of the Tsar?

Embarrassment and puzzlement changed to pity. The man had made a fool of himself. His fanaticism had overreached itself. He had made public what should have remained private. All this was clearly a personal matter to do with the Tsar. Pathetic and unforgivable to have exposed it like this.

All eyes gazed discreetly into some distance.

Relieved at the ending of his own speech the Tsar heard the familiar fervour of Constantin about the future of Russia with some satisfaction, even with something of a comforting security. He heard an unfamiliar tone but the attestation was ever the same, still there, still the living conscience of Russia. Still as strong as any man around him. But this painful foreboding insisted. Constantin's 'the future of Russia!' resounded with increasingly unpleasant implications. That confrontation with Nikki – of course respectful as ever! – had revealed an obstinacy, opposition, beginning to threaten most unpleasantly this future of Russia. No longer his Russia alone. But that future Russia which he was creating as an absolute, inviolate, his through and through, was beginning to tremble, so slightly, in its certainty. It was no longer wholly in his power, hands. His plans were being challenged. And that was the most important happening of all as far as the future of Russia was concerned. Not Constantin's well meant droning.

But being so challenged by that callow youth. That was the most unspeakable aspect. Enemies outside were bad enough. But that could be coped with. But enemies within! Yes enemies no less so close. From his own loins. That was intolerable. The boy's sheer dumb insolence. Out then! Out with him. A tour. An educational tour to knock some sense into him. Abroad – – and then the East! Let him see, learn, recognise who and what he was – a future Tsar! Railways? How right Witte was! Let him go to Vladivostok and start the line – see what the English were up to – realise that this question of marriage wasn't a personal thing at all.

He stood up and left the chamber as everyone quickly came to their feet. Pobedonostsev held tightly to the rail of his lectern, trembling as he let himself down onto his seat. Rostovksy and Danilevsky had decided in meaningful glances to each other that the Tsar was very angry with Pobedonostsev's outburst and accordingly made a hurried exit with the rest. Everyone was forced into some interpretation of the Tsar's countenance, mood, gestures. Discreet alliances would hopefully help towards some objective assessment.

Pobedonostsev sat alone in the empty council chamber, not

wanting any of them near him, anywhere near him. He'd been talking into a vacuum, catching even now the dull echo of his own words, falling emptily, unreceived. Seeds on stony ground. Words sounding the abyss that so clearly separated them all utterly from him. It was far worse than he'd ever suspected but it was good that he now knew. Bitterly he began to regret, recoil from with disgust, his attack on Witte. This public confrontation in front of these fools. Exposed – unholy – unclean. But it had been absolutely unavoidable. Never till now was such an action remotely conceivable in such circumstances. But for the Tsar himself. Even five years ago he could never have imagined that 'but for the Tsar', and with such bitter resignation. Yet with courage he'd done it – in front of them all. Them all, who by their very nature were in no way admissible to that holy place at the centre of Russia's destiny. From there he'd exposed himself to their crass, ignorant stares, their sniggering, deceitful glances. But never again! He'd dared to think possible that they'd respond, awake and see what he could see. It had been extremely unpleasant. But now beyond all doubt he was clear about the Tsar's ignorance, stupidity – and even questionable fitness for holding the supreme office. Weak – weaker and weaker these vessels.

Indifferent to his waiting coachman he walked back to his apartment, this city pressing in from all sides. Deeply saddened, yet gratefully knowing this return through the city as the return to a haven of purity, solace, amidst a polluted world. A haven served so faithfully in all his comings and goings by Catherine's pure, modest soul. How blessed he was. What did those whoremongers in the chamber know of such matters? They'd all be burned to a cinder in the presence of her purity.

Catherine had known that once again this morning would be her ordeal. Dear Constantin, leaving so gravely, so burdened, so frail after this recent flu, damp wretched city! no use to him at all. Yet so keenly felt his power of will. So grave this morning, yet almost smiling as he reminded her of this momentous news. That Captain Valentin Baranov was coming and she should entertain him till he returned from the Council meeting.

Pobedonostsev had come to know a rare sharing with Baranov. Not so much that Valentin understood or even could understand his situation but – even beyond understanding, a lightening, a relief, to be with, to have this man, honest, light hearted, yes a little light hearted – and speak with him. There it was. There it must be left. An acceptance, an ease of relationship that he had not known till now.

But strange, for Valentin was clearly an innocent in that world of evil and corruption. Strange for in spite of that Valentin was somewhere so close – almost like a trusted son. Son! that was it – in acceptance – the name of this long moment's yearning.

But wondrous the ways of God! A philanderer for years! – justified? – wife's betrayal – a philanderer – wrecked career – self destruction – the abyss – masked in that boredom – and then to him. Wondrous God's ways!

Not only himself! No question Catherine's tetchiness moping – those wretched swollen red eyes – that – whatever was its preoccupation – indifference? had gone!

Recently, whenever Constantin left the apartment a gentle, warming space began to beckon, to let her breathe. Frozen desperation dissolved. The tears came slowly, pressing forward. The suffocating constriction was released. Lightness, expansion drew her up away to glide to fly on this wave. That was the strange sound coming from her – herself – breathing free. That finest mask of frozen resignation yet seeming calm, fast dissolving in this warmth, heat, fire, kindling fire, leaping flame of breath, of life.

She groped for the chair, to sit, dizzy, float down, letting the silent tears press forth, knowing, pitying that own poor dear self.

Baranov had come to realise that he was needed by both of them. Seconded to a shore post after heavy drinking when his wife left him for a brother officer, he put his name forward out of boredom as a volunteer for the Commission headed by Pobedonostsev to report on the state of religious welfare in the Navy and Army. His antipathy on first meeting with Pobedonostsev gradually changed to an attraction, a challenge, a serious challenge, something emanating from this thin wizened man whose like he had never met before. Dimly sensed was the feeling that from this man there was something important to be gained, learned. That this other had something to give him. The initial embarrassment changed to sympathy, respect, very intimation of Pobedonostsev's inwardness and values, reaching so far beyond those which had molded Baranov himself. An uprightness, principled, a worldly disdain, a strength, purposefulness, certainty which awoke him to his own looseness, stupid, wasteful drifting to no purpose since her betrayal. He must put it behind him and set course anew, independent too. Like this man who relied only on an inner strength.

When at Pobedonostsev's invitation he entered the apartment for the first time he was fascinated, in it stillness and gloom, by a strange absence. He felt that Catherine's words, gestures, very presence, were elsewhere. Sensing her call, her yearning, he indulged and answered. He pitied that withering flesh and justified himself as bringing a little pleasure and lightness into her life. Unlike the many women who had enjoyed his company, vigorous, handsome, for Catherine the thrill was not just that of knowing it all as a delightful game. In her was awoken something new from the slow wasting. That another man showed interest in her. Till now unthinkable! Something awoken so overwhelming, so quickly!

She grew fearful, dear Valentinov saviour blithe fresh unknowing – a cruel joy what he was doing to her – carried so far beyond herself each time he visited – cloudless blue – yet whenever he left disaster felt lurking – audacity, song – yet fear and shame before her trusting Constantin upright old – deathward.

Before Pobedonostsev left for the State Council meeting, Catherine tried to warn him of the unspeakable danger that threatened. Dark freedom so yearned for so feared. A culmination, that this would be the fatal visit. That Constantin should not leave her, should protect save her from all this. But her tongue was bound in a cruel spell. And now it was already happening again, hearing that charmed music of his greeting to Anna, hastily drying her cheeks, her eyes, with him thrusting into the apartment, smiling, bowing, drenching the sadness with green growth of his sparkling life. At every point uprushing, bursting madness uncontrolled. And she wanted to. O how she wanted to. In a mad terror. If Constantin did not return soon it would be done. They would do it.

Baranov was alerted to the seriousness of Catherine's flushed face as he sipped his tea. In quick controlled recoil his smile ceased, his tone cooled, his gestures became extremely cautious. The game was surely over. He must withdraw, somehow transform the situation but with utmost subtlety. Catherine's lips were slightly parted, dreamily smiling 'You can see I'm ready'. He sipped awkwardly, stared at the floor, knew that every word and gesture needed utmost consideration in this dangerous situation. Knew, bewildered, that his normal reactions were fraught with disaster. He had never expected anything like this. Till now all previous players had known the rules. But in this one he now knew an anguish, a real presence that cut him to the quick. No game this but the freeing of a desperate captive.

The tension was becoming unbearable. Baranov felt paralysed by uncertainty. Both of them hoped desperately for Constantin's return. She felt Valentin's withdrawal as chilling emptiness and yearned for that age-old stifling.

She uttered a weird, sobbing cry, clenched her teeth, struggled to her feet and hurried upstairs to her bedroom at the sound of Constantin in the hall. She knew it all as an audacious risk, an exposure of most hidden treasure – but never again! Agonising abortion that this treasure had become. Dire warning, shock that pointed her harshly back to the old lifelong path of serving that good man and never being tempted thus again.

Baranov had failed her. But they were accomplices. Never must she have to do with him, with anyone in that way again.

That door must remain shut forever. Utterly sinful. Lure, fascination, disaster. What ghastly bubbling nonsense had she glimpsed with this sinful accomplice to their utter shame before this good man who trusted them both.

Baranov, shaken by that ugly cry, very edge of human, was afraid of what she might say or do. Unexpected career possibilities were opening through this work with Constantin Petrovich, whose trust might now be shattered in a moment.

Wheezing a little, Constantin Petrovich was being helped off with his coat by Anna.

Remember! He's come back from that difficult Council meeting.

Sympathy! Seriousness!

But what more serious than her piercing cry – his guilt? shame? responsibility? Piercing to such seriousness – sadness – so joining them together!

All so strange!

Pobedonostsev, trembling slightly as he entered his living room, at last on terra firma, welcomed the comforting presence. Valentin knew clearly the ordeal through which he had been.

"My dear Valentin you can stop worrying now. The Good Lord has been with us. When you stand in the truth you can take them all on."

Baranov, smiling weakly, struggled to make an adequate connection. He helped Constantin to settle down comfortably into his armchair and to feel secure amongst his own. He was pained to feel that trembling body and that frailty - pitiful. Sitting opposite he felt Constantin as somehow shrivelled, swathed, uncannily swathed in that eternal black suit. He forced himself to say something for fear that speech had left him. For fear of what she might say at any moment where was she? bursting in screaming about what had happened, about all that had ever happened, surely a dream fast fading. Yet strangely he didn't care - why! even wanted such an outburst and to brave it, as just needed right for him to suffer through, confirming, truly confirming their coming together once in that real place.

"How then did it go?" he asked having to feel his way for a normal phrase, then quickly mastering the essentials of Constantin's account to enable a response that would console and encourage.

The events of the morning had made both vulnerable to an unfamiliar loosening. Both, as they talked, were touched with the knowledge that the well trodden paths of their relationship had become a threshold beckoning into new realms. A door, waiting. Now or never.

As to a trusted son Pobedonostsev spoke though not even now daring to express his deepest pessimism about the Tsar. Baranov heard a new note, felt a new intimacy, a new responsibility - and shrank back from it all.

He must withdraw from both of them for good.

As revelation he discovered his other life in all its seafreshness, to take over once more, far away from this gloom. Already taking his leave he let the old man talk on, slipping further and further away on this new stream of quickening time.

Anxiously aware of Catherine's absence he grew desperate for a quick clean departure. He wanted only to cease all involvement with them both as soon as possible. Those were surely movements from the bedroom above. That dreadful cry again - when would it strike, accusing, witnessing to all?

"Enough of these miserable affairs," said Pobedonostsev, tenderly aware of that threshold touched. Sufficient, sufficient that glimpse, to be savoured, gratefully savoured in its plenitude and promise. Return now to the old, the familiar but strengthened.

"The Wittes – they come and go. They'll be forgotten soon enough with all their baseness, manoeuvrings, stupidity. Our work is Russia's truth. At the Commission's next sitting I'm going to announce the readiness of your report for publication. I've written an introduction praising it highly. Nothing less than its due – and be assured my dear Valentin that the very first copy will be on the Tsar's desk. In spite of everything I know that he still takes me seriously."

To Pobedonostsev's surprise, as he concluded, Baranov came awkwardly to his feet having waited tensely for the words to stop. He scurried frantically for excuses at leaving so unexpectedly. But somehow out with the truth. No other way! Deep need, a rightness involved. Straight out to the puzzled Constantin frowning from his chair.

"Constantin Petrovich, I've decided to finish my work with you on the Commission. I shall be reapplying for a sea post. Immediately. That's where I belong. That's where I must go."

He stopped abruptly, warned. His tone was unfamiliarly brusque, his gaze was through the window out to a far distance. Still without looking at Constantin he went straight from the room and called to Anna for his overcoat.

Constantin struggled anxiously to his feet, trembling, unable to grasp what was happening, not daring to express his feelings, clear that Valentin did not want him to come close, yet unable to stay back.

But there was one who could help!

Where had she been all this while?

Desperately, gratefully remembering he called her.

"Catherine! Catherine! – Anna where's your mistress? Why isn't she here? Our good friend's leaving you know, Catherine! Come show your respects – what rudeness is this?"

Unprecedented, that she wasn't here whenever Valentin took his leave – but now?

Baranov heard the distress in Constantin's voice and hurriedly buttoned up his naval greatcoat.

"Catherine! Catherine!" Pobedonostsev shouted desperately up the stairs, "I insist. D'you hear me? I insist that you show due respect to our Valentin."

In the shocked silence as the bedroom door opened from above Baranov knew that he had to see her for the last time, to meet her eye to eye before he could leave.

Since Constantin's return Catherine had lain on her bed, wounded, in a numb trance, thanks be to God, for ever and ever. From time to time Anna entered quietly, watching her mistress with deep concern. From time to time Catherine was touched by the dark weight of the room, drawn down again to that cruel centre of dread threatening to engulf her. Helplessly now returned to herself, chill self, by that name, her name, her self sounding from below, and the one calling whom she heard through that name still there. His voice calling, still there, to return. His voice demanding, anxiously demanding. So be it. Above all else! If she could not hide or die. If she could not have it so. He whom she was here to serve tearing her helplessly away from her hiding, her death. But lord, as she groped her way down the stairs, clutching the banister, swaying, towards the caller who wanted her. Swollen with weeping, blindly her master insisting that she see her awakener once more – cruel awakener – o so grateful! – better it had never been – shameful accomplice against that good old deathward man.

Let him see then this shattered weakling she had sought to hide – that he had made of her.

Let them both suffer, her master and he who had so cruelly created her.

Pobedonostsev was shaken by her appearance and retreated from the foot of the staircase. Catherine stopped before reaching the bottom, held by the once warming gold of his epaulettes. See what you've made of me! Revel in your power! Cruel. Saviour.

"No-o-o," she wailed. Never must that abortion be recalled – glorious – dreadful birth!

Baranov stood his ground barely breathing, to receive her desperate tearful stare with affirmation, acceptance, with pledge that he might somehow carry away, as part of himself, substance of her suffering. Quickly he turned in departure, flight and shut the door hard behind him. But the gold still floated in her trembling vision, wanly, so wanly dissolving away.

"No! Never!" she called out again, fiercely from beyond herself, yet so keenly centred at the heart of it all. Turning around, she returned to her room, to her bed, overcome with an emptiness and exhaustion.

In the hours and days that followed amidst his pain and

confusion Pobedonostsev sensed what he must not do, not know. The questions that threatened must be held at bay, neutralised by any makeshift strategy. In the last resort to acknowledge their sheer existence but through a willed, practised blindness to refuse acknowledgement of their actual content. In the last resort their life together must continue as if that scene, that past, that stranger which Valentin was fast becoming, had never been. Deep, raw was that wound laid open. But he knew when to forget. Catherine's behaviour and the other's behaviour – the door on whose threshold he had once surely stood was shut tight for ever. A memory. A dream. A painful forgetting.

In the strange time that followed, of her wan, hesitant appearances, he must hold steadfastly to the Christian way, refusing to judge, for love, says the Apostle, is ever patient and kind. Hold steadfastly also to the old, tried way of salvation – work!

Slowly Catherine emerged from some nether world, that flush of gold finally quenched by the arid light of Constantin's life. Gradually the weeping ceased, his old familiar Catherine reappeared, as answer to his prayers. Gradually she returned to the one she served, knowing her place, never to flee it again.

Pobedonostsev knew in work, as ever, the healing way. In that same measure of gratitude for its healing power, to draw from it the strength of understanding which let him see all that had happened, yes all, as good. As the Lord's guiding hand. As the Lord's chastisement. As His rod and His staff. No need to feel shame over his outburst in the Council. No need to feel shame over that door which had begun to open with Valentin. Through both came clear confirmation that he stood truly alone. Such weakness would never occur again. The Lord had given him a sign. None clearer. Could his task, mission, be for one who could not stand truly alone?

Refuge and salvation in work as he shut his study door and took his place before his desk piled with reports and tasks awaiting. He would tackle first the proofs of his introduction to Baranov's report. Nothing after all could diminish the value of that report and its contribution to the nation's well being. Or was it really so? Was it really objective, his introduction? Enough enough! – let him turn to something else.

In spite of his iron resolve, doubt and pessimism were taking strong hold. This intimate ritual year in year out at his desk, felt mechanical, brittle, drained of reality. This doubt and pessimism was the Adversary at his most dangerous! Not for a moment must he let go his hold. Work! and work again! saving grace. But this growing indifference - vague - vast - to everything! Such a weariness as he fiddled with his pen and helplessly watched the words on the paper dwindle to meaningless shapes. The great mocker at work! And still the wretched sobs of her upstairs. Quick source of himself, very will ever at call, drying up, vanishing?

Late each night he went to his bed, so weak, his chest so sore. Awakening in the early hours he knew, as he trembled still with the shock of that raw encounter, that he had come so very close to something. Something ominous, vast. A dark reality of shattering power.

As one afflicted he knew himself, for everything was sealed with the stamp of death. All about him transparent with its own dissolution. Petersburg, the power-seeking, glitter, sensuality. Madmen possessed! All of it momentary, passing. All of them doomed, pathetic, sucked into this abyss. Dreadful vanity of things - futility of men - inexorable passing - sweep of time. All our doing a stench in Thy nostrils. Of no avail! Only faith in the Saviour can spare us.

All about him become appearance, very marrow of being, sucked away. Resolutely he gathered himself against this relentless force dragging him down, lit an ikon candle and prayed on his knees till the first dawn light.

"Lord, O Lord help us Thy servant,
Jesus Christ have mercy on my soul!"

Numbed still with the touch of that fearful reality he fought back from the strength of his prayer over against that groundless depth dragging. Depth beyond all pessimism known till now. But he would not be broken, even now when forced to stare through the watery light at this skull-like mockery of himself in the mirror. Oh how he felt his years! This feebleness of body, irascible, brittle. This inexorable passing through the tides of time.

"Lord, Lord, help thy servant
Have mercy on my soul!"

Slowly, in purest inwardness, beyond all appearances, terrors, threats, to sense the quiet tide of his strength returning. Yea though I walk through the valley of the shadow of death Thou art with me! Thy rod has chastised me Oh Lord - and it was good! Thy servant liveth again Oh Lord.

Yes - it was passing.

The Adversary was retreating.

He had stood his ground.

With gratitude he glimpsed his work anew, released from that dreadful spell. A vast forgetting ended. Gladly the Adversary would have him abandon that task once and for all. Thanks be to Him who had heard His servant's prayer, as stream of will returned to this old body that he serve the Lord once more.

Gird your loins Constantin! Rise up, spirit invincible! the vista opening, the busyness of it all, the plans, meetings, decisions in all its fullness. There was the meaning, there was the life. This very morning Nicholas Ivanovich Chulkoff would be here with his report from Moscow. My Moscow. Petitions to be dealt with! The wretched Solovyev publications business again.

Enemies, detractors, indifference, the Adversary, Death itself - to the end! To the bitter end he would run the race just as the Apostle proclaimed. He would endure. He would bear his aloneness in the face of it all.

Chulkoff had been given increasingly responsible tasks by Pobedonostsev, and he carried them through with thoroughness, dedication and his lawyer's precision. As official appointee of the consistorial chancery of the Moscow diocese, he was Pobedonostsev's key man, both for general information from Moscow and for observing just how thoroughly Synod directives were being carried through. He knew that for Pobedonostsev, living and working in St Petersburg was a heavy cross which he bore faithfully on the Lord's behalf. He knew that for Pobedonostsev, Moscow, his beloved birthplace, was true home, and spiritual heart of Russia. The news he brought this morning would surely lighten this cross. But Constantin's unfamiliar distance made his eagerness, exuberance, out of place. He sensed a sadness, tiredness, frailty, not at all the Constantin Petrovich for whom he had boarded the Moscow train with such extraordinary news. In this uncertainty he kept to strictly official issues. First, the splitting up and transfer of two bishops to distant provinces in accordance with Constantin's policy of quickly cutting down to size any senior cleric who was becoming too big for his boots. He reported in detail how both men were continually thwarting Constantin's directives. In apparently minor ways but pointing to something dangerous.

Trickier and more important was the problem of the priest Makarios. From his living to the west of Moscow he was ceaselessly attacking corruption in high places. Official warnings only intensified his angry outpourings and popular support was rapidly spreading. Pobedonostsev and Chulkoff were fully supportive, Makarios spoke as very servant of Holy Russia. His purgatorial voice was a much needed warning. But the line must be drawn. Authority as such must not be endangered though the cleansing was essential.

"He's proving extremely obstinate," Chulkoff explained.

"The drawing of the line. That's where skilled judgement, real insight is needed," mused Pobedonostsev, drawn to the issue with relish.

"Not a simple either – or here," he went on, as Chulkoff felt relief at his loosening up.

"Makarios a man in our best Russian tradition. He frightens the wits out of the hypocrites, liars, office seekers. Let them indeed tremble before his chastening tongue. But – Makarios – and a thousand Makarioses must know that the Church is the servant of the State not its master."

Chulkoff was hearing his old familiar Constantin.

"In principle the issue's like the pogroms. Though of course the question of the Jews is much more complex. The people must be allowed even encouraged to express their feelings. But it mustn't be allowed to reach the stage of anarchy."

"Constantin Petrovich, at last," said Chulkoff, unable to hold back, "this most complex question – let me tell you what I saw with my own eyes last night - absolutely no complexity there – but a sight – such a sight that none of us ever expected to see in our beloved Moscow. They were leaving in their thousands! Down to the station and away. Isn't that an answer! Isn't that the answer to this most complex question?" Eagerly, excited he told, released at last of his blessed message.

Pobedonostsev was puzzled and irritated.

"Is it really that complex? Or does it simply need a Sergei Nikolaevich to cut the knot of all our dithering?" he questioned.

"The Grand Duke? But what are you talking about? What's been happening? What did he do? Tell me exactly," demanded Pobedonostsev, caught up by Chulkoff's excitement, sensing something extraordinary - even momentous. Chulkoff could only and simply describe, let live again and so release himself of the furious energies still resonant from the previous night's experience. Describe create discover.

"What a sight, what a victory, what a feeling. Those strangers, those alien creatures at long last sent packing through our Moscow streets - packing - marching - slinking - no there simply isn't a word to describe it - 'because when you see them all together like this, it's only then you realise how they all belong together - so odd, so foreign - not simply unRussian - but - well I felt - unhuman. Dare I say it - but it was with me. Not altogether human. I asked myself standing near the Grand Duke - so strong - fierce - I asked myself just what are they doing here? I mean not just here in Moscow but here on this earth altogether? I've simply never experienced it before - this not quite human quality. Of course individually - I mean we've all known some individually. But that's an individual impression. You don't quite notice it. But together - all of them! It was just overpowering. And now they're out! Our Moscow is free of them. And it was your Sergei! as you've always called him - rightly so! - who did it."

Your Sergei - alien creatures - the freeing of Moscow - each theme, picture, meaning, fused living in the fervent stream of Chulkoff's experience, drew Pobedonostsev to the very edge of a revelation knowing only as yet that it had happened. He wanted only to know more, hear more.

"Constantin Petrovich those Jews looked right in their manacles. The clinking chains seemed absolutely the right noise for them to be making. And what an inspiration - the Grand Duke's offer to all loyal citizens. Ten roubles for tracking down illegal Yids! And don't forget said the Grand Duke - all Yids are illegal - in spite of my revered ancestors' nonsense about useful Yids. There's your complex question solved! And there's your Sergei Alexandrovitch! That generous offer absolute guarantee. Hauled in in their thousands. Nowhere to hide. A matter of hours before they were all rounded up. Some gendarme idiot thought that as soon as the news spread a lot of Yids were bound to run away. Run away? Set up a cordon! roared His Highness.

What? round the whole city? - of course round the whole city - right now! And it was done! Just imagine what he could do here in St Petersburg!"

Chulkoff stopped for breath but Pobedonostsev asked questions, wanted details - when, where and how had it all started?

Constantin was becoming more animated, fresher, younger than Chulkoff had experienced for a long time.

"When?" repeated Chulkoff.

"Yes when? What was the first intimation that you, you personally, had?" demanded Pobedonostsev, irritated that Nicholas Ivanovich had not grasped how essential it was for him to savour, deeply to savour this fruitfulness of seeds planted long ago. Such a fruitfulness of earnest words given and so received into that soul's depths. Very balm of consolation. What was a Baranov in this light?

"The first? The very first? That's interesting now that you put it like that," answered Chulkoff, surprised by Pobedonostsev's question, yet led on by it and others to patiently create, discover for both of them, a picture of the whole affair in some purity, moment by moment. After careful consideration Chulkoff concluded that apparently - he repeated - apparently - it had come out of the blue as things so often did with the Grand Duke.

"Just so," nodded Pobedonostsev recognising inspiration in that blue, and beginning to feel the very tenor and timbre of his faithful pupil through Chulkoff's ardent retelling, reliving.

And again, as so often with the Grand Duke, went on Chulkoff, there was something so fantastic about the idea that no one present took it seriously. They should have known better. Especially General Savich who actually demurred next morning when pressed for action, even though at the time he had committed himself. From then on he was a marked man in the Grand Duke's eyes. As for the officials, security and transport, who'd have to deal with the basics - when they dared to put forward so called technical - well not even objections rather doubts - the Grand Duke's roar of 'Why not!' brought them quickly to their senses.

Pobedonostsev pressed Chulkoff to return to that actual beginning out of the blue. Chulkoff told of the regular monthly meetings with a circle of intimates. That particular evening they included Bishop Anthony and Chulkoff himself who handled some legal work for the Grand Duke's estates near Moscow. The Grand Duke was thoroughly worked up - yes, still after four years - over the Ulyanov affair. But something was coming to a head we all felt that. "Incredible - criminal! - the mother should have been hanged too - the whole rotten lot of them!" he'd shouted, "Not five but twenty - thirty should have been hung. Those creatures regard the slightest concession as weakness. When will my brother ever learn? He's got this authority this power! He must use it! That's why he's got it. If he doesn't it'll destroy him. It'll destroy all of us. It's not to be played with this power. If you don't grasp it with a grip of iron it'll cut you to pieces" - - we'd never heard anything like that before - and to realise who he was referring to! a kind of embarrassment - as though we shouldn't have heard it. Our closeness to him couldn't really bear the weight of that. Perhaps he'd never intended saying it - but he did - and we simply had to share it with him - - then he turned on St Petersburg. That place was the reason for his brother's stupidity and weakness. Just to live there made a man crazy. Thank God that things in Moscow were very different. Then he praised Moscow in words with which all present felt close. All that is except General Savich who begged to differ with His Highness.

Recalling now Chulkoff wondered whether there wasn't something intentionally provocative about General Savich's remarks. Anyway, General Savich suggested - only suggested - that here in Moscow before one could praise its sanctity - purity - one must recognise that the whole city was contaminated by a vile source of corruption - the Yids! And this some nine years after Ignatiev's grand offensive with his May Laws.

"At that - the Grand Duke's eyes narrowed - his voice went harsh - we waited for the storm."

My Sergei - make them tremble!

"General Savich," he leaned far forward and looked hard at the General "how many Yids are there in Moscow?"

"Well your Highness - one can guess - perhaps -"

The Grand Duke was on his feet, stock still.

"Guess? I'll give you forty eight hours for a list of every single Yid in Moscow - and then - out! out! out! D'you hear? Yids out!"

"Of course he was getting right out of himself with talk like this - some great leap with this image - some great anger frustration - deep - something none of us ever suspected - but it took him into the blue - to a place where he could see overlook something - courses of action not given to us lesser mortals."

"No one dared to speak or move. Eventually in a voice less fearsome he blamed our present troubles on his revered ancestors' nonsense. All their talk and laws about categories of so called useful Yids. That had brought nothing but confusion! It was all much simpler. All Yids are Russia's misfortune. Just imagine! A synagogue - a den - praying to their own accursed Yidgod - right in our Moscow. We've let them get that far."

"But no! it didn't completely end there - Bishop Anthony informed the Grand Duke that within those same forty eight hours their Yid Passover Festival would begin. The very idea seemed to draw new fervour from His Highness. Excellent! he shouted - we must descend like their god himself - smite them with a great shock!"

"General Savich was holding his ground. How exactly Your Highness d'you propose shifting all those thousands of Yids off their ugly backsides?"

"Constantin Petrovich - I think that was the final challenge for your Sergei's inspiration to sweep all before it. I doubt whether he'd ever thought of this 'how' till that very moment. I look at it like this. His original inspiration knew from the start, in all its certainty, of the rightness of the deed - and therefore that it could be done. General Savich's how was the opportunity to reveal more of its knowing, in showing -"

"Well? Well?," demanded Pobedonostsev impatiently, "What was his answer?"

"How? the Grand Duke answered beaming at General Savich - haven't we just the thing to carry out an 1891 miracle eh? - we were all baffled - the railway of course my dear General! the whole bunch back to the Pale. Moscow cleansed in one night - by the coachload. When Moscow wakes next morning - a miracle! Pure Russian air to breathe in! But most important! no warnings of any kind. It must fall on them - a stern and terrible shock!"

"Of course for years everyone knew that the Jews had no right to be in Moscow - and of course everyone had his - well - not so bad Jew. You know - some doctor or other. It took the Grand Duke to do something about it - and what? - kick them out! as simple as that. His simplicity – plus his will. With him seeing – knowing – doing – all one."

Chulkoff told how quickly everything went after that. How everyone became brisk, purposeful, into battle. His will driving everyone into furious action. In all departments, surprise, delight, relief at doing this extraordinary but obvious thing. Unusual good humour all round. Men at odds with each other for months – all vanished. The mood buoyant but deadly serious. Inspiring all, the Grand Duke's gusto, certainty – once decided, no compunction or hesitation – and harshly laying about, its appearance in others – his fever of enthusiasm – interest in every detail – immediate solutions!

"I remember Controller Fabritsky – do you really think he'll get away with it? – isn't it incredible what one man can do? – Fabritsky of Transport who co-ordinated the timetables so brilliantly – as one train left another was steaming up to take its place – as though even he couldn't quite believe that what he was doing was real – it was the obviousness that struck us more and more," concluded Chulkoff, "once it was all going I'm sure everyone felt the same – that it should have been done long long ago – and don't forget – imagine! Constantin Petrovich – amongst them many lawyers – doctors – merchants –"

"That's it," enthused Pobedonostsev, "the obviousness of the inspired – but the Tsar thinks him shallow – such is Russia's misfortune."

At Pobedonostsev's request Chulkoff recounted the scene at the station. Officials scurrying about, checking lists, conferring with one another all under the watchful eyes of the Grand Duke himself. "Of course he was there, a rock, by the station clock tower. The fact that he was there – his huge presence – essential. The real inspiration. We all knew that he was there – could see that he was there. Far beyond the giving of an order. His presence fed the flame of our zeal. It made the whole difficult business absolutely meaningful. Bound us to him. He would stand so still watching the waiting carriages, the shuffling Yids under their guards – Cossacks patrolling on horse and foot. There he was here there everywhere, questioning, hurrying men on if he saw signs of a slowing down. He'd issued a strict order – silence must prevail. No sound from any of them – or truncheons at their heads in a second. But as the first trainload steamed away Moscow's bells rang out – and went on ringing till it was all over.

He timed it like that. Our glorious Moscow bells driving us forward keeping us at it. Our Moscow our Moscow our Moscow – they sang again and again. Just what everyone needed – that mighty voice from above – rousing and praising – – but I've forgotten something Constantin Petrovich. I suppose it would have been unnatural if it hadn't happened. Before the bells started, an extraordinary howl went up – very odd! At the time I couldn't tell whether it was one or all of them. It made the Grand Duke furious but nobody could trace it. Very odd – stopped just as suddenly – all too quick for whip or truncheon."

"Of course there'll be the familiar criticisms of the Grand Duke – about his cruelty, arrogance, megalomania – etc. – etc. – but for those of us there it was something extraordinary – especially with those bells ringing away. Somehow I don't think any of us will be quite the same again. Oh yes! just before the first coachloads left Bishop Anthony appeared. Everyone was surprised. The Grand Duke looked annoyed. But the old man, with a couple of priests, insisted on being there and offering his blessing. He praised the Grand Duke as one zealous in the Lord. He reminded us all – who had crucified our Lord. That it would be failing, to be less than merciless. In other words that it was all beneficial for their Yid souls. The old man seemed very moved. He declared it a blessed new day for Moscow."

Chulkoff had finished. Pobedonostsev reached out his hand. An unfamiliar gesture but Chulkoff quickly responded, gently holding the freely offered hand for some moments, seeing in Constantin's eyes a lightening, in the mouth a softening, and sensing in the hand itself, thin, dry, a need to confirm, thankful.

After Chulkoff left Pobedonostsev knew a deep gratitude, to have learned of himself as a begetter. Cool shadow of a living sharing in this parched place. The fulness and sweetness of begetting. A hint, that's all it had been. And out of that hint what possibilities revealed by Sergei's audacious will. My Moscow restored – purer shelter now for men's souls. Shelter where men can humble themselves before the dark wisdom of God.

A man at last to counter the Wittes! A man to give confidence, hope, in this dry time. Sergei's Russian will giving the lie to Nicholas the First's abstract nonsense about useful Jews. Their Jewness an essence of the creature. Sergei understood!

The cleansing of Moscow – but to realise only now that at

the time of utterance he'd had no idea of the real implication. It had taken Sergei to disclose its true meaning and courageously go through with it.

But feel out now delicately how he'd felt at the time! How much of it was himself – how much Sergei? For did he not meet himself in this other and this other in himself? A mystery here. He was not alone. Delicately in the recalling to feel his way into something beckoning, substance other than himself, something mysterious.

But now one thing was painfully obvious. Even the Grand Duke could not have set about this business without the Emperor's authority. Likely enough the Grand Duke had in no way conveyed to his brother what he had in mind. Or was this the Emperor's underhand way of letting the Grand Duke do what he knew very well should be done but without taking full responsibility. Whatever the case, he had not been apprised. He had been purposely kept ignorant.

"I insist you see me tonight before returning to Moscow."

Chulkoff was surprised by the telegram. He would have to cancel an appointment. He hurried round from the hotel to Pobedonostsev's apartment. Constantin seemed very upset. Yes of course there had been a ukase signed by the Emperor. Chulkoff himself had helped the Grand Duke finalise its brief content. In essence – that the illegally present Jews of Moscow now return to their legal places of residence i.e. the Pale. Nothing to make the Emperor think twice. In fact he declared it was a long overdue measure. No particular timing was mentioned.

"I thought the Emperor would surely see through it – that return meant be returned. But the Grand Duke insisted that in these matters his brother was an idiot. See how he treated the Ulyanov woman – he always kept harping back to the Ulyanov business. For myself I didn't think the Emperor was an idiot in that kind of way. I think the Grand Duke underestimated his brother. However, that was the Grand Duke's way. 'We must do his work for him – in spite of him' – he often declared."

Chulkoff took his leave for the second time, still puzzled by Constantin's upset and questioning.

Pobedonostsev accepted the account. Hadn't he fought the Tsar to get the Grand Duke appointed Governor of Moscow in the first place – just at the time when the siren voices – the traitors - were beginning to lure him. Yes Alexander had yielded - but reluctantly.

That once brilliant dawn was over!

Alexander Alexandrovich - Sergei Alexandrovitch - Baranov - now even Chulkoff - all of them - entangling, untrustworthy.

Von Plehve alone left.

But how real was any of this - petty pathetic personal business - his petty personal pride no less! - compared to that vision - creation - organisation!

Dreadful weakness.

He must look beyond the throne and its present occupant to his real enduring mission.

But that Ulyanov affair!

After four years and still so affecting the Grand Duke's mood. Even decisive for the Jews' expulsion? Then he must look closely again at the affair. Sergei's continued concern was surely pointing to something.

Then send for a copy of the trial report and go through it again.

About twenty students involved - planned to kill the Emperor March 1st, anniversary of his father's assassination - bombing team arrested March 1st as a result of a letter intercepted by the Okhrana - organisation amateurish - bombs prepared by Alexander Ulyanov, biology student. Ulyanov took full blame and did not ask for mercy - hanged in the Schlüsselburg with Shevyrev, Andreyushkin, Generalov, Osipanov - all familiar dreary stuff.

What then? - only this long speech by Ulyanov himself.

Well - go through it for Sergei's sake - must be there what fired his will!

Same old impudent student business - - what! what!

"Only by terror can men achieve the right to think freely in a society where nothing is published until it has received the imprimatur of the government, and where no one dares to think at all without first acquiring government approval - -

"Our intelligentsia is physically so weak and disorganised at the present time that it cannot embark on open war. Only the terrorist is in a position to defend the right to think freely and the right to participate intellectually in the life of society. Terror is the sole defensive weapon which a minority can resort to in order to demonstrate its physical strength and the consciousness

that it is fighting for justice. Russian society is so constituted that we can defend our rights only in these duels with the State power - -"

"- - Among the Russian people you will always find ten men so devoted to their ideals and with such a burning sympathy for the sufferings of their country, that they will not consider it a sacrifice to lay down their lives for the cause. Such people cannot be intimidated."

Just there!

Again and again to hear more clearly, face up, of dire necessity recognise! this voice of assured fundamental strength. Recognise in this voice your truly matched adversary. No simple minded fanaticism here but a strength, resolve that he had surely underestimated.

The Grand Duke was right!

This Ulyanov voice was turning him once again to fundamental things, strengthening his resolve. This battle was Russia's destiny and this wretched, misguided youth merely a mouthpiece for the real enemy.

VI

Vilna

Within ten years the enforcement of Count Ignatiev's May Laws had achieved the compulsory relocation of one and a quarter million Jews into towns and cities within the Pale. Thousands of Jews from the surrounding countryside of Vilna province had been forced into the city of Vilna's Jewish quarter. Survival for most of the refugees depended entirely on charity of various kinds. Most native Jews of the city, themselves only managing to eke out the meanest living, were severely challenged. In the three and four storey overcrowded dwelling blocks on Navleski, Krochnalna and Ostrovski streets, rooms had to be vacated and given over to large refugee families. Food and clothing had to be found and education for children.

From deeper, deeper, was that response felt, called on, the real nature of the challenge, by Vilna's native Jews who were often uncertain about their own next day's meal. Apart from Litvinoff's, Lossky's and Rosen's factories, most were crammed into the quarter's back streets; locksmiths, shoemakers, watchmakers, carpenters, tinsmiths and tailors lived and worked in a competitive jungle which slashed earnings to bare sub-sistence. Long, hard toil hopefully provided a herring and a slice of onion.

Not simply the age old tradition of charity as duty but more was at stake. Survival? yes! – and dignity? yes!

Each single kopeck dropped into the little collection boxes for all the various charities was somehow finally intended to maintain both. For the destitute, sick, handicapped, and ever their own – the refugees.

Each single kopeck extracted from their sweat and blood, for the fuel charity, houses of shelter for destitute vagrants, fund for poor students' clothes, kosher food for Jewish soldiers, medical treatment for the destitute, dowries for poor brides, education for orphans – all – all – a challenging response to the enemy who clearly now – had death in its sights.

Only now to realise so keenly how the age old giving ensured their survival.

The threat was clear enough – death by starvation. The challenge clear enough – to show themselves and God and the authorities just what the Jewish bond meant.

In spite of despair conflict arguments, the bond must be strengthened through duty and sacrifice.

We shall not be turned into starving beasts.

We must maintain the dignity of our brethren through this bond of charity, righteousness, as never before.

From whatever we have we must give.

These wretched beggars at every step, men, women and children searching, daily searching for food. No! Not beggars! We could be them too. Not beggars but victims of this cruel power. No fault of their own.

As a Jew, for one's own sake, we dare not allow them to fall into utter despair and degradation.

This dreadful blaming that they make things even worse for us – that too the enemy's devilish tricks.

And his power hangs over us all!

Our lives as much at stake as yours before the tyrant's whim.

No Jew is going to starve!

But how much should a man give! – till it hurt!

Pain of their pain – till it hurt – needed salve – salvation – for our survival.

Now shall we know what our duty means as Jews – above all to help one's fellow Jews with a joyful heart. No! not at all so easy this joyful heart.

There'll be no shortage of time for sorting this out.

They're here to stay.

Telling of what?

The thread of a slow dying intended for us all!

And that only the pain of maintaining this bond can prevent it.

For over one hundred years, since the Gaon Elijah's illustrious leadership, Vilna had been the great centre of Jewish religious study. The Rabbinical Academy was founded in 1847, fifty years after his death, as tribute and honour to the outstanding Talmudist of European Jewry, who strictly maintained the validity of every detail in the Torah. In 1873 Alexander II closed it down. Several small seminaries replaced it.

For Rabbis and students the unambiguous meaning of this new disaster demanded a renewed cleaving to the Law with all one's strength, from dawn to dusk, as a matter of life and death for the whole community. What else, of this magnitude, could it be but a sign from HaShem, the unutterable Name?

Rabbi Mendel's Seminary was a grimy, dilapidated building near the old fourteenth century synagogue. It housed himself, his wife Esther, and eighteen students. Up rickety stairs were two sparsely furnished dormitories, some small storerooms and the large, poorly lit, study room.

Daily life was strictly ordered. From 6 a.m. to 8 a.m. morning prayer with various supplications and meditations. From 8 to 8.30 a.m. breakfast, followed by five and a half hours of study. From 2 p.m. to 4 p.m. dinner and afternoon prayer followed by study till 9 p.m. Evening prayer and moral instruction followed, till 11 or 12 p.m. Nothing was allowed to interfere with this timetable.

Night and day they sat in the musty room at the long bare table strewn with worn Hebrew tomes. Resenting the hours of sleep they returned palefaced at dawn, to enter that world of infinite wisdom. Late each evening they withdrew from the presence of the opened tomes, sore-eyed, bent-backed, strangers to the fallen world about them. Often Rabbi Mendel, alone, studied through the night. Since youth his task had been clear. To study the Law, understand the Law, and live by the Law.

Those words in large print, centre of each page, the Godgiven text of Torah itself, dazzling in its primal glory, ever fertile source of true life. Pressing in on it, thickets of zealous progeny, in smaller and smaller print, commentary on commentary according to rank. Meaning. Meaning of meaning. Meaning of meaning of meaning till no interstice be left in this weaving flux of Torah and Talmud, Mishnah and Gemara - yet its miracle - that the newly present - even Vilna's now - demanded - and too be answered, in its particularity - progeny of this moment's meaning too - revelation granted if Hashem so blessed him.

Each vowel, each consonant, of those Holy Torah words in the centre was the threshold of a mystery. God's ever-living speaking with man. This text, in the world, yet ground of the world for he who devoted his whole soul and life to it. To this text our greatest sages had dedicated themselves in preparation for the Messiah and the final redemption of mankind, when all the nations would turn to the One true God of Israel.

For this task alone the waking hours of one lifetime were insufficient. Yet another task also called urgently. The constant interpretation of dangerous ideas to ensure that his students and the community kept their feet on the ground of the Law and were neither seduced nor corrupted. Such loose ignorant talk about so-called 'Zion' - a so-called 'Jewish working class' - so-called 'rational Judaism' - anything and everything except cleaving to the Law.

But this continuous anxiety of recent weeks - telling of what? Their barrenness - still! after all these years. Did he accept - didn't he? Still no one amongst his long-standing pupils after all these years, as a sure successor - Yehuda Liebman? He did accept - didn't he? Then what was this anxiety?

The roofing over one corner of the study room was beginning to gape open. The draught annoyed him as did the wet, dripping through. Esther kept prodding him about it but he did nothing. The funds for the Seminary from the community covered only the barest necessities. Nevertheless he knew the time had come when he would have to mention it to Chaim Litvinoff. Perhaps next Sabbath eve would be a time to sound him out, when he and a favoured student would be going to the Litvinoff mansion to celebrate the New Year.

In preparation for the New Year he would speak to his students on the opening verse of Genesis.

In the dawn light of Thursday morning he dressed quickly and uttered the prayer of awakening, "Blessed are You the Lord our God, King of the Universe who removes sleep from my eyes and slumber from my eyelids.." The hours since midnight had not been fruitful for that preparation. Instead a restlessness had prevailed, a foreboding which he could not overcome.

Quietly, not to wake Esther, he went to the study room and stood by his chair at the head of the table. The Torah lay open at the first page, left so the night before in joyful expectation. The first illustrated letter of the first word - opening word - beginning word - Berashis - branched, budded, flowered to shelter birds and beasts in its sweet shade.

He sat before it finely attuning to surrender, yield that familiar spaciousness within, that the sap of life from this, Torah's very first letter, B, stream through him. But this brittleness would not yield. The harder he struggled towards the text the more elusive

it became. In resignation he turned away to salvage some fragments whose vagueness, formlessness, experience had taught him
to let be, but which he now clutched at. Simply now to collect,
hold together these odd scraps and somehow shape them into a
theme of renewal.

They would not yield!

He gave up. Perhaps this afternoon when they all began to
read the text together, the Almighty would befriend, hear him
again. Perhaps the theme would take hold spontaneously as had
happened before.

Yehuda Liebman, usually first up, appeared in the study room.
He went to the other end of the table and began his morning
prayer. Glancing upwards he was held fast by a face grinning
through the enlarged gap in the roof. Rabbi Mendel had taught
that only the need to save life should stop one's prayer. Yehuda
jerked his head down, unfolded his praying shawl with leaden
arms, afraid, not daring to look again at it, wanting to call out.
Only with greatest effort did he make sound the words of the
prayer. But so thinly.

The man on the roof changed his position with a grating
movement.

Yehuda heard the Rabbi begin, "Hear O Israel, the Lord our
God, the Lord is One," and he followed in unison, to feel secure.
The skidding and sliding of a heavy body thumped across the
roof, followed by a desperate cry and a loud thud. Violent
cursing, shouting and hurrying footsteps broke out. Yehuda's
heart pounded. Rabbi Mendel never ceased for a moment from
the intensity of his prayer. Yehuda followed again as best he
could.

At the afternoon meal the affair was discussed by some of the
students who had heard the man fall down into the yard. Yehuda
said nothing. Not the incident alone but the hint of something
far more disturbing had left him uncertain and anxious.

Naphtali his closest friend was chosen to watch from the
Prayer house entrance for the evening star whose first appearance
marked the beginning of the festival. After the service in the
crowded synagogue the students gathered in the study room to
await the Rabbi. With joy he had felt that surging of a greater
reality towards the end of the synagogue service. Surging wave
of inspiration which he tenderly cherished on his way to them,
already speech of his being with them, overflowing, eager to

begin as he entered the study room.

"Yes, yes, the New Year, the New Year! For Nature never fails us. With what joy and relief we greet it. Ever changing and moving towards fulfilment in the light of God's laws. Seed, stem, leaf, flower, fruit and seed. Yes, with joy and relief. But with sadness and anxiety too. And why sadness, why anxiety? Because somewhere, my students, my friends, my brethren, somewhere in spite of all its tender beauty, its richness and strength, its most subtle power, this change of Nature, of mighty Nature, is no more than a dim image, pointing at, questioning, challenging – us. Yes Us! You and me. Sadness and anxiety because we cannot answer the challenge.

"Nature repeats. Mighty Nature repeats. There, is the sadness. Man – man alone – you and I – is called upon to renew. When man grows old and stale – that is Nature in him. When he renews, renews himself and all around him – that is the true power and essence of God. 'The Messiah will make all things new,'" he felt the words singing out, streaming forth from their communion.

"And how does man renew? How does man make a new beginning? How can man make a new beginning? Mystery of mysteries. Listen to that first verse. First last and only verse!

"In the beginning God created the heavens and the earth."

"Students, brethren, it is said of Rabbi Ezekiel that he never read beyond this sentence. In fourscore years this pillar of Israel never got beyond it. Not even to the end of it. No! It is said even that he never read beyond the first word – Berashis – in the beginning. It is said – he entered so deeply into that very first word – was consumed so fiercely by its life, that he experienced the whole world creation, its beginning and its end.

"God's words are mighty deeds. They are life – everlasting – inexhaustible. Berashis – this word is not about creation. It is the word of creation. Creation itself – the power and the spirit.

"God's words are sparks from the cosmic foundry congealed by his mercy to hover in the heaven of mind. Cling and cleave to these words – to this first verse like the great Ezekiel – till your yearning for succour and truth, the ground of Israel's strength, bursts out into triumphant light, warming the heart of all mankind.

"How then does man make a new beginning, create new worlds, transform life? By becoming nothing – a vessel for creation.

"The very first letter of the very first word, the B of Berashis – greatest mystery of all. The B. Into the sanctuary, the nothing, the holy place, goes man. Into the fecund nothing, the nothing surging with life. And the point arises – the dagesh – very centre of that sheltering enfoldment – centre of new life – point of yearning – expectant – raised to a new key in the world's harmony. This is Berashis!

"This is creation. This is blessing – and this is true prayer – Bera – Bora – Boruch.

"Why did God create the heavens and the earth? Love knows no why. Creation – this blessing – this prayer – this space – place – made ready for man – is a boundless love. And these – these deeds of love are the true beginnings. This is the mighty power of God and man. For is it not said, "Let us make man in our image and likeness.

"Yes – we too have this power of being smelted down and livingly recast. But we are the anvil – the hammer and the substance. Out of the flux and chaos – out of the fiery heat and light – we can do this.

"In the beginning – may the blessed Ezekiel's light be with us too – let us return each year and renew this beginning. Beginning, dear students, which should be the real life of each moment. For such is God's beginning, eternal and ceaselessly new. And we in His image must so strive. Still at the centre, yet ever new. Possibility – becoming – this is man.

"Let Us make him in Our image and likeness. Is it not said that Rabbi Gamaliel, a Father of Israel blessed be his name, jumped for joy and danced whenever he heard this. Who are we? What are we? Images! Images of His mercy, glory, power. Hear it! Feel it! See it!

"And tomorrow when you eat with our people, see in each of them an image of God. Dwell in that image. Whoever you are with, renew your vision. See all things living and aflame, ready to burst its bonds asunder and sing for joy at the glance of an upright man. My sons – open their prison gates and free them all for the New Year. For this have we been chosen. To be abroad. To shine with His Light amidst the darkness. This is Israel's responsibility and mission – world redemption."

Yehuda was painfully aware of his inability to enter worthily into his Rabbi's exaltation. He listened, he sang the hymn of praise, but at an uneasy distance.

"Let Us make man in Our image!" rang out the words. But the grin confronted them starkly. Each time Yehuda tried to resolve the tension between the words and the grinning, he became confused. Each time the wordless question, so urgent, turned unreal.

Aaron Liebman struggled with the riddle of his I. At one moment a question. The next, chaos. Something vast beckoning, challenging, that withdrew whenever he seemed within striking distance. Something hovering each time he set out. In the light of his Rabbi's words, "Let Us make man in Our image," this something seemed immeasurably closer, all about him. He knew he must make a move. But still not what move to make.

Around midnight he left his bed, dressed and went quietly to the study room. Rabbi Mendel was there sitting, still undecided about taking Yehuda with him to the Litvinoffs'. Esther's involvement, her anger so unusual, would not leave him.

"Yehuda! at a time like this? You know there'll be trouble. Naphtali - of course! But Yehuda? - a fanatic! And you know it."

"That's not a reason for choosing Naphtali."

"How can you? Our needs come first - and a new roof before the whole place falls round our head."

"Esther - in this matter I must be left free. My decision is not going to be influenced by - by -"

By what? - needs? - roof? - Litvinoff? - A fanatic! no! - essentially a true witness! - so clear now?

"Free - free - since when are you free -" she left the room, very upset.

He tried to become clearer about his ambiguity and uncertainty but became entangled. He decided to go ahead with it and risk -yes a necessary absolutely necessary exposure of this.

When Aaron appeared in the study room he felt tired and irritable. He struggled for a measure of patience before Aaron's diffident yet earnest presence.

"Rabbi, I'm sorry to disturb you but it's a matter of life and death."

"What is it Aaron?"

"Please don't laugh - don't be annoyed. But that's just it. I don't know what it is. Now I'm here with you it all seems nonsense. But when I'm alone - when I move in a certain direction - or when I'm moved in a certain direction - the difference isn't very clear – then I don't know who or what I am any more."

"Aaron be assured. Our sages have left no questions unanswered. Didn't the great Gamaliel, blessed be his name, tell us that the very questions are from God Himself – His gift – yes gift to the searching soul," answered Rabbi Mendel, called, listening.

"But Rabbi," Aaron went on, encouraged, "This very question of questions – the one which keeps looming up in front of me – is just the one I can't put. That in fact seems to be its essential nature. There it beckons – I set out towards it on an easy path – and in a moment I find myself dazzled – bewildered – struck dumb."

He paused in concentration.

"Rabbi can you tell me why we feel – I don't know – so uneasy – yes uneasy – I mean in the very depths? Tonight when you spoke of the image I glimpsed a clarity – something – somewhere. But it all remains vague – beyond me. And now you see – I feel again that it all sounds nonsense."

"On the contrary Aaron – your questions teach me as much as they teach you. The image! The image! Yes! Yes! You see – into us, the image, He has poured and breathed Himself in love. So we say 'I' – 'I' – but so faintly, feebly, elusively – always aware of this strange gap– Aaron we stammer 'I' but somewhere within is the real one – Adam Kadmon – Man! The real one – from eternity – yet only becoming. A great mystery! We have to create him from ourselves. There from eternity but become sundered – disunited. We must reunite him from out of ourselves. That's why we call one another by different names – but ourselves we call by the same name – I. Because we know that the inmost self of all is the same – the One – the I. "I am the I-am," He said in His blessed mercy to his great servant. The voice of the Highest who alone can say I and be I."

In the silence that followed Rabbi Mendel prompted Aaron.

"There's something else Aaron?"

"Where is God?" Aaron blurted out.

"Where is God not? What is not God? To what can man say mine?"

"Aaron it's very late. Think on these things. Don't hesitate to come to me. We're both students," he held Aaron's hand warmly, gratefully aware of being newly restored to himself.

In the morning he informed them all of the particular families with whom they would be sharing the customary New Year's meal. Yehuda would be accompanying him to Chaim Litvinoff, wealthy president of the community who lived on the outskirts of Vilna. Most of them would be going to poor families, a few to the fairly well off.

"Remember then – the rich man is different only by this, that he has a far greater responsibility to the community than the poor man. But his riches can be a barrier. So it is with the poor man. His poverty – bitterness – misery can also be a barrier. With a warm and understanding heart – learn to see in both the spark, the image, yes, the image of God."

At six o'clock Rabbi Mendel and Yehuda left the Seminary in their long black coats, flat plush hats and top boots. The air was almost freezing, beneath a hard blue sky. Outside the high walls of the Litvinoff factory a carriage was waiting. A short elderly coachman was whacking his sides and stamping his feet. As Rabbi Mendel approached he stood aside and opened the door.

"Good evening," said the Rabbi stepping in.

The coachman smiled obsequiously and lowered his head.

Yehuda saw the smile hovering on the edge of a grin.

"Come on Yehuda," urged the Rabbi.

At the Litvinoff mansion they were welcomed by a robust man of authority and charm, with the respect, deference, which he considered the Rabbi's due. Chaim Litvinoff's wife and children all greeted him with much respect, pleasure, a gaiety at the way his presence so customarily completed the festive evening.

Rabbi Mendel began the prayers and blessings, everyone standing at their place by the laden table before the great log fire, beneath the shimmering candelabras. Yehuda, feeling an unpleasant constraint, kept carefully to himself. After Rabbi Mendel had made the blessing over the wine, and offered the prayer for the gift of life, Miriam, the lively, eldest daughter, fervent supporter and activist for the Lovers of Zion movement quickly took the measure of Rabbi Mendel's much too standoffish student.

"Rabbi we've had wonderful news – just this week from Mani in Jerusalem. A real New Year's greeting for all us Jews still here – don't you think?"

Litvinoff and his wife knew that look and tone of hers.

Rabbi Mendel listened, expectantly.

"Mani reckons over fourteen thousand Russian Jews – our very own people – have now settled in Palestine. Rabbi could this be the beginning of the end of the Exile?"

"Never! Never!" shouted Yehuda, "gravest error – on whom judgement will fall. Where? – Where? In the Holy writings does God through his servants say that we, by ourselves, arbitrarily, from our own paltry human intelligence are to decide when and how to return to the Holy Land. Nowhere! We must continue as we are until He reveals to us all that is necessary in this matter. Until He appoints the Messiah, the Chosen One, to lead us back. That is the Promise – the divine Promise. Nothing but misfortune can come from this present madness. Lovers of Zion indeed! Auto-emancipation indeed! Pride and vanity. Our task is to carry out the Law – cleave to Him night and day as our respected teacher does. We are nothing. Only the Law makes us something –"

On and on he rushed.

He'd taken the bait.

The children were smiling, smirking. Litvinoff was smiling though becoming impatient for this harangue to stop. Rabbi Mendel lowered his head, stroked his beard, deeply embarrassed and guilty. Yes! this whole violent exposure, his crisis of conscience. Compelled to bring Yehuda just here just now for this very reason.

Yehuda's zeal for the Lord to be witnessed – the burden of his own compromise be burned into him. No escape allowed now – pleased at Litvinoff's annoyance! – The compromises forced into on behalf of the community – how selfish his customary enjoyment of Litvinoff's abundance – taken as his due! Be grateful to Yehuda for these insights. Strengthen him in his discomfort!

".. Not through Eretz Yisrael but through Torah alone we've survived 2,000 years – No!" Yehuda shouted,

"No! – Jews without Torah disappear in a few years. Eretz Yisrael is important for Jews but without Torah there won't be any Jews. Without Torah we are vulnerable – helpless – with Torah we are the most powerful in the world! This is a fact! proven by our three thousand years of history – –"

"Enough! Enough!" Litvinoff interrupted angrily. But Yehuda

would have his last word, "The greater our persecution – the greater our salvation!"

"Enough! I insist!" shouted Litvinoff staring severely at Rabbi Mendel, "We're here to celebrate the New Year."

Miriam was upset at the way it had gone, watching her father's powerful hand tightening on his chair arm, afraid that he would resort to physical restraint. She quickly dipped her apple in the pot of honey and began the prayer, "May it be your desire, God of our ancestors, to renew for us a sweet and good year – –"

The family quickly followed her solution pretending that Yehuda wasn't there.

Yehuda, his forehead sweating, felt very tense, trapped. He made a jerky move which knocked a plate from the hand of a servant standing right behind him. The servant bent down for the broken pieces. Litvinoff called out angrily "Fool!" Yehuda fumbled about on the carpet to help the servant.

"How shall the mighty fall

And the humble be raised," Yehuda quoted back loudly from below.

Litvinoff was incensed. The dining room door opened noisily and a dapper youngish man hurried in. He bowed gracefully.

"Greetings to you all," he said smiling charmingly. He turned to Litvinoff, "Forgive me! But I must beg your presence on an urgent matter."

"My dear Saul!" Litvinoff hurried from his chair, surprised and relieved. After a quick embrace he led his friend up to his study. He poured out two large tumblers of brandy whilst Saul Kaplan took off his fur coat.

"Chaim, be prepared – I've bad news for you."

Litvinoff kept still and listened intently.

"Neubergers have collapsed. I've come straight from Vienna. One or two managed to pull out in time – but you, and the rest here, haven't a chance."

Litvinoff gripped his jaw tightly.

"Even that's not all for you. In Hamburg I discovered that Kreitman your German agent has been defrauding. In fact he's in with the English manufacturers. Don't be surprised if your whole German market dries up in a month or two."

Litvinoff paced slowly up and down, hands behind back.

"You still think God's interested in business?" Kaplan questioned lightly to ease the silence.

"They're both important," Litvinoff answered eventually, with irritation.

"You still need the Rabbi at your table then – to make you feel comfortable?" ventured Kaplan, further.

"I've nothing to be ashamed of."

"Well – I've said it before and I'll say it again. You're too sentimental. Give God his due – by all means. But watch your business. For me sentiments are a luxury. Take my advice. Close the factory for a few weeks. I'll try and get you into the American market – and sort out the Kreitman affair if you're agreeable. I know someone in Hamburg who'd be very happy to put Kreitman in his place."

"Close the factory? – Then they'll all starve here."

"The market isn't all that concerned with the feeding problems of Vilna workers. Not with charitable institutions. If you don't trim your sails soon the lot could go. You know what happened to Dubrovsky – overnight! But what's the good. You'll also perhaps have to learn the hard way – like I did. Only one thing – in the old days you weren't so concerned with the likes of those downstairs."

"Alright! Alright!" interrupted Litvinoff, "we've reached this point enough times. There's nothing more to be said. I still consider myself a Jew. And these are Jewish people!"

"Nothing personal please!" cut in Kaplan, flushing, "Consider yourself what you like. I consider myself a realist. A person who has learned most of the rules and plays the game accordingly. God – sentiment – parasites – even learned parasites – don't fit into my game at all. For me it's hard against hard. That's why I warned you months ago to leave Neubergers – in spite of the old man's title and decorations. Well, I must press on – but don't forget what I said about Kreitman and the American market. I'll be back in Hamburg in about four weeks and you can write to me there."

Litvinoff returned to his study in growing unease as the reality of Saul's news dawned on him. The meal – family – Rabbi – young fanatic – another world to which he had no desire to return. For long he stared vaguely at a sheet of figures on his desk. A gentle knock sounded on the door and Rabbi Mendel entered aware that something very important had been involved between the two business men.

"Well Rabbi what can I do for you?" he questioned brusquely

in quickly changing mood.

The tone immediately warned Rabbi Mendel of the price to be paid for Yehuda's presence.

"Well Chaim–," he began hesitantly, upset by Litvinoff's stance, "the Seminary roof is breaking up – a gang of ruffians is pulling it apart – we can barely feed the students – – we must have some help for the roof – – of course I realise – –"

"Rabbi I don't know what world you live in!"

"World? – how many worlds are there Chaim? I know only of many viewpoints – – I – –"

"Good! Good! And I'll tell you my viewpoint. From a world of humiliation and degradation I've raised myself up. That world – you're right – which always has been and always will be. The world which neither you nor anyone else will change. From that world – with my own brains – energy – willpower. And now you see I'm in a position to help my brethren – fellow Jews. To give them work! To speak up on their behalf. I'm taken notice of Rabbi – serious notice! by the authorities – by our rulers. D'you see all that? So! I don't want any upstarts and fanatics sitting at my table – whether they come from the Seminary or Paradise itself."

He thumped the table. Rabbi Mendel sat quietly, resigned to the harangue.

"The Seminary needs a roof – ruffians are breaking in – more food is needed – more work is needed – of course you're right, there's only one world – a very hard one! Either you fight or go under. I fought – I alone – I have made myself what I am – and now I'm taken notice of – speak for my people – not shoved into the gutter by any Goy lout who cares to – like you and the rest. So! I don't want that damned fanatic of yours in my house again ever. Fanatics like him will destroy us all. It's common sense we need. That's up to you – isn't it? The Seminary is responsible to the community. It's there for the sake of the community. Not at all intended to become a breeding ground for fanatics. Well enough of that! I'm sure I've made myself clear. And as for the roof there's nothing available whatsoever. Repair it yourselves! As best you can. As things are I may even have to close the factory down for some time."

Rabbi Mendel accepted the attack as retribution for his continued failure – cowardice? – to clarify his relationship with Litvinoff. Late that evening he glimpsed unsuspected depths to the conflict, an uneasy feeling of having somehow betrayed Yehuda. And behind the betrayal – fear. A real enough fear of Yehuda's readiness to stake his life on the Torah, in the certainty that it was absolute truth!

The news of Yehuda's tirade was soon circulating. He was condemned as an arrogant fool and blamed for Litvinoff's hardened attitude to the students and their needs. Rumours were spreading about the possibility of the factory being closed down. Yehuda became a scapegoat for the helplessness and despair never far below the surface. In the Seminary antipathy grew towards him.

Yehuda regarded the evening as a battle fought and won. Amidst strong opposition, even mockery – yes he knew it – he had testified to the Law. Naphtali, his closest friend, broached the subject.

"Is it really necessary to antagonise people? Doesn't that turn them further away from the truth?" he inquired cautiously.

"On the contrary, the truth is mean to upset us – make us unhappy, shake us out of our selfishness," Yehuda insisted.

"But what's more important the truth or the person?"

"No truth – no person! no real person!"

"Yehuda, are you sure you don't get pleasure – selfish pleasure, from your way with the truth?"

"Naphtali, you can think what you like. For me the truth is fire. A destroyer. A destroyer of what's rotten. I'm not going to pat Litvinoff's head or anyone else's. I don't believe in talking about the severity of the Law and leaving certain privileged people to carry on just as they are."

The hole in the roof had reached alarming proportions, but Rabbi Mendel never referred to it. The intimate refuge and security of the Study Room was being torn apart. Shimon and his fellow students found it unbearable. After four men had been seen on the roof late one night, and something ugly was clearly being prepared, they decided to take their own action. The harassment was increased with grinning faces staring through at unexpected moments, calculated to unnerve them. Bits of tiling were heard clattering down into the yard. Still Rabbi Mendel kept silent.

One morning, two weeks after New Year's day, whilst they were waiting quietly for the Rabbi to come and expound on the expulsion from Eden, the familiar grating sound was heard on the roof. Tensely they listened. Shimon watched the sneering face, hand – glint of blade! Grabbing a heavy tome good Rashi! –he shot up from his seat and hurled it with all his might. The knife fell to the floor. A wild cry, of rage and fear rang out. No one dared move. Yehuda went over to pick up the knife. He set it down carefully amidst all the books.

"That is not the way," he said looking sternly at Shimon.

Shimon was infuriated by his certainty.

"Faith in the Almighty is more powerful than that," Yehuda continued pointing to the knife, "Don't you know what it says? Vengeance is Mine, saith the Lord. His! Not ours."

Shimon trembled with rage.

"So! The Messiah's at it again," he sneered, "You stupid lunatic! Are we staying cowards all our lives? We were warriors till the Temple fell. Not cowards, to shiver in fear while they spat on us and killed us."

"Those wars were led by the Almighty, blessed be his Holy Name – that Israel do His will. Baba Mezi'a – Baba Mezi'a! If two men claim your help and one is your enemy, help that one first. If you know your enemy's coming to kill you – kill you! it says – nevertheless prepare food and drink for him," countered Yehuda unperturbed.

Rabbi Mendel who had been listening outside the door, came in, took his seat and began immediately.

"You see, Adam broke his covenant with God and disunity began. The primal unity of Creation and Creator was shattered. The Shekinah, the Divine Presence amongst Mankind, was exiled. This was the price for Adam tasting good and evil. And since that very moment in time, which is now – for all men the task has been one and one only – now knowing good and evil, to re-bind creation to God, to redeem the fallen world. To help create a new world. To prepare for the Kingdom which the Messiah, blessed be He, will usher in.

"But", he continued, glancing at the knife on the table, "answering evil with evil is not creating unity.

"In the Commandments – God's very own words – and in the words of our sages, the way has been clearly shown to regain the lost unity. The true unity. Because there are false unities, just as there are false kingdoms and false Messiahs.

"Assimilation is certainly not the true unity. That is the abyss. Nor will the kingdom which we must prepare for the Messiah be some other world. But this very earth, here and now, transformed. The eternal now become the eternal new. The eternal here become a bower for his presence.

"We Israel, the partners, the builders chosen to establish it with Him. And the Messiah will be of flesh and blood, a great leader, as a clear sign that the Kingdom has begun. Meanwhile whatever is done in the Almighty's Name and for His Glory, is a preparation.

"Of false Messiahs we have often spoken. There was the one called Jesus – pure yet most dangerous. In his teachings the nation, Israel, our very substance, is destroyed. Utterly destroyed. Nor is there anything in his teachings which is not in the Torah. And though he is called the Prince of Peace, he cursed mankind. And his seeds for the future were seeds of hatred, violence, and war."

"But Rabbi how long, how long have we to wait? Two thousand years – almost two thousand years have passed since the Temple was destroyed. Countless generations have been spat on, humiliated, butchered. Must we do nothing for ourselves? Not move a finger in self-defence?" insisted Shimon bitterly.

"The Law is our self-defence."

"What? when God Himself destroyed utterly destroyed the Egyptians in the Red Sea?"

"God's deeds are not man's deeds."

"What? when Moses himself killed the Egyptian?"

"Not even Moses, the blessed servant of God, was perfect. No! Our task is to hallow, to make holy, to redeem the daily life. To overcome the disunity, the separation, the fall. For this, man is called the Crown. The Crown of the King. But to do this we must follow the Law, the word of God. And into every aspect of daily life we must make a place for that word to pour. Only thus can we help raise up the fallen. And this – this recreation of man and world is what the Torah means by love."

"Rabbi! Rabbi! come quickly," shouted Esther flinging open the door of the study room and hurrying down into the courtyard with her husband close behind.

A small crowd, many of whom he recognised, were watching with curiosity at a respectful distance from two blue-uniformed officials and two policemen. Approaching he became aware of the still body on the ground.

"Well? What d'you know about this?" the taller official asked him brusquely, waving a notebook in the direction of the body.

"Very little," answered Rabbi Mendel slowly, looking calmly into the official's eyes.

"Indeed?" said the official doubtfully, rubbing his lower lip, frowning.

"Rabbi! Rabbi! I insist! I saw it all. I insist! I was a witness to the Almighty's power and protection, "shouted a voice excitedly from the crowd.

"Shut up Jew!" ordered the shorter official, staring fiercely at the crowd, "Speak only when you're asked."

"Is this man a dependable witness?" asked the taller official, "Remember," he stabbed an accusing finger, "you'll be responsible for his evidence. Any lies from you Jews will be dealt with accordingly."

"The man is perfectly reliable," declared Rabbi Mendel, "Vitebsky - the grocer."

"Jew! Come forward! Speak!" commanded the shorter official.

Vitebsky hurried to them, outstretched hands gesticulating in warmest greeting.

"Well? What happened?" demanded the taller official drawing back his head and narrowing his eyes disdainfully before this wretched, skull-capped bony head and waving ragged beard.

"Ah sir! What happened? I, a reliable man, a perfectly reliable man will recount to you sir. I stood by my shop door. I do, this time every morning to offer up my prayers - my humble prayers sir - to the Almighty blessed be -,"Vitebsky began excitedly.

"Come on Jew - to the point!"

"As I say, a reliable man your honour, offering up my prayers and looking at the roof of our Seminary as I always do because there -"

"Idiot! Come on! What did you see?"

"See - yes indeed. I saw a man crawling up that roof like a great spider towards that dreadful hole. Nearer and nearer he gets, my heart beats faster and faster - he grabs the hole - all closed up over it - and then, why, believe me sir - this spider is rolling down the roof faster and faster screaming - crash! Impossible to understand such miracles. Thus did the Almighty in -" he turned to the crowd.

"Shut up!" shouted the taller official grabbing Vitebsky's shoulder and violently shoving him away towards the crowd.

"Enough about your damn God!"

A horse and cart appeared at the courtyard entrance.

"He got what was coming to him," called a voice.

The police ordered three Jews to pick up the body which they then heaved straight into the cart. Rabbi Mendel addressed the crowd who were watching with satisfaction.

"Brethren bind your soul to his - or this hell will never end. Let us make life out of his death. Otherwise this vessel of God's highest creation has been utterly wasted."

"Nonsense! This man came to kill us and you know it. God has punished him! D'you know better then?" challenged the voice.

"Jews! disperse!" ordered the police as the horse and cart moved slowly away.

The officials left, annoyed by the dead man's stupidity, crude way of doing it.

On the first Friday evening in April after Passover had ended, Yehuda hurried along Ostrovski Street to celebrate Sabbath eve with the Bruskin family. The street ran near the Litvinoff factory where most of its inhabitants worked for up to fifteen hours a day. Each room of the grey blocks sheltered at least one family.

Ignatiev's May Laws had forced Jacob Bruskin, a cobbler, to leave Yonava village, to the northwest, with his wife and daughter. He hated the factory work but was grateful to earn his bread and have a roof over their heads in these dark days. His faith had not been shaken. Every Saturday afternoon he participated in the Talmudic discussions at Rabbi Mendel's Seminary.

Underfoot the slush was freezing into crunching ruts and glassy surfaces. Yehuda swept on with the Talmudic problem which he would expound tomorrow, and the questions which he would put to the Rabbi. On along swift currents of inspiration he gloried in God's greatness - the plagues - the miracle of the Red Sea - the Promised Land - borne - right along into the rousing words which he would speak to the Bruskin family after the meal was finished. Words for the humble, faithful, hardworking children of Israel.

But falling, in a flash, thrown down onto the icy ground with a sickening thud, back wrenched. Momentarily paralysed he stared up at the sparkling diamonds of the blue-black sea so close. Vile cursing forced him painfully to his feet. Shaking his head to check a threatening faintness, concentrating hard, he realised that he had passed the Bruskin's building. Slapping and shaking out his gabardine he turned back. The three men who had been following, ringed him, smirking. Hurrying behind his very swift strides and trying to mimic them, they had barely managed to keep their balance. Now as Yehuda advanced one tried to trip him. Failing, he shoved Yehuda in the back.

"Into the gutter Yid!"

"Leave him! - let's get down to the inn - some fun there tonight."

After spitting at him they hurried away. Yehuda made his way back carefully to the Bruskin's entrance, sore from the fall but knowing it all as one continuous sign, of course painful - of the captivity - the price which all Israel must pay for its backsliding - continuous sign - be roused - be joyful! that God's loving care - God's endless patience - how long O Israel - was real enough.

The ignorant offspring of Ham, very instrument of God's chastisement.

He climbed the dark, dilapidated stairway to the Bruskin's room on the second floor. Leah Bruskin, a small, worn, yet bright-eyed woman warmly welcomed him in. One part of the room was curtained off for sleeping quarters. In the other was a small stove, and a table laid, with the Sabbath candles burning, and delicacies, nuts, raisins, Halva, especially come by for this visit from the fearless Seminary student. The student whom Jacob and many others supported in his stand for God's word. His behaviour on that evening was not at all fanaticism and they let it be known by their invitation for him to grace their table.

Leah pointed to the basin, for the ritual hand washing before meals. Though tired from recent nights of restless anxiety and the nasty pain in her chest, she had made a great effort to have the room clean and orderly for him. A saucepan of beetroot soup was on the stove. She stirred it from time to time. Yehuda studied the Sayings of the Fathers, not a moment of God's precious time to be wasted.

"I'm sure they won't be long now. But you see - even our own Jewish factories, our very own people, won't let them home early on Shabbes eve," she ventured anxiously, trying to excuse Jacob's and Ruth's lateness.

"So it is," answered Yehuda, nodding seriously, "Men give less and less time to God. But your husband is an upright man. A man fearing the Lord. With such as him Israel will never falter until such time as the Almighty, blessed be his name, shall lead us from our present captivity. Then no more shall we say each Passover, 'Next year in Jerusalem'. For then we shall be there." His voice rose enthusiastically as he warmed to his theme but Leah went close to the door, hearing some commotion below. She left the room and went down a few steps to listen. In the entrance hall they were talking excitedly. Lightly falling snow was blowing in.

"Why aren't they back from the factory yet?" she called down anxiously.

"Don't you know? They've had a fight there."

"When are they coming back?" she asked again, not understanding, descending to the top of the first flight.

"It's that bastard Aleinikoff I'd like to get my hands on!"

"Every day another one!"

A thin sharp-featured youth pushed his way in, wild eyed, dripping.

"The gangs are out!" he panted desperately.

All talking stopped.

Levi Genz a squat, balding man in leather jerkin and muffler, who lived on the ground floor, gripped the youth's shoulder and stared into his anxious eyes.

"One of your jokes Moshe? – I'll flay you alive if it is."

"I'm telling you!" the youth screamed out struggling against that grip.

"Alright – alright," shouted Genz, releasing his hold, "then get on with it – quickly!"

"I saw them outside the inn– twenty at least – poles – torches – clubs – Yids out! – Yids out!"

A sharp eyed elderly man, with a dry cough, moved cautiously to the street entrance. He peered out, left and right.

"I don't like it. And there's a red glow somewhere – Levin's warehouse," he said in a low voice, stepping back inside.

"Of course!" said Moshe, "didn't you know? There's a fire near the Ostrovsky Bridge."

"That's the Lossky factory!"

"Exactly – a lovely one to blame on the Jews – the Governor's just waiting to call the Cossacks in," said Genz.

He swung round and briskly steered Moshe to the entrance.

"As fast as you can down the street and warn everyone. Don't miss an entrance. David! Yitzhak! Schneour! Everybody! tables

– chairs – whatever – get this entrance blocked! – all the children upstairs!"

Before they could fling themselves into action and check the threatening panic, Leah, now downstairs with them, cried out, "My Jacob and Ruth aren't home yet. You can't shut them out!"

"Rubbish! there are ten families here," shouted Rebecca.

"Wait!" ordered Genz as footsteps were heard along the street, laboured steps that seemed on the point of stopping at any moment. Sharp cooking knives appeared. Leah pushed her way through, glanced at the approaching one and ran towards him shouting "Yakov! Yakov!" But the broad shouldered, bald headed man whose grimy forehead was bloodied, plodded on, distant, alone. His head was bowed, his jaw clamped tight against the pain and the sickness. She hovered around him hysterically and they came in together.

"Look! Look! They've started on him already. Almighty God! Jews! Jews! The Sabbath eve!" she shouted, trying to make a way for him. The others were unmoved.

"He had it coming," sneered Schneour.

"Boss's man!"

"Are you mad?" screamed Leah, bewildered.

"Shut up you screaming idiot!" threatened Schneour raising a fist, "He got that in the factory – today!"

"Come on everyone! To work!" ordered Genz.

Jacob and Leah were pushed roughly aside as the barricading began.

When they entered their room Yehuda put down the prayer book and stood up. He knew what was happening but was determined to keep calm and preserve Sabbath sanctity Sabbath peace. Jacob slumped into a chair and shut his eyes. Leah began fussing. Jacob spoke painfully, threateningly through gritted teeth, clenching his fists with the effort.

"For God's sake shut up! Stop your whining. I've had enough. Enough!"

They kept silent. Jacob blinked open his eyes at Yehuda. From downstairs sounded hammering, heavy things being pulled about and orders given.

"Well! d'you know what it means?" he suddenly challenged with a bitterness, aggressiveness which badly confused Yehuda. Yet – it was more to himself that he was speaking.

"It means a generation of vipers – blasphemers. Fools! Fools!

Don't they realise what they're doing? And d'you know what's the most terrible thing?" he seemed to be challenging Yehuda again, "It's when your own turn against you, attack you. That's when you know that Satan has won."

"But Yakov – my Yakov – why did they fight? Why did they attack you?" whispered Leah fearfully.

"Because they're mad. Mad! And they'll destroy themselves and us too. And that's the price of transgressing the Law, of living without the Law. Of putting God's word to one side. It'll kill us. But wait – that's nothing", he jabbed at his scarred forehead, "a bang on the head – a trifle. But when I realised that she – my own flesh and blood was over there, shouting their nonsense – and that she could see, yes see me – then I went sick and dead inside."

He shut his eyes and let his head fall on his chest, breathing heavily.

"Honour thy father and mother eh? It's all nonsense utter nonsense," he flung out.

"Yakov Yakov," soothed Leah hysterically, "let me bathe your head. As soon as Ruth comes in we can begin prayers with the Almighty's blessing."

At her mention of prayer Yehuda found his bearings and prepared himself. Jacob stood up trembling, forced to hold on to the chair. He stared at Leah for a long while, through some mist, till her lips began twitching on the verge of a scream.

"Roooth!" he sounded the word slowly, bitterly.

"Who is Ruth?" he asked.

"Come! Come!" he broke through it, shaking his head and stamping on the floor. "We shall continue to serve the Almighty, blessed be His Name – come what may! Leah pour out the wine! Yehuda Liebman who so honours our humble table, please say the Kaddish."

Leah poured out the wine with trembling hands. The fear that Ruth would be cut off, unable to get into the building, was making her distraught. She wanted to speak about it but dared not. Jacob was so strange. All her normal reactions and words seemed dangerous. She tried frantically to think up some story which would take her downstairs. She felt that Jacob had been profoundly upset but the actuality of the situation eluded her. Dread and confusion dissolved into a dull paralysis, some release.

Jacob rinsed a handful of water over his face, scoured his palms against each other, dried, and followed them to the table. Voices from below were raised angrily in argument as Yehuda began the blessing. He strove to bind them heavenwards. Hurried footsteps sounded on the stairs. The door was opened and a dishevelled young woman, mouth set tight, strode stiffly through to the curtained side. She moved with a nervous violence, purposefully, thrusting the curtain aside, bundling up some clothes. Yehuda felt compelled to watch her. His prayer had almost petered out. Jacob forced himself not to look at her.

"Please Yehuda Liebman! the Almighty is not to be interrupted," he demanded.

As she tied her things up Ruth knew a burning guilt and shame which she strove to beat back. Her fury and violence would have blotted everything out including the guilt and shame. How often in the past had she imagined this situation and the impossibility of going through with it. But now, out of the blind sweep of something beyond herself it was happening, in spite of the pain. As she tightened the string she swiftly rehearsed her exit, only wanting to feel their presence dimly. Not at all to confront this one or that one, him or her. Yet she wanted to speak. But not to see them. Yet she would have longed so much to speak gently to them. To be understood. To be known by them.

She strode out unseeing towards the door where a young man waited quietly outside. Leah jumped up from her chair to touch, to hold that sad stranger fast vanishing. The burning candles fell to the floor but she thrust on wildly, to save.

The men fumbled about to save the candles, to restore them reverently. Ruth, clutched at by her mother, pale and tearful, watched the men with contempt. Jacob, up on his feet, was furious.

"Blasphemy – blasphemer!" he shouted.

"It's not good, not good," said Yehuda, shocked by this sign.

"It's come to this – that my own daughter attacks me with a gang of hooligans. That my own daughter turns on the hand that feeds us and spits on the Holy Name. Well – good! Yes good I say! Isn't this a proof that the Messiah must come soon," he challenged Yehuda.

"Rubbish! Utter rubbish!" called Ruth from the doorway. "There's nothing personal about any of this. Can't you understand?"

"But – my child my daughter – eat eat – this nonsense – forget – Reb Yehuda is here – Reb Yehuda has come here – respect him – of course don't respect us – not your father – not me – but Reb Yehuda respect – God respect!" stammered Leah.

Amidst the haze, violence, hysteria, Ruth stared at him, that third one, focussing with a savage strength the urgent desire to connect, perhaps finally but to connect.

"So-o-oh – that's who he is!"

Her voice was pitched high in feigned surprise as she screwed up her eyes to stare through him but never at or near them.

"Little Reb Yehuda – fancy! Did you hear that Joel? Reb Yehuda is here! – So! That's Reb Yehuda! And from this parasite with his greasy sidelocks you want respect from me? – While he mutters that drivel all day long – and we're expected to come back from Litvinoff's prison – dear – our dear respected Chaim Litvinoff's own special prison – and respect him? You fools – both of you – utter fools!"

She had dropped her bundle and stood white faced, furious.

"Almighty God what evil have we done to deserve this," Leah sobbed.

"Get out out! – and never come back," ordered Jacob, staring at the floor.

"I will I will, once and for all – but not until I've finished. Not until you've heard – once and for all. Especially this clown with his little cap. He's your real child not me. Holy? I'll tell you what's holy. Truth – reality – and there it is," she bent slightly and slapped her buttock, "which Aleinikoff touches up whenever it pleases him. No! – not this god and messiah lie which lets this parasite lord it over you. You believe that your god is everything. We! believe that man is everything. For you only Israel's glorious past is real – for us – only Litvinoff's prison is real. Of course the old ones dream like you. Their illusions are your illusions. Beloved father Chaim does best of all out of your illusions – he thoroughly enjoys returning the fruit of your sweat as charity.

"Listen you ancient mummy – at Lossky's a boy of fourteen had his head bashed by the foreman's fist and nobody dared stop him. D'you think your quotations from Hillel are going to help him? D'you think your stupid god will stop other youngsters having their heads bashed or women having to take their drawers down for the foreman? This is our present slavery! These are our present taskmasters! Don't you dare presume to preach to us till you stand where we stand. In the midst of the evil under the taskmaster with his fine book and his pinching fingers - behold it was good eh? - if you stopped wailing over that petrified rubbish you might notice there's nothing good about any of it. We think its bad - very bad - only we don't blame it on Satan - we blame it on men! Men - are the slave drivers - exploiters - murderers. And we Jews aren't being oppressed for our holiness. That's a lie which suits your lousy Rabbi Mendel. Punishing the Jews suits the Tsar - nobility - bureaucracy - and it's never been any different."

"Ruth we must go!" called Joel.

She had never intended to go on for so long. Both men had kept perfectly still with their backs to her. Leah sat in her chair bewildered, blinking her wet eyes. After looking at each of them in turn, especially Yehuda, she hurried out and down the stairs with Joel. They left the building by the backyard and along a maze of alleyways.

They stood by the canal's scummy waters in the moonlight.

"What a strange business - me speaking like that - as though they could understand a word of it. It was that idiot from the Seminary made me. I felt furious pity for him - strange!"

"You spoke well Ruth," said Joel cautiously. He knew how much the break had cost her and how gently he must proceed.

"Ruth I can tell you a little more - Kremer - Alexander Kremer is going to speak to our group tonight."

They walked quickly along the canal bank, past the pauper burial ground, and the Lossky tannery, to reach Znamenka Street on the west side. A wealthy young man had given over the top floor of his apartment house to the young people working with the new ideas. Other workers from Litvinoff's who'd been involved in the fight made their way there.

At the Bruskin's the Sabbath meal was eaten as calmly as possible, by each in a knowing unity, eaten slowly, deliberately, the men to acknowledge Leah's heartfelt devotion to the Sabbath's sanctity through her cooking, above all, act of some desperate necessity to restore, recreate some sort of sanity.

They finished sipping their glass of tea, a calm, a victory, a wonder. What! they were to stand firm - through daughter Ruth the attack had come, closest, closest, most taken for granted - through daughter Ruth their resistance would gather.

Jacob talked and muttered, half to himself as though in answer and justification.

"They should talk to Lossky's people - to Rosen's people. They'd soon find out how well off they are. Fools! What can he do if the market's bad? Don't they know? Rich and poor there must always be! No one can change it. Anyway what do they know? Drink and bed Do they keep up their religion? Don't they know they'll starve if he closes the factory?"

Yehuda nodded in sympathy though uneasy. During Ruth's harangue he had felt strengthened and confident. Her words were so alien, almost senseless, like any blasphemer. Yet soon after she left, in the difficult silence at the table, subtly, from that power, fire, integrity, the world about him was blurring, loosening. Certain words - ideas of hers - kept returning which he knew he would have to come to terms with. Kept returning with a life-powerful life of their own, to exert a fascination, to intensify that looseness, uncertainty. Intensify till he felt his inmost grip shaken, himself in danger.

Touched at an unknown quick of himself he longed to be up and away. While Jacob went on he grew irritated, to his surprise and embarrassment. He thanked them for the meal and said that it was time for his return to the Seminary, yet even while doing so felt uncertain about his destination.

Leaving by the backyard he began to wander along alleyways and deserted streets, challenged still by those words of hers, feeling strangely carefree.

He stopped dead.

He pulled off his black hat - then plucked off his black skull-cap, shocked, feeling it between his fingers like a live thing. He felt guilty, naked, vulnerable. Everything around was demanding something from him. Confused, joyful, he was aware of forms moving, of men watching him, and he trembled with fear.

Ahead in little groups, men were hurrying towards the station entrance. One of the men looked round and watched him with suspicion in the shadowy moonlight. In a second transformed, he was hurrying too with their aggressive swing, shouting drunkenly, well back in the shadows, on the knife's edge. Others coming up in his rear were from a nearby village and like the rest had a rendezvous at the inn.

The leader and organiser was farrier Melnik. After the Seminary incident last autumn came the call for swift revenge. Melnik, sniffing the air sensed that the Yids in Vilna were beginning to organise themselves. He warned the wildest ones against any more such stupid attacks. They must plan properly and wait for a big moment. Things were in the wind and they would eventually exact a bloody revenge. Last week he'd been informed that a large party of Yids would be arriving on the night train from St Petersburg to view the city sights. Could he and his friends arrange a suitable reception committee?

Chaim Litvinoff had been alerted during the Sabbath meal by a note from a sympathetic informant in the Police Prefecture. Brief, urgent the message. Litvinoff ordered Aleinikoff to keep the factory open – every inch of space to be made available. He sent servants to Jewish families – just keep knocking on the doors! – asking for readiness to take people in. He sent a servant to two young Jews whose activities he did not publicly recognise. Then he ordered his coachman to take him to the house of the Prefect, Colonel Badaev, in Znamensky Square, close by Police Headquarters.

"Well Litvinoff – and what's your problem?" said the Prefect, alerted by the other's presence at just this moment.

"Colonel Badaev, I believe that some Jews are arriving on the night train from St Petersburg – and that they're going to be attacked," he began immediately, as coolly as he could, having learned that obsequiousness with this man resulted in subtle forms of humiliation.

The Prefect listened politely, raising his eyebrows at the news.

Forced to breathe deeply in the effort to sound as casual as possible Litvinoff continued, "Of course I realise that you're going to intervene and ensure law and order."

The words a wall in whose shadows each stepped.

Litvinoff quickly took out his wallet and deftly conjured the fifty rouble notes, quietly, onto the table. He turned slightly away to stare at a large portrait of Alexander III. The Prefect looked vacantly through the several green pieces of paper.

"Really! I've heard nothing of such a matter," he said slowly, precisely, extremely irritated at this evidence of a sympathiser in the department.

He tugged at the bellpull and a brusque order quickly brought his adjutant over from Police H.Q. Colonel Badaev immediately mentioned the matter and Major Pogorsky raised his eyebrows, smirking emphatically.

"Frankly Colonel, the idea of any more Jews in Vilna – utterly impossible! There's simply not a square foot left. Someone must be joking," he insisted, enjoying himself.

"Nevertheless," said Colonel Badaev looking at the green paper with a certain interest, "there's no reason Major Pogorsky why we shouldn't send a platoon over to the station as our friend Litvinoff says – law and order must be ensured."

"Thank you Colonel Badaev," said Litvinoff, very relieved, yet keenly aware of such obsequiousness – such! a bowing down low – humiliation.

As he made to go Colonel Badaev began gravely, "Litvinoff – I must warn you. In the future you must not expect – too much help from me. Things are changing. But for the moment – you needn't worry. We are after all sensible men – are we not? So a drink then! to show that we understand each other."

Litvinoff was confused. He downed his drink awkwardly and left.

Major Pogorsky returned.

"Colonel Badaev our friends are steamed up to boiling. They want to taste blood."

"Pogorsky, keep calm. Try thinking occasionally – and a little tact too," said Colonel Badaev, smoothing his thumb over the roll of notes in his pocket. "Simply send a troop to await the train. It should be in within the hour. When the Jews get out – they must not be allowed to attack or harm in any way our brave loyal citizens. Our troops must as ever do their duty and defend – carefully defend – our Tsar's brave loyal subjects from any Jew danger."

He turned to a box of cigars and carefully extracted one.

Major Pogorsky grinned and left.

Near nine o'clock some forty Jews, in late teens and twenties, were making their way to a rendezvous in Station Street, two blocks away from the inn which stood opposite Vilna Station entrance. They would gather and wait till the train arrived. Then they would attack the enemy whose strength was unknown but whose savagery must be expected. With the gangs fully engaged a few could get to the platform and help the refugees to safety. But nothing was certain except their readiness to fight to the bitter end, come what may.

The gangs, informed that the train would arrive at eight, were becoming impatient as they drank inside the inn and on the street outside. Whatever happened, train or no train, the Yids were going to get their lot tonight.

Major Pogorsky decided that his chief's little joke could be disregarded. His men had little enough time off these days – certainly not going to waste it on scum like that.

In the Seminary everything had been done to clear as much space as possible. When Shimon and Namen heard the news from Rabbi Mendel they decided to make straight for the Station. They approached from the east side, past the high wooden fence of the sidings, unaware that within a couple of hundred yards David Mintz and his men were waiting in the darkness on the other side of the street. Keeping well into the shadows their footsteps rang clear and loud.

"How far?" whispered Namen a little afraid.

"To the station of course," said Shimon in his normal voice.

As they approached the bend which would bring them into full view of the Station and the inn, Namen held back. A low sound from the other side of the fence made him stop. He waited. Shimon's brisk footsteps ahead halted. Again he heard that low sound. A moaning sound.

"What are you stopping for?" Shimon called back.

"Shimon, come here!"

Reluctantly Shimon came back to him.

"There! – listen! – did you hear it?"

"Well – what of it – sidings! – they're animals!"

"Animals? – stuck in sidings – when it's freezing up – the –"

A trembling took hold of Shimon.

"No! – right! – animals they don't – Jews they do – to the fence!"

Namen closed up to the fence. Shimon, drawing in his gabardine, swung up on Namen's back and peered hard at the engine and coaches, dark and silent. Holding his breath, in utmost stillness, gripping the fence for balance he heard it again. Poising himself he sprang over and down into the shadows. A loosened board snapped back, its crack echoing along the tense silent street. Melnik, in the inn, was alerted by a couple of his men who heard. Mintz and his men were alerted for a possible attack or feint from the sidings side. He darted across the street and through the shadows crept up on Namen, recognising him immediately as a Seminary student.

"What are you doing here you bloody fool?" he hissed.

"He's gone to see –"

"Who's gone to see – see what?"

Shimon, landed over the fence, saw ahead in the moonlight an engine and coaches still silent – and heard it again – now sounding surely like some No-o-o!

Still silent coaches shunted onto the sidings long ago by the Station Master's orders. No intention of getting involved in St Petersburg affairs, high decisions. The line clear – let their own deal with it!

Still silent coaches crammed tight with St Petersburg Jews in shock since the dawn rounding up, dispossession, manacling by zealous St Petersburg officials, inspired by Moscow's example. Crammed tight into cold, dark coaches crammed sitting crammed standing no word of where they were going.

Admirable this Moscow way!

Doors locked.

Children! – the children? – well – all to their advantage – no illusions from an early age!

How we've been brought together like this

Did we never imagine?

On probation

Living a lie – illusion

After Odessa? After Moscow?

To have fooled ourselves that much?

Fooled? – betrayed! betrayed!

Now only to survive

Survival – surviving – me – survival me! lightness pearl what they can't take away.

I am – alone salvaged from the wreckage

Someone said Vilna

Someone heard 'Vilna'

Can only be Vilna

Luga – Pskov – Rezekne – Daugavpils – can only be Vilna

Only overheard – never told plainly the swine

Away from St Petersburg

All that now my past – forever now past – forever

But Vilna!

But only Jews will let you survive!

This that keeps returning – no longer mine me

Must be made past – to survive

Work esteem apartment – bitter wounds you memory

Taunts you memory

Lure – bittersweet lure – must be made past

Pain of that bitter still warmth – of what is no longer mine

Only memories – telling of what! – this whole life as only a memory – but most meaningful memory of all

Only these fragments

On the savage sweep of this tide – lifesaving fragments – lifesavings flotsam from this wreck of myself

home career esteem servants

very sparkling of finest details endless infinite – to table's proud grain – that it is finished – warning sparkle of its fragility

We!

New knowing

This we

The same for all of us!

All of us locked in our loss

We – so many strangers – reaching out to what we have in common why we are here

beyond friends strangers enemies

beyond

Jews! – such a simple truth sounding this dream – wherein we float dreamfully – lightly here – former certain selves shrivelling away

only Jews Jews

only that in this dream all are the same

At whose mercy now?

Former selves – as permitted by them

in their grace and favour

Of course we knew we were Jews

But how did we know it?

Hopeless this struggle to understand

Pressed this close – find that forbearance endurance – pray! – Almighty God of Israel save us – In Your Name it all is

We

All of it ours – ours!

smell – feet sucked into this wetness spreading – our wetness

Shimon peered through the misty windows, pressed harder to make out – make sure – from their strangeness – people – forms – people – yes! men women children crammed silent still!

so still!

What stillness was that! – some final waiting – faces – eyes – that he dared – must search out through the mist.

No!-o-o!- where was it coming from? – a human No! – a wind – a groan – sound of sounds – from where?

Questions – as in a dream – all so close – yet – slipping away as he reached out to it.

Standing crammed jammed to the coach doors whose handles he tugged at.

Everything here jammed tight.

Knowing only one thing – they must be released!

The lowing again – more keenly now – a No-ing

Yes – a No-ing!

Don't dare respond to that face pressed hard against the window

Tricks dreams made proof against!

Yet – yet – forced reluctantly to allow this meaning to break through

Yes

Somewhere it meant this dream had come to an end that misty staring face pressed through the silence

But sternest lesson insisting warning

How dare trust anything to be what it seems

But this is Vilna – the Station board reads

We're here as Jews – that's all we have now

To start again from the beginning

Only this one sure identity – branded left us

We are all – all – Jews

Cold cramped dream

Who we thought we were

Not dare believe this staring face is Jew

That Jews are around

No assumption about anything

Not dare the least gesture of affirmation after this deathvast No-ing of whom we thought we were – I am –

Exiles not of this earth – Zion not of this earth

Lesson learned. Story

Stay prostrate before that power

Then how awaken from this dream?

Damn that old fool's wretched No!

"For God's sake grandad stop your moaning!"

"How dare you –"

"Because we've got to find another life – stop mourning for the one we've lost."

Watch!

Wait!

Warily – ascertain whether we're dead or alive

still in the world of men – or demons

It reads Vilna Station

So swift! In one moment all revealed – the power – dependency – illusion – forgetfulness – fragility

our privileged St Petersburg Jewishness!

one moment – exposed destroyed

to now sense the foundation

forced to sense the foundation – accept – beginning of a strength

to be what we are

taught – forced to be Jews – only life thus liveable – bearable

What then does he want this staring face

What is he doing there

A Jewish face

So what! – and gone!

By ourselves – the time must soon be

This world here in so-called Vilna is settling

To smash the windows?

boots – hands inside boots will do it

His face again!

Two – three faces – all Jews

Don't move!

Watch – wait!

But this hope defies

Why are they staring at us

In whom what to trust

Trust!

If not in Jewish faces

Then whom?

This dark strength for survival will not give

this desolate place of resistance – suspicion

New guardian – prison

Shimon began tapping on the windows – anything to get a response from these uncertain forms.

Were they alive?

Such a strange stupor – these stiff forms

No response whatever – as if they didn't see him – hear him – tapping harder – tugging at the door handles.

Mintz peering through beside him was being drawn deep into some awful despair - out of which he summoned some ultimate strength to wrench himself away from that fearful real Jewish dream.

Wrench away - back! - fight back!

Fight - fight it - on all fronts!

Action!

Back out - right out!

Melnik Melnik Melnik!

Saved - saved!

Yes - right away from all this - to save them!

Not die with them

Only this away

Turn

Fight like this - on all fronts -

One two three - up and over

Again! much harder - one two three - and over this bloody fence -

Ankle!

Run feet run!

Lives

Jewish lives for us to save

Saving fury - saving fury - never leave me!

Blood must flow whatever the cost

From the inn commotion gathering torches being lit

"Mordecai - decoys! - attack! - anything! - but those bastards mustn't reach here - keep them down by the inn - for God's sake get going - Dov - Asher - hammers! - chisels! - anything! - those bloody manacles - God in heaven strike dead the bastards - Nathan! run - to the Seminary - with these two - get help - we'll get them through the sidings' gate - but go! go!"

Melnik had formed his men loosely across the street and sent a couple forward to investigate. Two heavy stones hit them. Melnik was thrust aside as the main body of his men began to stampede forward. A bloody fight broke out at the place decided by Mordecai. The Jews fought as men possessed knowing what was at stake. Melnik's men, many groggy with drink, retreated back to the inn after the first onslaught, mauled and confused. The fighting went on for three hours till all the refugees were taken to safety.

Slowly, painfully, Yehuda came to, after a savage kick in the head when flung to the ground, had left him unconscious. One last hard kick at the Yid's lousy head before hurrying off to the gang.

Above so close flickering splendour of dark sea. Above yet here. And he with them.

His body as breathing form yet not him. Such heaviness down there. Earth. Yet not him. Cool, calm, he outside. Spacewanderer.

Trying to feel with the knees, legs, arms of this body. Will's slow subtle infusion. Ghostly twitches and jerks. Burning stiffness his head. Lifewill's steady persistence, the movement gathering to raise off the ground. And at last drawn up to a sitting position, supporting columns of arms, hands splayed. Sore head his now, throbbing, as he held it, stroked it. And at last up onto his feet – in a puzzling place.

Several bodies lay stiff about him in the powdery snow. He recognised it all. But the meaning eluded him. Moaning and wheezing drew him to one of the bodies. The situation flashed into meaning. Yet he felt aloof, remained spectator.

He knelt beside the badly wounded man and summoning all his strength raised the man's head and shoulders. The man's breathing came easier. He blinked, to watch his helper. Hazily he recognised a Yid and twisted his mouth in a snarl. He dug his nails into Yehuda's wrist. Yehuda lowered his head back and prised his wrist free. Before walking away he wanted to look at the man calmly – draw in – to calmly take it in – that obscurity – enigma – but a profound embarrassment shame – to do with all us men – prevented him. He made his way back to the Seminary, pained, amazed, profoundly puzzled by the encounter.

"This way – quickly – quickly – just follow us!"

Out – out – along the platform to the sidings' gate, helpers everywhere, hustled through backyards alleyways to the waiting Seminary and apartments standing by. Jews! This is what it meant – with the most humble overwhelming thanks – for survival – for refuge.

Made welcome! – as ours – of us – no judgement – made room – made room – space – a place on earth right here.

Two of the younger St Petersburg men knew addresses in Vilna. Not prayers but all this as a signal, meaning, confirmation of a new action. Jewish action. Jewish workers' action.

Our history as Jews - unchanged!

Ever the torment - exile.

We shall change it!

During the confused days which followed, when the rigid discipline of the Seminary was forced to give way, Yehuda became obsessed with the desire to enter Litvinoff's factory as a worker. A desire which at one moment was felt as absolutely right, and at another as madness. A desire accompanied by guilt and fear. The fear of betraying Rabbi Mendel if he went secretly. The subtler fear, premonition that entering the factory would intensify his strange looseness and dreaminess of these last few days, somewhere there an abyss and he recoiled. Danger, challenge, the unknown, the certain, an inextricable confusion somewhere there. Yet there could be no turning back. The looseness prevailed.

Yes, he knew that he must go there. Must enter into something there. Must confirm something for himself by his deed alone. Knew too, fearfully, that this going, this confirmation would increase the loosening between Rabbi Mendel and himself.

The general disorientation through the refugees made it easier. Prayer times and study times were disrupted, absences unnoticed. He had twice walked past the factory and stared through the high iron gates without being missed. He asked Naphtali to cover up for him should he vanish for the day. Naphtali's refusal was a relief, for he felt guilty at the idea of dragging his good friend into the betrayal. Naphtali could not conceive of any justification for such an act when Rabbi Mendel needed the support of his students more than ever. Yehuda found it impossible to offer a coherent explanation.

Early one morning before dawn he got up, dressed quickly and left as though going for solitary prayer. For the first time he knew with fear the necessity of acting a part. Acting for the sake of something, some passionate truth calling him on, yet at every point uncertain, at every point balanced, held to the heart of his freedom. He in this deed creating himself felt as never before this self, as he crept past the sleeping refugees from St Petersburg huddled on their assorted bedding given by the community.

Into cold greyness he set off, soon joining a slow grey

procession of silent ones on their way towards the Litvinoff iron gates. Many were youngsters in their early teens, boys and girls, sallow, thin, one hump-backed, one bowlegged. The grown-ups leaned against the high factory wall, its top spiked with large glass splinters. He had worried about being recognised but none of these tired creatures - no! - worse than tired! - seemed to acknowledge another's existence. But to his surprise some young people were talking loudly, freely. He kept away from them.

At six o'clock precisely a large, heavily built man strode across the factory yard and unlocked the gates, slowly, gravely. Everyone moved slowly forward into the cold, dark building, whose four sheer blank walls housed that stillness of pistons, pipes, valves, arteries of the great engine wheel beginning to turn in slow vibrating thuds.

Following the others across the factory floor Yehuda looked back as foreman Aleinikoff was shouting at the same young people.

"Now then you bastards get out of here! and stay out!"

He quickly noticed Yehuda standing about by one of the long weaving benches.

"You!" he snapped, sizing Yehuda from head to foot, "from the Seminary - eh? - yes! - the boss is very taken with you Seminary lot - crackers! - well then! - you want to work for him? - alright I'll give you work."

He grinned, swung round on those watching and shouted, "Stop staring! You're here to work. Work!"

He moved off, swearing, shouting orders wherever he went.

The engine beat faster. Belts to the wheels mounted over the benches flapped and whined into life. Soon the building was one gigantic vibration, hammer blow pounding on pounding on, wild, brutal. The older hands could lipread. Others yelled into ears with little effect.

Foreman Aleinikoff appeared with a numbered card which he shoved into a slot attached to Yehuda's frame. Thirty-six.

"Get on with it! Thirty-six rolls for first shift. We're behind - behind!" he bawled, smashing his fist down on the bench, staring threateningly at the men and women struggling to keep pace with the ceaselessly clicking frames.

Yehuda copied the man on his right, simple enough, winding wool round cardings which fed the loom.

In sudden dread he discovered his lost self, compelled to insist to himself – I am here – This is the place. I. Compelled to call on name create guard an I that old vanished I. I I I compelled to so hear itself against that pounding. No simple affirmation but – I? I? I? against that ceaseless pounding heart of this prison.

From deep within to scream, to fight back at the attack. But such a numbing helplessness, a terrible isolation. Ghosts he and the rest – impenetrable this heaviness swirling cowering ghost.

Let us make man in Our Image– man – man – man in the roaring raging waves from that hammer beat pounding away in its own eternity.

He struggled to reassert familiar reference points, to find concepts that would name, hold off this attack, vague passages from the Talmud about master and servant. Helplessness and rage alone prevailed. Only to keep up with – serve – these ceaselessly clicking frames – everything him till now erased – no signposts in this desert.

The young man on his left was beginning to close his eyes. His movements were slowing down. Aleinikoff, striding from bench to bench, anxious, threatening, came up from behind and clouted his head viciously. The youth fell to the floor banging his face on the bench. Yehuda knelt down to him. Aleinikoff opened his fines book, spat near Yehuda and shouted, "You're paid to work!"

Yehuda gritted his teeth, to be kicked out now would achieve nothing. With a ringing in his ears he realised that the engine was slowing down to a dull, clanking thud. A metal dish was being banged as a gong in one corner of the building. Workers trooped frame by frame, in a certain order, quickly, toward a huge cauldron of hot tea into which mugs were dipped. Yehuda helped the youth onto his feet and towards the cauldron. No one was interested. He untied a mug dangling from string round the young man's waist and dipped it in.

"Hurry up loafers there's work waiting! This isn't a hotel!"

Yehuda went up to him, compelled to convince himself of what he suspected, yet dared not believe.

"Have you not heard?" he began, intoning as if in Talmudic disputation, "that in Derekh Eretz Zuta it is said –he who hateth man hateth the Almighty – Have you not –"

Foreman Aleinikoff narrowed his eyes and thrust his face very close to Yehuda. He grinned slowly, stood back, and raised his arms high in mock respect.

"There you are! – A Rabbi! – A preacher! – A holy man! – God help us!"

Yehuda faltered, bewildered as workers gathered round grinning with the foreman for they well knew their parts.

"Do you know what Rabbi?" Aleinikoff went on in a hushed mock-serious voice, stroking his beard, "you'd best meet our beloved governor the blessed Chaim Litvinoff. He's very keen on holy matters."

"You!" he roared, "back to work – hurry – hurry!"

As they scattered back to the benches he sang to himself,

"Derek Eretz Zuta – oy yoy yoy!

Derek Eretz Zuta – goy goy goy!"

By five o'clock Yehuda was utterly exhausted, a brittle shell, drawing strength alone from the pride that he had held on and won through to some connection with these others – fellow workers.

His eyes were strained, his hands stiff and trembling, his feet burning, and he could hardly straighten his back. For long after he returned to the Seminary that evening he tasted the bitterness of that iron reality. He knew again that rage, helplessness and enigmatic ghostliness of those at the benches.

Nathaniel assured him that he wasn't being missed –yes others too were absent from prayers –nor was Rabbi Mendel his usual self.

Yehuda went again for two more days. On the morning of the fourth day he remained in the Seminary. The reality of that factory world, though not absolutely enduring yet, he tensed himself to face Rabbi Mendel in confrontation.

Amidst the confusion, rearrangements, fears since Friday, Rabbi Mendel was well aware of Yehuda's absences and of an estrangement. He would wait, watch, not force the issue.

The thought of questioning Rabbi Mendel confounded Yehuda. Never before such fear – any fear! – on the contrary – that strength of their absolute necessity when asking deepest questions – yes! – all engendered by Rabbi Mendel's way so clearly felt now.

But this question marked the boundaries between two worlds – two lives – nothing less– this fear.

This question threatened everything that had given him substance so far. Profoundest hope then that Rabbi Mendel could answer it. But nonsense! It would be a question like any other question.

That Litvinoff himself would be there for the customary Sabbath afternoon discussions! Nonsense! a question like any other question.

But this was from a distance he had never known before – a freedom – a new risen formidable self. The very formulation of this content in its questioning form – which had risen up – Ruth – all centering on Litvinoff – Rabbi Mendel – the whole way of life – asleep till now!

Everyone knew that this Sabbath afternoon would be something special. Much was in the air. Underlying conflicts repressed by the immediate necessities of feeding and caring for the refugees, would surely come into the open. Litvinoff had warned Rabbi Mendel that he was going to announce something important. Many were coming apart from the regular orthodox, hoping that the dreadful anxieties could be somehow allayed, shared. Matters could not go on as they were. Chaim Litvinoff would surely sort something out.

Few of the Seminary refugees were truly orthodox. Most were felt from the beginning as an embarrassment, a threat to Seminary life. More than one student had declared, out of their hearing that God's chastisements were by no means unjust.

The few orthodox had tried to participate in the Seminary services. The majority felt embarrassed. Certainly they were amongst Jews. That was a relief, a security. Of course gratitude, yet this guilt, antagonism because they were not like them. A resentment at being drawn into an awareness which they refused. They had been thrown out from a world, their world, their way of life. But they could not accept their Jewishness as the reason. They had surely dealt with that business long ago. But all attempts at trying to reason things through proved futile.

Disorientated, uneasy, in an unfamiliar world, at least a kind of security and care. The plight of the St Petersburg Jews roused difficult anxieties all round, all in all an entanglement, confusion, kept at bay with difficulty. Beyond the age old caring, an intractable awkwardness, questions surfacing, feelings which Rabbi Mendel and Chaim Litvinoff must bear, confront, bring into the open.

The St Petersburg Jews marked a turning point for Litvinoff. He now recognised seriously that even the very possibility of some sort of secure future for the Jews, was in question – was in fact fantasy? The talk with Saul had also made absolutely clear just how much his power, status, wealth, were part of that question - fantasy? Clear too, looking back, how each time such painful incidents had happened to others, an optimism - naive hope -helped to ward off true recognition of the evil. This time optimism and hope felt unreal. This time he absolutely accepted that the powers above would stop at nothing.

Many of these St Petersburg Jews had professional status, a measure of wealth, good connections. It had availed them nothing. Worse than nothing! in chains - as criminals - doctors, lawyers, merchants - all criminals - and God help them! - God help us all - that they'd made their decisions so long ago to be something they were not. To fashion themselves according to the image which they believed the enemy found acceptable. The hypocrisy, obsequiousness, betrayal availed them nothing. The reckoning had come - as it could do to all of us at any time!

Our only strength - hope - as Jews - is in unity. Nothing new but pressing with such urgency, demanding such a clarification. Yet! without the help of the same authorities - same power! - he wouldn't be able to deal adequately with the factory agitators - all of them Jews! But his very power to support the community - help it stay united - depended on the working of those looms - on the very fact that he could trust all his workers.

Unity?

With Aleinikoff's young criminals! Troublemakers! - how resolve - impossible - in this historical hour of need and desperation. Age-old the measure of it - in the very blood - these young wreckers destroyers, who would split divide - for whom Jewish unity was as nothing - for whom their wretched class unity was all - Rabbi Mendel - useless - that Yehuda Liebman a crazy fanatic!

And he dared admit - deep it was - dark it was - the St Petersburg Jews weren't wanted here - their ways - every effort must be made to disperse them West.

Well then - God of Israel - some help please!

When he arrived at the Seminary on the Sabbath afternoon the study room was crowded with students, the orthodox, and many of the refugees who'd been told that important matters were to be discussed concerning their future. He pushed his way through with Rabbi Mendel and began speaking in a voice unusually grave, lacking its familiar buoyancy and authority.

"Brethren – those coaches which ended their journey at Vilna can also mark the beginning of a new journey from Vilna. Because the question is one of survival – for all of us. No more illusions. We must strengthen ourselves here in Vilna as best we can. And we must be prepared to emigrate. All of us."

"No! no! honoured Chaim," interrupted Vitebsky excitedly, "The Almighty must be loved for His own sake. Fear of death is base. Survival is in His hands alone. Did not Akiba the blessed –"

Litvinoff, usually indulgent to Vitebsky angrily broke in, raising his voice, as others rebuked Vitebsky into reluctant silence.

"Once again in no uncertain fashion we learn that to be a Jew – one of God's chosen – is a burden. A terrible burden – that cannot be escaped! We can only endure this burden in certain knowledge of God's higher purpose. I know that some of our most unfortunate brethren who sit here amongst us and for whom our hearts bleed have tried to do what others in their same plight have done. And I do not judge them! I state the facts so that we can all learn from this catastrophe. They imagined that one who is a Jew can pretend not to be a Jew. That one can go into perpetual hiding. But the Almighty sees deep and far. I know! From my own life I know! And we see how terrible has been the retribution."

Litvinoff was beginning to enjoy the stride of his theme in spite of some restlessness and shuffling. A loud fart emerged from the back of the crowded room. Its forcefulness and timing was surely intended as an appropriate comment. Those in the front faced Litvinoff with extra concentration. Some scowled. A few young people at the back were definitely sniggering. Litvinoff himself heard it indifferently and continued earnestly.

"My brethren – like a providence Herr Fischer from Frankfurt is visiting at this very moment. He is ready with his respected organisation to discuss all available possibilities – and help – for those thinking – I say only thinking – of emigration. One thing is absolutely clear. None of us will ever be safe here again."

"Utter nonsense!" shouted a voice from the back.

Litvinoff heard that clearly, stared at the back and fixed on Yehuda who was standing where the voice had apparently come from. Yehuda, concentrating on his Talmudic question, was waiting for Rabbi Mendel to open the discussion.

"You – you!" Chaim shouted back fiercely at this unprecedented insult to him in public.

Yehuda heard him, saw him, but did not comprehend. Those standing close to Yehuda began to laugh at the speechless, furious Litvinoff. From the front came hissing disapproval. From the centre, shouting and cursing at the back rows. The whole room was in uproar. Litvinoff pushed his way through to the door, shaken and bitter, followed by several others.

Vitebsky got up on a bench shouting hysterically and beating his chest. "This is God's house – God's house – God's house of study! First the enemy destroys us and then we destroy ourselves. Is this to be? – Is this to be?"

In his right hand – for God's sake! that's a knife!

Shut up! – let him talk!

"No! No! Israel shall not destroy itself. That would be Satan's greatest triumph. I shall be the sacrifice that Israel cease destroying itself. That peace and wisdom flourish."

Rabbi Mendel caught up with the situation.

Standing near Vitebsky he began chanting the prayer of prayers loudly, as calmly as possible.

"Hear O Israel, the Lord our God, the Lord is One!"

Many immediately stood up quietly and joined in, praying earnestly, yet daring to glance at Vitebsky who was staring stupidly at the knife which he brought close to his face. Soon the whole room was on its feet. Before the prayer finished Vitebsky let the knife drop to the floor and sat down on the bench, dazed, sobbing.

Yehuda, deeply moved, held grimly to his question. After the prayer, with everyone sitting again, Rabbi Mendel spoke.

"Brethren, let not passion and stupidity rule us. The important questions concerning our St Petersburg brethren will be discussed later on. But calmly. With patience. I suggest that Herr Fischer, our respected Chaim Litvinoff and myself will take up the matter here tonight with those who so wish to. Certainly – it is the case – some hard decisions will be unavoidable. Meanwhile as is our custom, let us try to understand a little of the lifegiving wisdom of our sages. Let us leave personal matters aside and search for the truth. This alone will give us strength and confidence."

He looked towards Yehuda certain that he would now put a question. But Yehuda felt confused by all that had happened. The voice of a young man from St Petersburg standing near him, rang out sarcastically. To Yehuda's amazement he heard his very own question.

"Please tell us - revered Rabbi - what our sages have to say about the master - the servant - and work!"

Calmly, quietly, Rabbi Mendel began to build up his answer with apt quotations from the Talmud. Yehuda felt unutterably relieved as that age-old confidence arrived, through its patient reasoning, at indisputable conclusions. Part of him was not even listening, simply joyful at the renewal of the bond, so reassured as the familiar wisdom flowed serenely.

Rabbi Mendel, puzzled by the questioner's attitude and aware of Litvinoff's mistake in accusing Yehuda, tried to answer the larger situation by bringing to bear a healing, peaceful power.

"- And so in the first place we see," he began his preliminary conclusion, "that the right of the master to hire workmen on his own arbitrary terms, is denied. The workman's standard of living must be safeguarded."

"- On the other hand -" he continued in that age-old chanting tone which musically pointed each statement, "the workman -"

"Slave!" snapped back the questioner.

"who either by slackness," went on Rabbi Mendel facing him without the slightest change of tone or pace, "or by deliberate lowering of output - or by unpunctuality - does not do his proper just part, is violating his master's -"

"Criminal exploiter's," snapped the questioner. Threatening cries of Shame! - Blasphemer! broke out at this further un-precedented behaviour. Rabbi Mendel raised his hand in a peaceful gesture towards his indignant followers.

"- rights of possession, and sins against his fellow man and God."

"Absolute rubbish!"

"Vile reactionary rubbish!" shouted voices close to the questioner.

"Well now," said Rabbi Mendel, smiling at the questioner, still puzzled, "our friend is clearly dissatisfied with our way of discussion which includes listening as well as speaking."

"Your revered sages and your almighty god," sneered the questioner, irritated, made wary by the Rabbi's patience and friendliness, "are quite clearly satisfied with the ways of the exploiters over the exploited."

Yehuda sat tensed, watching both, in this moment of challenge to the Rabbi who did not grasp any of it. In the angry, bewildered silence many wanted to shout the questioner down, throw him out for his blasphemy and nonsense, sensing in his incomprehensible insult to the Rabbi a threat to themselves, yet feeling in the Rabbi's calm and dignity, their refuge.

A silver-haired man, aristocratic in stance and appearance shouted out angrily, "Shut up you lunatic! Don't listen to him anyone! He's my lunatic son. Siberia's too good for him!"

"Hypocrite!" the questioner snarled back.

"My friend - continue!," insisted Rabbi Mendel, raising his hand again, still master of the situation, "as fellow Jews we can hear what you have to say."

"That arrogant windbag who stamped out - he'd really like to believe that the reason we're all here - stuffed into this god-forsaken hole is because some of us don't believe in his rubbish. I tell you - he's the reason we're here."

"Blasphemer!"

"Lunatic!"

"Can you understand that? you friends and disciples of the sages. Don't you know - dear brethren from Vilna - that we were rounded up and chained by the police - criminalised like all those sent to Siberia - exiled from that dear common Russian humanity - of the Orthodox kind - precisely of the Orthodox kind - and don't you know that the high officials and police got their idea from the great Moscow Duke - and all the gentlemen who served him. Religious gentlemen like yourselves who pay their priests to butter up their god. Same god! who's well satisfied with the way of things - exploiters - exploited. But I'll tell you something else - the St Petersburg gentlemen are really frightened in spite of their police and their priests - just like you are really - because their god is dying -"

"Lunatic! Blasphemer!"

Rabbi Mendel wanted to hear it out.

"- your pious saws, Rabbi, don't answer my question. Out there - in the factories of Vilna - St Petersburg - Moscow - Paris - London - thousands are being crushed in body and soul. Your wretched god approves - because he's a god of power - hatred - fear. But our god doesn't approve - the day of reckoning will come! Their despair and rage will be answered - our god will lead the slaves to something more befitting men."

He paused to glance round.

"Sleep well Rabbi - dream your dreams. Come on Lev!"

Before anyone realised, the questioner and another young man from St Petersburg had pushed past into the vestibule and were on their way to the apartment in Znamenka Street. Litvinoff had cooled down a little and was returning to the study room, noisy with shouting and argument. Two men hurried past him, Yehuda, and to Yehuda's surprise Shimon. Litvinoff was furious, forced to one side. He pushed his way through the disturbance to the front.

"This place is a madhouse!" he declared with disgust to Rabbi Mendel. A black mood threatened him. He could willingly have washed his hands of it all - Seminary lunatics - St Petersburg lunatics - this weak Rabbi!

"Ungrateful blasphemers - stoning's too good for them - let them be cast out of Israel!" howled Vitebsky.

"Imagine! our own Chaim Litvinoff who struggles night and day to give us work - food - clothing," shouted Bruskin taking in all the St Petersburg Jews present.

They were beginning to feel - victims again - what! - by fellow Jews? Was it possible? How find a way through this?

Rabbi Mendel raised his hand again for quiet.

"It's not for us to insult those who've lost their way. Especially those young ones in Satan's power. Their conceit, arrogance, emptiness demands - yes demands as duty - our pity - compassion - our prayers. Nothing less can restore them to Israel. Our God is the God of Mercy and Compassion. Justice is not enough - to endure as human requires compassion."

Yehuda and Shimon had soon realised that they were both following the questioner and his friend Lev. Without exchanging a word they kept together in their hurried stride. No longer the old contemplative pace through fallenness and sinfulness, but now through a robust world, charged, beckoning with the future. Awareness of one another strengthened them in their strange daring leap. After crossing Ostrovsky Bridge they followed on to Znamenka Street, watching the two men enter the apartment house. Momentarily they both halted, then as by inner agreement set off again.

They stepped into the hallway and began climbing the stairs, hearing voices from a room on the top floor. They stood on the landing poised between amazement and yet the profound rightness of being there. The door of the room, in which several young people were listening to Arkady Kremer, was ajar. As Yehuda and Shimon approached, the one vaguely guarding it, opened it and stared incredulously at the two Seminary students in their shabby caftans, panting for breath, looking somehow desperate.

"Good god – what d'you two want here?"

"Truth!" Yehuda shouted back, very presence, search, being challenged.

"Look everyone – look what we've got here!" the one guarding called out.

Kremer stopped speaking and with his listeners came to the door.

"Who are they?"

"From the Seminary – Mendel's – must have followed us here," said Asher. "Yes! that one," he pointed at Yehuda.

"They've come spying for Litvinoff!"

"Kick them back!"

"Go on – get back to your books!"

Yehuda and Shimon refused to budge, unable to respond with words.

"No! No! – welcome them," called out Ruth and Joel pulling them both into the room, "at last! – Rabbi Mendel's – the fortress crumbling – unbelievable!"

Reluctantly they were let into the sparsely furnished room whose table was covered with books, pamphlets, biscuits and glasses of tea. They were watched with curiosity and suspicion.

"You don't mean you're just going to let them walk in like this! The Seminary is pure reaction – Litvinoff's conscience money. What are they really doing here?"

"Didn't you hear what he said – he wanted truth," said Kremer, in his thirties, recently released from prison, "and our truth is for all including Seminary students. The caftans and sidelocks easily shed – Why – I nearly wore them myself once!"

"– Still that difficult? – alright – I'll personally take sole responsibility for them. But can't you see they're in earnest. They've sniffed something beyond their prison – so! – let's start from the beginning again – for their benefit. We must be absolutely clear about what's involved."

His listeners sat down, some on the few chairs, others including Yehuda and Shimon on the bare floor.

"First - no more illusions. Our Jewish workers here in Vilna are not responding to our propaganda about the class struggle - it's not touching them - it remains abstract - theoretical - we've got to concentrate on their actual daily experience - which means - working alongside them in their struggle for a better life - all our grand calling for the end of exploitation - the overthrow of the autocracy - etc. etc. means nothing in the context of their daily struggle for bread. We've got to concentrate on helping them to win back economic concessions from their employers - and it can be done I tell you - but we - you - must be there - in the factories with them - sharing - knowing exactly their daily, hourly situation - the everyday struggle - that's where we must start - grand theory is of no help to them whatsoever - their class consciousness will come - but through the daily struggle for better conditions - not through books - Marx or Plekhanov. It's going to need cunning courage and careful planning."

In the wide ranging discussion which followed, Yehuda and Shimon heard again the world of human suffering out there given voice and meaning. But in this voicing there sounded an answer. This questioning reverberated with a future, a new humanity, if accepted, affirmed and taken up with courage. Yehuda and Shimon returned as often as possible to talk with Kremer and others in the group.

With Kremer, Yehuda knew a clarity, authority, and slowly he gained the larger historical picture of class struggle with growing confidence.

Slowly, sounding out each new concept for its sure ring of truth.

Such parallels revealing themselves - age-old contemporary pressing - the slavery! - and the liberation!

The Leader - and the Redemption!

Very strange!

The Rabbi, the Seminary, all that life were being transformed. He could not make the final move nor utter the decisive affirmation in himself until the new foundations were secure. The more he read, questioned, the stronger grew his faith in this new law, very point where he sensed his truly own destiny being born.

"Societies are integral wholes whose histories obey discoverable laws."

That, the vision which shone so fiercely.

Not redemption in some vague distant future when it should please Him. But the kingdom of justice now within our own immediate possibility. Worked out for ourselves with our own freedom. Redemption that would alleviate the suffering of those around him right here in Vilna. Not some abstract pain of the Shekinah in exile but the desperate poverty and sickness of those right here in Vilna.

Now crystalline the world around him. The ground beneath a confident spur to action. People and things easily read. Litvinoff defined, understood, no longer uncertain challenge and threat. The Rabbi too. "Of course he condones things as they are," said Kremer, "he seeks security above all. The only risks he takes are with words. His particular kingdom of righteousness allows the Litvinoffs to get away with murder."

Yehuda began to experience the Seminary ritual as a spectator. He longed to begin in the factories along Kremer's lines. With Shimon he tried hard to win over others, insisting that studies in no way touched the misery of their fellow Jews outside. Those who spent up to sixteen hours a day at the bench. Those ignorant ones who failed to concern themselves in the way the blood of burned offerings some two thousand years ago required four sprinklings at opposite corners of the Temple altar! What madness were they wasting their lives on - supporting?"

"What are we here without this Book - ghosts!" he challenged. "The only way we can become men is by plunging into our people's daily misery - and end this vicious separation. Out there they're still slaves. The Litvinoffs, Losskys, Rosens control their whole lives. This community Rabbi Mendel keeps praying for only exists in his head. There isn't a community, only the haves and the have-nots. And everyone for themselves - to survive."

But to the last such a painful confusion insisted - Rabbi Mendel's humanity was so very real! The man himself, he did not want to leave. But the teaching, he had to leave. The final break was not at all as certain as he would have liked. Something crucial unresolved. He could never truly relate Rabbi Mendel to that hypocrite - parasite - exploiters' sop - so venomously attacked by Asher and the rest.

Within weeks Yehuda, Shimon and five others from the Seminary were working in factories on the west side of Vilna.

They had shaved off sidelocks and beards, changed their names and dressed as working men. They found rooms near the factories and met with the group.

Yehuda assumed that the factory workers would immediately respond. But for most, hearing their desperate daily situation so nakedly uttered proved frightening. To Yehuda's astonishment, from many it called forth a barrage of objections. The very thought of actually changing things was a madness. To curse the owners and foremen was one thing. But to take action! To enjoy sporadic outbursts of rage and violence was one thing. But to wilfully organise! That meant the painful embarrassment of standing out alone. That meant breathing the raw air of a new experience. New thoughts - new deeds - new world!

He began to understand that nightmare experience in Litvinoff's factory. The terror, the helpless desolation, had been a confrontation with some vast impersonal power, as yet unnameable. Terror, from the human nullity in the face of this power. Only now could he begin to stand back from it even whilst in the factory, and conceive the possibility of eventually mastering it, transforming its destructive violence into constructive energy for fulfilling the genuine earthly needs of human beings.

He knew that for most workers that power was un-questionable, like Nature itself, whether lived directly in the factory or in the suffocating net of their overall existence. Marx had indeed grasped the nature of the workers' essential experience. The inhuman economic situation was the rock bottom reality. The religious life was a cynical shadow-show, kept going by the exploiters and parasites. That profound terror was in confronting the desolation and superfluity of man. An order of things which had no place, no place at all for man in the truly human sense. An order of impenetrable darkness through which human creatures tried in vain to reach out to one another.

When it was realised that seven students from the Seminary, including Yehuda and Shimon had apparently disappeared for good, there was much consternation. Rumours traced it all to the two young St Petersburg blasphemers, Asher and Lev. Litvinoff criticised Rabbi Mendel harshly, in private and public for much of what had happened. What sort of purpose was the Seminary serving if this could occur under Rabbi Mendel's nose.

What was going on there? Was it entirely due to these alien troublemakers or had it been brewing for some time? If either was the case how effective was the Rabbi's teaching? Many who felt likewise stood firm in the Rabbi's defence because of the awful implications if the charges were true. A committee was set up headed by Litvinoff. It proposed that any student behaving in a questionable way by word or deed, should be expelled immediately.

Rabbi Mendel never attempted to defend himself. He recalled to himself that strong feeling of something critical happening during those tumultuous days of the victims' arrival. Something certainly related to this departure of certain students, yet of far more significance. He remained bewildered and despondent. That Yehuda should have done this thing! And how much more was illusion? But Shimon – Ruben – and the others? Wasn't it just as incomprehensible? When had he ever cause to suspect even the shadow of such an abyss as had revealed itself? So what of those who remained? Must he suspect them all?

Aaron Liebman for instance? Quiet, deep, most faithful of Jews. Was it really so? Did he really know Aaron? Aaron whose questions were so unusual, so searching. Aaron for whom the Almighty had inspired him with the answers. What nonsense! Yet, just with Aaron, in this very thinking, to know now, this dread, sadness, something mighty passing away, irrevocably passing away.

What was all this?

In his last days at the Seminary Yehuda talked to Aaron and tried to win him over. The brothers had grown distant and Yehuda hoped, expected, that this would bring them closer. By nature he expected others to see immediately what he had seen, and had little patience for any reservations. Aaron admired Yehuda's courage and stand for his truth but he shrank from his brother's arrogance, domineering certainty and inability to let others find their own way.

The hatred and bitterness in Yehuda's voice, reviling all that he had lived for, shocked Aaron. He accused Yehuda's new teaching of setting Jew against Jew. It could only lead to the destruction of the community, which the goyim were already trying to achieve by every means in their power. Couldn't Yehuda see that these ideas were simply playing into their hands?

Above all Aaron was shocked by the violence of his brother's attack on their father for the years wasted in this "graveyard". Behind Yehuda's anger Aaron sensed a groping, a freewheeling violence towards his brother's so-called new future. Aaron's foundations held firm. Yehuda grew angry with himself for having even expected to convince this fool of a younger brother.

Within months Kremer's way, replacing socialist class propaganda by agitational activity focusing on daily working conditions, was proving increasingly successful at the Jewish workplaces in the Northern district of Vilna. Pamphlets were appearing, not in Russian but in the Jewish workers' own Yiddish, concerned with their daily struggle for shorter hours and better working conditions, the strike as ultimate deed. Kremer, Martov and other leading activists, were learning in the process just how real was the Jewish workers' Jewishness, their stubborn identity in cultural traditions as against Marxist universal aspirations. That consequently some form of compromise was becoming the inevitable challenge.

It could well be that Jewish workers would eventually have their own separate Jewish labour organisation to lead them. But Kremer was convinced that they would eventually be forced by the system into a revolutionary confrontation with the autocracy. That their class consciousness would indeed mature but only through the daily struggle. Yehuda, not alone among the activists, began to doubt this concern with its increasing emphasis on Jewishness. It surely meant a radical split - radical! - in that very unity of the international working class which was their goal.

He would put himself to the test and find out whether working class unity - working class consciousness - was fundamental to identity - or whether the cultural trappings which seemed to serve the masters so well were in fact truly fundamental.

Colonal Badaev was kept closely appraised by informers. He was determined that the new Yid troublemakers would not be allowed to affect Russian workplaces in the southern districts, especially the Bunin metal works. It was arranged that one Ossipov alias Akayev should apply for a clerical post. If trouble started he would join the troublemakers and report accordingly. Bunin himself reluctantly agreed to the plan.

At Gendarme H.Q. St Petersburg, the negative aspects of Ignatiev's May Laws could no longer be doubted. The Pale cities were in fact becoming centres of socialist infection. Vilna in particular was becoming a major link for the widespread distribution of illegal literature. Especially dangerous was the promulgation of the enemy's new strategy, so-called Agitation, with its cunning use of Catherine's old laws which actually provided the strike movement with a legal base. Caught them napping! What he'd dug out! Only a twelve hour day for apprentices - two hours for lunch - two hours! And never repealed. Yid cunning if ever - several steps ahead of us every time! The employers caught on a hook. Well let the Yid employers be impaled on that hook. Let the government lawyers learn from it too. Meanwhile agents would be sent to Vilna and Russian factories protected from this infection.

Yehuda's unease increased, nor could he easily explain it. Marx and Plekhanov were surely, ultimately concerned with man. Beyond class - ultimately beyond class - nation - race. Wasn't Kremer's and Martov's direction somewhere a regression, betrayal?

He argued fiercely with Shimon for what he assumed all had taken for granted, that the Jewish question would cease to exist with the fulness of socialism. Hadn't they both agreed on it absolutely that these religious traditions are fantasies, useful certainly for the so-called priestly caste but responsible for holding back humanity's forward march.

Shimon countered assuredly that only with the eventual genuine international fellowship of socialism, could every national and ethnic group be true to itself - contribute its particular gifts to the whole. That was the reality, not theoretical abstractions called man. Yehuda must accept this actual experience! How strong a driving force and binding power this Jewishness would give to a Jewish labour movement - on the basis of Marxism.

Yehuda could not accept it.

Not Jewish workers but the working class were the bearers of man.

Then he must prove it for himself - must cross the line.

Must test himself out purely as a human being - with those others across this line, so-called non-Jewish workers. Must call on them purely as human beings - man to man. Nothing less would do!

To experiment!

Know it humbly as experiment - adventure - leap - but it

must be done.

Had he not lived, tested that old law, old way – on this same radical level? A new truth was at stake and a line had to be crossed.

The non-Jewish workplaces were mainly in the southern districts beyond the railway line and he would make his way there.

Not Marx – not Plekhanov – not Kremer – not Martov – but himself.

In quest of what? some illusion – called man?

Nothing to lose. Not Russian man – not Jewish man – but man – will o' the wisp – nothing to lose – let's see.

To begin with nothing – other than this direction.

From nothing – for him to make contact with the 'Russian worker' – yes precisely – at first according to Arkady – Russian worker – from nothing – dreams!

Begin – and be brave. The theory immaterial – the life reality – to be lived.

Man.

This 'man' which kept insisting, soliciting him – was that the Rabbi's Adam Kadmon which he had to discover for himself? Seemingly innocuous when mentioned but now – profoundest of all – mentioned – but now called to – was that it?

Russian man – Jewish man – working class man – boss man – Tsar's man –

man

to be discovered – created.

Man – very sun of being!

emptiness?

or radiant fullness – this man –

all dross of lies and illusions burned away in this sunblaze of truth.

fierce flame of 'Jew' dwindled vanished in this universal light.

Enough – of theory!

He must cross from North to South.

Start again as a man to men – rather than a Jew amongst Jews.

As socialist man.

Turn to those others – Russian workers – but as men.

To find seek out that common denominator. In action to find it – which was their common humanity.

This new law of Marx was for all men – Man – or none! And

only one way to prove it scientifically! – do it! Prove it to and for himself alone!

He could take nothing for granted – yet a direction – a structure was there.

Consciously to move towards the Russian workers – come to terms with them – join forces with them.

As yet somewhere they were strangers to him – goyim indeed. Unknown somewhere. Then consciously he would plunge into their life trusting in that call of man, purely man, not Russian man nor Jewish man – he would find his way towards them – discover just how universal is this class – begin again weak uncertain – yet holding to this one insight – summoning the courage to be what he was becoming, in the light of this new horizon.

To test it as he had once tested the old Law.

Whether fantasy – or truth – for him!

Not at all logically explicable.

From the will alone demanding – will that was himself.

An ultimate demand – directive – direction – destiny –

question put – answering –

as to what he was – and to be

as to who he was – and to be

and all – in a place that was his alone.

Painful this increasing isolation, this finding of his way to the strength of aloneness, beginning to sense himself, autonomous, needing no other.

VII

Bunin's

On a bitterly cold November evening Yehuda stepped out into Yelfinov Street and made his way towards the railway line. The snow was beginning to settle. He tugged his cap tighter and pressed on. He made for a part of the line well beyond the station, near a dilapidated warehouse. By the fence he sensed keenly the threshold which he was soon to cross. Pace by pace approaching it – creating it. Some limit determining his everyday identity and that of all Vilna Jews. A limit firm, secure yet always hinting disturbingly of the enigmatic beyond.

Uncanny place this, across the falling snow.

Here ever-present the threat of attack. Yet security too in knowing that precisely here their territory began and ours ended.

Had that attack on him occurred near here! He must have approached the place from some completely different direction.

Yield! Let it enter, begin to feel yourself freed of – beyond in that muffled stillness, whitening halt of life. Hushed, drifting whiteness, softening all sharpness, gently levelling, dissolving all into a rounded silence.

Vilna life muffled, gently covered, withdrawn.

He awoke to recall who he was, his task, his whereabouts. And this gate!

Here! could it be? through which they'd been helped to safety that night.

This place – no-man's land.

Since that night, anyone venturing here only attacker or attacked.

Us or them, still to know thus.

To linger in this misty whiteness was to risk being pounced on and beaten. Only the most destitute haunted these dilapidated buildings bordering the line here.

He stepped it out. A form flitted past. Flitted but a threat halting him momentarily. Enmity flitting through him – fought against but unable to effect reconciliation. He glanced back. The form was halted. Feigning an aggressive stance he stepped it out again to stand by the track itself, very midpoint, midpoint!

Confirmed – very midpoint confirmed – beyond its sparkling thrust – surging – from edge to edge of the world – by that flitting form.

An approaching train hooted in the distance.

A greater reality approached in this dangerous moment to awaken confidence, hope. A fullness lighting up this whole white wasteland with the truth that these men of Vilna, North and South were one. And that this place track line cutting through its heart was illusion.

The hooting train close now as he hurried across the track into enemy territory. No plans no directions other than to see whether he could survive.

Only realising now, pace by pace, into which he was stepping, that out of this call he was having to approach, very paces themselves affecting, this nearness, touch, reality so long veiled.

Enshrouding darkness the same, piercing cold the same, snow beneath his boots the same. These twisting gloomy alleyways, muffled shouts, dimly lit windows, lurching drunks, the same. But now he was amongst them.

Was it his feet that had brought him here? Had they crossed that mysterious threshold kindling this fierce elation, amazement that it was happening at all?

Into the surging unknown, to go with it yet to stay master. Elation yet the keen tang of danger. Almost adrift, dissolving but a task, demanding form, plan, self remembrance.

Drifting through these alleyways not daring yet to question anyone about night shelter, wanting to let the strangeness penetrate. But this bitter presence of Shimon Rabbi Mendel Aaron Litvinoff Ruth must somehow be shrugged off. Simply thoughts! But no! Their absence burned. He must not yield to these ghostly forms beckoning – back – back!

But this moment's heartbeat making their wraithly presence so deeply felt. He must stand firm in this ring of their absence. Myself! Alone! Kindled – this fiery strength. Flame that must endure laying waste those wraiths.

No longer the same Yehuda?

Who were they to him now?

Bitter the break but confident this rising strength.

Friend teacher brother receding to distant shores as the alleyway opened onto a market square crammed with snow-laden stalls. A low-lying mist hovered over the far side of the river. So small that world they'd been living in for so long, imprisoned by that book.

He would make for this workman's eating place. Enough of dreams, hopes, memories, doubts that all would know Yehuda the Jew - flame so keenly burning.

The traktir was a low sprawling wooden building fronted by a cobbled courtyard. Its regulars included many local coachmen and some nearby factory workers.

A man crashed out through the doorway running straight towards him. He stepped aside just in time as the man vanished into the maze of stalls, blood pouring down his cheek. In seconds another crashed through, shouting, brandishing something, stopping dead in front of Yehuda, one bony hand gripping Yehuda's arm, the other threatening with a thin blade. The man's bony, close shaven head was reeking of vodka and squinting into Yehuda's face, eyes narrowing, whole head puckering, quizzically, desperately, squeezed by some huge question. The eyes blinked, the head drew back, the grip relaxed as he swayed, slumped prostrate in the snow. Yehuda stood stock still, trembling, staring down at the poorly clad body. From nowhere a policeman was approaching, one of the two who ruled the area, knew everyone, only arrested if a fight, or orders from above. Yehuda made straight for the entrance, copying the man in front, bowing before the icon which hung on three silver chains lit by a nightlight.

Dense raw fumes compounded of sour sweat, tang of steaming boots, coarse catch of cheap tobacco, engulfed him as he found his way through the shouts, laughs, arguments, oaths. He joined men at the counter, for food and a glass of scalding tea. Crowding shadows flickered into being, gesturing grotesquely, leaping menacingly, vanishing in the fitful glare of the kerosene lamps.

He spotted some men at one of the trestle tables, apparently engaged in serious conversation. He would sit there if he could force a passage through. In this crowded world where every step had to maintain and advance itself by force, where every entity pressed so hard, questioningly, on every other, he felt a rough, buoyant intimacy, a give and take that was very lightness, and ease of movement. Strange! This denseness, this crowding, emanated a warmth, a fulfilment, a dark but friendly future. Wave on wave advancing this ocean of life, its teeming gestures, to seek out the shore of his being. This life - the warmth of it - sheltering power - this dark oneness with these others.

But then - so swiftly wrenched clear - to observe, plan, listen, size up.

Pushing his way through yet carried by some lightness, he carefully eased himself onto a space at one end of the table. Head down to his platter he spooned out the steaming food, grateful to be seated and eating, realising through the penetrating warmth how painfully hungry he had been. Each sip of the hot tea restored him to a balance, self-remembrance, distance, call of a task. Distant task - and this sheltering warmth. Both so real. So distinct, unconnected, as he listened to their talk, was drawn into their reality which was his reality, every phrase and word of it, striving to catch every meaning, feeling for mood and attitude.

The six men around the table worked in the Bunin metal plant and met here every week. They spoke bitterly about the cursed fines which management inflicted for misdemeanours. Damn their swinish power! making anything into a mis-demeanour. Yehuda listened keenly as one of them, Khodeev, made much of the mutual assistance fund, a rapidly spreading practice in the new industrial districts.

Lensky, a worn man with steel grey hair, cut through impatiently.

"You're a young fool Pavel. Mutual funds won't help us one bit with these bloody fines. Can't you see? The bosses keep screwing our wages down, always down no matter how bloody hard we work. But they keep screwing their profits up. Always up! Can't you see? We've got nothing to check their power with. Power! that's what we need," he shouted slamming his fist down on the dirty, littered table.

"You can shut your face Grandad," shouted back Peshkov, "we can all bang the table. The mutual fund at least means that the old and the sick won't starve if we're in trouble."

Tempers rose. Yehuda, of whom they had taken no particular notice, felt their bitterness at what they were having to endure, and with the argument which drove them angrily around.

He forcefully checked his most powerful urge to explain radical meanings behind what was happening, and instead strove to concentrate on what could be done in this immediate situation. He must make things as simple as possible. Their questions – the same questions! Out of this sameness he could speak without calculation, subterfuge.

When the argument reached an impasse and they were about to break up, he spoke about a way forward. A way which was being tried and tested, of which he'd had some experience. They turned towards him, surprised. They watched him carefully. They sensed his seriousness of purpose and integrity, heard words and syntax forged in the same fire of experience. He felt them following, encouraging, and on the tide of that encouragement grew more confident, more aware of the balance that had to be struck. All of them, except one.

"You must challenge management – that this system of fines is not on the Statute Book – is not lawful – and that you'll go to the Court over it. They'll realise they're dealing with thinking men who know about the Law. If they don't respond – you must be prepared to go through to the end. A strike! – we must have no illusions as to where this way leads if it's to work – otherwise we'll have no success at any stage."

He heard that 'we' with its resonances uttering this bond with these men in all their peculiarity, simply through the ideas, the truth.

"Strike! Strike!" challenged Peshkov, "What d'you mean? Are you an agitator? – a troublemaker? – we're married men – a strike means starvation – it means –"

"– that's where the fund comes in!" shouted Pavel Khodeev.

"Of course we must have a fund – but be prepared to strike even without a fund," explained Yehuda, but was he pressing too far, too quickly and losing them?

He was clear that preparedness to strike would alone make effective whatever they did – give it authority, power – demand serious recognition from management. But they weren't yet ready to hear it that clearly. Yet he felt they were accepting him along his path, which, through withdrawal of labour would teach management the real value of labour.

Pavel was with him. The others were sympathetic, but cautious, impressed by the sharpness and determination of one who knows where he is going and can lead others there too.

"Where are you from?" asked Akayev, silent till now, whom from the beginning Yehuda had felt to be different.

"Yes – where do you come from?" asked Lensky.

Akayev, alias agent Ossipov, immediately changed course at

Yehuda's embarrassment. Fool! The very last thing was to challenge him at this stage. Too clever by half.

Everyone was looking at Yehuda who was forced to face the fact that he had prepared nothing of a false background but not made any clear decision as to telling the truth.

"From Vilna of course - like all of you - what else?" was the best he could do.

The man had been thrown. Of course he was an agitator but he must quickly get him off the hook.

"Well that's good enough for us. What's it matter to us where a man comes from? It's where he's going that counts - what he stands for," said Akayev, smiling, relieved at finding a way out. Yehuda was grateful, those words telling of the man, surely helping to alleviate suspicion.

"Sure it's good enough," said Khodeev, "What he says makes sense to me - good sense. We've all got pasts haven't we? Eh?"

"Where you fixed?" he asked Yehuda and seeing again Yehuda's uncertainty continued, "There'll be some room with us in a couple of days. Come and join us - my wife and I."

"Thanks indeed," said Yehuda, all so swift, unexpected - but this gap this flux of identity!

Akayev felt it pathetic - the way these idiots were being so easily taken in but good! they'd have this agitator in the bag - for him!

"But what's your name?" asked Khodeev.

Yehuda heard himself saying, "Mikhail Karpenkov", by some flash of knowing which had lit up at the sound "your", soundlessly, forming name in a timeless moment of fear, out of a nameless world calling it forth. And with it an absolute seriousness, a firm decision as to his new identity.

"Karpenkov," he repeated to consolidate its fragile existence, "student - ex- student - father - a clerk -" he went on as though reading from some book. As though a whole story was at hand, telling itself with little effort on his part.

"Alright Mikhail - any fool can see that you're from good stock like our Semyon here," nodding in Akayev's direction and getting up from the table.

Akayev had sensed that subtlest hesitation affecting a man when he mouths another name instead of uttering his own name, pleased with himself at registering it so. Perhaps one did grow into the job as Badaev had said encouragingly. Yehuda felt burdened with the lying – happened simply thus – no going back – what necessity? – the cause knew what it needed – be resigned.

Outside Yehuda was together with Akayev whilst the others hurried ahead for the late shift. Their footsteps crunched down rhythmically through the freezing snow. The friendly glittering above, so firmly planted, dissolving the near and far, reassured Yehuda for his task ahead. Sharply breathing in the fierce sparkling air he no longer felt alone, the Bunin men ahead, known, familiar, with them together, the fiercely braced life of men to master it. Themes crowded in from this whitely glittering night. But all was not right. This man at his side must be told the truth.

"Semyon let's stop here a minute," he said as they reached a bench.

"By all means," answered Akayev, determined not to force anything, to play a waiting game, things were only just beginning.

"Semyon – Mikhail Karpenkov isn't my real name. If we're going to work together you must know the truth."

Akayev nodded in agreement.

"My real name's Yehuda Liebman."

As casually as possible Akayev asked, "That's a Jewish name – eh?"

"Yes – of course."

Incredible! This one of all a Jew!

Make appropriate gestures – for god's sake listen! – his voice – flesh – so shadowy – through the brilliance of this hate.

Yehuda went on about his activities in the Jewish factories and the group led by Kremer, relieved, encouraged, to be sharing it with this responsive and surely key man.

That this agitator – a Jew as well! – had to wait till he told you – such a cunning!

If he didn't damp down this flame all would be lost – listen! – listen to his words from afar! – get their general gist – all so very interesting!

He must look after this creature – keep him close – help him – see what makes them tick – that little debt to be settled! A job – a job! – at Bunin's!

"Semyon Akayev – a great question for me – that the others must know too"–

"Not at all, rest assured, it'll only confuse them. Our concern – yours and mine – is not Jew – or Christian – but workers' rights!" he confided, very anxious for the whole business to ripen undisturbed.

The man's clarity, forthrightness – that 'yours and mine' – strongly reassured Yehuda.

"You're quite sure of that?"

"Absolutely!"

"Semyon – it would be good to hear about yourself sometime," Yehuda suggested out of a suddenly awoken curiosity.

"Of course."

You'll hear about myself, rest assured Jew. And let's make sure we stick together.

A place for you in the goods' yard too, right under my caring eye.

On leaving he knew he must somehow try to feel out this most delicate path ahead.

Akayev was a clerk in the department responsible for handling the transportation of Bunin products, housed by the sidings. His appointment had been finally agreed by Bunin after discussions with Colonel Badaev. Bunin agreed reluctantly, by no means fully convinced that an informer should be planted in his factory. He trusted his workers, had never the slightest reason not to – fathers and their sons were working for him, in case the Colonel didn't know.

Of course he would help, would play his part, if, as the Colonel insisted, Russian industry was under threat.

Agreed then, provided results were forthcoming.

Everyone at Bunin's expected to work efficiently and productively including informers.

He wanted to be kept well in the know. The clerical job was simple and gave Akayev scope for nosing around.

He was alerted when first hearing a discreet mention of the traktir group. They were spoken of warily, and encouragingly. No question trouble brewing but no one prepared openly to back them. He began to appear at the traktir and cautiously approach them. The hostility and suspicion of the factory floor to the clerks, demanded a very sensitive strategy.

Patiently feeling his way he let sympathetic words and apparently confidential information nurture their trust. He encouraged their grousing, appeared fully on their side, emphasised that what they hoped to achieve would benefit all the workers. They grew to respect him, began to feel him as leading.

He became fed up with the whole business. Essentially just grumbles and would never be anything else. He was beginning to despise them.

The Jew's appearance had changed everything. What a fantastically long shot. Colonel Badaev had been right about the threat of Yid agitators from across the line.

Back in his apartment he let that flame blaze up again in all its fury.

Good flame! Good flame of my hate leap up, higher still, comforter, burning voice of my father's blood.

Darkly blazing power greater than me - to set the balance right! Blood - crying out in the heat of its raging desire - for revenge. Consume to ashes these devils till your pain is assuaged.

That a Yid, a real Yid had turned up!

One of them!

Not one of, but the very oneness itself. Jewness. They were all that one Jewness. That one had done it too. They were all that same one. No differences.

Dark flame of hatred fusing them all into sameness.

At his mercy. Ha!

This one that was them all. This one had destroyed his father and mother. What! This naive little swine. Pathetic! That his father, soldier, hero, Russian hero had been trapped by a swine like this. A Jewish money swine - but like this!

What! That the authorities were worried, anxious, afraid of such swine! On the defensive with them!

Good god! Then I, Valentin Ossipov must show you all who I am. What power I have. How I shall destroy them all like insects.

But this game is too easy - a trial perhaps - this one merely a shadow of the real thing - the Real Jew.

My power disdains?

Where is the Real Jew lurking?

Once and for all - Real Jew world's woe.

Lead me there destiny - that truly worthy of this hate - with the great ones - I'm ready - and for Father's sake.

But admit it! This particular Jew had something. He could bring something off. Give him enough rope to hang himself and all the rest of the swine whom he's taking in. Ensure that any suspicions about his Jew background are allayed. Encourage him and ensnare them all.

After Akayev left him Yehuda sought a place at two night shelters without success. He was directed to a grim two storey building near the river. A surly man drew back the heavy door which he had unlocked with a huge key tied about his aproned waist. He stared suspiciously at Yehuda in the feeble light of his oil lamp and stiffly thrust out a dirty palm.

"Two kopecks," he growled.

Yehuda followed him along a bare corridor which opened into a vast dark cavern vaguely receding. The keeper's swinging light dimly revealed, near and far, close packed bunks on which lay poorly clothed motionless forms. A sudden shift of the light plucked from jealous obscurity other forms below the bunks, on the bare floor. As he followed deeper into this receding void he had the uncanny feeling that these were not properly men, nor were they properly alive - some hall of the dead. Forms from another world not to be disturbed. The low creaking sounds, fitful movements, belches, farts, curses, moans, weird cries, strangely seemed only to give the appearance of human, not bear direct witness to it.

Of course these were men. But not completely men.

Nor was it simply this corpselike posture.

Steel yourself to accept - and the need to understand just what this keeper's swinging light is exposing fitfully - now glaringly - this reluctance at being drawn forth into visibility, at being conjured away from a nether obscurity, unwillingly drawn forth from some elemental darkness.

Men!

Who are these creatures? What are these creatures? Whence come these creatures?

Amidst this fierce stench, wasting of flesh, crippled limbs, filthy rags, openmouthed stupor, had he entered some twilight realm of man? What! that, precisely, which he knew marked the edge of the human abyss - some bitter dream.

Repulsed because they told of the not fully human- in man?

But in himself he must find it - in himself!

The keeper's feeble light gently, reluctantly glided over them - so uneasy, he felt their stirring - their exposure to light by light - their wishing to remain unseen.

The keeper, muttering to himself, bumping into bunks, cursing and being cursed, stopped and stiffly thrust out a hand towards an empty space. Yehuda squeezed himself under the bunk, wanting to yield to fatigue, yet feeling threatened, trapped by pressure closing in from all around. He fought to hold back the panic and need to escape. The evil smelling presence threatened to throttle his very life's breath. Beery fumes, sour vomit, foul farts, stinging stench of urine - more - some ghastly odour of disintegration itself soursweet knife-edged.

Stench of despair, dying.

These are human beings!

These are human beings!

The Litvinoff dining room! ablaze - light - warmth - servants - daughters smiling - telling me what? what?

Dozing off fitfully he returned time and again to an anguished awakening. Stiff, chilled on the damp floor, he knew that if his knowledge, that knowledge which he was to make his own, was to prove adequate at all to the task ahead then it would have to do so faced by this. It would have to explain and integrate this.

He would have to enter deeper.

These creatures were surely the truth of the social order, its touchstone. Unless their existence was thus taken into account, that knowledge was yet not mature enough to achieve anything of lasting effect.

Creatures?

What! - some uncanny self-deceit that he was different - of a different order? On the contrary - only by discovering - letting be revealed from its obscurity what was common - the common to in them and him could he begin to explain why they were there.

This deceptive appearance as totally estranged entity - to be revealed - to reveal itself as the crux!

Not reflections of a grotesque whole - Marx -

but reflections at all!

That much glimpsed this night - but no more than glimpsed.

Glimpsed - as already putting Marx to some kind of test

that there was a most profound level of explanation - as presence - not attainable by the theory

but - the theory potentised action - and that too a crux - that something could be done

but - so did that other knowing generate a doing - a doing which was in transformation - inner transformation -

glimpsed.

Man as God's partner eh? creating worlds - such worlds indeed!

But such a fury, bewilderment threatening that men put up with any of it - or - or? - this causal web of a seemingly absolute fate in which they were caught up - economically trapped.

How grasp, categorise, harmonise through that all-embracing theory?

How ultimately make transparent, orderable, controllable, redeemable, this elusive flux, everywhere yet nowhere?

Sternest challenge to thrust into its very depths. To discover the hidden humanity so grotesquely distorted beneath this grim mask. To grasp it in a practical everyday way as an aspect, necessary aspect of the capitalist order of things.

Pavel Khodeev's apartment was one of many rented by workers who preferred to fix up their own living quarters rather than be crowded into the communal rooms of bleak dormitory blocks provided by the factory owners. Pavel had two brothers who migrated every springtime to the mines or railway construction sites, returning in the autumn. But the new Land Settlement Acts had caused much conflict amongst the peasants and each time the brothers returned, furious arguments broke out over rent payment and taxes, over who was responsible for what, over who was doing the real work on the plots. Pavel finally decided to leave his village and let them go to the devil.

His invitation to Yehuda, to whom he had so readily taken, was further prompted by the decision to kick Sychkiv out, hopeless alcoholic and their second disastrous lodger. He didn't tell Dunia about Yehuda till the very day when the maudlin elderly man had to be pushed out onto the street howling and pleading. He sprang it on her in the evening, reminding her casually what the extra roubles meant. As though she needed telling! When he mentioned another one seeking accommodation who was different, she cursed herself at being taken in once again helpless victim - no way out!

So this new one was different. They were always different. A man of quality - whatever that meant with his fancy words. A man who could not only read but write as well. A long way that would take them! A man who would really do something. Do what? Pavel was always talking about doing something. "Doing something for us," Pavel answered. Us? What could he do, this man? In the forest the trees are unequal. So are men.

So what was this marvel going to do - this reader and writer?

She met Yehuda with indifference, a barely veiled sullenness intended for Pavel. While Pavel talked with the stranger, talked and talked, she remained extremely wary, a wariness burned deep by her time at Varnashev's, of all this world beyond Dimitrovka village.

At Varnashev's swingling factory where the flax was cleansed of coarse woody particles by beating and scraping, her dumb horror had never reached him, as she slopped her way through the black sticky muck on the floor, the bundles of dripping fibres hanging from the ceiling to clammily clutch at her face.

Meekly she had copied the other women, found rags to drape around the frame of their machine for breaking the fibres and made a cage in which they worked, ate and slept. A dreadful dream in which they lay together, the child born in front of everybody, and suckling it in dirty rags on an upturned crate. Pavel insisting that it was all a good start. Helpless before his grinning her into anything.

Night and day, never ceasing the clack, clack, click clack - clack, clack, click clack - such awful power this never-stopping. Night and day the tireless jaws of that monster. Ratchets, pulleys, teeth, ribs, in whose belly they lived.

Enduring all. But calling, endlessly calling on the Merciful Virgin as they clung together in the thicket of heat and stinking filth. What evil spirit had lured them out of their home in Dimitrovka? Dragged them into the belly of this monster? A good start? Merciful Virgin - she must have been mad!

All that - and the Virgin Mother's answering help!

That Pavel had found good work at Bunin's.

That they were here in this room of their own with a table, chairs, beds and money for good food. And she must keep praying, thanking the Virgin for her Blessings and ever wary for the Evil One. Pavel knew little of the Evil One's ways, who had lured them away like this. She did. And she would listen would watch.

The stranger stood straight. He was sober. He looked kindly. But all those words flying about were no good. They buzzed with trouble.

If Pavel were arrested because of the strike, she and the child - Varnashev's again? Never! But how the men loved these words words words.

Around ten o'clock on this first night, Pavel, still involved in conversation with Yehuda, dragged out a tattered folding wooden screen. Yehuda watched him unfold its three sections and fix it around the end of their bed. Dunia went behind the screen whose wings she opened wider, and never reappeared. A faint tension stirred Yehuda as Pavel turned down the lamp and also went behind the screen, still in conversation. Yehuda went to the other bed in the far corner covered with threadbare blankets and various patched materials. Unable to relax, dozing off, oppressed by their presence, he watched the screen which seemed only to intensify their closeness. Undisturbed by his presence they wrestled, panted, cried out.

Each day he confronted the only conclusion, some kind of total acceptance if he was to stay with them. Day by day living in a unity binding them all. A unity centred on Dunia. Not Pavel but Dunia.

A loosening, expansion, yielding, beyond the conflict of sinking within himself and distantly observing or being completely sucked into their life. No longer that need to withdraw behind the screen of his privacy. A new need kindled, to expand into this family, the more so doing, the more know himself – anew.

No – they were not indifferent to his presence at night but accepted it, took it into and with what they were doing as natural. Certainly they did not experience him as he experienced them. They felt no need to shut him out. What then was the screen for them and him? What needed to be screened and from whom?

What in man from whom in man?

What presence this? – his? – as they both seemed to float away – nameless ones – who were they – who?

What in him demanding secrecy – hiddenness – which they knew not – had not?

Not indifference but no difference? Like the sun, the harvest, the rain, uncanny. But not completely, for a screen, the screen was there but only as the thinnest of veils, the merest suggestion of a separation, some ancient cleavage of the heavens from the earth – not from him.

Dunia's sullenness – softening – the smells, grunts, cries – all being accepted by this newly awakening affirmation, her silence revealing itself as a fulness of life.

In her, finding a formidable strength. She knew something that he did not. She was drawing from some source whose reality was but confirmed by the poverty and grind.

While waiting to be fixed up at Bunin's by Akayev, he began to help her silently, with the child, with the piecework which she often fell asleep over, strength sapped. This silence a new knowing.

He found his way to little Yuri with stories. Whilst helping her he felt the vastness of necessity, of formidable destiny, so elusive yet so dense which hemmed them all into this world, this room. Simply to abide in this silent doing with them both, centre. From her something so strong, compelling, fraught with significance for the future as to overshadow that adventure on which he and the others were setting out.

Or could there be a connection?

Woman.

Mother.

Shy heart of the world's becoming.

Timeless – yet mighty truths from Dunia in her shyly glancing way.

Yehuda referred to Akayev's insistence that they must begin right now to organise a strike fund. Pavel lightly laid his grimy hand over Yehuda's mouth.

"That's a bad name here," he said nodding in Dunia's direction over by the stove.

Yehuda was very surprised.

"She doesn't trust him."

Later Pavel explained that Dunia had dreamed a bad dream about Akayev. And Dunia's dreams were true. Always.

Yehuda suppressed his anger, sensing a dark realm, of actions, gestures, words whose significance he had not taken seriously till now. Especially the bowing and crossing before the ikon, and Dunia's especial care for that Bible which neither could read. Was Pavel implying that for the sake of domestic peace they must play up to her dreams? Or did Pavel in fact believe in them?

He'd taken it for granted that Pavel, as all the Strike Committee, judged Akayev central to the work. A man who shared so much, risked so much.

He felt compelled to keep questioning Pavel on the bad dream. Pavel grinned his provocative grin, at once disarming, charming and seemingly fooling, beneath that grimy greening cap always stuck in place. Pavel mentioned Dunia's guardian spirit, a wise ancestor who told her many things. Yehuda pressed him further but he would not say any more.

No! Certainly not even for Mikhail. That was treachery. That was danger, to speak about it. Nor did he really like the way that Mikhail Karpenkov was thrusting at him.

"But what do *you* think Pavel?" Yehuda tried him out on the spur of the moment.

"Me?" sounded the dissolving substance of that singleness which seemed to doubt itself, deeply disturbing Yehuda.

"Well – my Dunia's no fool you know. Anyway she doesn't really trust anyone. You're an exception. The first time he came here she had bad dreams."

Very serious the note – and of fear? – and that 'he' confusing, frustrating.

Was Pavel talking out her thoughts for her?

Yehuda dropped the matter, frustrated and confused, for he had come to believe in Dunia. He felt pressed to think seriously about Akayev, but soon realised that precisely through doubt, every act, gesture, word of Akayev's was vulnerable to varied interpretation. This whole undertaking was fallacious. At this threshold trust was the only way forward. He'd never had any reason not to trust Akayev and from that he must start. Reason – this reasoning – secondary – must serve.

This trust – surely – grander – greater – than any memory – any reasoning concern about incidents – gestures.

But Dunia's dream would not let go.

He must try and come to terms with this whole business of their superstition – superstition itself. Dunia's dreams – the bowing before the painted picture, all of a piece. And he must get beyond the irritation, frustration.

But – wait!

He too – the great Yehuda – who'd been more superstitious?

Bowing – prostrating – bent double eh?

Before what?

Who'd revelled in it more? preparing to become God's chosen one, eh?

Stripped off in one fierce go – that night!

Then you know the madness how deep it runs. You who presume to help, to lead! – bear with them! – caught fast on this hook – held back in this twilight – but for how long?

Such a contradiction – radical truths as facts of nature – "bread and water that's our food" – "what is ours is the land, which belongs to God" – all so acceptable – and then this dreadful superstition – illusion – that their situation nothing to do with the Tsar – only his evil counsellors who wanted to keep him away from the people for their own evil purposes. Thank goodness he had heard and drawn back in time! Tread carefully here! the very measure of your inconceivability of such a gap – something here so important to simply accept let alone account for – at being the same traktir argument – only there, justified – leaving him exposed vulnerable off balance – alerted to their suspicions. Those laws of Catherine were the laws of a wise Tsarina who wanted to help the workers! And last night Pavel's casual – innocent – why casual? the word came of itself! – this suspicion of mistrust – that they're both making a fool of him?

And again flung right off balance – such a gap – when Pavel mentioned the stranger who'd appeared in Dimitrovka village talking about capitalism and socialism. These gaps – could he ever be sure? – know them? – establish anything here with certainty – or ultimately total strangers?

Were these two holding back what they knew?

Was Pavel's grin beneath that greening ancient cap which sprouted from his tanned, bony head, not really benign, friendly, but in fact making a fool of him? And when he'd tried to discover what more this someone, apparently a newcomer to Dimitrovka who set up as a tailor before moving on, had actually been saying? Then impossible to pin Pavel down to facts. Simply – and simple enough – that the peasants were entitled to take all those things of which the rich have too much. Fundamental enough that! No superstition there. Need to listen more than seriously – in Pavel's recounting he surely heard that resonance, word of earth's justice. Same resonance in the way they shared food with him, accepted him. Resonance kindling in him a profound gratitude at simply being with them. Out of this we, an elemental sense of justice, goodness, felt, known.

That you are in unknown territory.

Call on trust – destiny's call.

You can do no more, come what may.

But these last months had been a lonely groping – lonely responding – on his own, no other way. And then this revelation

fullness gratitude – that a threshold had been crossed
    beyond all else
    he was with them
    sufficient!

Who who who? as we stand at the machine.
Earth's bond gone.
Earth's rough friendship
Binding us in truth
All gone
Only your unyielding touch
No past   No future
Empty present

Who – you –
Tyrant
Grinding our life away

Standing at the machine
Lured
Flung into this void
Painful inwardness separation   new strength
Being born.

Secretly
In the dryness of this ceaselessly booming void
A newly wakening one
New tone in the way of man to man

Such bitterness tasted
Such confusion
And the struggle ahead
What rhythm is this
In the ceaseless turning and booming
Not of growth and ripening.

But this is the measure
The beat to which you must work
This bitter power from the West

New power of man the maker

Drawn forth from most secret source

Elementals
Avaunt!

New bond being forged from this dark unnameable
From the very threshold of death
Who Who Who?
Standing within.

Such anxious loneliness. Such anguish of being brutally torn away, exposed to a chilling void. Loneliness, sadness for that setting sun. Fear at being so sternly abandoned, orphaned. So bleak this present yet meaningful future being born from out its womb. Womb whose brooding burden was this meaning, was themselves. Bewilderment, despair yet borne knowingly.

Deep deep from this loneliness arising a striving to unite with all these others who out of this ordeal are reborn too – separate, independent, equal – brotherhood – it's brotherhood! that hovers so ethereal over all this new becoming, as unity in freedom, so near and yet so far, so strange yet so well known.

The strike was Yehuda's all embracing goal. It alone meant lifting clear into the open, the awareness of men through living experience. Above all with regard to the meaning and value of labour. Plekhanov's great theme his inspiration. To beat a path forward that would lead to the emancipation of labour. To lighten the crushing weight, this bitterness that pressed men to the ground like oxen, yoked. Not simply the burden of sheer physicality but this social form through capitalism and the machine.

This manmade imprisonment, necessity – the ultimate burden and bitterness.

To begin on this way of freeing labour, the first, the crucial testing ground was the strike.

Brotherhood, towards brotherhood, through a struggle woven out of sacrifice, courage, leadership, trust. Struggle whose essence was the strike itself, turning point, when flux of feelings wills and thoughts are forged to enduring shape. Forged by the hammer of confrontation, new moral substance created, shaped, only the real, the essential remaining.

Yehuda and the others cautiously felt their way towards those workers who were confident enough, courageous enough to show sympathy and support in varying measure. Yehuda insisted on ensuring that men understood the situation as it was developing, and that nothing foolish was undertaken simply for the sake of doing something. Only when they had gained the backing of enough skilled men in the Casting shop, key men, did they feel the crucial moment approaching when they must put the measure of their unity to the test.

A Strike Committee was formed in secret with each member taking on specific tasks. Yehuda knew that the average sentence for strike leaders was a minimum of twelve months imprisonment. A failed strike could lead to despair, disintegration of the unity so painfully achieved. Just this either – or had to be risked. But even through a negative experience something positive would be gained. A much sharper, more bitter yet more realistic awareness of the masters.

Akayev was reluctantly impressed by Yehuda's caution, thoroughness and organisational skill.

Nicholai Vuchina who'd been involved in a strike at Minsk tugged open his shirt to show how the ugly weal along his cheek flashed snakelike down his neck, across the shoulder to halt in a snarled angry knot. The puckered skin made movement sore and awkward. Like other workers in the yard that day when the Cossacks rode them down, he'd been marked for life.

"No!" he shouted in panic, seized by that past, and pointing at Yehuda.

"Have you seen what they did? No! It must never come to a strike again."

Yehuda held his ground. Didn't Vuchina's experience clearly demonstrate just how important their labour must be for the employers that they had to go to such lengths, to ensure it was maintained. Their work was far more important than themselves! Their work fed, clothed, housed the whole employer class, the whole system. It must continue at any cost. And, as important, we know now that the Minsk strike failed through lack of organisation, direction. Strikes did not have to fail. Organisation was the key to victory.

Yehuda held firm to Kremer's strategy, dealing with the everyday issues as they arose, showing that everything possible was being tried in a lawful way. Management, marking him well, responded to the demands with contempt and disbelief. The strike then, implied Yehuda, as something inevitable. He did not want the workers to feel that they were being led to strike by him but that the course of events gave them no alternative.

He often felt an awkward gap opening up between his theoretical knowledge and this daily activity. Somewhere, but to be held off as unreal – a distant horizon where it was all leading – parties – parliaments – democratic legislation. Kremer? or Plekhanov? – when it seemed that the very density of the immediate situation was a maze leading nowhere – and that precisely, activity on that distant horizon alone would prove far more effective.

His leadership had been accepted. His dedication and purposefulness generated optimism but the unanswerable questions created doubt and diffidence for himself. Another critical turning point was ahead. A broadening experience which in turn would demand clarification, continued re-testing of the very concepts which had made it possible.

The new answers, but the new questions – and the new answers yet again – some spiral's ever upward striving life.

One evening in early June the Strike Committee members made their way separately to the woods north of Vilna. They used the rough track which followed the river bank and was pocked with the footprints of the barge haulers who trod it from late spring. Roped together, sight sweat-bleared, they strained forward with "a one – and a two!" – "a one – and a two!" charming the black hulks laden with timber along the tributary. On the path these summer evenings lovers and loners dreamed their way.

The meeting place was near a mighty stone pine famed in local legend when a young monk saw flames burning steadily from the branches one Christmas, whilst on his way with food to Father Feofan who dwelt somewhere in the woods. Everyone appeared at the appointed time except Akayev whom they awaited impatiently. Knowing that the crucial moment had arrived he would have liked to put it off.

At last he appeared with a show of confidence and Lensky, who knew these woods well, led them to a clearing near a lichen covered sandstone outcrop. After the angry heat and fury of the workshops the sweet evening air soothed. Darkness drifted, veiling the waning sunlight's lingering glow, in living tinctures of purple, blue. Gentle yielding of light and night to each other, glowing resonance, hailing the ripeness of their moment. Moment of human time yearning to ripeness from that first dark seed of hope, of constant striving.

Seed of courage in the womb of will to ripen through endurance and resolve.

Earthly and our human time with their moments of ripeness. This darkness and light whose play of colourings lingered, away.

"Everyone! Let's begin immediately with reports from the shops. How is it in Casting?" said Pavel.

Yehuda hardly dared believe that at last it had come to this, very touch of a power, as the reports were given, all together declaring a clear readiness, workers prepared to down tools knowing well the risks, within the next forty-eight hours if management refused to negotiate on their terms. Only about the rolling mill some uncertainty.

A power, at first no more than a breath, but gaining substance with each utterance, report, and raising to a higher key the groundnote of each one's being. A power, a voice, a will, their own, no longer dream, insistent on its absolute right to be.

No! not at their mercy but masters too – we can take them on!

A power expanding far beyond the words yet centring, Yehuda knew, on him. Each word fraught now with gravity but with fulfilment too. Very centre, focused, sharper, bearing the weight of their dependence, his decisions, his leadership, the absolute pivot. Yet, this weight a fulfilment, his life's very meaning. This power reaching out to those friendly lights above.

It was concluded from the reports that if management pounced first with arrests, most shops would be even more determined, especially Casting, the most militant of all.

"Nothing will stop us, nothing, not even those cowards in the rolling mill," Yehuda said fiercely, the note new to himself.

"Cowards! that's the word – cowards!" spat out Lensky.

"What the hell! They're fellow workers like us –"

"Traitors!" insisted Yehuda vehemently, "we're either united or lost – as simple as that."

Everyone heard that violent note from across the threshold. A ruthlessness, that any such obstruction must be removed.

"Damn the rolling mill! What about the strike fund?" Pavel

pressed on.

Peshkov the treasurer calculated that they could last out for about ten days.

Korovin brought up the question of arrests. Supposing management had the authorities arrest the Committee as soon as the formal demands were presented.

"That'll guarantee an all-out strike!"

"You're very sure - where d'you get your facts from?"

"I've asked - I went with Feodor right through the Casting Shop - furnace men - drawing mills - they'll come out to a man - they've said so - what more d'you want?"

"Anyway all our number two's are ready to take over," reminded Pavel. He turned to Akayev.

"What d'you think Semyon? D'you think they'll arrest us all?"

Pavel was disturbed by Akayev's silence. He felt an unease - hesitancy - afraid? now that the test was on them? Why of all nights so late?

"They're not complete fools - they're more subtle than that," answered Akayev, feeling the threat in Khodeev's voice and the need for some quick response.

He had worked things to ensure that everyone experienced Yehuda as the leader with prime responsibility, so that when retribution came he could be blamed for everything. The moment had arrived and he must seek help this very night. But he must tread warily. Whatever the hour he must see Bunin. The moment was now and he did not know what to do next. Dimly he felt his place in all this called to account.

Yehuda recapitulated the main issues and their final decisions, emphasising that it was impossible to cover every eventuality. Risks must be taken. There remained only to decide who should present the formal demands to management.

"Who? Who?" burst out Pavel in disbelief, "who else but our Semyon? What? D'you think that Ivan - Sergei - I? - could make out our case to the boss," he stood up mimicking gestures of pathetic obsequiousness, "he'd make mincemeat of us!"

Akayev did not immediately connect Pavel's words with himself. When he realised the obviousness of the situation, that there was no way out, his consternation intensified.

That the possibility had never even occurred to him!

Vanish!

Collect your wits you fool! What the hell have you been thinking about?

Pavel was puzzled by Akayev's failure to confirm his proposal immediately. He felt a distancing, an uncertainty about this man called Akayev. This man there and his Semyon were beginning to float apart.

Dunia!

"Not so fast everybody," said furnace man Shavrov gravely, "and what about your Cossacks?" from out the circle of faces, subtly changing in the shifting veils of dusk.

"What Cossacks?"

"Come off it Shavrov - why didn't you bring your damn Cossacks up before?"

"Shavrov what are you on about? It's late. We all want to get back," demanded Yehuda, yet Shavrov's rare contributions were generally of substance.

"I'm telling you that Cossacks were seen near the Casting Shop this afternoon," Shavrov continued, unperturbed.

"So what?"

"Shavrov's right! What were they doing there just this afternoon?"

"Of course he's right. They haven't been near the works for months!"

"Semyon have you heard anything?" demanded Pavel of Akayev once again.

"Yes - Semyon - anything in your office about the Cossacks?"

Yehuda felt the keenest touch of alarm. Something tightening, constricting around this centre of responsibility.

"Shavrov - did *you* see the Cossacks?" demanded Yehuda.

"No, but I'll tell you who did -"

"Not good enough," returned Yehuda sharply, "there's bound to be rumours everywhere. We must have facts."

Shavrov stayed silent. He nodded gravely in disapproval and narrowed his eyes as he looked round the circle.

Pavel had been intently watching Akayev, determined to grasp something tangible, some answer to his insistent question. He caught a grotesque, fleeting grimace from Akayev's direction, Akayev's barely mastered tension, feeling trapped in some abysmal complexity. This new part to play, out of the blue! Strike negotiator! Hang on to it - as best you can. Cossacks? What bloody fool had been responsible for that at this moment! wait

318

till he saw Badaev!

In the moonlight's sheltering shadow play his bewilderment befriended him. It took on by itself the part demanded, though tainting his voice with an awkward frenzy. He stood up.

"Forgive me - I'm not really myself. Now the moment's come - why! it's simply overpowering. Don't you feel it so?" he winced into the darkness.

"I ask myself - am I, Semyon Akayev, really up to this great responsibility that you ask of me? But rest assured I shall do it," he faltered, sitting down again, weak at the knees, relieved to have come through. In the darkness he reached out desperately for that power which had so elusively withdrawn, leaving him in this chaos of informer-negotiator. That power lost, but momentarily, only. The power was not the yid's nor his minion's, but his, Ossipov's. And he knew it would return.

"Good, Semyon - You just put the case - and we'll smash them, Cossacks and all."

"Smash them! That's it!" repeated Akayev taking the cue, "We'll bring Bunin to his knees. We'll show him where the real power lies."

Yehuda reconfirmed that they would all meet in No. 3 Casting on the six o'clock shift tomorrow morning, openly, as the official Strike Committee.

Everyone was standing. Akayev sensed their elation, that at last they were expressing their will. Sensed too as revelation the very crushing of it by that far mightier power, Bunin power! How this excited little yid would be stamped into dust! Strike - no strike - what matter! That the yid would be crushed was enough!

They returned separately along the path.

Pavel followed Akayev and kept him in sight. In growing unease, each turn and twist, through darkness and shadow, that one moving ahead - was become unknown.

A strange isolation, no longer at all his old Semyon but as one unknown, whom he would have to deal with. Some inexorable reckoning so deeply felt within himself. He must stay with this man.

Akayev, hardly aware of Khodeev, knew only that he must turn to Bunin.

Pavel felt something was playing tricks with him. As they reached the outskirts by the Old Cemetery he hurried to catch up with Akayev. This was the old Semyon at his side as they both made for Elizavetinskaya Street together before parting. Pavel was anxious for a familiar word to break the silence. Akayev, having decided to go straight to the Bunin mansion was irritated by Khodeev's presence. Some glimpse of the other's suspicions, some danger, forced him into clumsy effusiveness.

"Well Pavel Grigoryevich – it's going well – isn't it?"

He grabbed Khodeev's hand, shook it jerkily, then turned down Elizavetinskaya Street to his lodgings.

The gesture and touch jarred on Pavel as he walked on, as naturally as possible toward his own room. He halted, hesitated, returned to the street corner and cautiously, in shadow, spied the length of Elizavetinskaya Street, at the far end, a figure, hurrying away which he must follow, left turn! vanishing down Varvarka Street, he must go faster, street by street, wherever it led, not at all certain whom he was following or even why, at moments enjoying the chase for its own sake, always carefully keeping his distance and shadowy coverage. And if it was Akayev, where the devil was he going? I must know!

The pace was brisk through the silent empty town. The scent of the chase keen, fierce. Lithe stride pressing lightly on in the moonlight – as in the old days! Arms swinging to lunge grip carry off goose duck chicken.

Who was that other? Only that he must be held firm – in this following.

Already out on the Kovno Road! – trees – houses standing so gently in the moonlight. Whisperings, breathings, caught up in this shimmering sea of ancient light. Dreaming moment of brooding fears.

Shake yourself free! Return!

What are you doing here at all?

You alone – there is no other!

This road?

The Kovno road?

Bunin's road! direct to the Bunin estate!

Something is happening!

Hurry on again! The driveway – on – on – can only be Bunin's at the end.

At the mansion arrangements were being finalised for the marriage of Natalya Bunin to Anatoly, the son of Pavel Pavlovich Romodanovsky, who was extremely reluctant to mix with the blood of this small, wiry upstart from nowhere. Romodanovsky could go back hundreds of years to ancestors who stoutly defended the northlands against the Teutonic knights, ancestors ennobled by Tsars, serving the State generation after generation. But the Bunin dowry involved was very large. It would help check the unending plunge into debt begun by the late lamented's misguided emancipation nonsense - treachery? Nothing less! This new-fangled Land Captaincy business was all a nonsense. He knew his power was dwindling ominously. Yes he remained on his very own lands, walked them, hunted on them, yet a chill shadow pervaded even during midsummer.

God's ordained order of things had been interfered with.

The reckoning was coming - would be catastrophic.

To Bunin, Romodanovsky's reluctant agreement was one more acknowledgement that a new and real power was being wielded by men like himself. The time must come when all would acknowledge with positive praise.

Throughout the evening Romodanovsky, bitterly resenting the whole situation, put the best face on it that he could but it grated dreadfully - this red-bearded oaf with his beady eyes - yes - beady eyes when you really looked at them - wriggling in their sockets - upstart's eyes - this oaf grinning so arrogantly amidst all this garish bric-a-brac. In fact if you really dared look hard, his face was covered with pockmarks, a crude face.

Through the many rich courses Romodanovsky kept himself inviolate, uncontaminated, only making reasonable gestures from the very edge, nodding occasionally, a word here and there but refusing to be drawn into this oaf's way. He absolutely refused to be impressed by the gaudy glitter and thrusting coarseness, the large cigars, rare wines, sweetmeats, proffered by the servants on the veranda, bathed in the evening scents of honeysuckle, jasmine and lilac.

His wife Eudosia withdrew into an icy formality, waving her fan with nervous shakes and barely uttering a sound. She could not come to terms with the marriage but she would never let her Pavel down. This widower Bunin liaised with certain young ladies. There was even talk of one living here in the mansion itself.

Not once had either of them hinted by word or gesture their distaste for the man and both drew some consolation from this. Their boredom and exhaustion with the strain were surely nearly over. There was nothing more to discuss. Bunin had covered every aspect with a frankness which had made them squirm.

"Well my dear Pavel Pavlovich. Now the business side's settled and everyone knows where they stand, we can enjoy ourselves," Bunin announced to their dismay at this late hour.

"Not such a bad deal, eh?" he winked at Romodanovsky, whose lips tightened almost to a bitter grimace in the pretence of not understanding a word.

Bunin bowed to Eudosia and led them both into the grand drawing room where more sweetmeats awaited with tea. By god he'd unstiffen her crush that damned stiffness.

Two gypsy musicians, guitarist and fiddler, were waiting apprehensively as Bunin stepped in gaily, clapping his hands towards them,

"Come on you hooligans," he shouted amiably, "strike up!"

They began a wistful theme.

"No! none of that stuff!"

He roared out a lively tune, stamping the rhythm, and they tried to take it up.

Eudosia was fascinated by the quietly attractive young woman in the gilt backed chair from across the large Persian carpet. Almost demure, yet the jewelled sheen of her low décolletage was already floating towards them as Paul found himself responding to Bunin's outstretched arm inviting,

"Pavel Pavlovich Maria's an excellent dancer, really excellent."

Eudosia, stiffening, found herself dancing with Bunin, unable to resist the swirl, noise, eddy and whirl, even smiling which he'd conjured up around them.

A loud banging from the front door of the mansion was heard through the music. Bunin frowned. The banging continued, and he shouted bringing Eudosia to a halt. She had felt unnerved in his dancing hold, Pavel and herself, gyrating round the room, disconnected, helpless. Now the wretched man had let go, stopped completely without any apology, those stubby hairy hands clenched at his side, his face fiercely flushing. A servant anxiously hurried to him in the silence.

"A man! master."

"Of course – a man! What man? Who at this hour in this joy stops our pleasure?" he demanded with the hoarseness of a rising anger.

"Ossipov, Valentin Ossipov's the name."

"Ossipov? Ossipov? What kind of a name is that?" he frowned, "Ossipov? - Whaat! That one! How dare he? I forbade him ever to come here. This is my place. Not for him at all. Exactly! Informers spies - mishmash! They take on airs. They become familiar."

Everyone listened in puzzlement.

"Master - he says it's important - very important."

"Important?" Bunin roared, "It had better be a matter of life and death - nothing less. Nothing less!"

He stamped out of the drawing room to the entrance hall and stared aggressively at Ossipov.

"That's exactly it Grigory Bunin. A matter of life and death," began Ossipov, relieved to see Bunin.

"How so?"

"It's a strike - tomorrow."

"You dog!" raged Bunin, "You cunning little dog! We don't have strikes at Bunin's. Never! till you appeared." He brought his face very close to Ossipov's, breathing out the alcohol and the fury as to burn him away.

"But Grigory Bunin - have you forgotten our agreement?" Ossipov managed, confounded, incredulous, "- that I -," he struggled on, faltering, that I crumbling away, overwhelmed by the power of the reality that this man insisted on presenting.

"What agreement?"

"Colonel Badaev -" Ossipov called on the name, surely a pointer for sanity, a power well known.

"Badaev! That swine! Bring him! Get him! Go get him! Strike? Who's going to strike? I'll smash them. I'll smash you too. I'll smash the lot of you!"

He ground his fist into the palm of his hand, again and again.

"Vladimir! Vladimir! where are you? - you lazy scoundrel!" he roared through the mansion, "So - so! - get the coach - go to Police Headquarters - bring Badaev here!"

"Colonel Badaev master? - Now?"

"Now! Now! Now! you swine," he shouted at his coachmen with accompanying thumps on the back and a fierce shove out of the mansion into the driveway.

"Oho! So they're going to strike are they?"

He strode back into the drawing room. Staring fiercely at the musicians he flung his arms toward the hallway, "Off with you - you hooligans! Off with all of you!"

Everyone escaped quickly. The gypsies scurried away not daring to ask him for money but managing to stuff their pockets on the way down to the Kovno Road. Maria hurried to her room, thankful that his anger was not being vented on her and preparing for the kind of arduous night that often followed such outbursts. The Romodanovskys went straight to their carriage, incensed at the man's rudeness, fearful of his violence. His abrupt dismissal of them astonished, humiliated, made them feel completely at his mercy. They vowed never to visit him again.

Ossipov still stood on the driveway, not daring to enter the mansion. Bunin paced up and down in the empty drawing room, stopping for gulps of brandy. Ossipov, shattered by the attack, hung about stupidly, bitter at the injustice. Or was the man simply raving mad! He would get his own back on this lunatic. So! he was being blamed by this lunatic was he? Right! Then he'd tell him all the facts. One by one. Rub his nose in it!

Bunin's pacing, to and fro pacing centred him ever firmer, in that fire of himself and that world of his creation. Ever firmer in that power, living potency which was himself – so challenged by these shrinking creatures who slunk away. The Romodanovsky creatures – and that one slinking outside. All of them. What did they know of his power over men? But they would. The time was coming. What did they know of that power which he had won for himself over men? Not inherited – or given or rewarded. But won. Proving himself in the battle with men. And with the earth. What did Pavel Pavlovich Romodanovsky know about the earth? His were the hands that had wrestled with it, forged it, hammered it into a new glittering Russian life stretching its way across the vastness. Life veins for a new Russian future. Black his men. Black the sweat. Black the forges. But gleaming pure the rails – Russia's new veins.

That was his claim and the source of his power. A maker of Russia's future which these others had yet to acknowledge, were afraid of – yes he knew.

Milked dry for taxes. Acknowledged only as a milch cow. Useful for His Highness and those silk-arsed swine at Court. But the time was coming! The time was coming!

Vladimir banged wildly on the door of the Badaev house close by Police H.Q, his very life at stake if he failed to bring Colonel Badaev back with him even at this late hour. Colonel Badaev, when informed, was furious at the disturbance and threatened Vladimir with arrest if he didn't go away immediately.

"Never! he'll kill me if I don't bring you back," pleaded Vladimir with a desperation which compelled Colonel Badaev to enquire further.

Breathlessly, disjointedly, Vladimir told of Ossipov's appearance – his mention of a strike – Bunin's terrible rage.

"Terrible!" he repeated, "terrible!" – in awe, pride – of serving an all powerful master who respected – revered – nothing! nothing! – certainly not you!

Colonel Badaev could not make any sense of Bunin's behaviour. What kind of a misunderstanding could possibly be involved? Reluctantly, to Vladimir's blissful relief, that pride confirming, he felt compelled to go. But whatever was the matter with Bunin? – he'd been kept in touch throughout in all essentials. Only this timing of the strike was earlier than expected. He himself had informed Bunin that the names of the Strike Committee were known, its supporters, its leading activist Karpenkov, pseudonym for Jew agitator Yehuda Liebman. Bunin had agreed – hadn't he – the correctness and success of the whole strategy – as well as the excellence of Ossipov's work! Hadn't he?

The man was even thicker than he'd imagined. Obviously hadn't grasped that more was at stake than his immediate satisfaction. That it was essential for St Petersburg to assemble as complete a picture as possible of the whole agitational pattern throughout Vilna. Simply couldn't see that the final killing would be so thorough that he would never have any more trouble.

As soon as he stepped out of his carriage by the mansion, Ossipov hurried towards him trying to explain the situation and express his bitterness.

"I can hear you Badaev – talking behind my back!" shouted Bunin, striding into the hallway at the sound of the carriage.

"– and he's staying out there. Not one inch further!"

"Grigory Yefimovich – Valentin Ossipov has done all we've expected from him and –"

"Arrest them! I order you to arrest them – all. Now!" shouted Bunin.

Colonel Badaev faced Bunin squarely.

"You're making a fool of yourself Grigory Yefimovich. I, Anton Constantinovich Badaev, represent the full power of the state. Any arrests will be on my terms. Either you hear this man out or we go."

"Go! Go! Go! I'm not afraid. I can face them."

Ossipov began speaking. Bunin listened, reluctantly, suspiciously. Ossipov, withdrawn to some pleasant neutral ground was enjoying them fighting it out. What did he care? Who were they to him? When he did speak he felt uncommitted except to the one task alone.

"Tomorrow the Strike Committee are coming out into the open. They're going to formally make their demands to management - shorter hours - more pay - etc etc. They're giving management a day to think it over. Then actual negotiations to begin on the twenty-fourth. Otherwise - an all out strike."

"Negotiations?" queried Badaev, "Through whom?"

"Through me," answered Ossipov, unable to resist grinning broadly.

Colonel Badaev was taken aback.

"I'm the negotiator," repeated Ossipov with enjoyment.

"This is madness absolute madness - am I Bunin? - are you Badaev? - and he?" asked Bunin, bewildered.

"Negotiations! and this is your damn scheme. Never! It must never come to that. That means recognition. We do not recognise them as anything but anarchists - criminals."

Of course everything was under control - but that word, entity, pressing to exist, burned within him.

"On the contrary," said Colonel Badaev with a lofty assurance, excited by a glimpse of the implications in Ossipov's dual role.

"What greater achievement - what greater compliment to Valentin. They must trust him utterly! If we keep a cool head - a cool head I say, Grigory Efimovich - this whole situation plays absolutely into our hands. With Valentin as negotiator we shall be in complete control. The screw can be tightened just as we wish. Till they're completely demoralised - crushed. All resistance can be choked out of them - now and forever. In one go - smooth - efficient - and they'll know what authority means."

"Crushed - demoralised - that's it - that's more like it," said Bunin.

Colonel Badaev proposed a plan of action. Bunin listened, answered questions of detail but became increasingly dubious about the tameness of it all. Where was it leading? No blood to be tasted in that. He could only see his factory frozen in a silence, an empty stillness of bricks and machines. That's what the wreckers wanted - to destroy his creation.

He'd do it for them!

What he'd built - he'd destroy - and no one else!

He'd stop the never ending life of men and machines with the greatest power of all which these hooligans still hadn't learned to recognise - Bunin power!

Never mind about your screws. This would be an explosion - of silence. Demoralise for sure - a million times over.

Let Badaev drone on.

Nurture this inspiration!

What else to expect from this fool with his fancy uniform?

What did he know of real work, of coping with these bloody minded hooligans? Eating well, signing documents, wearing uniforms. That was about it. Sitting on their arses all of them. Not such a bad thing if Badaev spent a few days in No. 2 Furnace for instance - with the sweat dripping down his fat arse.

Listening carefully to Colonel Badaev, Ossipov realised just how much power he had. Be damned, Bunin! That you dare so intimidate me! No! It was not we who were in complete control- but I. I'm the one who can direct things in any way I choose - the fixing of the Yid Liebman! Vengeful arrow's finality for Father. Immediately he must spread confusion and mistrust - rumours of theft from the strike fund - theft of the workers' hard earned money - then a handbill - to tell the world who Karpenkov was - to tear the mask off that swine - a tool! the whole affair a yidplot. That was it! All there! Given to him! Simply to get on with it!

Colonel Badaev was well aware of Ossipov's discomfiture and hostility. On their way back together he stopped his carriage before it entered the town and praised Ossipov's work. Lofty work, worthy of a loyal Russian. Of course the Bunins of this world were pretty crude fellows, but in their way loyal Russians too. Yes, in a sense all the threads were in Ossipov's hands - a great responsibility. Much more important assignments could be expected.

As Ossipov got out and walked to his room he was filled with the righteousness of his course.

Coachman Vladimir was well on his way to Colonel Badaev when Pavel passed through the wrought iron gateway and quietly advanced along the wide well-kept drive. Reaching the avenue of sweet-smelling lime which led to the pillared porch, he moved cautiously, in the shadows, tree by tree, watching ahead intently.

He halted, recognising the figure near the entrance. The Rodomanovsky carriage rolled past and he ducked right down to the moist night earth. Shouting and roaring reached out in the chilly air, unmistakably Bunin's. Another carriage clattered past and again he ducked. He recognised Colonel Badaev stepping out. Bunin appeared in the hallway, shouting, gesticulating. A few words, repeated, sounded clearly. Negotiate – arrest – crushed – choked – Bunin's anger – Colonel Badaev's gestures of pacification – Akayev's appearance out of the shadows at Colonel Badaev's beckoning – all very puzzling – but no question – the three of them involved over the strike! At this very moment – with Akayev! Meaning – meaning? – impossible confusion.

But none of that his concern. Only the one thing! This one thing, returning to his room, not alone but with her, irresistibly with her through this whispering world of shadowy presences. Whispering presences with whom he would willingly linger through these empty streets – Dunia – shadowy source.

Yehuda was sleeping as Pavel eased himself into the bed beside her. To breathe in as strength their closeness.

No longer tired, puzzled, agitated. Not seeking sleep. Becoming the shaping, sharpening point of an irrevocable purpose. Not sleep but this warmth, Dunia's warmth, glowing, a flame, consuming through him the treachery, rottenness. In her, her warmth, the fire, measured, unwavering. Fire burnishing through the pale night hours to a purpose, so pure, so sharp.

Ossipov slept lightly. Colonel Badaev's words suggested a new, exciting mastery. He got up early, eager to be at it, blithe. Today the killing. Today his creation. Slow down or speed it up at will. What idiots they all were!

At 7 o'clock the Strike Committee met together openly for the first time in No. 3 shop, the most militant. Men from other shops were quickly informed and crowded in expectantly. In the open now for the first time, face to face with all these men, their being, very substance of the deed which had brought them all thus far. Yehuda's words, hesitant at first, gained strength, confidence, an exultation wrought from their affirming, united presence, wrought from his work, his experience.

The forges and presses ran idle, their muted rhythms potential with new themes in the changing awareness, no longer tyrannical counterpoint, as men pressed forward to hear, question, discuss. New possibilities were hinting of work, machines, world. A new perspective was daring to shape itself into being.

Yehuda explained carefully the demands that were being put to management; that they would give management till the end of the day shift for a satisfactory answer; that any response would be circulated immediately by their representative members, the strike committee, and that for today everyone should keep working as normal.

A vote on it then!

All hands were raised, most with enthusiasm.

Any questions?

"If management want a showdown, how's the strike fund – and where's it held?"

"We're going to win!"

"Shut up!" shouted the questioner angrily, "I'm not a child! I've got a wife and three kids – and I want an answer."

Yehuda, standing on an upturned crate, sensed the need for an immediate, firm response. Looking straight at the questioner and then taking in the whole assembly he said, "Rest assured – everyone. The fund stands at nearly 380 roubles. Your strike committee will distribute the money as and when needed – in your presence. It's your money! We'll decide all together just how it should be handed out."

The questioner was satisfied.

"And now," Yehuda continued raising a sheet of paper and turning to Ossipov, "Semyon Akayev from the Goods Department will take our demands to management."

Amidst cheering Ossipov took the paper, waved back cheerfully, and left. They all returned to their work.

On his way! What a fantastic business! Cheerful indeed to lead the poor devils right on into the shit! But now, very serious, to confront management.

Pavel Khodeev's mood held sombre throughout the excitement. He had awoken to the day reluctantly, a great sadness in his soul.

For him and Dunia alone.

Relentless, brilliant, the light in which he saw Akayev. Light that had to be endured, exposing in all its duplicity every gesture, word, of Semyon. Within its focus Akayev's every move revealed its untruth. Night grimace – evil – present still! In that cheerful wave on his way to management – a gloating wink, a cunning sneer in eye – lips – hand – implacable line of that grimace – low – bending low – lope – smoothly lope! as he left, of that old gamey creature that he knew so well from deep deep within. Dimitrovka days – ways.

The chase under way – very scent of it underway at last!

O yes cunning snarling one – your measure at last!

But then – but then! – all that hope – expectation of something new for them all – finished. Utterly finished!

Ossipov, hurrying on his way to Bunin's office was determined to do for both of them – the Jew – and that swine Bunin for his insults last night. And why this breathless hurry? To whose tune was this? Stop! and saunter. Just saunter along. He was the timekeeper in this performance. Let them all wait a little longer – on him.

Inside the administrative block he climbed the stairs slowly, up to the office on the first floor where Bunin was sitting at a green baize covered table with his three plant managers. They had been called without explanation and sat waiting uneasily while the boss read from papers in front of him, frowning from time to time, clearly in a rotten mood or worse – ready to explode.

Clerk Akayev from Goods, walked straight in without knocking, cheerful, at ease. They were baffled. Bunin looked up slowly, his mouth pouted threateningly at Ossipov's bearing, attitude.

"What happens here is absolutely secret," Bunin ordered.

They nodded dutifully, their bafflement increased.

With a flourish Ossipov opened out the sheet of demands and handed it to Bunin.

"Here Grigory Bunin – is –"

"Don't dare give me that rubbish," said Bunin, pounding the table with his fist.

"Let *them* see it and learn from it. Learn well gentlemen just what you're dealing with here," his voice rose angrily as he stabbed a finger in Ossipov's direction.

Ossipov recoiled sharply at the unexpected attack and thrust the paper down in front of senior engineer Rudnev who read it and silently passed it on. None of them were sure of just what Bunin expected them to learn from it.

"Exactly what are we supposed to do?" demanded Bunin angrily, extremely reluctant in the light of day to accept that this Ossipov was indeed directing the affair, and blaming himself bitterly for having given in to Badaev.

"Deliberate - consider - discuss - negotiate," answered Ossipov with some relief, or was Bunin going to repeat his nonsense of last night?

"Negotiate! I alone - my sweat blood brain! Deliberate! Are you mad? I told you last night, never!"

Bunin pounded the table again making the papers jump and his three subordinates cringe.

"Impressions! Impressions!" Ossipov shouted, "Don't you see - that's what we've all got to do. Give impressions!"

He shouted with such passion, desperate to protect his fragile, inspired improvisation from this idiot, that Bunin was momentarily forced to listen.

"Listen! Listen Bunin," Ossipov almost whispered.

"This approach of mine is like litmus paper," said Ossipov, in the very effort to convince, becoming clearer himself. "The exact shade of every worker can be correctly judged. Right up to the moment of crisis. Those showing even the faintest red - out! You gentlemen surely understand that."

He turned to the engineers but they could hardly understand any of it and remained silent.

Something about his words impressed Bunin.

"And how long's it all going to take, this - litmus business?" he demanded.

"Till tomorrow. Tomorrow morning. Then we'll bag the lot. I'll make out a list for Badaev tonight - in order of importance. There's your shades for you. At least four who must be arrested on the spot."

"Shades? Shades? What are you talking about?" shouted Bunin, confused, feeling tricked, "It's men we want - names - workers - not shades."

"Names eh? Here's names then - to be going on with."

From a pocket he pulled out a grubby list which included the Strike Committee. He jabbed it at Bunin.

"There! Names - men - workers - wreckers. And there'll be more tomorrow, providing you do what I ask."

Bunin stared at the list and passed it to Rudnev. That at least was something real.

"Alright. Alright then," Bunin said grudgingly, "but mind you, tomorrow morning. That's the limit. The absolute limit. Not a minute longer. And now gentlemen – as we've nothing to do but wait here most of the day –"

"Not quite nothing," intervened Ossipov, "At about – let's say three o'clock – I want you to call me back."

"Back?" queried Bunin, annoyed.

"Yes – to clarify certain points about the demands which you will proceed to see in – shall we say – a more positive, a more hopeful light. Don't forget – don't forget," he warned, sensing Bunin's increasing annoyance and the need yet once again to spell it all out to this idiot, "it's impressions we're talking about and you promised to do what I ask. So Grigory Bunin – thus Grigory Bunin – we can give a little hope to the workers, can't we? We can loosen and tighten – loosen and tighten – till they're utterly demoralised. And that's what we're after. That's what Colonel Badaev was talking about – wasn't it?" he finished excitedly.

The patronising tone made Bunin bristle. He could see no way out. Had he suspected such a preposterous entanglement with this creature he would never have undertaken any of it. But how then? The whole business was Badaev's. And on Badaev's men all ultimately depended.

Ossipov returned slowly to No.3 shop, letting his frustration over Bunin simmer down and feeling out the mood, gestures, words for his meeting ahead, with the men. Mood, gesture, words, partly to be created, partly discovered in the thrust of this play, his, yet not completely.

As soon as he entered the workshop four members of the Strike Committee hurried over to him, including Pavel, who watched him carefully.

"What did Bunin say?"

"Who was with him?"

"D'you think he'll agree?"

Ossipov smiled confidently and raised his hand for quiet, feeling in that gesture his power over them as they looked to him expectantly.

"Come on Semyon – details! Details! How did Bunin take it?"

"I bet the old man was bloody surprised."

"Bloody angry you mean!"

Other workers downed tools and began to crowd round.

They wanted details eh? Good enough!

"Bunin, my friends, stood up – actually stood up when I went in," began Ossipov.

"Never!"

Careful! Don't overplay your hand.

"Of course! that means he acknowledged Semyon as the workers' representative – what else?"

"Imagine! the boss stood up! That's half the battle won already."

"Well done Mikhail! You timed it well."

What a good humoured mood. The whole business bounding along by itself!

"And then, Semyon?"

"Then – he took the paper from me very gravely – read through our demands with utmost seriousness and asked the others to do the same."

"What others?"

"There was senior engineer Rudnev."

"That sod!"

"– engineer Fevralski – engineer Levik –"

"Big stuff! imagine! They were all there to hear."

"Bunin questioned me on certain points – closely," Ossipov continued, "he wanted to be sure that he understood them properly – oh yes! and this is how he finished up – I'm sure that your committee will act sensibly and that the tradition of good behaviour amongst Bunin workers will not be besmirched."

Out of the blue it came, surprising, delighting with its potential for misunderstanding and conflict.

"But what about negotiations?"

"Didn't they say when they'll answer us?"

"Good behaviour? We're not children!"

"What points did you discuss with him?"

"Fellow workers!" called out Yehuda, "These questions won't help us very much. We've given them a time limit. All we can do is wait."

They went back to their benches mulling over Akayev's account but unable to draw any clear conclusions. For some, an optimism prevailed from the very fact that the boss had read through the demands seriously. For others, pessimism and suspicion were aroused by Bunin's reference to their behaviour, their good sense, but no mention of negotiations.

Ossipov sensed the uncertainty with satisfaction. Yehuda went with him to the other workshops where he repeated his performance with more polish, more enjoyment, and similar results. As three o'clock approached he was very tense as to whether Bunin would go through with his plan. No question that Bunin hadn't really entered into the spirit of things but he dared not risk going back to the office and checking up. Yet so far everything was moving with a swing and he felt increasingly sure of his touch.

At three o'clock precisely a stooping elderly clerk, Anatoly Kuprin, appeared, unfamiliar spectre in the heat and din of the workshop. Bunin, determined on some absolute minimum for Ossipov's crazy litmus business, had insisted, "that for nobodies a nobody - and let nobody tell me otherwise," he roared.

A worker stacking coils of heavy wire noticed Kuprin.

"Off your arse uncle?" he wondered with some curiosity and amusement. "Don't be afraid, this is where the work is."

"Which one is Akayev?" asked Kuprin, still trembling from Bunin's startling choice of him, Bunin's command to leave the office and venture into this hostile territory. Bunin had never addressed him in all these years. Why now? Why not his chief, Nikitov?

"Akayev? Akayev? Why? Who wants Akayev?" the young worker questioned excitedly.

"Our good master Grigory Bunin wants him immediately," answered Kuprin, relieved at having uttered that last word which Bunin had so insisted on, "Don't dare forget - you must say immediately! - dogs!"

"Akayev is wanted immediately! Bunin wants Akayev immediately," the young worker shouted.

Men came crowding round.

"Immediately?"

"That's more like it."

"There's your negotiations for you."

"Well done Semyon. Tell him what's what."

Broadening grins acknowledged each other, strengthened each other, yet cautiously. But clearly, surely, the boss then was beginning to take the true measure of them.

"Semyon! Semyon!" the cry went up, "Semyon! Semyon!" steady yet exuberant with their fervent support for this man who advanced towards Kuprin, this fighter through whom each felt himself doing battle with Bunin.

Ossipov had for some time been glancing anxiously towards the entrance of No.3 shop. Through the chanting praise something of the men's mood unexpectedly touched him.

"Fellow workers, this could be the turning point," he announced dramatically, but the catch in his voice sounded to him uneasily, nor truly what he wanted, some chaos, the two worlds, his theirs, not at all clear. As he left the workshop behind and made his way across the stacked yard with Kuprin the two worlds separated out clearly again. The plan reasserted itself.

In Bunin's office he found everyone busily engaged. Bunin was dictating to his secretary and discussing with his chief clerk. The engineers were involved in writing up reports. No-one showed any interest in him.

He went over to Bunin.

"Well - everything is going according to plan," he tried cheerfully.

Bunin stared up annoyed at the interruption.

"Grigory Bunin I want you to call in Bakhmetyev - from No.2 Rolling Mill," he said, well aware of the antagonism.

Bunin's fist flew up, and was stayed above his head by Ossipov's violent reaction, before slowly descending.

"Bunin you're a fool! I'm not one of your workers. Don't dare treat me like one. None of your shit! My father was a Russian officer. D'you hear? An officer!"

He was white with fury as the pride of his mission awoke and stormed through him, for all to hear and know who he was and who his father was, an officer of his Imperial Majesty.

"I'm here in this wretched works of yours for one purpose only. To weed out, destroy, exterminate the workers who're disloyal. I'm not doing it for you personally. You personally don't interest me that much," he snapped his fingers right under the amazed Bunin's nose. "I'm doing it just as my father did his task -unappreciated - unrewarded - even reviled - yes reviled - sacrificing his all - for Russia. And you should know - all of you here in this office - what's being done for Russia - this weeding out of the loyal and disloyal."

He swung round wildly on them, exulting in this torrent of self-righteousness, and the power of this last indictment which applied to everyone!

"D'you understand you dimwit? You've got disloyal workers – lots of them – and you've got a few loyal workers. Bakhmetyev is a loyal worker. And he's going to help us. And you're going to call him now – your part of this damn bargain."

The engineers who had glanced stealthily at one another when Ossipov shouted that he was not one of Bunin's workers, had paled at the onslaught, not daring to look at the boss. Bunin was shocked by the power, virulence, suddenness of the attack into a wary respect for Ossipov.

"A few? loyal workers. Why haven't they made themselves heard then – these loyal workers?" he asked, with something of self-pity, confused, chastened.

"They have and they were threatened for it! Bunin – you know nothing about your workers. Nothing at all! Now – I insist. Have him called and you'll see how he can help."

When Bakhmetyev appeared Ossipov briefed him to set in motion certain rumours about the strike fund, before the evening shift took over. That it didn't amount to the figure given out by the Strike Committee: that it didn't amount to two days keep let alone two weeks; that the fund was being drunk away; that it was missing, any serious accusation like that would do. And when Bakhmetyev returned to his shop he must give the impression that Bunin had called him in to see whether he, chosen at random as an ordinary worker, actually agreed with the terms set out by the Strike Committee.

Back at No.3 Shop, Ossipov told how Bunin was engrossed with his chief clerk and seriously considering whether the business could support the wage claims. He told too how Bakhmetyev had been called in to confront him, as Bunin wanted to satisfy himself that the men were genuinely behind the claims and the threatened strike action. Ossipov's account generated considerable optimism, and praise for Yehuda's tactics, to which he added his carefully directed share.

Yehuda was surprised and delighted at how well things were going. Didn't it prove, he explained confidently, that when the boss was faced by the facts, he did indeed see the light. He obviously realised that the workers meant business, and weren't frightened, even at the cost of withdrawing their labour with its threat of starvation. Again questions were asked about exactly when negotiations would begin and Ossipov answered calmly that it couldn't be long now.

Around seven o'clock rumours about the strike fund reached No.3 Shop. Yehuda refused to take them seriously. Lensky wondered whether it might be a trick on management's part. Ossipov countered that surely even management didn't think the men so stupid as to be taken in by such rubbish.

But where was it coming from? And why?

With two hours to go there was still no sign from Bunin. Neither no nor yes. The Strike Committee were unprepared for such a situation. Ossipov was thoroughly enjoying it.

The light in Bunin's office, closely monitored, was reported still burning. Most unusual at eight o'clock. They must still be sitting. Couldn't be long now. But what plans regarding the night shift? The rumours were circulating in plenty, not simply rumours but so-called facts now to whose seriousness Yehuda was alerted. All highly accusatory about the Strike Committee members. That Peshkov had done two years for fraud. That Korovin had been inside for arson. That Mikhail Karpenkov wasn't his real name. Could such be trusted as workers' representatives? The Strike Committee countered swiftly with total denials. Yehuda was forced to recognise an enemy determined to spread mistrust and confusion. The Strike Committee remained pledged to the task ahead and to one another with the tempered elation of men on the threshold of a critical, far reaching event in their destiny.

By ten past nine, most shifts having changed and still without an answer, they would have to wait till morning. The night shifts were confused by the rumours and counter-rumours, including the very latest, that management would definitely see the Strike Committee at nine in the morning, with a clear answer. Bunin himself had contributed this one. In spite of the Strike Committee's dismissal of it, feeling the whole business moving beyond their control, someone had apparently overheard senior engineer Rudnev remarking to engineer Fevralski as they left the administrative block together that nine tomorrow "would see it through".

Bunin and his engineers had learned much from Ossipov, had come to see the comprehensiveness of his strategy and were contributing to it with much pleasure. Bunin intended to see the workers at nine, intended to show Ossipov how to make disloyal workers loyal, very quickly. Meanwhile let the wretches stew in uncertainty overnight.

Ossipov was well satisfied. Not Bunin, no-one, was going to stop him from tightening the screw, from choking all resistance out of them. That much Badaev had got exactly right! The Strike Committee and the Yid were in for a real shock, and he'd put that ruffian in his place. Most instructive how that fist had been stuck fast in mid air by officer! – loyalty! – Russia! – and with what conviction he'd uttered them. Words of such power to threaten – sober up that windy oaf. And who knows? perhaps he did have a special gift for this kind of work, just as Colonel Badaev had said.

Everyone on the Strike Committee was coming to realise that a deadly serious enemy was confronting them. In spite of endless discussions they could not decide how to measure up to it. So much obscure, elusive. How hold back these swirling waters of rumour? – this wild, destructive glee – these creeping poisons. Pavel knew what they were dealing with. Foxy was radiant, simply could not hide his happiness. This vicious hidden attack – their helpless responses – all coming from him. Pavel's intent, cautious watch had brought him certain knowledge. This creeping harassment, this sly destruction, very quick of blood all Foxy's – these darts of gamey cunning from his red-tongued flick.

But no slavering revel to be allowed this crafty swine.

Deeply drink it in his cunning to the very dregs. Brace yourself, point inflexible to his lair in this moonlight haze.

Keenly now to know this trail as of old. Just the two of them. Taking Foxy on. Running him down to his lair.

Fierce breeze of awakening whetting him, keening him.

This bitter-sweet scent yes! to what must come then off on his own. The challenge was good. No he hadn't lost his touch. Now was the time to strike.

Sharp, quick, stealthy with Foxy as the moon's very light drew him out from their bed – away, far away from Dunia thought he fought, fought back hard to stand firm and look down at her, long? long.

But a world pressed in. Great trouble was coming. The others knew nothing and it must be done.

Dunia knew!

Sharp, quick, light he left them, drawn away.

Left Dunia, the little one, Mikhail, all. He had to leave them.

It had to be done.

Ossipov, up very early, was drafting a handbill for distribution later in the day. Colonel Badaev had offered to help with the printing, using Headquarters' press. It would be a final settling of accounts. The workers would know once and for all who was behind their troubles – who was behind everyone's troubles. The Jew traitor unmasked!

Bunin workers! wake up to the devil in your midst.

That Jew arrogance, smug satisfaction, jewgrin – torn away like a foul plaster. The poison, corruption beneath, revealed.

Appearances! Always appearances! And all the rest of this bunch of self-appointed representatives too.

A gentle tap on the door checked the ardent flow.

Opening cautiously he was surprised to see Pavel, finger on lips, warning to keep silent. Pavel went straight to the window and Ossipov followed to see where Pavel was pointing, along the empty street. His eyes followed the direction of the pointing arm but saw nothing of note. About to question, he was again checked by Pavel's warning gesture and allowed himself to be edged in front of Pavel whose arm pointed over his shoulder in order apparently to direct his searching look more accurately.

He focussed harder.

Pavel's arm snapped back to squeeze, shear at his throat in an iron vice, whose closure was fused through Pavel's other arm, vice charged with a will beyond all mere life, pure, unbreakable. Pavel diffused, encircling, in this glowing round of darkness, fury's fullness.

Fierce is Foxy, snapping, snarling.

But down!

Grit, bend, yield, crush. Down! But down!

What bright red cheeks. Game old fellow.

But down you swine. Come on now. Down!

Blazing circle of fiery will, lair scorched away, fire fiercer, to wither every last breath of Akayev-life. Splutter and froth as the flames lick forward on the charred ground of your going.

Burn fire! Burn! Nothing can withstand you. Life shrivels flees before you, dread will indomitable.

Vast me grim burning, Foxy threshing – vast me! – ready to die too – but there! – victorious! – the moment passed – this great fire dying down – this body mine once more –

But don't let go yet.

Not even yet!

Beware the Foxy one.

No letting up. But it would soon be over.

Foxy had fought hard, like the old days.

You made me work Foxy - good for you!

What! Another gasp - but now you know who's master.

How Foxy had thrashed about gasping and grunting!

Now you can smile with pride at the power - that old power, unquenchable in its fury.

So heavy limp this Foxy's body hanging - still keep your arm tight round his rotten throat - then now let go his soft sack of flesh.

No glitter now in those eyes bulging back.

Foxy's face was blue and pinched and sad.

It had to be done.

He sat down in the chair, watching, the pink tipped tongue and the darkly blue shadow draining away to let settle a stiff ashen pallor. Only slowly did that fierce struggle withdraw, die into faintest echo, releasing him to himself, yielding him to a great sadness, everything in desolation as a fine trembling took hold.

The Bunin factory hooter brought him to his feet. Sadly he stared at the silent body bathed in the fresh daylight. He looked round the room. He picked up some papers and saw a list of names headed by the Strike Committee, with ticks and other signs against them, and a call to Bunin workers exposing the Strike Committee as criminals.

A fierce anxiety for the others waned just as suddenly in the growing brilliance of this daylight. Papers - names - the others - become wraiths in this light.

In this day-radiant light on the Kovno road, away back, his way calling.

Away from all this sadness. Just the road itself, the way, horizons, blueness calling.

The Open calling
No longer shut in
But the brothers gone too
Calling
Ivan - Sergei - Mikhail
But ahead above around
Sky land brightness calling
Away! Yes away from Dunia too - but with her forever.

Yes he'd take to the road once more, calling. Away from this gloom and corruption as the green drew him on.

Back, back to Earth you go, you rottenness!

But I to freshness seeking.

Yehuda, still clothed, just as he had lain down, exhausted, after midnight, was dragged awake by the Bunin hooter's raucous blare. Painful anxiety yielded to renewed zest for the struggle ahead which must culminate soon. Realisation of Pavel's absence puzzled and alarmed him as he hurried along with the first shift to join the Strike Committee in No.3 shop. Puzzlement and alarm spread through them all at the realisation of both Pavel's and Akayev's absence. They felt caught up in a dangerous, obscure situation. Nothing was as left the night before. They felt threatened, fragmented, drifting in a heaving swell of rumours, contradictions, accusations.

The strike fund was missing!

Pavel Khodeev and Semyon Akayev had disappeared!

All too obvious.

We've been fooled.

And what about the rest of our so-called representatives?

No longer rumours, unpleasant implications, but sheer lying with whatever lay to hand.

"Machinery had been badly tampered with in the Rolling Mill."

"Cossacks had been seen nearby."

Hectographed sheets were circulating, attacking 'the evil criminals and anarchists who want to destroy our work and force our families into starvation.'

The Strike Committee insisted that this was all a management plot to create confusion - out of desperation, stooping to such lies and nonsense. But where were Pavel and Semyon?

The pamphlet awoke Yehuda most painfully to the depth of his naivety. He tasted, as for the first time, bitter reality of enmity, right here, in this action, and out from this very bitterness he must nerve himself to strike back.

In rage to strike back. In rage, pain to strike back violently against the force speed mastery of the enemy who seemed to be everywhere.

Around eight o'clock great excitement accompanied a new rumour, that management was ready to negotiate soon, which could only mean the nine o'clock deadline. Yehuda wanted the

Strike Committee to be extremely wary. A new rumour had it that the Committee were to be questioned over the missing funds.

Rumours, counter-rumours, lies, suspicions, hatreds, spawned forth to entangle every effort by the Committee and those supporters who still remained loyal, to ascertain and declare the truth. Those workers last to be won over were wavering, withdrawing support. So much was now beginning to be seen at stake, but with the odds apparently as far less certain than ever suspected.

Bakhmetyev had done his work well. Now he brought the issue clearly into the open by quickly, with his supporters, organising a large gathering in the yard itself, soon crowded with uncertain, confused workers from most shops. He asked for a show of hands on whether to down tools at nine if no answer were forthcoming from management. One after another, beginning with close supporters, hands were raised, to become a total decision against.

The news of this turnabout was immediately conveyed to No. 3 shop where the men were preparing to stop work and shut down the furnaces. Bakhmetyev's messenger left to cries of, "Cowards! - Bastards!"

"What are they up to?"

"Are we going to be the only ones - the only ones?"

Kuprin appeared again.

Nine exactly!

A cheer went up - no rumour this!

Kuprin came over to Yehuda, trembling, desperate to remember every Bunin word exactly.

"That's it! That's it!"

"Negotiations!"

"They've seen the light."

The elderly clerk breathed in deeply and pressing his lips tight, raised his head towards the roof.

"Grigory Bunin the owner himself - and the management - himself - themselves - will now see you personally."

He lowered his head and wandered away in confusion, those exact words?

"He was right you see - he was right!" they cheered as Yehuda followed him out of the shop into the yard, proud that Bunin, no less, had recognised him as the leader, as the one to deal with.

Lightly he trod, now that the goal had been achieved – and really so quickly.

The men returned to their work with a confidence, dignity, brightness that related them to its sounds, smells, fierce demands, even tyranny, in a newly expectant way.

Let this power thrive – the wheels turn – the sparks shower, faster, fiercer. They need no longer fear. This tyranny being tamed at last. Their voice was being heard.

"Are these negotiations? Why don't they call us all – the whole committee?" Shavrov insisted.

"Stop complaining! They're afraid of us all together. Who better than Mikhail to speak for us all – eh? – or don't you think?"

As Yehuda neared the office block he felt the reality of his power. Long awaited moment, he must sternly check this exultation. He must not overplay his hand, presume to take advantage of a chastened, even frightened management. Be cautious, compromising, consider the hurt to Bunin's pride. Make clear to Bunin that the workers are sober, reasonable men, but that they must be treated fairly.

He followed Kuprin along a ground floor corridor into a small room. Kuprin still anxiously trying to carry out his instructions exactly, was, through his very bewilderment, beginning to worry about Yehuda. He explained that someone would soon be along. Yehuda was grateful for the extra time in which to prepare himself – here in this quiet room – something very discreet then – even in secret – with Bunin.

Three gendarmes entered briskly, grabbed his arms, pulled him violently to his feet, snapped his arms behind his back into handcuffs, propelled him along at the same brisk pace without a word and bundled him into a waiting carriage with blinds drawn, at the work's entrance, which had been kept cleared for hours.

The same procedure was repeated at brief intervals for the rest of the Strike Committee. Rumours had it that they were being interrogated over the missing strike funds, one by one, to prevent any further trickery. Of course the carriage was taking them to jail. They were guilty men.

Bunin was very impatient to begin his personal settling of accounts. But the officer in charge of the operation which had thus far proceeded smoothly, was an obstinate, precise man. His list of arrests was not complete. Where were Semyon Akayev and Pavel Khodeev? A tall, thin suspicious man, he thrust his list of names at Bunin, showing his pencil line neatly through each of the nine arrested and insisted that he would not leave until the two were found, the operation properly completed. Bunin worried little about Ossipov, though remembering that he was to be arrested for appearance sake. As for Khodeev, the man might be ill or dead damn him! What matter!

He was becoming desperate to begin right now, fearful that the moment, the whole timing would be snatched away. On the point of actually pleading, offering any way out possible for this idiot to leave with his men - a large bribe! - he was inspired to write a note, explaining the situation to Badaev and taking on himself full responsibility for insisting that the operation now cease. The officer studied it carefully and eventually decided that it would be a sufficient safeguard when he reported back to his chief.

At last then, his moment had come.

As with his dogs he'd teach them a lesson they'd never forget. Who the master was - once and for all. For their own good.

Badaev was right, this isolating the leaders. Now he'd show them who the real leader was.

At last the absoluteness of his power could express itself openly, beyond all doubt.

A little while after the second coachload of Committee members was on its way to the jail, the power supply to the workshops was shut down. All workers were ordered to assemble in No.3 Shop where Bunin would address them.

All of them. To see, to hear, to fill themselves with his presence.

In the unprecedented silence of No.3 Shop, no-one dared to speak, to risk uttering or hearing his own unfamiliar voice. In this space before one another, glancing about in embarrassment they waited, suspicious, touched with some obscure fear. That tough shell within which they shouted, lip-read against the furious gale of blasting power hour on hour, was dissolving. All of them together as presence, purely human presence, were threatening to break through. Fierce blood of this presence, such a lively potency.

In this painful space of a new awareness dawning, many looked around tentatively at the iron web about them, knots, coils, tentacles as for the first time, and so high above, at the grimy skylights. Men from all over crowded in. Only a decision from the top was responsible for this. Viktor Belov, scowling foreman of the Rolling Mill, climbed onto a bench and began to speak, on Bunin's orders, to which he had reluctantly agreed. He stared solemnly up at the roof as the murmuring died down. He began uneasily.

"Our esteemed employer Grigory Bunin - I repeat - our esteemed employer Grigory Bunin will soon address us all."

The words boomed out as he drew himself up but the silence echoed a faltering tone. He looked anxiously towards the entrance of the huge shed and with relief saw Bunin striding in briskly. All eyes focused on Bunin as he stopped sharply some twenty yards inside the entrance, similarly distant from the nearest workers.

What had been threatening so dangerously to break forth was violently pressed back, with bitterness yet relief, by Bunin's presence. Their familiar selves quickly restored. Grumbling, suspicious, but in whom no danger smouldered.

In one swift, all-embracing glance, Bunin sensed what he knew well as normal, the cowering, the sullen resignation. Slowly, decisively, he turned his head to look right round the building, taking in the workers, the machinery, the walls and roof, his building, that each pair of eyes fix, confirm, endure him, unmistakably. A most meaningful unhurried gesture, that magically reaffirmed it all, that whole woven unity of men and things as substance of his very being. What had tenderly dared to be - gone!

As of old each knew his place and was it.

Bunin's gesture sealed again their bond with him.

Who and what he was - and who and what they were.

"Loyal workers of Bunin's," he began, referring to something greater than himself, than them all, he and they together. Not appealing, or describing, but commanding, warning.

"- these machines - this whole works -" his arm swung slowly round, hand pointing beyond these walls, "have never - I repeat - have never stopped before."

Pausing he stared momentarily with the slightest narrowing of eyes at a group whom he associated with No.3 Shop.

"Rest assured - they will not stop again in my lifetime. The men responsible have all been arrested. Evil men, anarchists who so easily deluded you - who so easily misused your trust. Men who won't stop at wrecking our works. They want to wreck our Russia as well. And what have they achieved? They've taken the food from your mouths and from your children's mouths. Because until these machines are mended there won't be any work here."

Angry murmurs broke out.

Mended?

Was that the reason they'd stopped? – All of them?

But who'd done that?

"But how long will it take to mend them?" called a worker in desperation.

"And who will suffer?" Bunin reiterated, felling with that worker's cry in absolute control, just as Badaev had said, his finger on the screw itself.

"I? No! You! And as for the money, the so-called strike fund you were so foolish enough to give them. Well! Where is it?" he questioned gravely, commiserating.

"Bastards!"

"Shame!"

"Scum!"

"And how else could it be when you give in to criminals."

"Down with the strikers!"

"Out with the strikers!"

"Blessings on Grigory Bunin!"

"Bunin's for one and all!"

He raised his hand for quiet.

"Learn this," the tone almost caring, "there will always be help available for loyal Bunin workers."

Bewildered, bitter, anxious yet hope stirring.

"In fact some strike money has been recovered by the police – they too have your interests at heart. And I shall add to it. And the money will be given back – fairly."

He had never intended any of this but the fierce outbursts of cheering seemed to justify it.

"When the machines have been repaired – which could take one – two weeks? according to Engineer Rudnev's estimate," irresistible that turn of the screw, "you will return to work."

"Learn this Bunin workers.

This here is your life – and my life. It must never stop again."

So swift this ebbing away of life's fullness. This void about her. Pavel's absence. And from this desert she must flee.

Homewards, homewards returning to the place that is yours.

Dimitrovka's sparkling waters of green life, youth, where she and her Pavel had laughed and splashed with the others through ardent summer evenings.

So swiftly Vilna vanished behind as she fled with her child from that desert of men, trudging along the dusty road that led back.

In the dream of late summer stillness, shimmering harvest, pulsing to ripeness, in that rippling corn, its gentle thrust and fulness, she was returning home. In that pulsing sea of golden life, returned to herself, the harsh expulsion over. Not just in what she saw around her, so truly there, the wooden houses, the distant spire, but the quickening, the ripening, the pulsing within.

With her child she stood - here right here! was Dimitrovka - in the warmth of this welcome, embrace, by her trees, her stream, her rainbow hued fishes and jolly frogs. Its green strength returning to endure that absence, to tenderly heal that savage Vilna wound. Green strength returning from the waters of life. And as the song from across the way reached towards her, around her, she knew in tearful joy she was back with her own once more.

Only at nightfall venturing closer, listening, watching, dreaming. With her own now under these friendly stars, wraithlike, past her parents' house, sister Maria's, Katya's, grandfather's, gladness on gladness, on up the street, to the far edge, slowly now, her heart beating fast as she stopped in the silence by their wooden cottage - home. Found again, as treasure lost, overgrown, empty, waiting. Mildew and rot its anguish, uncared, abandoned for that deadly mirage, yet waiting, enduring. This odour its emptiness, waiting, needing her return.

Awaiting the touch of her presence that could bring it to life once more. Tenderly she entered its bitter-sweet sadness, womb, shelter of their glowing young life, so painfully betrayed. No, brothers of Pavel - me you will not break!

As she sat with the sleeping child she knew she too could wait, could endure.

The unfinished wooden bowls still there! their incompleteness hers.

Was it ever more than a spectre that went to Vilna?

Only for his sake wrenched away - his frustration and bitterness - but leaving herself behind.

His absence no more than the moon's swift shadows till the radiant sunlight returned. Already from that far shore the strength approached her, reaching out. The strength which no mere stream of time could weaken. Dimitrovka's strength, of father and mother and stream and birdsong and corn that would bind them both together, as one, enduring, evermore.

VIII

Aaron's Way

Each night, the empty beds a constant reminder, as a righteous remnant, Aaron Liebman found himself caught up in a strange harsh realm of question, beginning and ending, always, with its own very riddle. What is Thought? What is Real?

Each morning thankful for being returned to the familiar. Rabbi Mendel, fellow students, the books, the study comforting, comfortable, not daring to let himself believe in their - unreality? Rather doubt that strange realm itself when returned to them, amidst them, back from that parched place. Grateful to them - yet.

Nights, again nights through which he wandered on some quest. Yet on awakening, a dream, enduring shadow of his daylife.

Arduously he struggled each night through grim landscape.

Thought!

Challenging call from the start.

First form given to that something so vague, so clear.

Threshold.

Simple awareness of the self-proliferating, self-creating.

Then then then in this lunar shadowplay, groping handhold by groping handhold - All is Thought!

Handhold by handhold.

Thought is not Real

then what is Real?

Directionless yet drawn on to call out and name for himself, at any cost to establish something for himself, these obscure lights in this weird demanding place.

Thought is not Real!

Then what is Real?

'Thought is not Real' mercilessly threatened prayers and studies with meaninglessness.

'What then is Real?' forced him to fling out desperate handholds clutching at the hard facts, as a very earth on which to stand upright amongst threatening chaos, annihilation.

This bedrail so felt, so fiercely gripped was real.

But, so lonely this peak – what is man when he isn't thinking – what is that space?

The bedrail is real – repeat! test out! consolidate!

Sitting up sharply he shook his head to free himself from it all, confused as to the time and his whereabouts. Yet aware of something long hovering near. Yes indeed the unreality of thought but a mightier affirmation – the Greater. Reality! whose very presence now known, true comfort, enigma, joyful enigma.

In the early hours a brief groan from the next bed awoke him. Lemel?

And again, so brief, and the sound of a word. He got up quickly and came very close. Lemel's face was flushed, his eyes opened and quickly closed. It could be – must be – "water". Get some water!

From what depths – what otherness disclosed – a warning? – what threshold sounding in that groan, as quickly, quietly, not wanting to wake anyone, feeling what was happening as so intimately bound to himself, he filled a mug, lifedraught, and put it to Lemel's lips. But Lemel had dozed off, hot, restless, some sort of fever.

Aaron knew he must stay close and watch. Others were awakening into the dawn light dissolving nightlight's familiar shadows. Quiet and concern prevailed during dressing and preparation for prayer in the study room. Daniel went to inform Rabbi Mendel of Lemel's condition.

Aaron knew that he was watching for something, but for what? And this helplessness?

Rabbi Mendel decided that if no improvement was noted by midmorning Dr Zaitsman would be called in.

Aaron began to recognise in the watching so ardent, enjoined, that something was taking over. Began to hear in that brief groan a voice sounding. Not Lemel's voice. No more pretence – the distance vast. Beyond the personal. Lemel beyond the personal. But where then?

He knew –must know that it was Lemel. So much then of what he saw, was watching, depending on him!

Riddler!

Groan scratching across him – a calling from somewhere beyond.

Wild thoughts gathering – about the one who was closest. Ending?

Ended?

What! that his face - him Lemel - no longer holding together. What was it what was it? this hardening dispersing - beyond him - happening where? The familiar one and only Lemel now no longer - what challenge this?

Refuse to be taken in - preserve! no not preserve! Lemel was - and was as always yet - yet - the resonance in all this turmoil - pointing to a greater reality -

challenged obscurely - yet to go with it - Lemel and he inseparable still.

He stood aside as Dr Zaitsman, Litvinoff's personal physician, took most careful account of the symptoms. The fever - that neck so rigid to the touch - the drowsiness - drowsiness? - more - comatose no question - three of these in the last two years - very serious but here thank God no sign of the red-purple spots. No threat of epidemic! Needn't fear reporting a Jewish epidemic but they're all so pale here - so badly nourished in spite of Chaim Litvinoff's beneficence! Should he offer some comfort amidst this whispering silence and anxiety as they stood back with respect, waiting, watching?

"Well," he began quietly to Rabbi Mendel, in front of them, as best he could of truth, comfort, adjusting his pince-nez, "it is serious. I suggest cold compresses - and an ointment which I'll write out. He should be moved to a quiet place - and I'll be back this afternoon to see how things are."

He left, to face up to such a rapid and fierce onslaught from this enemy. But time - time would even the balance. Only a question of time for medical science. Wasn't their traditional response the best, for the moment?

All concluded what that return visit really meant. All felt that Lemel was no longer properly with them. All heard the challenge and were ready to take it up with God.

The small baggage room on the dormitory floor was cleared, Lemel moved in and a vigil rota established.

Dr Zaitsman's afternoon visit was expected to be conclusive.

When he left the room with Rabbi Mendel they knew from his sad nod towards them, wanting to face them, to somehow confess a helplessness, a doctor's helplessness. They knew Lemel was dying. They knew from that nod it was only a question of time till the turning down of the eyelids. They knew that Lemel was dying.

But they were not helpless.

On the contrary. The Lord of Life and Death was their Lord. Each one of them now in the Seminary personally called. No!

They must through their prayer make real if ever, a way to the Lord of Life and Death right now.

Pray pray pray, ancient response, the most real.

But why, why them? why the Seminary again? just now at this time of healing over, leaving behind them the dreadful betrayal.

One more attack on their faith. To be tested again then?

Accept!

Accept then – and pray!

In the study room many members of the community had come to join in the prayers.

"These days there are worse things than death for a Jew. The Almighty will decide," declared Vitebsky.

Aaron, to his consternation, felt unable to join in the prayers.

Dark flame of Vitebsky's word, bitter this knowing, as he changed places with Ruben to maintain the vigil beside – what?

Not! – to resist – deny – those – eyes – line of mouth – all a narrowing – twisting apart – discordant – no longer his Lemel. The Lemel that he always and only knew.

Was that the challenge – from the dark flame?

What he saw with eyes was unreal – before this – which he alone must sustain – meet – create – his Lemel.

But – but – where now that hope, that fullness shared?

It – was happening – which nothing could stop.

At nine Daniel took over.

In the study room voices were hushed, speech faltered. Aaron wanted to cry out against this pathetic attempt to seek shelter from the chilling loneliness. He wanted to expose the whole feeble illusion.

The rota of vigil and prayers was maintained through the night. Aaron slept fitfully.

He awoke to the startling realisation that Lemel's parents had not yet been informed. As though Lemel's actual existence had been wiped out for these last hours by this Other. He hurried to the Rabbi's room, bewildering the abyss between the two.

"Rabbi I'm going straight to the bakery for Lemel's father," said Aaron.

Rabbi Mendel had long been in prayer and stood composed yet weary.

He sensed keenly Aaron's alarm, desperation.

"Yes - of course. His father," he answered slowly.

As Aaron set off a shock of uncertainty, loss, something so close and precious pulsed through him. Along Tcherikover Street, chill, empty, in the direction of Moshe Kuperman's bakery, he felt himself in a whirling movement of flight, flight and yet return, stupid, small, in this dream, whole being, stance, movement, transformed.

Of course!

Vitebsky's death is the real.

This ending.

The rest is make-believe, frantic business to hold off this all engulfing space.

At the dilapidated gates of the Old Jewish Cemetery he halted abruptly. New resolution empowering, he walked slowly through the desolate maze of leaning, lurching, crumbling gravestones, to the grave of Rabbi Meir ben Baruch.

Now he must call each thing by its true name.

The crumbling stone.

The rotting paper wads of pleas crammed into every crevice.

And this bent shaking form approaching, mouthing and whining to the dead.

True name - for it all - Illusion!

Crossing the bridge in the freshening breeze he recalled a recent conversation with Yitzhak and Lemel. Looking down at the briskly rippling water, the very tones sounded clear amidst the sadness of the grey, hushed town. Tearfully he heard Lemel's voice, passionately recounting Akiba's martyrdom by the Romans. "That's the way a Jew should die," concluded Yitzhak.

But this was something very different!

No glorious meaning. No example to sustain the generations. Just this miserable blotting out.

But most were mercifully unaware. Theirs a simple coming and going.

Turning into Starobin Street, the bakery almost in sight, the words on which he had decided so long ago, the simple statement "Mr Kuperman, Lemel is dying," now eluded him. He was unsure, afraid of them, for a moment about to flee.

Two beggars stood outside the bakery door, waiting for the

stale pieces that Kuperman gave away. Aaron entered quietly. Kuperman was bending before the open oven door and deftly drawing out the new loaves with his long-handled wooden spade. His sinewy arms glistened with sweat as he passed the loaves onto a large table where his young assistant Eli sorted them. Aaron coughed to attract attention.

"Aaron! our Lemel's Aaron - delighted!" Kuperman called out, smiling warmly, without stopping.

"Hallo Mr Kuperman!" said Aaron, wryly aware of the false tone. Aware of his face as a mask through which he anxiously watched this other world. He glanced distantly at the rows of newly baked loaves, aware of the power of his message and what it would do to Kuperman. The more he steeled himself to blurt it out the more impossible it became.

"Here Aaron!" Kuperman called out, pointing to four large oval loaves set apart from the rest. "You see these! They're what I like baking most. Wedding loaves. And when I make the braid on the top - crossover and crossover and crossover again - I think that will be good for them. You know who it is? Schlomo Kossky and Rachael Yadin. A fine pair! A well matched pair. That's how God arranges it too. You'll know it also one day Aaron. She there - you here - then the braiding - the crossing over. And didn't I think with gratitude when I was doing it of our dear Lemel. His goodness - his respect for his parents - his learning - and his dear friend Aaron. Didn't I think what a blessing he is to us? Didn't I think of all this with gratitude? Didn't I think when I braided these loaves how it'll be for these two - Schlomo and Rachael? Children to bless them and make their life rich. Some learning here in the bakery eh Aaron? - how the yeast wants the dough to rise up with joy and live - and how the dough just wants to lie there - sad and heavy."

Kuperman shut the oven doors on the trays of unbaked loaves which his young assistant had been pushing through with a long wooden pole. Wiping his hands down his smock and glancing at the next batch of loaves which Eli was preparing, he came over close to Aaron.

"And now Aaron! Tell me what you're doing here at this time of the morning."

Aaron smiled weakly, pretending not to hear. His mouth was dry, his tongue stiff.

"What is it? Rabbi Mendel sent you along for some rolls

before prayers," Kuperman went on jokingly.

Aaron smiled again as if acknowledging the joke.

"Well I only wanted to tell you that Lemel's ill – and we think you ought to see him," he risked, as casually as possible.

"Ah, I thought you weren't your usual self. Worrying over your dear friend. But you mustn't. The Almighty is with us in illness as in health. The Almighty –"

"Mr Kuperman, you must come now," Aaron insisted urgently.

Kuperman set his large wooden mixing spoon down on the table. His brawny arms hung limply as he looked straight into Aaron's eyes.

"Aaron," he whispered, "what are you saying?"

Aaron opened his dry mouth. He felt his eyes filling with tears.

"Aaron – I'm a man – I –"

"Lemel is dying Mr Kuperman. Our dear Lemel is dying."

Aaron kept his eyes to the floor as Kuperman stood so still for some time, his arms hanging slack. Slowly he went over to the oven door and turned the draft right down. Arguing voices sounded from the street.

"Dying?" he nodded grimly to himself, "So!"

Aaron heard resignation – challenge – hope!

Kuperman swung round, apron off and strode out into the street, to Aaron's surprise not turning right towards the Seminary but left towards the town outskirts. Aaron found himself following, simply following, so close, so drawn to this other, thinking it all so strange. Where were they going? Breathless he followed, often forced into a run as Kuperman stepped it out faster and faster.

Everything around him was staining with palest washes as the dawnlight yielded to the buoyant blue above. Form, substantiality awakening amidst the springing lightness, passing the church, behind Kuperman who was already crossing the bridge. Leaving the river, glinting in greygreen coolness, Kuperman took the coach road running east from the town and curving through the woods.

Aaron ran in spurts trying to keep abreast of Kuperman whose eyes were fixed on some distant goal. His head was held high and rigid. His lanky legs were thrown forward ceaselessly as he gritted his teeth, sweating and breathing forcefully. Fixed on Rabbi Pinhas. Rabbi Pinhas the Healer! Rabbi Pinhas the

Reviled!

Through this bitter space hurled forward knowing only the direction - the tales - the rumours - the attacks. Aaron at his side was a form friendly form but no more.

Aaron ran and caught up once again.

"Pinhas!" threw out Kuperman, his features fiercely set.

Aaron fell back. Each time now, try as he would to concentrate on Kuperman, the life around him, of the words, the vista of pastureland opening out, grew ever more insistent. An unfamiliar buoyancy rippled through him, streaming around him, a looseness in his limbs, expanding, joyful in this unknown land, living this dream of the earth.

Distant Kuperman, he small in this enchantment. But the straight road ahead was empty and his alone. Running and walking he reached a fork. A vague image of the dying Lemel dissolved elusively. A growing desperation and confusion could not grant it reality. Elsewhere it belonged. Dry, wistful, utterly elsewhere was its enigma. At the fork he prayed that the path he chose would be the right one. Checking doubts about the act of prayer itself, he went on up the rough rising track to the right. A grizzled old man with a scraggy beast appeared round a bend.

"Why so worried?"

"I'm sure I've lost him," answered Aaron anxiously.

"All paths lead to Him. Rabbi Pinhas will show you where He is," the old man indicated with a nod towards the rise ahead.

Over the ridge Aaron halted. For the first time the name related to happenings in the Seminary. Fierce arguments, rumours. Something more? A violent attack by Rabbi Mendel.

A vista of low lying land opened out and in the distance some humble wooden dwellings.

As soon as Kuperman had crossed the ridge he had run all the way to them. The street, a beaten earth track, was silent, empty but for some children playing at the far end. Kuperman was struck by the dreadful uncertainty that his Lemel might already be dead. And he had not even told his wife Hannah. He had run off like a madman in a nightmare from which he would surely awake.

"Rabbi Pinhas children!" he panted.

They looked at him with curiosity.

"Take me to Rabbi Pinhas children," he pleaded desperately.

Did Rabbi Pinhas even exist?

A confident little red-haired fellow jumped to his feet from the game of bones and led Kuperman by the hand along a path to a wooden house standing alone. Several men and women stood about in a rough circle before it. Others were close around the entrance. As Kuperman approached the boy ran off back to his friends.

A voice from the open window ceased.

The circle broke into movement with song and handclapping. The movement grew faster, wilder with sudden shouts, laughter, rhythmic stamping. It all seemed a mad din rousing Kuperman to bitterness, throwing him back in isolation, afraid of being torn from his life's only task.

As he made for the entrance the circle tried to pull him into the dancing but he grimly shrugged them off. The jostling press at the open doorway confronted him, solid, indifferent. The dancing stopped and the voice began again from the front room which he now saw was also crowded with people. He screamed out,

"Rabbi Pinhas help me!"

"Let him come," answered the voice, in the stillness.

Kuperman pushed through as people squeezed aside.

"Let him through!" commanded the voice.

Kuperman stood facing a chubby faced man with a red, straggly beard and large, tender eyes. He was sitting on a chair whose high back was carved with Hebrew letters.

"My son is dying Rabbi Pinhas."

"So! You've come then," holding out his hand in greeting and smiling gently.

"Levi! some bread and cheese for him – he's come a long way. And wine too yes, wine too."

Rabbi Pinhas turned aside to speak to another.

"Rabbi Pinhas my son is dying. Save him!" Kuperman pleaded desperately, his face twitching, his clenched hands shaking.

"Why?" came the response, calmly.

Kuperman, hearing an indifference, was so shocked that he stood there with tear-filled eyes and chewed stupidly at the bread and cheese.

As Aaron hurried in the direction of the singing he remembered clearly Rabbi Mendel's warning about this man.

The Rabbi hadn't actually used the word 'charlatan', but he had declared that this so-called Rabbi was replacing God in the eyes of his misguided followers. Instead of following God's Torah they were worshipping *him*.

Aaron was determined to be critical, aloof, ready for any tricks. He pushed his way through. These last hours were surely some kind of madness. Lemel must be dead by now and the sooner they returned the better. Amidst whispering and shuffling he reached Kuperman's side, grasped his arm and declared in a loud voice, "Mr Kuperman we must hurry back."

"And who is this?" asked Rabbi Pinhas leaning forward to Kuperman.

"Why! this is my Lemel's dearest friend, our Aaron – our Aaron," answered Kuperman tearfully, his arm still held by Aaron.

"So!" said Rabbi Pinhas looking keenly at Aaron who grew increasingly suspicious.

"Well then," he continued almost curtly, "we shall indeed do something for your Lemel. Yes! Yes! but not because he's your dear one, your only one. Not at all! But because our God is the God of the dead as well as the living."

He turned again to Aaron.

"And how dear is your friend? Are you prepared to give back your life so that he can live? Eh? then we can indeed do something for your only one, your dear one."

Aaron let go his hold on Kuperman's arm. A word had been uttered which forced him to listen with utmost seriousness.

"Where is your son?" Rabbi Pinhas asked in that curt tone again.

"In the Seminary. In the Seminary at Vilna," answered Kuperman smiling blissfully.

Rabbi Pinhas sat straight up in the chair, hands gently held together, eyelids slowly closing. Aaron watched alertly. Had he stopped breathing? His lips were compressed. His body jerked forward slightly. The faintest smile touched his lips. His hands clenched. His body shook, once, twice.

Aaron felt himself nodding off.

When he looked out again Rabbi Pinhas was sitting relaxed, his gaze gently resting on some space between Aaron and Kuperman.

Rabbi Pinhas looked through the open window up at the clouding sky.

"Levi – it is so! Let us go to Vilna. Now!"

A chant went up from all around,

"The Rabbi is going to Vilna

Reb Pinhas is going to Vilna

May the God of the living and dying

Uphold him, be with him, always!"

A few women remained behind with the children but the rest excitedly followed Rabbi Pinhas, Levi and Kuperman on the way to Vilna.

Kuperman, smiling and frowning alternately, soon thrust ahead alone with the rapid nervous strides which had brought him to the Rabbi. But Rabbi Pinhas walked slowly, almost sauntered, steeping himself in the countryside as Kuperman scurried back panting.

"Rabbi Rabbi, hurry please," he pleaded.

"God heals with love not time," answered the Rabbi, not altering his pace. "The love from which Creation stemmed. The love which sustains Creation."

"But he'll be lost if we don't hurry," insisted Kuperman hopping about at his side.

"Lost? What can be lost from His sight? Haven't the Fathers said, the living for death – the dying for life, eh? Life! Your Lemel for Life!"

Kuperman scurried ahead again.

On the way Rabbi Pinhas uttered words to Levi and those nearest, words whose music was taken up by all, to sound forth spontaneous, in verse and chant. Living warmth of his communion with earth and heaven, living song of his joy and praise.

Aaron had withdrawn to the rear. Rabbi Pinhas' few words had intensified his conflict. At one moment, in earnest quest, he sensed the mystery as he strove to track down this his elusive self. At another, suspicious, sensing deception, a whole show of make believe, he hardened himself in sullen distance against this whole nonsense. Then, watching Kuperman's antics he wanted to run to the front and shake this so-called Rabbi in violent challenge.

Nearing the outskirts of Vilna he recalled words from Maimonides on the sacrificing of life. He halted in concentration. Those nearby stopped. Rabbi Pinhas was walking towards him.

"Not words but deeds! The only answer my son. Books won't

help you," he waved his arm for his followers to advance again. "Love is for the simple," he went on at Aaron's side as they walked together. "Your questions will grind you to dust. They come from our friend the Adversary - learn to recognise them. Only love can conquer death and fear. Only love can heal - not learning. And love is simple. Love is God's gift to Israel. Faith is Israel's gift to God."

Lightly he held Aaron's arm and Aaron knew something burned away as dross. He felt a new confidence as together he and the Rabbi stepped forward into the lead.

In the Seminary Aaron's absence had not been noticed till late morning. Rabbi Mendel was finding it difficult to connect himself with the immediate situation. Something was moving to a climax with a will of its own and he felt himself no longer at the centre. When his wife Esther demanded that for God's sake Lemel's parents be called, he remembered Aaron's departure early that morning and realised that Aaron should have returned by now. He immediately sent Ruben to the bakery to find out what was happening.

Kuperman's wife Hannah, a quiet capable woman, had taken charge as soon as Eli had told her of Aaron's visit and the two men's hurried departure. Eli had not dared to speak of Lemel dying, of being very ill or any of that. She was puzzled. But it wasn't the first time that Moshe had walked off like this, sometimes into the woods alone for hours.

When Ruben appeared and told her simply, and strictly according to Rabbi Mendel's instructions, that Lemel was not very well, she left Eli in charge of the bakery and went with Ruben to the Seminary. She made him take her straight to Lemel though Rabbi Mendel had expressly told him to bring her to him first.

This hush!

This special room!

So!

Quietly she ordered Nathan, in vigil, to leave.

So! This silent still one her Lemel, as she knelt to kiss what she knew as hers, to pour out her love for the life that was her very own, through these warm flowing tears. Her Lemel affirmed from deepest love within.

Dr Zaitsman unexpectedly appeared in the Seminary. He wanted a final look, the symptoms still questionable, the possibility of epidemic still unresolved. He warned Rabbi Mendel to carry out the necessary arrangements discreetly and quickly.

When Hannah Kuperman heard both men approaching she stood by the bed, ready to defend. Dr Zaitsman watched the body again as keenly as possible. Rabbi Mendel was confused and upset by her unexpected presence.

She stared at them each in turn, hostile.

"How dare you! Have you no respect for the sick? My son is ill here. Keep quiet! Keep away!"

Rabbi Mendel alerted, pretended to listen sympathetically. Dr Zaitsman began to edge awkwardly by her and look closer still. She turned on him, as some creeping violation.

"Liar! Keep away from my son," she hissed coming at him, ready to attack.

They left quickly, down to the courtyard. Vitebsky rushed up gesticulating wildly, shouting to one and all.

"He's coming. Pinhas the blasphemer's coming! Gird up your loins you faithful, your enemy approaches!"

Dr Zaitsman hurried away from the growing commotion.

Beside the bed, kneeling, Hannah Kuperman returned to her task. She knew what she had to do. From birth this Lemel had been a sickly one, a shy one and she had ever helped him into life. Long nights she knew of tears and love. She spoke to him now as then, as forever, out of the eternal bond. Words of her ever renewing love.

In Vilna Rabbi Pinhas had many secret followers. The secrecy necessitated by Rabbi Mendel's declared intention, should the least provocation arise, of having him arrested by the authorities for causing civil strife and disorder. Among such followers were rumoured important persons. Litvinoff's own wife claimed healing help from him, it was said. But many were ready to attack him in the name of the true faith.

Rabbi Pinhas knew that he had to come. He knew since Aaron's first appearance that this young man's destiny was profoundly involved in the decision to come to Vilna. As they set foot on the bridge it could even be that his followers might have to engage in a bodily struggle. Once across, he told them to scatter and meet again at the Seminary. Something essential had to be achieved and revealed. Nothing must prevent it.

They were soon recognised and the news travelled quickly.

Something was in the air and people hurried to the Seminary, milling about in the courtyard, arguing, singing, looking for him. Aaron sensing the urgency, quickly led Rabbi Pinhas, Kuperman and Levi past the courtyard, along a little used passageway, up some stairs, through the study room and out onto the dormitory landing to the room which had been cleared for Lemel. He told Kuperman and Levi to keep guard by the door.

He and Rabbi Pinhas went over to the bed where Hannah Kuperman was kneeling, head couched in her arm, as she whispered to it through her tears. She looked up. Rabbi Pinhas smiled and nodded confidently. She noticed Aaron who too smiled, borne on a tide of compassion, great tide, binding him, them all.

Rabbi Pinhas beckoned to Aaron. They both drew back. The Rabbi sniffed the air, once, twice.

"He's not dying – he's choking with all this rubbish. Barren! It's all barren here!" he pointed at the walls, indicating something.

Slowly he lowered his head, his arms hung loosely. Aaron watched him, drawn, expectantly, uncertainly. The commotion from below was becoming distant, sweetly distant, a soughing, a peace, a life pulsing peace, his eyelids closing in a mellow twilight, he vast, now shrinking, shock on shock into body, back, on wavesway of shimmering light, then, then, looking once more through his eyes, finding his familiar self, breathing noisily, in a tremor of awakening, smiling with some strange knowing at the Rabbi's smile. From a distant shore a muted harshness sounded, growing louder, arguments, heavy footsteps as the door was pushed open against Kuperman and Levi, and Rabbi Mendel appeared with his students.

"Who let him in?" he shouted angrily in the crowded room.

"I did," Aaron answered.

"Are you mad?" hissed Rabbi Mendel, agitated as Aaron had never seen him before. As though he were facing a stranger, a desperate stranger.

"But he's here to heal," insisted Aaron, bitter at some grave injustice.

"The unity of Israel is more important than all that nonsense. He's a charlatan – a destroyer. Don't you understand?" shouted Rabbi Mendel. Aaron was dumbfounded.

"For the Almighty's sake remember the dead," Vitebsky called out sternly.

Everyone shamefacedly quietened down. They became aware of Kuperman, and his wife kneeling by the bed. They watched, as the eyes in that couched, swollen head – moved. Yes moved. Lemel was there! Lemel was with them – here. A faint smile shadowed that head. Yes Lemel was there.

"My son! My Lemel!" Kuperman whispered hoarsely.

"My son, my Lemel," he repeated.

Swinging round to face them all he called out loudly, clearly, joyfully, "Reb Pinhas! – Reb Pinhas!"

Remembering, they looked about them but Rabbi Pinhas and his followers were nowhere to be seen.

Lemel's recovery was rapid. Hannah Kuperman refused to leave his side. All sorts of people insisted on seeing him. Rabbi Mendel felt threatened, more than ever confirmed in his suspicion that the whole affair was a sinister attempt to disrupt, destroy the Seminary. The man was extremely cunning. Vitebsky suggested that he was easily capable of bringing on the illness in the first place, for his own dark purposes.

Within days Lemel was on his feet, smiling wanly and then home – for good. His father had felt, from that moment he entered the room, that the Seminary was not at all the right place. Rabbi Mendel's violent reaction to the man who had saved his son's life confirmed him beyond doubt.

The news of Lemel's healing, rumours and counter-rumours, spread rapidly. From Rabbi Pinhas' followers in Vilna, that Rabbi Mendel informed for the authorities, lied about them and received payments. The old conflicts were out in the open again.

Lemel's presence was daily proof of another power in Israel. People visited the bakery merely to set eyes on him, and Kuperman never lost an opportunity to declare who the real Rabbi was. Lemel took it all, calmly, modestly. When Aaron cautiously questioned him, well aware that it was delicate ground, Lemel, after a long pause, as though uncertainly recalling a dream, spoke quietly about a struggle. Yes, there had been a struggle, in which he had been deeply involved. Yet strangely, he had been watching the struggle at the same time from somewhere outside. He recalled something else, the strong presence of another and of receiving help from that other.

His return since then seemed to him like a convalescence. He no longer felt so intensely involved in life. A note was sounding, pitched more peacefully, reassuringly.

No amount of reasoning could lessen, alleviate Aaron's shock at Rabbi Mendel's reaction. He questioned the Rabbi in desperation, with a new freedom and fearlessness. He had to be satisfied. But Rabbi Mendel's answers could not satisfy him.

"Where had that healing power come from if not the God of Israel?"

"There can be no proof that he healed him. We have seen trickery like this before in Israel. The black arts have been practised since our father Moses came down from Sinai. These men seek first and foremost power over their followers. Otherwise they would follow the precepts of the Torah exactly instead of following their own personal whims. I tell you my son, they seek to divide and destroy Israel."

Aaron listened with respect to the man whose words, whose life, had taught him so much. But he could not accept it and realised how much he had changed. When Rabbi Mendel spoke, Aaron felt with sadness his teacher's weariness and resignation, felt the farewell they were bidding each other.

Lemel began helping in the bakery. He felt no desire to return to the Seminary. Each week, Kuperman, Lemel, Aaron and others went to Rabbi Pinhas with loaves and other gifts.

Aaron was spending more of his time at the bakery. He knew that it was leading to a final parting of the ways, drawn on by the secret of that healing power and deed. Of course Rabbi Mendel was correct. Rabbi Pinhas did not worship or celebrate ritual exactly in accordance with the precepts. There was too an awkwardness with Rabbi Pinhas' followers. Yet in Rabbi Pinhas' presence he experienced a power, a directness and an inner strength convincing beyond all words and arguments. The thought of endless study in the Seminary no longer satisfied. He knew definitely that he must change course.

Whenever Rabbi Pinhas answered him he listened in the light of that healing deed. Then always came the questioning, the disillusionment, the frustration of still not knowing where the truth of his life lay.

One day, casually it seemed, Rabbi Pinhas said in the course of a conversation, "My son you should stop asking questions and use – work with your hands. Let them think for you. You should learn from the earth – the fruitful one – and move much more amongst men. It's not – surely not – for you to stay with us here."

The words touched him to the quick. A desperate shock – disappointment – to make a decision, throwing him into his own aloneness. Shock – but – own – and with it – a warmth, encouragement, belief in very own destiny! Painful – but healing gift from Rabbi Pinhas then.

Rabbi Pinhas knew that only Aaron would be able to answer the unanswerable questions with his own destiny itself and that in this very answering would he create himself.

One March morning Aaron decided to make his way south to Odessa.

Hands? – move amongst men?

Go forth then – into their great unknown – with his trusted encouragement!

IX

Livadia

Tsarevich Nicholas with his dear brother George stood on the taffrail of the battleship Pamiat Azova as it steamed out from Athens billowing dark smoke, thrusting through freshening seas towards Egypt. The Eastern tour planned by Papa had really begun. Gaily the foaming waters streamed away as Nicholas' protective arm embraced George's shoulder. Smiling into the lively breeze they watched with delight the sparkling furrows, dissolving renewing, dissolving renewing as the mighty vessel carried them away.

Away, ever away from those dreadful studies. Towards, oh towards what unknown! Away, with friends of the heart, banter and roguish fun. And through this pure and eager air towards new hopes and quickening skies. Movement, change, freedom. New sights, new sounds, the company of sailors, the eagerness and buoyancy of youth. Released, and the sparkling waters alongside streaming.

In his cabin Nicholas felt compelled to record this release. To record and in the very writing down to establish the ending of that captivity which had grown so hateful. As though if not named and thus sealed off from the present, this new space, it still had the power to make him captive again.

'Oct. 1890. Now I have finished forever my education.'

Those hours days months years of tedium and the dour faces of Pobedonostsev - Minister Bunge - General Oldenburg - Professor Karkunov and the rest of them so dour! - threatening?

For what?

For what purpose? - right now this dark menace threatening to overwhelm.

He snapped shut the gold clasp of his diary and sprang up thankfully at George's knock. They went off to the officers' mess, joining cousin George of Greece and three other travelling companions, princes of the nobility.

Exhilarating, endless, the new sights and sounds. Pyramids, camels, cataracts, belly dancers, tiger shoots in India with the English redcoats everywhere! cherry trees in Tokyo. But made so much more real by just this earthly show whose delights so soon, so sadly waned, was that constant presence about him, shy, so pure. Her white muslin dress and the roses wreathed in her hair very scent, tenderly leading his yearning heart. Empty, slack that writhing brown flesh in the light of this presence. Chuckling and grinning with the rest at the belly dancers, he yet felt it shameful, sad.

Dear Papa as ever.

Papa had made it possible to discover just how close they were. To know how much he longed for her.

But she?

Yes, give yourself over once more to this story - yours and hers - with tenderness and devotion - memory by memory - that seeks to be sealed by you with love - those glances of hers in the chapel at Uncle Sergei's wedding - each - still now! such a tender, quickening of his life. Not challenge, curiosity, barely appraisal those glances, simply gentlest recognition, shy calling to one already known! And see that brooch which she had returned, so clearly now, as gentlest reproach. Such coarseness, stupidity his flustered response. Only now to know what she was saying even then, from her girlhood's radiant soul. Simply wait in the silence trusting. In that protective shade let it grow. Let it come into being. Force nothing. Neither jewels - brooches - coarse gifts are needed. Only your faith, your yearning heart. And when they had skated together at Tsarskoe Selo no words were spoken. Thankfully he had grown wiser. He had dared to know. It could never be other than her.

But stark was that sternness which had yet to be braved.

In the desolate frontier town of Vladivostok he turned over the first spadeful of earth to inaugurate the great Trans-Siberian Railway project as symbol and reality of Russia's Asiatic mission. On the journey back through the vastness of Siberia, at town after town, the peasants appeared in their hundreds to cheer and praise him. He was overcome with an exultation and bewilderment. With a joy and a fear, a great fear.

A question resounded, momentous, mysterious as the echoing cheers died away. For whom? For whom was it all being done? Between the for whom? and he Nicholas, a fear, a great fear prevailed.

To Alexander's increasing irritation the Tsarevich's Far Eastern tour had not apparently resolved anything. He swung from trying to take it for granted, to hoping somewhat despairingly that the trip would mature his son, make him grow up, become serious. He could have put it in many ways, though even then they would have left untouched that something deeper which alarmed him.

After four months back in St Petersburg it seemed that the Tsarevich had not changed in any essential way. He was spending most of his time at the ballet, art exhibitions, opera and theatre, with frivolous young friends. Or carousing at too many regimental dinners. He showed no concern for those matters of State which were his future. Something was indeed lacking. It was becoming unacceptable.

Had the whole trip been nothing more than a gay jaunt for him? Did Nikki not grasp any implications from what he had seen and heard? Did he not realise yet who he was? How else could the Alix business be explained? For the wretched thing was still there. Nicholas had turned over the first spadeful of earth at Vladivostok. He'd been told often enough what this railway line meant for Russia's future. That French money, French interest was vitally important for its construction and success. That a marriage with, for example – alright, only for example! – the Bourbon Hélène, could greatly strengthen the Entente Cordiale and as well prove so fruitful for Russia's Asian future.

That it had been necessary to spell it out so emphatically was deplorable. Everyone knew that negotiations for an alliance were in the air. Was the unthinkable happening – that – what was it? – a sullen obstinacy lurking behind his seeming obedience – that – on this matter of Alix the boy was not going to yield!

Impossible!

But maddening this obstinacy – politeness– something there impenetrable.

Policy! – real decisions! – future! – with this boy on the throne – God help Russia!

But what was the matter with him?

So sudden – awful. This enforced confrontation with the future – and his helplessness – lack of power before it.

But what was the matter with the boy?

So uneasily this very question pointing more to himself than to his son!

Who in heaven's name could he, dare he put it to? He must hear, have something, from someone else. No! Surely it hadn't come to this. That he was thinking of asking other men for help. Help – in dealing with his own son!

Yes!

Desperate this need to open his heart to someone – but this shame, sense of failure – defeat!

Whom?

Only Witte or Constantin Petrovich even remotely to be considered.

Nicholas had come to realise that on this issue his whole life was at stake. The very thought of upsetting dear Papa and dear Mama on this of all issues was unbearably painful. Yet he knew that he must not yield. That he must live it all through, must bear all their arguments, hostility and indignation.

Alexander's frustration entangled with his feelings towards his younger brother Grand Duke Sergei. The Moscow Jew expulsions had at first alarmed him. Something a bit – frightening? about Sergei. People spoke of capriciousness, derangement, even madness – he knew. Madness which Constantin Petrovich had begged to point out Russia could do with a little more of.

But might it not also bring the dynasty into some disrepute?

Admit! your administration – no less – your wanting such a deed to be carried out.

Ultimately justice for those criminals who had spilled Our Lord's precious blood. Or had Sergei outwitted him over the ukase? Sergei flaunting a measure of power – a clear challenge. Something there which had made him reluctant in the first place to grant the Governorship in spite of Constantin Petrovich's insistent proposal. And anyway it wasn't just Sergei. Most of the family lacked the necessary tact in their ways of authority. Were Sergei and Constantin Petrovich making a fool of him? Yet the whole affair could only strengthen the loyalty of true Russians who detested the Yids.

Yet again of course – Alix as Ella's sister certainly had every right to be staying with them from time to time. But knowing his and Maria Fedorovna's strong views, they both could have – had they really wanted – done much towards backing them up and turning Nicholas aside from this stupid choice. Or were they actually encouraging him? Then to what end?

After ten years Gatchina was still Alexander's favourite residence. All the royal excursions from it were closely guarded by troops and police. The yearly itinerary included summer weeks at Peterhof on the Baltic coast, Krasnoe Selo for the Guards' summer exercises, and hunting on the royal preserve at Spala in Poland. Occasionally they took a trip to the Crimean estate in Livadia. The children loved it, but Alexander found the southern air too relaxing and never stayed for long. This year the move to Peterhof had been planned for the second week in June.

Most ministers were called from St Petersburg on a monthly basis to report but Witte was a familiar visitor every week. Alexander asked for and listened carefully to Witte's opinion on a wide range of issues, many outside his official ministerial field of Communications. In Witte's presence Alexander was keenly, admiringly aware that sheer individual merit alone had raised this man up. His increasing trust in Witte had reaped its reward of a frankness which he experienced with no other man. He felt that Witte's appraisals were far and away the most realistic, practical and needed just now more than ever, with the dreadful drought in the central provinces and the thousands of peasants dying of starvation and cholera in spite of the provisions being sent in.

And just now! the damned liberal rabble was daring to attack the government for its so-called inhumanity, backwardness - in dealing with the situation. In particular Finance Minister Vyshnegradsky's doing his very loyal best for the nation - his devoted concern to balance the budget and continue exporting grain. Of course painful difficult decisions but putting the nation first. And the fact that Witte never wavered on this.

And of course! the sheer impertinence when the nation was in crisis - when else? of that damned traitor to his class Tolstoy! Calling for action by individuals! - and the locally elected councils all over the country! Witte was emphatic! Those damned liberal councils were using all this relief business for subversive ends.

Then strict instructions must ensure extreme caution in this matter of relief distribution.

The death toll was unpleasantly high. But Witte continued to stand absolutely firm in his justification of Vyshnegradsky's policy.

"Nothing else Sire will stabilise the economy. And *that* we must have. A stable economy as a basis for industrial development – if it's your intention Sire that we truly enter the ranks of modern nations."

Indeed my intention. And that you soon – very soon – replace Vyshnegradsky. Your assuredness – firmness is knowing where and how to draw the line.

On a fine May morning at Gatchina, Alexander was in a very irritable mood. An unfamiliar mood but increasingly present and tenacious. The empress, though certain of its cause, felt helpless in the face of it. Till now her robust, good humoured nature dealt with the tension between father and son to its own fair satisfaction; loyal and consoling to Alexander, protective to dear weak Nikki, somehow mediating between both. She felt as deeply as her husband his need to share this problem with another man. She trusted none of the Grand Dukes. No question but that Witte stood closest. But she felt something not right there either. Even now as Witte bowed, she sensed an over-familiarity which pained her. Witte waited expectantly.

"The Emperor is not quite his usual self this morning – so – I beg you to –" she began out of her uncertainty.

"I understand, Your Highness – perfectly," he responded, naturally, spontaneously, upsetting her more as she recalled the "I beg you".

"The Emperor works too hard. He carries the whole country on his shoulders. The sooner he relaxes at Peterhof the better," Witte went on, dimly suspecting that she had wanted to communicate something else, something very different.

Marie Feodorovna had heard an opening in his words for what she would have liked to say about Nikki. But she withdrew. She dared not risk coming any closer.

On the wide bank that sloped gently down to the lake Alexander was sitting in his wicker chair under the great oak. Simply to be near this tree, loved since boyhood, was strength, consolation. On the lacquered bamboo table a silver bowl of his favourite lemon ice cream was replaced when empty by a discreetly watching footman. At regular intervals a soldier of the Guards regiment passed by discreetly on his patrol.

Alexander was determined to read through Tolstoy's latest tirade against the government for its handling of the famine. Marie Feodorovna had even in her anxiety, considered momentarily hiding the pamphlet away, somewhere in his study, in order to protect him, help him relax.

Alexander let the mood hold sway, take over, infuse him with a savage stance – yes! face up to the worst, the most despicable surrounding him, like the ravings of this vile aristocrat, traitor to class and country. A few paragraphs were enough. He flung the pamphlet down, incensed, stood up to feel the earth firmly under his feet and himself master of the situation, as he began to pace his path around the tree, centre, centred, head bent, hands clasped behind back. With that consoling strength now joined, he stopped, his gaze drawn up high, higher, himself, above into this mighty thrust of green life, which scorned such pitiful creatures and their crimes.

Approaching him was Witte followed by a footman carrying a garden chair. Here was a man! Faithful to the uttermost – loyalest – and of such sound judgement!

The footman placed the chair near Alexander's, bowed towards the tree and withdrew.

But in spite of that consoling power, rooted, enduring, this bitterness prevailed. With only a glance in Witte's direction he returned to his chair, keenly aware that his faithful one was here.

Witte walked across the lawn with a buoyant, jaunty step, stirred by that surely? attempted confidence, ready with facts and figures to cheer his Tsar. All was well under control. The famine was over. With industrialisation Nature would be increasingly mastered.

His jauntiness faltered. This was no welcoming gesture as he bowed and sat down.

"How is it that Durnovo allows this vile trash to circulate?" Alexander demanded angrily, pointing down at the pamphlet on the lawn where he had flung it with disgust.

Witte immediately picked it up, glanced at the title page and let it drop again.

"Sire I can't speak for Durnovo – but as for the famine itself," his voice rose with confidence.

"Enough! Enough of the famine," Alexander cut him short,

"Sergei Yulyevich I want a frank answer to my question. What – exactly what d'you think of the Tsarevich?" he kept jabbing his finger directly at Witte, peering intently into Witte's face.

"The Tsarevich?" said Witte, taken completely off his guard, playing for time.

"What do I think of the Tsarevich," he repeated slowly, holding off what pressed so hard, that none felt in Nicholas a future ruler - lack made glaring by this one here!

"Good enough, good enough!" declared Alexander impatiently, "An honest soul indeed. I can hear it all. Useless! Let's not mince words. Useless! My own son. Not simply useless but an idiot. He understands nothing. He has no sense whatever of who he is. I'm at my wits' end Sergei Yulyevich. He lacks all seriousness. He's been right across our great empire - and what d'you think? He comes back and spends his time playing - art exhibitions, ballet, opera - that's what he thinks life's about. It's unbelievable!"

Witte was shaken by the disgust in Alexander's voice and shocked into an awareness of what was really happening. The man opposite. A father's desperation! A call for help. Unsure how to proceed he wavered but his forthrightness broke through, his responsibility to this man whose acceptance and recognition had encouraged his talents to flourish. He owed it, risky, audacious as it seemed, to fearlessly tell him the truth. Manly part of the pledge which bound them so together.

"You asked for frankness Sire," he looked firmly at Alexander, "the Tsarevich will stop being useless when you give him something useful to do. Tasks. Responsibilities - real ones - serious preparation for what lies ahead. Make him chairman of the Trans-Siberian Committee," he threw out on the instant, "see! - see Sire! whether he won't rise to the occasion. If he thinks you don't trust him why should he show responsibility?"

"Alright alright!" shouted Alexander, wincing at the very thought of Witte's proposal, holding the man off yet listening.

"But what of this damned Alix business, tell me that," he shouted, on his feet, striding up and down, for now it was out, wildly, threateningly. He halted near Witte's chair and lashed the words down in a fury. "I tell you I won't give way. That little fool knows nothing of raison d'état. Is he a Romanov? He thinks his private life is more important than his country. It's unbelievable!"

That was it! There, was the violence, bewilderment, despair. Witte dared not look up. He sensed danger in this whole situation, knowing still that this unhappy man wanted to hear the truth as he saw it. That and that alone.

"Well! come on – don't sit there! Let's hear. Let's hear!"

Witte heard the urgency, menace, in that imperious order. Before he could speak, for an answer to the raison d'état attack had quickly formed, he was startled by the sight of the Emperor gasping for breath, forehead creased and eyes shut hard in a gesture of wincing pain. Alexander's broad hand was spread shieldlike over his chest till the sharp pain lessened and his eyes blinked open.

"Stop staring! Let's have your answer," he said with gritted teeth. Yield he would not. Damn the pain.

Witte knew that he must keep true to himself, stand his ground, yet be tactful, very tactful.

"You insist Sire that he change, that he give her up for reasons of state. But just for reasons of state –" glimpsing something momentous, "for future reasons of state, would it not be – sensible – to have him on your side – as soon as possible."

He could have said more. That only such real responsibilities would enable Nicholas to experience for himself the reality of state reasons. But he felt it dangerous to do so unless Alexander insisted.

"Yes yes! You've all the answers. But what d'you know? Nothing!" Alexander answered back defensively.

He had heard that word, that tone of truth, bitter truth in his most trusted one's answer. But enough! It was enough! He'd exposed enough of himself. Sullenly he turned about to shake off this other and found his way down to the lake's edge, the way to his own lonely world. Why should he have to do that, expose himself for that wretched boy? Own proud implacable will he would remain.

Halted at the lake's edge he looked down at his gentle reflection, selfless gift of the stillness of waters. Stirred, dreaming this gentleness. The faintest shadow of pain drifted over his chest. He straightened up against it and walked slowly back to the palace.

The other had proved his worth. Of course there was something in what Witte had said but something else was involved about which Witte knew nothing and never would.

One man did and he must hear from him too.

But the thought of Constantin Petrovich made him uneasy.

Things had changed, had been let slip. It should have been simple enough, once decided, to call him to Gatchina. Yet a painful uncertainty prevailed. With five days to go before the summer trip to Peterhof he grew restless and undecided.

The children, Xenia, Michael, Olga were excited, eagerly looking forward to the holiday by the Baltic ·sands. Marie Fedorovna had the considerable packing arrangements well in hand. As was usual since the Borki incident, when the whole family had very nearly been blown to pieces, two identical trains would be used, travelling at a set distance from each other. Till the last minutes of departure no one except the security guards would know which train carried the family.

Behind her show of cheerfulness Marie Fedorovna was very uneasy over Alexander's irascibility, sullenness, and a withdrawal which she could not reach. This was a holiday which he always enjoyed with its walking, swimming, boating and bracing air. She could only suspect the one cause, Nikki's intransigence which was tainting so much of their lives. The matter was far too painful to bring up without the most careful consideration.

On the day before departure Alexander reached a crisis. He told her curtly that the trip must be delayed for a few days. He sent a messenger to Pobedonostsev summoning him to Gatchina. Marie Fedorovna knew better than to ask for an explanation or even when exactly he had in mind for the new departure. The security officials were thoroughly put out, but the empress quickly arranged some outings and parties for the children.

Pobedonostsev read through the summons very carefully, several times, listening, weighing. It had come out of the blue with no indication of its real purpose. *"We go to Peterhof soon. I wish us to talk as soon as possible."* He sensed an awkwardness, and yet the personal note as of old. Though telling himself that bygones must be bygones and surprised at the apparent ease with which he made the decision to go straight to Gatchina, he continued throughout his journey there to consider the possibilities behind the request. Then accordingly to prepare himself should any of them emerge. That first excitement at being asked and that pleasure of wanting to go at any cost, had soon passed. He decided to take any opportunities offered for making a firm stand on the issues dividing them and which had been for so long condemned to silence. For it could well be, must be, that the awkwardness, the brusqueness of that note, was a sign of Alexander Alexandrovich's coming to terms with his conscience. An awakening at long last. Was it too much to expect that Alexander Alexandrovich had begun to see through Witte? That what he had long awaited could only be a matter of time?

On the Empress' way out with the children to a party at the Dolgoruky's, the thin black suited figure of Pobedonostsev appeared in the hall. Pobedonostsev bowed gravely to her and the children. Michael could barely suppress a gesture of mocking imitation. As soon as Pobedonostsev went on up to Alexander's study, Michael's face lengthened, lantern-jawed, his lips tightened and he ringed his goggling eyes with finger spectacles to the merriment of his sister. Marie Fedorovna had barely responded to the bow. She could never feel easy with this man. That eternal black suit and bow tie - prowling around here just this moment. After such a long absence which had helped to reassure her that Alexander was at last rid of him! Something was going on not entirely accountable by Nikki's intransigence.

Pobedonostsev entered Alexander's study ready to discuss many issues, including Synod policy, over the last two to three years; the Ulyanov affair with its still unresolved implications for his higher education policy, and the Moscow expulsions. Prepared above all to answer questions on his speech from one who at last was apparently ready to come to terms with the truth of his situation. He had decided on a neutral attitude, courteous but wary. He would not make it too difficult for this belated attempt of the Emperor to salve his conscience. On the other hand there was a lesson to be learned by the man, that trust was something to be cherished, not taken for granted or turned on and off like a tap.

He was very surprised when the Emperor came straight over, warmly shook his hand and asked with heartfelt goodwill,

"Constantin Petrovich is it good to be back at Gatchina?"

The old Alexander! no stratagem here.

"Indeed Sire," answered Pobedonostsev with heartfelt response, looking squarely into Alexander's face, touched immediately by a sharpening of features, a tautness, same Alexander but changed. He waited, hearing the Empress' carriage on its way to the Dolgoruky's.

Alexander was finding the situation more painful than his spontaneous outburst with Witte. He had formed the question in various ways, mostly intended to conceal the real depth of his concern, despair. But then if so concealed, what hope that the answer would help him, would measure up to his real need. And how to come to terms with the lapse in their relationship. Lapse, drift, only now in the summoning so awkwardly felt. No - not at all intended like this only borne along with it - the moment - Russia's needs - that Witte was as much Russia as Constantin Petrovich. He had to work with and through them both. But both had their times and their seasons, the drift unavoidable.

Pobedonostsev waited, looking down at the carpet. Alexander breathed in sharply and the question, framing itself with care, yet burst out from a brooding uncertainty.

"Constantin Petrovich, what are we going to do with the Tsarevich?"

Pobedonostsev heard the desperation in that what? and though immediately attempting to console the Emperor, yielded willingly to a pleasurable satisfaction. And that 'we' - eh? A truly shared responsibility? or what suits the moment?

"Why Sire, the Tsarevich is in every sense a true Russian. Respectful - more - reverential towards his heritage and towards your achievements," he began reassuringly, cautiously.

"As far as the old traditions are concerned he's absolutely reliable. I know that his attitudes towards the Jews - Poles - the peasants - are most correct. Your very own," he hesitated, watching Alexander carefully, unsure of the effect his words were having.

"Yes, true! But it's not enough Constantin Petrovich. He lacks something. Don't you see! He can't assert himself. He's afraid to take responsibility. What is it? You taught him for years. You should know. He lacks firmness - backbone? I don't know. The older he gets, I just can't see a Romanov in him. I don't know. I simply don't know."

Alexander did and did not want to hear any more, to share any more. The frustration, the violence, were beginning to threaten again. Pobedonostsev felt it and tried once more.

"Sire, you've done all that any dutiful father and Emperor could do. The rest is in the Lord's hands. Know Sire, and yield willingly. That's for Him in His great mercy. He who has the welfare of Russia in His hands. You'll reign for many a year Sire because you're doing the Lord's work. See how the five murderers were caught. See how you saved your own family at Borki, it was a miracle. Trust in Him! He'll teach the Tsarevich as well. When the time eventually comes he will be ready. He will have learned."

The meeting had come to an end. Both men knew it and had no need to pretend otherwise. Pobedonostsev left with much relief, saddened, disturbed and not at all clear as to its real meaning or purpose. Whether Alexander hadn't wanted to talk about something very different? That note of desperation so clear! But the Tsarevich simply did not justify such despair. Yes he had been taken by surprise but all in all he seemed to have managed a fair response – his holy truth – then down to earth – and a touch, faintest hint, of what? – some rare closeness dared allowed – permitted! in such an – unprecedented situation.

But – what he didn't say! Good Lord – how dare resist your Light. What he was afraid? to say. That your son Sire is deeply affected by your dissatisfaction with him. More – of the same – that you've lost the ability to trust those most worthy of trust – that! sinful is my nature – Your Mercy alone my help.

Alexander realised while Constantin Petrovich was talking, that these soothing words were not at all what he wanted to hear. They didn't touch him. Beyond all doubt the summons to both men had come from weakness. It hadn't been advice that he'd sought but that someone else should relieve him of the problem once and for all.

Weakness had led him to do it!

Then he'd deal with this weakness.

He must and would bear this wound, this pain alone. He would hold out the longest. He would never accept that this son of his could not be bent to his will.

Dreadful this humiliation over Russia's very future.

Of course he knew but hateful to admit – not! for his sake but for Russia – that he must die! Then God help Russia! Till then he would strain every nerve for Russia's welfare. But already senselessly his plans were being thwarted by this son. And what did those two understand of that? Absolutely nothing with all their sanctimonious and clever talk. What did they know of this unbearable aggravation? That his power was already being bled from him, undermining that future. What could they know of this bewilderment, resigned desperation? Trapped! That the boy was somehow beyond his reach, some elusive cunning at work, outwitting him. The boy did everything correctly just as expected but that was it! Some emptiness – some real involvement lacking - for all - all! - to sense. The derogatory comments reaching him - weren't they justified? No one respected - took seriously - a future Tsar?

The departure to Peterhof was on again but the family knew soon after their arrival that Papa was not his familiar Peterhof self, enjoying the brisk early morning walks along the shore with them, riding and bathing with them, all such intimate response to Peterhof's enchantment, call.

Alexander became aware of an unfamiliar fatigue which daily began to threaten, delicate shadow, veil. Disdainful indifference towards its persistent presence and intensification, yielded to the need for some explanation. Well! he was forty-eight, not thirty-eight, not twenty-eight. He'd known tiredness before this year, after all. Too much sitting at that wretched desk with those pieces of paper. Not enough exercise.

But the nights were becoming awkward. No longer a sleep sea-scented sea-centred, from which he would arise invigorated, to enter the day as a great hall of the world, sensing a source of strength which would carry him through the coming year. No longer for granted that each evening as the stars shyly appeared through the deepening veils of the wide summer sky, salt-tang quickening in the gentle offshore breeze, he would stride along the sandy beach inhaling the fruitfulness, serene, preparing to cross that age-old threshold and yield in perfect trust to those great friendly powers of strength and life.

Now, in spite of the evening walk, he found himself awake during the early hours and unable to return to that place, to cross that friendly lifelong threshold, to that source which he had so long taken for granted. Awake in a dismal unfamiliar light, shut out. Bound, in this brittle, questioning greyness. And throughout the following day he felt as though something vital had been stolen from him. He wanted to beat back furiously with all that sheer strength he could muster but there was nothing to come to grips with.

After the Peterhof holiday came the annual army manoeuvres to be held this year in Kiev province. He regarded the occasion as of utmost significance. A renewal in fullness and brilliance of that sacred bond with those who were touchstone, foundation of the empire. General Staff always sent him detailed plans of the manoeuvres beforehand, which he studied with deep interest and enjoyment. During these last August weeks as the Peterhof vacation was nearing its end, he became, to his confusion, increasingly intent on returning to Gatchina and staying put there. At Gatchina he would be secure. This vulnerability needed protection.

Once back in Gatchina he felt relieved but very upset at not being with the army. He could not come to terms with his unprecedented indecision over attending the manoeuvres. The matter was very sensitive and no one dared refer to it. He ordered General Bykov and General Koblinsky to report personally to him as soon as the manoeuvres were over.

In spite of his determination to the contrary, the matter of Nicholas would not leave him alone for long. Then he would simply wait for the young fool to come to his senses, which he eventually must do.

General Bykov and General Koblinsky had returned to their headquarters at Smolensk after a discussion lasting several hours in Alexander's study. He had insisted that they go over the manoeuvres in detail with the large maps spread out. He questioned them searchingly on dispositions, tactics and strategy. Their strategy for this meeting included yielding to his criticisms after some show of bluster so that he would feel his superiority. No attempt then to defend Hussar General Golovine's appalling blunder on the right flank, in case the Emperor ferreted out that General Staff itself was responsible. Absolutely no reference to the Emperor's absence and to the deep disappointment of officers at all levels, even the feeling that it had had a detrimental effect on the manoeuvres themselves.

Once the maps had been laid out and the battle plans explained, Alexander became so passionately involved that the two generals were puzzled, cautioned by a note in his voice which seemed to indicate not simply manoeuvres but some real battle situation. Over refreshments which at last appeared, the discussion moved to the French and German armies, to Napoleon's fantastic error of judgement, to Russia's lack of natural defences which made her so vulnerable. At which point Alexander emphasised the immense strategic importance for Russia's future of the Trans-Siberian railway. It would eventually make possible, if necessary, a Russian withdrawal, in good order, of such an extent as to utterly overstretch any conceivable enemy from the West.

"Yes indeed Sire," praised General Koblinsky, not at all sure of this dazzling implication.

"Such tactics of course would need an iron hand at the helm," he added innocently.

Alexander frowned sharply and for a long silence stood staring at the map.

"The future will be the future," he said stiffly and they knew gratefully that the discussion was ended.

The books and maps were carried from the study into the private living room. Alexander wanted to look again at certain aspects of Napoleon's Russian campaign, the subject fascinated him. But as he approached the table and looked down at the books, a veil, yet of steel, a muzziness, took hold.

He reached out for his chair and sat down heavily. A fine trembling crept through him. Marie Fedorovna looked up from her sewing.

"General Bykov just had to tell me how much you and Nikki were missed by the army."

He listened and looked back at her. The tension in his head gathered into a painful fog of thought. He knew, as he sat staring at her, wanting to answer, wanting to gather the words together that she was already out of reach, that the words were darting fireflies on the edge of his mouth unreachable, that his body was floating away, no longer fully his. She, words, limbs were loosely withdrawing.

Marie Fedorovna alerted by the quizzical gaze hovering over his eyes and the trembling of his partly opened mouth, watched carefully, touched with a pain, his pain, yet knowing she was on the outside, forced to watch something unfold. Fearful, not daring to intervene, knowing that he was in a place of his own, utterly alone.

Bearing that pain, watching, yet, yet tenderly in the waiting, hoping, her own substance pledging. He as never before, eyes shut, jaws tight, summoned his word from the depths, a shuddering force to claim back his body from the enemy's hold, somehow up lurching onto his feet, trembling violently, breathing noisily, gasping for life. No power of his would overcome this enemy. He was the one forced to yield, sit down again, as his breathing became more regular, the drifting waters of life, slowly, in their good time, returning him gently to this homely shore, this more familiar land of himself and her.

She waited, and watched those veiled eyes and tiny beads of sweat, gently being with him once again, knowing the worst was over, so delicate this return, to be so tenderly protected.

The musical chime of the clock and a restrained tap on the door recalled them both to this other world. Marie Fedorovna was astonished that only minutes had passed. She still watched him intently, ready to stop the servant from entering with their late night tea and biscuits. His face was touched in a shifted light with a presence, fullness, yes himself, and he nodded gently, affirmatively towards the door as she read in the line of his mouth a smile, a greeting, a courageous resignation.

The following day he felt almost his usual self. Frightening how his limbs were taken from him – the words beyond his reach. No question of fighting back. His body was being taken over and he had simply to go with it.

Follow it – he – follow! And the world about him went on – without him.

Annoyingly he found himself looking into the mirror all too often.

No casual glance but a holding steady demanded, a definite watching, searching. Yes, a definite thinning of nose, chin, a loosening, looseness of skin round the neck. Or was it so? Was he watching himself, or really watching, really interested in something else, happening there, unfolding there?

Puzzling and disturbing was that current which dragged him helplessly from a past focused on Papa's dying, through a drifting, ghostly present towards that enigmatic future called Nicholas.

Marie Fedorovna told no one about the attack and though at first desperately anxious to discuss the matter with Dr Spiridovich, their physician for several years, she held back. She wanted to know yet dared not. In a strangely calm and matter-of-fact way she took it at its worst, a warning stroke, and her thinking turned to Nicholas in a more thorough, determined way than ever before. A crisis was unavoidably nearing in which she alone could play a crucial role. Now the Alix business would simply have to be resolved positively. Stability there, was essential as soon as possible.

Alexander was refusing to acknowledge the implications of the attack. Until he did – was forced to? – she would watch and prepare herself. The utmost care, finest tact, would be needed.

He might not yield till brought to his knees.

So desperate for both of them, father and son!

Since returning from his trip abroad Nicholas had come to dwell in a calm knowing that if he could not marry Alix then he would never marry at all. Clear, simple, final.

Out of that calm he had told his mother who held it at a distance, not daring to tell Alexander. Nicholas knew that Mama was for him. Mama was very loyal to Papa but he knew deep down that she was for him. She was always available, attainable in a way that Papa never could be, never was meant to be. Yet oh if only he could come to Papa as he came to Mama. But that would not be Papa any more!

He knew that this struggle with Papa was a crucial struggle. The bitterness, pain, had to be endured, for her. This was the ordained battleground where finally he must and would stand to fight for his own. In Alix, his life and salvation. Deepest need! Ecstatic yet dreadful need! demanding that he stand firm even against Papa. But how could anyone assert themselves against Papa? But dear Lord, he knew that Papa wanted him to assert himself more. Such a dreadful trap! Nothing that he could do would ever satisfy Papa. He himself – he just as himself – only! That, he knew, would never satisfy Papa – that! – the dreadful anguish.

Marie Fedorovna began to feel in her husband's continual carping and barely contained disgust with Nikki, a threat to herself. Touched to the quick, irrespective of the Alix business, her support for Nicholas, fiercely willed, secret, was a fight back on her own behalf also, against an injustice. She was determined not to abandon her boy, but to protect, arm him.

Alexander's sleeplessness grew worse. Daily a fine web of listless fatigue settled over him, disempowering. Daily, frustration, wondering at a man and a life which had been, so recently had been. That strength at Borki ensuring their survival – the kind of strength a Tsar needed even with God's merciful help and blessing. Yet no more. Wondering, in recall, at that well-being, blithe fullness, abundance of energy, ever taken for granted. Such a darkness this reality, inmost secret, refusal of limbs to respond, all the time that something vital was seeping away from him.

Then take up the challenge!

No pampering whatsoever!

One first step in that direction – and on the downward path! Downward path about which he didn't want to know.

Everyone quickly learned that not the slightest intimation of his condition was allowed.

An absolute taboo.

Or a frightening outburst risked, worsening the condition.

Dr Spiridovich diagnosed overwork and worry as the main causes. He prescribed teas for liver and kidney, more outdoor exercise and general relaxation. Alexander took the teas and tightened his hold. He took particular interest in the detailed reports on the exiles in Europe, from Rachkovsky in Paris. Everything abroad and at home must continue to be kept under the very firmest control.

Marie Fedorovna knew that the iron strength, confidence, will, were, unbelievably, weakening. That power, for so long shelter, bastion of their lives, she, Nikki, George, Xenia, Michael, Olga. Proud, chosen, alone, it was withdrawing.

Strong hints forced Nicholas to consider a direct connection between his father's illness and the Alix issue - and Alix herself - so threatened! Forced him into feelings of guilt and shame. Obvious solutions were offered. "Give her up now - and your father will surely get better." He sensed a cunning threat, a trap, and drew on a bitter strength. His newly awakening self knew that its survival, very deed of self-baptism must never yield to any of this.

Certainly Papa was not getting any better.

Papa was getting worse.

And that worse was leading to himself, to Nicholas, to a Nicholas whom he could not avoid being yet never wanted to be. All he wanted was his Alix, the two of them together. But whichever way he turned seemed only to tighten the painful grip of this fatefulness.

Never anything else so clear that she was for him and he was for her. Papa, even dear George, had insisted on reasons of state. But those first two meetings were gentle radiance ever with him, as close as his own self. No! If Papa continued to refuse then he'd go further still. Not simply give up the idea of marriage altogether, but take nothing seriously.

No! Those hints, rumours were vile and stupid. What could they know of this life, light, calling? Beauty! - Treasure! - Life!

No!

Before God, never never to hurt - hit back at dear Papa dear Mama.

No!

But this was his very foundation.

Never to add to Papa's burden - but - to bear witness to the fact - absolute certainty - that whatever the future brought, with her he would be saved.

After some comparatively restful nights Alexander again awoke in the early hours, but from a height serene, watching the waters of life receding, gently receding. Light with the knowledge of a fullness clear and pure, he reached out to his Marie, his hand gently over hers in awakening pressure.

"Marie dearest - should anything happen - - we must give our consent - now!"

Something insisted she memorise the words. They were so unexpected and uttered in, yes, his voice, but such an unfamiliar voice. Each word, its very placing, intonation, felt significant. As was his hand, still protecting, yet seeking assurance. She had heard it, felt it, was sure of that.

Alexander slept on. She stayed awake. She must follow through this decision, started to life by those words. Words which already seemed not fully to be his. Nikki must be invited round before - strong this premonition - Alexander might want to retreat. This time, more than conciliation. Somehow she must will it so. Alexander, remembering the words he had spoken, his own yet not his own, moodily, warily, let her lead the way.

Nicholas read his mother's message, *'Papa wants to see you about something very important'*, and trembled. Only one implication was possible, and so overwhelming. Any activity to hold it off. Fortunately the next two days till the meeting included an opera, and a regimental ball which went on into the early hours.

When he arrived at Gatchina Mama made a brave attempt at lightheartedness. It jarred. Alexander was in a sullen mood and she was prepared for the worst. At lunch, from the start he was hostile, intimidating, regarding his son with wariness and suspicion.

Marie Fedorovna began small talk with Nicholas as the tension increased. She tried to bring Alexander into the conversation but he managed no more than a perfunctory nod. Nicholas had given up any attempt to understand the situation. Mama was here at his side as he had expected, dared hope. But it was looking ominous.

They moved into the living room.

Marie Fedorovna managed somehow to hold at bay such an inner confusion. Still unsympathetic to Alix - but that it might bring Nikki some independence - happiness - and Alexander's bitterness at being thwarted, that Nikki was doing it solely for ulterior motives

and now

right now in this silence!

that Alix would not be a suitable wife for - a future Tsar -

future Tsar Nikki which now he might be.

Convinced that Alexander would never speak out to break this intolerable silence she began nervously.

"Nikki - your dear Papa wishes you to know that he gives consent - full consent - for your proposal to Alix."

Alexander nodded in Nicholas' direction as convincingly as he could, relieved that it had been said.

"Yes yes, of course," he muttered. Suspicion of some ulterior motive on the boy's part would not leave him.

Nicholas, tearful, went towards Papa. Carried forward, light, freely, in obeisance to dear Papa. In deepest gratitude carried with this decision into the timeless. No sense of victory, only purest gratitude from those depths which at last had been granted hope. Lightly now to bow low, hold Papa's hand, kiss his dear hand. But as the bow began before father all powerful giver, something straightened him up, drew him back to see in Papa an other, to stand firm with proper respect, finding the only possible words, with a calm that surprised him.

"Thank you Papa."

Marie Fedorovna saw Alexander's wincing recoil, in those compressed lips, the sharp cough, that hand gripping his jaw. As soon as Nikki returned to his chair she began discussing some practical aspects in as matter-of-fact tone as she could, much to their relief.

"Nikki, your dear Papa who has your welfare so much at heart - he's decided that you shall represent him at the coming marriage of Alix's brother Ernst. That'll be your opportunity to make your proposal. In Coburg itself. What better time and place," she finished almost gaily, taking the risk, though none of it had been properly discussed with Alexander.

Tearfulness again threatened Nicholas.

"Thank you Papa," he said as calmly as he could.

"Uncle Vladimir, Uncle Paul, and Uncle Sergei will be going with you. Victoria, the Prince of Wales and Wilhelm will all be there. So we must put on a good appearance."

"Of course Mama."

A good appearance! And Papa who had planned all this for him – that it had all come together like this – was listening, was waiting.

"Mama they must hear our singers then."

Both of them were warned by Alexander's frown.

"I mean of course our soldier singers, our warrior singers. The glorious choir of our Preobrazhenskys. What a sight that'll be for them," he went on enthusiastically.

Alexander still frowned. Mention of Sergei had upset him and now this stupid singing business. He stood up, clasped hands behind back and snorted loudly. The meeting was over. Marie Fedorovna began to leave the room with Nicholas. She wanted to say some words of consolation before he left for St Petersburg. Alexander would not have it.

"Marie!" he called sharply, forcing her to return. Nicholas shut the door behind him upset by that call and the unexpected separation from Mama, yet tremulously aware that every step forward now was carrying him into a new life.

"Marie!" repeated Alexander, looking hard at her, determined that she should answer for what she had done. She heard the accusation. Of course she should have expected it. But she would stand her ground, come what may.

"Marie does he think he's beaten me?" Alexander demanded, threatened.

"Sasha! How can you? Didn't you see his utter gratitude? No one could feign that," she felt forced to add.

"Well – let's hope it'll make something of him," he nagged at it, surlily, still questioning, wanting confirmation, consolation, "give him some substance, some stability, what he needs."

"Of course that's what he needs," she said encouragingly, carried forward audaciously, "should anything happen –"

He did indeed remember that strange night truth, as from another world, hearing even now resounding, its rightness – no chiding her for that. Even that this thing had to be done in spite of all his disgruntlement and resentment. But the nagging struggle to explain, to justify just why he had given in, continued long and fruitless.

Out of this wretched debilitating weakness? Because for Russia's sake there was simply no alternative? So strange that night-truth. The only real reason even if he couldn't properly understand it?

"Sergei – and she especially, will be very pleased I'm sure. But I tell you he hasn't won."

Was his hand being forced?

"Of course not!"

Within a few days of the meeting her relief that the issue had been resolved this far gave way to anxiety. Her longstanding dislike for Sergei's wife Ella, thrust itself forward, encouraged by a dark awareness, for the first time! that the two, Alix and Ella were sisters! Were close, very close! Ella had never shown the tact so necessary for one in her position. A tact which knew to a fineness the correct balance between rank and sociability. Alix's stiffness was just as incorrect. The two together augured something unpleasant – for the future – that future – 'if something should happen'! The two sisters were very close. Never mind, she herself would be needed more than ever. That future involved them all including her. All those remaining! For goodness sake! how these thoughts ran on.

Calm, steadfast, faithful to her Sasha she must face up to the unthinkable. Nikki as future Tsar!

No, not betrayal, on the contrary, taking it into her thinking bravely, this thought – for the very sake of Sasha's Russian future. Not to would be the betrayal.

Nicholas was clear that Papa had yielded reluctantly. But yielded he had. Consent had been given through darling Mama in that sullen, nodding way. And that was enough.

Painfully recalling Papa's very presence very gesture, he sensed with amazement, behind that sullenness, Papa's struggle! Papa's great struggle and overcoming for his sake, for his Nicholas' sake alone. How closely it brought him to Papa to be shown thus the great effort, sacrifice that he had made, in his own way. But he had done it. This difficult thing. And he would show Papa yet in his solemn gratitude that much good would come from it. Dear Papa would be amply blessed, recompensed for that difficult decision. That was Papa's way that hard sullen way. But already blessings were ripening in tenderness as he reached out towards his true life. Blessings would flow to them all in time, yes all, from this lightness, this fullness of being. He'd stood his ground and Papa – in the only way he knew, gruffly, why, even disparagingly, but that was ever Papa's way – had yielded, confirming recognising.

At last he was free.

Only now to go. To be with her. To say it to her. To offer himself to her. For that, he knew now, was what he sought. To give himself to her. Not at all to ask for anything, but to let himself be made hers.

That dark dread at last driven back by the light of this gentle hope, heart beating ever stronger with joy. Shyest note barely daring from that first moment when he saw her at Uncle Sergei's.

Vast dread shrinking back from Grandpapa's fearful deathday.

Knowing it so clearly now – and daring to face it in the light of this hope – so slowly ascending the marble stairs

behind them bearing poor dear Grandpapa

the bright blood dripping drop by single drop

all around him vanished!

even now

only himself – a question

calling – dumbly calling for Papa's help – protection – strength –

but only the awful loneliness

and that! – then? – yes then now –

his day yet to come

some dreadday

His day!

Inevitable – incomprehensible

It must be so but he could not and would not accept

Stern memory demanding his witness over the years, mysterious, confused, in dread.

And once in his study Grandpapa gently laying a hand on his shoulder and saying some words about Russia – to do with himself?

How? – to do with himself

Dream? – that bright falling blood lived through year after year

It's brightness –yes!

That Papa would live for ever

That no one could replace Papa

Who else could rule Russia?

Only now with Papa's consent, with this hope, to dare admit the dread – his fate. But Godwilled! Himself? – becoming –

beyond all understanding – that fated self.

Papa's consent meant a strength, a light which would enable him to bear it. With Alix at his side he knew he could face all.

A power that had sought him out from afar? but had given her to him too.

Life of its own – this fate now in the open before him – and the hope the strength too given –not to be overwhelmed somehow stand firm – even to bow with this strength before that sacred image enduring – drop by single drop.

Nicholas' call, intimate, certain, inspired Alix's long hidden self with the hope of daring to be. His gentle, unassuming presence, broke the dreary, self-willed spell, since Mama's awful death. Wonderful darling Mama nursing her and Ella and Louis and Ernst through their diphtheria – and then – exhausted, ill – dying. Year after year Mama's bitter absence. Void of unbearable sadness. Some never ending punishment from Above?

Slowly she learned to ease the pain, raw wound of herself. Nothing the others said or did could touch it. Only to withdraw beyond reach, wild, truculent, melancholic, so angry that they even dared think to console her. Poor fools unable to bear the weight of Mama's death. "How Alix has changed!"

Poor fools who went on simply busily living.

She would never cease mourning, bereft of that loving warmth, Mama, once very source of her happy, lively growth, her dimpled smile, her merriment which brightened the life of all around.

In this desolate world she grew wary, aloof, protected but trapped.

She must acknowledge his awakening glance, somehow receive, contain it. To truly respond was to yield. Oh so to yield, let go this brittleness. His glance a door gently opening her to herself. Reclaimed, able at last to be revealed.

His presence recalling to life with painful tremulous touch. Beckoning her to his land – the wide expanse – the incense and choral litany calling, to return – to stay. He and he alone, but to know already that her religious faith would make it impossible.

Four weeks before the wedding of their brother Ernst, Grand Duke of Hesse-Darmstadt, to Victoria, daughter of the Duke of Saxe-Coburg and Gotha, Ella wrote to Alix at Coburg that the Tsar had given his consent, that Nikki would be coming to Coburg as the Tsar's representative and that he would be formally proposing to her, then and there. Her beloved, for she could call him none other, had fought then and won. Her beloved was coming to Coburg - to her. He would come to her as quiet victor who had won through, and she guessed at what cost. But she must say No!

She who had longed for it, must say No. Her vow, given over with her life, was to the only true God whose Word is revealed in the Gospels alone. She knew her faith in Him as sole sustaining power through these desolate years. Nicholas' Orthodox faith and beliefs were not hers. Yet, at Ella's wedding as the incense and the litany filled the church whose golden gated iconostasis dazzled with its radiance, she was drawn through that strangeness, glimpsing a fervent light, pure, of such reverent exaltation.

If he came and asked her, touched her, she already felt the saying - No! as impossible, unbearable. But the Yes, flowing so easily, too easily - was betrayal. Impossible desertion of God who had given her very life.

So painful this puzzle.

When she thought of that sweetness - presence - loved one - purely himself - purely that loved one - himself alone - where then - what then - of his beliefs and faith? - of belief and faith?

If Nicholas looked at her, touched her, as his hand had done so gently, affirming, protecting on their sledge gliding across the frozen ponds, she knew she would yield, melt away as she so wanted, into that Yes. So she must not speak at all. For the only word she felt she could utter was Yes. Even to think of saying the No in his presence was a darkness, an awful annihilation.

For long she knelt on the cold stone floor of the family chapel at Coburg, praying to God that the way be shown. She longed for some miraculous intervention. But a grave understanding knew that the decision would be, must be, hers alone.

Nicholas and his uncles arrived in Coburg at the beginning of April, a week before the wedding, taking Alix's acceptance as a matter of course, as did everyone. Public interest over the proposal was beginning to overshadow Ernst's wedding, for it involved a great power, not simply a small German princedom.

The day of their arrival at Coburg was filled with formalities including a lengthy banquet at the Grand Ducal palace in the evening. Nicholas suffered it with increasing impatience which in no way affected his habitual charm and politeness. His gracious, modest way, enabled him to dwell with his Alix amidst all this clamour.

In truth there would be nothing to say. His presence there, with her, alone, ever had been and would be sufficient. How could words add to that or touch it. But his heart was aflame as he knew that at last he could say this thing - these words which were truly deed of deeds, true gift of himself. Words aflame with a life, even now as he thought them and lived them.

"My dearest Alix - I am yours - will you be mine?"

Such a verdant delight all about him, such a smiling happiness within that he knew in blissful trust, whether he spoke or did not speak - all would be well!

Theirs was this something greater abounding, all sufficient - security and strength.

At the sight of Nikki's visiting card Alix despaired. During these last days of prayer she swung violently from one extreme to the other. She conjured up innumerable variations in the way of putting him off entirely, from hiding, fleeing Coburg, insulting him, forcing herself to be horrible to him, convincing him that she was not the person he thought yet dreaming, ever dreaming, of being his forever. The conflict exhausted her but the very exhaustion made her anxious with its threat of carrying her forward, helpless, yielding.

In his blue and green Colonel's uniform of the Preobrazhensky Guard, Nicholas followed the footman along the corridor to Princess Alexandra's apartment in the east wing of the palace where she had lived since her mother's death. The footman was about to knock on the pink, gilded door when Nicholas impulsively waved him aside and stood waiting until the man had disappeared back along the corridor. He tapped gently three times and entered, closing the door on that other world.

Simply to be here in this so substantial world of her presence was all sufficient now. Unsure, whether awake or dreaming, she reached out her hand as he approached and held it to his lips. He sat closer on the chair she had made ready for him, still with her hand in his. Unrestrainedly their tears welled forth. Beyond words. But he must speak to establish that conventional con-nection, orientate them with the rest of mankind, or else in this bitter-sweet dumbness they would drift away entirely, never wanting to return. Words then must be spoken, made. But he uttered them huskily, whispering, diffident as he reverently sensed the import of this worldly affirmation, through which their love would be sealed once and for all. Born, brought into the world of all men, so shy, so exposed now, yet strong enough so to be.

"Dear Alix - Papa has given his permission - Alix my dearest," he smiled, joyful and with a deep breath, "I ask for your hand in marriage."

From the moment he entered she wanted to, dared to, let herself be for him, not daring to speak, wanting to drift with him, anxiously awaiting the question, and now it had come, able only to shake her lowered head from side to side, saying No! Not daring to look at him. That was the question and this was what she must, had determined to do. But, so gently, she remained with him. Terrible this challenge, not to betray God in his very presence. In spite of the wounding, the pain, she must not yield.

Nicholas drew back covering her hand with his, waiting. Her tearful face and drawn lips and that insistent shaking of her head made him so uncertain, uneasy, desperate at the unexpectedness of it. Something dreadful was happening and he must know.

"Are you saying no - No? - What d'you mean? Alix - tell me - what are you saying? Dear Alix - you're my life. You must tell me!"

Still he held her hand in his and would not let go. Bewildered and anxious he waited, holding in that hand, those slender fingers a source of his life which he would never give up. A shuddering breath drew her out of a tearful stupor. She knew she must speak, must force out the words through a tear-dimmed haze. She had been drifting clear away but at the shore's edge of this longed-for release, so tenderly whispered the quiet touch of his life. Ever there. Insistent. Touch telling of that which endures and is true. Touch telling of that which waits, so sure, so pure.

Her drifting must cease. Cowardice! She must speak, she must tell, whatever the cost, as she felt his pain.

"Nikki," she whispered, "How can I? It's my religion. It's impossible," her voice strengthened.

"Your religion? But our religion is the same - the same my dear. We are both Christians."

"How can I?" he repeated, distressed. "But why! - your dear sister has found it possible. Is she less good than you?"

The question alarmed her and she fought back. But the more she argued on concerning doctrinal differences, the more she felt his sadness and distress as by far the greater reality. The words paled before that radiance in which she lived his love for her.

"You just don't understand Nikki. For you the Church, its tradition, the service, the priests are so important. For me, a Lutheran, it's the Bible itself. God's word. Everything else is secondary. Dear Nikki, if I became your wife I could never do what was expected of me."

Though standing as firm as she could on what she knew, Alix sensed that she was losing her grip. They were indeed both Christians. Could they not meet there as one too?

With relief they heard the knock on the door, and the footman entered with a tea trolley. Silently they drank. Nicholas stood up and she stretched out her hand which he held and kissed before leaving.

Numbly he returned through a joyless world to the ducal Palace of Rosenau especially made over to the Russian guests. He went straight to his own apartment and immediately confided his distress in a letter to Mama, the one whom alone he could ever confide in. But he felt compelled to tear it up and begin again, writing this second time less effusively, at one point wishing he had not to write at all, at another certain that Mama, if only she were here now, would have an answer, a happy answer to this dreadful situation.

At the evening meal in the gloomy banqueting hall in which Luther himself once ate, Nicholas' older sister Xenia complained about her cramped apartment, comparing Rosenau unfavourably with the magnificent Callenberg Palace given over to William and his Germans. The small talk soon died down as it became clear to his aunts and uncles that Nicholas was thoroughly downcast. Everyone knew that the proposal had taken place this day and they were awaiting a happy announcement from him. They could only assume something unfortunate and left him alone. Grand Duke Sergei had much at stake. After the men had finished their cigars and brandies he must speak straight to the point.

He linked arms with Nicholas and led him away, protective, forceful.

"Nikki my boy, things haven't gone too well. Come back with me."

Sitting opposite his uncle in Grand Duke Sergei's apartment, Nicholas stared down at the floor. Uncle's presence somewhere so like Papa yet easier. But shouldn't it have been Papa right here - was he committing some betrayal?

"Well! Tell me! Then I can help you. I also had a proposal refused once," began Grand Duke Sergei, brusque but friendly.

"I can't believe it," said Nicholas quietly, shaking his head. "I know she loves me. She knows I love her."

"Then what's the problem my boy?" asked Grand Duke Sergei impatiently.

"Religion! She insists that her religion makes it impossible. But we love each other!" he said in desperation.

"Religion? Is that all? My dear boy stop worrying. No problem at all. Leave that to your aunt Ella."

"What d'you mean? no problem," asked Nicholas.

"I mean that Ella will show her dear sister from her own life, her own example that it's not impossible. That for a Christian all our roads lead to Christ - our Saviour and Redeemer," he crossed himself. "Now say no more. Worry no more. Leave it to me. Be assured that all will be well."

Grand Duke Sergei went straight to Ella. From the beginning he had taken most seriously the implications of a relationship that might lead to Ella's sister becoming the Empress. That, he felt and told Ella, could lead to the kind of Russia that he wanted so much to see, to help build.

At Nicholas' news he felt the successful outcome of the proposal now become a most urgent challenge. When he told Ella, she trembled at that all too familiar tone demanding immediate compliance.

"The proposal must go through. Must, I say. Must, Ella!" His gaze was on some far horizon.

"Of course my dear. I shall see her straight away in the morning," she answered immediately.

That 'must' meant do everything possible to achieve success whatever the cost! Failure would risk that terrible rage, very thought making her feel faint.

So urgently fearfully pressed, she became newly aware of her sister. A sympathy, understanding awoke drawing her close, unveiling tenderly, from such long years we two sisters - alone - together - after Mama's death. A force drawing her so close, come of itself, truthful, she would yield, let do its work through her. Out of it she would speak to her Alix.

Such unease now - yield - confess it - about the way she'd

been towards Alix since Mama's death. But how difficult Alix was. But then! how deeply Mama's death must have affected her. How drastically it had changed her. How impossible she'd become. Clearly now, the pain never assuaged.

"It's the religious business that's causing all the trouble. You've got to knock some sense into her," Sergei ordered.

The religious business - knock it in - with Alix?

How then?

With herself the change from Lutheran to Orthodox hadn't been difficult - just because! - it wasn't such a serious matter for her.

She would plan nothing. Simply speak from the heart. She could do no more.

Ella's unexpected appearance so soon after breakfast, which could only have to do with her rejection of the proposal, made Alix very wary. Through the night she had been fighting a harsh battle which must be won alone. On that high place, in the light of those principles, she must beware of any well meant but naive solutions - betrayal!

"Dear Alix," Ella began, barely allowing herself to notice Alix' appearance or attitude, striving only to remain true to that heartfelt impulse, trusting in its goodness.

"Who is offering you this treasure, this happiness but God Himself? Nikki's a true Christian. A good pure kindly person. It's been hard for you since Mama's death. But Mama above all would only want your happiness now. And we shall be together again. You, Nikki, Sergei, myself. A family. Happiness. And that's all from God - the only God. What a hard life you've had Alix. It was easier for me being older. But look now. See what God - Who else dear Alix? - has brought you? A cup brimming over with joy. Who else could have brought it you? The dry years are over my dear. And who would be happier than Mama herself. Isn't this God's day Alix? I tell you dear sister, the two of you together will bring you even closer to God. That's how it's been with Sergei and I."

Alix could only yield, let the tears flow as Ella held her hand. O let him come again. Now. Soon. Uncertainty still there. Not prevailing but still there. So he must come soon and she would give him her Yes. For she had Ella with her too now. Her Ella. In all truthfulness! awakening out of that loneliness. Joyfully awakening to this bond, one with them all.

Downwards, downwards into this warm, welcoming place, to Ella's comforting heart yielding. This deeply buried one coming forth - the yielding. For this she was yearning, ready. Recognised. Gently affirmed. Not fiercely striving will straining to Him, but bathed in this gentle affirmation by Ella sister, Ella mother. Cling tightly to Ella speaking of Mama like this, let the tears flow, Ella's tears too, cleansing, restoring. This deeply buried one coming forth - the yielding.

Smile - through the tears - childhood's sunny smile - radiance daring to be, once again.

Ella saw Nicholas and told him to ask again.

When he knocked on the door of Alix' apartment and entered, there was no need to ask, to speak. He entered into that new awaiting world of their own, his hand on hers. Through the tears her smile was entrance to a life, so long awaited, so magically here.

Timeless existence.

Eternal pledge.

Each in the other.

Timeless existence, stillness of gaze, each seeking itself in the other's yielding space. With effort they must leave it and return to that fallen world.

Nicholas left Alix for that poor, needy world, walking back through Coburg whose buildings were now recast in some powerful radiance. Alix, serene, in this fullness of being, knew him beyond all leaving. And what need of doing, in this finding, confirming of each other, as all in all.

Back in his apartment he knew a certainty, a peaceful joy which would bear him up no matter what life had to bring. Whatever prevailed. He knew he was not alone.

How dare believe such happiness possible in this world - such a feeling of unity between two mortal beings.

A mutual joy, a mutual hope, the source not of one but of both together. All about him, gentler, friendlier, transformed by this radiant joy, hinting some beauty of its own.

From this world he must write the news to Mama and Papa.

His letter arrived at Gatchina two days after the decision had been taken to move the Tsar to Livadia, royal residence in the Crimea, on the advice of Professor Adolf Leyden, the famous specialist from Vienna. The Tsar had taken a considerable turn for the worse with dreadful headaches, insomnia and a weakness in the legs which forced him to lie on his couch for several hours a day. Professor Leyden had been urgently called in by the Tsar's own doctors who were alarmed by his condition and his failure to respond to their treatment. The eminent professor diagnosed nephritis and was optimistic, insisting that a complete rest in the sunny Crimea would do the trick.

Marie Fedorovna was deeply disturbed. The failure of Dr Spiridovich's and Dr Melgunov's medicaments and their petulant disagreements in her presence when she had angrily to remind them that the patient's well-being was more important than their professional vanity, left her with a mistrust, a lack of confidence, in no way dispelled by the arrival and authoritative pronouncements of Professor Leyden. His magisterial certainty and benign optimism in no way related to her shock and distress though she had no alternative but to follow his directives.

Never before had Alexander been laid low like this in the blue bedroom which overlooked the lake and whose curtains he preferred well drawn for most of the day. She sat by his bedside for hours at a time watching his unfamiliarly quiet form, dozing fitfully, moaning occasionally with the pain in his head, and the room, such a sombre, eerily hushed, shadowy world. Everything in it, bed, chairs, desk, bric-a-brac, becoming tinctured with a finality.

One time his face looked puffed up. Another, thin and drawn. He was changing, elusively changing. Sometimes a listless lethargy, sometimes a delicate pallor, aura of extreme exhaustion, sometimes the haunting gaze of wan resignation as he clutched at his throbbing head. Gently she held his other hand, ghostly, limp, willing him life and love through her anguish. In this hushed sombre world, she felt around her, a new presence, another person, yet Alexander. She could not prevent her thoughts, her whole being, turning with increasing strength towards Nicholas. A turning, a forcefulness, whose implications she dared not fully confront.

She had received Nicholas' first desperately unhappy letter with mixed feelings. Relief that the German girl with her stiffness, arrogance, awful dress sense and dreadful French would never be his wife, and that, out of her very own mouth, justifying so clearly Papa's and her own attitude. Yet upset too at the dear boy's dreadful unhappiness.

Nicholas' second letter arrived amidst hectic packing for the journey to Livadia. Once the decision had been taken the tension at Gatchina eased. A vague hopefulness was aroused in Marie Fedorovna herself by the busy activity which momentarily countered her feelings of helplessness before that inexorable Other. Professor Leyden's 'do the trick', which so upset Marie Fedorovna, passed humorously round the palace, his German intonation jokingly imitated – to hold off a growing desperation?

She kept her doubts and distress to herself especially not wanting to upset the children and managing somehow to maintain a cheerful face. Nearly everyone, close entourage, officials and servants felt reassured at the news that the eminent Professor Leyden had diagnosed nothing worse than nephritis which a good rest at Livadia would cure soon enough.

Nicholas' second letter with its utterly unexpected news, made suddenly so real, absolute, impersonal, all that she barely dared to feel in her deep distress – that an implacable fate was already decreeing it. Give way, stand back, be pleased. Hadn't Alexander Alexandrovich himself – himself? – said 'Should anything happen'. But what were those words? What had he been saying? And wasn't it so now? That Nikki would have his wife. And wasn't it good now – his joy and happiness that simply radiated from this letter? *I cried like a child and she did too. The whole world is changed for me: nature, mankind, everything and all seems to be good and lovable.* Wasn't that what they'd had in mind, his well-being at last, his stability – should anything happen.

But this bitterness, suspicion, could not be held off. Through Ella it had come about! That naive boy had not spared her the details including the part played by Sergei. *'If it hadn't been for Uncle Sergei it would never have happened.'* But this praise for Ella was worse – 'Dear Aunt Ella, so understanding, so ready to help, to explain to my darling – she has really saved my life.'

So then!

A warning a warning!

In what lay ahead Nicholas must be near her and she near him.

She began to write, in the very writing pulling him towards her.

'Papa is very ill' – she began but soon became annoyed, confused at her continual crossings out, uncertain as to what she was aiming at, afraid, wondering even whether now he might not take it very seriously. She began again on a fresh sheet, 'Papa

is seriously ill and tomorrow we go to Livadia for a cure. You must come too.' That 'must' she would not alter. That's what she wanted, that's what must be and so it would stay. Gratefully she received an afterthought which she added but with such confused feelings.

'*Papa and I are of course very pleased at your news.*'

The letter arrived in Coburg during the week of festive celebrations following the wedding. Celebrations heightened by the general excitement over the news of Nicholas' successful proposal which was soon being discussed across Europe. Nicholas had decided to stay on for a week or two after the Grand Dukes returned home so that he could be with Alix as long as possible. He didn't really want to leave Coburg at all, feeling that simply being with her was home. All the cousins from abroad and more distant relatives too were being so kind to them, wishing them such happiness, especially dear Victoria, Alix's Grandmother.

The letter was handed to him on his way to a performance by the Preobrazhensky choir, at which Victoria, cousin William of Germany, the Prince of Wales and cousin George of Greece would be attending. He intended to merely scan the contents for this hurried moment, in the happy expectation of confirming his parents' pleasure at the news, swiftly adding one more great joy. But the tense message from Mama, so unfamiliar in tone, struck deep. He left the letter opened out on the desk, went over to the window, returned and read again those hard, dry words as a meaning broke forth darkly, anxious, ominous. That he must go straight to Livadia now! But each time he thought about leaving, about saying Goodbye to her, a blank refusal, an immense resistance overpowered him.

Livadia.

Livadia the future his future!

Never before had Mama said 'seriously ill'.

But Alix too his future never to be left – never to be away from her. The very thought so fearful. He must go to Livadia but leaving Alix? – a dangerous threat. Papa must be dreadfully ill for Mama to have written like that. He should be off to Livadia immediately.

He sat through the concert racked with anguish and guilt. Straight after he went to Grand Duke Sergei, who sternly told him where his duty lay. Soon telegrams were alerting the Grand

Dukes themselves to the gravity of the situation. News arrived of a further deterioration which followed a deceptive improvement. At a gloomy family conference it was decided to cut short their official leave-taking at Coburg and entrain immediately for the Crimea.

Nicholas dared not accept the reality of what was happening in Livadia, yet knowing as he journeyed through a dreamlike world that something overwhelming was unfolding around him. On taking his sudden leave from Alix, so distressed, he referred to Papa's serious illness as briefly, calmly as possible. But unexpectedly, urgently he asked if she would follow him to Livadia - soon - as soon as she could - because - because my darling Alix, things seem so uncertain, so confused. Of course she would. She would follow him anywhere, her smile, concern love his strength. Whatever awaited in Livadia he could endure.

The wooden palace stood near the cliff and commanded a glorious vista over the Black Sea between Yalta and Simferopol. When the Grand Dukes arrived there had been a constant coming and going for days of ministers and officials from St Petersburg. Soon after his arrival Nicholas was shaken to see Father John of Kronstadt, the famous miracle worker, little, old, whitebearded, summoned by Marie Fedorovna. Yes - he knew.

The great waiting had begun for all. Inbreath hovering on the edge of existence. Each suspended in the timeless moment, powerless, before that mighty Other. Each now knew the time for doing was over. Now only was the time for kneeling, the time for praying, the time for yielding in prayer to our Lord and Father of our Saviour Jesus Christ. Now only to turn, to do with one's inmost. The presence and prayer of Father John filled the great waiting, transforming its first painful emptiness through wisdom-wrought ritual into the substance of hope. Ritual binding heaven and earth, preparing, strengthening those below with that heavenly presence descending, from above. The presence of Father John told of the process begun and that heavenly One with them here and now. Earthly hope was yielding to the greater hope in heaven, roused, recalled. The prayer of Father John was become true life for the living, while the doctors continued to watch and consult.

But everyday life, the running of the empire must continue at any cost. Some ministers and senior officials began handing documents to Nicholas for his approval and signature. Necessary, vital gestures, but gestures only as yet.

Marie Fedorovna, aware of Nicholas' arrival didn't yet want to see or even speak. In this moment gathering, the tides of time withdrawing, the silence alone resounded and was real. Her life, suspended, was in that room which she rarely left, as she watched those stricken eyes, searching, delicately charged, gentle. Helpless at what was happening, angry, rebellious, why? why? this to her beloved who had worked so hard for his people. And those wretched useless Romanovs filling the palace, daring such arrogance – presumption!

The Grand Dukes were grumbling openly about Alexander's failure to delegate and the administrative tangles which were quickly becoming evident. Piecemeal they were taking over imperial tasks with a pomposity and heavy-handedness which made it clear to the unprepared ministers and officials that they were in charge now and expected to be consulted at every turn. They could make no real rapport with the many issues which Alexander had kept so intimately under his sole control. Had he expected to live forever? They quickly intimated that Nicholas was to be consulted only as a formality, creating uncertainty and embarrassment for the officials concerned. The real authority and power was to be regarded as theirs from now on. For the moment they held Nicholas of no account, loathe to admit that he was involved significantly in what was happening.

Admitting the reality of his presence meant accepting the fact that the Emperor was dying and incredibly that he would be the next Emperor! The formidable reality of the Emperor even in his passing was overpowering, very ground of their identity and doing. The 'and then?' petered out in a void before that ghostly youth.

Nicholas felt himself to be watching a scene in which he was not involved, yet somewhere was the missing central actor. He realised that people were going out of their way not to notice him, sometimes as tactfully as possible, sometimes not at all tactfully. All of which he simply, gratefully accepted. Outside, the anxious consultations, arguments, prayers, his uncles' curt orders, but knowing, from depths ascending, that all of it was beginning to centre on him. That long dreaded implacable future was reaching its culmination. Out there yet himself. That Papa was leaving him. This vast space opening up about him was Papa's absence which Alix and Mama alone could help him bear.

Only to wait, an embarrassment to them all, an embarrassment to himself.

But the Godwilled doom which he'd fled had sought him out. Chosen him - elected. These funeral preparations were for his own future too!

This doing of theirs could not avoid it.

But the him they were referring to was not him at all - only his darling spoke to that.

Alix arrived within a couple of days amidst despair, incredulity, that so unexpectedly, at forty nine, in the very prime of his strength and leadership, it was happening and that it would soon be over. On arrival she asked how Papa was. He explained that he didn't exactly know Papa's condition because no one had yet told him. Immediately alerted, angry, she demanded to know who had refused to tell him. Flustered he said it wasn't like that, no one had actually refused. "You must demand to know straight away. You mustn't let others forget who you are!" she insisted, defending against the attack. Forget? how else put it - their terrible refusal to acknowledge his reality. She was quickly alerted to the way both of them were being treated. Of course! something amiss in her reception at the station - not at all the recognition due to her rank. Quickly she grasped what was at stake - who her Nikki really was.

Nicholas spent much time in his room or wandering about the grounds, greatly distressed that he still had not seen Papa. Twice when he went down the hushed corridor to the sick room, guarded by two silent household officers, some awful force gathered making it impossible to continue. In confusion he returned to his room certain that his presence, this painful presence would only upset Papa. Alix was shocked when he told her but her presence, look, words, reaffirmed that newborn self of their coming together, which transcended all this. A bliss being wrought as their armour which this stupid unworthy world would never know. A bliss sounding forth in everything - yes everything? - because it was theirs alone.

He went again to the sickroom, inwardly gathered, sad. Marie Fedorovna was dozing off in her chair at Alexander's side, in a stupor of exhaustion from the days of ceaseless vigil. She noted Nikki's quiet entry, to stand at the foot of the bed. At last he had come. They were together. The three of them.

Cautiously, reverently, he gazed at Papa drawing even now!

403

on that strength, calm, majestic in the stillness, mysteriously different yet very substance still of this world about. Never had he wanted to see Papa like this, so still, so quiet, so thin. Daring to look into Papa's eyes he saw so sadly – but surely only for the moment – stricken giant. But more, he glimpsed something more, a call, a gentle challenge, a helpless resignation – what was it?

Alexander's eyes saw revealed spoke with a primal speech, since a stroke had stilled his tongue. Newborn meaning eluding all, son there, wife, doctors, Father John. For them he remained the centre, still giant of familiar appearance though shrunken and wan. But he was out there, not centre any more.

Out there wistfully wondering, glimpsing with some amazement that other man who had hunted so strenuously, taken part in manoeuvres and held up the shattered roof of the Borki train with fiery strength. But no longer roused by the sight of this man that he was, to fight back in desperation. For where had it gone that power, that strength, gone in the prime of his life, making no sense at all. Now calmly this wistful wondering for a line had been crossed. Now was acceptance as he lived this great withdrawal with affirmation. Positive, calm.

Drifting on a summer's day across the lake with Nikki – George – Michael – Marie and Xenia waiting there to begin the picnic meal – the oak tree – so warmly intimate – such peace flowing this yielding.

All the challenge was over now, from Nicholas, from death itself, felt as a calling to him, such a rightful calling. For during these very last days given over, accepting, at last graciously accepting, he had begun to live the painful unreadiness, inadequacy of Nicholas as though it were his own. With a tender compassion he lived it, seeking only to strengthen, to call down blessing for this poor boy who so uncertainly stood at the foot of his bed. And all the time drifting, carried backwards, drifting on a gentle rhythmic tide. Backwards to beginnings, steady pulsebeat of the world, the power leaving.

Fear, disbelief, intensified about the sick room. The drastic change in the Emperor's appearance could not be accepted. The threat to each one's identity was too great, too sudden.

What was coming?

To contemplate, even begin to turn one's thoughts in the direction of that pale, nervous youth creeping around, was extremely painful. To dare believe that he would – replace? – take over? – was sacrilege, a nonsense. And now this creature who had appeared with him. Surly indeed! taking on such airs! Does she dare suppose amidst this catastrophe that she has some right to acknowledgement? Wasn't it she who had so aggravated our lord's troubles? Then shun her too. Cut her too down to size!

In the watching and waiting by Papa's bedside, the gentle breathing, so still, there wove an ebb and flow of contending uncertainties affecting the lives of all in the palace and the country beyond. Alix kept determinedly at Nikki's side helping to hold at bay that vast dread threatening. He felt dreamily suspended beyond the business and bustle outside. Necessary business which had to be kept going for the administration of the empire and which helped to protect those involved from the enigma of the sickroom, sanctum.

Alix insisted that she and Nikki keep ceaseless bedside vigil with Mama. Marie Fedorovna, puffy-eyed with exhaustion, dozed much of the time, drifting drowsily and returning to the anguished watch over her beloved. Nicholas was coming to know Papa anew. No longer that stricken giant which at first sight had so shocked him, which he had starkly refused to accept was Papa. Now, tenderly, he was seeing that quietly breathing one, so distant, as his Papa, such a different Papa, but Papa.

He Nicholas compelled to know himself as centre forming, the currents of meaning, shifting, swirling, delicately reweaving the textures of earthly life.

In the waiting by that softly breathing form Alix glimpsed, as stern revelation, what and whom she would become, inexorably carried forward on this destiny's tide.

A loud gasping and shuddering struck at the three of them with shock, panic. Alix's and Nikki's hands, long clasped together, squeezed painfully tight.

So fearful!

From what place!

The shuddering breath repeated that ghastly sound with its clear note of struggle, desperation. Alix trembled uncontrollably and rushed from the room for the doctors. Nicholas held Mama close as they watched helpless. Papa, his old Papa, had come to life, struggling, fighting. Oxygen was hurriedly brought in as the doctors took over. Someone had called for Father John and his robed presence pervaded the room before the ikon of the Blessed Virgin of Mercy. His low steady chant was of man's plight, God's saving grace, calling now, rising from sadness and calling on God's great mercy for them all. For all present, family, doctors, servants, Father John's prayer sounded the true voice of what was happening, drawing them, hope, sad joy, away from some last urgent gestures – the awkward metal clips, stubborn rubber tubes, whispered orders.

The frantic efforts of the doctors were in vain.

The struggle was over.

That barely perceptible trembling died away. Nicholas and Alix still watched but borne along on that prayer, beyond, to new beginnings, dimly, consolingly, to 'husband', to 'Emperor', who belonged to all Russia now. All of them drawn upwards on those words which sought to resolve, to unite each one with an other and them all with him, Alexander, and with God.

Nicholas suddenly withdrew, followed almost immediately by Alix, along the corridor and through to his own room. He was numb with despair at the realisation that Papa had abandoned him, finally abandoned him. Had gone. Had left him behind, naked, vulnerable, with no place to hide. Centre now of this empty space which threatened on every side.

They embraced tightly. Alix felt him trembling all over and gently led him to a chair. He stared blankly, shaking his head from side to side in bewilderment, as the tears started down his cheeks.

"No! No! No! I can't. I won't. It's impossible. I never wanted it," he sobbed.

Yes, this was his destiny, his doom, himself. But he did not want it, could not bear it, felt utterly incapable before it. Yet before her he could cry out and confess.

Alix felt his pain as her own, the very bitterness of his abandonment and despair. She willed her very life to him for him seeking only to become one with him in everything. To share completely all his terrible burden. Terrible – but Godwilled!

From now on she would maintain a stern watch on his – on their – on – yes already she could think it with wonderment, as most meaningful presentiment – Russia's behalf too.

"Courage! Courage my darling," she whispered again and again. Through the open resolve from this courage, Papa's encouragement felt. Mysterious this strength from Alix and Papa – Blessed Papa watching over, protecting. Papa more needed now than ever. In bravest purest dedication he would follow, call on Papa now. Papa who had consented – yes consented in his saintly rising – very blessing surely – with that gentle awakened smile, she at his side, making all well.

All was well!

In this desolate space of Papa's withdrawing Alix and Mama were with him, even though this space was his alone!

Watching them erect the altar on the lawn he must simply do like them. Like them in their uncertainty, he knew that this doing, these ancient actions were the wise, well tested ways of abiding through the darkness.

The sure ordered sequence of rites touched all, mystery concealing and revealing the passing away and the coming into being. Rites through whose grave rhythms all could discover, create that weaving texture of being shimmering with becoming. So fine, so little there, yet so palpable, heavy, with that body of death.

Family, courtiers, officials, servants, formed a semicircle round the altar and Father John administered the oath of allegiance to, "Tsar Nicholas the Second!"

Could it be?

Guns boomed from the harbour, saluting, warning, as wave on wave of a new reality drew towards him.

Hidden was this transformation. Already the new naming uttered, its object conjured into being.

"Long live Tsar Nicholas the Second!"

Mysterious this ritual, each present, spectator and creator.

The coming into being, so fraught for Nicholas, was over.

The so long dreaded moment, of himself as Tsar was past.

Weight now of this destiny – but Godwilled!

Godwilled!

Joyful revelation!

Gracious revelation – strength – foundation – to submit in humility!

God was with him!

Strength from God!

Strength from Alix!

The uncles led by Grand Duke Sergei, continued to express themselves in a way that implied a new independence and assertion. They had no intention of being deferential to this nephew of theirs, and went straight ahead in planning for the funeral. Family mourning at Livadia would last a week, after which a special funeral train would carry the coffin across the Ukraine via Kharkov, Kursk, Orel and Tula. At each of these cities nobility, officials and the peasants would take part in services by the halted funeral train. In Moscow the coffin would lie in the Kremlin for one night allowing Muscovites to pay homage. Then on to St Petersburg and the Peter and Paul Cathedral for its final resting place with all the Romanov Tsars.

Suddenly, urgently, Nicholas felt the need to be wedded in the Livadia family chapel before Papa was moved. To have Papa with them during the marriage ceremony would be such a right, such a holy resolution and fulfilment of all – all the difficulties, that had gone before. But uncle Sergei was adamant from the beginning.

"My dear boy whatever are you thinking of? You and Alix don't belong to yourselves any longer. You're Russia's. Your wedding is for all the Russian people – to see – to live through. You're a lucky fellow Nikki. Your dear Papa has set this nation on its right course. You've simply got to look after his work. That's your heritage and your task!"

Nicholas gave way immediately, trusting Grand Duke Sergei completely, mastered by his uncle's confidence and decisiveness especially at this moment. Yet, inexplicably to himself he felt uneasy. He needed all the family help at this moment – and yet.

"You have simply to follow in his footsteps," Uncle Sergei had concluded emphatically, reassuringly. So each day in the chapel, for a week, with Mama, Alix, Olga, Michael, George and all the family, he bent over the coffin to kiss Papa's lips and pledged himself through that kiss, quick of bitter-sweet seal, dedicated himself to following in Papa's footsteps and to being a faithful custodian of Papa's great work.

All the uncles were keen to press the message that he must continue with his father's sound policy, which had created such stability. Men around were looking at him with concern for their future, who would go? who would stay? Obscurely he struggled for some distance from them all.

Grand Duke Sergei played his hand carefully and tactfully strengthened his relationship with Nicholas at every opportunity, to ensure that this immature youth follow his lead from the start.

Alix's conversion, and consecration to the Orthodox Church, was proclaimed by Nicholas' 1st Imperial Decree, which confirmed her as, "The truly believing Grand Duchess Alexandra Fedorovna."

Through the incense, candlelight, litany, shimmered a world of incomparable radiance, glory and warmth. A new world, ancient, holy, mysterious beckoned with a gentle power, for which she yearned. Raised up, ascending through this beauty which so drew her once she had begun to yield. Floating on this golden-hued ocean of colour and sound, away, away from that ugliness below. The radiant light of this new world casting the shadows about her more deeply. World whose gateway was love.

She felt immeasurably strengthened, their love so protected on high. Closer even would they surely become, blessed, cherished from that high place. But light from that high place showed clearly too, the doubt and disparagement directed against Nikki and herself. How vulnerable - timid? - he was. But she was ready. Through her independence, wrought long and hard, she sensed that she would have to fight her way forward for them both. This was not what she wanted or expected but the fight was on. Well! a worthy task - to care for, - defend her loved one.

For his very own sake, in spite of the distress it caused him, she must tell him clearly who he was and make him fight them too.

"You must insist - demand!" she kept repeating, "You mustn't let others forget who you are!"

Forget? - that she dare not put it more truthfully - let others try and pretend you are not a real Tsar.

Reluctantly she was forced to admit his timidity. But let them all be assured, those who were thus conspiring, confident that they could get away with it. The fight was on - for herself and her own!

Now indeed a worthy task for her lifelong burden of wariness - yet turned - to care for, defend - more, with this newborn strength infuse with lifewill her loved one - task she would joyfully bear for ever.

She knew what they were saying, the spiteful things that she was even intended to overhear - that he was wholly unfit to reign - good! - good! - and with such blatant license - let them! But she knew what power was at work guarding that bliss, that joy.

Power preparing them both for Russia's future. Power far transcending this petty world of intrigue, scandal, lie.

Marie Fedorovna and Nicholas emerged from their compartment into the gloomy November afternoon. On the platform of St Petersburg's Nicholaevsky Station, silent ranks of soldiers, and small groups of high officials stood waiting. Slowly, with great care and effort the immaculately uniformed Cossack pallbearers in their crisp white jackets, black caps and black breeches, positioned the large black-draped coffin of their beloved master onto their shoulders. Grave, firm, bearing their sacred treasure, they slow-marched to the beat of a muffled drum. All heads were bowed as they moved across the platform in the chill gloom, followed by the immediate family, Alix, and the Grand Dukes with their wives. At the station entrance, lined with men from the Guards and Hussars regiments, the pallbearers transferred the coffin to the funeral carriage as the drums beat steadily and the long line of waiting carriages readied to move off.

Marie Fedorovna and Nicholas took their seat in the leading carriage, exhausted, overwrought after the week-long vigil in Livadia, the gruelling journey north to Moscow stopping for services en route, and then the night long service in the Kremlin.

Painfully slow the procession moved off, pace of some never ending dream whose hidden pulsebeat was the muffled drum. On towards the Cathedral of St Peter and St Paul, through the mist and the slushy streets lined with men of the Pavlovsky, Volynsky, Litovsky and Semyonovsky regiments, and behind them the silent waiting thousands. Thickly veiled, the Empress leaned forward into view, knowing that those waiting, those outside, wanted to see to acknowledge and to share.

Dry implacable drumbeat, each one marking an end of earthly time. The one and the one and again the single one, separate, always separate and alone. In its dryness reminding, warning and reminding of that chill and airless realm which each must cross.

It took nearly four hours to cross the city and reach the Cathedral entrance which was flanked by men of the Preobrazhensky Regiment, behind whom, waiting patiently, were more thousands, Petersburgers, and people from the outlying districts who had been trekking into the city for several days.

The presence of these thousands waiting patiently for so long made the authorities extremely anxious. Every possible security precaution must be taken, but the anxiety persisted.

Pallbearers carried the coffin, draped in cloth of gold, up the wide entrance steps and into the shimmering candlelight, setting it down on a marble plinth before the iconostasis of St George and the Dragon. Priest and choir ceaselessly chanted weaving litany's ladder from earth to heaven. A guard of four men took up positions, arms reversed, heads lowered, at each corner of the coffin. The lid was lifted off and laid below on the cloth of gold. Led by the Empress, drifting in some trance, swaying awkwardly, only held by Nicholas's support, the ritual kissing of the corpse began.

Each morning a special service was held for the family which included the European dynasties whose representatives continued to arrive. This was followed by the homage of senior officials from all over the empire. Then in due course the main Cathedral doors were opened wide and the waiting thousands, strictly supervised by the soldiers, were allowed to pass through and pay their homage. Day and night the chanting of the litany never ceased as priest replaced priest, and choir replaced choir.

The patiently waiting thousands, shuffling forward, tired, hungry, to wait yet again before moving forward once more, were determined to see him, most for the first and last time, anxious to establish and confirm his reality, in its very passing elusive.

The final leavetaking, and they would never be so close to this most distant one. He very centre to the last, available to every Russian still. Never closer than this - nor more distant. Strange and sad and sweet then were the ways of this life.

From cities, towns and villages, from remote dwellings in wood and forest they came, by foot, in rope-girt cloaks, by horse, by cart, mile upon mile through muddy tracks, through slush and snow. Called to come because they must and could do no other. Called, recalled along the myriad streams to that mainstream and its source. To the Father who even now sustained them and their hopes.

Called, inexorably called, by the slowly tolling bells of monastery and church across the whole land, penetrating the paths and lonely places with their lamentation. Called from this petty, forgetful life, quickened by the unanswerable question, to face the palpable body of death, very hand of God on his servant, recalling. But yes quickened, borne up, great ocean of our life together, in facing, acknowledging, this call from God, toll of death.

Each morning Nicholas with the family, the women veiled, descended the Cathedral steps after their service. He saw the silent thousands, four and five abreast behind the barriers, waiting in their endless queue, watching him, bowing and crossing themselves as he passed. A tension began to resolve itself through the warm acceptance that Papa's body, Papa, belonged to everyone – to these, these Russian people, each single living one of them. They too had lost their saintly father, just as he! Recalled – father whom God had recalled. Papa indeed belonged to them too and he could accept it wholeheartedly as a living truth. With gratitude he could greet them, strengthened, uplifted by their presence. Daring, already daring to think them his people too.

Each came close to that open coffin in their own way, breathing in the growing stink of death's raw presence, that he, the Tsar, was a mortal man, like oneself, but raised, raised by God's own hand, destined to rule over us. To watch and care for us. Close binding this mortality, sharp the stink. But mysterious, so mysterious this raising up by God.

The royal family, including those from all Europe, had to acknowledge their special closeness through that ritual kiss. Kiss that tasted this mortality, a giving and receiving which acknowledged one stream, one source sustaining their earthly being. That they too were subject to death and raised up by God. That they had not simply to watch but to commune as flesh to flesh in the passing. Bitter, pallid the taste of those lips. Musty, putrid that stink. But embrace confirming above all, and with courage, the strength of their bond, and their love for him, for their own. The features no longer his but peacefully changing into some other wholeness.

Provincial governors and high officials came from all over the empire to pay homage to the passing of a blessed man and to ensure anew that unity which had centred on him. Seeing one another and being with one another helped towards restoring some confidence. Eagerly, anxiously, they saw, watched for the first time, the one in whom their future hopes, their trust, their very life would lie. They noted this slight, all too modest, pale, drawn young man. Wan sapling. No mighty branching strength here. That the Grand Dukes had to bend down low – bend right down! – to speak with him.

Why has the strong lord been taken from us like this? Why has the one who kept the nation so firmly on its course been plucked from us like this in the prime of his life?

Not terrorists this time!

And to leave in his place?

Where are we going from here?

From the first day of the lying in state Grand Duke Sergei was surprised and impressed by the size of the crowds. He felt uneasy about their silence and would have preferred a little noise, even some untoward behaviour. He conferred with von Plehve to ensure that security arrangements were adequate. He was emphatic with Metropolitan Nikolsky that the coffin should be kept open for as long as possible so that as many as possible could pay their homage.

On the fifteenth morning of the lying-in-state, Prince Michael of Serbia was overcome by the stink as he leaned over to kiss. He grabbed at the coffin for support. Colonel Gurkov was quickly at his side with an arm round his waist to lead him away, trembling. On the sixteenth morning it happened again to Crown Prince Henry of Prussia. Metropolitan Nikolsky decided that the coffin should be closed and lowered into the family vault of the Romanovs the following day, even though the crowds were as great as ever.

"Weaklings! our womenfolk are stronger," declared Grand Duke Sergei, loud enough to be heard by many.

Up till these final moments Nicholas, at times on the verge of total exhaustion and tears, at times carried forward by a power beyond himself, struggled to hold firm in utmost dedication to the seriousness of it all. Grimly he was determined to do his duty for all here, for Russia. He felt their vast presence sustaining him. He knew that he simply had to do what was right. He knew that all, high and low, rich and poor were watching him, more – were already beginning on that transformation, recentering of their hopes, expectations, lives – on him.

As he watched the coffin being lowered into that deep shadowy darkness a fierce loneliness singled him out, cutting him off from all around in an icy silence.

Appear Papa! End this nightmare!

Such dizziness threatening!

A hand clasped his in the press of the tearful family. The stone flags were replaced and the gaping hole blotted out. Her hand, her life with his as he yielded. They had endured it, through to the end. It was over and they already daring to turn to this new life, light of that future now pouring in on them so swift as they led out of the chapel with Mama leading. Mama, so erect, courageous before the watching, waiting thousands. But all eyes were now turning on him and her, as they descended the Cathedral steps and slowly, so slowly drove away on that final leavetaking, yet already entering into their heritage. Delicately entering yet confidently, strengthened by this presence of the people in their thousands, strengthened by having seen it through to the ultimately earthly end.

It was over!

It was over and they knew that at last they were free to turn to one another in the fullness, richness of that long-gathering bliss. Dare to celebrate each other. The shadow of Papa's death persisted, bitter, painful still for those around them, but this gathering bliss would not be thwarted.

Regardless of all they had one another.

Golden ark which would keep them safe.

A week later they stood before Metropolitan Nikolsky in the Winter Palace to be made, become, man and wife in the sight of God.

Large crowds cheered their carriage on its way to the Anitchkov Palace where the newlyweds were taking up residence. The mourning period for Alexander forbid a honeymoon or even a reception. But that night their love was sealed in blissful consummation, their life for one another.

Bliss in the touch of living lips, the gentle flames of living desire rejoicing, expanding, fusing. To their bliss they yielded, fulfilled and blessed. For they had one another, found, given. Each through the other claimed, made of worth.

Radiant this ark of their shelter and warmth. Breasting the ocean of life it rode resplendent. Ark invulnerable on this ocean's ecstatic surge. Ark made holy through the sacrament, blessed in the name of our Lord and Papa too. For Papa had truly blessed them, she knew it now, and this bliss was that blessing fulfilled.

All will be well!

And if for them – for Russia too.

Tenderly, shyly, so long awaited his hand reached out to trace, create, discover herself-for-him. Gentlest flow of his touch refining, her and him, this now, eternal. Touch melting re-sculpting with ardour, sweetly pulsing current which was them both. This speech more delicate, intimate, deep than anything uttered yet.

Seeking, exploring, all secrecy to be revealed in the light of this fire. To be known like this, freed he and I to be revealed at last so joyously, to him, through him, mysterious one yet so well known. You through whom I have touched that quick of my being, hope and promise of which was awaited so long. Enter, enter my dearest all for you alone. Taste, grip, fill, do more, for you alone have made me. Through you alone reborn. What I am becoming.

Lip to living lip, thigh to thigh, she opening to his fierceness, that nothing any longer be held back, hidden. Yielding with pain blood touched bathed in the assuaging warmth.

Fearful the urgency of his demand. Stern, cruel this grip to utterly blot out. But she surrendered, surrendered into the wildly threshing waves, trusting, carried trusting through this wildness and into these sweet waters floating. On his arm her resting head, a gentle, sure foundation, peaceful, poised, in the balance of the love he was creating.

He had revealed himself, tender hidden self which was for her alone. Now was a steady flame enkindled of entrustment which nothing could ever quench.

This, Papa's doing - through him these fervent waters freed, made pure, blessed.

Through him this celebration.

Papa taken - Alix given - only God.

God's will ruling.

He knew in this glowing fullness that what had passed between them this night in its purity and strength could only be for the good of Russia too.

He glimpsed a confidence, absolute, source to draw from and make decisions as mediator for the Russian people, alone in his conscience before God Who had willed this destiny.

Alix felt compelled to mark it down on this earth as sign and seal of this miracle. She took his diary and entered it. *"I love you! These three words have my life in them."*

Thus declaring it thus marking it was all in all. Her life now sealed with a joy inviolate. True love the gift which God has given, daily, stronger, purer, fuller.

At last united, bound for life and when this life is ended we meet again in the other world and remain together for eternity. Yours, yours.

X

Khodynka

For the newly married couple, Dowager Empress Marie Fedorovna had six rooms hastily prepared in the Anitchkov Palace on the Nevsky Prospekt. Nicholas' refusal to have the wedding postponed meant that nothing had yet been adequately planned for their needs. As Tsar he began to work on official business from a small sitting room whilst Alix began to study Russian in an adjacent bedroom. Another room nearby was set aside for petitions and audiences.

During these first weeks they were deeply grateful to Marie Fedorovna for her arrangements, advice and welcoming attitude. Nicholas especially needed her invaluable hints, suggestions, comments and directives on matters of protocol. Alix's apprehension gave way to a feeling of being accepted as one of the family.

Nicholas' workload was far heavier than either of them had ever suspected and the long hours of separation were broken only by meals. Alix grew bewildered. That the work had to be done, she could begin to accept. But beyond the demands of the work, she felt him, increasingly during the day, out of reach. Only at night did they truly meet. Most painfully it dawned on her especially at mealtimes that it was not acceptance but indifference. She waited nervously, tactfully for a word, a sign, but they went on conversing so busily together this older woman and young man. Two strangers. Not her Nikki.

Her throat tightened, her seeing wandered uneasily but she fought to keep it hidden. Those modes of address had fooled but now enhanced the annulment. Obscurely she knew what was happening and that the night brought victory with it. Day-life was become bitter, dry, to be endured. Night was return to that freshness.

When soon after Alexander's consent to the marriage, Nikki told her that Marie Fedorovna wished Alix to address her as 'Mother dear' and no longer as 'Auntie-Mama', Alix nodded tearfully, not daring for some time to utter that sacred name.

Bitter-sweet was that name. Long had she yearned to sound it again. Openly, simply now to be allowed to call someone by it, was balm, surrender. Name of that radiance, smile of loving care. Born again as daughter through such yearning to dear dear Mother dear. Sounding that name was a sharing with his love for Mother dear, a strengthening of their love for one another.

But now each mealtime when she mouthed the words 'Mother dear', bitterness was their taste. Brittle these once sacred words, tainted, her betrayal so guiltily felt. That name should never have been given to another. How had she let herself be fooled to say that name so glibly, so lovingly, so utterly forgetting that Mother dear from the start had been firmly against the marriage. Fool! To have imagined that she was willingly accepted! She never had or would be.

Day highwalled yielding no handhold.

But she'd fight back against it – this making of her an intruder – outsider – a nothing. Nikki was blind to it, nor dare she trouble him. Her struggle was with Mother dear alone. And she would win.

That ark of night would carry them to victory when he came to her, tired, resigned, needing what she alone could give. In a darkness ever radiant with that bliss which broke on the shores of her being, through that touch, his touch, weaving the inmost texture of their ark. There, was the reality in which she would and must believe. There, could she find him once more. From there came forth a Nikki Mother dear knew not of.

To return was his hidden longing through the drear stretches of day. The magic of that nightworld, deepest yearning, ever finer drawn.

From that nightplace of peace and secrecy, Alix looked down serenely on poor Mother dear – so pale, wan. Mother dear's day was passing.

Fierce this struggle to defend her own, to be acknowledged. But from her womb Russia's future. She alone would be crowned Empress.

Marie Fedorovna found it extremely difficult to accept the new situation. The protocol which gave her as Dowager Empress, precedence over Alix, made it doubly difficult. Everything had happened too quickly, too suddenly, beginning with her beloved's death. That this girl whom she had never really liked was now not only married to her son but soon to be the new Empress, was beyond her. A stranger still, in the house

– at table – in that bedroom and at night. Her poor weak boy had been beguiled. He was so vulnerable. The Kishinskaya affair had shown that. But at least the ballet dancer was a real beauty – not this awful stiffness – arrogance. Well she'd protect her boy even now.

But it couldn't continue like this.

*

When the official twelve month period of mourning ended, planning for the coronation went forward with much zest. Traditionally the Minister of Court, elderly Count Vorontsov - Dashkov was responsible overall. Grand Duke Sergei as Governor-General of Moscow where the coronation had taken place for centuries, took effective charge from the start. His imagination and drive left no aspect and no department unaffected.

His strong impressions from those thousands patiently waiting to pay homage at the funeral, had inspired the feeling that the occasion must be used to express something special, beyond the traditional ritual. A great opportunity was approaching, missing it criminal! To display the power, the glory of the dynasty in a dazzling, breathtaking way. He would create a spectacle of sheer magic with this new wonder, electricity. Starlight on earth to excite and amaze the people. And not only the people in their tens and hundreds of thousands who would be encouraged to come, but all the foreign visitors too! Russia would be seen as a great power in this modern world. Here in Moscow our ancient holy heart, Russia would be seen and felt, glowing glittering in blue red green yellow, strong, fierce against the night sky. And God help Zlotnikov if his promise of coloured bulbs didn't work out!

How amazed all would be when the lights went on and struck out with Russia's strong future blazing into the darkness. Throughout the long coronation night this second crowning, of the city itself. Moscow's grandeur! Russia's brilliant light – from of old! Moscow's modernity! Moscow's place among the nations, seen and never forgotten. That we here in Moscow do indeed recognise your progress and your science though you sneer at our ways. But we don't make an idol of them. We have our priorities. Just so, this new magic serves the old, sure truths.

The entire city sparkling forth throughout the night! That was the vision which the people and the Europeans must take away. Moscow light prevailing against the darkness. Beacon of strength, of faith in the dynasty's future.

By order of the Grand Duke no expense was to be spared. Every public building to be freshly painted, scaffolds erected for smaller illuminations in gas and kerosene, and platforms for spectators.

The letters N and A were appearing everywhere, on restaurant table cards, on windows, on walls. That these two become part of our seeing, knowing, life. These two. Names which we must complete. N - standing for Nicholas, which we have to make stand, and her too - that A - lix - the one who will reign over us, which we read properly.

"God save the Tsar
Glory Glory Glory
To our Russian Tsar"
Give yourself to it - sound it out!
Let it sound forth!
What else?
Rare - a rejoicing.

Hundreds of churches and public buildings were surveyed and orders sent in to the Zlotnikov factory for tens of thousands of bulbs. They were wired to light up at the touch of a button which would be pressed by Alix herself on the coronation night.

Food and drink for the people must utterly surpass the traditional coronation fêtes. The best of course, would have been for every single Russian to have come, eaten, and drunk their fill, learning directly of their Tsar's concern for their welfare.

The plan for second best involved a huge open air feast on Khodynka Meadow, a military training ground on the outskirts of Moscow, near the Petrovsky Palace, where Nicholas and Alix would be in retreat, fasting and praying before entering the city itself on the coronation day. It was intended that hundreds of thousands should make their way there from Moscow itself and the rest of Russia.

"Hundreds of thousands of loyal devoted Russians. That's what we must welcome, encourage. That's what's needed," enthused the Grand Duke.

Tons of food and thousands of gallons of beer and vodka would be freely available. Tens of thousands of red and blue enamelled mugs, initialled, 'NII' and 'A', in gold, below a double-headed eagle and the year '1896', were to be given away as souvenirs.

The Grand Duke ordered strict security. Every building along the ceremonial route from the Petrovsky Palace to the Kremlin, must be thoroughly checked. Attics in particular must be searched carefully, and an identity check made on all porters, janitors, and any painters still working on the decorations.

In late April at a final meeting, departmental heads reported to Grand Duke Sergei on the state of preparations. Everything was coming on well. The Grand Duke was particularly pleased to hear that all the electric light bulbs were in place and that thousands of spares were available too. He was also well satisfied with a report from the Supplies Department that 286,272 mugs had been completed as from April 16th. He stood up, looked round the table and in a rare, fulsome mood, hinted strongly that he would mention their achievements to the new Tsar and commend certain of them for specific recognition. But one face irritated him.

"Pavel Ditiatin you look unwell," he said accusingly.

Ditiatin, responsible for the Royal Pavilion, was alarmed and smiled back effusively.

"Not at all Excellency. Not at all. No more than a little tired," he anxiously managed to counter with enforced cheerfulness.

Everyone else was alerted and smiled too.

"Tired? Good! That's the price of hard and honest work. Russia could do with more such tired men."

Back in his office Ditiatin was appalled at the madness that had nearly possessed him during the meeting. That he had actually considered speaking out to the Grand Duke about his anxiety! But it would not leave him. Was he the only one? Or were there others too?

Hundreds of thousands! Surely something had been forgotten? But nothing else was mentioned. Only those hundreds – and hundreds of thousands. Surely something was missing? But nobody else had said anything let alone ask anything. Perhaps he simply hadn't heard. Perhaps he'd missed something, dozed off. It must have been mentioned – and settled. He certainly wasn't going to make a fool of himself now. Or even so much as question anybody after the meeting. After all it wasn't exactly his business. His business was the Royal Pavilion and everything there would run like clockwork. It might be taken for a criticism! It might even, for there were people, get back to the Grand Duke and that would be finis to any promising future - special recognition eh? Nor did he intend to be sent to the provinces one fine morning and spend the rest of his life rotting away thank you!

But it wouldn't leave him.

Then try again, harder, much harder, to recall any mention whatsoever of the question of how these hundreds of thousands were going to be controlled, organised, looked after.

Not at any meeting he'd ever attended.

Presumptuous fool!

That matter of crowd control, organisation, is so obviously taken for granted as first priority by everyone, as well as you! that it must have been dealt with automatically, without it even having been considered necessary to mention.

Councillor Buryshkin wanted to remind the Grand Duke that Khodynka Meadow was scarred quite deeply and deceptively in places with old crumbling trenches from decades of military exercises. But what of it? Why bring that up? Everyone knew what Khodynka Meadow was. Some others were aware of the point but not at all inclined to mention anything that might cast even the faintest shadow on the Grand Duke's so rare and fulsome mood.

Very disturbing for Grand Duke Sergei was Nikki's reluctance - anxiety? - about being crowned with Catherine's great crown. That he preferred - preferred? - the Monomakh crown of Vladimir I.

He must explain in simple language what was at stake.

The boy was choosing the easy way out. Lack of trust!

Lightweight Monomakh cap for a lightweight ruler - lightweight Russia - primitive beginnings - that would be the message to the world.

Never!

The people would be shocked!

Monomakh was for Russian beginnings.

This was no beginning - but a great continuity - of expansion - Power - Russian glory - which only Catherine's great crown could crown.

Nicholas and Alix spent April 24th at the Petrovsky Palace in solemn preparation and purification through fasting and prayer. A cleansing and a lightening that the consummation which they were approaching and soon to enter, be achieved with utmost intensity and commitment. Prayer and supplication, for only with strength from above could they see it through and carry this mighty burden of what lay ahead. Through the fasting, the bodily lightness, the distancing from the busyness around them, they knew in painful purity – themselves alone, weak, and the Power above. Through the praying was wrought humility before this destiny, that all be in His hands and His alone.

On the following afternoon in accordance with the sacred tradition they entered the city. Beneath the cloudless, radiant blue, Nicholas, in a plain army tunic, rode on a white horse into the city that was becoming his city, past the waiting thousands who were becoming his people. Leading ahead of him along the four mile route to the Nikolsky Gate and into the Kremlin, were the Imperial Guard, the Cossacks of the Guard, the Moscow nobility, the Imperial Orchestra and the Imperial Hunt. Behind him, the Grand Dukes, the foreign princes and the carriages carrying Marie Fedorovna and Alix.

All of them with their glittering orders and medals seeming mere appearances, ephemeral brilliance, lent, only lent reality by that presence, simple, luminous source in their midst.

Reining with his left hand, saluting with his right, Nicholas was given over to something greater out there. Slowly he progressed through the brilliant sunlight for the cheering thousands who had lined the route for hours. From Poland in the West to the regions beyond the Urals in the East. From Archangel in the North to Tiflis and Baku in the South they had come and now saw him, golden, revealed by the Lord of Light above. Their seeing a needy hunger, this sustenance appeasing. Such confirmation, proclaimed by the cloudless blue above, all the powers of heaven and light and life.

Our jewel, our crown on this day of days, never nearer in us. Our king, emblazoned, between heaven and earth. See how the Lord of Light creates him, reveals him, illumines him for us!

See how this pale youth rides!

Nicholas, drawn away from himself, lost in this dream of their wanting was yet held to his course. Pure symbol, golden symbol of their hopes, needs, expectations. Symbol lit to such brilliance with Alix, following in her golden carriage drawn by eight white horses, white gown strewn with jewels, diamond necklace ablaze with the sun.

The following morning, blue above still cloudless, they rose at dawn, nearing the very threshold, prayerful, resolved, a strength for each other.

In due course, Nicholas in the blue and green uniform of the Preobrazhensky Guards, and Alix in a silver-white court dress, followed by trainbearing attendants, descended the crimson velvetted Red Staircase leading to the Ouspensky Cathedral, watched by hundreds of high dignitaries crowding the wooden grandstand and the unseen thousands beyond, sustaining him and he them, but such sustenance from her! what goodness Papa had done - he knew it even now through this radiance all around, her closeness, enabling him to bear this dreadful burden.

They entered the Cathedral, glorification of the Light, so built that men see, know, praise the Light in all the richness, fullness of its eternal being. In the gentle flowing and shimmering of myriad candlelight. In the golden blaze of the iconostasis. In the serene luminosity of the frescoes. In the jewelled mitres of the clergy, gleaming, sparkling with iridescent hues. Light flowing, Light's bounding sea in the fullness of its life. Light speaking to all of its all pervading radiance and its Source.

After the Mass, the robing, Nicholas' prayer for Russia and his anointment with Holy Oil, he swore his oath to preserve autocracy as Emperor and Autocrat. The Metropolitan intoned the ancient formula affirming the God-given nature of autocratic power and confirming once again the God-given right of the Romanovs to the throne of Russia. Nicholas, in his oath, through the very utterance, bound himself to the Higher, before and with them all those present, and the devotion of those unseen thousands.

Those present, in his utterance, heard their unity resounding, re-established, transported in spite of doubts. Those millions, presences, unseen, in their fullness abounding this most spacious moment. Nicholas gave of himself to the utmost, into the ancient words, that the higher power which of old spoke through them could accept - make of him - a true servant. Binding moment of this utterance, that, with his very life, he bind himself to the Highest, the people to himself, all in a golden unity.

After the receiving of the sacrament, he took the huge Imperial Crown of Catherine the Great, thickly encrusted with diamonds and pearls, from the Metropolitan and set it on his head. Its iron heaviness bearing down, no longer feared but accepted with an upsurge of strength – that, was his burden! his pain – pain – with relish! – under the weight of this hardness, bearing it firm. And this awful throbbing begun again, as it pressed down on the assassin's scar – mark of saving grace for all this! – so with resolve borne too – all – heavy touch of destiny – acceptance!

It rested, glittering focus in the tense silence. Balancing up to it squarely, gaining the feel of its implacable weight, he raised it up with both hands and placed it on Alix's head. Willingly head firm and erect, she felt that weight thrusting down to crush, momentarily unforgettably sharing, till he replaced it back and a smaller crown was set upon her head.

At last to be seen as theirs and to see them as his. He, sung now as Our own dear Father, Father in the flesh. Alix borne on this shimmering radiance knew them as her people, her children, her own. Raised up through the unanimity, massiveness of the gestures, laden, age-old, flowing around over in the shimmering golden lights, of jewels, golden surfaces, floating lightly above them all, these people seen and unseen, with her hers, hers, in this place of meeting penetration consummation.

Near midnight after the long banquet attended by several thousand guests, they stood on the balcony of their bedroom in the Kremlin, looking out over the illuminated city whose life and light flooded its way into their room. A brilliant shadowplay of the city permeating, flickering on the walls as the bells ceaselessly rang out. Throughout the night they felt bathed in the radiant warmth of that loyalty, trust and praise, beyond flesh, beyond passion, Moscow's Russia's. So much greater than they.

Empowered, changed, carried up to a new strange place, ancient, great, enduring. Place of service in dedication to His Will, for the people. Those distant yet so close ones. Unknown yet deeply known – the mystery of it all. A night of sanctity that they live steadfast servants of His Will.

Pain, where the great crown had borne down on the would-be assassin's scar. Mingled pain of scar and crown. Destiny's weight, soothed by her fingers through the night, the sweetness to bear it all.

Painful this memory of the heavy St Andrew's chain silently slipping and slithering away from him, leaving him lighter but disturbed with that lightness.

Onto Khodynka Meadow tens of thousands were streaming.

Around the blazing bonfires they danced and sang to balalaika and guitar. Through the night they gathered and waited expectantly for the feast which the Tsar and Tsarina would attend.

Right across the Meadow, halfway, stretched wooden railings. At the northern end several wooden pavilions had been erected and decorated with gaily coloured bunting and flowers. They included the Royal Pavilion for which Ditiatin was responsible and from which many of the day's festivities would be conducted. Scores of tables and food stands had been set out ready for the feast.

South of the railings where the thousands were assembling, Captain Lukomsky, in his late thirties, with a patrol of sixty police had been assigned to keep an eye on the crowd. He'd been told that the carts would be arriving with the souvenirs, mugs and free beer at nine in the morning. This to be followed later by the festive meal.

Even after midnight the friendly star brilliance of the warm summer sky held the darkness at bay. Captain Lukomsky noted the singing, dancing, everywhere excitement and good humour. But from time to time as he crossed the Meadow alongside the railings and looked around and across he sensed an entity, a vastness, no more than that.

His hand rested on the wooden railing which wobbled. He felt attuned to their mood of excitement, expectancy in the dawn light but questioningly. As the light increased he watched warily. All was orderly.

A cheery voice called out from near the railings now taking pale yet frail form.

"When's the beer coming?"

"And the grub, eh?"

Questions – that surely querulous eh? – which so swiftly transformed that vastness, that entity beyond the railings into a warning – threatening – ominous life. Such grim possibilities – overwhelming!

All was orderly still.

Staring hard across the greyness from left to right into the creeping stirring chaos of vague forms he realised with a profound shock that he was facing thousands upon thousands of people. Major Rudnev had never indicated such a possibility. Only a crowd had been mentioned. So what? What was the matter with him?

What was he worrying about?

All was orderly.

He made a sudden decision and sent Pypin to police H.Q., as quickly as possible, for urgent reinforcements. An hour passed but no reinforcements appeared. Lukomsky veered from increasing anxiety to fear that he was making a complete fool of himself and consequent relief, that the reinforcements had not arrived.

But now in this clear morning light something definitely was happening. Each time he looked across the railings, those in the very front of the crowd, good humouredly chatting and singing were definitely coming closer to it. A movement was taking place, perceptible, intangible. What harm in that?

He told his men to order back those nearest the railings.

"Back! Keep back there! Back I say!"

They appeared to be retreating. Lukomsky realised that it was not really so. The forward movement was still continuing. The order was given again, louder, more threateningly but taken with much good humour by the crowd. Lukomsky realised with a shock that he had no control over them. His men reported that more and more of them were asking when the beer and mugs and food would be given out. He told them to explain to those in front who were again inexorably creeping forward, that in due course, not long now, the mugs and beer would be given out in orderly fashion. No one would go without. But why hadn't the reinforcements arrived? Lukomsky and his men looked across the Meadow in growing anxiety seeing, as for the first time, the entire vista in every direction alive with people, thousands upon thousands, a vast overwhelming something and their own presence, each man to himself now in the face of this vastness, increasingly questionable.

Those in the front nearest the railings were finding themselves caught up in this slight, obscure but definite movement forward. They were finding the space between themselves and the railings decreasing. Ever nearer the tables beyond the railings, laid out, inviting, as they heard and repeated to one another that talk of mugs and beer and food.

They were coming closer not quite by themselves but already borne forward, slowly, yet knowing uneasily that this movement forward was not to be stopped. Those behind them were pressing so closely! This forward movement of those in front was imperceptibly taken up and become an advance, wavefront of the whole, advancing to that out there beyond them, the waiting tables, the mugs and beer – beyond that too – to something more. O wonderful magical more – awaiting, charging this pressing and pulling with such excitement – an infinite expectation! Everyone now caught up, pressing forward, forced to press forward only forward, great wave surging onwards over the railings collapsed, splintered underfoot. Everyone pushing and thrusting, ruthless, relentless, cursing, screaming in terrified flight from the wave behind, engulfing.

Where are we moving to?

Where are we running to?

Where are we going? – going – dark wild ocean this we?

Simply now to survive, to keep moving, free, alone, ahead in some space. Somehow blindly to thrust ahead over falling, fallen bodies, kicking, trampling, sidestepping the gaping jaws of those trenches below. To keep surging ahead and survive for how much longer, clambering over the smashed overturned tables and benches. Out at last, clear of earth's deathchoked jaws, the front wave, its desperate fragments, within reach of the Pavilion, tinted with pinks and glowing reds by the rising sun.

The rearmost, first to waver were forced to take note of the dead, the dying, the injured – that something terrible had happened! The wavering spread till the foremost were halted in their mad flight, to find themselves in a desolate space echoing with screams and cries. Forced to awaken out of this nightmare, as the momentum drained away and people stood staring, unbelieving at each other and the torment around them.

Just before the railings had started to give way, Captain Lukomsky ordered that it was every man for himself. Apart from two who were badly bruised, all the patrol managed to reach the edge of the Meadow unharmed. Captain Lukomsky left Sergeant Strakov in charge and hurried back to H.Q. Something dreadful had happened. He stopped momentarily at the Pavilion end to look back across the Meadow. All strangely still, sculpted, as in slow motion. Clouds of dust were rising slowly all over and through them he could make out people standing in small groups, crying, calling, searching but all so very still. Just people now.

Captain Lukomsky was grateful that old Strakov was in

charge. He felt so overcome, so failed. He knew only that he must rush back and tell them all immediately. Everyone must know and come and help.

Distraught he ran and walked along the highway which led back to the city outskirts. Pounding wave of death relentless eddying terror, Moscow's festive decorations were gleaming and glinting in the early morning sunlight as crowds of excited people, chatting volubly, passed him on their way to Khodynka Meadow. Panting and sweating he pressed on to H.Q. in Tverskaya Street, up the wide stone steps and straight into Major Rudnev's office. There to his surprise also sat Police Chief, Colonel Semevsky. Like many a senior official during these hectic days the Colonel decided to be up and about, to leave nothing to chance and to descend on his subordinates without a word of warning. Commendations were after all in the offing and might not be again for many a long year. Captain Lukomsky's surprise changed to reverent gratitude.

"Colonel! – generals! – Majesty! – let them please all be here. It's Khodynka! Khodynka!" he pleaded tearfully to his two astonished superiors.

"What the devil's the matter with you man?" demanded Major Rudnev sternly, "Pull yourself together! This is Colonel Semevsky here! Have you been drinking?"

"My reinforcements – where are they?" shouted Lukomsky desperate to communicate, explain.

Aware that his superior was watching the whole business very carefully and that his words were having no effect on this wretched officer, Major Rudnev grew furious.

"Reinforcements Lukomsky? You've sixty men. Sixty! And all you have to do is look after a picnic party! A jolly picnic!"

Lukomsky gripped Major Rudnev's wrist fiercely and stared desperately into his face, "It's a graveyard – can't you understand? A graveyard!"

Major Rudnev, trembling with rage, wrenched Lukomsky's grip away.

"How dare you! You're mad Lukomsky!"

"His Majesty will see a graveyard – a graveyard," repeated Lukomsky in a low, weary voice.

"Lukomsky! You'll pull yourself together and go straight to your quarters. And stay there till further orders," ordered Major Rudnev finding a voice of some authority. He was considerably flustered but at least Colonel Semevsky could see that he was dealing with a madman.

"We'll go," said the Colonel curtly as Lukomsky left the room, relieved yet still distraught.

"Go? Go where Colonel?"

"Khodynka of course!"

Colonel Semevesky did not like that word 'graveyard' and on this particular day he was taking no chances whatsoever. Horses were quickly saddled and when they arrived at the Royal Pavilion, Sergeant Strakov and the rest of Lukomsky's patrol were waiting around anxiously. Within some three hundred yards, where the old army trenches had finally ceased and the first wavefront had died away, survivors were struggling to disentangle the bodies jammed into the trenches and ravines, and to tend the wounded. Colonel Semevsky looked right across the Meadow thick with thousands woefully searching and wailing. He turned violently on the bewildered Rudnev.

"You bloody fool! what's going on here?" he snarled, "What's behind it all eh? Why didn't you send him his reinforcements?"

He quickly checked his fury. Within a few hours the Emperor would be here. As far as possible downfield, the place must be cleared up immediately. The bodies must vanish. Vanish! Those damn corpses must be out of the way well before the first delegations arrived. He bit his lip hard. Come on Semevsky!

How? How?

Major Rudnev and the patrol watched him intently as he walked right round the Royal Pavilion then through the garlanded entrance. Just inside he stopped, looking, to the large wooden dais at the far end, standing well off the ground and almost the width of the Pavilion itself, on which the Emperor and his party would be sitting. He strode quickly to it. The front was boarded down to the ground but the sides were merely curtained with heavy material. He pulled up one edge of the curtain and peered through the slender uprights supporting the platform. Space! Yards of it! For dozens!

"Rudnev!" he roared.

The major came running in and saluted.

"There – down there!" he pulled back the curtain, "Pack 'em in Rudnev – and God help you if you mess that up," he warned. "When his Majesty arrives – that whole area," he indicated out through the Pavilion, "must be cleared of all bodies from as far downfield as possible."

Major Rudnev, utterly shaken, was filled with admiration and relief at the rapid, masterly way in which the Colonel had dealt with this catastrophic situation.

The idea of the Emperor and those on high actually seeing the corpses was too appalling to contemplate. Thank God that the Colonel had been with him, for such would never happen.

Pavel Ditiatin had risen early for the great day, anxiously going over the timetable of events – the various delegations, the bands, the choirs, the royal arrivals – whilst on his way to Khodynka. He had surely covered everything to the very last detail. There could be no possible hitch. He rode proudly along in his carriage beneath the cloudless blue, satisfied but not too satisfied, at having carried through this weighty responsibility with utmost dedication, not sparing himself in any way. He nodded in amiable salutation to the hundreds hurrying along the streets in the same direction. Sometimes he noticed wagons piled with large wooden crates occasionally passing from the opposite direction.

As the Pavilion came into view, he saw numbers of gendarmes and Cossacks, more and more of them, all over the place, around the Pavilion and to its rear, all in some purposeful way. Strange this! What the devil was going on? A squadron of Cossacks galloped past him. He could see figures in twos and threes carrying what? between them and laying them awkwardly down. Tables and benches were strewn about – on their sides – broken. Another cart came towards him laden with wooden crates.

At the Royal Pavilion entrance he stepped down hastily and went straight inside, where several gendarmes had been ordered to methodically search the whole building. The true nature and cause of the catastrophe, though not yet understood, had quickly resulted in the intensification of security. Ditiatin was distressed to see them in the building at all, let alone the way they were poking about, pulling at curtains, shoving chairs around, thrusting sticks into the huge ornamental flower bowls holding thousands of blooms, disturbing their meticulous arrangement and scattering earth all over the brightly polished floor.

"Leave it alone! Leave it alone! Don't you know the Emperor's coming?"

But in spite of his red sash none of them took any notice. He hurried outside in confusion. Colonel Semevsky spotted him immediately.

"All the dirty work's been done. It can all go straight ahead as planned," he advised.

Ditiatin was perplexed and alarmed.

"What's happened – tell me please! What's happened Colonel Semevsky?" he pleaded amidst the noisy bustle of gendarmes and soldiers.

"Happened? A brawl of some sort. What else? Free beer and their grub. It was the same last time."

A brawl? But the beer and food weren't to be distributed till ten o'clock. A brawl? What? All these people being carried about and laid down, lying so quietly, so many of them! all over the place – had been hurt in a brawl? Nearer still, running, he approached a dreadful tangle of arms heads legs, spilling out of a trench. Around it stood distraught ones, watching soldiers pulling at the bodies, black with dirt, terribly bruised, to somehow sort them out. Earthdeath, mouths noses stuffed choked with earth grit dust.

In desperation he swung around and rushed back. Soon enough now the Emperor would be here. The Colonel was right! There was no need at all to spoil the Emperor's day. No need at all. Smile now! – greeting smile for H.M. – come on! – it still works!

He gave orders to his subordinates for the place to be put in good order in readiness for the first delegations, making sure that they were absolutely clear about the seating arrangements. He looked at his watch. By God it was a near thing! The Colonel had done a wonderful job. But just in case questions were asked – a brawl then! Of course – the Colonel was right. It was the same last time at Tsar Alexander's coronation fête – what was it? about thirty was said. A good natured brawl. To be expected. But why should any questions be asked – at least at this particular moment. And this particular moment was the only one that concerned him. Let each worry for himself. All was well here.

The first delegation arrived, artistes from the Moscow Imperial Theatre, and Ditiatin, calmer, himself showed them to their places. Whilst other delegations appeared, representatives of the Moscow Old Believers, the Moscow German Colony, the Georgevsky cavalry regiment, he glanced cautiously across the Meadow. Nothing really special to be seen from this distance now except for some carrying, and then only if one looked hard. Anyway by the time this whole ceremony was over even the carrying would have finished. But there was an awful lot of carrying. In fact wherever he looked there seemed to be nothing but carrying.

Colonel Semevsky ordered a thorough reconnaissance of the whole Khodynka area. He was very clear that this was no ordinary brawl. The reports coming in had already put the count of dead bodies in the hundreds and the injured at far more. Dozens of carts would have to be commandeered to carry away the corpses. But at least some semblance of order should be restored in time around the Pavilion. With that underway he must immediately inform Grand Duke Sergei.

He trotted his horse away to a quiet spot and walked him up and down for several minutes. A great deal was at stake. He'd have to think this through, carefully and smartly. He himself would have to confront the Grand Duke. No question of anyone taking a message, especially that idiot of a major. The Grand Duke would demand facts. He must tell him all the facts as now known. For if the news reached the Emperor first there would be hell to pay. If the Grand Duke asked what had happened? He didn't know - nor did anyone else. So far no one could give any coherent explanation. One thing of course was absolutely clear. Sixty men on duty! Any fool could see now that it hadn't been enough. Even without anything special happening. What had they been thinking about?

They?

He - Colonel Semevsky was responsible! Directly!

How proudly he'd declared during that final planning session that sixty of his men could easily do the job at Khodynka!

But no one had indicated that the whole of Russia was going to be there! Only by chance he'd heard the figure of four hundred thousand mugs being distributed. And even then no one was clear about whom, for what, when, where? He certainly wasn't going to cross swords with the Grand Duke over that - or anything else.

And imagine! it was always the Grand Duke who so prided himself and beat into everyone else his concern for the details always the bloody details. Well he'd got the details wrong this time - somewhere along the line there'd be a price to pay for this little lot!

At Ostankino Palace, while a groom led his horse away, he was shown into the spacious lounge whose parquet floor and furniture had been made by the serf craftsmen of Count Sheremetyev in the eighteenth century, and from whose painted ceiling hung ornate chandeliers. Uncertainty had prevented him from using the word 'urgent' in his request for a meeting at this early hour. The Grand Duke was in the very best of spirits after the previous evening's innumerable congratulations on his magnificent spectacle. Those from the foreign ambassadors had particularly pleased him. Though surprised at Colonel Semevsky's request he kept well disposed, merely expecting a report that all was well in preparation for the day's festivities. He came in briskly and the Colonel saluted.

"Well! What did you think of it eh? The Europeans were dumbfounded. That's how it should be. They've seen the wonders of Yid-free Moscow. They've seen loyal Russians in their thousands paying homage. That's good! Your men are doing a good job Semevsky. No trouble eh? No hooligans about? It won't be forgotten either."

It wasn't going to be easy but time was short.

"Another magnificent affair this morning," enthused the Grand Duke, "just look at that sky again. Blue – such clear blue – day after day. The whole of Nature's happy. What else can it mean? Our new Tsar's making a tremendous impression. Better than expected – I dare to say. Our late Emperor would be proud of his son, very proud."

"Indeed Your Excellency!"

"Well, on your way Semevsky! Your place is at Khodynka now. His Majesty is particularly looking forward to receiving the delegations – to meeting his people."

"Your Excellency," began Colonel Semevsky.

"Yes?" answered the Grand Duke impatiently on his way out of the lounge.

"There's been some trouble at Khodynka," continued the Colonel, determined only to get the message across immediately.

"Trouble?" questioned the Grand Duke turning back to face him. The Colonel was unsure how to proceed and the Grand Duke raised his voice sternly, unpleasantly.

"What trouble?"

"Well – it's a – it looks like a –"

"Looks like a what?" shouted the Grand Duke.

"Your Excellency – I don't know what's happened. But the facts – the facts are several hundred dead – and far more seriously injured."

"What the devil are you talking about?"

"With my own eyes - I've seen them. But I simply don't know how it happened."

"Several hundred dead? On a day like this? You damn fool! What are you and your bloody men for? Several hundred dead - on his coronation! What wreckers are about? You bloody fool letting a thing like this happen. Can't you even look after those damn peasants for a few hours? Let me tell you one thing Semevsky. One thing only. Nothing - absolutely nothing of this must reach His Majesty. I shall be responsible for that. I shall be at his side. You fool - get the place cleaned up! Out - out man! Get on with it! And keep me fully informed."

For several minutes after Colonel Semevsky had left, the Grand Duke, enraged, stamped about from one end of the lounge to the other cursing from time to time, "Fool! Damned bloody fool! - Fool! Damned bloody fool!"

He went to the staircase and in some panic shouted,

"Ella! - Ella!"

She came hurrying down the stairs from her dressing for Khodynka. That dreadful shout and the fixed stare and the clenching of his fists made her tremble.

"Stick to Alix's side - every second - don't leave her! - and don't let any news reach her," he ordered.

"News?" she dared question, prepared for a storm because just at moments like this he never explained himself.

"News woman! News! Khodynka's covered with corpses according to that idiot. The man must be mad? Don't worry - we'll soon find out. Then there'll be a reckoning."

Ella hurried back to finish dressing and prayed for the strength to face whatever lay ahead. The Grand Duke ordered his coachman to drive like the wind and throughout the journey he kept muttering, "Several hundred dead? Several hundred. The man must be mad!"

Colonel Semevsky had left the Grand Duke, relieved at last to realise that he had in fact given the right order - rapid disposal of the bodies. On his return to Khodynka, he drove the gendarmes and soldiers into an increasing frenzy of activity. Corpses already at collecting points were carried away at a fair trot by men in twos and threes, straight through into the Pavilion where others were waiting by the platform whose curtained sides had been drawn right back. Collars were undone, tunics stripped off, as the packers, panting and sweating, hauled, pushed and thrust the bodies back as tightly as possible.

By the time the Grand Duke stepped out of his carriage the job was finished. The men were dressing properly, joking and downing some beer. Everything appeared to be reasonably shipshape. The wooden floor was being swept clean, and on the Colonel's orders the curtained sides tacked firmly into place.

Grand Duke Sergei walked quickly around the Pavilion keenly aware of the considerable numbers of troops and police. He scanned Khodynka Meadow downfield. The weather was changing. A lively wind was blowing dust clouds right across the field. Through them in the far distance, momentarily, small groups of figures were revealed, but indistinctly, something unreal. Otherwise no obvious signs of disturbance.

He strode back, angry and puzzled, to confront the Colonel. At the Pavilion entrance he was met by Ditiatin, distraught, wringing his hands.

"Don't you start! Enough with one madman!" bellowed the Grand Duke thrusting him aside.

Ditiatin had been watching horrified as the men had pounded to and fro across his floor, shaking the place to pieces, covering it with dirt and shoving corpse after corpse underneath the royal platform without so much as a word to him. Almost in tears, he would not be rebuffed.

"Excellency! Excellency!" he shouted hysterically, pulling frantically at the Grand Duke's arm and managing somehow to drag the bemused man to the platform at the far end. He drew back one of the side curtains.

"Look, look Excellency! It's packed – packed with them. A graveyard! They've turned my Pavilion into a graveyard."

The Grand Duke didn't believe what he saw and immediately took up the challenge.

"Pull yourself together Ditiatin. Put your Emperor first. Stop your whining! Damn your snivelling little self. Don't dare to mention anything," he ordered.

With survivors hurrying back into the city and meeting the crowds on their way to Khodynka, news of a dreadful disaster spread quickly through the city. It soon reached the royal couple's entourage. Immediate, unspoken was the decision of everyone around them to conceal the matter at any cost. Sooner or later they would have to be told. But when and by whom was beyond thinking. Still vibrant with the coronation deed, a fervent desire prevailed to protect the royal couple from being disturbed, sullied in any way by such all too wretched earthly events. They should be allowed to remain inviolate. This above all, beyond the natural reluctance to disturb the young couple's obvious happiness.

Somehow the news seemed so utterly incongruous as not to belong to the same order of things as the coronation celebrations. So much so that it needn't, shouldn't, couldn't be mentioned. Where had it come from? From what other world? What had it to do with the Tsar? With any of them? But amidst the rapidly spreading rumours of dreadful catastrophe, fear grew that soon it would be impossible to prevent anyone from knowing including His Majesty. Within hours the banquet and ball at the French Embassy was due to begin and it was unthinkable that His Majesty should first hear the news from the French.

Anyway, one or two I could mention now lording it - certainly be taken down a peg. No bad thing either. Getting away with it far too long.

But goodness - and God help us - but God gave us eyes too - and what did we see - didn't we? - the St Andrews' chain - holy holy - slither away off his shoulders like a snake - onto the floor - by itself!

and - and -

how dare you!

and - and -

then does not all depend on you too - traitor!

The festivities at the Royal Pavilion were a great success. Only a few of those attending had heard of some trouble at the far end of the field. After the last of the delegations were presented Nicholas addressed them warmly.

"The Empress and I heartily thank you for your expression of love and devotion. We do not doubt that these feelings are shared by all Russians. Care for your welfare is as close to my heart as it is to that of our Father and Beloved Saviour."

Tumultuous cheering rang out led by Prince Trubetskoy, and the massed choirs sang, "God save the Tsar!"

On their return to the Kremlin apartment Alix felt something in the air. Two ladies-in-waiting and the hairdresser were helping to change her dress and touch up her coiffure for the evening ahead. Princess Zinaida and Princess Irina who had been recommended to her by Ella, were very subdued. She felt it keenly, this absence of their familiar, friendly courteousness, so puzzling at such a time. In the awkward silence the hairdresser nervously scraped the jewelled hairclip across the nape of her neck. Alix flung her hand to the back of her head as the clip fell to the floor and the hairdresser jumped back, alarmed.

By mid-afternoon all the city's hospitals were crowded out with the wounded. Incredible figures were circulating. Most reluctantly Grand Duke Sergei admitted to himself that something big had happened but was determined to keep a grip on things. He ordered an exact count to be taken throughout the afternoon from all available sources, including hospital and mortuaries. Then at least he would know. Nor was there any reason why anyone else should know. One or two were growing nervous. Of course this would show up the weaklings pretty quickly. And not just pathetic creatures like Ditiatin. Not at all. Witte – the great Witte! had had the effrontery to declare that the French Ambassador's ball should be cancelled. Witte! The strong man! And Nikki himself? They'd see soon enough whether he was a real Romanov. An excellent start really to test a man. But if Witte was already gabbling along these lines he must busy himself.

Messengers were sent urgently to his brothers, Grand Dukes Vladimir, Paul and Alexis. Their grateful acceptance of his offer to break the news crossed with a message requesting him and Ella to join the royal couple.

The latest figures to reach him were unacceptable, around twelve hundred dead, over a thousand badly injured. Utterly absurd! typical – sensational rumour-mongering – the enemy already at work – at *you* fool! at you! Strike a figure now and make it official! – and for seeing Nikki – around around six seven – seven hundred will do. A lot! – but not too many.

Ready, he set off immediately with Ella to the Anitchkov Palace.

Nicholas wanted right now to thank and congratulate him for the way everything had gone so well.

"You were right Uncle Sergei. I'm indeed a fortunate man – above all to have you with me."

Grand Duke Sergei tried to nod with modesty.

"Your Majesty," title still against the grain! "there's something that needs to be mentioned before the ball tonight – just in case the subject comes up," he began, as casually as possible.

"There's been a mishap – an unfortunate mishap at Khodynka this morning – but it's all been sorted out. Well really these things are to be expected. It happened on your father's coronation too."

Nicholas was puzzled.

"Khodynka? A mishap? What exactly Uncle Sergei?"

Grand Duke Sergei kept up his light tone.

"You know what it is with the people. Plenty of free beer. High spirits all round – high spirits all round," he made a smile, "That's what it always is – a brawl broke out. There were some casualties."

Nicholas remained puzzled. It all seemed ordinary enough.

"Uncle Sergei – are you trying to tell us something?" Alix interrupted.

Grand Duke Sergei, still determined to play it down, was grateful for the opening.

"Yes! There are rumours about. Fantastic rumours. Malicious rumours. It's important that you know the truth. You mustn't be embarrassed or compromised at the ball tonight."

"Of course – I appreciate that. But – what is the truth then?" Nicholas asked, still puzzled.

"It seems – my dear Nikki – there are about (eight) seven hundred dead," said Grand Duke Sergei as evenly as possible. "Of course those responsible will be dealt with!"

"Seven hundred dead?" whispered Nicholas looking straight into Grand Duke Sergei's eyes.

He stood up, looked above and to Alix, reaching out for her hand, standing in a far realler world, revealed so suddenly by that truth. World of God's very nearness where he must bear himself in dread and humility. Prayer, ceaseless prayer to the All Highest in supplication for His mercy. That must be his life. No shows. No grandeur. On his knees in supplication. For now as never before was God giving him the opportunity to strengthen immeasurably the bond with his people. To pray for them. To drink to the depths the cup of their suffering. What greater sign of God's nearness than that God let him come forward and do this thing. To know his people in this very different way, their wounds and their pain. He must go to them now. Join with them in this new, harsh reality, to be lived, accepted from the All Giver. Not to question His will but to know how comprehensive, All searching, His will was. Know – know – know. That his power was in God's hands from this very first moment of his reign.

"Alix," he whispered, still holding her hand, "this is God's doing. We must be grateful for this proof of His nearness – this chance He's given us of showing our love for Him. We must go to Optino monastery immediately and seek His mercy. We must pray for our people and ourselves – that He make us worthy and give us guidance."

Alix nodded tearfully, for both, the world become mere appearance, this pain within, reality.

"Uncle Sergei thank God it was you who brought us the news. Make it known straight away that all festivities are over. We shall go to the Optino monastery. Make that known too. Let services begin everywhere – forgiveness – repentance – purification – for all of us."

"My dear Nikki that's quite impossible!" Grand Duke Sergei countered emphatically, appalled by Nicholas' weakness, ignorance, dangerous flight of fantasy. Back to reality immediately!

"You're the Emperor of all Russia. Not just a few hundred peasants who went wild with drink. The Russia which the whole world has come to see and celebrate. If the celebrations are stopped at this moment, the very next day after your coronation just like that – the whole world will feel that some dreadful visitation, some awful evil has been afflicted on us. It'll cause confusion and apprehension everywhere. Especially the French! There can be no question of you not attending the ball tonight. France! Our great and only European ally. It'll be taken as a dreadful affront. An outrage. They're crucial in our undertakings. And all of it begun by your dear father. Just remember Nikki! The French fleet visited Kronstadt and your dear Papa stood bareheaded as they played the Marseillaise – all for Russia's absolute need."

He simply had to spell it out word by word at this vital moment, to this naive boy, take nothing for granted.

"No Nikki! We must show them that we take such things in our stride. Out of strength! Of course we won't pretend it's a particularly happy affair. But we mustn't go to pieces in front of their eyes. It simply isn't for you to run off to a monastery – to escape. Necessity demands a harder way."

No! Uncle Sergei not escape but given over totally - to God there.

"Of course I respect your Christian feelings," he continued in a milder tone to the shocked, desperately confused Nicholas still holding Alix's hand, "but it'll be seen as softness. They're a private matter. Much more difficult than running away to any monastery is to keep them private - in the greater interests of Russia. There are plenty of other ways to show your feelings which the world will respect and understand. The families perhaps can be compensated. Instead of a mass grave individual coffins could be provided and so on," he advised sympathetically from one of his ready inspirations.

Overwhelmed Nicholas could do no other than follow Uncle Sergei's certainty and make the appropriate gestures. But what had France and the French Ambassador's ball to do with this pain, sadness, dread which made his very breathing difficult. Right here - tender pain - trapped.

Right here - secret place - only - to remain so - shared with her.

So unreal Uncle Sergei's words about the world and the French Ambassador. But he knew too that Uncle Sergei was saying something very important, very serious and that somehow - yes, he knew it already in his anguish, indecision - he would follow, must trust and follow Uncle Sergei in spite of the burning pain, the need for salvation. Would follow with the acceptable gesture of state! - diplomacy - dynasty -but not of himself.

Caught up so obscurely - yet caught up in this great unease.

Impossible to carry through - inescapable!

If only Papa was here now!

He must put on a brave face and hide this burning heart. Both of them. What strength, hardness would be needed! Hide it! Follow numbly.

"Alix - what? - what shall we do?" he kept asking.

"We must trust Uncle Sergei and do as he says," she answered in a tearful, desperate way. A dreadful loneliness from which to draw away into that only certainty of their love for each other.

For the ball, priceless tapestries and silver plate had been sent by the French government from Paris and Versailles. Tens of thousands of roses from the south of France were set out in the ballroom steeping it with red and pink. No expense had been spared. Much was at stake. Ambassador Count Montebello's brother-in-law, a brigadier on the French Headquarter's Staff had recently explained to him in some detail that the huge low interest loans floated on the Bourse for Russian railway development were not going to benefit the Jewish financiers alone. The French government had stipulated that any railways built with their money must run right up to the German frontier. General Staff were thinking in terms of a Russian mobilisation that could be at the German frontier within fourteen days, if and when the next confrontation took place. Alsace would be revenged!

The embassy had their own sources of information and knew by late afternoon that the death toll at Khodynka was well over a thousand. By the minute they anxiously awaited news of cancellation. But with less than an hour to go it was clear, to their surprise, that the Tsar was coming. Montebello was deeply moved to realise just how highly the alliance was regarded. Of course it was a painful business but time was a great healer.

Nicholas was to open the dancing with Countess Montebello, watched intently by the hushed, glittering gathering who packed the four sides of the vast ballroom. Stiff and pale he began, merest shell of himself making the correct gestures, display, the raw pain burning, blasphemous the music's very sound. If this ghastly display was his duty towards Russia - Uncle Sergei - then he would carry it through whatever the cost. And he knew as he glanced at Alix following onto the floor with the Count that somehow his darling would carry it through too.

Alix felt her limbs as lead, quicksand around her. At each desperately willed moment, movement a voice cried out to stop. To simply leave this glitter, shameful frivolity. Quicksand lapped by that chaste joy of the roses so wanting to bathe her - them all! in its warmth wave on wave of it - gentle rapture very sweetness purity drawing her pain more fiercely still.

Only to keep going for Nikki's sake. For him alone she must suffer this dreadful pain. Him she would never desert, never scandalise by flight. But she so wanted it.

As a puppet whose master has much to learn she moved round the ballroom floor, on the verge of stagger here and a blind lurch there, hardly caring.

Others stepped onto the floor in spite of their embarrassment and soon it was crowded with dancing. Alix and Nicholas knew they'd seen it through.

Grand Duke Sergei was greatly relieved. Informed that Grand Duke Mikhailovich had just walked out noisily with some friends, he declared loudly, with disgust, "What else d'you expect from a follower of Robespierre?"

For many during the evening, Nicholas's pale, drawn features indicated a creditable stoicism. But Alix's red-rimmed eyes, blotchy cheeks, stiff posture, were felt as tainting the evening's enjoyment, tapestries, roses, exquisite plate and superb food. They were there to see and be seen, curious to discover just how Nicholas and Alix would behave – in yes of course a touchy situation. But she'd spoilt it all.

Montebello knew it as an historic occasion. No matter what his sadness, the Tsar's presence in the embassy was what counted. That presence alone confirmed and sealed the alliance. That presence strengthened hopes and plans for revenge. And it had all taken place while he was Ambassador.

Nicholas and Alix spent much of the following day visiting the hospitals crammed with injured, he so wanting to see and be with them in their suffering. With them in their suffering all were as one – bond of bonds. Had Uncle Sergei's advice prevented them from making this explicit? From his private purse, he ordered that every family involved receive one thousand roubles. He took the Grand Duke's advice and at his own expense ordered separate coffins for the dead. But the significance of the disaster could in no way be alleviated or diminished. Its ultimate inexplicability – the scale of it! – cast an ominous shadow far beyond the more immediate issues of responsibility and blame. That such a happening had occurred, of such proportions, on such a day, was the all-embracing reality. It was no one's actual doing. But nor was it a natural disaster. There was something uncanny about it.

The anguished gesture that evening which Nicholas had made, out of such uncertainty, against his inmost feelings, letting himself be led into a painfully false situation, was seized on by many. It could only mean that the lives of the common people were of little account to him – the hospital visits – the coffin business – all sickening hypocrisy. That gesture had for his enemies and critics, stamped his image with utmost heartlessness.

For a few it was a heroic gesture. For others, spelling doom. A pamphlet appeared depicting him dancing with the French over high piled mounds of corpses.

And how could it be? Months spent by high officials on the minutiae of coronation protocol, but no planning at all on the tens of thousands to be given free food and drink!

How?

Because the people were of no account in official minds – utter indifference.

And that he danced on with her?

Only an inescapable catastrophe would answer that! For these others, everything he did would be scrutinised intently, interpreted to that end.

Nicholas had known the shock of dread, the overpowering need to humble himself, yield in compassion, identification, yes identification with them before Him. But if at this moment, of all moments, the trained response was required, not the heart of compassion, then once and for all that heart, that self, would be hidden. To be revealed before one, and one only, in its joys, its deepest pains before her, who had cried and cried. From now on no man would know that hidden heart of his. But they were his people and his father's people. The same who had thronged the wayside as the cortège passed.

The question of responsibility and blame would not go away. A human cause had to be established. In the last resort there were only two men ultimately concerned. Grand Duke Sergei and Vorontzov-Dashkov. It was argued that as Minister of Court, Vorontzov-Dashkov was traditionally responsible overall for the occasion. But everyone knew that he would have had no chance of overriding the Grand Duke even had he been dissatisfied with the latter's arrangements. In the actual context his function was purely formal.

Grand Duke Sergei had never for one moment thought of himself in terms of blame. From the beginning he had never changed his opinion that Colonel Semevsky wasn't fit for his post. He'd decided to have the idiot packed off to the provinces or given the chance to retire. But the question persisted in court and government. The magnitude of the disaster was far too great to load onto a police chief's shoulders. The subject was strictly taboo in the royal couple's presence. Nicholas was extremely sensitive about any reference to it. Ella, through her ladies-in-waiting, knew all too well what was being said about her husband. She had no hesitation in telling Alix pointedly, how in the very highest places, the Grand Duke was being openly attacked and denigrated for his main part in the affair. He who had made it possible for the greatest show of popular acclaim ever known for any Tsar. But, explained Ella, Sergei would not even think of defending himself in public, it was out of the question. Only a word from Alix, said at the right time, in the right place, was needed, dear sister. Alix, only now began to realise from this how she now stood, crowned, with many simply waiting on her words, and she gave just that word. And in the giving she felt a newly emerging independence, a sharpness. She made it known clearly, that she regarded any talk of Sergei's responsibility as absolutely reprehensible. That what he had achieved for their coronation and for Moscow was beyond all praise. She spoke out of a new independence, wrought, claiming her own. Which could only mean that Vorontzov-Dashkov was to blame. Vorontzov-Dashkov had already decided to offer his resignation as the best resolution, out of loyalty to the dynasty. A decision which would gain him much esteem. Alix's outspoken intervention drastically altered the situation. Ominous implications were drawn as to the unbelievable arrogance on the part of this foreigner, barely crowned, for daring to interfere in such a matter. Marie Fedorovna's antipathy towards Alix came into the open. Vorontzov-Dashkov had served her husband and herself for years most conscientiously, and she let it be clearly known where her support lay.

Nicholas would not commit himself but his unease persisted over Uncle Sergei's advice that dreadful evening – and his response. The feeling would not leave him that a wrong decision had been made. Alix concluded from the gossip reaching her that Mama dear was drawing up her battle line and that the fight was to continue. Those first impressions at Livadia had been true. What naiveté! That she had wanted to excuse the family attitude because the Tsar was dying and all were in shock.

They did not accept her, then or now. Nor did any of these creatures around her! Nothing but lying and flattery.

The lifelong wariness came once more into its own, sharpened, needfully sharpened, become suspicion, ever-present suspicion. A hardening, a wall once more, to protect this sacred place of him and her – and Ella – and Sergei. All and enough. If it had to be – so be it.

To whom? with whom? had she been borne that day, that hour, that moment in the Ostrovsky Cathedral. Was it for these creatures? Were these court creatures the Russian people whom she had known in that radiant moment, which lived so strong in her? How ready she'd been, happy, opened, awoken by her prince.

But it was not to be. Her prince had released her for himself alone.

Towards against all others from now, only protection and concealment.

Protecting, concealing but sadness in knowing an ultimate loss.

XI

The Ulyanovs

Pobedonostsev was not alone in his unease when reading and rereading Alexander Ulyanov's courtroom speech. For those who could hear, for those who dared secretly to acknowledge, for those taken unaware and unable to prevent recognition, Ulyanov's words in the courtroom and now set down on paper, resounded with the force of a wholly committed life. Words charged with a calm, a certainty, whose existence none in the courtroom had even suspected till then. Intimate, potent words of true being, even in print, presence resounding, through the magic of sacrifice living, enduring. Deedwords of purity consummated, through fine wrought decision, from the silence wrested. That place of truth to which Alexander Ulyanov ever turned, knowing it as the source, his life itself. Having heard, ensured, decided, he would not shift for to shift was betrayal of life itself. All this, dimly, was heard in the courtroom as very tone, essential meaning beyond the obvious content. All this pure, total commitment of a young, ardent life was the real challenge.

They heard the self-assurance of one who has overcome this world. Even one who has already quit this world. Even as though such quitting were a normal enough affair, deepening further their consternation.

Court president Deyer insisted several times that the accused should not speak in theoretical terms.

This impersonality was infuriating, spectral, as though he wasn't talking about himself at all. Much cunning here! To what end? To unnerve him, disorientate him?

Where was the confession, plea, recognition of wrong doing?

"I do not deny the facts. Therefore the right of defence consists exclusively in the right to present the processes of thought which led me of necessity to commit the crime.

"Only the terrorist is in a position to defend the right to think freely and the right to participate intellectually in the life of society. Terror as a form of warfare, originated in the nineteenth century: it is the sole defensive weapon which a minority can resort to when it is only strong spiritually and when it is conscious of fighting for justice against the majority's knowledge of its own physical strength. Russian society is so constituted that we can defend our rights only in these duels with the State power.

"Among the Russian people you will always find ten persons so loyal to their ideas and so filled with the misery of their country that it is no sacrifice for them to die for a cause. Nothing can frighten such people."

On and on his wretched excuses - our so-called educated youth - ah! sounds as if he's coming to an end.

"That's all I wanted to say."

Uttered merely as one more statement of fact. Simply as it was from the place where he spoke.

As simply, he took all the blame. Blame borne lightly by the power he had become. A power embarrassing the prosecutor who chided him for taking so much on himself.

In these last months of his life Alexander Ulyanov was convinced beyond all doubt that only in working towards that goal of the good through scientific socialism did earthly life have any real meaning. And to know the truth was to do the truth. Out of this truth he acted and spoke in such calm assurance, witnessing to it as that by which he lived. If it was truth, the knowing was itself an enlightenment of the will, very birth of a doing. One must had to do it to preserve one's life - that earthly life now raised, enriched by the light of this very truth.

Alexander Ulyanov's purity of soul and firmness of will had long been felt by his family as a blessing and a sustenance. Yet dimly sensed, especially by his mother Maria Alexandrovna, was a strangeness, some distant goal, as though in judgement. Gentle judgement, but judgement. And for Maria Alexandrovna the possibility of something unexpected.

Alexander's inwardness, remote yet friendly, and his gentle acceptance, were an ever-present source of warmth to all around, calling forth respect, in acknowledgement of standing before something special. Out of this respect, this needful halt before their Sasha, each found new sources of love. Over the years each had been enriched by that concern, tolerance, letting-be which was Sasha's special gift.

Within the family and to close friends he openly expressed

as an obvious matter his gratitude for the treasure and preciousness of life. Self-giving alone could acknowledge, justify, be this gift's very fulfilment.

Self-discipline and sacrifice is our Sasha's life – making space for us – encouraging –helping us to grow – ripen. It was good to be near him with him the best in us brought forth. His ways so thoughtful, his words so caring. Thus the treasure of life.

Yet for his mother, Maria Alexandrovna, despite his gentle intimacy – the strangeness, a stranger. The strangeness, shock, of his decision two years ago to cease attending church. Utterly unexpected but told them both in such calm assuredness. Told in that special way of his, not the slightest hint of criticism towards their faith. On the contrary – yes it was so – affirming it, but with an affirmation enfolding both his beliefs and their faith, a harmoniousness to which he attuned them, beyond them, yes with a wisdom seeming beyond their years.

But this time, Ilya Nikolayevich Ulyanov could not hold off a sense of shock and increasing dismay over his son's decision. It was not at all good that the eldest son of the Educational Director of Simbirsk Province suddenly stopped attending church. Something ugly had appeared. Was it a judgement on himself? Would important others so see it? Of course it was true as she pointed out that one of Councillor Berkhov's sons had done the same. But this was Alexander. Never had he considered the possibility of Alexander doing such a thing. Something essential in the family life had been weakened, gravely, in-comprehensibly weakened.

Alexander respected and admired his father's uprightness, dedication to work, pursuit of knowledge and high sense of social responsibility. He had to choose between the inevitability of upsetting his parents and the failure to live transparently that truth of himself.

The decision was made during his last summer vacation before going up to St Petersburg University. Every summer the family stayed on the Blank estate at Kokushkino near Kazan. Maria Alexandrovna's father, Grandfather Alexander Dimitrievich Blank, had been a doctor who gave up practising in his forties and bought the estate of some thousand acres with its manor house, stables, and peasant village of estate workers, in order to live the life of a country gentleman.

Alexander, Anna, Vladimir, Olga, Dimitry and Maria loved

these summer weeks at Grandfather Blank's large house with its white-columned portico and veranda overlooking the rush-lined river Ushna, the woods and the wheatfields. Everyday some new adventure, bears and elk so suddenly encountered with startled delight. From early morning, fragrantly scented, the urgent call to be out in it all and doing, testing their strength and skill, boating, swimming, climbing, exploring ever fresh world of Kokushkino, expansive, free.

When twelve, Alexander had decided to study zoology and over the years in their Simbirsk house on Moskovskaya Street, his room had been transformed into a laboratory, museum and library. One holiday, during his seventeenth year, whilst wandering through Kokushkino's woods, sparkling, lush with dew, he glimpsed in the clear early morning light, portals, radiant portals of that temple which he was approaching, and at long last, as though carried forward - no longer by his own effort advancing - in humblest gratitude, to enter, there, in that same place, where these had dwelt and worked - Darwin - Spencer - Mendeleyev - Botkin. To enter and take his place, humbly yet surely, dedicated, a servant to science, gaining for mankind truth, certainty, clarity.

In this cool morning light so expectantly awaiting in its infinitude, service, servant, and this he would willingly be. Knowledge, clarity, certainty alone that could help, could save mankind. Its foundation right here around him in every detail of what is actually seen and rationally thought about. Haeckel, Darwin, Spencer - great edifice arising. Exaltation as he trod the sparkling grass, to think that he too would be such a servant, no matter how lowly, would win such a knowledge no matter how small. Exaltation enduring, sweetness sounding, in this outermost court, feeling, judging himself as worthy of entry.

Each morning at dawn he left the house, swept by that cool breeze freshly into the his future. Raw, chastening, a needfully felt vigour. One, one with it all this Nature with him. A harmony, invisible harmony. Music, sweet foundation, sustainer of his life in its becoming. This harmony the pledge, surety of his decision. His path of knowledge. Light. Freshness. Freshness beyond all. In that other building Mama and Papa's solace - good people! - was no freshness for him - nothing that carried him forward, breeze-swept. It smelt of decay.

When he returned from these walks before breakfast the

question was simply, when to tell? These walks took him over the threshold and there could be no other way.

News of unpleasant disturbances on the Viazemsky estate to the north awoke some obscure dissatisfaction in him. Apparently buildings had been burned down and people threatened. Those vague dreams, yet insistent in this fleeting way, to do with all that other outside, haunting, outside family, home, room, intimate life.

As he concentrated behind his microscope lens, observing, comparing, sketching, noting with scrupulous care till his eyes watered with the strain, and he drew back with aching neck for relaxation, so that enigmatic other pressed in on him. As he brought into focus the sharply outlined from the mist of obscurity, uncertainty, form, fact, data, joy of birth, he knew he would have to come to terms with it, but as yet – its vagueness. There must be a key, a way of focusing on that too, a way of beginning somewhere.

Before going up to the University, accepted in the Department of Natural Science, he spent each day studying in his room. The duty each day to thrust back the darkness, and to know. Maria Alexandrovna regularly sent Anna up at midday to call him down for lunch. Over the meal he heard mention that vespers this evening would include special prayers for St Tychon, a saint particularly dear to Papa. He returned to his studies but the light had dimmed and this pain, this heavy pain of a knowing must be borne. Birthpain familiar of decisive deed. At last to know that vespers – church – were no longer for him. All that shimmering candlelight a void. Those fumes of incense become an unwanted past, a casting off leaving him vulnerable but newly present to himself. Some ill lit cavern, a shrinking back, a trap. Only what man was achieving in that dawn clarity could be truth for him. Out of this certainty, given him, which he could not, must not betray, because given him, he would utter his No to Papa, that it be heard and known by others. But always the pain in giving up, that had to be, and always the pain of those he loved to be suffered as his own. But carefully – think carefully! Not 'I shan't be going to church again!'

Ilya Nikolayevich Ulyanov sat at his desk preparing a carefully documented report for his superiors in St Petersburg. It concerned the disturbing lack of zealousness on the part of the village priests in the teaching of the catechism. Though well aware that strictly speaking it was a synodal matter he felt he had no alternative. Through the catechism the spiritual roots of education were established and the firmest foundation for life was assured. What could be more comprehensive for a truly Russian life than:-

Question :   What does religion teach us as to our duties to the Tsar?

Answer   :   Worship, fidelity, the payment of taxes, service, love and prayer – the whole being comprised in the words, love and fidelity.

Though beginning to strain his eyes in the deepening shadows he put off lighting his lamp. He liked to savour this gentle dissolution of forms, of separation, as the bells of St John the Divine began calling through the gathering darkness, gently drawing towards that very light, very height from whence man came.

Alexander tapped lightly on the study door, entered and waited respectfully. Ilya Nikolayevich put down his pen. Being thus disturbed meant the matter was serious.

"Papa, I shan't be coming to vespers tonight."

Ilya Nikolayevich, on the verge of asking 'Why not tonight? Aren't you well?' heard the note of finality, the note of Alexander. Self-discipline enabled him to receive the announcement with outer calm. But it was a shock. It showed as such to Alexander for Papa settled quickly back to his writing as though nothing had been said.

Before leaving for vespers the family as always gathered waiting in the hallway. Olga asked where Sasha was and should she remind him because he was studying so hard. Ilya Nikolayevich would not reply. Nor did Maria Alexandrovna, wanting somehow to support him in his mood.

"It's time to go children," she said as they went off in customary order, she and Ilya Nikolayevich leading, greeting friends on the way to the Church of St John the Divine.

"But what can it mean? What can it mean?"

She heard an unprecedented note of uncertainty, anxiety in her husband's voice. They both knew that nothing they said would make him change his mind. That the decision had come out of that communing with himself which they were learning to recognise. But in this instance Ilya Nikolayevich anxiously needed to know why Alexander had made just this decision within three months of his twenty fifth anniversary year celebration with the Ministry. Maria Alexandrovna could only, for help, remind him that Alexander had been awarded the Gold Medal at the Gymnasium, and that for years his reports, for academic achievement and character did honour to the family. She believed in, trusted in Alexander, in that truth of his, which she dared know lay beyond any conventional immediacy. But to none was this utterable. She must abide with it all, hope and pray.

But Ilya Nikolayevich felt somewhere threatened and at odds with his son. When asked by Father Gregory why he hadn't seen Alexander at church for some time, Ilya Nikolayevich found himself vaguely referring to some nervous indisposition as the result of too much studying.

Maria Alexandrovna struggled to attain some more certain knowledge about Alexander.

So self-contained.

Too self-contained?

Yet such a serene giving. Such a modesty in spite of his gifts and achievements.

A warm, a gentle depth. Which somehow all could share.

And the smile that he smiled from his sadness – yes sadness – what did he know? – was so forbearing.

What depth had he touched in that inwardness? What gentle wisdom known?

And how Sasha calmed his quick tempered – awkward – growing very awkward! brother merely through his presence!

Ilya Nikolayevich's churchgoing, large comfortable house, esteem in which he was held, and his title of nobility, were the substance of a life lived from the sense of a deep gratitude. An all pervading gratitude expressed through loyalty and dedication to Tsar and Autocracy. Expressed through the commitment to help those below him, that Russian life progress, all in good, steady time as those above, in their wisdom, judged right. His own life, ever present touchstone of the autocracy's beneficence which made it possible for a humble orphan to be raised to Actual State Councillor holding the Order of St Vladimir.

Pledged, sacredly pledged, he would likewise never cease in his efforts to help those below him through the spread of literacy and education, nor in his efforts to defend against all subversion, this autocracy to which he owed everything. For loyal, earnest subjects there were just rewards. Whenever he looked back and saw from whence he had come, he was amazed – from humble teacher to Inspector to Provincial Director of Education. Yet – simply – what else than but simply – by giving of his very best he had reached such heights, helped, encouraged at every turn by goodness, recognised for his loyalty and integrity by discerning superiors. 'Would there only be more Ulyanovs and the schools would soon enough be cleansed of all subversive elements'. That was his good fortune – their recognition. Not at all immodest. Their recognition of what he had to give to Russia – that was his good fortune.

Near the end of Alexander's first term at the University, a celebration evening was planned in the Simbirsk Gymnasium Assembly hall to honour Ilya Nikolayevich Ulyanov's twenty-fifth anniversary year. From St Petersburg an important official was coming. His presence acknowledged at the highest level, esteem for the man who had been responsible for the opening of nearly five hundred new schools in the province.

The hall was crowded with teachers, old colleagues and local dignitaries. Director Ulyanov's praises were sung by many including the president of Simbirsk Council whose long rambling speech was especially fulsome. Golden references were made to Director Ulyanov's exemplary family life and to the Ulyanov children, especially Alexander, who were clearly following in their illustrious father's footsteps.

Generally Directors of Education were retired after twenty five years service but in certain cases men with outstanding records had been employed for a further five years and even longer on full pay. Ilya Nikolayevich, like everyone else, took it for granted that it would be so in his case. With Alexander at University, Anna soon to follow and young Vladimir almost certainly in due course, his salary would be essential.

After the celebration, reported in detail on the front page of the Simbirsk Messenger, he waited day by day and week by week for the official letter granting the extension of his tenure. His working routine continued unchanged, including the inspection of distant schools in the province, which kept him away from home for several days at a time. On returning, first thing, he would anxiously look through his mail.

It came one afternoon in late September when he was relaxing on the black leather sofa in his ground floor study, which was papered in pastel yellow and looked out onto the garden. Relaxing but never far these days from an unease. Even the pastel yellow which he had chosen years ago had begun to irritate him.

Maria Alexandrovna brought it to him as soon as it arrived. She had given up trying to reassure him, with reminders of that high official's presence, and of several instances when St Petersburg had delayed over important matters.

When he saw the letter in her hand he sat up sharply and reached out for it, unable to check the surge of anxiety, unable to open it in her presence. She quickly left. He carefully slit through the envelope with his paper knife and opened out the stiff sheet of official notepaper. Four brief lines announced that his services would no longer be required and that he had been placed on the retired list.

Signed by – whom?

Impossible to decipher this elegant flourish.

And – whatever did it matter?

It was so!

It was so! – relief! – in this knowing it was so.

Now at least he could do something. For clearly there was a misunderstanding.

He went to his desk and began to draft a letter. But even as he wrote, humbly requesting an interview, for surely there had been some misunderstanding, he knew, feeling the very emptiness, feebleness of his hand's movement. He knew well enough and from the beginning that the decision had been taken and was irrevocable. An instinctive knowing, as with surprise he was reminded of just such irrevocable decisions about the lives of subordinates that he had made over the years.

He stared again at the announcement.

No explanation. No warning.

Simply that fact in front of him.

For he knew it was a fact, a deed accomplished!

But it couldn't be!

The celebrations! His services!

What was happening? What did it mean? This surely was a judgement being passed. Everyone would take it so.

Can it be? Can it be that same power – same power that had raised him up now so dealt with him?

But what? in heaven's name. He had no enemies. His record was untainted in any way – absurd – impossible even to begin thinking like this – about himself!

Everything was against such a decision.

Then – it could only mean – he was not – not – for them – what he thought he was.

Hold to this – point by painful point – courage! – its logic, stern truth.

Then what had he thought he was for them?

And what was he for them?

There – just there – the humiliation – that he had taken the result for granted – beyond all possible doubt

because

he had taken it for granted that he was thinking – as one of them – very source of his fullness.

And it was not so!

That – had been his security.

It was no longer so!

But – possible – possible even? – that Alexander's abandonment of church and this rejection – surely no less? – were connected? He must find the connections. He must know. This not knowing would destroy him.

No formal finishing date was mentioned in the letter and he continued to work. But Semion Ustrialov, an old trusted colleague who sometimes accompanied him on his tours of inspection, realised the change in him. Ilya Nikolayevich's moroseness and distractedness were unprecedented. Ustrialov learned the reason from Maria Alexandrovna and though surprised at the decision from above, considered his old friend's reaction as most disturbingly out of proportion.

St Petersburg was St Petersburg!

He dared to remind his senior colleague whose strange mood was so upsetting, of some old advice. Why? – Who? If you want to know the reason, see who the new man is in the Department. Ilya Nikolayevich heard out the words with bare politeness. Reason? What did Ustrialov know of reason?

Pure coincidence? that it had happened at the same time as Alexander's apostasy, Alexander's betrayal. His son's staining of his own unblemished record. That could not be chance! His superiors simply hadn't wanted to mention the matter. Too embarrassed. Very understandable. God's punishment for his sins. Well and good. Fool! Ilya Nikolayevich. Had you imagined yourself sinless? Woe! Be thankful that God in his Mercy has woken you up to your sinful condition.

Twisting, turning, he could only shrink back from that power which till now he had served, given himself over to, believed in. Power which had now rejected him into this darkening nullity, shrinking back on himself in despair. Shrinking back to the black leather sofa, recalling his proud, warm days. Back, away from garden and street, to his study, to this last place of refuge, the black leather sofa. Raft on the threatening seas. This alone left of himself on the wild ocean of life. Forced back to this fearsome blackness beneath whose enshrouding he cowered. Where at last he felt safe. From where alone he dared venture forth to see his very own, dear ones.

Driven back, driven inward as one marked, abhorred amongst men. Had not his own son rejected him too? What then could be trusted? One thing alone. This blackness, bleakness, this darkness of welcome.

Back, back, at last to his very own. Where alone he felt safe, untouchable. Tiny raft - tiny - point - but untouchable - where alone he felt free from it all.

Sweetly to yield to the sofa, to dream of the children. Here was his own. This and they were his to muse over, old files, friendly smell of the leather.

Terrible silence of that impassive power which he had served so well.

Merciless injustice, burning, through his mutterings.

Maria Alexandrovna soon gave up trying to reason, sensing something which she could not come to grips with. Helpless she turned to prayer, ever sure way. Wordless prayer of her very being offered up to the Giver of All. Offered up for her dearest one's sake.

She noted clearly, alarmed, his gaunt appearance, shrinking step and reach, smile wan ghostly, refusal to leave the sofa, odd mutterings, but felt too something greater involving them all, which she must bear. Even yes even her Ilya's death which was but part of it.

Behind her sadness and tears which she feared to let the family see, she could but say Yes Lord, and Yes again. Enduring and bearing and being with them all until the end, the very end.

All this, coming to know, in these strange, harsh days.

Strength O Lord - only strength to endure Thy Way.

For so long he had been their centre. There at his desk, facing the window onto the garden. There, working into the night. Working, always working, at the centre of things. But now the sofa, a dark uncanny burrowing. Something that they were harbouring within.

Wanly appealing his look, but she was afraid to speak the wrong word. He would still sit at his desk but as though puzzled.

"Finished," he would mutter, "all finished."

Working in the garden she anxiously noted his blank gaze through the window, not at all that familiar smile of recognition. Working in the garden the earth itself became more precious than ever, touchstone its darkness, binding, healing as she prayed. "Dear God who heals and sustains us – heal him, sustain him as well. My good one, my close one, do help him. You – and You Alone!"

She wanted to call in Dr Zaslavski but Ilya Nikolayevich reacted angrily. There was nothing wrong! Everything was alright, just as it always should be. Nothing was wrong, he kept repeating.

She yielded as to some strange paralysis.

Of course St Petersburg's decision was unexpected she told herself over and over again, but the higher authority often acted unexpectedly. It wasn't a matter of life or death, simply that his expected retirement had been advanced a few years. And he'd said more than once how he'd like the chance to write a book on education. But the awful thing was, even while so thinking, that she'd never even managed to begin discussing any of these simple, obvious things with him. That, so quickly, he seemed to have crossed a dreadful line, into another place, where she, where nothing of the familiar, the intimate could reach him.

Where could he be? talking about them soon all starving!

She felt guilty. She could not forgive herself. She hadn't been awake enough. A coward for not having broken through the seeming barrier on such subjects as his future, his salary, his pension, his relations with the higher authorities. But all already too late!

She must do something. Must tell someone that her husband was acting strangely. Must get someone to convince him that he was seeing things in a wrong light.

One afternoon, having watched him staring blankly through the window then slowly turn back to the sofa, she stopped her gardening and in desperation, after quickly tidying herself, hurried off down Moskovskaya Street to the Veselovski's house. Ivan Veselovski as Chairman of the Simbirsk Council on which her husband had faithfully served would surely help! When a servant told him that Madame Ulyanov wanted urgently to see him, he was surprised.

As soon as he entered the drawing room she was on her feet.

"Please, please – could you reassure my dear Ilya Nikolayevich – you know him well!"

"Reassure him? About what?"

Veselovski did not at all like the sound of her voice.

"Oh I don't know – about everything."

"Everything? Ah – yes! We can all fall prey to that. Dr Zaslavski is the man to see. He's excellent for nervous conditions."

With great effort she broke through.

"No! No! Not that! He keeps saying he's been rejected."

"Rejected," Veselovski whispered, "What nonsense! By whom? For what?" he questioned sharply, angrily.

"A lifetime of overwork my dear. Exhaustion! Rest will cure it all," he went on hurriedly, soothingly with a note of praise and admiration for Ilya Nikolayevich's dedicated service.

She wanted desperately to describe her Ilya's actual appearance, condition, in all its dreadful reality, but it was beyond her. She thanked Veselovski for his advice and to his relief quickly left.

The most important thing had not been said. How could she put that, to the point, just as she felt it to be – My husband's worrying himself – to – yes – to death! But really – to death! The demon of worry is eating away his very substance – but was there some truth in Veselovski's advice about exhaustion – overwork – a lifetime of it?

Why hadn't she persisted? Why had she suddenly dried up, coward that she was? She would go to the Ministry! She would confront the Minister! She would and must find out. She would have it in writing, a letter signed and sealed, so that Ilya should see that no blemish or doubt was attached in any way to his reputation. But everything was happening so quickly. She must act quickly too. That Other was – already had outpaced her, along a road that was branching right away.

But – but – what delicate issues behind all this, which she knew right now – at least for this once she must acknowledge to herself. Unspoken delicacy which they all lived, of this power – mysterious – graciously granting – ever hidden – yes – and now see its ugliness – its refusal to reveal itself.

Fruits – gifts – blessings – bestowals – and this too!

Oh – endless possible reasons for this early retirement but – it remained hidden!

Through Papa the great world beyond Simbirsk entered into them, grand flush of life connections from his tours around the province. But now its sound had dried up in an awkward silence, isolation. Papa shrivelled up, within them too.

They saw, knew that something strange was happening to Papa, asked no questions, knew that this was no ordinary illness.

Maria Alexandrovna knew that he was leaving them.

One evening in July Anna was reading to him from the Simbirsk Messenger. She did it because Mama asked it of her. She knew with Vladimir so deeply that she must help Mama – that, beyond all else – feeling Mama as the very certainty of their survival. She read as best she could each evening though never sure whether he was really interested or even listening, so passive he had become, so small, this evening his gaze so empty. Yes, nodding to her when she began but it could have been a nodding to himself.

She read on about the new extension being built onto the Gymnasium. She thought it might interest him. She heard a strange mumbling, a language, words of some kind. She stopped. It went on. Sounds like words, like sentences. Apparently coming from Papa but somehow not really coming from Papa at all as he sat with that distant look, his teeth making faint clicking sounds, saliva threading his lips.

She was afraid. A stranger was voicing that weird sound with a rhythm of its own. Her Papa.

She looked hard at him, to find him, to force him and he back to her with those no-one's eyes. Dropping the newspaper she rushed out into the garden past the flower beds, into the orchard where Mama was picking the first cherries of the year from the three trees near the arbour, known as Papa's trees. A family ritual ensured each year that no one should touch the cherries till Papa had first tasted and eaten for they were his favourite fruit.

For Maria Alexandrovna, working in the garden these long summer evenings was a solace, a blessing, alone or helped by the children, weeding, trimming, watering, picking. Her basket was filled with the resplendent fleshy globes, crimson, shining yellow, purple, in all their eager fruitfulness as Anna clutched at her wrist and pulled towards the house.

"Mama come quickly – it's Papa!"

Maria Alexandrovna was surprised at the way she was standing so firm against that fierce pull, earthgrounded, earthstrengthened, skysoaring affirmation, in spite of being prepared some days now for a possible shock.

"Mama come – it's Papa!" repeated Anna, straining hard against her mother's resistance. Maria Alexandrovna gently, firmly, put her arm about Anna's trembling shoulders.

"What is it with Papa my dear?"

Anna shook her head, bewildered by her mother's attitude, yielding to the comfort and security of that arm.

"Come then. Hold my hand. Let's go and see Papa."

Together they walked through the orchard, Maria Alexandrovna, steady, sustained by she knew not what, in the realisation, now, that she was already the sole mainstay of them all. And why! everywhere around her for her such rootedness assurance, such an intimate assurance in these trees, this fruitfulness of late summer air's streaming

Earth ever renewed, renewing
Ever the flower the fruit
Earth so sweet your silence sounding
In the fullness of sunlight ever abounding
And the blue yearning
Summer's blue above

Close to the house she let go Anna's hand and said calmly,

"Why! we've forgotten Papa's cherries."

Anna waited, tearful, trembling.

Maria Alexandrovna returned with the basket but when they reached the study Anna held back. Papa was sat there hunched in a stiff, awkward posture, muttering and apparently indifferent to Maria Alexandrovna's presence. She braced herself against this indifference not her Ilya's at all!

She put the basket on the table. Their fruitfulness so palpable, their blessedness ablaze.

"Ilyushenka, my Ilyushenka, it's cherry time, your cherry time," she called tenderly, then rousingly.

"Ilyushenka, it's cherry time. Look at them Ilyushenka. The crimson ones your favourites– and purple ones. Your own, your very own. Ready at last for you. Your joy my Ilyushenka, your joy."

He had heard and was faintly smiling as he pressed his eyes tight shut and opened them to focus and see in the world of her presence. Awakening – to her presence, fruitful scent. Awakening to the hopefulness, the fruitfulness that shone to him from these tender ones.

He straightened up, took one from her hand and let it rest in his mouth before biting and tasting once again that juicy flesh which he so enjoyed. She had called and awakened him and he turned to her, taking another from her hand. And she knew him here with her now, rescued, reclaimed, frail his presence, but sufficient.

"As good as ever," he said weakly, smiling, the juice a quickening, a pulsebeat, dreams – hopes – cherrytime.

"But I need a plate my dear," he said with a full throated resonance which surprised and cheered her.

"Anna!" she called excitedly, "bring a plate for Papa – and one for yourself – and call Vladimir!"

"But Mama he's insisted on not being disturbed. His exams – on Monday! You know how angry he'll be."

"Anna please do as I say," Maria Alexandrovna insisted, anxious that they should all be present as of old, for the cherry eating with Papa.

Anna brought the plates in but Vladimir was nowhere to be found. Late the following morning Maria Alexandrovna was carefully moistening and tidying her potted palms and aspidistras in the hall when she heard unusual sounds coming from the living room. A step, then silence. A step or two, then silence.

Quietly she edged in behind the partly opened door and watched. Ilya Nikolayevich was in front of the opened piano on whose music rest was a piece by Tchaikovsky, which Anna was practising. Silent, immobile, he stood there, somehow poised, his, this very silence, stillness, challenging her. A stillness and silence binding, charming the whole room, whole house. Centred in him, his, then hovering elsewhere.

She drew breath as quietly as possible. Cautiously, his fingertips reached out to make contact with the mahogany body, to stroke it, before gently pressing down a key to make a bleak sound. Then louder. Louder still and as the note died off he reached out again, for middle C – E – G, sounding the chord up and down the keyboard, firmly, at steady intervals.

Moving slowly round the room he gazed at the family portraits set squat in their ebony frames. Grandfather Blank. Grandfather Ulyanov and Grandmother Ulyanov. Gazing, touching with outermost – to remind – take with – carry away.

He neared the doorway. Maria Alexandrovna decided to stay put, wanting to know something, wanting to act against this uncanniness. Openly she set her face in his direction, not daring to do more. So near he was gazing at a favourite painting 'Mountain Path'. Then he simply passed her by. She felt him as a blinded man, no longer belonging here. A child, a stranger standing at the doorway of the dining room which he had not entered for weeks, gazing at the table laid for lunch, before returning to the sofa, at one moment so certainly here, then timeless, hovering, as she had never known him before.

At lunch she struggled to maintain a calmness with the children. They felt her anxiety, distractedness, and were upset.

"Mama for goodness sake tell Anna to leave me alone about yesterday."

"I simply asked him where he'd been," insisted Anna.

"Absolutely none of your business!"

"Stop it, both of you! Anna you should treat Vladimir with more respect. Vladimir you're becoming a rude person."

She was very irritated, even angry. Her response had reassured them.

So strongly living with her now this one, trying with such difficulty to find his way through a strange world. A world to which he no longer truly belonged, yet yielding something here and there of a once lived intimacy. All she could do was to watch, be aware, moment by moment. "Dear God help my Ilyushenka. Lead him. Lead us both."

After his light lunch from a small bamboo table in his study, he took from her hands the medicine prescribed by Dr Zaslevski. Glancing up regularly from the flower bed she knew that he had settled down for a doze on the sofa. Normally she never cut flowers till late afternoon but she so wanted at this moment to fill his study with the colour and scent. So wanted to counter that withering black with life of flower freshness. Kneeling, she cut slower and slower drawn into the radiant blue centres. Gentle blue come down to darkening earth, sweet ones. Such pain! heart, beat on! – beat on! – what was this anguish? this heavy stone of pain?

Drawing herself up against some overpowering force she hurried giddily to the study window. So still he was there on the sofa and she knew as she entered the house, the study and knelt down by his side that her Ilyushenka, the stranger, had left them.

O Earth's pure ones comfort my sad Ilyushenka! Comfort him, heal him! Carry him on the stream of your green life. Earth's darlings, earth's treasure, earth's blessed gift. Fill this black corner with life - light - your pure healing breath.

Confused, she hurried back to the garden to cut flowers, more and more flowers. She knelt down, disturbed, that she should be doing something else? not this! - but something completely different. Vladimir strode energetically towards her along the path which led to the orchard. The cherries were free now to be picked by everyone. She straightened up immediately, his presence sounding what had happened with an absolute clarity. As he neared her she said gently, appealingly, yet more,

"Vladimir - my son."

He slowed down, irritated at the threat to his plan for a little mouth-watering enjoyment before a final concentrated bout of history revision for tomorrow's exam, in which he fully intended to come first. Reluctantly he came to a halt. He had heard something unusual in Mama's tone, and had sensed something altogether unusual in her. She was looking at him in such a sad, knowing way and on her cheek some moisture glistened.

"Vladimir - my son," she repeated.

So much against his will, at the sight of that moisture he felt tearful himself as she reached out for his hand, holding it and they walked slowly back to the house. He following her as he knew he must yet at her side as an equal. Together they passed through the silent house, hand in hand, Vladimir increasingly uneasy, strange to himself. Together they passed through the living room and into the study. Immediately he knew, almost without looking, that the stillness of that body on the black sofa was final. Together they stood looking, Maria Alexandrovna strengthened by Vladimir's presence which called forth so resolutely for her, that note of endurance for the task ahead. Vladimir not wanting to look but knowing he had to. A vague look which struggled to keep all meaning at bay, as soon as it threatened. 'Papa is dead' which he knew to be right must be acknowledged as the sky outside must be acknowledged. But even that no more than a word, a phrase.

Still they stood looking. Mama's hand was warmth, comfort and strength. She put her arm around his shoulder and gently kissed his cheek, reaching out, seeking and finding in deepest gratitude.

"Dear Vladimir," she murmured, so sad, for what he, her son had lost. So tenderly concerned and resolute to help him. Through Vladimir's presence – the children, she sensed a task, a reality, all one with Ilyushenka, with Ilyushenka's presence. All one and onward together, she holding firm, the centre.

So strange to be drawn thus from himself to her, yet so right, so wanted.

"Vladimir my son," she said sounding the word with its yet new and gentle knowledge. "Go straight to Father Gregori and tell him what has happened."

He left the house and walked along Moskovskaya Street, thankfully, away from Mama, freed from that strangeness as he passed the Bakhtin's, the Golikova's, the Bolotov's houses, along Strelitskaya Street, past Karamazin's Library and the Gymnasium with its scaffolding round the new extension, each and all so familiar beneath the warm, blue Simbirsk sky and yet as they stood about him, touched with a hardening, ominous hardness. Each and all speaking of limit, finality. No longer their warm familiar hope, pointing beyond, expectantly. No longer that friendliness whispering ever till now, enter! Live with in and among us!

Only silence now, empty, threatening.

As the gleaming dome of St John the Divine came into view he felt the shock of a sudden shrinkage. Most painful, absolute its voice.

There's nothing else but this.

No beckoning beyond.

Nothing else but this stark encirclement.

This starkly outlined world, dense, bounded like that body lying so still on the sofa.

This blue-roofed space above never more unyielding. Unyielding to stiffen his glance and stride. An unyielding that suited him!

Overarching truth resounding from all sides as he entered the church.

Nothing else!

Nothing else but things and the end echoing through this dim cavern with its flying angels and saints. Its mere bricks and mortar.

Men?

Men cowered away from that unyielding truth.

Bricks and mortar and wherever he looked - things.

Hard, limited, simply put together. Just as so simply Papa had died.

That dense, still body.

That's all.

Nothing else but that.

What the church had been still present wistfully, beside this new stern truth.

Father Gregory, stout kindly man, no longer so familiar but even in his vestments one like himself, like Papa. If only he could speak to Sasha, ask him some questions about all this right now.

"Papa has died," he began, lost in the simplicity. That's all there was to it. Stark, rigid, shrunken that body on the sofa and that's all there was. And what did any of this mean now? Father Gregory and these burning candles and the intoning.

"Mother asks that you come and visit her," he said sadly.

Nothing else.

Nowhere else.

Papa's end will be for all of us.

Icy this knowledge, barely waiting for Father Gregory to express his sympathy and consolation. Outside, he stopped by the low wall surrounding the church and kicked out sharply at it. This! This! This! He felt ashamed yet relieved. That pain in his toes confirmed his new knowing, proving deed. That was the pain of the dense, dark limit. Stiff still silent steeped with that hardness which everything around him had become.

His five - top marks - for religion! but only words. But words were all that it was, merely words.

Grateful? dared be grateful for Papa's death for exposing this hard reality!

For feeling cleansed, stripped down, alert, ready to endure - to fight back!

To these familiar faces greeting, on his way home, he would respond politely.

"Good day! - Good day!" Good indeed. Such happiness.

Such cosiness. Should he tell them. Tell? How tell this knowledge dawning. Happy ones – simply not knowing what was going to happen. Not having seen, taken to heart that stiff still thing on the sofa.

Along Moskovskaya Street as a revelation it struck that Sasha's finishing with church had something to do with all that he was experiencing now. So strengthening, this connection with Sasha, so easing his isolation. If only Sasha was with him now. Why had Sasha stopped going to church? He must find out. Sasha must know all this. Sasha knew what he was doing. Thank goodness he would soon be home.

Meanwhilst, he would do these things for Mama, politely and decently, if this was the way things were done. He would keep it to himself and upset no one. Mama least of all.

Then this was where Papa's strangeness had been leading.

He'd been tricked!

Nature! Great and mighty Nature to whom we were as dust – our little moment of glory – then puff! – the candle blown out!

But – that it had happened to Papa was a sad business, confusing.

Of course he would help Mama, this calmness sustaining him.

But so much heavier, more cautious, sad, he felt.

The news of Ilya Nikolayevich Ulyanov's death was soon known throughout the town, and then the province. It was reported in both St Petersburg and Moscow newspapers. A memorial meeting was arranged in the Simbirsk Council hall where educators and teachers came from far and wide to pay their respects. Once again a high official from the Ministry was present. In the order of speaking were several teachers, young and old, who had been trained or personally helped by Ilya Nikolayevich. They were to be followed by three Council members and the Chairman Ivan Veselovski. But early on and out of turn Veselovski stood up.

What finer death could any wish than in the knowledge of a life loyally dedicated to Tsar and fellow countryman? What more peaceful death? What finer example of death as a very culmination of life, a very flowering? A life that will ever live in the hearts and minds of all his fellow citizens in Simbirsk. A truly exemplary life. A life of which all Simbirsk province can be justly proud.

We know all that Veselovski!

Veselovski, warmly into it, lightly fingered his neat beard, pulled his jacket tighter about him in a businesslike way and launched out to show the man from St Petersburg where loyal Simbirsk stood. To take the opportunity right here and now to warn, as he knew our revered Ilya Nikolayevich would expect him to do. Else all this praise would be but empty words. And a few old scores to pay off – what better time.

"Friends and colleagues – to remember him truly means never to forget his guiding imperative – that teachers above all have a tremendous responsibility for ensuring loyalty to the best and the highest – to remember how he cleansed the teaching profession – right here in Simbirsk in his persistent methodical way. Yes cleansed – not too strong a word! No detail too small, no stone left unturned that Russian youth be brought up and educated correctly. Friends, colleagues – I know I'm not saying anything that everyone here isn't aware of – when I emphasise on this sacred occasion that even now there are teachers – even in Simbirsk – even in spite of all Ilya Nikolayevich Ulyanov's lifelong efforts – teachers who are not – I repeat not – maintaining that standard of loyalty. Your beloved Director died from his loyalty – if I can put it so. Let his death not be in vain. Died from his highest standard of dedication, conscientiousness, self-sacrifice. His own family are exemplary products of his dedication. Let his death not be in vain."

And yes stupid woman!

"His was a life which to the very end his dear wife and children can only but remember with the happiest proudest memories," he added out of some sudden necessity.

He stopped abruptly, stroked his bald head, sat down and smiled benignly. Many present felt bemused and irritated. The interrupted speakers felt outflanked. As though Veselovski had said everything possible in one go. Yet there was something not right about it – something very provocative – fantastic – most unnatural to the family – absolutely out of place – what good would it do Simbirsk?

A young teacher, very agitated declared loudly, "Doesn't our Council Chairman know the difference between a memorial service and a court of inquiry?"

The next two speakers told in some detail of the training colleges and libraries begun by the Director. But Veselovski had sounded an uncertain, unpleasant note. Once more, after the speeches were over he stood up and called for, 'God save the Tsar!' It was sung with fervour.

From all over the hall people came to pay their respects and shake hands with Maria Alexandrovna, Anna, Vladimir and Olga. Veselovski's soaring praise about her Ilya dying from his loyalty, which provoked some to conclude that he couldn't even speak the language properly, was a cruel thrust into that wound which Maria Alexandrovna was coming to accept.

Yet with wan bewilderment she was deeply comforted by this whole presence around her. Waves from her Ilyushenka's world, from far off shores returning to bathe us with warmth and pride in all that he was and did. Presence of the greater then we the family, for which he worked, unseen but now streaming about them, claiming them too as its own. Drawing them out of their sadness, loss into this presence of all – through him – all his.

Strength, hope – but painful the connection between his death and all this.

Meeting this world, these people from far and wide, Vladimir knew Papa in a new way. Strangers they were yet somehow Papa. Each single one here because of Papa. World of so many strange faces warming him with pride. Wide world that he belonged to with Mama, Anna and Olga. World extending to the Tsar's very own domain. Yes! Papa was known and praised from afar. And he was Papa's son. Warm, high, proud, one with them all as they walked home with the Veselovskis and the Demirovs. But soon after they turned in Moskovskaya Street and left the Veselovskis, it all vanished. With chill consternation he felt the presence of that hardness, everywhere about them in the hush of this late summer afternoon. There is nothing else but this – that body on the couch sternly demanding. And how was it possible that Sasha hadn't come to Papa's funeral?

Sasha must have had the most tremendous reason possible for not coming.

What?

What? could it possibly be – what strength? – power? – that let Sasha say No to Papa's funeral – then – Sasha is not with us any more! Sasha why have you left us like this?

On the stone flags to the front door he would no longer contain himself and stamped down hard for the relief and confirmation he needed. Good this sound of that hardness, clear, brusque.

It was so! – fixed – finished – trapped. So clear and yet a struggle. A fighting against something, a struggle in which he was not himself – a real struggle nevertheless.

"Well Mama," Anna noted discreetly, "at least he played it decently while we were there – let's be grateful for that."

Maria Alexandrovna knew that had Alexander wanted to come, nothing would have stopped him. He had not wanted to. His own father.

A dreadful business at the memorial ceremony – how everyone had gone out of their way not to embarrass her. But who could have been thinking of anything else? Some awful judgement!

Could it possibly be? – Ilya Nikolayevich's reference to Sasha's refusing church as a personal attack.

Was this absence at the funeral Sasha's final gesture of denial – abandonment? Sasha?

Sasha?

A terrible riddle!

Such terrible thoughts trapping her – taking her further and further away from her Sasha.

But – in this numbness – to glimpse momentarily – beyond – beyond all this pain of the personal, a call, a voice as from Sasha himself. Not her Sasha not Ilya Nikolayevich's son. With this very note, this call, she must come to terms.

Yes distant he was, but he was not denying her.

His own he was, but not against her.

Stranger whom she would have to make hers in a new way.

A new connection, something greater.

A new connection with a new son.

No – not a separation – denial by Sasha! It is something he has to do. In spite of this pain she must find that in herself which can accept.

Alexander knew simply that he must not, dare not return home for the funeral. The distance that had opened up between him and the family through Father's death was immense, but he must yield to it, live with it, know it also as himself. Held to in guilt and shame but he must live with it.

Released, blessing – and burden of guilt. But turned to all that world outside.

That outside whose bearer, veil had for so long been Papa

himself. For much too long, Papa as representative, messenger, guide. Irresponsibly too long.

Only now to feel with this fact of Papa's death - free enough, strong enough, audacious enough to turn to it. To acknowledge for certain, that the life outside the precious sanctum of his studies was as crucial a reality - and as needful of himself!

There was no conceivable justification for not attending the funeral. Only simply this knowing, grimly, sadly, that it would be dangerous to see any of them at this moment in time. This bitter loneliness must be sustained. In spite of the sadness, shame, desire to be with them all, share with them all as in the old days, these were no longer the old days. This loneliness was a fierce new source of strength to be guarded, endured, kept pure.

To no one now did he owe any justification. He was himself, beholden to nothing. Justification to himself alone and none other. Not even to Mama.

As one entering on his rightful heritage, so natural to himself at every turn, he joined the Don and Kuban students' Society and was soon elected General Secretary of the scientific and literary section, speaking and writing on a wide range of topics centring on social, scientific and political issues. In Marx's writing he met a knowledge which clarified, delineated, focused that diffuse outside - gave it logical structure and definition. Scientific socialism! Evening after evening in his room, over bread and tea, he studied and discussed it with Lukashevich.

At last to be answered. That there did exist a way, a clear knowledge of that outside - so long veiled by Papa's protective presence.

At last come into their own - those feelings so long obscure insistent - very sounding now, loud clear assured. Liberty! Equality! Fraternity! - no longer dreams but a new reality calling - here - right here in Russia - for him.

At last to know in this turning - this painful turning of Papa's death - what he was here for. That outside now become within.

More - much more - that his very own work take on a new meaning - this gaining of pure knowledge for a new and better world.

Faculty members watched alarmed. The University courtyard was rapidly filling with hundreds of students, all orderly, forming into ranks, ready, eager to pay homage at Dobrolyubov's mouldering gravestone in the Volkhov cemetery.

Sound it again! Dobrolyubov is where we're going!

A taboo on his grave? not really supposed to be approached? Well – we're going to approach him – his grave. Imagine! a taboo on a mouldering gravestone.

Strange! Did he do anything wrong? Not at all! Not an official. Not a practical man. Not a useful man. No power. Simply a writer. Words, words, words. Only words. A literary critic. Writing about characters. Characters in Russian novels. Nothing real about any of it. And we'll pay homage to his literary acumen. We'll go there as students of Russian literature. No more, no less. The point? Well – what is literature? What are our Russian writers? No more, no less. Teachers, prophets, guides. Singers of that freedom song whose eagle flight has settled yet again in our hearts. The point? – aha – listen to this friends, 'The point where word becomes deed, where principle becomes fused with the inmost need of the soul, is dissolved in that need and is transformed into the single energy that moves man,' – that's the point friend – and that's Dobrolyubov! A fighter for liberty of mind – for light in the darkness – for an end to falsehood. His words stand for man's freedom and independence. Our homage to him will too.

So now you know friends why you're joining us in the ranks – and it's all of us together – as one – confronting one – get it?

No more talk after six years of hangman Frolov. But a deed. An answer to this deadly quiet.

An answering deed.

Our beacon to kindred spirits across the darkness. Our duty towards that brotherhood of truth.

A pious ceremony to his memory. Homage to the worthy dead. What possible offence in that? To reach his mouldering grave in some far corner.

With decorum we'll do it.

But in our hearts – through the wreathlaying and the prayers we'll stand quietly on the damp earth – steeping ourselves in the source of most earnest aspirations. By his mouldering grave!

Be you in our hearts, bright flame, sustained by our timeless pledge.

Alexander left his laboratory work for the rear ranks at the very last moment. Of course he must be with them moving together as others came hurrying to join – his meaning, his life too.

As the march swung forward out of the courtyard, binding momentum vibrantly roused, some had already crossed a threshold. Looking back up at the faculty members staring anxiously through the high arched windows, they waved a challenging, audacious wave. A mocking, threatening gesture. Goodbye to you! From our budding youthful strength, goodbye, goodbye to you!

"Note them! Note them Lumin! - Fischel! - all of you! - Take their names I say - every one!" ordered Rector Andreyevsky.

Rector Andreyevsky was upset and puzzled. Days ago, appraised by a student informer, he'd told the police about the proposed march. The district commandant brusquely requested him to let the students get on with it, and not say a word.

Colonel Melganov, Police commandant of the University district had decided to teach these young bastards a sharp lesson. He intended to put an end to this particular game very quickly before it got out of hand. Hundreds of students on the march right across the city! A very sharp lesson was needed!

When Rector Andreyevsky had described this Dobrolyubov, then he knew something serious was involved. The mouldering bones of a scribbler! That was obviously an innocent sounding ploy. Before the meeting ended both men agreed that expulsion of the ringleaders was essential - all disorderly elements to be utterly rooted out - a severe lesson to ensure no further trouble. Expelled from the city too, emphasised Colonel Melganov.

Whatever was afoot would be crushed before it had a chance to go any further. No bloody students were suddenly going to disturb these good years of peace and order. Even a good side too. This little exercise would keep his men on their toes, provide some fun and give the new men some experience in mob control.

Something about Colonel Melganov made Rector Andreyevsky feel a little vulnerable - no! not afraid - but it was that self-assuredness which he - no! - had not attained. But with gratitude he would take advantage of it right now. Ringleaders did he say? Indeed there would be many of those. Many faces that he would be only too pleased - and not he alone but faculty heads too - to see cast out, stamped out - but out! Out for their insolence. Yes he knew it when he saw it - and threatening looks no less. Why! all the subtleties and deceptions were so suddenly revealing themselves in the harsh light of Melganov's certainty, and warning - no less! The students only? A clean sweep! A wonderful opportunity. A meeting soon enough with faculty heads and let lists be drawn up. Let the slightest signs of suspicion be aired. Let every student's record be re-examined, on the march or not. Careful! Careful! It can reflect on you! Forty or fifty'll do then from the march. That'll settle the rest to their studies. Once and for all.

The front ranks struck it out along the University embankment towards Nikolayevsky Bridge yet surprise still that it was even happening like this at all. Till the last there had been some disagreement as to the actual route. Nothing seemed really certain, still something dreamlike about it all as from the start in that frail space of the courtyard, the six wreath-bearers had taken up their position, others immediately joining, strengthening, sensing in and with each other that growing whole.

Power! Foreboding power of buildings gathering against them. Threatening grimacing power of the watching staff. This low grey sky bearing down. But together - towards Volkhov - moving together - space, that light, that freedom. So fragile sweet feel it now, men moving together - a life - a way - our unity.

Many felt awkward before the puzzled stares of passers-by. Many moved with confidence, not provocative but with pride, daring to believe, borne up by this surging movement forward, knit, sustained, each and all, that they were carrying this city's very treasure, that in spite of all this city was theirs.

An entity newborn had found itself, rejoicing, purposing in its vibrant waves of space, bolder, more audacious, beyond, so far beyond these granite blocks. Each now part of this stream's resolve, hope. Youth's testing strength against this threat surrounding. Yet afraid amazed, uncertain giant.

At Sadovaya Street the leaders decided as of one accord to turn right, advancing through Stasov's Triumphal Gate commemorating the victories over Persia and Turkey. Its thrusting gesture of victory their very mood and pace. Thus quickened and confirmed, who could now stop them? Who would? as ever more confident they stepped it out across the Obvodny Canal, down Moskovsky Prospekt towards Kievskaya Street, the grey drizzle itself become friendly, its touch, its taste, the cheering scent of life. A tender flame, a warmth to charge, to change this greyness.

But where, where are we going?

Keep moving, keep moving with joy.

But where, where are we going?

To remember, only remember as they watch us, surly, suspicious.

To remember one who fought the battle unending for Russian light.

In spite of a deeper urge from many, order was maintained, a line of tact and caution unspokenly agreed. No unnecessary provocation, bearing themselves neither humbly nor aggressively, the impulse delicately tempered. For even bigger things could be involved. Where indeed might it not all end? And they were after all doing nothing wrong, merely visiting a Russian writer's grave.

Until Moskovsky Prospekt they had been watched by plainclothes police especially posted. Their turn into Moskovsky Street was unexpected. Radev, disguised as a waiting droshky driver, was urgently hailed to follow the marchers at a discreet distance, pretending to ply his trade.

The drizzle turned to rain, the mood sharpened, something implacable was felt in that steadily falling greyness. A song started up of strengthened resolve, come what may, hail or snow.

As the leaders turned into Kievskaya Street which ran long and straight past three apartment blocks to the high wrought-iron gate of the Volkhov cemetery, their pace faltered, slowed, awkwardly, the word quickly passed back. At the far end could be seen through the steady veil of rain which streamed down forehead, nose and cheeks, a line of gendarmes, cloaked, shoulder to shoulder in front of the Volkhov gates which were shut with heavy chains and padlocks.

"Keep going! We keep going!" went swiftly along the ranks.

A sternest note was sounding – welcomed – most real counterpoint – way now of grimmest implications.

Coming closer into view the line of gendarmes was seen to extend far on both sides of the gates. The wreath-bearers leading, halted at the junction with Semyonovsky Street which encircled the cemetery. The student ranks spontaneously regrouped themselves across Kievskaya Street to watch the gendarmes.

Arms folded menacingly across their chests, with no officer in sight, they stood as one. Sharpeyed, disdainful, ready. Unnerving this feeling of one there, not many. So still, so silent in the falling rain, shoulder to shoulder, before the spiked cemetery wall. And the look of this one was disdain.

Finished! your flight, movement, hopes, sneered this look of disdain as the students fell back on themselves, uncertain, feeling the streaming, eddying rain as a veiling, a grey dissolution. Absolute was the gesture of that one.

"Don't panic! Don't go to pieces!" called a voice through the uncertainty. One of the wreath-bearers, a chemistry student, raised high a dripping, bedraggled leafy shape.

"They want us to provoke them. We must return but with dignity – with dignity fellow students," he declared.

"Coward! we must face them! – with dignity."

"Don't be ridiculous Lozovsky, it's time to go," called back another standing near Alexander and turning about with a friend, as did many others in twos and threes to retreat back up Kievskaya Street. The whole group began disintegrating, to follow these first few retreating who halted, held fast in shocked confrontation. Slowly advancing towards them from the far end of Kievskaya Street – horses close pressed across the street – one – two – three – four! ranks of mounted police.

They were caught in a well planned trap between the advancing police on horseback and the gendarmes guarding the cemetery. Each fell back on himself seeking that dignity, seeking to stand erect in this narrow place. A serious business now. Deadly serious. Everyone felt it, surrounded, isolated. To what end? But that too, though fearful, sounded the measure of their deed. That the enemy had approached in such force to meet them. They could take pride in that.

As the mounted police advanced the gendarmes guarding the cemetery gates advanced, to fan out into a semi-circle at the junction. The trap was closing in rapidly.

The word went round 'No heroics. That's just what the bastards want.'

The front rank of the mounted police, close strung across the street, sternfaced, hands on reins and whips, were mere yards away. The well groomed chestnut horses, flanks dripping, in precise formation, showed no signs of slowing down. The student front facing them began retreating into those behind. The movement gained momentum.

"Back back! – get back – get back!"

The high chestnut wave of proud moving flesh came on them,

implacably, threatening, to touch, to sweep, to overwhelm from on high, where their erect cloaked riders were borne forward. Back! Back! went the blind retreat, furious shoving, panic. Quickly the whole body of students were squeezed right out of Kievskaya Street into Semyonovsky Street where they were held fast by the encircling cemetery gendarmes.

The students were completely surrounded. They stood about bewildered, helpless, utterly relieved that the horses had halted. A lean sharp-nosed mounted police officer raised his whip high. Immediately the horses advanced again and the whole encircling cordon tightened, till every student was forced up against another. A jammed knot of uncertainty and fear, sodden and chilled. No spaces? Good! let them choke on each other!

The lean lieutenant longed to give this student rabble a word-lashing too. But the order was to keep silence throughout, and they'd stuck to it proudly.

"This is ridiculous!" called a voice which became a fierce scream of pain as a whip cut deep into cheek and neck. The lieutenant stared fiercely at the tightly packed students and pointed sharply down at the ground with his whip. Swiftly aimed truncheon blows from the men on foot and a continuous pressure from the men on horseback left no doubt what was meant. Squatting, kneeling, thrust back to back, the students somehow managed to force themselves down. No one dared to speak. One whipped, bleeding face was enough. Lieutenant Postnikov felt relieved, surprised, disdainful. The Colonel had said, "Don't hesitate to make examples! It'll be you or them. Be ruthless!" But he'd never expected one stroke of the whip to achieve this.

Down! down! - victor's primal gesture felt by each - relief in this knowing and the pain of searching for, calling on the strength needed to prevent one becoming what they want to make of me.

In this watery pit, sodden, twisted up against each other, some knew only a swift descent into a numb hopelessness, their selves become wraithlike, vaporous. Those encircling beings now sole source of the real, of power, their very life. Some magic charming the will from them, sucking their souls away, to leave them underfoot, staring up feeble, void, at these lords of creation.

Uncanny silence of this dark disciplined inhuman purposefulness.

Choking so tight this knot of all our flesh.

Thinged - they would make us - thinged by that disdainful stare into this darkening void - and all planned! - and our naiveté!

Hold fast to this knowing sheer cliff-face grip.

They would reduce us by this silence, this violent immobility to the dense nullity of things. That was the aim, threat. They would - it would - have us know that our humanity? - human dignity - was at their - its - disposal. Their very horses our superior.

We are of the cesspit.

We in this dumb helplessness to learn whose was the power here in St Petersburg - here on this earth.

Down! Down! - and back sucked back into this grey streaming downpour. We - of that future so lightly sketched - sucked back into its primal greyness all embracing. Fragile self sucked away into its all-engulfing sway.

Cold streaming painful earth - befriend us!

They would have us yield utterly to this formless void - fragile spark of knowing - not - not to be extinguished in this strange passing of time - as I - begin returning - I returning to something of myself - humanself - quickened!

In this very pressure of each against the other, meant to confuse, violate, subdue, meant to breed, inflame some seething larval hate disgust, here and there a tender glow of confidence.

A sustenance as each sensed in the one pressed close, unsmiling, yet a strengthening of his own quickened self, telling somehow, somewhere from the sodden depth of this pit, of a final - yes final! victory.

At intervals the mounted police, still maintaining the silence, walked their horses around the students with finely calculated closeness forcing the students to keep pressing harder back in order not to be trodden or kicked. Several students had been bombarded with horse droppings which they tried to shake off into the streaming road, without altering their position. Alexander was one of those wedged in the exposed outer edge, unable to resist the pressure pushing outwards, then forced to savagely elbow back those behind as the horses came closer and closer. His clothes were sodden through by the incessant rain and puddles afloat with horse turds.

In spite of the constant tensing and ducking aside he was

learning to yield in a way which encouraged that calm, observation, first begun when the wreath bearers confronted the cemetery gendarmes and the marching had wavered.

From that calm place of observation he had come to realise that in this confrontation, a knowledge of great importance was revealing itself, was available to but only to an acceptance of it, a total acceptance of it in all its stark, painful reality. In this acceptance he tasted an acid withering power which he knew he must swallow down to the dregs in spite of fear and revulsion.

A bitterness he tasted in this greyness.

To do with these men yet not of them.

Man against man. An order, power, inhuman, implacable.

He had seen police before but this fierce, bitter knowledge was different. An entity sensed - evil - to constrict all movement life growth.

Something was shifting, quickly happening. Students were raising their heads and looking in all directions as the mounted police were already making their way back along Kievskaya Street. The horses so steady, dignified, aloof, wincing reminder of the constriction in which they still lingered.

The gendarmes were forming up in two lines and stepping it out along Semyonovsky Street, keen to dry out and drink some hot tea.

"The little sods - fairly shitting themselves - a clever man our Colonel!"

Only some minutes after the gendarmes were out of sight, did they wryly come to their feet. They had re-found, discovered, come to that power of rising up, but shakily, feeling themselves standing upright, returning but with a new painful knowledge in that stance. They felt their way towards the fullness of their humanity - through this attack on it. They shook themselves down as best they could, meeting each other's eyes in needful confirmation, seeking to re-centre on an uprightness which could no longer be taken for granted, against these buildings, hostile, stark. Upright once more as men. Moving forward again but warily. Tempered now that exuberance. Fraught with dangers now that youthful potency. No longer charged with the future was this erectness but a wan, cautious stance, making each so mindful of himself, touching each with deep uncertainty.

They walked slowly back in twos and threes, the sense of

encirclement still present. Their sodden clothes oppressive but merest husk of this knowledge branded deep within, restraining their step. The sense of encirclement still present, in the very houses, hostility of the city itself. This sense of encirclement, Alexander knowing, as the reality crystallised out of Father's world – a fact – impersonal – to be simply accepted – simply – all personal antipathy transcended – its pure state accepted.

All the marchers quickly came to realise that blame and argument were pointless. They had been completely outwitted, naive idiots in the face of this enemy. The news on the following day made the lesson absolutely clear. Forty of those taking part received notice that morning of their immediate dismissal from the university. More, they were instructed to hand in their identity cards to the Police Department in Smolensky Street when they would be franked with an expulsion order from St Petersburg. All to be completed within forty-eight hours, no discussion.

Most of the students now accepted this power as absolute and acknowledged their ultimate helplessness before it as far as their futures were concerned. The forty, in a public declaration, referred to by the authorities as 'ringleaders of a demonstration clearly planned to threaten public order', must obviously have been selected well before the march. Some of them had been involved in an earlier incident. Some had been at odds with their tutors. But regarding the majority, the choice seemed arbitrary. It meant that no one was secure. Not being expelled – not having one's whole future annulled, depended entirely on the whim of the authorities – on a dreadful – inhuman power. For a few, including Alexander, this arbitrariness was an injustice, an inhumanity, that could not be simply tolerated.

When the expulsion notices were posted up, Alexander was in the laboratory setting up a slide and bringing it into focus. As the patchy shadows shrank and darkened into definable forms, he sought with intense concentration for that elusive significance which would yield something of itself to him. That living moment of cognitive tension, expectant, brooding warmth – a fire! – become tender flame of meaning. But he was forced back, away from the slide, the instrument, in frustration as if slide, instrument, notebooks, whole field of that activity were separated from him by the finest of veils. An indifference was settling over them. They were becoming less important than they should be, slipping away.

He went out into the courtyard. Small groups of students were in earnest, restrained discussion. He decided to return to his work. No sooner had he settled down than the laboratory door opened quietly and Michael Turanov, a close friend, went over to his bench near Alexander. To Alexander's surprise Turanov opened the locker beneath his bench and began clearing everything out, textbooks, notebooks, instruments, specimens, into a large leather holdall. He did it as quietly as possible so as not to disturb Alexander. Finished, he stood up and held out his hand.

"Well, that seems to be it," he said as calmly as possible.

"What are you talking about?"

"Haven't you heard?" Turanov replied, showing his expulsion note. A flimsy bit of paper with two brief lines in type, signed by the Rector and the Head of the Natural Science Department.

"Good god! - but why you?"

"They had to get someone! Count yourself lucky," Turanov said bitterly.

"They must be mad - a first class scientist in the making!"

"They don't seem very interested in first class scientists my dear Alexander Ilyich."

Through the bitterness and the shock Turanov could no longer restrain himself and they embraced tearfully. Alexander felt the touch and taste of that bitter power - keenly - in this very arbitrariness - an inhuman whim. While talking on to Turanov and trying to console him, he knew irrevocably that he no longer belonged to himself, that the events of the previous day were absolutely crucial, that nothing less than total commitment would assuage this present anguish. Something must be done.

"Where are you going?" he asked Turanov.

"Home."

"I assure you," said Alexander, not knowing precisely what he was meaning but that he had to say it, "that something will be done."

"Done? What? another memorial ceremony. Alexander stick to your work. That's real. Read the signs my friend. You've been lucky. All this other business is hopeless."

"Michael give me your address."

There was no more to be said but Alexander now knew that

he belonged to Turanov – to the rest of the forty, to all who were present at Volkhov.

That on so fine a thread his own future hung.

Luck?

On their gracious mercy?

Father's world.

There was a path.

All.

Mysterious all, yet reality. So intimate yet so elusive.

All is one. One is all.

New meaning, fullness, warmth through which to find himself and this other work which he knew he had to do. In this anguish over Turanov, over this blind, cruel destruction of his dear friend's future, this inhuman stamping out of promise, he sensed the existences of all those involved.

Each of us at Volkhov was responsible for what happened. Each of us is responsible for the forty. Something must be done.

A small group found each other and set about planning some form of protest over the expulsions. They decided to inform society at large about this stupid, intolerable injustice which had destroyed the careers of Russia's gifted sons who when trained would serve her so well in many fields. And the reason behind it? simply remembering an undistinguished critic, one Dobrolyubov, not a line of whose work had been read by most of the students involved.

The group decided to simply detail the bare facts of the police action at Volkhov cemetery. A straightforward account yet too a deed of resolve and determination in an atmosphere being felt in their daily lives as a threatening intimidation.

Headed, 'A Protest', it was copied and posted to notabilities in administration, business, journalism. Anyone with a name. Anyone who might listen.

It was assumed, hoped that all or some would take note and make known their views to the high authorities in no uncertain fashion. Something surely would, must happen as a result of it by those out there in society. Deeds would surely be done, meetings convened, words spoken, articles published. People out there after all must really know what is being done in their name. Once they do know there can be no question of what will happen.

The silence must be broken.

People out there must be made to listen.

Of course no newspaper would publish any criticism of the police or university administration.

Mysterious that society out there as name after name was added to the list making it more real. It was signed 'Fellow students' though Alexander felt strongly that their own individual names should have been appended. Their conviction of rightness in what they were doing and the assumption that others once informed would support them surely made anonymity unnecessary.

Two weeks passed, of anxious but unfulfilled expectations. Their growing disappointment made necessary some kind of explanation. Personal replies after all were not really important. It was the general effect that mattered. Nor were many of the names really expected to respond – they'd just been possibilities. But still after five weeks there was no discernible response out there of any kind.

Pyotr Shevyrev from Kherson was ready for this silence. He had gone along with those vague unreal assumptions. He had bided his time. He had known it would come to this.

When it became obvious that no response would be forthcoming the group dwindled. Soon not more than nine were left to meet, no longer certain why but feeling that they should not yet cease completely. Alexander became increasingly frustrated. He could no longer give himself properly to his work and yet that for which he had re-orientated himself was leading nowhere, becoming unreal when reliving the packed sodden pit's void dense silence encircling.

For the first time Shevyrev suggested his room instead of Ulyanov's where they normally met.

"What's the point of going on like this? The others were right. There is nothing more to be done," insisted Vasily Generalov.

"Absolutely right. Let's not kid ourselves any longer," said Shevyrev. "There is nothing more to be done – in that way! But my friends – that way has taught us a lot eh? We know now don't we what surrounds us – nothing but cowardice and fear."

Till now he had rarely spoken. They were held by this unexpected note of certainty. He waited. He Pyotr Shevyrev would measure them for worthiness. Time was short but worthiness was essential, and few, very few were truly worthy.

"Well then Shevyrev?" queried Govorukhin embarrassed at

the long waiting and he not the only one. "What more is there to be done?"

"We must arrange another ceremony – another act of homage –" said Shevyrev, his deep set eyes narrowing beneath his high delicate forehead, the line of his mouth tightening.

"Stop having us on!"

"Homage my friends to the men of '81 – the men of the deed – the real deed," Shevyrev's voice had become a tremulous whisper.

"Homage my friends not with words and wreaths and graveside prayers – not with letters of protest – but with a real deed. A deed that will shatter to fragments that wall of cowardly silence!"

He looked intently at each one, weighing up for the task ahead.

"The question is my friends – are you ready? Are you able to work with me? – to do something that has to be done?"

That 'me' sounded with authority.

"If you're ready – and if you're committed – then the Executive Committee is ready to go ahead."

Executive Committee? Already established?

And Shevyrev a member?

Shevyrev knew they were listening. That he had them with that name – no! – reality! He had leaped. No more room for doubt. This moment, these people simply proved it. That he was indeed what he had long suspected, the link, inheritor, of the People's Will – the men of '81 – with new forces, new followers ready to carry the movement forward.

The pale delicate skin of his gaunt head flushed with the flame.

"What exactly are you," began Generalov challengingly, caught up by Shevyrev's conviction but uneasily, "and your Executive Committee getting at?"

Aha! So! The Ex. Com. were behind him! He Shevyrev truly spoke in their name. They were fully recognised. The Ex. Com. lives wherever men seek freedom.

He lowered his head, his voice often near a whisper, he, the one to transform legend, hearsay into reality, here and now. Speaking to these. Communing with those.

"In five months time on March the first – will be the anniversary of '81. The Central Executive Committee of the

People's Will," he said slowly, "plan – with your help – to repeat – no not repeat but renew – the deed of those heroes of '81- Zhelyabov – Perovskaya – Kibalchich – Mikhailov – In other words my friends – in case you're not absolutely clear – in case you want to withdraw – we plan to assassinate the Tsar."

He looked around from face to face. No one moved. Each sought to respond to the challenge of that searching look by drawing on an inner strength and resolution. The sound of deeply drawn breath registered the momentous challenge, the realisation that Shevyrev was taking them across an ominous threshold. Barely mastered was an exhilaration that this indeed was the task, the way. Not for others, not for legends but for them here and now. Fire indeed had Shevyrev struck and he felt it.

"What they did to us at Volkhov, and the expulsions, and this silence – it's all part of the system. And the system must be smashed. We know it – all of us in our hearts. We know we can't leave it to anyone else. That's sheer cowardice. We must do it ourselves. In full consciousness. Men they'll meet – as they did in '81. And whatever they throw back we'll take on our heads."

He explained that unlike the isolated deed of '81, their deed would at one stroke smash the present system and ignite the revolution. The revolution scientifically predicted by Marx. Several questions were put to him and he gave a confident, authoritative answer to each. One flash of inspiration, improvisation, followed another. Why did the men of '81 fail? They didn't fail they were too early. Now the revolution is ready and will answer the new deed.

"To renew the deed of '81 my friends means the terror. The only language they understand. That's when they realise there are men who won't be cowed – won't remain on their knees."

"But –"

"Yes of course! but but but – but don't you see – we're the proof that these buts – these cowardly hiding places are of no avail. All that avails my friends is the call of destiny. What you are – that, you have to be! – and do! And this is what we have to do – for ourselves, or we shall never stand upright again. And for the men and women of '81 through whom we find our manhood. And for Russia – to find her true self through us."

On to a lofty place Shevyrev drew them and imbued them with the exaltation of being chosen for a momentous task.

We agree to what has to be done.
We respond to the deed of '81.
We carry it forward to greater heights.
We declare to those of '81 that you didn't call in vain.
We at least shall not be ashamed.
We at least shall accept destiny's call.

Shevyrev's intensity was a feverish fire, consumptive, desperate that nothing would come to fruition in this time of his which was burning away so fast. This absolute moment of transformation he must live – to inspire – to see!

"My friends," he said, the note unexpectedly personal, "d'you know how it was with me? My uncle Sergei had been in St Petersburg for the hangings and liked to tell the family – so righteous – so indignant about the abominable Executive Committee. I knew then and there I'd be a member of it one day. The Executive Committee which lives wherever men seek freedom. When I heard dear Uncle Sergei speaking away like that, I felt I was with a total stranger. But – very close to those he was talking about. Strange eh? I felt *they* were my family. I took such a holy oath, never to forget them!"

His hacking cough abruptly checked him, to leave him trembling, exhausted, sweating.

But at any cost to make incarnate the Absolute's moment, the final transformation once and for all.

Alexander listened in most delicate of ways, to something beyond the words, most intimate, that inner tone, as if resounding from himself.

Shevyrev's intensity, incantation, inspired them all with the rightness and vision of a seemingly absolute purpose, bound them to that ever-present past of '81 beyond life and death, revealed momentously the meaning of their coming together, drew them mysteriously into a brilliant realm – no graveyard ceremony but a new beginning.

Shevyrev's intensity charged Alexander with that same pressing necessity to act, and act quickly. Conclusive for him, demanding his total commitment, was the tight link with a socialist revolution. He was aware of crossing a fateful threshold but beyond all doubt there was no other way.

No other way. The logic unassailable. Acts of terror inevitable in the present situation. A painful logic, yet pure, impersonal, demanding from him the final sacrifice.

To herald the birth of a scientific socialist society.

The final sacrifice - which meant - know it now as a blessing. That what you have been granted to know, taste, of that boundless realm whose majesty and beauty fill you with such tranquil joy - a blessing, for even that - this very thirst for life itself must be done with.

The struggle against this evil –
beyond science
beyond the pain to family
beyond life and death
the final sacrifice.

To come to terms with the social as a whole - that once distant vague outside. But in which also - so much also now he knew - we have our being. Structure web atmosphere mysterious - but now given incontrovertible form through Marx' concepts. And demanding necessary action.

A knowing here too that is a destiny.

Members of the group proposed themselves for various tasks; getting information on the Tsar's movements; procuring money; getting technical assistance; organising a squad of bomb throwers and signallers. Around this central group and its close associates, others of revolutionary inclination willingly carried out assignments without being aware of the actual aims.

Lectures were attended and studies kept going so as not to give the slightest grounds for suspicion.

Alexander began reading up on explosives and bombmaking in the University library. He would design the bomb. Destruction for the good. Opening up a space for freedom. He enjoyed the challenge of beginning from nothing in this new field of ballistics. His design consisted of a metal container holding the dynamite, and packed around with hollowed leaden pellets filled with strychnine. Andreyushkin's pharmacist friend supplied the strychnine. Lukashevich made the dynamite. The nitric acid for triggering the explosion was obtained through Kancher. Andreyushkin, Ossipanov and Generalov would be the bomb throwers. Alexander made some of the nitric acid, dynamite and lead bullets.

During these weeks of working on the bombs it became ever clearer to Alexander, when he struggled to define the essence of the matter - Volkhov - Dobrolyubov - the pit - the expulsions - the wall of silence - that, to his great surprise, it was precisely this very struggle in thinking – this thinking itself! – that was the essence. This very thinking activity was what they wanted to control.

This ardent stream, fresh, from ever fecund source. Himself! His very significance. All this is what that bitter, ruthless power would stultify, poison – corrupt through fear – force to shrink back.

But this thinking was himself.

Only in this clear light of one's own thinking could one stand erect – be truly man – Arise!

That was a great evil – preventing him from being himself.

Bitter evil already tasted now known in this radical way.

That evil power must be destroyed. That power which worked through individuals.

Those individuals must be destroyed through whom it worked.

And the first to be destroyed must be the most important of all.

Unassailable this logic!

No man must have such power. That was an absolute evil.

Life was a precious gift. But life meant flowering – being free to become oneself.

Life worthy of man meant generosity each to the other. But the life allowed by this power was timid, fearful, grey. A thinking cowering before that wall of silence.

"With this deed, this death, Russia will awaken, a space will be cleared and the new life begin," declared Shevyrev.

New life through which he could give himself entirely to that sanctum once again.

Bombthrower Andreyushkin lived the future deed as giving absolute meaning to his life. That he, intensest point, would be the instrument of death and destruction, decisive for Russia. An audacious exhilaration barely containable as he lived the deed again and again. A huge Andreyushkin, his arm alone, righteous, merciless. Bringer of death and destruction. Cleansing. Astride the mountain peaks of destiny. Beyond mortals. Friend and servant of death. And as the hills and the streams and the meadows were beautiful – so was death.

In Alexander's room he noted with admiration how the metal fruit of destruction was ripening beneath Ulyanov's hands. He soared above it, the details and the substance, soared, ablaze in this spirit's black fire.

By day in the zoological laboratory Alexander worked intently on his vivisectional studies of marine cockroaches, now a preparation for that new future when his work would be more truly needed for all men. By night the bombs, notes, sketches, calculations were pored over in secret. This double life, this hiding was painfully accepted as part of that ultimate sacrifice.

He enjoyed the discussions at night with Andreyushkin concerning the size, weight, shape and throwing curve. He was impressed with Andreyushkin's grasp of the problems involved and with his enthusiastic concern for detail. But oddly to himself over the weeks he came to feel that – yes! – with Andreyushkin there was a strange vagueness. From time to time the man was saying odd things about death – beauty – the futility of political parties – the joy of terror for its own sake? – which left him uneasy – No! he didn't like any of that.

Increasingly he took responsibility for overall planning and organisation as it became depressingly clear that regarding these most practical aspects, Shevyrev was not simply incapable but, distressingly, seemed to have opted out. In late December when a network of over twenty active sympathisers had been established, all ready to help in the most varied ways, Shevyrev announced that he had been called South on urgent work for the Southern region Ex. Com. Also that he'd been suffering a lot with his chest recently and the southern climate would help him pick up. But all said with a bewildering indifference to the momentous task in which they were involved – task inspired by him!

That he even taunted them for their sloth!

Everyone was relieved. His indecisiveness and inability to provide sure direction had led to increasing frustration. Alexander's ability to communicate clearly, simplify, organise and maintain a balanced judgement, were recognised in the acknowledgement of him as leader. He took on more and more tasks, procuring finance, recruiting people, finding accommodation, well aware that he was becoming the pivot, strong centre.

Shevyrev, fired by his success with this group had decided to awaken elsewhere the Ex. Com. spirit. The whole of Russia was waiting to hear from him. That was his real task. The mere details, actual organisation, were for lesser ones. Rousing the Ex. Com. spirit – that was his mission. How easy it had all proved to inspire with his talk. But elusive this power. There in all its fulness. Then gone!

Alexander's realisation of Shevyrev's weakness was painful, yet his own awakening through thinking's very own light enabled him to take the entire task on himself in an ultimate responsibility. On this his very own ground he stood, upright, irrespective of the men of '81 and of Shevyrev's invocation. From this ground, simple and right, there could never be any question of feeling guilty for what he was doing. And only through this total commitment of himself would such a flame arise as gave fruitful meaning for others.

Poor weak Shevyrev. He knew not of this deed of rightness which I have taken into my being. How I have strengthened, permeated myself with this absolute responsibility. How I have answered my Yes to the world. A Yes that lives in me, through me and forward, to the men yet to come. Poor weak Shevyrev. This new I of mine can – will, take it all on with a strength which cannot be taken from me. This fullness is what Shevyrev has led me to – but himself could not attain.

In late January Alexander decided that a Programme must be prepared. Together with the assassination their voice would have to be heard. So he must prepare an account of those aims whose achievement would result in a just, free and democratic Russia. Shevyrev had seemed to think that the assassination would by itself be sufficient to start off the revolution. Alexander considered the Programme to be an essential part of the deed, an urgent necessity. It covered, freedom of conscience, speech, press, assembly, association; democratic elections, a bill of rights, local self-government, the village council as the basic economic and administrative unit, education for all, nationalisation of land, factories and production. In it he declared the group's respect for the liberals and Social Democrats.

Andreyushkin, watching from his heights waited impatiently as Alexander's deathfruit ripened. One could only join forces with those prepared to serve death. The purest courage was needed here. The blissful potency of total sacrifice. Nothing less would do.

Even the Social Democrats would have to be destroyed. Their timidity would prevent men becoming such as he, the real cleansers of Russia.

He felt sad for those not yet touched by the bliss of his life, the sweetness, and he wrote out of sorrow, pity, to his student friend Ivan Nikitin in Kharkov, who was sympathetic to Social Democrat ideas.

> *My dear Ivan,*
>
> *Outside - fog as usual. But me - you wouldn't know today. Few do. But soon enough the world will know and hear of the deed for which my whole life is but preparation. The deed that will signal anew the start of the final struggle. This is life! Watch for this deed. It will strike a chord in groups all over Russia. The Ex. Com. will continue the work. Our leader has gone South for this. The day of days approaches. Finish your triflings with the S.D.'s and their childish theoretical games. Join us. Be baptised in blood and cleanse Russia white. Ours will be a truly merciless terror to purge, purify, baptise our dear suffering Russia. O the beauty of death. The beauty of being cleansed and purified. Father and son likewise. There is so much more I could say. I hold sway over new eternities. And when you hear the news remember your dear friend. Take courage. Go on with the work. For Russia's sake. For the sake of long suffering Russia.*

After the briefest hesitation he signed his own name with pride, with an exalted fatalism and invulnerability. He felt himself break into a poetry, surge and potency carried forward as the white foam of life breaks on the shores of death. A poetry gleaming, ahead, obscure, calling sweetly, beyond all this. A poetry telling of unknown things with a luminous joy. In the rhythm of the words he knew the power that would carry him through and beyond, beyond.

The censors responsible for the University district had been requested by Colonel Melgunov to intercept all outgoing mail. Things had been a little too quiet for too long. Student informers had reported nothing of substance throughout the autumn months. Rector Andreyevsky was well satisfied and told him of a marked change in student attitudes as a result of the expulsions. But Colonel Melgunov was not convinced that what lay behind the Volkhov affair - still surprised by the numbers involved! - had dissolved harmlessly away into nothing. He was determined to keep a delicate finger on that almost silent pulse.

Beletsky, a junior censor clerk, opened Andreyushkin's letter, fairly certain that it was the work of a crank. Ex. Com. Executive

Committee? The People's Will business, all finished with years ago! But, appending a small slip with his comment 'Crank?' he decided to hold it back in one of the General files for the attention of his immediate superior Simonovich. Some weeks later Simonovich chanced to glance through it. 'Father and son likewise,' intrigued him. An awareness gently intensified of the various ceremonies arranged for the next few days, to commemorate the sixth anniversary of Alexander II's assassination, including the main one to be attended by the Tsar himself at the Peter and Paul Cathedral. Awareness of the two Tsars themselves – themselves! as father and son! – the connection impossibly obvious! But – but – listen harder! – not that simple – not at all! – just this obviousness could be the trick – the possibility – or – was Beletsky right? That only a crank could have put his name to something so obvious. But Beletsky's question mark? Wasn't that pointing to the same possibility?

To discuss? – share it with Beletsky? – some sign of weakness – especially after his recent blunder.

Nor could he afford to risk another – as – possibly – big as this!

It must be Dyakin – whatever the outcome – but even – much glory might be his too!

Department head Dyakin listened impassively to Simonovich's cautiously prepared approach. Quickly sensing a huge security risk he brusquely criticised Simonovich and Beletsky for not informing him sooner. Simonovich left frustrated. Dyakin decided to act immediately. The stakes were very high.

Only now though – to dare admit – that the 'obviousness' might have tricked him too!

Rector Andreyevsky gave him details of the student Andreyushkin, and he then conferred with Colonel Melgunov. Three plainclothes gendarmes were detailed to monitor Andreyushkin's activities.

On February the twenty-seventh a final meeting took place in Alexander's room, with Andreyushkin, Osipanov as second bomber and Generalov as reserve. On a recent practise run in the countryside south of the city Alexander had successfully exploded some dynamite with the nitric acid. Three bombs were now ready and false passports were on their way from Vilna to enable the whole group to escape abroad.

A letter arrived from Maria Alexandrovna asking Alexander

why he hadn't written for so long. Her voice, her writing made him realise just how distant he had been from the family and just how close to them he was at this moment. How vulnerable he felt them with Mama. More, anxiously much more glimpsing over some abyss a dark future for them, through him. Future till now most hidden but making them more vulnerable still. There was no other way! He dare not, must not think about it, so far away, so other was the realm of this doing from all that life.

But memories persisted, intimate memories to claim him, bathe him in the warmth of that most personal stream of life. Walking along Ushna's banks with Vladimir gathering specimens, feeling now! so keenly the pain of Vladimir's arrogance and prickly pride, yet the fine tempering bond which held them so close. Elusive this struggle throughout the day to resist the memories but reluctantly, for such a sweetness there as would overpower him.

Andreyushkin arrived for the meeting and fervently held his hand. He went over to the table on which the two cylindrical bombs were waiting beside Grinberg's Dictionary of Medical Terminology whose pages were glued togther, hollowed out and packed with dynamite. Generalov and Osipanov arrived a few minutes later. As they went over to the table, Andreyushkin picked up one of the bombs, gently gripping it, lifting it up and down with a light spring as if beginning a throw. He felt in his grasp already the very substance of that power, that righteousness, the deed itself. Felt almost as if there was no need to take any precautions whatsoever, for those fools would never know.

"Perfect! Absolutely perfect! He's a genius," he smiled broadly at Alexander, with the bomb held out in his hand at arm's length towards them. He put it down gently on the table.

Generalov's doubt would not leave him.

"I'm sorry to have to say this again," he began almost apologetically, "but d'you really mean that we're simply going to wander round the Nevsky for - what, days! - waiting for the Tsar to turn up - with these?"

They'd had all this out more than once but still to Generalov's increasing alarm nothing specific ever seemed to be concluded, let alone planned. Generalov knew at this late moment that he had no alternative but to believe in Andreyushkin's certainty

"The Tsar will be there. The Tsar must be there. And we shall destroy him," said Andreyushkin with benign resignation.

"My dear Vassily," he went on, to more lowly matters, "we know that he's most likely to be coming from Gatchina on the twenty-eighth, and most likely to be driving along the Nevsky for the remembrance service. All this is common knowledge. All we have to do now is get the feel of the place – get the feel of the bombs, these excellent bombs – and be ready."

Certainly put like that it seemed straightforward and reassuring enough.

Andreyushkin having for some time now recognised Generalov's mundane attitude, was prepared in this resigned way to appease it. The fellow had a willing heart and that's what mattered. Had any of them really grasped that the deed alone was sufficient? That its power ensured – would master everything present and future. That the Tsar would turn up. That this deed was alone the real – would alone infuse new life new blood into the world. Old blood must run that new blood be infused.

Best of all would be to carry the bombs naked – openly – for all to see or not to see.

Alexander had begun to suspect – what was it? – an emptiness? – lack of seriousness in Andreyushkin.

He had begun to accept the possibility of a nothingness on the far side of all this. He was preparing himself to stand before the tribunal, to confront them face to face. The stance would not leave hold of him and he was ready for it. There did seem something unreal in what was happening and the way it was happening. That Andreyushkin had still not decided when and where. Generalov was somehow right. On his part – a closer confrontation would be called for. But here were the bombs. Here were the hands that would do this deed of deeds. And all Russia was waiting.

On February 28th it was decided by the three bomb throwers that they would make their way separately along the Nevsky and slowly reconnoitre past the palaces, churches, public buildings and shops. Once in the morning and then again in the afternoon should enable them to size up the situation with some confidence. Andreyushkin reassured Generalov when he emphasised that they must walk purposefully, though not too purposefully, as if innocent passers-by. Their main task, he instructed, would be to look out for vantage points, places which gave a particularly clear and lengthy sighting along the road, places suitable for taking up positions in readiness. Generalov wondered why it was necessary to carry the bombs on a reconnoitre. Osipanov carrying the thick bookbomb was surprised at Vassily's ignorance. The information circulating was certainly not to be trusted. The Tsar could appear at any time and they must be ready for him.

On their afternoon reconnoitre, closely trailed by several police agents, Generalov's doubt returned, soon near despair. In the morning, so long ago, he had felt a space invulnerable radiating out from that cylindrical hardness, hung on the hook of a cord slung over his shoulder beneath his overcoat. They had been the moving centre, secret lords of life. Now the Nevsky itself was sucking at them with a power of its own. The deed for which Russia was waiting! Russia? Russia? Where? these little people on the Nevsky? It was all shrivelling to nothing. Were they going to throw the bombs – or the book – or the bombs and the book? Good God! It was ridiculous. But they'd never discussed it. And how could he ask Andreyushkin now, on the Nevsky, like this.

This was a wandering – a separation – most unpleasantly alone – losing contact.

Drifting.

Where indeed were the others?

Alone!

What was it this drifting – holding them together – drawing them apart?

They were not the men of '81.

Watching Andreyushkin from this distance – that figure didn't seem to be looking at anything in particular – vantage points or anything else. He seemed to be just walking alone cut off, sure of something.

They were trailed back to their rooms. The police agents reported in detail to their superiors who instructed that if the suspects continued to patrol the street where the Tsar might pass, they should be arrested. Meanwhilst, the situation permitting, to await further instructions.

The following day His Majesty was due to attend the commemoration service in the Peter and Paul Cathedral at eleven o'clock. Andreyushkin, Generalov and Osipanov set out and were arrested.

Generalov lived this ending as a dreamlike dumbplay.

Handcuffed and led away Andreyushkin remained calm,

smiling faintly. Let them do as they would. Their reality but dross. His remained invulnerable, brighter than ever.

Generalov, through most painful deflation, yielded passionately to this world's reality from a dire necessity. His refusal to accept it had been his sin, which he would somehow make good. Easily he named names to prevent any other fools from being taken in. Such a naming, heartfelt, might not be without its rewards.

The whole business had been so absurd.

No – not at all confession but an overpowering. That a greater reality was the victor to whom he they all involved must yield in the long run, so better now.

No – not betrayed – not doing anything wrong. Merely addressing that reality.

And to hear that none of the bombs would have exploded – hopelessly amateurish! – that was the valid sign over their fantasies.

Within hours fifteen were arrested.

That evening in his room Alexander was surprised that Andreyushkin hadn't come round to let him know how things had gone. He stayed in his room next morning still awaiting a visit rather than going off to the laboratory. He tried to study, all the while wondering what was happening. From time to time he went to the window, looked down onto the quiet street, then across Neva's broad waters, the Fortress rearing rocklike, so briefly veiled in limpid washes of pink through a break in the clouds, to vanish into that ghostly grey grimness – blank brooding bastion – darkest presence pervading St Petersburg – and his way.

He turned to his books wistfully but could not make contact. He turned again to the window, drawn across Neva's gleaming waters. That high black wall – Pestel – Bakunin – Chernyshevsky – Karakozov – Nechayev – and the five – the five – Grinevitsky – Zhelyabov – Kibalchich – Perovskya and Rysakov – poor Rysakov! Names it had endowed with earthlife eternal – living memorial in letters of fire at the heart of your darkness. Those names, every one recalled, not one to be missed, resounded as a faithful deed, inspiring on the way. Across what distance calling? – by what time separated? – why! – none!

From what inmost necessity had Peter built it – to immure his own son in it? So crammed together – these souls left to rot – the Cathedral – the Romanov tombs – what Russia was that?

He picked up Mama's letter, pulse of family beating so strong – abyss – searching for Father?

Those eleven o'clock church bells – he must have dreamed his way through them! What was the matter with him, stuck here in his chair well past eleven.

Why wasn't he on his way to Kancher's as planned, for news of how things had gone?

He must stick to the plan!

Then what was holding him back like this?

Anna's regular Wednesday visit – Anna! – what! – more important than Russian destiny, the ridding of an unjust Tsar?

Yes! – she would come – so vulnerable – she would be dreadfully upset by finding this room empty for the first time – he knew it!

Uncontrollable these thoughts of her, this feeling of her acute anxiety before the emptiness.

At a time like this! To be overwhelmed – threatened – by feelings of her pain – this dreadful sense of loss rejection – hers! But now so strongly his. What would she do? – suicidal she said last autumn.

Impossible to leave a note of any kind.

Why impossible?

Because this immediate future now to be faced was – uncertain.

So puzzling still that after all these months of regular visits she had never indicated any awareness of his terrorist activities.

Anna! – Anna! – forgive me! your succour – lifeline – closest one not there for you. From my heart prayed – stand firm Anna – stand firm!

Stuck even faster – threatened even further – this intimate irresolvable of family – nation – death flashing in – only to helplessly yield.

Hopefully she wouldn't be too distressed – it all began with Papa's death – but how much had his absence at the funeral contributed. Guilty. Guilty.

Generalov Osipanov Andreyushkin – repeat! Those names that have sounded at last so thankfully to call him back to that reality. Hold to them, their warning that all this other is seduction, temptation.

Generalov Osipanov Andreyushkin have already risked their lives, their dedicated lives – know this Anna business as a dreadful temptation.

Now!

Now!

With Generalov Osipanov Andreyushkin go! And just keep going to good dependable Kancher.

Hard, shut against all other feelings, keep going. Make it your only focused goal, last trial, across the bridge, looking neither to left nor right but wary to spot anything unusual.

No! Passers-by, carriages, even the timber barges below – everything its familiar self.

Off the bridge, towards the Nevsky but somehow holding at bay the thought – would it? could it all be so normal if the assassination had been successful?

In Kancher's street, his pace quickened as if now to some uncertain ending. The sight of three black carriages flashed with a shadowy sense of unfamiliarity, this, in Kancher's street, as he made for the entrance of Kancher's apartment block.

He should have left Anna a note – any note! So vulnerable she was since Papa's death – so sharp this pain of her.

No caretaker about – so what? just keep going, this is your road, up two flights, yes something is there. No, not really surprised now as you two oafs close in on me.

Police agent Svergunov whistled down loudly and two more plainclothes police agents took up position by the street entrance from which the caretaker had been ordered to retire. Yesterday evening, the arrested Kancher, threatened with torture and the gallows, broke down and named many names, always beginning with this one.

Agents Svergunov and Sverzdin knew who they were waiting for as they grabbed his arms.

"Alexander Ilyitch Ulyanov?"

Alexander was not entirely surprised, it was some deep culmination.

But had the bombs actually done it?

Had it worked at all?

Svergunov and Sverzdin were amazed at the sheer amateurism of this lot. Dozens of names! And here in Kancher's room simply to wait for the rats to stick their noses in. The carriages were waiting.

"Yes! I am," Alexander eventually replied, unexpectedly calm to himself as the handcuffs were locked in place and they led him, one in front, one behind, down the stairs to the waiting black carriage at the entrance.

Some people were gathering nearby to watch.

Alexander knew he was now crossing into a place where all would be made known, transparent.

"Swine! - it didn't work," he thought he heard.

"They're catching them like the rats they are."

No matter. No matter.

It was into the open now. Here, outside, on this irrevocable path. This only path for the closer confrontation still. He could and would take it all in his stride. Nothing went off! But this was what he had wanted, deeply wanted, and it had come about. This testimony, this witnessing which he would surely have to give. Not the bomb but the words. Words. His words must be the final deed, seed. Through him others would hear what he had heard, in all purity, and that would be sufficient. He knew once more, pure, in this adherence to the truth, the proud glory of this I and what is beyond world, beyond death. Now he would be free to say it all. All that had to be said. In this saying was his life. In this truth and the witnessing to this truth was his destiny. What more could be asked of it?

A report on the arrests was on the Tsar's desk when he returned from the memorial meeting of the Council of Ministers. Written by Colonel Melgunov it presented the police achievement in glowing terms. Thank God for the police! Their acumen, dedication, swift response. But damn this vile germ and damn it again! Who and what and why were these creatures? It was like original sin - some ancient affliction? They were clearly beyond learning the lesson of '81. Colonel Melgunov's remarks connecting the arrests and the plot with the Volkhov business once again put in question the higher education policy.

He stood by his study window, turned, turned he knew to face directly enough the Fortress, bastion thrusting from Neva's broad waters. Of course! How wisely the ancestors had built. Great Peter - of course! There were those for whom death was too good. Let those not properly human be immured in that darkness below where they belonged. Not death but back, down, to the darkness silence from when they came. Unfit to share in human speech or light. Let them linger out their twilight existence. Great Peter had known all this. Pestel - Petrachevsky - Bakunin - Nechaev -not Russian men but aborted creatures all of them.

There would be no public trial. No public communication of any kind. They would simply vanish. Hanging too good! People would wonder whether they had ever existed, been real. Simply vanish into that silence. A warning. The Minister of the Interior must ensure from this very moment that all knowledge of them be blotted out. All police must be forbidden to mention them in any way. The Fortress guards must be sworn to utmost secrecy.

But in the living with it, the thinking through, some doubt persisted. By morning he had reluctantly decided on a kind of compromise. The ringleaders would be given a trial but in camera. Their hanging inevitable! – but to be carried out in absolute secrecy. The very briefest of press announcements. Neither time nor place to be indicated. Merely the barest fact, in a timeless, placeless void.

Vera Kashkademova, a retired schoolmistress in Simbirsk, widow and close friend of Maria Alexandrovna, received a news cutting of the affair from her sister in St Petersburg. From the Government Herald, it simply named the seven arrested plotters including one Alexander Ulyanov from Simbirsk, leader of the attempted regicide. Her sister recalled Vera's many warm references to the Ulyanovs in her letters, and especially her respect and admiration for Ilya Nikolayevich. Could there possibly be any connection?

The letter also mentioned some of the rumours about in St Petersburg. That dozens more people were involved. That a new wave of terrorism was beginning. And that the Tsar was going to deal ruthlessly with them all.

Vera stared at the cutting unable to relate it to the Ulyanovs, to the Alexander she knew. But these facts must be shown as quickly as possible to Maria Alexandrovna. The implications were terrible but she could not connect them with the Ulyanovs.

But! – absolutely impossible to tell Maria Alexandrovna after all she had been through and borne so magnificently. If it was true! Maria Alexandrovna would of course be informed soon enough in the official way. But that was cowardice! That official way would be even more devastating and the news might by then be circulating through the town from others with St Petersburg connections. No! Maria Alexandrovna must be given the facts now. Just the very strength of their friendship would make it possible, bearable. No! unbearable. Young Vladimir then! That was a way, a closeness that she could bear.

At midday she walked to the Gymnasium to catch Vladimir on his way home. Much tact was needed since his father's death – it wasn't at all easy with him.

She waited as casually as possible some distance away from the main entrance, near the Anchovsky memorial. He came hurrying alone, head lowered, his satchel bulging with books. Final examinations less than two weeks away and he intended to win the Gold Medal. Absolutely no time to waste.

"Vladimir!" she was forced to call out sharply as he came abreast of her. He stopped reluctantly and raised his head to stare at her. She managed a smile.

"Good morning Vera Kashkademova," he said impatiently, "but if you'll excuse me please," and began striding on.

She hurried after him, caught him up and grabbed hold of his arm. He twisted fiercely out of her grip. Whatever was this creature doing, wanting. She was very flustered.

"Vladimir – I have important news for you," she almost pleaded, her face pale, her lips trembling slightly.

"What news? What is all this?" he demanded angrily.

Two classmates were approaching.

She mustn't attract any more attention. But she knew she must mention Alexander's name, in the open, now, against her deepest instincts. She had never wanted it like this.

"It's about Alexander," she whispered loudly, "do follow me!"

Mystified and annoyed he went with her to her apartment. Important news? Sasha? from Vera Kashkademova? Perhaps she was a little dotty – those wretched 'mi' verbs still needed constant practice – night and day – and they'd get it – and he'd master them!

"Please read this," she said quietly, handing him the cutting. He thumped his satchel down in her front room and read it through, once, twice, three times, staring at the blank print whose message fiercely quickened his heartbeat. He looked at her distantly, his eyes puzzled, narrowed.

"Sasha? – a terrorist? – the leader?" he said in a hushed voice to himself as from another, attempt to come to terms with his bewilderment, disbelief.

"This is serious – very serious Vera Kashkademova." He

breathed in sharply, handed her back the cutting, his hand trembling slightly, picked up his satchel, which felt so much heavier, and slowly made his way home. Sasha? A terrorist? The ringleader?

So sheer these facts, so vast, unassailable, across this new landscape of his life. Just this bare naming of them, in stern, most serious acknowledgement of their existence, let alone their implications, making him tremble. And this naming, these facts, these bare sounds, he must simply, somehow pass on as messenger to Mama.

Sasha. A terrorist. The ringleader. Regicide. These facts become the very pulsebeat of his existence, in spite of his disbelief, yet trembling with their implications. He and Sasha and Mama now one. All one.

Unbearable, this anguish, chaos.

He went straight up to his room and took out his Greek grammar ready for revision immediately after lunch. At last, reluctantly, he went downstairs to the dining room where Maria Alexandrovna was sitting at the table set for lunch, waiting for him, surprised, for he was usually very punctual.

"Vladimir! It's your pancake day. They won't keep for ever you know," she gently chided as he sat down at the table.

"Vera Kashkademova asked me in to see her," he said curtly.

"Really? Vera? How nice of her." She was well aware of the awkwardness between them and curious to know more.

He still had not begun eating and looked anxiously at her.

"She had some news for me – it's about Sasha – he's been arrested." He drew breath sharply.

"Sasha arrested? Nonsense!" she smiled. Vladimir was looking deadly serious, frowning.

"What for then? – and how does she know?"

"It's in the papers Mama – the St Petersburg papers. She showed me the cutting."

Maria Alexandrovna waited, tensed.

"It's for terrorism – a bomb plot."

"Sasha?" she exclaimed incredulously.

"It's serious Mama. He was the organiser. They tried to kill the Tsar."

If this was true then Sasha's life was at stake. This thought anchor point – road forward – centre and goal of her existence from now. Nothing else mattered. She too must see that piece of paper. One task only. To save Sasha' life.

"Vladimir I'm going to Vera's. Wait for me!"

On the way she reminded herself of the official contacts available to her in St Petersburg as the widow of a State Councillor. There were too some well-placed relatives on the Blank side living there – and – and – yes already – that final petitioning available – to the highest himself.

Hurrying, struggling to hold off the incredulity of the situation, the wild questions, the dizzying bewilderment that the one she knew, was a total enigma. But only the one, the one she knew counted and for him she would give her all.

Vera was extremely glad to see her at the door of her apartment. Since Vladimir's departure she had thought of nothing else.

"Whatever I can do my dear," she said gently holding her dear friend's hand.

"Just let me see it," said Maria Alexandrovna. She had never doubted Vladimir's account but she had to see it with her own eyes. When Vera handed her the cutting, without reading the details she immediately saw and knew that it was so.

"Vera I'm going to take the train to St Petersburg, from Syzran. Please look in on Vladimir and the children for me. I know you don't quite hit it off with him – but he's a good boy at heart."

She left, not daring to yield to that vastness of feeling which threatened to overwhelm her. Vera understood her tautness, her awkward reserve and prayed for her.

Maria Alexandrovna now knew what had to be. Those that wanted to help, let them help. Vladimir – Vera. But she had work to do and must get on with it.

On the walk back from Vera's the enigma forced itself on her again. Her Sasha must have been fooled, misled. But it couldn't have been so. Her Sasha could never have been misled. And he was the leader!

Some important Simbirsk families including the Veselovskis also received the news from St Petersburg that morning from relatives and friends. They reacted with astonishment and horror. Enough that it should be Alexander Ulyanov, Gold Medallist – but that it should be the son of Ilya Nikolayevich! And if this could happen to the son of Ilya Nikolayevich then who and whose son was safe. Safe? Suddenly the name Ulyanov became a danger signal for many in Simbirsk. The implications were extremely grave. Each was compelled to assess their relationship to the Ulyanovs and take action accordingly, however painful and embarrassing. We loyal citizens of Simbirsk have unwittingly been harbouring a monster in our midst, a potential regicide, one committed to the ultimate horror. From this very moment for our own sakes, the world – the authority must be vigorously made aware of our utter revulsion. No more contact with the Ulyanovs. Best of all for Simbirsk that the Ulyanovs vanish as quickly as possible from her loyal and peaceful bosom – children too must be instructed accordingly. Indeed who knew whether the authorities were not already in Simbirsk beginning their investigation. Dr Arefyev was right of course – now you could see why the young scoundrel – a dark one if ever – always secretive – you could see clearly as anything – of course he couldn't go to the funeral if he was plotting all this dreadful business. They'd been right all the time. Only a monster wouldn't have gone to his father's funeral, let alone if his father had been Ilya Nikolayevich. And they could let the authorities know all this straight away.

Vera told Maria Alexandrovna that Lydia Vorontsev the tea merchant's wife and Elizabeth Veselovski were making a coach journey to Syzran sometime this week. The Syzran coach ran twice a week and it was usual for people making the journey to arrange to travel together on the same day if possible. The hundred and twenty mile trip was arduous, much less so in friendly company.

Maria Alexandrovna asked Vladimir to go to the Veselovski's and ask if Elizabeth would share the coach with her tomorrow. She'd certainly understand her awful predicament. He went off cheered that his mother would be with friends on the journey, very thought a warmth tempering that fearful isolation.

Maria Alexandrovna began packing with the help of Annushka the maid, vaguely assuming that she would be in the capital three to four weeks. Vaguely. If she thought about it too intently a kind of possibility marking the end of that period touched her with a trembling, a dizziness.

On his way to the Veselovski's Vladimir sensed his mother's departure with dread. But nothing must be allowed to weaken his most earnest resolve. To come first in the exams. Resolve renewed in this very moment, feeling something secret, maturing, of himself, a responsibility, yet so real, for them all, as one. Sasha, Mama, Anna, Olga, Dimitry and Maria, the Ulyanovs – as one! Strongly, firmly, he would conduct himself here at home in Simbirsk while Mama went, so bravely went. He here, but at her side. He here, but at Sasha's side, more responsibly, more resolutely than ever.

The thin elderly maid showed him into the Veselovski's drawing room which he had last been in eight months ago for Gerasim's sixteenth birthday party. He could hear the voices of Veselovski and his wife talking and arguing in the adjoining dining room where they were still sitting after their lunch. Ivan Veselovski had eaten little. The news from St Petersburg had upset him considerably.

Elizabeth reminded him of his funeral speech and of the fact that she had warned him at the time that it was too fulsome. Warned? She had never warned him! Absolute rubbish! She had praised it! On the contrary. He -he was the one who had done all the warning. Couldn't she see, foolish woman. He must have had a sixth sense. Somewhere he must have known of this viper in their midst. His speech was one long warning, thank God!

After a sudden quiet the maid returned and without looking at Vladimir announced, "Madame Veselovski is ill. She cannot see you."

Vladimir was puzzled.

"This is a serious matter," he said sternly looking straight at her.

"Go please and tell your mistress that my mother Maria Alexandrovna has to go on the Syzran coach and would she please join her. My brother Alexander is in trouble in St Petersburg. The matter is urgent," he said, feeling thwarted and awkward in his way of putting it.

With a sigh of impatience, even disdain, the maid left the room. Vladimir listened intently, still puzzled, and heard a brief murmur of conversation. She returned and once more announced without looking at him, "My mistress wishes to tell Vladimir Ulyanov that she has no intention whatever of travelling to Syzran. Today or any other day Master says."

Vladimir stepped straight past her out of the room and reached fiercely for the handle of the adjoining dining room door.

"Whatever's going on here?" he called out, bewildered,

gripping the handle and turning it.

Most urgent danger had shot Veselovski to the door at the sound of that turning handle which he gripped with all his might against against – suddenly slack – and the footsteps leaving thank God!

Vladimir, letting go with disgust after that first immediate test of strength, strode out of the house, trembling, shocked, deeply hurt that this should have been done to him. Furious to hit back. How dare Mama's friends treat him like this!

He turned about in the street, and about again in sickening indecision. He would go straight back to Mama and complain bitterly about being subjected to this treatment. It was Mama's fault. The Veselovskis had gone mad. He'd tell them so right now. No! He wouldn't cross that stinking threshold again. He'd report them.

Again he turned about and went along to the Vorontsev's house. He'd ask Madame Vorontsev about the Veselovskis, first thing for he had to have an answer. Lydia Vorontsev's carriage was waiting outside the house and the coachman stood holding the door open as she came down the path to step inside. She turned her head momentarily to glance down the street. Vladimir waved cheerfully and called out loudly,

"A moment please Madame Vorontsev!"

She jumped into the coach ordering the startled coachman, "Off! Off!"

Vladimir quickened his pace in desperation, knowing that she had recognised him. As the coach clattered away he stopped, turned about and made for home striding faster, running.

What the devil was happening? He must know.

He hurried into the hallway where the cases were lying open and packing well under way.

"Mama what's going on – what's the matter with your friends?"

One of his difficult moods? just at a time like this.

"What d'you mean?"

"I don't know – I don't know. They were all odd – very odd towards me."

"How – odd? Tell me Vladimir – exactly – what d'you mean?"

"But Mama – the Veselovskis wouldn't see me – they – they held on to the door handle to stop me going in. And when I called out to Madame Vorontsev, she jumped into her carriage and drove off. What's the matter with them Mama? Whatever's going on?"

He was very distressed and angry.

"You shouldn't have made me go Mama. It was wrong to let them treat me like that. I'm not going to stand for it."

Maria Alexandrovna sensed a connection – within the bounds of possibility! She must tell him straight away. But how to tell him? This was Vladimir! To excuse them? – a betrayal of him!

They were being called to draw on something deep – Vladimir too.

"It's to do with Sasha – that's all it could be. They must know too," she said quietly.

"To do with Sasha? What d'you mean?"

"They're afraid. Just be strong Vladimir. Take no notice. They'll get over it. I'll write all the news from St Petersburg and be back soon. You just work for your exams. Take no notice at all. You're the man of the house now. Look after your sisters and brother. I won't be long away."

Grigori the coachman drove them to the coach station. No one else boarded the Syzran coach. Vladimir told Grigori to drive back home without him. As he walked home, each house passed, or friend or acquaintance threatened with uncertainty and confusion. The whole neighbourhood, once so intimate was holding him off. His mother's words hadn't really helped him. He still couldn't see a connection with Sasha. Her words did not touch this bitter experience of treachery, hostility, some poisonous venom permeating the whole place.

The pain of this rejection – it was nothing less – struck deep. Incomprehensible injustice! He had done nothing to any of them. At last his own house in sight. House, home, our home, refuge, bastion, as he went into Father's study for long kept well clear.

Whole house emptier than ever now with Mama gone, flame of a grim anger slowly kindled.

Maria Alexandrovna watched him, as the Syzran coach drew her away, standing there, not waving but raising his arm and holding it in a kind of salutation. Yes, he knew how serious it all was. Whatever is going on Mama? Whatever is going on?

She hadn't properly answered him – couldn't from this whirl of her life.

With sweet relief borne into a light doze. Into that warm

family place of – oh how long ago? Or was she dreaming? Turning wheels bearing her painfully, blissfully – some happiness? – pride of children – husband – children's games – stories – Gold Medals – endless reverie – and bitter! Back – out! – wrenched back! to this present. To this life of his now on trial.

No matter how fantastic, impenetrable his appearance, she knew that it was still him there. He beyond all appearances, all timetricks. So quickly their withdrawal, shunning. She was as one unclean. Through and through. Tainted by her own. But she would stand by her own – in spite of this burning shame.

Their shunning was intended to weaken her bond with Sasha. Intended to make her blame him, curse him for bringing about her rejection by society. But she would stand by him more resolutely still. Now more than ever he needed her. And now more than ever she would be there for him.

Ilya Nikolayevich my dearest one it would have killed you.

"How anyone could have murdered that saintly man in cold blood is incomprehensible."

Beyond comprehension, only prayer, just as – just as? – then – Sasha – participating – participating! – so reverently in the family prayers for the poor murdered Tsar.

So contradictory overwhelming – incomprehensible – yet a power – her life was spreading, deepening – something theme-like obscurely felt – a meaning – which she herself was beginning to shape, to utter, to live.

On arriving in St Petersburg she went straight to the apartment of her cousin Mikhail Blank and his wife Olga, having to assume that she would be made welcome – supported.

Over the years a warm friendship going back to childhood Kokushkino days, had endured, even though rarely meeting since then.

The Blanks, especially Mikhail were shocked by the news of Alexander's arrest. Their immediate sympathy for Marie Alexandrovna was deep. Her ring and appearance at their door was an utter surprise leaving them to painfully realise that they had never considered even the possibility of her coming here – so soon!

Of course there was a room for her – help in every way!

But where did it leave one?

What could should one do say to with for her?

The longer she stayed with the Blanks the more uneasy

Mikhail became. Maria Alexandrovna confided in them and sought their advice concerning her daily dealings with the authorities. But increasingly Mikhail found himself trying to hold something off – something most unpleasant – something that he dared not truly face.

But it would not leave him alone. That Alexander, that quiet dedicated student son of his dear bereaved cousin – had done it.

Saying what? this Alexander – saying what?

Calling into question what? – just what?

All of yourself!

Of course you know well – that this moment of truth is not to be betrayed.

Calling into question this Alexander your whole wishy-washy so-called liberalism.

You are the spewed out.

Where do you really stand?

Who the devil was asking this question?

That it would ever come to that for him? – being even forced to face it in his thinking?

Of course a dreadful business – the very worst.

And yet – that Alexander – most promising career ahead – whole life yet to be lived – but what kind of a life? – had done it!

Asking such questions?

Had he never considered – looking back – forced to look back – never considered – even as most infinitely distant possibility – any idea like that?

Never?

And – if Alexander – what then of his own son?

Who then could be trusted?

Ridiculous! – not at all ridiculous!

This sympathy for dear cousin – a danger in it?

For his life's fullness and future – for Olga's – for his son's?.

Maria Alexandrovna set about seeking interviews with anyone whom she thought could usefully advise or use influence in any way on Alexander's behalf. These included high officials in the Ministry of Education, including Minister Delyanov himself. Tirelessly she went the rounds from one office to another gleaning as much information as she could on the case itself and her best procedure. She was treated with the respect and sympathy due to the wife of a State Councillor and provincial

Director of schools whose reputation stood high in St Petersburg. But most unfortunate that he had sired a monster.

It was soon made clear that her most immediately effective act would be a detailed petition to the Tsar, setting out her husband's career and her son's, with supporting affidavits from the relevant authorities. A lawyer at the Ministry of Education would help her in this.

The Tsar received her long petition a few days after he had decided on a trial in camera, by handpicked Senators whom he could trust, to be followed by a secret hanging. Reading carefully through Ilya Nikolayevich Ulyanov's record, he was considerably impressed. Almost exemplary subjects in their way - to be pitied - a dreadful outcome! having spawned such a cunning criminal. The son's record showed clearly that he'd fooled everyone. Kept his criminal instincts hidden till the very last moment.

This hiddenness was the most devilish aspect. That no-one in this loyal family had grasped till far too late what they were harbouring in their midst. The best way he could help this poor woman was to let her see this son of hers - *'Gold medal graduate - so absorbed in his scientific studies'* - as he really was, for the very first time.

'if my son's mind and heart have become blurred -'

if? if? - poor creature - what else could she - dare she say -

'I shall set him on the right path again -'

too late! much too late poor deluded creature!

Let her see his criminality nakedly exposed in its natural surroundings, unable to hide. Let her visit him in the Alexis Ravelin, wisely built by his forbears, to house that whole brood of such wild beasts. Her awakening would be painful but merciful. She would soon realise that for such criminality there could only be one possible punishment.

Alexander directed, in the margin of the petition, that she be allowed to attend the trial as well. Let her see just how merciful and understanding he was in these matters. Let her be granted this privilege of attendance in order to see the accused in his true colours, cast out, already held in abhorrence by all.

Two weeks before the trial was due to start Maria Alexandrovna received a letter from the Minister of the Interior, Count Dimitri Tolstoy. The Minister informed her of the Tsar's merciful permission to visit her son in the Peter and Paul Fortress, and also to attend his trial which would not be in public.

She was surprised, encouraged and humbly grateful. She would see Alexander, would be with him. Nothing must be left undone. Nothing else mattered except that he live. She answered the Minister, asking that her most humble gratitude be conveyed to the Tsar for his beneficence.

The Minister wrote another letter to General Subkovsky, the Fortress Governor, ordering him to ensure that the prisoner was not informed ahead of the visit. His Majesty certainly knew a thing or two. Likely indeed that this mother could be persuaded to get the wretch to speak out frankly on those who obviously were behind this whole affair. The People's Will – or whoever. A cosy room then near the Governor's office – tact – discretion with her – but Subkovsky? – nothing tactful about him!

Maria Alexandrovna excitedly showed Count Tolstoy's letter to her cousin. He was alerted by the reference to the secret nature of the trial and felt pessimistic. He kept it to himself and encouraged her in every way.

Since their arrest the seven had been kept isolated in different parts of the Fortress. Alexander had been taken to the Alexis Ravelin, itself isolated by a moat from the rest of the Fortress. The grey arching wall of his cell, No. 5, was thickly draped with webs of living and shrivelled spiders. Beetles and centipedes wandered about. Through the stone flags crept Neva's slime. The bed and table were bolted down. A perpetual twilight filtered through the high barred window painted over with lime.

The silence, at first felt as nothing particularly unusual, was taking on a deepening, a permanence, overpowering presence of a strange realm. A silence established over decades on orders from above. Prisoners were not permitted to speak. If they coughed, moved about or knocked loudly on the wall, the guard would quietly lift the green felt curtain covering the judas-eye glass, and peer through. This silence, ordered from above as active deed, as profound gesture made the very guards ever more spectral.

Alexander felt fatefully overcome, reduced to this spectral life and fought back hard to maintain some balance, to resist being sucked away into that void, on the edge of a madness. Dense, hostile this world from which the word had been forcibly withdrawn. Echoing, hollow as the very body of things was sucked away into that emptiness which crept about him, menacing.

This was the enemy's gesture and somehow he must find the strength to fight back. Somehow he would, turn, turn to that sure flame of himself and believe in its own reality. From those depths, old, friendly depths, he knew resolve, resolve being forged by himself yet not entirely by himself. A strength welling up which he could join with and claim as his own. Resolution ever clearer, fiercer as he saw how he could turn all this to his own advantage.

Into this very silence of theirs would sound out the purity, sharp uncanny even for him to himself, of his words. Their silence had created a space for him to test out the very timbre of himself.

His struggle ceased as the menacing presence around him became transformed. His strength renewed, place within inviolable, truesounding silence of himself, the gesture of those around become pitiful, of last resort, as he set to work on his trial speech with words which of course could be his last. With words felt not entirely his, rising ahead of him, wrought from the warmth of this encouraging silence, this friendly presence, human? – impersonal? – mysteriously, sweetly, enduringly beyond both.

More – this manmade silence ringing with the men about him.

With words which he felt were his very life substance, the work itself very life-deed. Truth – logic – clarity – light – a weaving through.

His words, destined to come into their own.

No Vasily! no anger towards you.

From the first this naiveté – this relying on bombs and revolvers!

Alexander Ulyanov – the great bombmaker!

Lesson if ever that this logic, reason – methodical labour of logic and reason cannot be shortcut. For the men to come – bullets and bombs will not convince. Truth-forged word alone – the real deed!

This was a calm, a peace prevailing, abiding in him, strong, joyfully strong he knew.

This pain – of his dear ones, he would endure – never seek to assuage but hold to it from the strength of this calm prevailing.

Maria Alexandrovna waited in the room near Governor Subkovsky's office. Had she heard correctly, that certain information – might be – a real consideration for leniency?

Could it be, such a possibility? as the Governor had declared so firmly – "Of course!" – of course? – "your son and the others were being used – manipulated – no question about that."

Pain of ever new uncertainty but at last to reach him, through that desperate maze of offices – pleas – humble requests, humble humble humble wherever it led, right through the great Petrovsky Gate, to find him again. But now these surroundings as nothing – made mere surroundings by this meeting.

Being thus allowed, and to attend the trial, surely some recognition by His Majesty! But what recognition?

Such arrogance!

Even to dare question!

Only, and only humblest gratitude to His Majesty.

Sasha was his accused would-be murderer!

Come to terms with that – on your knees!

Just to see him, be with him – gratitude!

Just to see be with and question. Question? Gently now – but somehow to get her bearings – just where he is standing? To know him – anew – but cautiously. Listen to this warning – cautiously!

Cautiously – with Sasha? And that 'information' of the Governor!

Was it Ilya Nikolayevich's life of loyal service?

Life?

Pray for composure! Composure!

Alexander's cell door was opened.

"Prisoner Ulyanov – outside!"

How unfamiliar that sound of a human voice. He could only follow, out of the cell, into the corridor, in some helplessness, feeling the presence of another guard behind him as they moved slowly along.

Feeling the presence of the guard behind him as they moved slowly along the stone corridors, turned suddenly right, ascending onto wooden floors, comforting human surroundings, a carpeted corridor, the door opened for him to pass through.

"Mama," he whispered, voice trapped weeping.

Pain of such guilt, deepest voice breaking forth with relief. She, source, focus, most bitter challenge.

Lifedeath from through her.

Papa! Papa!

Yield, embrace through the flood of this pain.

Down down on his knees for forgiveness to embrace – cling tight through this weeping from intimate ones each to each.

Her Sasha!

When will words come? what words? how words? this fierce storm weep through together.

Living affirmation of each other beyond all judgement.

But even as they embraced the pulse of the tides of withdrawal gathered, to himself, to his very own.

She knew she must stand firm, so desperate this need of his to be taken back. Stand firm for him, he is yours, is telling you now he is yours – and ever so remaining – ever so – what more?

Only for both to wait till the weeping ceased of itself.

He stood up.

They sat by the table turned to each other, awaiting words.

"Mama I do know. It's terrible – terrible – what you and the family have to bear. But – how can I tell you? – Papa too, Papa too! what I owe my country – my people – so wretched here in our Russia. It's – it's – that my life must make things good. I can't live in any other way – how can I explain? How can you understand?"

"Yes! – I do, I do – but this way – it's so horrible."

Said! Said so! Said then.

"But what can one do if nothing else works – if there's no other way," he challenged, already on his guard, distanced, that all this had been planned by their desperate cunning to unnerve him. No warning! Just through Mama, who else?

She heard the challenge, threshold crossed, warned – no other way!

Sasha's truth – prepare yourself somehow.

Alexander knew he must hold his ground and take the initiative.

For her sake no illusions. He knew her strength, her truth.

"I wanted to kill a man Mama – no other word for it. That means that I too –may – may be killed."

The may for her sake – thankfully managed. The deed must take its course.

He wanted her to come to terms, begin to come to terms with this truth right now as a measure of his strength and her strength.

Just as he was reconciled to his destiny – so for her too that there was no other way but to be reconciled to it also.

No! not at all to stifle hope – her hope – but that this hope abide by this truth.

That she must try and come to terms right now with the end, with his acceptance of the end.

He knew her strength.

He would turn their talk to the family. Those left living are what she must concern herself with.

She, after it was all over, would know, believing in him as ever she they all did, that he did what he had to do. She knew, Mama, well, that it would never be – have been! – any other for him. So he lived the truth of himself – and what more for a son of hers could she have wished? And that pain never to leave her was the pain of the world.

So warmly restored to the familiar human by her presence. She still felt by him as source of self-giving life of his life. That was Mama! But this other him, stern, aloof was compassionate too.

Both knew to bear this tension in a communing.

This his guilt and this his truth could only be lived, never resolved.

Accused under Articles 241 and 243 of the Penal Code, the fifteen were seated behind one another on three benches, flanked by gendarmes. In the front row sat the seven main accused, watched intently by the senators. Final speeches were due and Alexander was chosen to make his first.

He had been memorising it for days, theme by theme and word by word, in order when he uttered it, without reading from the paper in his hand, to be present in it fully, with the court, facing them. Only then, he felt, would his total commitment be present in the sounding words themselves as a very force. Keenly aware of the impatient, hostile judge, the pitiful evasions of Shevyrev, the firmness of Osipanov, the unexpected appearance of Mama, and the embarrassed distaste of the government appointed defence lawyers for their task, the moment approached for him to speak into all that and beyond it, and in that moment he sensed for himself, a destiny, culmination, completion. These unknown Senators – Russia's way of facing him. That all was as it should be. The bombs had not exploded. Only the word was left. A final confrontation through the word as he prepared to stand up before them, these unknown ones, naked to their nakedness. Final confrontation there from the beginning.

All was as it should be.

"Prisoner Alexander Ilyich Ulyanov!"

He stood up feeling in what was happening a fullness, meaningfulness transcending past and future time itself. In this moment of completion these externalities were but signs, gestures. Head held high, his deep-set eyes took in all those who watched him so intently, feeling through that look a fragile boundary, no more, and then beyond.

The senators leaned forward. Judge Deyer tightened his lips, pulled off his spectacles in one hand and stared sharply back at Alexander, suspicious of his every move. The five were culpably guilty,. There remained only to hear the sound of contrition and permissibly, the excuses of their unfortunate lawyers about being misguided by criminal ideas etc., etc. Thank God he'd never had to endure being picked from the rota and playing that game. Still, loyalty to the Tsar made all things possible.

Calmly Alexander told the court that he disputed none of the facts about the plot. But that was of little concern. Of crucial importance for Russia now and for the future was that the court understand the imperative need for freedom of thought and speech – the right to think freely as an inalienable right – its requirement an obligation to all human dignity.

He continued in the same calm manner of one whose task, with all the time in the world, is to explain something of great importance to those who simply haven't grasped the simplest of facts. The only right way to influence society, for the development of society, for the bringing of light into the consciousness of society is through word – thought – ideas, the press, writing, speaking. Thinking must be left free if it is to be true to its nature. The dignity, the uprightness, the very meaning of man centres on this ability, this need, this right to think freely, openly in public exchange. To defend this freedom, this right, against a powerful State which would deny it, deny man this dignity, is a great honour, a worthy sacrifice.

He stopped because he knew he had to but more, much more he could have told them. That in the very process of thinking he'd learned to recognise an ultimate – a teacher – objective – impersonal – universal – which these here now and eventually all, would come to understand. Universal or it is nothing. Come to understand directly like himself by approaching the process from its immediate inwardness, or through some painful labyrinth of experience.

In response to close questioning by chief prosecutor Neklyudov, Alexander, slowly, sought to clarify as accurately as possible his changing role. As accurately as words would allow. That he was not the initiator or organiser. That there had not been a definite initiator or organiser. But, that he was one of the very first, not the first, but one of the very first to advocate the founding of a terrorist group. Later, certainly, he and Shevyrev were central.

Neklyudov, listening very carefully, listening in some way to his equal and match, determinedly aiming at just such accuracy, decided on Ulyanov's overall role as an - indispensable - accessory. And indispensable means all. Yet he could not forbear in his summing-up - as equal to equal? - almost rebuking Alexander for insisting that he had taken on by far the greatest responsibility. Alexander, listening as carefully, heard clearly that he had taken on nothing. On the contrary, hearing that he alone was the pivot on which all turned. Had he withdrawn - all would have dissolved away. In this looking back he saw with some amazement how he had infused with his whole substance - planning, organising, making, writing - energetic beyond measure - and the others kept going by him.

The Senators heard Ulyanov with increasing impatience and anger. His arrogance, presumption, beyond belief.

He would instruct them, correct them!

His 'of course' he'd committed the crime! - as though they were imbeciles to have imagined for one second that he would have pretended otherwise, like that pathetic creature Shevyrev. No! That wasn't his game at all. Nor were the crimes the important thing! - Eh? - a madman!

There was something more important than the crimes - thinking!

Literally - a madman!

And his tone - his tone!

Where was he standing - to speak like that? - so erect.

Perverse - rambling - his justification.

That stance, arrogance - to be cut down to size!

Undoubtedly a kind of madness - shutting himself off from reality - from any sane respect for authority.

Clearly he hadn't grasped that he was on trial. That his life was in the hands of the highest one and that contrition alone was the only meaningful act left for him. Only madness could explain it.

This refusal to plead for mercy, for the continuance of his life, repeat, repeat, the continuance of my life, was a plain case of insanity. Or was it all a pose, sheer bravado? But that too could only be a form of madness.

Still ranting on, poor Judge Deyer.

"That will do! accused Ulyanov," ah, thank God he's had enough.

"You've already told us what brought you to this crime –"

"I wanted to prove –"

The swine's not stopping!

"– that terrorism is the inevitable result of the prevailing conditions and contradictions in life. Is it not a fact that whereas we have the opportunity to develop our intellectual powers, we are deprived of the possibility of exercising them for our country's benefit. An objective scientific appraisal of the causes, such as I have given, however strange it may appear to the Prosecutor, will be much more useful for those who reject the idea of terror than mere indignation. That is all I wanted to say."

All!

Incredible! to the very end! And not a single word to suggest his own position, his fate.

Just watch Judge Deyer's face. Now he'll give it to him. His Majesty has certainly chosen the right man to deal with this lot.

Alexander sat down grateful for the completion of his task. Osipanov nudged him comfortingly. Judge Deyer delicately adjusted the bridge of his spectacles and pursed his lips, slow, gestures of a power, gathering, focusing, preparing to strike. Alexander heard the inevitability of it all from the judge's moving lips, the power of that speaking-I, his highest, purest, still with him. That I which had discovered itself in the very speaking, him and not him, savouring it still as the judge's thin lips moved. Risen, expanding, invulnerable, transparent, one with that here, as yet beyond them all. I, voice of this ardent desire through the broad stream of his being to quench their dryness with light. Light!

I, forged in that sanctuary of silence, where he'd found his true voice. No! not of separation – but for a real unity with these ones around him. Sanctuary, to which he could at any time withdraw.

I, responsible for all that has happened, been done. That truly these others should not be found responsible, punished.

"This, members of the court is surely the ultimate. So-called scientific reasoning, so-called objective logic used to prove that murder is a necessity. This is surely the criminal mind in its most cunning and diseased form. The posture, the audacity of the accused Ulyanov beggars belief. What we have seen is a display of megalomania - no less! This strutting, prevaricating Ulyanov is an impostor and must pay the price accordingly."

Mock on! Mock on!

Me you touch not!

"We are not interested in his development towards socialism made out as of necessity. Necessity? There was nothing necessary about such a development. But of course a diseased personality will try and excuse itself - more especially if it has intellectual pretensions - instead of seeking contrition and confessing its evil nature. But far more frightening gentlemen as a symptom of utter degeneration and self-deceit, he blames the very process of thought itself. He even abjures responsibility for his own thinking. Surely the ultimate prevarication. The implications, though that is not our task here, are appalling. Let those responsible for the higher education of our youth note them - with utmost seriousness."

"On the one hand we were lectured on some so-called autonomous development of society according to some so-called higher scientific laws - knowledge of which of course the accused alone are privy to - and on the other - of the individual necessity for avenging deeds - to be carried out gentlemen - by these self-appointed avengers. Such evil prevarication. Such pernicious fantasy. Sick minds? Satanic seduction? You may well wonder. Certainly I heard a sympathetic note regarding the accused's 'appalling inefficiency' - 'obvious amateurishness' - and such like excuses on the grounds of youthful misguidance. Excuses I'm sure intended out of - what shall we call them - decent motives. But we are not here to concern ourselves with such decent motives. We are here to ensure the security of our great Russian nation. That nation for whom murder is murder."

"This attempted murder at its basest and most criminal. Pure and simple. The guilt has never been in doubt. Nor can there be any other possible punishment than death by hanging. The

Tsar, most sacred of our nation, has been threatened and by God's great mercy spared. For Ulyanov and his fellow criminals there can only be one possible sentence. A sentence which merely confirms what the accused themselves have already accomplished – their complete removal beyond human society with whom they are not fit to live."

"Nor shall I desist from insisting once again that those responsible for our country's higher education take serious note of what is happening here. What! Dissertations on terrorism! – no less! from this Gold Medallist Ulyanov – not to be encouraged, eh? Russian society will not be terrorised by these insane young criminals. They will be rooted out and destroyed with all their insane casuistry."

The Senators felt jovial.

Judge Deyer's words – absolute triumph – some great fear exorcised – that Ulyanov's daring to mouth about our country – sacred – shown up as purest blasphemy. Such a shield, saving grace, men like Judge Deyer.

As Judge Deyer's speech ended Alexander was aware of a loss, of a painful emptiness at the back of the court where once – once! – had been Mama. Having spotted her just before the proceedings began, utterly surprised and consoled by her unexpected appearance, the very intonation of his speaking had been modulated by her presence for she above all was the one whose burden was greatest. How could she reconcile it all? This Alexander with her Alexander?

When he looked into that space, that emptiness, on the back bench between the heads of two Senators who had joined in the spontaneous burst of clapping for Judge Deyer, looked, searched ever deeper into it, he knew desolation. Why had she gone? Had she heard his speech? Had she really been there?

That emptiness told irrevocably of what could never be! Such sadness from that place out there – of those so close – and that Kokushkino morning light. He had done what had to be done, but such sadness, desolation of that and those which never again would be.

Much strengthened by Alexander's composure and words, in which they heard their ultimate justification, Osipanov, Andreyushkin and Generalov managed briefly and calmly to make their final speeches. Generalov had learned so much, so quickly about this power which had treated him no differently from the others in spite of his confession and the names he had supplied. He knew now that he was indeed no different. Alexander's speech, composure, and warmth towards him in the courtroom had shamed him, drawn forth once more an avowal for their common aim.

Judge Deyer looked sternly at Shevyrev. He had sat throughout head down, next to Andreyushkin. The gendarme at his side, responding smartly to the judge's meaningful nod, shook him by the arm. His head lolled. The gendarme let go. Watched intently by the court Shevyrev breathed in sharply, hoarsely, slowly came to his feet, tentatively drew his face toward the Judge, blinked, shaped his lips and hovered in that posture, a look of anxiety, desperation taking hold. Swaying, he sank down again, head dropped.

Dispossessed, fiery vision gone, feeble ghost of himself, he was unable to account for what was happening since his arrest in Yalta. His plea of not guilty was interpreted by the court as extraordinarily naive or barefaced or pitiful.

Some senators were sympathetic, approving of his gestures. That slumped figure demonstrated a very real awareness of the supreme power's omnipotence. Or was he pretending insanity - in line with his unbelievable protestation of innocence in face of all the evidence. That he'd had nothing to do with it. That 'nothing' made everyone smile. For him it was just that. When he looked back and tried to establish a connection with what they were all saying happened, it was like trying to establish connection with a dream. And the one they said had done this that and the other, the one they said was him - he simply could not relate to meaningfully.

Alexander could only wonder at and pity this Shevyrev with his "No - never!" - "No - never!" repeated again and again, fearful, desperate. Where was Shevyrev hiding? He had been the inspirer. Did he think one could placate that power? That at the last minute he could turn it into a game with words? What dreadful selfwounds he was inflicting with this lying and cowardice! What awful corruption was this denial!

For Osipanov and Andreyushkin this whining creature told of what they could never be. A dire warning - the slumped one beside them, that this struggle was deadly serious and Alexander's words its voice. Men were watching - Russian men - how they bore themselves. Just as they'd watched the five before them.

And this stance, must, as the highest of which they were capable, speak to others likewise - likewise.

Maria Alexandrovna listened to Alexander in growing confusion, such authority, dignity, but he was making things worse for himself, for them all!

Of course his life was at stake!

She dared not be seen by him, hiding in the back row somehow behind the Senators. Such pain to be here at all but must, to show to all around, her own, the Ulyanovs' deepest gratitude for the Tsar's benevolence in allowing her to be here. Torture! Allowing her to be tortured.

To win some favour for the whole family's future.

Awake! Awake! to that voice those words - calm lucid - at peace with himself. I know who it is - the voice words of that secret one, silent one, speaking at last. Secret Alexander yet ever dimly divined, sounding in all its fullness from the start, vibrant with a destiny, certainty, necessity.

Had she expected pleading?

What was she doing in this strange place?

She here he there awful abyss between them.

He was telling of the end unbearable.

Her secret Alexander long divined, heard with aching heart.

My son. I have born you. Your death will be my death.

Oh that he'd had to do it. But in that 'had' she knew, for him, was that same truth which had been strength for them all.

No! No weeping here - leave this place!

Bend low, somehow creep away from it - or on this edge go to pieces.

She must not go to pieces.

This will be a different dying to Ilya Nikolayevich's!

No! not to be warded off in any way such a thought - a visitation.

Only hope in God's Mercy and Goodness in for all things.

Olga, waiting anxiously on this day of Alexander's final speech, was very upset at Maria Alexandrovna's unexpectedly early return, pale, trembling, unable to speak. Whatever was it?

"Impossible - impossible -" was for a long time all Maria Alexandrovna could manage in desperation.

Eventually that evening, Olga and Mikhail grasped from her painful efforts to recount something sounding coherent, that Alexander's final speech was in no way a defence. On the contrary, he simply explained the principles on which he firmly stood and from which he had acted.

Didn't he want to live then?

Mikhail was forced to realise - it could only be something like - seeing he was a Gold Medallist, with a brilliant academic career predicted - something like - that there was for him something more precious than a brilliant career- than life itself!

What a sharpness piercing through so stubbornly from his own past in the light of this realisation.

What light was this?

And what light then lights my day now?

Sentences of death by hanging were passed four days later. A further seven days were allowed for clemency petitions to be submitted, which the Special Session of the Senators would consider before sending His Majesty their final report.

The Senators had decided that the five must be made a clear example.

The five were not prepared to submit petitions.

Mikhail pressed Maria Alexandrovna that she go to the House of Preliminary Detention and insist that Alexander write a petition. In spite of her depression, moments of incoherence, nausea, she must do this thing for her very own sake.

Do it because it could and must be done. Anything that could, must be done. How allow ourselves to think otherwise?

Never to forget, insisted Mikhail, grasping at anything, that she alone of all parents involved, had been allowed to attend the trial, surely a beneficent sign.

What else could one do but insist that she do what had to be done. In spite of her despair - on the very edge!

Somehow she prepared herself, even with the ever present courtroom memory, the knowing of what she had endured.

She knew she must go, even knowing that Alexander's whole stand - so praiseworthy! could only point to one possible outcome.

In the House of Preliminary Detention, Alexander knew that the waiting had begun, that the days could be counted, that towards Mama and the family the pain of this anguish was to be borne to the very end. But let his words be known clearly, spoken, heard,- through this writing down - letter of life -by those he loved.

"I realise my dear sister Anechka, that I am endlessly to

blame for all the grief I have brought down on you and mother -
that is the first thing I must say to you and beg your forgiveness.
I need not enumerate all the suffering that I have caused you
both, for everything is so obvious. Please, forgive me if you can."

But that too - yes! - to relive - be relived through him - with a new gratitude as a life ended, as the life of another, all the good things - all the very goodness that life itself has given freely.

At very short notice his young State attorney Knyazev informed him that his mother was coming to visit. Some more desperate cunning? with sentence passed! It could only be again to weaken him.

Resigned to death, and the authorities were letting her visit him? Letting her? what was he thinking of? She was Mama! Whatever was he trying to wriggle out of again - coward!

This pain of being forced to face Mama was also his truth.

But they the family were Russia too, all of them, and it was for them too he had done it.

Maria Alexandrovna prepared herself, learned it by heart, refined it down to the simplest possible that she must simply utter as a messenger, but as herself, herself's awkwardness, impossibility of being with him.

Because I want you to live - to live - can't you see? That's why I've come, why I'm here, why I speak.

Alexander knew he must be gentle with her, but truthful, gently truthful, he must make things good for her. But only the truth, relying on the truth to make all good in some way.

"Mama, I did see you there," he began after their tearful embrace, all to mean brave Mama! bravely become reconciled. After that first meeting it could only mean that. She had been allowed at the trial - and she had come.

Simply now for her to speak it, that he hear it from her.

"Alexander - have you sent in your petition?"

Gently now!

"Petition Mama?"

Same tone! But this time she must take it on - this life of her life was not to be extinguished. This she would not have.

"Of course - you must begin immediately. Ask forgiveness of the Emperor. Confess your sinful deeds. Explain to him how you were led astray against your better judgement - how - Sasha? - can't you see what you have to do?"

So painful her desperation but that tide of withdrawal was

gathering him back, pure, stern. Gently, calmly he spoke, "But Mama – none of that is true. I have no sin to confess. I don't seek his forgiveness. I wasn't misguided by anyone."

Such invulnerability!

Words unutterable, from some vastness approaching – but unutterable. Don't you want to live? My son. I have born you. Your death will be my death too.

No – it was not to be, meaningfulness of her womb – this abrupt ending of such promise. That he would be – would have been compensation for Ilya Nikolayevich's miserable ending – that dream broken!

She was pleading beyond herself, beyond all knowing, even that such pleading with Alexander was of no avail.

She felt stupid, needing desperately a way to that distant place where she could only sense him.

"Mama – can you imagine me stuck away in Schlüsselburg for life – surrounded by religious books – the only possible alternative," he said smiling.

Of course she could imagine it! and even there managed a feeble gesture.

"Alexander you're young – your views may well change – we all do – –"

"Mama!" roused – gentle! be gentle, "d'you really want me to become an imbecile rotting away in Schlüsselburg for the rest of my life?"

A numbness took her over and she gazed emptily.

He was gathered in confusion and tried again to make a contact. But he was no longer able to face her. This numbness was telling that reconciliation was impossible – had no part in any of this.

After she left he felt threatened by that numbness, forced to let it reveal itself in confrontation – as a veil, veiling that which he knew simply to resist. That which he knew he must from the depths acknowledge – in all its unfathomable purity as son – purely as son.

That you are my mother, but as if said now for the first time, the power, awakening, closeness – threat.

That through you – – that the Tsar too had a mother who was still alive.

Bow – bow low.

A petition to the man – only a man! – whom he had planned

to kill – whom his truth assured must be killed! That couldn't be done.

As mother, Mama had spoken, turned it from her to him as son. She could do no other. He could do no other but bow low in all humility – and resist.

She would learn to be proud, let him will it so. Trusting, proud that her son –just her son – was one of those who – generation after generation of sons – whose task was to help Russia. Our still greater mother? – source of all our way in the making?

Yes a sacrifice. But what else? Her sacrifice for him. His sacrifice for Russia.

An example – the inspiration of example, irrespective of success.

When Mikhail Blank returned from his office, late afternoon, and heard through Maria Alexandrovna's distress, of Alexander's resistance to any idea of petitioning, he grew anxious for her mental state and very angry.

Such an ugly selfishness! Alexander's fate was surely sealed – and that he couldn't even do this much for his mother.

This the high minded selfless Sasha?

Time was running out.

Two days left for the petitioning.

She would break down completely – die first!

"My dear Maria do rest assured. I shall visit him this evening. It will be done I assure you. I won't leave him until he's agreed," he said gently but firmly, holding her hand throughout.

"Please – please don't say anything harsh to him."

"Don't you want me to save him?"

Save him! surely, try and save him – such bitter contradictions glimpsed, such an unease growing that he was being caught up in some awful confusion.

Whatever, whatever, he'd quickly bring Alexander down to earth, remind him in no uncertain way that far from revolutionary martyr he was in fact the son of a devoted greatly burdened mother – there! his true duty – humblest of all obligations.

Soon after his arrival at the House of Preliminary Detention, Alexander was asked whether he'd agree to see Mikhail Blank. The matter concerned his mother and was urgent.

To that alone Alexander responded, not at all sympathetically to the remembrance of his much older second cousin at Kokushkino some years back - such a superiority - arrogance.

The same exactly again as soon as Mikhail Blank entered the small barely furnished room where Alexander was waiting, reached out brusquely for Alexander's hand and began immediately, absolutely assured, justified.

"My dear cousin Alexander I come straight to the point. Very lofty your ideals but except for a few lunatics - yes - you'll go down in history alright - as a monster twice over. The Tsar nearly murdered - our Tsar nearly murdered - and your mother too I tell you. Almost out of her mind right now. It's killing her too because of you and your wretched principles. Great achievement! And the rest of your family - brother and sisters wherever they set foot - kin of a regicide! Much! Much to be proud of!"

To the bone he would cut. Not heroics of a martyr but killing his mother - in spirit killing his mother.

Alexander was somewhere prepared to hear this more terrible charge. It was true! He helpless and to this his destiny must answer.

"Now I tell you straight. This is, you know as well as I, this is your last chance to redeem yourself - and to let your mother remember you as a human being - a natural son - by writing a petition for clemency. For your family's sake - that your country remembers you showed a sign of repentance for your awful crime," he thrust on tasting an enjoyment in the very fullness of this denunciation.

"In less than forty-eight hours the cassation ceases. I'm going now. I'm returning to your mother. I intend telling her that you've agreed. That as I left you took up pen and paper. And don't imagine that she sent me to see you. I came for fear that she'll go mad."

Yes yes so it was, the self-righteous indignation. Let it be put into words - the cost, the sacrifice for Mama and himself that this devilish system was exacting.

He was killing her!

Nor could would he refute that. And that too would be made public - and what example would that provide? No! Only to show up the devilishness of the whole system by writing a petition. Let others - who will surely follow the same path - know only too well how devilish the system is. None of us can extricate ourselves.

Yes – he'd petition but on his terms. But then at least the Senators will learn – of course it'll get no further – just what a petition is – something – a speaking – as from – towards – equal to equal! Strike what spark it will.

He set about it with bitterness but knowing that neither he nor she could do other.

He began to write and the words took on that familiar truth-ordered life of their own, very twist and turn into a form that would try and do justice to the impossibility of this human existence.

Same familiar life of their own in the light of his truth.

Even though a sacrifice was necessary for Mama and the family, in its ultimate form, its, the greater than him, the compromise was evaded and refused, was transformed into a petition of another kind.

Still to somehow sound a note of truth and freedom, possibility glimpsed, only glimpsed, for above all else it was felt as helpless surrender.

The truth through language prevailing, where his life began and ended, would end, was ending, towards which this calm. But not towards Mama, Anna, Vladimir, Olga, Dmitry, Maria – no calm allowed – leaving them forsaken.

Every word weighed in the balance, obscure balance of his destiny.

The petition was handed in by his attorney Knyazev the following afternoon. The Senators read it in turn, horrified, outraged, by the blasphemy, mockery, from the very first words.

"I fully realise that the nature of my act and my attitude to it give me neither the right nor the moral grounds to appeal to Your Majesty, with any plea for leniency."

Trickery from the start.

"But I have a mother whose health - etc. - etc. - -"

That 'but' – such a brazenness – such an obvious brazenness so to use his mother – lowest of the low!

Words, phrasing, implications, word by word, just as he had written it, forcing them to interpret it word by word. He was challenging them directly. He knew well this murderer, that it would never be passed on to the Tsar. He was signalling to them a final insult, out of his arrogance, that same madness as in the courtroom, even his four minions hadn't stooped to that.

"Your Majesty's condescension to commute my death

sentence to any other form of punishment, will relieve me of the torturous realisation that I would otherwise be the cause of my mother's death and of my whole family's terrible plight. Alexander Ulyanov."

Torturous realisation eh? How misguided is it possible to be?

No sign of repentance, humble pleading, promises, nothing with which a loyal subject addresses his sovereign.

And what of the torturous realisation of the whole nation's suffering if the evil had triumphed – nothing! – not a word!

Torturous realisation? with twenty four hours to go! And who put him up to that?

The whole business – malevolent – or mad.

Very late in the day to try and fool us that he is so concerned about his mother.

She's been shown extraordinary beneficence by His Majesty in being allowed to attend the trial.

Anything yet about who's behind this whole gang?

The five accused were transferred from the House of Preliminary Detention back to the Peter and Paul Fortress. Their existence became a waiting, a hovering uncertainty. The prosecutor's demand for the death sentence had been clear cut. Those guarding them were certain. It could only be a short time before a public execution. The Tsar would repeat his decision of '81, which had provided six peaceful years.

The prisoners felt a gentleness in the guards' attitude, even respect. Each time they entered the cells under strictest orders to keep an extremely close and constant watch, the prisoners felt a reticence, a gentle acknowledgement, purely as from human being to human being. These guards might almost be the last men, and they were not rejecting. Not mocking. No!

We too are men – and we know, could be felt, gently felt from them. Solace, a kind of solace for this harsh waiting – listening – ever keener listening – inwardness – wrought – fiercely wrought – sustained – the once great world around drained of meaning – this bond alone enduring.

We are together.

Strong word of being – waiting for words from the world of men telling of life or death.

Twice a day they were allowed to walk together in the small triangular garden of the Alexis Ravelin. Conversation was tried and found wanting. Enough, to see, to be with each other. The birch leaves' delicate greenness shone with comfort, grace, telling of something purer than the world of man, something consoling as they returned to the silence of their cells, drawn, dreaming into the shadowy dusk, merging into this rhythmic tide of night and day. And the morning light spreading newness around, hope, tasks.

But no words from the world of men. Words that must come. And in that 'must', a power refining, enhancing wanting to needing to make of every act, sound, sight – a blessed giving. Each yet still willed something of the old familiar life. In this waiting their books were still at hand. But the reading, Andreyushkin of his mathematics, Alexander of his zoology, Generalov of his law, was no longer the same. Against that ultimate unfamiliar, which those words awaited from the world of men had called into being, the reading was willed with a desperation, as a refuge, a reassurance that all was the same.

The promise held out – the sanctum of knowledge awaiting – blurred – veiled by this anguish.

Magical infinitude of knowledge – once intimate partner for a lifetime – but now utterly beyond their reach.

After two days in deep depression Shevyrev felt the need, sudden shock of optimism, to join them on the garden walk.

"What are you all looking so upset about," he shouted as they walked quietly round in twos.

"No priests – no lawyers! Days gone. They won't hang us. It'll be life – life!" he laughed.

He pointed his thumb in the direction of the birch trees.

"Life!" he shouted, winking.

They watched and listened warily.

"Well then! – what's happening to us here?" he shouted to the duty guards – what they had not dared to articulate.

Only in the presence of the others had he found it possible. But still that wasn't it yet.

"What are they going to do with us?" That was it and he would hang on to it.

"What are they going to do to us?" he repeated, sharply, anxiously.

"Prisoner Shevyrev – we don't know. We simply don't know," answered one of the guards quietly.

Since the trial ended no news of any kind was officially forthcoming. Only rumours. Everything in a limbo for families and friends, all towards that terrible silence of non-existence especially intended by the Tsar. Let the whole rotten bunch of them sweat it out, feel his authority over life and death for Russia's well-being.

Let the rumours spread, purported leaks from those in the know. That the accused were misguided students - it was really most pathetic - hopelessly amateurish - the so-called bombs were useless, would never have worked. Obviously a salutary warning to youth was needed. Life sentences certainly possible, most probably stiff twenties for the five. Tenners and fivers for most of the others rounded up.

When Maria Alexandrovna knew from Mikhail Blank that Alexander would petition, she applied to visit him in the Fortress. Permission was granted. By all means let her see him again, in the direst circumstances, lest she still had in any measure, a false picture of him. Let her see him and know him once and for all as condemned.

All so different this time as she was brusquely handed a card enumerating the strictest visitor's regulations, and managed, almost desperately to grasp at least one of them forbidding any mention of the prisoner's legal situation or risking an increased punishment. Her confused reaction was itself the cause of distress. It was strength and hope she had come to bring him.

Along bleak stone corridors she followed the guard, trying to explain to herself the reality that Alexander was a man on trial for attempted regicide, trying to recover herself. But worse and worse it became till they entered a vaulted chamber. Something bewildering here. Yielding, she simply followed the guard's pointing, and sat on a chair behind a huge metal-barred screen.

"Fifteen minutes only!"

Exactly opposite, as she looked through the close set bars, another huge metal-barred screen, several feet distant, and Alexander being led in to sit down, exactly opposite, to look back at her and he smiled, across the gulf of the guard's steady pacing between them, ten steps this way, ten steps that way.

Time?

No - of course no - it's already run out.

Whatever we say through this showing - whatever words he could quickly find to lighten, sensing her confusion.

"Yes, of course Mama - the petition has gone in - so we'll see."

Mama – what are they trying to do? – so to harm us – separate us – such pitiful illusions.

Everything to be risked now in this silent embrace Mama – time has already run out – their time.

She so wanted to mention the rumour of leniency.

He so wanted to give her cause for hope.

Yes – yes – we both are smiling –

We both are smiling – well beyond the distance of these screens.

Not wanting daring to speak words here both knowing them as the last.

He knew a freshness in being with her, their life's precious enduring.

Such a prayerful strength called up, gloriously called up by this power which would have them suffer such pain, welling up in her as they communed in this way, welling up into such a fullness, bursting out,

"Courage – courage Alexander!"

The guard had stopped his steady pacing, and raised a hand, that time was up.

Back in the Blank's apartment she endured a waiting whose very harshness revealed itself as a purging strength, to leave her seared, wrenched free, naked on its open plane, turning to him alone in prayer. The memory, burnished, a kindled flame, no longer fearful. He speaking to the world, that's how it seemed now. And he speaking to her now with a warm strength in whose soaring flight was born her prayer.

Only possible response, her very substance, so she could return and live with those who meant so well.

They would still be together. She must go a little of that way too. Not condoning but an acceptance of his way in all its impenetrable otherness.

More than memory, still living, on the threshold of that secret place where he was truly an other. Threshold, tension, glad tension, spark, culmination, even –yes! – culmination was this life-giving warmth.

Acceptance, challenged to seek out that place of acceptance! for whatever he's done.

His suffering mine, yet he is his own. And as I feel it – from acceptance of this mystery is born my strength for the future.

Acceptance! fruitful challenge for the future – and such solace from his calm in the face of death.

On May the fifth, five days after the Senators submitted their report to His Majesty, the Fortress Governor, General Subkovsky received instructions which surprised and disappointed him. He was ordered to dispatch the prisoners that same day with 'speed, discretion and efficiency' by steamer to the Schlüsselburg Fortress some sixty miles to the north, on the west bank of Lake Ladoga. His own plans were drawn up to the last detail and would have ensured a first class execution fully in keeping with the Fortress's praiseworthy tradition for despatching regicides. Since when had Schlüsselburg been used for such occasions?

His abilities in doubt?

Getting too old for the job?

Discreet enquiries as soon as possible!

Efficiency?

An unfamiliar word from above. His reputation was for efficiency!

Study it. Study it!

Good Lord! Something worse still. How had he missed it? *"I want no bungling!"* Bungling? Since when had he bungled? He must get to the bottom of all this. Meanwhilst speed - discretion - straight away!

At nightfall a small river steamer tied up to the wooden platform off the St John Ravelin. Without warning the five were shackled, put in leg irons and led aboard. The ship untied immediately, turned about and headed north through the Neva's moonlit waters to the fortress town of Oreshok.

The guards detailed for the escort were surprised and could only assume that the sentences were life imprisonment in an out-of-the-way place. General Subkovsky in his anxious concern for that discretion, had ordered that the steamer escort be made up of guards who till now had no dealings with the prisoners. But the bearing of the five and their youth, had aroused a respect, a word of praise, which circulated through the Fortress. So the prisoners were allowed to stay up on deck for an unusually long time, stretched out, in their leg irons, leaning back against the rail.

The guards had indicated discreetly, life sentences in Schlüsselburg. As far as they were concerned it could only mean that.

Lying on the deck beneath the night sky it meant returning,

being returned, allowing oneself to let that life flow back, knowing once again as friend, the great world out there. Returning, responding with purest Yes, over Neva's broad night waters, ceaseless onward current, sinewy, blackness glittering, will, striving will. Above, gleaming fullness, ripening of a pink-gold moon through gliding banks of cloud. All that, they could embrace again with their Yes. All that which surrounded and met them they could acknowledge as they swept along, beneath the world's great arch. More than acknowledge - let yield in joy and expectation.

Once again drawn into world's glowing, fruitful possibilities. Once again to let themselves become men on earth. Even though constrained, sore from the biting iron of their shackles, this seeing released as of old, ceaselessly budding, fecund with world.

In this moonlit friendliness they dared speak as earthmen. Yet warily, feeling out the language, as men returning from afar. So thin, frail it sounded, yet through it they must achieve their earthliness once again. Through it that reborn hope, that expectation. Through that voice reclaim themselves anew.

"I love thee - Peter's creation!

I love thy austere lines,

The regal Neva's stately flow

Between her granite banks."

Shevyrev recited again the lines from Pushkin, enhancing them with a simple tune as the others joined in. Their attitude had changed from hostility to pity, to a realisation that his whole bearing was a misfortune. The gap couldn't be bridged. Yet, when he struck up they joined in, adding fresh lines of their own. His voice grew harsher uglier and they stopped.

General Zhirov, the governor of Schlüsselburg, a large florid man with thick sideburns, received his orders on the same day as General Subkovsky. He was surprised, honoured and anxious. 'Speed' - 'efficiency' - and 'utmost secrecy' were required of him in carrying out the execution of the five condemned. Assistant Attorney-General Shcheglovitov of the St Petersburg Regional Council would be witness in the name of His Majesty.

He felt honoured at the responsibility so conferred. Not at the Peter and Paul? Whatever the reason and it was not for him to so much as surmise - he would rise to this unique occasion and respond unreservedly to the trust granted from above.

But! – five at one go! – was the courtyard large enough?

He sent for Major Verikeyev and hurried along with him to the courtyard, a small square surrounded by fortress buildings and whitepainted walls.

No matter which way they calculated, length, breadth or diagonally, the largest gallows possible would only take three men. That would mean two separate goes. First three. Then two. And all the messing about in between! By no stretch of the imagination could that be regarded as efficient and speedy.

It could only be the five at one go!

The '81 gang – five at one go! – as ordered by H.M. He'd never put up with a three and a two – and all witnessed by Assistant Attorney-General Shcheglovitov. Besides, there was something quite wrong about doing it in two goes.

Never!

This was a providential opportunity to really prove himself – the Peter and Paul governorship in his sights – why not? – the rumours about Subkovsky's 'retirement' – and something already fouling it up for him! Unless of course he had those damned courtyard walls taken down! What more to show those responsible for shunting him into this lousy post that nothing was impossible for him when an order from the Tsar was involved. And the Tsar would hear of that direct from Shcheglovitov himself.

That evening Shcheglovitov arrived unexpectedly. He had decided to take the opportunity of visiting a kinsman on his nearby estate, and came earlier than planned. In spite of his inspiration General Zhirov felt confused.

"Welcome! Welcome to our humble Schlüsselburg. We're deeply honoured to be chosen by His Majesty for such a task. But – but I tell you Shcheglovitov – this order can only be carried out properly – I say properly – if I smash the walls down. Of course that's no problem. Walls – bricks – that's nothing for us here at Schlüsselburg!"

Shcheglovitov was puzzled by the man's agitation.

"My dear General what's your problem? Be clearer."

"Problem? Why, don't you see Shcheglovitov? We can only hang three men at a time here in Schlüsselburg. This order requires five at a time. We simply can't do it – I mean unless of course I –"

"Calm yourself my dear General. A loyal conscience like

yours has nothing to fear. Providence works in strange ways. What else dare one call it? The Emperor particularly requested in his wisdom that the two ringleaders – Ulyanov and Shevyrev – shall not be hanged with the others. On the contrary, as extra punishment they shall witness every detail of their accomplices' deaths. Those whom they led into this evil."

General Zhirov was as given life again.

"In fact," continued Shcheglovitov, "His Majesty thinks that if this had been done in the case of the Decembrists or that '81 lot – these criminals might well have had second thoughts. In other words – a more subtle approach is needed."

General Zhirov could hardly wait for Shcheglovitov to leave him. 'Utmost secrecy' – right! First, the courtyard to be made out of bounds from this minute. Second, the prisoners, expected between five and seven tomorrow morning, to be confined in the Razumovsky Ravelin – the four tenners out! Third, apart from Major Verikeyev, no one to be informed of the time of execution – and the condemned not till the very last moment. 'Speed and efficiency' – carpenters to be rounded up immediately in Oroshok! The main units for the scaffold to be made in the town – brought in and fitted up just before the execution. 'Speed' –Yes indeed! Here in Oroshok, Nikolai Borodulin. Twenty minutes – twenty five minutes for the lot. Would the Emperor think that speedy enough? Borodulin could certainly do it. A providence working for him? To make good? This Schlüsselburg posting never adequately explained, but definitely a downgrading.

Alexander sat down on the low iron bed to take stock of his cell. Yes. Somehow he would make of this his place. Unyielding these bleak mouldering walls but he knew that he could make it into his own. Only this stony emptiness left him, in man's world, pressing in from all around, concentrated, dry. Somehow he would resist being thrust into a void. Resist being squeezed between these threatening walls, enshrouding. Somewhere he glimpsed that he could make it his own and be. He could come to terms with it as these others had. If they let him have his books his work could go on. Others had done it and so could he.

A booklist beginning, his gaze rested on the graffiti strewn across the wall. Full names, initials, single words, lines from poems, geometrical patterns, marks of all kinds.

Almost sinking away beneath entangled layers of more recent marks, he deciphered, bridging, extrapolating, 'Have courage – all of you –'

He went close, focused intently, traced his finger gently over it, to touch, to make sure. Just here too then he must have stood to scratch it.

Deeper still – live into these signs! It was we that made them!

We – all of us together – these scratches – signs – this speaking from one of us to another of us – this reading and speaking is the voice that endures.

The spectral space held back transformed – these speakers with him – courage.

Even for a three-er Borodulin found the courtyard a squeeze. He told General Zhirov straight that he didn't want the priests fussing around too much. He would make marks where they should stand in order not to get in the way. On the eighth of May he and his assistant shared an evening meal with the guards and napped a little around midnight. The prisoners were to be woken at 3.30 in the morning and taken straight to the gallows.

Alexander was in a restless sleep when the hand insistently shook his shoulder. Puzzled he looked up to the serious face of the guard. With effort he drew himself up, turned back the thin blanket, felt urgently the need to have his feet on the ground. He shook his head briskly to awake – awake! The guard stepped back and began reading from a document.

"Prisoner Ulyanov, in accordance with the sentence imposed on you at the Special Session of the State Senate between April 15th and April 19th, 1887, you are now to be executed."

Of course! Of course!

The truth! – awaited all along.

There – where he had remained so finely attuned, and as the voice continued he drew himself upright, breathed in deeply. Alone. Stand firm. Have courage. Courage in the presence of destiny, so awful yet bearing the weight of such reality.

Listening, acknowledging, beyond this voice, far beyond this voice, this man, in this pale light for this final word from the world of men. Dawnword set apart from all others.

"Prisoner Ulyanov make ready immediately!"

The guard left him and waited outside the cell.

A priest entered to receive Confession and offer the Sacrament.

Now preparing, he knew in rarest calm that this was inmost truth and destiny. The fullness of that which had to be done - being done. Osipanov, Andreyushkin and Generalov, in rarest calm, bestowal, were led into the chill greyness of the courtyard minutes ahead of Alexander and Shevyrev. They were allowed to embrace each other and kiss the proffered cross.

Once in the courtyard Alexander faced immediately before him the gallows platform, the three standing on stools with ropes round their necks. Puzzled only momentarily. All intended! This whole presence speaking through these forms standing about in the raw uncertainty of this fragile night hour. Governor, high dignitary, officers, doctors, priests, guards - forms - only forms, felt so keenly. Final, yes final confrontation with the power, same power. These forms around him spectral, of little account in the sharpening awareness of this gathering presence.

He could lower or shut his eyes as he faced the three. In this very way of his watching he knew the battle continued.

He would take up the challenge.

He would indeed look with a seeing more alive, stronger, more selfless than ever.

Lovingly to absorb every detail which the light was blessing him with. Selflessly to absorb that they become his. Let me yes let me, enter into, bear your suffering dear Vasily, Pakhomy, Alexei.

To gladly face them and unite himself with them. Strength upon strength from them that he bear himself thus.

They three held their gaze onto him, resolved, strengthened, in final salutation. Borodulin's strong sensitive hands made a final slight adjustment and in the same smooth movement he kicked the stool aside. Andreyushkin last, called out in a clear rousing voice, "Long live the People's Will!"

Well done Andreyushkin!

Good to be reminded.

Borodulin had done an excellent job. The convulsions had been very brief.

General Zhirov became engrossed in Borodulin's way of working. Quietly, quickly, deftly adjusting a rope here, a knot there. As though nothing resisted his touch, all working with him. The condemned themselves responding so naturally - a real craftsman. How good too that they'd all kissed the cross - acknowledged God and sought His mercy before the stools were pushed aside.

Throughout the taking down of the bodies and preparation for his own hanging, Alexander had watched resolutely. Anything less, a betrayal. Watching still he touched, yielding to a nearness – Mama – Anna – and Vladimir – and Father – suffusing his pained, purged vision of the world with gentleness sweetness brightness.

The wooden cross at his lips – he could do no other, kissed, tasted, that sweet hardness, emblem of a final trust in man. Touching tasting a rightness of being which would carry him through.

Shevyrev grimaced angrily when the cross was near his lips. He tried to butt it aside with a furious gesture of his head. Nothing could assuage the raging fire of his desperation. How had he been lured into this ghastly cul-de-sac?

Yalta! Your sunlit boulevards – Oh Life!

Since the trial ended, day followed day, still with no official announcement of any kind. Families and friends desperately awaited a word, a sign to trembling hearts that men could not simply disappear. A word, a human word surely, at the very end, to allow them to bear it. Was it possible that they were never to be told? That they would be left to tremble, as a dire warning? Left in this awful unknowing to stare with aching hearts into the void.

Many others in St Petersburg were drawn into the long waiting for sentences to be announced, glancing at the Fortress, looking into themselves, anxiously wondering where each truly stood.

Before the power itself, life was not to be taken for granted. Then you! how pure within? – very asking – of itself somehow implying that I too am on trial – for what? Ridiculous!

But it won't go away, this questioning, uttered by their deeds in me?

Just how pure – straightforward – is your support for the autocracy?

And you dear friend, now when we meet – can it be so eh? – every day of this waiting, our meeting and greeting a little more awkward eh?

Whatever is it? – that we've been forced to stop taking for granted – stop trusting – stop trusting what? each other? ourselves?

Why this long silence? The Tsar must have decided by now.

Why still no announcement?

Only to know that the announcement will be a relief.

No question at all we too are on trial, and found wanting.

Aren't the five our accusers too?

Mikhail Blank's unease about himself took ever stronger hold. From that very first ring of hers on their door his responses had been unavoidable. Why then? was he thinking they should have been avoided? Unavoidable - his cousin - a widow - in great distress - what! that he was beginning to have to justify his actions - before whom?

What judge - what court?

But he was not going to check with the Post Office. He was not going to let himself be dragged down to that level. He could do without the annual invitation.

But five days now - five! and still no renewal of the Leontev contract.

That was serious, he dare not pretend otherwise. Something was happening. Connections - connections - were insisting on their reality.

He must immediately check again with chief clerk Gradovsky. Make sure he wasn't talking himself into things.

Opening the door to Gradovsky's office he was forcefully halted, to listen, to catch -

"- it's odd, to think this Ulyanov murderer is also a Blank - on the mother's side -"

"- pretty close really -"

Close to what?

"- the mother's been staying with them all the time -"

He must go through with it.

Their heads went down over their ledgers.

He almost forgot what he'd come for, somehow willed it back.

"Ah of course! Gradovsky! - the Leontev contract - what's happening?"

"Why?" responded Gradovsky with unprecedented brusqueness, caught up in some obscure embarrassment, "nothing -nothing - nothing at all."

"Nothing at all - eh?"

He felt forced to simply withdraw with dignity.

Why odd?

Hadn't he Gradovsky thought till now that the young fool

led astray was a Blank – partly a Blank?

Of course Gradovsky knew that the Ulyanovs were his cousin's family.

Clear as daylight what Gradovsky was saying! I've realised there's a regicide in your family. Your family. Well? That was a fact. Simply a fact. Face it then. Your family. Not a comment – a fact. My family. How very strange? And that we live here in St Petersburg. She doesn't. And that she has conveniently used our home – and that we have to go on living here.

But it was a difficult fact Sergei Gradovsky. Have I been hiding it from myself till now? Pretending that – that he – they – were not that close?

Simply a fact. But what a fact! Family? My cousin's son. Impossible to disentangle myself from this wordnet dragging down over – that Alexander was a Ulyanov – and a Blank. He'd been fooling himself that general excuses floating around would do, like 'a dreadful misfortune'.

From the beginning – that ring on their door – a veil – of naiveté – cosy family familiarity – veiling that he was so closely related to a whole nation's would-be murderer – that's how he'd go down in history!

Seduced – almost!

Diabolically fooled – almost!

But from the beginning that feeling too, so recklessly disregarded, that he was forgetting who he was – Mikhail Blank.

Responding spontaneously? No – insanely surely in the context of a Tsar's life.

And he had a wife, a son, who must be protected and who had been drawn into his delusions.

Impenitent woman – impenitent son!

She was smug, complacent.

The Blanks and the Ulyanovs were utterly separate – and all the world would know that he had got rid of her. The world must be made clear about the absolute difference which he had been seduced into forgetting.

That right feeling from the beginning!

It was Olga who'd kept insisting on all that Kokushkino family drivel.

Why! even that getting him to write the petition could be judged awkwardly.

From the beginning Maria Alexandrovna's attitude had been

totally unacceptable. Never so much as a word of criticism about her dear son. Actually, living with us and condoning it all. Absolutely no awareness of the price everyone else was paying. Right now! Being cut - tainted - unclean - being also considered responsible through that wretched son of hers.

Thank God - thank Gradovsky! - woken up from your trance! to learn that tsaricide is connected - connected in this way with our boss - and so no renewal of contract - no invitations - and action - take action!

Such a fierce light cast on these recent days - on looks - that odd pitch of voice - strange shyness from friends - all saying No! keep away!

Contagious your disease!

She would be going soon.

She must be sent packing now. Back to Simbirsk.

He must clear his name, make it clean from all that Ulyanov mess.

That was an accusation, a personal accusation. He hadn't done it!

What was Gradovsky daring to say, to reproach, to insult the Blanks with - the Ulyanov murderer! Good God - then just what was the rest of the world thinking about him?

In a trance these last days! Had she cast a spell over him?

The young swine was an Ulyanov.

Should he go straight and inform his chief clerk - shout it to the world, "Here in St Petersburg my home, is my family, my future!"

Wretched fate - she would remain his cousin.

He should never have taken her in.

Tricked!

Make good now quickly!

Everyone sees you as a regicide's kinsman. That's what they want, what they like. All of them pointing the finger away from themselves. That he was responsible, he was the cause of Russia's woes. No contract - no invitation - an outcast!

Becoming some kind of accomplice!

What madness was this?

Reward eh? Sickening reward for the times in company when he'd so modestly referred to Ilya Nikolayevich Ulyanov - my cousin's husband - Maria Alexandrovna Blank - as an exemplary educator of Russian youth!

Leper!

He must remake who he was is.

That he is not who he thought he was.

No! No!

Blanks don't go round murdering Tsars.

Surely he wouldn't have to go round telling people that. Then what was branding it into him so fiercely? – that unless he spoke up – confessed? – the world accepted, took it to be the case.

On trial himself now!

A petition then to the Tsar for mercy – for an end to all this – on his own helpless behalf?

Nothing would even begin to assuage any of this except ridding them of her. He'd be branded for life. Cousin of the murderer's mother.

"May I have the pleasure – may I introduce you to the cousin of the murderer's mother – Mikhail Kyrillovich Blank."

Watched closely from now on, no question.

Let Olga know they were under threat, being watched.

Even if the sentence were commuted to life it would do him no good – could be even worse.

Only being rid of her – her smugness.

Why! she seemed proud of her murderer son.

On his way home from the office earlier than usual, agitated, he walked through the Mikhailovsky Gardens and on down to the embankment near the Troitsky Bridge, feeling the need to look long and hard at the Fortress. In this looking, yes, yes, such a containment, relief in this reality, letting himself be warned to the quick, of the limits for a man.

"Hallo Mikhail Kyrillovich – early for you isn't it?"

Keep calm! Aralov was smiling – in a friendly way – surely? All as it ever was – old friend!

"Mikhail Kyrillovich – I think there'll be something for you tomorrow," said Aralov, an old student friend, in the Ministry, wanting to indicate that the waiting was coming to an end.

"O thank you – thank you so very much Sergei Petrovich," he burst out with humble effusiveness. The world was such a friendly place!

The man had confided in him?

Had he been imagining everything?

On his way home the questions pounded at him.

How odd just now this meeting with Aralov?

Relief was close!

Tomorrow! Tomorrow! One must trust in something.

"Something for you"?

Coming from where? – it was said in a friendly way. Friendly? Keep alert! And keep it to yourself.

All morning next day he found it extremely difficult to take seriously any of this office life. Without informing Gradovsky he wandered out, along the Nevsky around midday. Wandered in some limbo.

At the Sadovaya corner he heard the newsboys shouting something.

Plotters – exer – cuted!

Plotters – exer – cuted!

Plotters – exer – cuted! went the steady rhythm, varied with satisfaction and righteous indignation. He bought from a brighteyed grinning fellow who was enjoying the quick rush of business. He folded the newspaper tight, tighter still into a roll and hurried back to his apartment. Several times on his way he wanted to stop and read but he kept thrusting on briskly. Olga was not entirely surprised to see him back so early. After last night's row, his pale angry face, trembling jaw, fierce shouting at Lev, she sensed some kind of crisis approaching.

"Some papers – I left them behind," he said with a brusqueness with which she had become uneasily familiar these last few days. He had never left any papers behind before.

Safe at last in his study but bewildered by these actions this savage thrust which he could not control. He cleared a space on his desk. Unrolling the newspaper he spread it out and column by column, page by page scrutinising, alerted only for one word, one magic sign – so foully mixed up with his existence here in St Petersburg – Ulyanov – found! – at the bottom of the last page but one – almost shyly present – as though not wanting to be there.

"The Ruling Senate's Special Session's sentence of death by hanging pronounced on the convicted Generalov, Andreyushkin, Osipanov, Shevyrev and Ulyanov has been carried out on May 8, 1887."

and Ulyanov!

Of course and Ulyanov!

The damn fool!

Then he would tell that creature right away! Her blasted

progeny. Destroying, degrading, humiliating the Blank name. Nothing less. Oh yes - he'd tell her right now. Give her something to think about. And let her pack and be gone by midday. The news would be round St Petersburg in no time. Good God - that it had come to this. Blanks! Regicides - common criminals - hangman's ropes!

But he must prepare himself. He couldn't go to her like this, trembling, his tongue not his own and these words flying about from his mouth stiff and savage. He could make a fool of himself. But impossible to struggle free from the angry violent words.

"That son of yours Maria Alexandrovna - he's been executed - it's official - here - see!" with finger thrusting - but he couldn't have stopped there. "D'you realise what it means for us here - damn him! Our lives have to go on and your wretched son has tainted them with his rotten blood!"

Yet he knew that he could not, must not do it. But she must be told now and she must get out immediately.

He opened his study door and called out as evenly as he could,

"Olga!"

"Shut the door," he almost shouted as she entered.

"I should never have listened to you," he charged angrily, thrusting the newspaper at her, "and I tell you - when I come home this evening I don't want to see her here. Make sure that she's out. Out I say. Out!"

Olga took hold of the folded newspaper, shutting her eyes to ward it off till she heard the apartment door closing behind him. She sat down, trembling, shocked and bewildered. He had been so hospitable, so understanding towards Maria Alexandrovna - they were completely at one in their admiration for her courage!

So desperate - desperate? - violent! that tone.

Dimly, she dared sense in that newspaper column - a the connection with what had just happened - *'The Ruling Senate's - - of - - death by hanging - - on - - and Ulyanov - - carried out'* - - 'and Ulyanov' - alone demanding meaning from her - all else a blur.

She leaned forward, held onto the chair, shut her eyes, gently shook her head from side to side. No! No! No! It couldn't be. In what dreadful place - in what ghastly darkness - she must - she must go with him - she must go with dear Alexander where he went - a rope - a hood - squalid - savage - where none of us could be with you – dear Alexander – and the cutting down of the body.

She could barely breathe. She opened her eyes, passively emerging into a pale world. Immediately, unavoidable to tell Maria Alexandrovna. She had never thought that it would have to be her. But how glad that it was her. But she could never do it. How even to sound the words within, as preparation. What should it be? – "Alexander has been executed – Alexander is dead," – impossible!

Yet she must.

It had happened like this and she knew that she must.

Sounding the words to herself she felt delicately, a strange impersonality in them, yet even in just saying them – guilt.

She could simply take the paper itself, point to it, let *it* take responsibility. But the cruel ache in her heart, the yearning that called from mother to mother knew that as cowardice. From herself alone she must draw this news, make her news as from dearest to dearest and in the very telling that courage would be forged. But she would never find the strength for it. Yet she must.

Only to share now as mother to mother, Maria Alexandrovna's loneliness, to take it on herself, sensing it unexpectedly beyond that noble independence.

She left the paper on the table and with it that dimly felt domain of power – which had brought about Mikhail's sudden turnabout – betrayal. Bewildering betrayal whose savage tone she still could not believe. Frantic threatening tone. Get her out! Get her out! That 'out' a knifethrust of fear and hatred making Maria Alexandrovna so vulnerable – charging her to share, to bind herself, to suffer it with Maria Alexandrovna.

Since her arrival Maria Alexandrovna had been writing home to Vera Kashkademova and Vladimir every few days. Sitting at the small bureau in the guest room, she made an especial effort to be positive and calm with no taint of forced cheerfulness, for she knew Vladimir too well for that. She noted any St Petersburg news that she thought would interest him, like the discovery of a prehistoric site some ten miles to the east of the city. More than once she referred to her prison meeting with Sasha, mentioning his courage and good wishes for Vladimir's exams, and the fine speech he had made in court. She could not find the right way to mention Sasha's tactful questions about

Vladimir's welfare - all too tactful! All very painful, Vladimir's need for Sasha's approval - Alexander's silent disapproval of Vladimir's rude churlish behaviour. No way of mediating!

Vera's letters from Simbirsk told in glowing terms how responsibly and efficiently Vladimir had taken over the running of the house. Everything going smoothly. Like a grown-up in charge. Nor was he letting up in any way on his studies. She also mentioned as discreetly as she could, guessing that Maria Alexandrovna would certainly want to know, that, yes, Simbirsk society was still put out but that Maria Alexandrovna would surely be pleased to hear how Fyodor Kerensky, Director of the Gymnasium had gone out of his way to keep telling people that as far as he was concerned Alexander had always been a truthful, dedicated and exemplary pupil. Nor was he the only one.

Since the trial Maria Alexandrovna had striven to maintain in purity the memories of the prison meetings and of Sasha speaking to the court. Sacred must they remain, suffused with the light of her love, touched with timeless presence, unmarred by hope. But for Vladimir and Anna and Olga she could allow herself to think about their future. And that future would not be in Simbirsk. They no longer belonged in Simbirsk. She knew it now. But the injustice of it was very painful. All that Ilya Nikolayevich had done for the whole province! And how long ago it all seemed. Another life. They would return to what was their own, their very own, Kokushkino. To the place where they could truly be themselves once more.

The tap on the door was timid. Olga came in, unusually diffident. Maria Alexandrovna was not surprised. Mikhail's angry voice and brusque, uneasy attitude over these last few days told of something wrong. She put her pen down and looked up in welcome. Olga, not daring to open her mouth, her tongue a burden, managed the frailest smile. Maria Alexandrovna understood. She saw the sadness in those eyes and realised that the trouble went deep. Come my dear, let us share your trouble. It was sad but it was good that she could be there for Olga.

Olga came close and put her arm protectively about Maria Alexandrovna, shutting her eyes, knowing that now she could speak. To speak now, she knew in all rightness was to speak as one willed in union, given over, to speak and yet to listen, to bear it all as one with that other.

"My dear it's good that you've come. We need each other.

We can help each other. Your Mikhail – he's a good man. I know he is. You mustn't take things too badly."

Maria Alexandrovna's hand rested on Olga's.

Olga dared not listen. She must speak now or never. Do this deed. Utter this pure fact.

"Alexander was executed two days ago."

She opened her eyes, so wanting to yield 'Oh my dearest Maria Alexandrovna – Oh –' but she knew she must not. Knew that she must taste once again in uttering this deed from the world of men – feeling in the very uttering the deed itself – and yet, having uttered it, having tasted, having been forced to taste the bitter estrangement in the uttering, now to return to this communion, enriched communion, the sure gentleness of that hand over hers and the strength of that shoulder beneath, enduring in the stillness.

Maria Alexandrovna's hand reached out to pick up the pen between her fingers, feeling its hardness and heaviness. She pressed her fingers against it, knowing in its unyielding firmness a relief, a strength awakening, a certainty that she lived through in dazzling light. That last meeting, his words, his uprightness, his very uprightness in the court and this gift of strength were alone the reality. In spite of the numb pain and the tightness in her chest she knew that this strength must ultimately prevail.

"You must see it for yourself," said Olga, unable to bear the burden of the words she had uttered, still standing with her arm on Maria Alexandrovna's shoulder.

"No need – I trust you."

But immediately sensing her cowardice she continued, "No – do bring it my dear. Do let me see it."

Olga returned with the newspaper. Despite the pain Maria Alexandrovna steeled herself to read the sentence, word by word, from beginning to end, each word and its meaning steadily accepted, their ultimate necessity and reality. Accepting in spite of the pain, through the strength that had awoken within. That pain which she would ever bear. But in just such measure, this strength, his strength would enable her to bear it. To bear this sharp thrust of a fierce world which was gathering itself about her. Strength raising her up, carrying her forward for their sakes alone now, knowing what she had to do.

"I must telegraph home immediately. I'll go alone," she said, standing up and embracing Olga. "My dear you have been so good to me both of you."

Olga, surprised, relieved, could only watch and wonder. Maria Alexandrovna put on her hat and coat and went out into that world of the streets where the decision had been made, knowing that now she could face this abrasive breath. The newsboys were chanting their "Plotters - exer - cuted!" as she walked past them to the Telegraph Office. She walked without hurrying, to let Vladimir, Anna, Olga, whose lives had become infinitely precious, know immediately the starkest truth. That this strength would somehow be theirs too? That this strength would be sufficient to resolve all that might beset them? *'Sasha has been hanged. Returning immediately. Mama.'*

Writing it out was abiding with the meaning again. Yet it was good to be writing those words for she could willingly absorb their reality into the yearning abyss of her pain. To write record create relive. This writing it thus in public for all the world to see was good - a coming to terms with that world.

Semyon Draudin the elderly counter-clerk read the words in one rapid glance. About to calculate the cost he read through again slowly, pondering it as a whole - as if one dear to him! This was Ulyanov the terrorist leader. This little worn but upright, so upright woman, was the mother. Such courage and pain in making this thing public! No ordinary telegram, her words, writing, no ordinary act. Such a sadness binding him with her, with all of them here together. He had to give her a word - in such a straightforward purely human way. He must do a necessary deed as he pretended to peruse the telegram officiously, glancing at her, yielding to what came from her.

As she put the coins into his palm, he held her wrist with swiftest touch and allowed himself to look into her eyes.

"Be brave Madame Ulyanov - be brave -" he whispered, wanting to say so much more.

When the telegram boy knocked loudly three times Vladimir was tutoring Okhotnikov in Greek and Latin. Yakovlev, Ilya Nikolayevich's senior inspector for Chuvash schools and good friend of the family, had seen much promise in this young Chuvash tribesman who wanted to go to university. He suggested that Vladimir might like to coach him.

Vladimir enjoyed doing it. He soon found in himself the teacher able to reduce complicated matters to simple essentials, a responsiveness and an encouraging firmness. Okhotnikov made rapid progress. He had grown to admire and respect Vladimir. In particular during these last weeks, when he knew of the dreadful things happening to Alexander in St Petersburg. Maria Alexandrovna's departure had upset him for he was very fond of her. During these difficult days he felt that perhaps it would be easier for Vladimir if the lessons stopped for a while. When he tentatively referred to the matter Vladimir cut him short.

"What are you thinking of? This," pointing to the open books, "has nothing, absolutely nothing to do with that."

Another painful incident made Okhotnikov realise that the matter must not be mentioned at all. Three days previously he had made a guarded reference to Maria Alexandrovna in St Petersburg, about whom he would so much have liked some news. But at the very mention of her name Vladimir frowned fiercely, paled, tightened his lips then brusquely asked Okhotnikov to continue translating.

Throughout these days Vladimir felt compelled to carry on as usual, at any cost, if anything working even harder, whether at his own studies for the final examination, tutoring Okhotnikov, helping Nanny Varvara or in generally running the house. Something vast was happening in St Petersburg to do with Sasha. Such a relief Mama's letters but each time he read them a most painful anguish gripped him. Nothing in her letters related to that vast unnameable! She had written of the trial but still as the days passed there was no mention of a sentence. Nor did he or Vera dare ask her about it.

The telegram boy knocked three louder knocks again.

Stark they sounded.

Okhotnikov looked up from his book.

Vladimir stood up, frowning, and went to the front door, his chest tightening.

"It's alright Nanny," he said as he met her hurrying on her way from the kitchen.

He slowly tore open the green envelope, unfolded the telegram, read the words, looked hard at them, nodded to the telegram boy, shut the door after him and without a word to Nanny Varvara found his way back to Okhotnikov, trembling, that same vastness threatening to overpower him. He managed to reach his chair knowing simply that he must go on, not betray any of this to the world.

Okhotnikov pretended to notice nothing but was clear from

Vladimir's long silences, strained tone, pale face and clasping of his hands that something most serious had happened. Grimly Vladimir carried the lesson on for another half- hour to end as usual at six o'clock. After Okhotnikov left, he took the books up to his room and set them neatly, very neatly in their places on the shelf. Everything neatly in its proper place as usual, as normal. Feeble dam against this floodtide gathering.

He told Nanny Varvara that he was going out for a walk and that he might be late back – should Vera appear on her evening visit, to let her know.

Not until he had passed all human dwellings along Sviaga's banks and was well into the open countryside of meadow and field, did he begin to feel sufficiently alone and ready. Only now, away, away from them all did he feel himself approaching this place which he could and must enter, but more purely alone than ever before. Bravely, fearfully alone to respond to dear Sasha's challenge. Only now, amidst these fields, their purity, necessity, dignity, by Sviaga's ceaseless waters streaming, could he, dare he yield to this anguish. Only now, out of this newly discovered, newly demanded treasure of himself could he, dare he begin to acknowledge the reality, bleak reality of a transformed world, announced by, ordained by those words. Only now, thrust thus far, away from all men to abide in this wordless realm of silent dedication, of meeting, of somehow meeting with Sasha. He knew that only through this aloneness could he reach Sasha which he wanted beyond all things to do.

Remote, impersonal, charged yet with fearful possibility, there sounded those words which had led him into this secret place. 'Sasha has been hanged.' He took the telegram from his pocket to read it once again. What dark magic in those signs. A tidal wave of meaning rose up towards him. In anguish he strove to stand firm.

He would never see Sasha again. Into the blankness of that swirling terror he was buffeted, waiting bound with Sasha, the rope round his neck, breath strangled, as trembling violently, his knees giving way, he dropped down on the bank.

All that – all that, Sasha had gone through. And he had been untouched. Sleeping, eating, studying, even joking.

What did it mean?

What did it mean?

Tears, bitter tears slowly welled forth as he stared through a mist at Sviaga's waters – the two of them together here along the path – but so clear now – ashamed – that Sasha was often – sometimes upset – offended by him – critical.

Distant voices along the path wrenched him into that other world. He drew himself up unsteadily, grimly knowing with a strength desperately drawn from his newly forged aloneness that they, and Simbirsk, must not be allowed to touch any of this. He hurried away letting be even again what had just passed before him. Even again the rope that had tightened round Sasha's neck. Feel it burning! Hold firm! No tears now in the face of Simbirsk. Yield nothing to Simbirsk. Absolutely nothing!

He pressed on, this strength drawing him deeper into himself, closer still to Sasha, a questioning out of the very earth, vast, weaving these fields meadows streaming waters path itself into a fervent challenging unity.

What?

What could it be for that Sasha had risked his life and been destroyed?

What? What was the measure of this struggle that men killed and were killed for it?

The Decembrists – of course – and those men of '81. But that Sasha had been killed in this struggle? That Sasha had been hanged? Burning unquenchable pain – this terror – the waiting – the rope – the abyss. Of course – the Decembrists. Of course to realise now that they and the men of '81 must have gone that way too. Pestel – Ryleyev – Kilbalchich – Zelyabov – kindled into life these names – all of them united with Sasha and himself! Vast presence of his nation's history.

Why – stopping! – this was just the place – this inlet – where he so proudly helped Sasha dig around for his specimens.

How starkly separate the town from himself just here – just now.

But what beyond this point, as the bank curved away into the distance? And when helping Sasha – that strong urge to go on further.

But Sasha was the centre of things.

But now – turning – he was ready to go on alone. To meet what lay ahead – this strength ready to take him along that curving bank. Simply to stride forward along it.

But he must return along the old path to them at home.

But the return the path the them the he – all were different.

Even that 'must' with which he challenged himself and answered victoriously, was touched with that new one he felt himself to be.

Head held high to confront any shunners he met!

Approaching the empty wooden shelter on the outskirts, he sat down, absorbed in the play of Sviaga's darkening waters, yielding to the enchantment of that pure, comforting realm.

In sudden shock an overwhelming reality about Sasha's suffering and death broke through in one raw flash and immediately extinguished itself. It left him dull. A numbness overwhelmed him and that world of 'nothing else but' was reconfirmed, in all its ominous presence. World which from this numbness he looked on so warily. World whose very texture was woven with this most serious challenge. The challenge of Sasha's absence. Sharply, was separating out those who had taken Sasha away from them for ever. That was a terribly serious business, most serious business of all as he stared into the darkening waters.

Dmitri Kudrin, a good friend in the graduation class, strolling along as a break from his studies, spotted Vladimir in the shelter and quickened his pace. In spite of his parents' hostile attitude to the Ulyanovs, the news of Alexander's arrest had drawn him closer to Vladimir. But all attempts to express sympathy were thwarted by Vladimir's prickliness.

Approaching close he was surprised that Vladimir, staring into the river, showed no signs of recognition. Cautiously he sat down beside him. Vladimir did not stir.

"Vladimir whatever's the matter?" he asked quietly.

From out of his numbness, desolation, Vladimir knew relief and gratitude that Dmitri was near, present, with him. Gratitude to this good friend at his side who had called him, roused him, joined him. Oh he would say so much to this friend, dear Kudrin and confide in him.

"Vladimir please! - what's the matter?" asked Dmitri gently placing his hand on Vladimir's shoulder. Vladimir drew in a sharp tense breath. "My brother's been hanged," he said, barely audible, still without turning his head.

Dmitri shut his eyes and tightened his hold on Vladimir's shoulder. The words were so devastating that he could not even begin to think about them.

Walking back through the deepening dusk with Dmitri,

Vladimir was increasingly distressed. Since uttering those words through which he had so wanted to confide in Dmitri, a feeling of bitter hostility prevailed, of violent antagonism, bewildering. At the corner of Moskovskaya Street, Dmitri held out his hand. Vladimir fought against refusal and gripped it hard, looking into Dmitri's face as into a strange question. Dmitri bore that look, gladly, for Vladimir's sake.

Nanny Varvara and Vera were waiting anxiously for Vladimir to return. Nanny had told her about the telegram but they dared not speculate. In spite of the lamplight from the downstairs room, Vladimir, nearing the front door, sensed such an emptiness looming that he did not want to cross the threshold. Vera heard his footsteps and came out into the hallway. He did simply what he knew he had to do and with some relief that the words need not to be spoken, as he handed the telegram to her. Exhausted, empty, he went straight to his room.

Only the thought of Mama could begin to assuage this emptiness. Mama's presence alone, even now, when he thought of her could ease, help endure this emptiness which bound him so closely to Sasha.

The night became a desperate longing for her.

Sometime after midnight he felt compelled to visit Sasha's room. He stopped on the landing listening to the voices of Vera and Nanny below. He went down a few stairs and listened again. Vera was reading from the New Testament. He braced himself, irritated, disdainful. Whatever were they doing that for? Didn't they really know? What was all that compared to this emptiness consuming him? of a world without Sasha. Final, absolute!

Quietly he went back upstairs and entered Alexander's room, partly to assure himself of its existence. Wanly withdrawn, in the mooncast shadows they waited, the books, specimens, jars, apparatus, elusive, sealed, yet watching – he felt touched so gently, so chastely with the knowledge of some future. He returned, to a restless sleep.

Maria Alexandrovna arrived in Simbirsk next evening. On the journey back as very companion, Sasha's calm, as balm and blessing, as strength through her sadness. She knew she had received something which would never leave her, could never be taken from her.

When the cab stopped at the house they were having supper. She had the driver leave her cases on the front path, and then waited till he was away off down the street.

The thought of knocking and entering through the front door was painful. There was a secret threshold which she must cross, leaving that strange terrible world of St Petersburg, to be with all this again. Nor could she force her way in. But already, thankfully, healingly, she knew that she was being reclaimed, made one with her own as she stood by the kitchen at the back of the house and looked towards the garden.

Held, by this earthy tang of the ancient rainbutt and the hoe still leaning against the kitchen wall just as she had left it. So intimate, binding, telling with such earthfraught sweetness, evening dew's fragrance, of this place that was theirs. Telling of those who were closest, dearest. Always that call from them to her, she heard.

Quietly she entered the kitchen, calm streaming round her, that strange world of St Petersburg gone, going away. Here the enduring, Vera's voice, Varvara's voice, thank God, she now so sure of her task.

Nanny Varvara came in with an empty bowl for more boiled potatoes.

Yes dear Varvara my hair has gone grey! – ashes – but a new strength also, to do with him.

Nanny Varvara's surprise at seeing Maria Alexandrovna yielded to a deep recognition that all was well. That this presence, calm, strong, was here amongst them once more. She knew as she smiled with tearfilled eyes that Maria Alexandrovna wanted no more than this as yet. Maria Alexandrovna nodded gently and followed her into the dining room. The children jumped up and clutched her arms and kissed her. Vladimir and Vera embraced her tearfully.

Beyond any immediate questions or explanations, her presence sufficed Vladimir. Simply that she was there. The grey streak in her hair, the dark patches under her eyes, even the wrinkles that he had never seen before – yet, the very set of her head more calming than ever. These last two days he had become so strange to himself, her presence healed, established the ground once more. Within her presence a new gravity awoke in him. He sensed as through a veil that something tremendous, ominous, was at stake in this whole woven texture of existence.

In the days leading up to the exams Vladimir kept asking her for details about her meetings with Sasha and how it was at the trial. He felt it as a matter of urgency that he knew as much as possible. In the hearing and knowing he felt enabled to face the shock of those final moments with a mutual strength and courage.

Maria Alexandrovna answered him frankly. She could not hold back any essential detail. She acknowledged his right to know everything as brother to brother, sensing the deep need of his questioning and the effect it was having on him. But she felt that she had to be careful about praising Alexander in the wrong way, a faint uncertainty.

Never once did she mention Alexander's critical reference to Vladimir. Vladimir dared not ask her outright, afraid of a negative answer and awoken by that fear, deep disappointment, shame, guilt, that he had never come up to Sasha's expectations.

The riddle of Sasha's life was becoming inseparable from his own. In spite of all that Mama was telling him something essential was eluding him. As if the riddle was only made more obscure by these facts which at first seemed to bring him so much closer. That the deepest – most real – how pose it? – Sasha – aspect of Sasha? – part of Sasha? had not belonged to the family at all. They had all felt he was their Sasha. But he belonged to something more important than the family. Unbelievably more important. Unto death! And there – that darkest of riddles which would not leave him. From that 'something' he had been left out.

He struggled to hold off this bitter involvement and concentrate on his studies.

Do your best in the exam – for Sasha's sake!

Do your best in everything – for Sasha's sake!

Blessed inspiration!

Once so clear, he spent hour after hour, pacing his room, the garden, meticulously working through each subject by rote again and again, having Mama question him too, and checking with his textbooks if he had the slightest doubt on any detail. Sasha had won the Gold Medal in his year. Anna had won it in hers. That a Ulyanov might win it again this year! A Ulyanov! That's what he could do for Sasha – for them all.

The examination room was isolated from the rest of the building, its entrance guarded by two stern-faced officials. Through the awesome silence was heard the approaching footsteps of His Excellency Fyodor Kerensky, Director of the Gymnasium, with the two invigilators from the Ministry. The Director carried the papers, brought from St Petersburg by courier and kept in a safe for the last three days. Dread scripts, words of such power on whose correct decipherment depended career, status, life itself. Beyond the tension, the seriousness of the occasion, Vladimir felt a hostility that had to be mastered for Sasha's sake.

Ten days later the results were posted up ceremoniously by two senior teachers as the twenty two examination students stood back respectfully, anxiously. Reactions to the results from the students and soon enough, their parents, ranged from incredulity to a certain suspicion in some quarters. Next to each name in fine copperplate were the details. Vladimir, at the top of the list, was first in all subjects, setting him well ahead from his nearest challenger.

It had been assumed, even hoped by some that the Alexander business would have pulled him down. But, in this particular context, these results, admittedly consistent with his record till now, were astonishing. Just as disturbing was the fact that this blessed – damned! – Ulyanov family had now won the Gold Medal for the third time! It had never happened before in Simbirsk. Of course! the papers were set by the Ministry in conjunction with Kazan University – no question about that! Nevertheless Director Fyodor Kerensky had been a protégée of Ilya Nikolayevich Ulyanov and owed his career to him. More, since Ilya Nikolayevich's death, he'd been entrusted by the court with the management of Vladimir's affairs.

Kerensky was very pleased with the result. He had long held Ilya Nikolayevich in the greatest esteem and regarded his way with both pupils and teachers as exemplary. In the court's entrustment to him of Vladimir's affairs he felt granted a sacred task, a duty, an opportunity to repay in some small measure what he had received from his father, as guidance and encouragement throughout his career.

His next official step was to write a personal report on Vladimir for university entrance. He looked forward pleasurably to the task, only to be soon checked by certain considerations, a problem, one indeed at the very heart of the matter. Apart from Simbirsk society and its hostility since the hangings, he knew well enough that this name Ulyanov would from now on be tainted throughout Russia, amongst officialdom of every kind, especially those directly involved in one's academic and professional advancement. Whoever bore this name would be judged by extremely harsh standards. Doubt and suspicion would always prevail as of a necessity, which he well acknowledged and understood.

Against this pressure he felt drawn deep into a struggle to clarify to himself who and what was this Vladimir when he really thought about him. That, was his concern. To that, he must hold fast. Purely what was Vladimir.

The pure person Vladimir?

This pure person Vladimir?

The countless reports he'd written over the years! - but this demand was something special.

He must present discreetly, not to overdo it, those truths, nothing less than truths, about the boy which would ensure that Vladimir would be, would have to be judged for what he was in himself. As far as possible in the circumstances. Judged on his own merits. This was the issue. But what then constituted his own merits? Here, the utmost care needed, for the boy's sake and for Ilya Nikolayevich.

But he had his duty to society and those very officials who upheld and represented it. To be truthful to that society which Ilya Nikolayevich had always praised for enabling him to achieve his own exemplary career. That same society which had enabled himself to achieve his career too. A duty then to Russian society. But also to Vladimir and Ilya Nikolayevich. He knew of something in both boys in spite of the whole catastrophe - which smug patriotic Simbirsk society knew not.

He thought again on the exam results and his own initial surprise at them, to become aware of just how remarkable were Vladimir's powers of concentration, dedication to a goal, and yes here - just here - what was it? - what actually was it? - in the last resort - his independence - isolation? - he liked the boy very much - something remote? - cut off? - what exactly was it?

Very difficult to say!

The facts? - definitely a certain reserve - avoidance of much contact with school friends outside school hours - so he had heard said - actual avoidance? - who knew that for certain?

And what really did these facts point to - mean?

Meaning? Meaning?

Goodness! he'd never had to bother himself about this kind of thing before. At this rate he'd still be writing his first ever report over twenty years ago. But one thing surely irrespective of meaning – these truthful facts all surely pointed to an essential characteristic – call it reserve – independence – isolation – remoteness – which was precisely not calculated to arouse in anyone's mind the picture of a troublemaker.

Wait a moment! Independence is not isolation. And independence is all very well but independence can be unhealthy – too much of it – even threatening – some kind of a threat? Was that so? – this too much independence – a glimpse of what entity here? – But anyway – who was he to judge at what point it became unhealthy? Questions! Questions! Questions! Where were they all coming from? Everything was turning into a question.

He must make an end to it. He would mention some of these things, but discreetly – the tone then a little critical – some things underplayed – not to sound too contrived. Let the reader judge. Reader? What reader? Goodness me Fyodor Kerensky who taught us to think like this?

"There has been no misbehaviour throughout his school career."

Never? It wasn't true! But this too coming from him Fyodor Kerensky would have to be accepted. As a lie it would have been considered impossibly blatant. In spite of the incident with the French teacher Monsieur Paul – but that was years ago when Vladimir ridiculed him mercilessly – and anyway Ilya Nikolayevich had chastised him severely for it. He knew that he had to declare it thus. He had to ensure that the balance was held for he would never have another chance to correct it. Through the irresolvable problem of that isolation–independence business, he felt that the balance was too heavily against Vladimir. Accordingly he would make this slightest of adjustments. After all, he had told Ilya Nikolayevich everything about himself at that first interview which had placed his feet firmly on the ladder.

Salutary, very salutary all this.

Very humbling!

And coming from where?

He read his report through again and again, finally accepting with dismay and frustration that he could never be finished with it. He sealed the envelope.

The most sensible course would be for Vladimir to apply for entrance at a regional university – why not their own Kazan itself where Ilya Nikolayevich had been a mathematics student under the great Lobachevsky – and he was friendly enough with the Rector.

Vladimir listened as politely as possible when Kerensky emphasised his father's connection with the university, and expressed frankly his opinion that in the present circumstances, acceptance from St Petersburg university was unlikely. He did not want to hear anything about his dear illustrious father, or that absent one. He did and did not want this fatherly gentleness of Kerensky, this deep concern, touching so acutely on what was lost to him. Angrily, as victim, he knew that all this manoeuvring about provincial universities was because of that sacred unmentionable absence.

Near the end of the conversation the question arose of what subject he would pursue. Kerensky had taken for granted history or languages in accordance with his previous advice and in which he foresaw a brilliant academic career. He was unpleasantly surprised when Vladimir mentioned almost casually that he intended to study law.

"Law? Whyever law Vladimir?"

"Why not?"

Kerensky heard clearly a note of challenge, provocation even, from which he immediately drew back. Vladimir felt pleased at Kerensky's surprise, at the effect of his assertiveness, but uneasy about the really abrasive note in his voice – would it cause distress to Mama? Not to cause her any distress was the imperative. Taking leave he went out of his way to be polite and grateful for all that his Excellency had done on his behalf since his father's death.

Yes Law! and thankful that it had come out like that almost by itself. No way of asking anyone outright. Somehow it would bring him into that place where Sasha was involved. Bring him in a more directly concerned way.

The trial – the rope – were all Law!

But that abrasive note with Director Kerensky was still worrying.

Abrasive? – no! – rough! rude!

Papa dead – Sasha hanged – the family shunned!

Sasha had been torn from them by force, not at all like Papa's death – that was Nature – this was man.

Rude Mama!

What has happened is terrible!

A note of ill grace could not be concealed from Kerensky. When Vladimir bowed so slightly there was – mockery? – yes it was – the ghost of a mockery in that sudden stiff movement. No, not quite mockery. But no other word would measure up adequately to that movement. Something there, which he had never noticed before?

No! He would not alter the report. But the content of that sealed green official envelope was again in question. This glimpse of a new ignorance was troubling. No! He would not alter the report. This gist of it was truthful and fair. He could do no more – no better.

But his feelings after their talk would not be denied. Looking back from the beginning of it, a sullenness, and at the end, on that question of studies, for the first time, something hostile. He would not change the report – remoteness, isolation, whatever – but something hostile.

It was not the leave-taking he'd expected and to which he'd looked forward. Not at all.

Once Maria Alexandrovna had received Kerensky's assurances and advice about Vladimir's future she put the house and furniture up for sale and Vladimir made his personal application to the Rector of Kazan University. Maria Alexandrovna wrote to Kerensky expressing her heartfelt gratitude for all his help. In these last two years and especially these recent weeks she had come to realise that such help was by no means to be taken for granted. She insisted that Vladimir write likewise, which he did. But much more for her sake than for his. In her unremitting efforts on behalf of the family he was beginning to taste humiliation. If that was what Mama wanted he would do it. If that was how it had to be done he would do it. But with resentment, questioning resentment.

Since Mama's return, the house in Moskovskaya Street had become a subdued place, painful, as though rejecting them all. But the house and furniture had to be sold and Maria Alexandrovna advertised them immediately. At the same time, she made enquiries for a suitable family apartment in Kazan.

Whilst they waited about during dismal days for the buyers to appear, Vladimir lived it again and again that Sasha was not here. And in that 'not' the very rooms were different. Thin and wan. The very furniture no longer really theirs, forlorn, slipped from its moorings, awaiting the buyers, in that vastness of space forcing everything, everyone apart in this bleak light. Somehow they must huddle together. But a new coming together, there would have to be.

In this waiting for the buyers to appear they felt lost, wandering through the rooms as though searching for each other. Maria Alexandrovna somehow held it all together, so fragile, against this threat of being burst asunder. But inexorably, the chairs, tables, desks, cupboards were falling away out of the warm stream of their life and love into a desolate kingdom of the unclaimed.

The past sucked them up as a quicksand. The ever-present past. Past that was Papa and Sasha, as they wandered about the house, sad, oppressed.

A new start had to be made elsewhere. The two absent ones filled the house with an overpoweringly sad desolation. As they sat at table she realised that together they had become something strange. Something forever without the other two. Something needing a new place for healing, for guarding, for yielding to that light of the future.

All those once loved tables chairs desks wardrobes cupboards – cold sad things now made public – helplessly displayed – to be handed over to anyone – nakedly orphaned – shamefully deserted – betrayed – torn away from our caring.

Horrible! what had brought it – forced it all to this!

They were being forced out!

She had never wanted this but it had to be so. In that 'had to be', the anguish, that power, making it so. Such rich warm, praiseworthy life had flowed in Simbirsk for them! But they were fleeing it. Their very lives were of the place but they were being torn away from it.

In order to make the move as quickly as possible she set a modest price for the house and furniture. Simbirsk society refused to be drawn. After days of anxious waiting a dealer appeared, a warehouse owner from the north side. A burly, red-faced man, cheerful and unpleasantly intimate. He was surprised to discover that nothing as yet had been sold. After thoroughly working his way through every room, briskly tapping with knuckles, inspecting underneath and looking into corners, he made her an offer for the lot, ten per cent below her asking price. She accepted. He was delighted but gave the impression that even that was too much. However as she was a widow he was glad to do her a good turn.

Early next morning three large horse-drawn carts drew up outside the house and several men began the removals. Vladimir hung about watching. The front garden soon became a confusion with furniture of all kinds lying around as the men decided on the order of loading up. Vladimir picked his way about this chaos which their things had become, not knowing where to put himself or what to do amidst the heaving and tugging and swearing and arguing. Maria Alexandrovna, glad at last that it would soon all be over, saw his distress and tried to cheer him with what lay ahead – Kazan!

They were being plundered!

Something should be done about it!

He must leave – go right away – by the river away from that dreadful helplessness. But this shameful exposure of their things – being torn away – was happening to himself!

Who were they these strangers? Why should they have these things?

That this much more was being taken from them – being torn away from them!

When he returned, the last of the carts was being piled high for a final journey to the warehouse. He stood by the front gate angered by the workmen's good cheer for a job finished.

The black leather sofa was heaved up, onto the very top and precariously roped into place. The men sweated and laughed as the tailboard was hooked up. Suddenly one of them leaped sheer up the side of the cart, again on up the hillock of furniture, to land on the sofa, wobbling it from side to side, grinning, and waving salutations to the cheers of his mates who accompanied the cart as it started off down the road.

The front garden was left trampled and strewn. Beds, a table and some chairs had been kept behind for their last night.

In Kazan, Vladimir made Maria Alexandrovna a solemn promise that he would concentrate entirely on his studies. That he would not participate in any student activities, even of the most innocent kind, rather than risk drawing the attention of the authorities to himself. The thought of bringing any more suffering on her made him recoil as from an open wound. He felt guiltily how Mama was caught up in some inextricable round of suffering because of them. Only to bring her some peace, protection, good!

His openness, direct avowal, meant everything to her after Alexander's bewildering secret, secrecy. She felt keenly how much he had matured, become responsible, that bitter arrogance subdued.

When the autumn term began Vladimir looked forward to being left completely alone and studying in peace. He had made his plans and wanted simply to move forward in that direction. If Russia was to be changed it would be through lawyers. The legal, reforming way was the right way.

This decision, this path, boundaries drawn, was security. More than this he did not want to, dared not want to know. Just this path forward, this goal, this world of study and nothing else. He could do it. He could do anything he put his mind to. The family were down, deep down and, just beginning he could pull them out of it, and he would. His path so far had been – first in everything. Doing whatever the authorities required, looking neither to left nor right . He seemed to have no rivals.

No question the authorities would be watching him. He must conduct himself as a model student. Well in that too he would come first. They would not be able to fault him.

Rector Rozhdestvensky read through Kerensky's report several times.

How the devil could one really assess it?

Impossible –insupportable – a second time!

What were they being marked out for punished for?

One Karakozov not enough?

Forced to count – forced to count! – twenty one years – only – that only! – twenty one years since that Karakozov swine of a student had blackened the university's name with his swinish attempt to murder the Tsar – all this time – to redeem – peace – make good – and now this dreadful business threatening.

A second regicide? – brother of a regicide! – well? – in their midst.

After twenty one years trying to get over it! God above! – insupportable!

Director Kerensky's report made it impossible to refuse the brother's application, especially with its reference to Ilya

Nikolayevich Ulyanov, but he would inform the Kazan police immediately that Vladimir Ilyich Ulyanov, brother of Alexander Ilyich Ulyanov, had been enrolled. He would not be caught out, especially with this pressure from the Ministry to stamp out as quickly as possible all signs of student dissent in the new term.

From the first Vladimir was both the quiet, industrious student who kept very much to himself and also the brother of Alexander Ulyanov, the martyr. Having him in their midst, the brother of the very one, the leader whose hanging and deeds had been a major instigator of widespread student unrest since the trial in March, was to have very guarantor of their hope's, way's, striving's reality.

Vladimir was soon aware of the tension between his planned way ahead and how he was seen by the other students. That he represented, somehow even was Sasha for them. But in an inspiring way, making him feel proud, and that all of it was Sasha's just due. He could not fight against it but he refused politely to attend any of the numerous meetings. They were honouring Sasha and his comrades – paying justified homage. But he must shut it out. He dare not be drawn in.

He knew moments of overwhelming numbness, a bewildering separation between himself and all their activity, towards which he felt so close.

Irresistible their homage to Sasha.

His non-committal attitude was not understood by those who approached him and who took it for granted that he would join them as Alexander Ulyanov would certainly have done. But just because he was Ulyanov a certain respect held them back from any serious criticism and helped preserve the neutrality, the space which he sought. Most likely he was still suffering deeply from the shock of his brother's hanging and should be allowed to get over it in his own way.

On the morning of December 4th at eleven, the main assembly hall began to fill with students from every faculty, called together for a mass meeting. The mood was confident, lighthearted. Provincial Inspector of universities, Borozdin, had unexpectedly agreed to come and hear their respectful petition. It had been as easy as that and for many, a clear acknowledgement that the authorities realised just how serious the students were. Rector Rozhdestvensky was most perturbed by the Inspector's response. Utterly contradictory to the firm line demanded by the Ministry! Borozdin's assurance in writing that the event would in no way prove contradictory and that he welcomed the opportunity to personally see exactly what was going on, and to show all concerned where the authority lay - was most confusing.

Borozdin had decided that the time was ripe. He'd give those Kazan criminals - respectful petition! He'd draw their fire. Make Kazan an example for all the eastern provinces. Indeed let them speak! Didn't that fool of a Rector understand? Kazan eh! that Karakozov swine still about? He'd find out for himself exactly who these respectful petitioners were - face to face - and none of the faculty to be present! including the Rector's own precious self. Draw all possible fire. Risk even a punch-up as happened so recently in Moscow University. Then pounce! Why! the Emperor risks his life every day. Let's show these weak-kneed cowards an example of how to act. And in the last resort who else was to blame?

Till the very last minutes when the hall was all but filled with nearly a thousand students, Vladimir sat in the empty Law Library in an agony of indecision. If after all, the whole student body was present, everyone there, nothing concealed, and if in addition the Provincial Inspector had agreed to talk to them, then there could be absolutely nothing wrong in him being there too. On the contrary! as possibly the only one not present, he would be extremely conspicuous - the most conspicuous student of all! Hurrying along but with considerable misgivings he entered at the rear of the hall where the last couple of rows were rapidly filling up, intending, as discreetly as possible to join them.

A watching student recognised him immediately and caught his attention, cheerfully flinging out an arm and pointing towards the front rows. Vladimir followed its direction bemused as another arm was flung out and another, all pointing onwards, and he in some desperation hurrying as the hall settled down in these last moments to an expectant tension, he given over to these knowing smiles, leading to he knew not where. Only that he could do no other but follow till he reached the very front row and the empty seat waiting for him. Although trying to remind himself, convince himself of the apparent innocence of the whole situation, he felt somewhere trapped, constrained to look rigidly ahead at the empty waiting platform and in no way to acknowledge the nods of recognition from students nearby.

Some plainclothes police from Kazan Headquarters had by now infiltrated the meeting. Borozdin advanced imperiously down the centre of the hall and onto the platform.

"Kazan students, I'm here to listen to your petition. Who's to present it?"

Borozdin stood facing them squarely and spoke slowly.

Confidence and high spirits were just that much checked by the firmness of his voice, not yielding anything though apparently not threatening either. The precise choice of his words and that assured stance told of one in control. Several students could barely restrain themselves. Their furious need to pour out their frustration on this figure representing ultimate, anonymous authority and power, was at fever pitch.

Mintslov, a tall bespectacled Physics student stood up and began to read from a sheet of paper.

"We, the students of Kazan University, present the following respectful petition to Your Excellency for your urgent consideration."

No sooner had he begun when loud interruptions broke out.

"Not petition! Demands! We demand as of right!"

"Rubbish! You don't represent us!"

"The man's a policeman nothing else!"

"We're surrounded by them – look here, can't you see –"

"Out with him! Down with him!"

Official eyes watched guardedly as the shouting, noisy shuffling and incitements continued. There seemed to be two groups, one in the front of the hall and one in the rear, at odds with each other. Borozdin pretended to hear and concentrate on Mintslov alone.

Vladimir kept as still as possible staring into the middle distance. To his great discomfort student Elensky, close by, jumped to his feet amidst cheering, looked round the hall aggressively and then faced Borozdin. He waved disdainfully towards Mintslov that he sit down. Bewildered, Mintslov did, to cries of, "Fathead! Idiot! Toady!"

"Students of Kazan – these, are our demands. Right?" shouted Elensky.

"Right! Right! Right!" acclaimed the chorus.

Vladimir stared down at his feet and tried to shrink in further on himself. Borozdin seemed to be looking almost directly towards him.

"First!" Elensky declared, pointing sternly to the Inspector, "no interference by the Ministry of any kind, in the running of the University!"

"No interference by the Ministry!" repeated the chorus.

"Second! no supervision of our private lives. Third! the right at any time to assemble and petition. Fourth! scholarships and fellowships to be distributed by student representatives. Fifth! any police officials responsible for brutality against students to be punished. Last! but not least! our ancient and honoured university rights to be protected at all times."

Carried forward on the waves of exultation Elensky had achieved, reached a fullness of demands, till this moment discussed only amongst disparate groups. A completion as of right, as natural, all barriers swept away.

Now it had been uttered openly to the policeman's very face and they knew a sense of courageous achievement, of being carried beyond themselves, on into the boundless the fraught.

Could it be? Look at the man! that something would yield now.

That something could, must happen. The rightness of their claims, so natural, so daring. It had been trumpeted forth by all. Even the timid acknowledged it in their hearts. What could, would, he do before that?

The students watched Borozdin with a profound curiosity. The man was clearly nonplussed, unnerved. His stolid stance was surely mere posturing, ridiculous.

Borozdin kept them waiting. He stood unmoving throughout the din. Only his eyes had narrowed. Many were on the verge of derisive catcalls but something checked them. They sensed, as he slowly looked round the hall, once, twice, catching in this steady sweep the subtlest of nods from the plainclothes police, that his waiting was not of one cornered.

From his fastness Borozdin was letting something take its course, as from the very beginning when he'd stood his ground and this howling mob was drawn out into the open. From his fortress he'd watched them, these unbelievably impudent little fools. Watching and waiting for all these barkings and screechings to die down. Pathetic. Painful. Dangerous.

These whinings dangerous?

Ulyanov and his gang had meant business!

Never forget!

Crush stamp out! Absolute firmness!

Ready now in his own proper time, all strength gathered from his centre of power and authority, unhurried, totally assured, he would reveal the law, teach once again – and always once again – these raw unredeemed youth, the lesson of lessons, the first lesson of life, the lesson which no faculty could teach. Unexpectedly he stepped down from the platform, opened a nearby door onto the adjacent corridor where the Rector and faculty had been waiting in growing alarm at the disturbance and summarily called them in. Led by the Rector they filed through uneasily to the back of the hall.

Many students heard that sharp summons of Borozdin with much enjoyment, freedom of broad grins. He returned to the platform.

"Students of Kazan University, what I've just witnessed is not a petition. It's criminal behaviour. Anarchy pure and simple. It will not be tolerated. If necessary the university will be closed down, indefinitely."

"Of course," he continued, with a new, almost personal note, "I know that most of you want to continue your studies in peace. That's why you're here. Be assured then that the criminal elements responsible for this madness will be dealt with."

"Watch him! He's trying to split us!"

"Who knows? These criminal elements may well be strangers, outsiders," Borozdin's tone a sharing, informal, concerned for their well-being.

Sergeant Kashkin in plainclothes had slipped out quickly to join a colleague waiting in the corridor to check all registration cards.

"Students of Kazan, return to your studies as the students of Moscow and St Petersburg have returned to theirs. We shall find these wretches who want to disturb and destroy your careers – be assured!"

Several students immediately stood up and began to make their way out of the hall. They found two tables in the corridor at which sat detectives demanding their registration cards. The word quickly went round that the authorities were checking for those very outsiders – troublemakers mentioned by Borozdin.

Most of the students were unsure of what was happening. Mention of outsiders was spreading confusion. The registration business all set up, when? how? had taken the activists by surprise.

Throughout, Vladimir felt himself to be in growing danger. He must somehow make it absolutely clear to watching eyes, especially those of Borozdin himself, by some gesture or other, that he Vladimir Ulyanov had no connection whatsoever with any of it. He sat as still and impassively as possible.

He felt trapped. He knew now that he shouldn't have been there. Somehow he must show that he wasn't there. The impassivity and stillness were not enough. He was desperate to show by a positive gesture that none of it had anything to do with him. Amidst this din swirling around him one truth whose savage thrust must be embraced. That Mama's well-being was under threat, at risk – yet again. But the more he struggled with himself to show watching eyes, Borozdin above all, that he was innocent, unconnected, the more he found himself hopelessly present, very surprised even amazed by those demands, present, drifting with it in strange currents.

He filed out without gesture of recognition to anyone, fearful of a wrong move. He showed his registration card to the police at one of the tables and returned as calmly as possible to the Law Library. He stared at the open volume and thought painfully through his conduct. At no point could he conclude any essential alternative.

Sergeant Kashkin had nodded that his colleague simply return Ulyanov's registration card. When Vladimir left the table, Sergeant Kashkin added the name Ulyanov to his particular list of ringleaders. According to plan, his particular attention had been concentrated on the front rows, and he had carefully noted the red-haired student sat there so stiff, sulky and odd. Ulyanov! That's who it was. That explained a great deal.

Back at Headquarters notes were compared and lists were finalised.

"D'you know who I had in the front row – that red-haired one – Ulyanov!"

"Ulyanov? What – the terrorist?"

"No – the brother –"

"The brother? – making trouble? – his own brother hanged – must be mad –"

"They even kept a seat for him can you imagine? as brazen as anything – how he came in at the last moment. Ulyanov! What else could he have been there for but to organise and incite?"

Inspector Borozdin had emphasised that punishment, to be effective, must be swift and severe. The Rector would shortly be informed of their findings and prepare a list of expulsions.

That evening thirty-nine were arrested. Four days in the police cells were intended to emphasise the seriousness of their offence. Summary expulsion would follow.

Vladimir was arrested in the apartment on the Pervaya Gora when Maria Alexandrovna was out. He was allowed to leave a note of explanation for her. Passively he let them lock the handcuffs on and stepped forward awkwardly into the waiting carriage. Passively, trapped, but in spite of this burning guilt towards Mama he was not responsible for what was happening. So soon all this happening again but now through him – him who alone was left.

Why was it happening to him at all?

Passively he submitted as he entered the cell to feel so keenly again that harsh ominous reality beyond which nothing else. Thrust into this bleakness he dared sense with dread that none of his efforts at playing safe had been of any avail. Something far beyond him was involved.

He must try and resolve the more immediate and comprehensible.

He was innocent. He had done nothing wrong. There clearly was some mistake. As soon as the authorities called for him he would have the chance to clear himself. What then was he worrying about? And Mama would not be touched by any of this. Yet it persisted. Something vast, about his very self and all that was happening to him and it would not go away.

They were all released late afternoon on the fourth day. They met outside the police station, cheerful, with bravado. It was clear that every one of them had been involved in the harangues and attacks on the Inspector. Ulyanov's presence was taken for granted as one of them. Vladimir felt awkward as they walked off down Spasskaya Street conversing loudly, aggressively and feeling proud. He had already decided to request an interview with the Rector and was concerned with how he would prove his innocence, how he would emphasise the flagrant injustice in his case.

On the corner of Yakovlev Street several student friends met them with loud hurrahs, handshakes, congratulations and news. That morning a black bordered list had been pinned up in the

Assembly Hall with the names of the expelled. It seemed as though all those arrested were on the list. As they sauntered back arm in arm the mood stayed lighthearted, jovial. When they entered the university precincts constant cheers of recognition sustained their pride.

Before they reached the board helpful information was forthcoming. Expulsions generally meant about a year. Eighteen months at the most. You simply kept studying under your own steam. Didn't you know that Professor Aliansky had been downed for a year in his student days? What? Professor Aliansky? You must be joking. The man's an utter reactionary! So? - Perhaps you'll be at his age!

"Ulyanov what d'you think you'll do for the next twelve months?"

"It seems my brother's decided for me," Vladimir answered vaguely, surprised by what he'd said.

Though aware of the suggestions and advice, he could not connect any of it with himself as he accompanied them to the hall, to look at the list. He kept at the rear as they pressed about the notice. Recognition of their individual names was expressed through oaths, sarcasm, groans, an uneasy mixture of seriousness and attempted unconcern.

Vladimir intended merely a casual glance. No more would be necessary. But almost immediately the casual glance focused on a name, three from the top, Ulyanov. V.I. A sharp constriction caught at his throat. He shut his eyes then looked again, squarely, out of deepest necessity, to confront, ensure incontrovertibly that it was so.

That, as he walked away, there could only be one possible reason for his name on that list - Sasha! Bitter, angry before this injustice he sensed for the first time the strength of that power, able to bring this about. He'd heard the complaints of injustice from other students who felt that they had been arbitrarily picked on. But he knew now that his situation was utterly different. He felt in the very strength of his failed efforts at good behaviour the vastness of that power against him. His whole future was involved. Helpless, trapped but far more keenly revealed than even this bitter injustice, the closebound destinies of Sasha and himself, drawing him forward.

Now it could only be for all of them back to Kokushkino with Anna.

But beyond all to know himself in this new way as Sasha's brother! What he had been trying so hard not to be!

So clear now their insistence that he was just that – the brother of Sasha – the brother of a regicide – a terrorist himself then.

Trapped – by the ruthlessness – utterly impersonal.

Then there was no need to flee to dread being Sasha's brother any more. Now he could be what he was. Be what he was taken to be. Be what they wanted him to be.

No more twisting and turning, be Sasha's brother!

Salutations Sasha!

All so mysterious – but thankfully embrace it now as inseparable from yourself.

They were clear who he was and had dealt with him accordingly.

He too then was clear, for now and the future.

Sasha's brother.

Very decision shaping his awareness of it – of them.

So much beginning to relate, coalesce, present itself through all its diffuse appearances as a single, formidable entity. What had entered deep into their home, ruthlessly destroying. Even Father's death had not been a straightforward matter. It too was somehow related to those who had taken Sasha from him for ever. Yes! out of this anger, bitterness, he could admit now that 'for ever', which would have to be answered.

Only now! – to have so little known Sasha but now he knew him, now he would come closer, much closer. No regrets – only resolve – somehow a resolve.

Not tears for you Vladimir – but an account surely to be settled – squared – balanced.

Not tears but response, brother for brother.

We becoming the hounded. Father's sheltering roof is no more.

A meeting was held in the Rector's office with Borozdin and Major Yerykalov of the Kazan gendarmerie, to finalise the expulsions on behalf of the Ministry of Education and the Ministry of the Interior. At the mention of Ulyanov's name the Rector asked what he was actually doing in the hall. The note in his voice was taken as a challenge on matters of fact and veracity.

"Actually doing?" Borozdin responded angrily, to the surprise and discomfiture of the Rector who had expected Major Yerykalov to answer.

"Just sitting there with an impudent smirk on his face from the start," Borozdin continued.

Fool! Of course! He was sitting right in front of Borozdin.

"Typical – typical," said the Rector self-righteously, instinctively, shoring up his threatened position, "deceit, nothing but deceit from the day he entered. And he imagined he'd taken us in."

Not enough! Had his very acceptance of Ulyanov in the first place become questionable?

"The fact is I was uneasy about Kerensky's report from the beginning," he explained apologetically. "I couldn't put my finger on it. You can read it for yourself. But we've all been watching him extremely carefully. It was just a matter of time before he overreached himself. Showed himself in his true colours. In fact he's proved to the hilt our worst misgivings."

Twisting about, the Rector realised hopefully that what he was saying was in its way a confirmation precisely of Borozdin's strategy – bringing them out into the open.

"Frankly Rector I don't think we can afford to risk such a generous approach as yours with a background like Ulyanov's. We're dealing with the brother of a would-be regicide. We can't afford any mistakes. You make your report out. I, mine. From now on there must be no question for anyone in authority as to who and what this Ulyanov is," Borozdin declared brusquely.

After consulting with the Law Faculty, Rector Rozhdestvensky began on his report, criticising Kerensky. His misgivings had been right from the start. But now he must be very careful with his words. From the Law Faculty what did we have? A certain 'off-handedness'. Off-handedness? for a Ulyanov? That was dodging the issue à la Kerensky. Rudeness surely – obviously. Rudeness! Controlled but calculated rudeness. And the other very important point – 'withdrawnness', a 'lack of attention', not 'properly involved'. Anyone could see behind that now. Ulyanov was clearly concentrated on something else! So there we have it – deceit, which we already know well, lack of attention, rudeness. But? Actual written work extremely good! So what! What does that prove? It doesn't prove what kind of student he is. That's what we're being tested for – and rightly so – yes rightly so – the more subtle aspects. So much for character.

Then to show Borozdin that he was well aware of what had taken place at the meeting – the empty chair incident. Clear that Ulyanov was an important instigator if not actual ringleader. Mention too the report of loyal students who had seen Ulyanov running along the corridors waving his fists – all unmistakable identification because of his red hair. Finally set it all in the context of the family background.

'During his short stay at the University his behaviour was deceitful and rude. He was often unpleasantly withdrawn and showed lack of attention in his studies. His behaviour during the meeting was grossly impudent. He was clearly accorded the recognition of ringleader by his fellow students.

When the exceptional circumstances of the Ulyanov family are taken into consideration, his general character and behaviour at the meeting - he is clearly capable of various kinds of legal and criminal demonstration.

I have no doubts whatsoever that his presence at institutes of learning constitutes a great danger.'

After several days of weighing and testing, phrase by phrase and word by word the report was sent off and entered into Vladimir's recently opened files at the Ministry of the Interior and the Ministry of Education.

JEWISH TERMS

Arba Kanfos
(four corners).

Ritual undergarment with fringes at
its four corners, worn by male Jews.

B.

In the Hebrew alphabet, the equivalent
of the letter B is written thus ב. The
dot is called 'dagesh' in Hebrew.

Baba Mezi'a.

Talmudic tractate on ethical and social
teachings.

Berashis.

Hebrew word opening The Old
Testament, meaning 'In the beginning'.

Bimah.

An elevated platform in the centre of
the synagogue where The Torah is
read.

Chmielnicki

Leader of the Cossack uprising in the
Ukraine 1698/9 – during which tens
of thousands of Jews were murdered,
and hundreds of Jewish communities
exterminated.

Cholent.

Sabbath dish prepared the day before
from potatoes, oatmeal and chicken
fat.

Chollah.

Whitebread loaf.

Derekh Eretz Zuta.

Talmudic tractate on economic aspects
of life.

Eastern Side.

Place of honour in the synagogue.

Gaon.

Outstanding scholar.

Gemoreh Kheyder.

Higher grade school for youngsters
devoted to the study of the Torah.

Goy.

Non-Jew.

Kiddush Hashem.

Holiness of the Name.
Death for a holy cause.

Mishna.

Collection of the oral law.

Mitsva.

Divine commandment. Good deed.

Moshe Rabbenu.	Our father Moses.
Pilpul.	Scholarly interpretation of rabbinical text.
Rashi.	Great mediaeval commentator on Bible and Talmud. Indispensable guide for all future students.
Reb.	Teacher.
Shammas	Beadle.
Shul.	Synagogue.
Talis Koton.	Ritual fringed undergarment.
Talmud.	The Jewish oral law, consisting of interpretation of Torah laws.
Torah.	The Old Testament. The Teachings. The Law. The Entire body of Jewish wisdom.
Zimzum.	Kabbalistic concept of contraction. God makes room for the world by abandoning a region within Himself in order to return to it in the act of creation and revelation.

RUSSIAN TERMS

Dessiatine — A land measurement.

Dvornik — Janitor of apartment buildings, whose work also involved keeping the police well informed.

Ilyushenka — Endearing form of Ilya.

Kopeck — The smallest coinage.

Sasha — Endearing form of Alexander.

Streltsy — Russia's first professional soldiers. They guard the Kremlin and were the key to power during the first half of Peter the Great's life.

Traktir — An eating place for the lower classes.

Volodya — Endearing form of Vladimir.

Zemstvo — Institution of local self-government, established in 1864 by the reforms of Alexander II. The aim was to provide social and economic services.